ANNABELLE ARCHER COLLECTION: BOOKS 1-4
WEDDING PLANNER COZY MYSTERY SERIES

LAURA DURHAM

BROADMOOR BOOKS

For Emma and Nicolas,
my best creations

FREE DOWNLOAD!

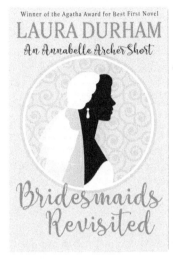

A LUXURY BRIDAL SHOWER.
THE STRESS IS HIGH.
THE PRESENTS ARE GONE.
THE BRIDESMAIDS ARE SUSPECTS.

CAN ANNABELLE UNMASK
THE THIEF?

amazon kindle

nook

kobo

 iBooks

Get your free copy of the short story "Bridesmaids Revisited" when you sign up to the author's mailing list. Go to the back of the book to sign up.

BOOK 1: BETTER OFF WED

Annabelle Archer Wedding Planner Mystery
by Laura Durham

CHAPTER 1

Planning a wedding can be murder. Planning weddings for a living is nothing short of suicide.

"Is there a patron saint for wedding consultants? Because I think after this wedding, I just might meet the requirements." I stood near the top of the wide marble staircase that swept down the middle of the Corcoran Gallery of Art's central foyer. Below me, dozens of tuxedo-clad waiters scurried around the enormous hall filled end to end with tables and gold ladder-backed chairs. After having draped ivory chiffon into swags on all forty tables, I massaged the red indentations left on my fingers by the heavy pins.

"Annabelle, darling, I may be a lapsed Catholic, but I'm pretty sure you have to be dead to qualify for sainthood." Richard Gerard has been one of my closest friends since I arrived in Washington, D.C. three years ago and started "Wedding Belles." At the time he'd been the only top caterer who'd bother talking to a new wedding planner. Now I worked with him almost exclusively.

"The wedding isn't over yet."

"At least your suffering hasn't been in vain." Richard motioned at the room below us. "It's divine."

The museum's enormous hall did look magical. The side railings of the staircase were draped with a floral garland, leading to a pair of enormous white rose topiaries flanking the bottom of the stairs. Amber light washed each of the three-story limestone columns bordering the room, and white organza hung from the ceiling, creating sheer curtains that were tied back at each column with clusters of ivory roses.

"I just hope the MOB is happy." My smile disappeared as I thought of the Mother of the Bride, Mrs. Clara Pierce. I started down the stairs to double-check the tables.

"I don't think she does 'happy.'" Richard followed, his long legs catching up to me quickly.

"If I'd known she would make my life so miserable, I wouldn't have taken this wedding." I brushed a long, auburn strand of hair out of my face and tucked it back into my tight bun. I wore my hair up to make me look older and more experienced, but it didn't make me feel any different. I still got butterflies in my stomach at every wedding I planned.

"You must be kidding, darling." Richard lowered his voice as we reached the floor and a waiter walked past us. "This event is your ticket to all the big, society weddings."

"If society weddings mean more women like Mrs. Pierce, then I'm not interested." I leaned over the table closest to me and smoothed one of the organza bow napkin ties.

"Well, sure, she's been difficult. . ." Richard came behind me and fluffed the bow back up.

"Difficult?" I narrowed my eyes at Richard and picked up another napkin. "I had to drive her fifteen-year-old, incontinent poodle to the church this afternoon."

"Her dog was a guest?"

"Not a guest. The ring bearer." I watched as Richard began to shake with laughter. "Turns out there wasn't enough room in the limousine for the wedding party and Muffles, so I got the honors."

"Look at the bright side." Richard ran a hand through his dark, choppy hair. "You're barely thirty, and you beat out all those older consultants for this wedding."

"Probably because I charge less than they do. The first thing I'm doing on Monday is raising my rates." I picked up an unlit votive candle, and Richard produced a long, butane lighter from his suit pocket.

"Then we're going shopping." Richard gave me the once-over and shook the flame of the lighter at me. "If I see you in one more pantsuit, I'm going to cry."

"But they're so practical for working." I looked down at my "lucky" navy blue suit. "Lucky" because the long jacket covered up the fact that I'd been eating way too much take-out. "And this one is silk."

"It's a blend." Richard shook his head as he rubbed the fabric of my jacket lapel between his fingers. "If you want to be an A-list wedding planner, then we're going to have to dress you like one."

"Fine. As long as you promise not to go overboard."

"When would I ever go overboard?" The spread collar of Richard's fuchsia and green Versace shirt peeked out from underneath his black four-button suit.

My eyes darted to his neck, and I cleared my throat.

"You don't like the shirt?" Richard extended his arm so I could see the French cuffs. "It looks just darling with my white linen suit. I'd have worn that tonight but I never wear white before Memorial Day."

"Thank God for small favors."

"Speaking of doing favors, I'm also going to take you to the makeup counter. What's the use of having great cheekbones if you don't accentuate them?"

"I appreciate the flattery, but you know I don't like to wear lots of makeup."

"No kidding." Richard studied my face. "I'm amazed you look half decent with that drugstore garbage. Imagine how great you'd look if you used a designer line."

"I'll think about it."

"It would be cruel to tease me." Richard formed his lips into a pout.

"If there's any teasing to be done, I should be the one to do it." My assistant, Kate, came down the staircase behind us, her high heels clicking on each step. Kate always wore heels to weddings to show off her legs and make her look taller. She said you never knew whom you might see at a wedding, and I was pretty sure she didn't mean old family friends.

"How's it going upstairs?" Richard asked. The nearly four hundred guests were being served cocktails on the upper level of the museum, which overlooked the foyer.

"Well, the sushi chefs almost quit because Mrs. Pierce timed them and took notes on their presentation."

"That damn notebook again." I rubbed my temples with my index fingers. "I can't believe she actually brought it to her daughter's wedding."

"Have you ever heard of someone making notes each time you do something she doesn't like?" Kate put a hand on my arm for support as she stepped out of her heels.

"There are a lot of things I'd never heard of before I became a wedding planner," I said. "After working for Mrs. Pierce, I've seen it all."

"Tell me about it." Kate flicked her short blond hair off her face. I noticed her perfectly painted nails and instinctively hid my hands behind my back. I couldn't remember the last time I had my nails done. "She finally left the sushi guys alone, and I haven't seen her harassing anybody else."

"Annabelle Archer!" A shrill voice came from above us.

"I spoke too soon." Kate fumbled with her shoes as she tried to wedge her feet back in them. We all turned around to greet Mrs. Pierce as she barreled unsteadily down the stairs toward us, a mass of overly bouffant blond hair and turquoise chiffon.

"Lord have mercy, she's drunk as a skunk!" Richard scurried out of her way. She plowed past us, pulling me by the sleeve as she went.

"I have some additional changes to make in the seating." Her words slurred as she staggered against the tables, craning to read the names on each place card. I averted my eyes at the mass of wrinkled cleavage barely contained by her strapless gown as she leaned over.

"The invitation clearly said 'black tie,' but there are some women here in pants, if you can imagine the nerve." She cut her eyes to me and appraised my outfit. "Of course it doesn't matter what you wear because you're just the help, but I won't have shabby guests sitting near my table."

"You want to change the names around now?" I felt a wave of panic begin to rise as I looked at my watch.

"Change names?" Mrs. Pierce paused then gave a harsh laugh. "Yes, that's exactly right. There will be plenty of name changing at this wedding. The ambassador does not go at this seat..."

"But Mrs. Pierce." I cringed as she knocked a water glass over. "The cocktail hour ends in ten minutes and the guests have already picked up their table cards. I'm sorry, but it's too late..."

Clara Pierce stopped me with a sharp snap of her fingers and turned to face me. I could feel my face begin to burn. After staring at me for a few seconds, she produced her notebook with a flourish and scrawled my name on the top page.

"You've turned out to be a great disappointment, Miss Archer. We'll discuss this matter later." She zigzagged her way back up the staircase.

"How much longer until it's all over?" I asked Kate, squeezing my hands into tight fists by my side.

"Four hours and six minutes, to be exact."

"Don't worry about it, Annie." Richard patted my arm. "She's so drunk she probably won't remember a thing tomorrow morning."

Kate punched a fist into her open palm. "I'd love to beat her to death with that tiny notebook of hers."

"That would take forever." I picked up a votive candle that Mrs. Pierce had doused with water and sighed.

"That's the whole point, sugar." Richard winked at me. "Now I've got to go check on the kitchen. We're supposed to invite guests downstairs in five. Are we still on schedule?"

I managed a smile. "Always."

"Good." Richard started down the stairs. "I'll tell the chef."

"Do you have your itinerary?" I asked Kate when Richard walked out of earshot. "I think I lost mine again."

Kate rolled her eyes.

"I know, I know. I always leave my schedule lying around." I searched my pockets. "I remember having it during the family portrait session in the Salon Dore."

"The room in the back that looks like it's been hosed down in gold foil?" Kate started downstairs. "Well, let's go get it before the guests start coming down for dinner."

"We'll go through the rear galleries. It's faster and we don't have to push past all the waiters." I started walking up the staircase and stopped so Kate could catch up. "I can't wait until this night is over."

"You say that at every wedding!" Kate followed me up the stairs toward the back galleries.

"But this time I really mean it, Kate." I reached a hand up to rub my neck. "I don't care how high-profile this wedding is anymore. It's not worth it!"

"If we survived melting wax to seal three hundred envelopes with the Pierce family crest, we can take a few more hours of this." Kate held up the finger I'd accidentally poured hot wax all over.

"Sorry about that," I said. Kate put an arm around my shoulder as we reached the landing between the foyer and the upper level. I could see that the cocktail hour was in full swing above us. The sound of the Dixieland jazz group we'd flown up from New Orleans could barely be heard over the din of the crowd. Body-to-body guests. Almost everyone in black. A typical Washington wedding.

"We never did talk about workman's comp," she continued as I raised my eyebrows. "All I'm asking for is one Friday night off to go out on a real weekend date."

"With the congressional aide?" I found it difficult to keep track of Kate's social life.

"No, I'm off politics for a while. This one's a lobbyist."

"How do you meet all these men?" Kate's ability to put in a sixty-hour workweek and still have an active social life amazed me. I felt lucky if I had time to water my plants.

"I don't find them." Kate shrugged, grinning. "They find me."

"Oh, right. I forgot you're the innocent bystander." I started to walk through the rotunda at the top of the landing. The lights in the back of the museum were turned off to discourage guests from wandering, and the room got dimmer as we walked. "Okay, I'll run next week's rehearsal, and you can take the night off."

"You're the greatest!" Kate hurried behind me. "I'll cover for you one night, if you ever want to go out."

"That's a pretty safe offer."

"Are you sure we should be going this way?" Kate held onto my sleeve. "The big statue back here always gives me the creeps."

"I think when it's this expensive they call it a sculpture."

Kate ignored my comment. "Why don't you let me introduce you to someone? How about the assistant to the assistant of the White House chief of staff? He's too tame for me, but he'd be perfect for you."

"Thanks, Kate, but I'm too busy to get involved with anyone."

We reached the top of the staircase that led down to more of the back galleries and each held on to one of the side railings as we descended.

"Who said anything about getting involved?" Kate's clicking heels were like sonar pings on the dimly lit stairs.

"Then I'm definitely too busy!"

"Come on, Annabelle, you haven't been out with anyone since that doctor who moved to Algeria last year."

"Armenia."

"Close enough."

"They're not even on the same continent!"

We reached a small landing, and I could make out the final few stairs barely illuminated by the red and blue glow of a stained-glass window on display.

"We're going to kill ourselves." Kate started down ahead of me, and then let out a small scream as she went sprawling off the last step and onto the floor.

"Are you hurt?" I knelt down next to her, my concern mixed with slight vindication that her absurdly high heels had finally gotten the best of her.

"I think I'm going to be sick."

"It can't be that bad, Kate. You probably just twisted your ankle."

"No, not that. I mean *her.*" She pointed behind me, and I turned to see a woman's body crumpled at the bottom of the stairs.

The woman's neck twisted so sharply that, even though she lay on her stomach, I could see the contorted wide-eyed expression on her face glowing in a mottled pattern of red and blue light from the stained glass.

Oh, God. I never meant it. Though I'd wished for it more times than I could remember over the past year, I'd never imagined it would happen. Not really.

The mother of the bride was dead.

CHAPTER 2

I pulled Kate to her feet as a waiter appeared at the top of the stairs.

"Get Richard," I called out. My mouth felt numb. "And make sure no guests come down here." Kate and I walked slowly up to the landing.

"Go ahead, Kate. I'll wait for Richard."

"I'm not going to leave you here." Kate motioned behind us. "With her."

"Just make sure nobody else comes back this way. We don't want to start a panic."

Kate paused, and I gave her a push. "Go on, and find a light switch."

She started shakily toward the main staircase, where guests began to filter downstairs for dinner. I watched her fumble along the wall and find the switch for the ambient lighting recessed high in the ceiling. It gave the room a dim glow. Better than being in the dark, at least.

When Richard appeared, Kate whispered something to him and he hurried toward me.

"What's Kate babbling about? What's going on? Who hit a big one?"

I half groaned, half laughed. "I think she meant 'bit the big one.' " I wondered if I'd ever heard Kate get an expression right. I motioned to the body at the foot of the stairs below me.

"Good heavens!"

"We found her just like that." I concentrated on speaking clearly as I felt my head start to pound. "What are we going to do?"

"Are you sure she's dead?" Richard didn't make a move toward going downstairs to check.

"Have you ever seen someone's neck do that?"

"We have to call the police." Richard shuddered and took his tiny silver cell phone out of his pocket.

"But the wedding . . ." I said. "All those people . . . the bride . . ."

"Annabelle." Richard grabbed me by the shoulders. "This isn't something we can fix with your emergency kit, and we certainly can't hide her."

"Nobody uses this staircase, anyway . . ."

"If you think we can carry on an entire wedding with the bride's mother lying spread-eagled on a back stairway, you're out of your mind! What are we supposed to do? Throw a tablecloth over her?"

"You're brilliant!" I ran past Kate and up the stairs to the cocktail area. I pulled an ivory damask linen off the nearest cocktail table and went back downstairs.

"You're not serious?" Richard stared at me.

"Come on." I started down the back staircase toward Mrs. Pierce. "I need help covering her."

"I'll have no part of this." Richard followed me down and stood on the last step with his hands on his hips. I unfurled the cloth over Mrs. Pierce and let it float down over her sprawled limbs.

"Damn," I said. "It's too small. We'll need one of the bigger linens from the dining tables. Do you have any extras?"

Richard folded his arms over his chest and shook his head. "No, and don't even think of using my hand-beaded silk cloths, either. They cost me a fortune to get cleaned."

"Okay, then, we'll have to make do." I tugged the fabric over one of her feet and it slipped off her head. "Can you fix your side? It's all twisted."

"I'm calling the police." Richard snatched the tablecloth off Mrs. Pierce and marched up the stairs. "Unless you want to set up a champagne fountain over her?"

"Wait." I started to protest, then stopped. My shoulders sagged. "I'm not sure what got into me."

"You can't help it." Richard pulled out his phone. "It's the wedding planner in you."

I listened to his side of the conversation with the emergency dispatcher. After hanging up, he led me away from the stairs to Kate.

"I'll stay here until the police come, and make sure no one sees the body," Richard said. "Annabelle, you're going to have to tell the family before they see the paramedics arrive."

"This just keeps getting worse and worse."

"I'll go downstairs and wait for the police," Kate said.

"Let's go." Taking a deep breath, I fixed a smile on my face as Kate and I made our way down to the foyer.

Guests stood milling around the tables, apparently continuing the cocktail reception from upstairs. I spotted the bride and groom near the dance floor as Kate headed for the front entrance.

The groom had his arm secured around the bride's waist and both were smiling, the bride gazing adoringly at her husband whenever he spoke.

I hadn't gotten very close to the bride or the groom while planning their wedding. As a matter of fact, I'd only met them a handful of times. Safe to say Clara Pierce hadn't liked to share the decision-making process.

My eyes rested on the bride. Elizabeth was a sweet, Barbie-doll blond girl as placid and easygoing as her mother had been argumentative and difficult. Usually mother-daughter wedding planning could be counted on for at least one tearful exchange, but Elizabeth had never objected to her mother's firm handling of the wedding. I'd never seen the two argue. Kate had claimed once, with some amount of disdain, that the girl was too love-struck to notice anything. Easy to see why.

Dr. Andrew Donovan was everything a woman, or her social-climbing mother, could dream of. Tall and darkly handsome, the young doctor had an intoxicating smile and an Ivy League pedigree that satisfied even his future mother-in-law's hunger for status. After hearing Mrs. Pierce extol his virtues for nearly a year, I wasn't sure whether Elizabeth or her mother loved him more.

"Excuse me, Dr. Donovan." I touched his sleeve to get his attention. He stared at me blankly for a moment, and then bestowed one of those famous smiles on me.

"The wedding planner!" he said loudly to the group around him. "Hasn't she done a fabulous job?"

"Thank you." I tried to make my voice sound natural. "May I speak with you for a moment?"

"Is anything wrong?" The bride tore her gaze away from her husband's perfect features.

"Of course not, dear. What could be wrong?" The groom answered before I had a chance to speak. "I'll be back before you can miss me." He kissed her on the nose, and then followed me to the middle of the dance floor, where no guests could overhear.

"There's been an accident," I tried to get the words out as fast as possible. "Mrs. Pierce fell down a flight of stairs." When he didn't respond immediately, I continued. "She's dead."

The doctor put a hand over his eyes.

"Where is she?" He pulled his hand away from his face. "Maybe I can help."

Before I could answer him, two uniformed policemen arrived, and I watched Kate direct them upstairs. The crowd buzzed with curious chatter and a few people tried to get past Kate to follow the police.

"Andrew!" Elizabeth ran up to her new husband and clutched his arm. "What's happening? Why are the police here?"

The groom put his arms around her, and I turned away. Wouldn't it be better if she heard it from him than from me? I didn't want to have to see her face when she found out her mother was dead and her wedding ruined. Knowing brides the way I did, I couldn't be sure which would upset her more.

I pushed through the crowd of wedding guests and headed toward the front door. I needed fresh air.

"Whoa, there, ma'am."

I'd run headlong into a man in a wrinkled, blue button-down shirt. Obviously not a wedding guest.

"Sorry." I stepped back, sizing him up. Dark hair, broad shoulders, and hazel-brown eyes that held mine without faltering. I sucked in my breath. Wow.

"Are you in charge here?" He'd apparently given me the once-over and then decided that I didn't look like a wedding guest, either.

"Well, I'm the wedding planner, so I guess . . ."

"I'm Detective Mike Reese." He held out his hand and I shook it. "You're the one who found the body, right?"

"My assistant and I both found her. My name's Annabelle Archer."

The detective nodded. "Your assistant already spoke to one of my officers. Would you mind coming back to the body with me? I have a few questions for you."

I followed him up the stairs to the back galleries. The sculptures that were so eerie in the dark seemed harmless with all the lights on. Detective Reese led me to the rear stairway and down to the middle landing. Several uniformed officers blocked the remaining stairs and another snapped pictures of the entire area. I waited at the landing while the detective went down the staircase and knelt beside the body. Two men in tuxedos followed a police officer down to the body and began examining it. One of the advantages to having lots of doctors as guests. A few minutes later, the paramedics rushed by me down the stairs.

Mrs. Pierce hadn't improved any since we'd last seen her. The blue of her dress cast a purplish hue on her skin and her contorted mouth had become pale and waxy.

"Not bad looking," Kate walked up to me.

"What?"

"He's hot." Kate pointed at Detective Reese. "Who is he?"

"A detective."

"You know, I've never dated a cop," Kate watched the officers working around her. "There are some cute ones here, too."

"And here I viewed this whole 'mother of the bride dying' as a negative thing." Kate didn't hear me. She'd wandered over to talk to one of the officers. My next assistant would be a little old lady with cataracts.

"Annie." Richard hurried up to me. "I've been searching all over for you."

"I'm waiting to be questioned by the detective." I motioned to the only person clustered around the body not in a uniform.

"Well, lucky you." Richard gave me a nudge, and then became serious again. "I'm not sure if I can keep these guests calm much longer. They want to know what's going on."

"Have you told them anything?"

"Well, I couldn't exactly make an announcement that their hostess is twisted up like a human pretzel, now could I?"

"I'll have one of my men make an appropriate announcement." The detective joined our conversation. He turned to Richard. "You must be the caterer who placed the 911 call."

Richard winked at me. "Well, we know why you made detective so young."

Detective Reese ignored Richard's comment. He wore latex gloves and flipped open a small notepad. "We found this on the body. Do either of you have any idea what these names and notes mean?"

"Those are Mrs. Pierce's recorded infractions." My stomach tightened at the sight of the familiar spiral notepad. "She always had it with her."

"Infractions?" The detective looked confused.

"Mrs. Pierce was . . . how would you put it? Well, particular about the way things were done." Richard gestured to the notebook with a wave of his hands. "If she didn't like what someone did, she would write their name down in that notebook. We called it her 'hit list.'"

"Interesting." Detective Reese glanced up at Richard. "What did she mean by writing the words 'skewers too sharp' next to your name?"

"Oh, heavens." Richard tossed his head back in a manufactured laugh. "She wanted me to dull the skewers I used on the Indonesian satay station so she wouldn't poke herself in the roof of her mouth."

"Did you?"

"Have you ever seen a blunt skewer?" Richard tapped his foot on the ground. "Defeats the purpose."

"Who's Maxwell Gray?" The detective turned to another page in the notebook. "And how would he have 'taken the wrong side?'"

"The photographer." I noticed that my palms were getting sweaty, and I tried to wipe them on my pants without anyone noticing. "Mrs. Pierce was compulsive about being photographed from her right. She had me remind him a dozen times."

"So what did you do to upset her?" Detective Reese's eyes met mine as he opened to the page where Mrs. Pierce had written my name in big, scrawling letters.

"I wouldn't let her rearrange the guest's table assignments at the last minute."

"I'm afraid I'm not following."

"She felt that some guests weren't dressed well enough, so she wanted them moved to the back."

"Naturally." Detective Reese cleared his throat. "When did this altercation between you two occur?"

"It couldn't have been more than ten minutes before we found her." I picked at a loose thread on the sleeve of my jacket. "But I wouldn't call it an altercation. I mean, she was pretty drunk, so I didn't take it too seriously."

The detective's eyes widened. "She appeared drunk when you last saw her?"

"The woman could barely stand up." Richard leaned close to the detective and gave him a nudge. "I'm surprised she could remember Annabelle's name, let alone write it down."

Reese turned to me and took a small step away from Richard. "Did you see her argue with anyone else tonight?"

"My assistant, Kate, mentioned that Mrs. Pierce had an issue with the sushi chefs, but I don't think it was serious."

"Why all the interest in the hit list?" Richard rested a hand on the detective's arm and lowered his voice. "Do you suspect foul play?"

"Just getting all the information." Reese returned Mrs. Pierce's notebook to the plastic evidence bag and backed away from us. "Excuse me for a second."

"He seems nice." Richard's eyes followed the detective. "Don't you think, Annabelle?"

"Richard." I grabbed him by the shoulders. "He's a cop."

"I know."

"Nice or not, I get the feeling he considers us suspects."

"Why would he even be thinking this is anything but an accident?" Richard readjusted his shirt collar. "The woman was clearly drunk and took a spill down the stairs. End of story."

"Not exactly." Kate walked up and motioned for us to follow her away from the group of nearby police officers. When we moved out of earshot, she lowered her voice to a whisper. "They think it may not have been an accident."

"How do you know?" Richard's face drained of color, despite all the hours he'd put in at the tanning salon.

"Do you see that cute uniformed officer?"

Richard stared over my shoulder. "Mr. Biceps?"

"Wait." I held up my hands. "Let me guess where this story is going."

"We were having a nice little chat until another officer pulled him away." Kate kept her voice low. "I overheard them talking about an odd rash that the doctors who tried to revive her found. The ME will most likely do a tox screening."

"The ME?"

"Medical examiner, Annabelle," Kate sounded exasperated. "The guy with the body now. Get with the program."

"They think a rash killed her?" Richard made a face. "What a horrible way to go."

I groaned. Kate wasn't always the most reliable source of information. Especially if it came from a man.

"She didn't die from a rash." Kate looked at us as if we were idiots. "You guys aren't the brightest balls in the box, are you?"

"Does she mean brightest bulbs?" Richard asked me out of the corner of his mouth.

Kate ignored him. "The rash apparently would've been caused by a medication overdose."

"So she overdosed on Valium or something." Richard shrugged his shoulders. "Not surprising in this crowd."

"That's not what the police are saying." Kate shifted her gaze from Richard to me. "They're saying this might have been intentional."

"Murder?" Richard went completely white and leaned back against the wall, his hand clasped against his heart.

"Murder." Kate nodded vigorously. "Poison."

Richard gave a tiny gasp before going limp and sliding down to the floor.

CHAPTER 3

"I'm absolutely mortified," Richard said after I fumbled to find my cell phone on the nightstand and pushed the button to accept his call.

"I told you a hundred times last night, it's no big deal," I said, my voice still scratchy. "I felt like fainting myself."

"Do you know how bad it makes me look?"

"Hardly anyone saw you."

"Annabelle, I'm not talking about what I looked like slumped against the wall. It makes me look like the prime suspect."

"You're just being paranoid." I sat up in bed and saw the suit I'd left crumpled on the floor after stepping out of it the night before. "Why would your fainting spell have anything to do with being a suspect?"

"Oh, God, Annabelle. Don't call it a 'fainting spell.' You make me sound like one of those Southern belles who wore their corsets too tight."

"Good thinking. You can explain to the police that your corset was too tight."

"You're an absolute joy in the morning." The sarcasm dripped from his voice.

"It's not morning anymore." I picked up my alarm clock and groaned. Daylight poured into the dark room as I opened the blinds next to my bed. "Why are you so obsessed about this, anyway?"

"Do you know why I had to close my restaurant?"

"That happened before I knew you," I reminded him.

"Food poisoning." Richard let out a long breath. "Imagine what it felt like to hear the word 'poison' bandied about again."

"That's why you fainted? Well, food poisoning is totally different from murder. Nobody's going to blame you for this one."

"Hearing anything associated with poison is never good for a caterer." Richard's voice became shrill. "You know how people in this industry talk, Annabelle. They're going to have a field day with this."

"You're right about that." I walked from my bedroom to my office and flipped on the light. Small Tiffany-blue favor boxes for my next wedding covered the floor, but I was in no mood to think about my next wedding. I held my phone away from my face and checked my text messages. "I have texts from seventeen industry people since yesterday, and it's barely two o'clock."

"No doubt all concerned colleagues," Richard muttered.

"Concerned with getting the dirt, you mean." I pulled the door shut and continued down the hall to the kitchen, promising myself that I would spend some quality time cleaning my office. Soon.

Richard gave a deep sigh. "I'm sure all the other caterers are celebrating my demise as we speak."

"What are you talking about? You weren't the one murdered." I turned on the fluorescent kitchen lights and opened the refrigerator door. A package of fat-free cheese slices, a browning head of lettuce, and a nearly empty plastic bottle of Diet Dr. Pepper. I added grocery shopping to my mental to-do list.

"Might as well have been," Richard moaned. "Once the word is out that a guest died at one of my events, the clients won't be lining up."

"Stop being so melodramatic. The detective said that they'd know more about the cause of death in a day or two. They'll find out that your food had nothing to do with it, and you'll be totally cleared."

"A day or two! I won't have any clients left in a day or two."

"Listen." I rolled my eyes and poured the remaining soda into a glass. I took a big swallow. Completely flat. I made a face and took another drink. "There's nothing we can do except wait until the police have finished their investigation."

"Aren't you the least bit curious about who murdered that horror of a woman?"

"It would be nice to know who to thank."

"Annabelle," he scolded me. "You have no respect for the dead."

"Come off it. I'm not going to pretend that I liked the woman. Okay,

I'm sorry someone killed her. Not a nice thing to do, but if anyone had it coming..."

"I wouldn't go around saying that since you were the last person to argue with her before she died."

"Whose side are you on, Richard?" My old-fashioned doorbell rang loudly. I put the glass down on the counter and hurried down the hall to my bedroom.

"Is that your door? Probably the press wanting an interview. I told you this wedding would put you in the spotlight."

"It's probably someone trying to sell something." I grabbed my suit pants from the floor of my room and pulled them on, then threw on the jacket and buttoned it up. No one would ever guess I didn't have anything on underneath.

"Whoever it is, they really want to talk to you if they climbed four flights of stairs. You'd think they'd have more elevators in an area like Georgetown."

"That's why it's called a walk-up, Richard, and it's supposed to be charming." I walked down the hall to the front door.

"Exhausting, is what it is."

"I've gotta go. Try not to poison anyone today." I clicked off the phone as I swung open the door, my mouth falling open a bit when I saw who it was.

"Detective Reese?" I fumbled to put the phone down on the bookshelf next to me. My first-floor neighbor, Leatrice Butters, stood next to him smiling. A tiny woman in her late seventies, she never left her apartment without a heavy dose of bright coral lipstick and her unnaturally dark hair curled up in a Mary Tyler Moore flip. She wore a multicolored striped blouse and matching hand-painted sneakers, which I recognized as one of her gardening outfits.

"I went outside to check on the tulip beds, and found this nice young man on his way to see you." Leatrice took Reese's hand and squeezed past me into the apartment.

Leatrice noticed the mounds of papers on the dining room table and the books in towering piles on the floor. She shook her head. "She's a busy career woman. No time for anything but work."

"Thank you, Leatrice." I tried to keep my voice pleasant as I closed the door.

"I'll make us all some coffee while you entertain your guest." Leatrice ignored my protests and hurried to the kitchen. "Happy to do it, dear. Happy to do it."

"Nice place." Reese sat down on my yellow, overstuffed couch. I pulled back the front drapes and light flooded the sparsely furnished room. I moaned inwardly as I noticed the herds of dust bunnies on my hardwood floors.

"Thanks, but it's a mess." I straightened a pile of wedding magazines on the coffee table. "As my very helpful neighbor told you, I've been swamped with work."

Detective Reese leaned forward and picked up one of the pink candy hearts that were piled in a bowl next to the magazines. "I thought these were only around at Valentine's Day."

"Those are special ones we got with the bride's and groom's names printed on them. We had a lot left over that they didn't want." I didn't add that I snacked on them constantly and had seriously considered ordering a private batch when I ran out.

He popped it into his mouth. "Pretty creative. So you plan weddings full time?"

"Full time and then some." I swept my hair out of my face and let it fall down my back. "Brides are pretty demanding clients."

"Mrs. Pierce more than most, I take it?"

"You asked me these questions last night, Detective. Why are you questioning me a second time?" I suddenly noticed that my suit was covered in beige lint from the area rug in my bedroom, and I felt my face flush. Fabulous. It looked as though I'd been rolling around on the floor.

"I thought you might be able to help me out." He smiled as his eyes traveled down my crumpled outfit. I hadn't remembered that he had dimples, too.

"Sure." I sat down across from him in the yellow twill chair that matched the couch, trying to brush off some of the lint on my suit without being obvious. Still grinning, he took a notebook out of his blazer pocket.

"We made a list of the guests in the Corcoran last night, but I wondered if you might have an original guest list."

"I have the list of names and addresses we gave to the calligrapher." I went over to the dining room table and shuffled through the folders to find it. I couldn't remember the last time I'd actually eaten at that table. "What are you hoping to find?"

"There's a name in the victim's notepad we can't match up with any of the guests or staff at the reception."

I located the thick list of names and handed it to Reese. "She didn't limit her infractions to the wedding."

"I'm guessing that some of her guests declined the invitation and got themselves written up." He gave me a quick wink, and then began studying the list.

"It sounds like you're catching on to Mrs. Pierce's style, Detective."

"Thanks." He held my gaze for a second before returning to the papers. I hadn't remembered his eyes having so much green in them. Not that it mattered.

"Coffee's ready." Leatrice walked into the room carrying a wicker tray with three mismatched mugs and set it on my glass coffee table. "You don't have a thing to eat in there, Annabelle."

"I'm never here to eat," I said, more to Reese than to her. Why did I feel that I needed to explain myself?

"So how did you two meet?" Leatrice handed us both a mug and perched on the couch. She leaned closer to Reese as he started to take a drink. "I already added some sugar and there isn't any milk to be found."

"We met last night when one of my clients died at the wedding." I watched Leatrice's face drop. "Detective Reese is in charge of the case."

"I'm here to get some more information from Ms. Archer."

"Heavens!" Leatrice put her hand over her mouth and shook her head back and forth. Then her eyes lit up. "A murder case?"

"We're exploring all the possibilities." Reese flipped through the guest list, his eyes darting from the paper to Leatrice. "It's not as exciting as it sounds, ma'am."

"I read mystery novels all the time." Leatrice took a sip of her coffee. "I'm always on the lookout for suspicious people. Isn't that right, Annabelle?"

"Any luck with the name?" I tried to steer the conversation back to Reese's investigation before Leatrice could launch into a lengthy chat about her methods of neighborhood surveillance.

He shook his head. "Does the name Phillips mean anything to you?"

"Not really." I picked up a stray rubber band on the coffee table and pulled my hair back into a ponytail. "Aside from the Phillips Collection."

He raised an eyebrow. "The art gallery?"

"Right. But I don't think Mrs. Pierce had any connections to it."

"It's worth checking out." He stood up to leave. Leatrice jumped up after him. "You should check out all leads, Detective. You never know what might turn up."

"Yes, ma'am, you're absolutely right." Reese turned to me. "Do you mind if I keep this list? I'll return it to you once we're done."

"No need to return it to me."

"Thanks, but I may have to return to ask you more questions, anyway." Reese walked toward the door.

"Come back any time." Leatrice followed him.

"Thanks for the coffee." He handed his mug to Leatrice, who blushed as she held open the door. She didn't close it until he'd walked halfway down the stairs.

"Isn't he charming?" Leatrice headed for the kitchen with Reese's mug. "And so handsome."

"Don't even try, Leatrice." I warned her. "He's not my type."

"I didn't know you had a type, dear."

"Well if I did have a type, it wouldn't be a cop." I rubbed my clammy palms on the legs of my pantsuit.

"Not fancy enough for you?" Leatrice returned to the living room.

"That's not it." I grabbed a handful of sugar hearts and tossed one in my mouth.

"Well, he's better than those young hotshots you bring around every so often. All those boys care about is their careers."

"How do you know?" I'd never let her know how right she was. I hadn't had the best luck with Washington men.

"I told you, I'm very observant. Comes from reading those detective novels."

The phone's high-pitched trill made me jump. I grabbed it from the bookshelf.

"Annabelle." Richard's voice crackled on the other end. He was on his cell phone.

"Where are you? I can barely hear you."

"I'm in the closet."

"What are you talking about?" I pressed the phone closer to my ear.

"I'm hiding in here so no one can hear me," Richard whispered.

"Who's going to hear you?"

"You've got to help me." Richard's voice faded in and out. "It's a matter of life or death."

CHAPTER 4

"For your information, a cocktail party for twenty does not constitute a life or death situation." I stood in the kitchen of one of Richard's clients, breathing hard from running the five blocks from my apartment. Richard barely glanced at me as he placed cookie sheets along the counter.

"It does for a caterer who's on the brink of extinction. This is the only client who hasn't fired me, and I'm not about to let her down."

"So where do I come into all this?" I ran my fingers over the cool marble countertop. "I hope you didn't make me run all the way here just to have someone to complain to."

"Why didn't you drive?" Richard sounded impatient.

"And try to find a new parking space in Georgetown on the weekend? The closest spot would have been more than five blocks away."

"Did you bring a black skirt and white blouse?"

I nodded and pulled the items out of my red nylon bag—a designer knockoff I'd bought from a street vendor. "I followed your orders precisely, Commander. What's this about, anyway?"

"As you're fully aware, I couldn't hire any staff for tonight. I'm technically supposed to be shut down until this murder business is cleared up."

"You don't think I'm going to play cocktail waitress for your illicit party, do you?"

"Fine, you don't have to be a cocktail waitress." Richard placed miniature beef Wellingtons on cookie sheets in perfectly spaced rows. "We'll call you the food-and-beverage distribution engineer."

"Hilarious." I took the white apron he handed me and tied it around my waist. "You owe me one."

"We'll consider it payback for your client who had me place garden gnomes on the buffets at her wedding."

"That happened three years ago." I put my hands on my hips. "I can't believe you're still upset about that."

Richard narrowed his eyes at me. "Are you forgetting that I had to dress the gnomes to match the wedding party?"

"Okay, but after tonight we're even."

Richard nodded. "I've been doing parties for this client for years. They like to keep things simple, which is lucky for us."

"So what's the timing?"

"Since it's a pre-theater cocktail reception, guests will start arriving at six-thirty and they'll all leave by eight to make it to the Kennedy Center."

"Then we've got plenty of time." I relaxed and hopped up onto a kitchen stool.

"Not quite." Richard motioned me off the stool with a jerk of his head. "Dr. and Mrs. Henderson like to make surprise inspections of the setup."

"Henderson... that name sounds familiar. Have you mentioned them to me before?"

"Maybe I did because they live so close to you."

"I've always wondered who lives in this house." I pushed the swinging door to the dining room open and peeked out. "I can see the front room lit up at night when I walk by. The artwork is gorgeous."

"They spent a fortune renovating the place." Richard lowered his voice to a conspiratorial whisper. "The moldings alone took three months to get right."

"Is it okay if I take a peek around?" I gave Richard puppy-dog eyes, and he groaned.

"Only if you make it snappy. We've got four dozen wild mushroom chopsticks to wrap, fifty Brie tartlets to fill..."

I let the kitchen door swing closed before Richard could recite the entire menu. The noise of my heels on the hardwood floors sounded deafening, so I slipped out of my shoes and padded in my bare feet from the dining room into the front parlor. A polished black grand piano covered with framed photographs stood in front of the expansive bay window. Dr. and Mrs. Henderson at a black tie party, Dr. and Mrs. Henderson on a sailboat with a group of friends, Dr. and Mrs. Henderson with a pretty blonde in a graduation cap. I looked at the photo on the boat again, then picked it up and walked back to the kitchen.

"You didn't tell me that the Hendersons are friends with the Pierces." I waved the silver frame in front of Richard.

"Dr. Henderson is in the same practice as Dr. Pierce. Isn't the groom in with them, as well?"

"No, he joined Clara's ex-husband's practice right after we were hired, remember?"

Richard nodded. "Now I do. Our MOB wasn't too thrilled."

"Were the Hendersons at the wedding?"

"Most definitely. Mrs. Henderson wore that silver backless dress that Kate drooled over all night."

I put the picture down and rubbed my temples. "This can't be good."

"What's the problem, Annabelle?"

"Catering a party against police orders the day after one of our clients gets killed is one thing, but doing it for a group of witnesses and friends of the victim is another."

"Relax." Richard held out a mound of dough and a rolling pin. "Rolling out some dough for the mushroom chopsticks will help you take your mind off things."

"Nice try. Let me put this picture back before someone misses it." I tiptoed to the parlor and replaced the frame. Before I could turn around, I heard a series of fast, clicking footsteps coming down the stairs.

"Of course we're still having the party." I assumed this low, cultured voice belonged to Mrs. Henderson. "Why on earth would we cancel just because of last night?"

I searched the room to find a place to hide. In a few seconds she'd be standing in front of me and I'd have to explain why I was wandering around her house barefoot. Not a good first impression. My eyes rested on the billowy blue curtains that pooled on the floor.

Thank God sheers are out this season, I thought as I slipped behind the heavy drapes.

Mrs. Henderson came into the room. I could hear pacing and could smell her floral perfume as she passed my hiding spot. "Yes, it's the same caterer and no, you have nothing to worry about."

She must be talking on the phone to one of her guests for tonight's party. I shifted my weight so I didn't lean against the window. I could imagine crashing through the glass and landing outside in the bushes.

"Of course I'm sure Richard Gerard didn't have anything to do with her death."

I heard some voices outside. I pivoted my body toward the window and realized that everyone who walked by on the sidewalk could see me cowering behind the curtains that covered the bay window. Like most houses in Georgetown, this one sat so close to the sidewalk that people could almost touch it as they passed. *Please let no one I know see me.*

"Because I know who did kill her, that's why."

My heart started pounding. I couldn't believe Mrs. Henderson was talking about the murderer.

"I didn't see anything, but it doesn't take a genius to figure out who wanted her dead," Mrs. Henderson said in an authoritative voice.

I felt a drop of sweat trickle down my neck as a man outside stopped to stare at me. I pretended to be wiping a spot on the glass and smiled at him. Perfectly natural to be cleaning the windows hunched over behind the curtains.

"I've got to go, hon." Mrs. Henderson's footsteps sounded as though they were in the foyer now. "Donald is running the water for my pre-party bubble bath."

I waited until I heard her walk upstairs, then I dashed back to the kitchen, scooping up my shoes as I went.

"Where have you been?" Flour covered Richard's apron and most of the floor.

I could smell the savory scent of the beef Wellingtons in the oven and heard my stomach growl in response. When had I last eaten?

I waved his question away. "I just overheard your hostess talking about Mrs. Pierce's murderer."

"How did you overhear that?"

"I hid behind the living room curtains when she came downstairs," I mumbled.

Richard opened his mouth to speak, then shook his head.

I held up my hand. "Don't start with me."

"Okay, so did Mrs. Henderson say who killed the wicked witch?"

"No." I took the pile of linen napkins that Richard pushed toward me and started folding them. "She didn't mention a name."

"That doesn't do us much good, Watson."

"Why do I have to be Watson?" I sat on a stool and swung my bare feet in front of me.

"Elementary, my dear." Richard gestured to his head. "You could never pull off the hat. I have a much better face for hats."

"The hat is all you," I said. "I want to know who Mrs. Henderson meant."

Richard wagged an oven-mitted finger. "Since it's only the two of us, there's no time to solve this crime during the party."

"I'm not trying to solve anything, but it doesn't hurt for us to keep our ears open tonight," I insisted.

"As long as your investigation won't interfere with your ability to pass hors d'oeuvres."

"Just think, Richard," I finished folding the stack of napkins into neat squares and stepped into my black slingbacks as I stood up, "maybe one of the guests tonight will reveal the murderer."

"Maybe one of tonight's guests *is* the murderer."

I gulped hard as someone began rapping on the door.

CHAPTER 5

"The guests, or should I say suspects, are starting to arrive." I stuck my head in the kitchen door and Richard glared at me. "How do I look in my uniform?"

"Stunning. You've got to hold them off for a few minutes. I still need to garnish." He shooed me away with a handful of parsley. "Take that tray of white wine with you."

I balanced the silver tray of filled wine glasses on my arm, the glasses clinking together slightly. "Perfect. The more they drink, the more they'll talk."

"I hardly think you're going to wiggle a confession out of someone with a precocious Pinot Grigio."

"I'll use what I've got." I winked at Richard.

"God help us."

When I walked back to the living room several more couples had arrived. The sound of big band came from the piped-in stereo system, but the high-pitched chatter of women greeting each other masked the music. A group of men clustered around the display of antipasto I'd put out earlier. Mrs. Henderson held court in the center of the room in a sleek black dress, her dark hair piled on top of her head. She motioned me over with a flick of her fingers, and I hurried over to proffer my tray. I tried not to cough as I breathed in the smell of expensive perfume that hung over the women like a designer cloud.

"You can imagine my shock." Mrs. Henderson turned back to her friends after taking a glass of wine. I stepped away from the group and hovered nearby, pretending to wipe a nonexistent spill from an end table.

One of the ladies leaned close and lowered her voice. "Did you actually see the body?"

"No," Mrs. Henderson said with some measure of disappointment. "But I saw a few things the police didn't."

"What do you mean?"

I held my breath and took a step closer.

Mrs. Henderson turned to face me. "How much longer until hors d'oeuvres are passed?"

"I'll go check." I hurried back into the kitchen.

"Good," Richard held out two glass trays edged in parsley and brightly colored edible flowers. "Let me explain what's on each one."

"No time to waste." I took the trays out of his hands and dashed out of the kitchen.

"Annabelle, get back here." Richard called after me. "You don't know what you're serving!"

I went back up to Mrs. Henderson with the trays in hand, trying not to breathe hard.

"Where was he when they found her?" One of the women asked Mrs. Henderson.

"Who knows? Probably with Bev Tripton. Try the Brie tarts."

"Her best friend? Do they have nuts in them?"

"Well?" Mrs. Henderson looked pointedly at me. "Do the Brie tarts have nuts in them?"

I glanced at the tray and tried to remember if I'd seen any nuts in the kitchen. I swallowed hard as the women stared at me, and my mouth went dry.

"No nuts."

"Good." The No-Nut lady popped the tart in her mouth. "If I so much as touch a nut, I have to go to the hospital."

Oh, God. I rushed back to the kitchen and slumped against the counter near Richard. I felt faint. "Please tell me the Brie things don't have nuts."

"I will not have my hors d'oeuvres referred to as things. They're Brie tartlets and, no, I left the nuts out this time. They do have a hint of saffron, though." Richard pulled off his oven mitts and raised an eyebrow. "Why?"

I motioned toward the party. "Nut allergy."

"I told you to wait for me to explain the food to you." Richard's face began to flush, and he threw the oven mitts down. "But, no. You had to run off and try to kill more of my clients."

"No harm done." I reached for one of the crab puffs that Richard had arranged on a hand-painted ceramic plate and he smacked my hand away. I jerked back and ducked out of the range of his swinging dishtowel. "I think I overheard something important. Apparently someone had a liaison with Mrs. Pierce's best friend last night when the murder happened."

Richard barely concealed his disdain. "You call that a clue?"

"It has to be someone important. Someone who shouldn't have been with her."

"Like who, her husband?" Richard started to laugh, and then stopped. "It could have been her husband. Now things are getting interesting."

"So far it's just a theory."

"Well you're not going to find out by sitting in here." Richard handed the plate of crab puffs to me.

"You just want me to get back to work," I grumbled.

"I've always admired your keen perception, Annabelle." Richard pushed me out the door. "Now go!"

I made my way through the ever-growing crowd, spotting Mrs. Henderson and her friends in the far corner, huddled together. By the gleeful looks on their faces, I'd missed a color commentary of the murder. I tried to push my way through a group of men, holding the plate above my head.

"Of course he did it." A man with wide sideburns stared at the plate of hors d'oeuvres as it moved past him. "Wouldn't you have killed that woman?"

I spun on my heel and swung the tray down. "Crab puff?"

"No doubt he had a motive." A man wearing a plaid tie popped a puff into his mouth.

"Motive? She didn't give him a motive, she gave him a mandate."

"They're excellent with the remoulade sauce, sir."

"Trying to ruin his career just asked for trouble." Plaid Tie shifted his eyes to me. "I don't like spicy food, thank you."

"It's very mild," I assured him.

"He wouldn't have been foolish enough to actually kill her, though. She's right, Glen. The sauce is delicious."

"Maybe he didn't do it, but he should have." Side-burns jumped in the conversation. "I prefer old-fashioned tartar sauce myself."

"We'll probably never know if he did do it. He's much too smart to get caught. Do you have any tartar sauce, young lady?"

"I'm sure I can find some for you." I turned and raced to the kitchen.

Richard had arranged the remaining hors d'oeuvres on trays. "How did the crab puffs go over?"

"We've had a request for tartar sauce."

"Tartar sauce?" Richard shrieked. "Why don't I just slap a bunch of fish sticks on a plate and they can eat all the tartar sauce they want?"

"I thought you'd feel this way." I tried not to laugh as Richard threw open the refrigerator door and began rummaging through the contents. I snuck a crab puff off a tray and ate it in one bite, chewing and swallowing the savory hors d'oeuvre before he turned back around.

Richard shook a fist in the air. "These are the same people that ask for A-1 with their filet mignon."

"What have you heard about Mrs. Pierce trying to ruin her husband's career?"

"Nothing." He slammed the refrigerator door shut. "Why would she do that?"

I tapped my fingers on the counter. "I'm not sure, but that's what the tartar-sauce guys were talking about."

"Are you sure they were talking about her husband?"

"I just assumed they were," I admitted. "But they never mentioned him by name."

"Knowing what we do of Clara Pierce, it's possible that more than one man had a reason to kill her. Pretty likely, as a matter of fact." Richard grimaced as he shook the contents of a plastic bottle. "Squeezable tartar sauce. What's this world coming to?"

Before I could respond, a crash of glass came from the living room. Richard jumped and squeezed the plastic bottle at the same time, sending an uneven stream of tartar sauce into the air.

Richard had bits of chunky sauce splattered on his face. Globs of white dotted the shiny copper pots hanging above him and dripped onto his head. I put my hand over my mouth to keep from laughing. "Well, now the only thing we need to make this party perfect is a dead body."

Richard narrowed his eyes. "The night's young, Annabelle."

CHAPTER 6

"Was that so hard?" Richard handed me the last wine glass to dry.

"Now I remember why I'm a wedding planner and not a caterer. At least I've never had to clean my clients' kitchens." I glanced around at the sparkling stainless-steel appliances and the white marble counter-tops that were cleaner now than when I'd arrived. I could almost see my own reflection in the copper pots dangling above us. No evidence of the chaos that had taken place only an hour before and not a single drop of tartar sauce anywhere. I had to hand it to Richard. He could break down a party even faster than he could throw it together.

"I've always said you wedding planners were a bit soft."

"Soft?" My jaw dropped open. "Who cleaned up that crystal bowl of artichoke dip that someone broke all over the living room floor?"

"I never said you weren't useful, honey."

"And did you see how much wine those people went through? I'm surprised they could still walk out the front door."

"I'm quite aware of how much wine they drank because I washed every last glass."

Richard picked up a red milk crate full of cooking utensils and trays, and I pushed open the heavy kitchen door that led out to the alley. When we reached the sidewalk, I looked around for his silver Mercedes convertible. Cars were lined up end to end along both sides of the street, inching over driveways and blatantly ignoring NO PARKING signs, but I didn't see Richard's car anywhere.

"Didn't you drive?"

"I tried, but the closest parking space I could find was the one I already had in front of my house." Richard shifted the milk crate onto his hip. "It's impossible to find parking on the weekend. Sometimes I wonder why I bother to live in Georgetown at all."

"You live here because it's fashionable," I reminded Richard before he launched into a laundry list of petty grievances.

"Well, there is that." Richard began walking in the opposite direction of his house toward my building. "Come on, I'll walk you home."

I knew it would be a waste of breath to argue. Living in a city hadn't affected Richard's sense of chivalry one bit. Anyway, he loved strolling around Georgetown at night and peeking into all the fabulously decorated row houses. "Window shopping," he called it.

"Where else in the city can you find homes like this?" He motioned with an elbow at a house with two ornate iron staircases leading up to a pair of lampposts.

"Mm-hmm." I alternated between looking up at the house and watching the uneven brick sidewalk. "Who do you think those men at the party were talking about, anyway?"

"The house on the next block is really something to talk about. Wait until you see the chandelier in the front room and the fresco on the outside."

"We already know that her current husband may have been having an affair and couldn't be found during the wedding, so don't you think that gives him motive and opportunity?"

"I wouldn't be surprised if it's Waterford, though." Richard ignored the taxi at the intersection, and I hurried across the street after him. "They have money, even if they don't have restraint."

"It could have been anyone. Everyone wanted to kill her. Even we wanted to kill her." I stumbled over a bit of tree root that poked through the sidewalk. "All we have to do is sort out the motives."

"Talk about too much!" Richard gazed up at a brick house with an enormous crystal chandelier dominating the yellow living room. The front room was almost entirely windows and the lights were on, giving us a perfect view. "Palladian windows weren't enough for them. They had to do double Palladian."

"Considering her winning personality, I think our prime suspects should be the people who knew her best." I tugged Richard by the sleeve, and we resumed walking. "Which brings us back to her current husband, who may or may not have been having an affair."

I ran the short list of suspects through my head as we turned up the next street.

"Sometimes you just wonder what people were thinking," Richard gasped.

"I know," I agreed, trying to imagine who could have committed murder. "It's awful."

"It's beyond awful." Richard pointed at a white lattice carport dripping with vines. "It's like the Hanging Gardens of Babylon right here in Georgetown. Have you ever seen anything like it?"

"I've never seen anything as awful as Mrs. Pierce's mangled body. But if the fall wasn't what killed her. . . if that rash on her neck means she may have been poisoned, then the killer didn't have to push her down the stairs. Anyone Mrs. Pierce came in contact with during the night could have murdered her."

"Now that's a real crime." Richard nodded at two enormous urns that flanked a doorway. They were ornamented with carved floral swags spilling down the front.

"A crime of passion isn't out of the question." I shrugged. "Especially if Mrs. Pierce found out about the affair. Let's not forget the ex-husband, either. I have no doubt she made their divorce as painful as possible. So I'd say those are our two prime suspects."

"You have to have both, I suppose." Richard shuddered and made a face. "It would be off-balance to have just one."

"I never thought about it that way, Richard, but they could've been working together. Why not? More than one killer makes a lot of sense."

Richard stopped short as we rounded the corner onto my street, and I bumped into him. "Are you expecting another visit from the police, Annabelle?"

I followed his gaze and saw a pair of squad cars and an ambulance with flashing lights parked in front of my building.

"Leatrice!" I grabbed Richard's arm and pulled him forward.

"That nutty old lady who's always trying to set you up with the UPS man?"

"Something must have happened to her." My mouth went dry. "She's old, Richard."

"She never seemed that old to me," Richard muttered as we ran up to the building. I went to knock on Leatrice's door on the first floor but heard loud voices and crackling radios coming from upstairs. I took the stairs two at a time and could hear Richard puffing behind me, the contents of his milk crate clattering as he tried to keep up. When we reached the fourth floor, I saw that my apartment door stood wide open and two uniformed police officers were in the hallway.

"What's going on here?" I could feel the panic in my voice.

"I'm dying." Richard reached the top of the stairs and let the milk crate crash to the floor.

Leatrice rushed out from my apartment and threw her arms around me. "Thank heavens you're home."

"Leatrice." I pulled her away from me and tried to ignore the fact that she had loosely belted a brown raincoat over what had to be children's pajamas, complete with feet. "What are you doing in my apartment? What are the police doing here?"

"What is she wearing?" Richard looked up from where he leaned against one of the officers.

Detective Reese stepped out of my apartment. "Ms. Archer." He placed a hand on my shoulder. "I'm afraid you've been robbed."

CHAPTER 7

"Ransacked is more like it." Leatrice pulled me by the arm into my apartment. Papers were scattered all over the floor and my couch cushions had been tossed against the wall. The shopping bag full of clothes I'd meant to take to the dry cleaners the week before had been ripped open, its contents emptied onto a chair. Tiny candy hearts littered the floor in bits and pieces.

Detective Reese walked past me into the room. "From the looks of things, they didn't burglarize you."

"What were they doing then, redecorating?" Richard came in to stand next to me and had his hands on his hips surveying the damage.

"What I mean is that it appears that your computer and TV were untouched. You'll have to check and see if the intruders took any jewelry, of course."

"I don't have any expensive jewelry."

"Now there's the real crime." Richard began picking my clothes up off the floor, and then spotted my dining table covered with scattered papers. "Look at the mess over here."

I glared at him. "Actually, the burglars didn't touch the table."

"Sorry," Richard mouthed.

"There's always a chance that the intruders were disturbed before they could take what they were after." Detective Reese leaned against the back of my couch. "Your neighbor made quite a racket."

I peered down at the tiny woman standing beside me. "Leatrice disturbed the burglars?"

"Well, I knew you weren't home." Leatrice patted my hand. "I saw you tear out of here earlier."

"An emergency?" Reese eyed the milk crate of cooking equipment that Richard had pushed into a corner.

"Something like that." I avoided the detective's eyes and turned my attention back to Leatrice.

"So when I heard someone throwing things around in your apartment, I knew it couldn't be you." Leatrice turned to smile at Reese. "She's such a nice girl. No parties or late-night guests like other young people have these days."

I heard Richard stifle a laugh, but I refused to look at him.

"Miss Archer is lucky to have such an observant neighbor." Reese returned Leatrice's smile. He probably loved this.

"Leatrice." I took a long breath. "How did you hear someone throwing cushions and clothes from four flights down?"

"Well, I came up to see if you were back home yet." Color began to creep up her neck and seep through the bright coral dabs of rouge applied to her cheeks. "I stood outside your door getting ready to knock when I heard the intruders."

"The truth comes out." Richard picked up a couch cushion and brushed the dust off, sending him into a coughing fit.

"Why are there so many cops here?" I asked Reese. "And why an ambulance?"

"Mrs. Butters requested every emergency vehicle in the city." Reese wasn't smiling.

Richard sat up from where he'd collapsed on the couch after his coughing fit. "Some people are so dramatic."

"Just trying to be helpful." Leatrice lowered her eyes to the floor. "I thought you were in trouble, dear."

Reese patted Leatrice on the arm. "Who knows what would have been taken if she hadn't called the police and set off her safety horn."

Richard lifted the arm he'd draped across his eyes. "Safety horn?"

"Half the neighborhood heard it." Leatrice beamed at me and produced the small red horn from her coat pocket. "Do you want me to show you how it works?"

Richard jumped up from the couch. "I'd like to see."

"No," I snapped. Richard made a face at me and sat back down.

"So what's the next step, Detective?" Leatrice reluctantly put the horn back in her pocket. "Should I come downtown with you?"

"We appreciate all your help, Mrs. Butters, but we've done about all we can do for now."

Leatrice cleared her throat. "But how are you going to find out who did it?"

"To be honest with you, we might not."

"What?" Leatrice and I spoke at the same time.

"We dusted for prints, but it appears the doorknobs were wiped clean or the intruder wore gloves." Reese slid his notebook into his blazer pocket.

"I hope your men are going to be cleaning up their dusting powder." Richard pulled a monogrammed handkerchief out of his jacket and waved it in front of his mouth. "One thing this apartment doesn't need is more dust."

"Or another smart comment," I said under my breath.

"Well, I'm just being honest, darling," he mumbled through the white linen.

Reese raised his voice. "I'm afraid without an eyewitness identification, we just don't have much to go on."

"You didn't see them leave?" I asked Leatrice. "I thought you were standing by the front door."

"They left through the back door and down the fire escape," Reese answered for Leatrice. "Probably the point of entry, too."

"I've been meaning to get a new lock on that door for a while." I sighed. "It's loose."

"Do you think they'll come back and try again?" Richard's eyes darted to the back of the apartment.

"I'm sure these are just petty criminals." Reese started for the door. "I'd recommend changing your locks to be on the safe side, but otherwise you don't have to worry too much about them returning. I'll bet Mrs. Butters scared them pretty bad."

Richard followed after the detective. "Are you sure this isn't connected to Mrs. Pierce's death?"

Reese shook his head. "Doubtful."

"So it's just a coincidence that Annabelle finds a body and gets robbed all in the span of two days?" Richard's eyebrows popped up so high they almost disappeared under his choppy bangs.

"I'd say so." Reese stepped into the hall and the rest of the police officers followed him out. "Feel free to call me if anything else unusual happens, though."

"First a dead body, then a burglary," Richard said over his shoulder to me, but loud enough so Reese could hear. "I forget what comes next. Swarms of locusts or water into blood?"

Leatrice followed fast on the detective's heels and tried to talk over Richard. "So nice of you to come down personally, Detective."

Richard closed the door behind her and started pushing a bookshelf in front of the door.

"What are you doing?" I sat down on the sofa and kicked off my shoes. "The back door is the one they broke into."

Richard took off his suit jacket and pushed up the powder pink sleeves of his shirt.

"I'm not protecting us from the burglars," Richard said and gave me a disdainful look, "I'm saving us from Leatrice."

CHAPTER 8

"So we're all secured." Richard swung the milk crate onto the kitchen counter. "I pushed a table in front of the back door and made a pyramid of those little silver bells on top. If anyone tries to get in tonight, we'll hear them for sure."

My mouth fell open in surprise. "You used the silver-plated bells for Saturday's wedding as a booby trap?"

"Relax. They're not breakable." Richard bumped into me as he opened a cabinet. Definitely a kitchen designed for one. "The pyramid is fabulous. I think you should arrange them that way for the wedding."

"How many did you use?"

"All of them."

I felt a huge headache coming on. "Are you telling me that at this moment two hundred bells are stacked up against my back door?"

"You don't sound grateful, Annabelle." Richard pawed through the contents of the plastic crate and produced an aluminum tray covered in cling wrap.

I pressed my hands to my cheeks and tried to look sincere. "Oh, I'm sorry."

"Don't mention it, darling."

Richard missed my sarcasm.

"I wouldn't have dreamed of letting you stay here by yourself after what happened." Richard patted my arm. Great, now I felt guilty.

"I told you that I'd be fine."

"Just because you're an independent business woman doesn't mean you have to do everything on your own."

"I know. I'm just used to it." I squeezed his hand. "Thanks for staying with me."

Richard batted his eyelashes at me. "I only hope Leatrice doesn't consider it inappropriate that you're having a man stay over."

I groaned. "She's like a chaperone and a matchmaker all rolled into one."

"I must admit that I'm enjoying watching her try to set you up with our detective friend."

"Don't you dare encourage her." I wagged a finger in his face.

"Encourage her?" Richard unwrapped the foil tray and tossed the wadded-up plastic wrap in the metal trash can in the corner. "She doesn't need any encouragement."

"That's the problem." I rubbed my temples.

"This will make you feel better." Richard began unloading the contents of the disposable tray onto a plate. "I saved some hors d'oeuvres from the party."

"Good. I'm starving." I watched Richard arrange a handful of crab puffs and Brie tartlets on a dinner plate and place it in the microwave. "Someone didn't let me eat anything all night."

"You're breaking my heart, Annabelle." Richard opened my refrigerator. "There's not a drop to drink in this house, is there?"

"Not unless you want coffee."

Richard closed the door with his hip. "That would calm my nerves and help me sleep better."

"I might have some decaf."

"Never mind. I think I have a bottle of leftover champagne." Richard emptied the rest of the milk crate and held up a bottle with a white label and heavy gold lettering. He made a face. "It's warm."

"That's okay. I've got ice."

"Normally I'd be horrified." Richard peeled off the foil and popped the cork into a yellow-striped dishtowel. "But desperate times call for desperate measures."

I pulled two fat mugs down from the cabinet and filled them with ice.

Richard eyed the mugs. "You must be joking. This is champagne, Annabelle, not Ovaltine."

"Sorry. I don't have much occasion to use fancy champagne flutes."

"Pity." Richard poured the champagne into the mugs and took them into the living room. I followed him with the microwaved plate of hors d'oeuvres, holding it by the edges with paper napkins so I wouldn't burn my fingers.

"You can put it here." Richard motioned to a space he'd cleared on the coffee table. He pulled one of the paper napkins from under the plate. "Who are Martha and Matt?"

"One of my couples who got married last year." I grabbed a cushion from the couch.

"And why do you have their cocktail napkins?" Richard held up a white napkin with shiny silver script.

"I called the clients for months but they never picked them up." I shrugged my shoulders. "One day I needed a napkin, so I started using them."

Richard dabbed his mouth with the napkin. "Remind me not to leave anything behind."

"Let's see how good these famous Brie tartlets are when they're reheated." I took a bite of one and the crispy sugar topping crackled in my mouth. "Not bad. Kind of like a pungent crème brulee."

"Be careful." Richard scowled as I dribbled some of the hot Brie onto the couch.

"It's okay." I dismissed his concern and scraped at the small spot of Brie with my finger. "This cotton twill is easy to clean."

"That's all well and good, but you're not the one who has to sleep on it."

"Richard, I said you can take the bed and I'll take the couch." I took a drink of watery champagne to cool my mouth from the hot cheese. "I know how your neck gets if you don't sleep on a proper mattress."

Richard nibbled on the edge of a crab puff. "I wouldn't hear of it. Besides, I should be near the front door in case the burglars come back."

"They broke in the back door, remember? The door near my bedroom."

"Which is all the more reason they'd try a different door." Richard's eyes disappeared behind his mug as he took a drink. "To surprise us."

"Very funny," I gave Richard a saccharine smile, and then got serious. "You don't think they'll try to break in again, do you?"

"No," Richard assured me. "I think we're safe for now."

I snatched the last crab puff off the plate. "What do you mean, for now? You don't agree with Detective Reese that it was a random break-in?"

"It seems too coincidental to me." Richard pulled his legs up onto the couch and folded them Indian-style. "How many times have you found a dead body? Once. How many times has your apartment been broken into? Once."

"Okay, so it's a bit odd that they both happened within a couple of days. I'll give you that."

"And why did the burglar take nothing?"

"I think Leatrice did a pretty thorough job of scaring the burglars off before they were able to get anything." I finished the last of my champagne and stood up, stacking my mug on top of the empty plate. I continued talking as I headed for the kitchen. "I'm thinking of buying a safety horn myself."

"Maybe she scared the burglars away, but why did they bother to throw things around? Not that you can tell the difference."

"Hey! I heard that." I refilled my mug with champagne and brought the bottle with me to the living room. "So what's your theory, then?"

Richard held out his mug for me to fill. "I think they were after something."

"If they didn't want valuables, then what could I have that any thief would want?"

"Good question." Richard let out a deep breath as he scanned my apartment. "Maybe this particular thief obsessively collects scrap paper and old magazines."

"Have I told you how hilarious you are?" I arched a brow at Richard.

He blew me a kiss, and then sat up straight. "If we're going with the theory that the murder and the break-in are connected, then they had to be searching for something to do with the Pierce wedding."

"Let me see if the file is gone. I left it on the table earlier today." I went to the dining table and began sifting through the mess of papers. I held up a purple accordion folder. "Here it is."

Richard hopped up and craned his neck over my shoulder as I flipped through the papers inside the file. "Is there anything missing?"

"I don't think so. Except for the guest list that Reese took with him."

"Maybe that's what they were after." Richard began pacing up and down the length of the room. He stopped at my large front window and began fussing with the curtain ties. "Someone could look right in here if you're not careful."

"I don't think they could see much. We're on the fourth floor, after all."

"You never know. People are so nosy these days." Richard pulled the curtains together tightly, and then peeked back out through a tiny gap. "Why, I can see right into the house across the street from here."

"They always keep their curtains open."

"Do you ever see anything good happen?" Richard pulled his head out of the crack in the curtains and glanced over his shoulder at me.

I shook a finger at him, and he stepped away from the window, mumbling something I couldn't quite hear. Knowing Richard, I wasn't sorry I missed the comment.

I tossed the Pierce file on the table and sank back onto the couch. "Maybe we're going about this all the wrong way. What if Mrs. Pierce's ghost came back to haunt me and ransacked the place?"

"It would be just like her to be high-maintenance even when she's dead."

"Putting the poltergeist idea aside, is the missing guest list our only motive?" I asked. "That wasn't a big secret, so why go to all the trouble to break into my apartment for it?"

"I don't know what they were after, but since nothing is missing, I think we can assume that they didn't find it. And if it has something to do with Mrs. Pierce's death, you can believe they'll be back."

"What are we going to do?" I felt a little lightheaded and doubted that the champagne had anything to do with it. Even if we had finished the bottle.

"We'll just have to figure out who's behind this little break-in before they can try again." Richard sounded more confident than I felt.

I swallowed hard and felt my mouth go dry. "If the killer and the burglar are the same person, we have to find them before they *kill* again."

CHAPTER 9

"Do you really think Mrs. Pierce's death and the break-in are connected?" Kate handed me a white paper bag as I got in her car. "Your favorite chocolate croissants from Patisserie Poupon."

I took a deep breath, inhaling the rich buttery aroma as I felt the warmth of the fresh croissants through the bag. Chocolate for breakfast. I'd have to start my diet the next day.

"Remind me to give you a raise." I pulled a croissant out of the bag and a shower of buttery flakes fell onto my lap.

"I figure you deserve indulging after what happened last night." Kate jerked the car into traffic, and I heard the cacophony of car horns that usually accompanied her driving. "Weren't you frightened to stay at your apartment after someone broke in?"

"With Richard to protect me? Why would I be afraid?" I took a bite of croissant and moaned as I tasted the dark chocolate combined with the flaky pastry.

Kate laughed. "If I were you, I'd want to spend the whole day in bed recovering from the shock." Kate gave me a sideways glance as she swerved around a van double-parked in the street. "Do you mind if I ask what those marks on the side of your face are?"

I swallowed a mouthful as I pulled down the window visor and examined myself in the tiny mirror. "Oh, great. I've got marks from the sisal area rug. I got ready so fast I didn't even check myself in the mirror."

"You slept on the floor?"

"Not on purpose." I flipped the visor back up and took another bite. "We ended up staying awake pretty late and just fell asleep in the living room with all the lights on."

"The illustrious Richard Gerard sleeping on the floor? Now that's a sight I'd love to see."

"Well, you missed your big chance." I finished the croissant, folded up the empty bag, and tucked it in the glove compartment. "He's off to the Phillips Collection to see if Mrs. Pierce had any connection there, then to the police station to try to clear his name."

Kate sighed. "I wish we had a reason to stop by the police station and see all those cute cops again."

"Sorry to deprive you, but we have to pay condolences and see if we turn up any clues." I wiped a smudge of chocolate from the corner of my mouth.

"After our cake appointment with Meredith Murphy, right?"

I slapped my hand to my forehead. "I almost forgot we had a meeting this morning. Good thing you reminded me."

"I'm sure Meredith's mother would have understood if we missed the meeting. She's so easygoing." Kate winked at me and we both burst into laughter. Meredith Murphy's mother had a facial twitch that I attributed to her being as high-strung as a Chihuahua. Kate insisted it must be a result of multiple face-lifts.

We burned a yellow light as we turned onto a residential street behind the Georgetown cemetery. Kate rolled through a stop sign and angled her car into a space on the street. I hopped out of the car and scanned the fronts of the nearly identical row houses until I found the one with the Christmas lights still wrapped around the top of the porch. Our favorite cake baker, Alexandra, had her cake studio in the basement of her fashionable Upper Georgetown house.

"With five minutes to spare," Kate sounded out of breath as we climbed the stone stairs to the house.

I leaned on the doorbell, and then brushed the last croissant crumbs off my skirt. "Are the marks on my face gone?"

She glanced at me. "Pretty much."

The front door opened and Alexandra waved us in. I'd always thought that bakers should be round, jolly people, but Alexandra had changed my preconceived idea. Thin and sophisticated, she spoke with a slight accent that I could place vaguely in Eastern Europe. She never claimed any one country. *Just a little bit of everywhere,* she said.

Today Alexandra had thrown her long brown hair into a loose bun fastened with chopsticks and wore a body-hugging turquoise dress with matching strappy sandals. Her talent for making clothes look perfect came second only to her ability to create stunning wedding cakes. If she weren't so nice, I'd hate her.

She motioned downstairs and rolled her eyes. "They arrived early."

"How's it going?" Kate whispered.

Alexandra picked up a glass of wine from the entryway table. "Do you want some?"

"That bad, huh?" I groaned.

"Well, they got better after my first glass." She nudged me and giggled. "Come see for yourself."

We followed her down the narrow staircase to the studio. Shelves lining the back wall of the room displayed sample cakes decorated in elaborate sugar flowers and swags of edible ribbon. A whitewashed wooden table dominated most of the room and held stacks of photo albums.

Meredith Murphy and her mother were sitting at the table flipping through pictures of wedding cakes. You'd never guess that the mother had the highlighted ponytail and too-tight top and the daughter wore a mousy brown bob and linen blazer. I always felt as if I'd stepped into a real-life *Freaky Friday* when I saw the two together.

Mrs. Murphy glanced up at us as we sat down across from them. "I'm glad you're here. Which is fancier, Annabelle, buttercream icing or fondant?"

I tried not to cringe as I imagined Mrs. Murphy's concept of fancy. I should consider myself lucky that she didn't want a Chippendale's dancer jumping out of the cake.

"For your July wedding, I'd go with fondant. Since it has an elastic texture, as opposed to the softness of the buttercream, fondant will hold up to the heat much better."

Mrs. Murphy nodded. "We like the big bows on the top with the ribbons coming down the sides." She held up a laminated photo of a five-tiered cake dominated by a cascade of bows and ribbons.

"I like the cakes with just a few sugar roses, Mother." The bride's voice hardly rose above a whisper.

"Don't be silly, Meredith," her mother snapped. "The bow on the cake will match the bow on your invitation."

"We haven't made a final decision on invitations yet, and I don't like the one with the bow."

This could get ugly. I'd seen fistfights break out over bows before. "Perhaps you could select two different cake designs and wait until later to decide which one fits the design of the wedding."

"I'd be happy to sketch out two options for you," Alexandra said. Her expression said she would do anything to get them out of there. A glass of wine was starting to sound good.

"Thank you." The bride's voice sounded louder, and she almost smiled.

"Whatever you want, Meredith." Her mother pressed her lips together and tossed her ponytail off her shoulder. "After all, it is your wedding."

Kate kicked me under the table. We always said that if we had a dollar for every time we heard that phrase, we'd be millionaires. If we had a dollar for each time it was sincere, we'd barely be able to split a latte.

We followed the bride and her mother up the stairs and said good-bye to them at the door so we could debrief with Alexandra. I marveled at how the mother could walk down the steep stairs to the sidewalk in her high-heeled mules. I'd never seen the woman wearing age-appropriate clothing and shuddered to think of her interpretation of a proper mother-of-the-bride dress. I hoped there wasn't a line of eveningwear tube tops.

Kate let out a long breath after the door closed. "What is it with these mothers?"

"They aren't all bad, Kate. Remember the one last year who baked us cookies?"

Kate counted off a finger. "That's one."

"I heard you got rid of our worst one the other night." Alexandra crossed her arms over her chest. "Don't forget I had to do four tastings for Mrs. Pierce to make sure the crème brulee filling for her cake had enough crackle for her."

In all the chaos, it had slipped my mind that Alexandra had done the wedding cake for the Pierce wedding. By the time we found the body, the cake had been set up for hours and she had been long gone.

"You make it sound like we killed her," I said.

Alexandra winked. "I just wish I could have helped whoever did."

I shuddered. "Don't joke about it. I think we're still on the suspect list. I know Richard is."

Alexandra's mouth fell open. "They think he had something to do with the death?" She knew Richard well since she created the cakes for almost all his parties. "Have they met Richard?"

"The only reason he's a suspect is because of the poison," I explained.

Alexandra shook her head. "Richard would never ruin his food, even to murder someone he despised."

"Did the police question you?" Kate sounded hesitant. "After all, you did bake the wedding cake."

Alexandra's face lit up. "Actually a cute detective came by yesterday. Since my cake wasn't cut or served, he said questioning me was just a formality."

"That must have been a short interview." I couldn't help hoping that Reese hadn't spent long with the city's sexiest baker.

"I did tell him about the fight I witnessed between Mr. and Mrs. Pierce."

I exchanged a look with Kate. "When did you see them fighting?"

Alexandra paused as if trying to remember. "I left the museum as the bridal party arrived to take photos. I remember seeing the Pierces in the entrance foyer as I went out the front door. I couldn't hear what they were saying, but they were definitely arguing."

"Did the detective seem interested in what you saw?" Kate asked.

Alexandra shrugged. "He didn't seem too surprised. I guess investigating all of Mrs. Pierce's fights is a big job. He seemed to be pretty focused on the food angle. Bad luck for Richard, I'm afraid."

"I'm sure he'll be cleared soon," I said with more confidence than I felt. "He planned to go talk to someone this morning."

Alexandra gave us a mischievous grin. "Tell him if he ends up in jail, I'll bake him a cake with a nail file in it."

"I don't think that would do any good," I sighed. "Knowing Richard, he'd just give himself a pedicure."

"I want to hear more about the wedding and the murder." Alexandra looked positively giddy. "Can you stay for lunch?"

"I wish we could." Boy, I meant it. Alexandra could cook as expertly as she baked. "We have a full day of appointments."

"I should get to work on those two sketches, anyway." Alexandra gave us air kisses. "I promise to make the drawing of the cake with bows hideous."

I smiled all the way to the car imagining Mrs. Murphy's face when she got the sketches.

"Are you sure you still want to go 'pay condolences'?" Kate made air quotes with her fingers.

"It's the least we can do, Kate. Who knows what we'll find out?"

"I think this is an exercise in fertility, but okay."

I shook my head as I stepped into the car. "Just drive."

CHAPTER 10

"I still don't understand why we're offering condolences for a person we couldn't stand." Kate sounded exasperated as she drummed her fingers on the steering wheel. If she saw me glaring at her, she pretended not to notice.

"Because it's the polite thing to do, Kate. Anyway, we've got a good reason. Self-preservation."

"Hey, it's not me they're after." She paused behind a line of cars waiting to turn left.

"If I get killed, you're out of a job, remember?"

"Good point. But explain to me again how this is going to help us find the killer."

"I'm willing to bet that one of her husbands killed her. Either Dr. Pierce or her ex-husband, Dr. Harriman. You heard what Alexandra said about Dr. Pierce." I motioned for Kate to turn before we reached Dupont Circle. "So I figure we should hang around people who know them and keep our ears open."

"But we're going to the bride's house first." Kate sounded confused. "You think she had something to do with it?"

"We're just acting concerned. I don't think Elizabeth could disagree with her mother, much less kill her." Kate shook her head. "You know what they say about the nice, quiet ones?"

"Not this quiet one. Park anywhere in the next three blocks. Her house is right behind embassy row."

Kate backed into a parking space and ran one tire up onto the curb. "Maybe she got fed up with her mother controlling her life and flipped out."

"And ruined her own wedding?"

"You're right. Murdering her mother is plausible, but ruining her own wedding is inconceivable." Kate stepped out of the car and smoothed down her black wrap dress. "Which house is hers?"

I looked down at the address on the slip of paper and pointed to a red brick townhouse a few doors down. Mrs. Pierce had run the entire wedding operation out of her home in Chevy Chase and I could drive there in my sleep, but I'd never been to the bride's house before.

"Do you think you could have picked a less somber dress, Kate?" I eyed her clingy dress with a plunging front.

"What are you talking about? It has long sleeves and it's black."

"I'm talking about the neckline. Doesn't exactly scream 'mourning,' does it?" I'd chosen a black crepe suit that buttoned to my collarbone and had a knee-length skirt. I felt like a nun next to Kate.

"I think it's a good compromise." Kate walked up to the front door and pressed on the bell.

"What kind of a compromise?"

"I'm sad that I found a dead body, but I'm not all that sad that it was Clara Pierce." Kate pulled the front of the dress closed a fraction. "It also transitions from day to evening beautifully."

The front door opened, and Dr. Andrew Donovan stood in the doorway wearing wrinkled chinos and an untucked green Polo shirt. He looked nothing like the dashing groom from the wedding night. I stepped forward and took his hand.

"Annabelle and Kate from Wedding Belles. Your wedding planners." I hurried my prepared speech. "We just wanted to stop by and check on Elizabeth. How is she?"

"Of course, I remember you." Dr. Donovan stepped back into the house and opened the door. "Please come in."

I pushed Kate inside and closed the door behind me. "We don't want to intrude. We're just so worried about her."

"We grow so attached to our brides." Kate had such a serious expression on her face that I had to avert my eyes to keep from laughing. Kate didn't grow attached to anyone who didn't have an Adam's apple.

The entry hall smelled like lilies, so I wasn't surprised when I spotted several flower arrangements in neutral shades clustered on an entrance table, unopened cards protruding from the tops.

"It's kind of you to come." The groom showed us into the den right off the entryway. Done in dark wood and leather, this was clearly the groom's domain. I perched on the edge of a wingback chair, and Kate sat on the burgundy leather couch. "I'm afraid Elizabeth isn't handling her mother's death well. You saw how she went to pieces at the wedding."

"Is she at home?" I asked.

"We've had to sedate her." Dr. Donovan shook his head. "She's not in any condition to see visitors."

I tried to sound solemn. "Of course not."

"We spoke to the police, of course." The doctor picked at a loose thread on the hem of his shirt. "But there's not much we can tell them. Did the police question you?"

"Yes, but we don't know anything, either," Kate said. "Aside from finding the body."

"In all the drama, I'd forgotten that you two found my mother-in-law. That must have been quite a shock."

"You can say that again." Kate shuddered, and I shot her a look. Before I could try to smooth over Kate's blunder, my cell phone began ringing to the tune of "Here Comes the Bride." I fumbled in my bag to find it.

The groom stood and managed a weak smile. "Do you mind if I go check on Elizabeth for a moment? I don't like to leave her alone for too long." Dr. Donovan backed out of the room.

I retrieved my phone, and Kate stuck a finger down her throat. She hated my personalized ring.

"Wedding Belles, this is Annabelle."

"Hi, Annabelle. It's Kimberly Kinkaid." The bride for this Saturday. I always gave brides my cell phone number the week of the wedding and not a moment sooner.

"Hi, Kimberly. Is everything okay?"

"Well, I know this number is for important calls, but I need your help with something." Her voice sounded even more tentative than usual.

I braced myself for a bridal breakdown. "That's what I'm here for."

"I've been thinking about the rose petals outside during the ceremony."

"The ones that the florist is going to scatter down the aisle?"

"Right," she barreled on. "What if the wind blows?"

"What do you mean?" I tried not to sound impatient.

"I don't want them blowing out of the aisle. I want them in a straight line."

"Well, there's not much we can do if the wind blows them around, Kimberly."

"Can you pin them down to the ground?"

Was she serious? "You want me to pin the rose petals in place?" I heard Kate stifle a laugh, but I couldn't look at her for fear I would burst into laughter.

"Or maybe there's a special adhesive to glue them to the grass?" It was official. She had lost her mind.

I needed to get off the phone before Dr. Donovan came back and heard me debating ways to adhere flower petals to grass. I kept my voice steady, despite Kate's muffled cackling behind me. "Why don't I check on that special adhesive and give you a call back?"

I flipped my phone off and dropped it in my bag. "Nice, Kate. We're paying condolences and you're laughing your head off."

"I couldn't help it." Kate stood up and walked around the room. "I'm sure Dr. Donovan didn't hear me and even if he did, I'll bet he wouldn't care."

My jaw dropped. "You don't think he'd care that you're laughing while his new bride is practically in a coma?"

"I just mean that he has so much on his mind that he wouldn't notice. I didn't catch him peeking down my dress once."

"I wasn't aware that cleavage is a test of how distraught someone is." I leaned back in the wingback chair and ran my fingers along the brocade fabric.

Kate faced the wall, studying a row of framed diplomas. "It's one of them."

I held up a hand. "Spare me the others."

"Check out this guy's credentials." Kate whistled. "No wonder Mrs. Pierce adored him so much. Princeton undergrad. Harvard Med."

I walked up next to Kate. "She wouldn't have accepted anything less. Both her husbands went to Ivy League schools, too."

"Talk about being label-conscious. At least he seems like a nice guy." She dug a small cellophane bag from her purse and extended it to me. "Gummy bear?"

I took a squishy red bear and popped it in my mouth, grateful for the rush of sweetness. "Yeah. With all these fancy diplomas, you'd think he'd be a pompous jerk."

"He's a bit dull for my taste, but nice enough, I suppose," Kate said as she chewed a mouthful of gummies.

"At least he isn't a groomzilla." We'd had a few grooms who could give crazy brides a run for their money.

"True, but this visit has been a total waste if we're supposed to be looking for clues." Kate tugged her dress together in the front. "What's our next stop?"

"Mrs. Pierce's house. It should be the perfect opportunity to talk to Dr. Pierce."

"So after that all we have to worry about is finding the ex-husband?"

"Right." I sat back down and leaned my head against the chair. "Dr. Harriman. I remember him from the ceremony, but only vaguely."

"I might be able to assist you in that regard." Just then, a tall man with dark, silvering hair stepped into the room. "I'm Dr. Harriman."

CHAPTER 11

"Now that you've found me, how can I be of service?" Dr. Harriman took a few long strides into the room and sat down in the armchair across from me. "Are you friends with Elizabeth?"

I let myself breathe again, and I could see Kate relax as she sat down next to me. He must not have overheard much of our conversation.

"Actually, Dr. Harriman, we're your daughter's wedding planners." I managed a smile in his direction. "We wanted to offer our condolences to the family."

"That's thoughtful of you." He pulled a cigar out of the pocket of his tweed jacket and rolled it back and forth between his thumb and index finger. "My ex-wife's death has been a terrible shock to us all."

"I can only imagine, sir." I shook my head along with him. Right. He probably couldn't wait for us to leave so he could light up his cigar and celebrate.

Dr. Harriman pocketed the cigar again. "Of course it's hardest on Elizabeth. She's been hysterical since they found Clara at the reception. I came over to be here with her and help her cope with the tragedy."

"Of course." I pulled my skirt down over my knees. I hoped Kate would get my hint and do the same thing. "Unfortunately, we're the people who found Mrs. Pierce."

He shifted his eyes from me to Kate. "Yes. I remember seeing you with the police."

"You were one of the doctors called to the scene of the crime, right?"

Kate's eyes darted to me. Surprising that she remembered anyone being around except the cute police officers.

Dr. Harriman looked at his hands and nodded. "I couldn't help her, though. She was dead by the time she hit the floor."

"So the fall caused her death, then?" I tried to make my question sound casual.

He glanced up at me. "What else could it have been?"

Kate gave a loud, hacking cough, and Dr. Harriman stood up to hand her his handkerchief. Kate's dress gaped open as she reached forward, and I motioned for her to close it as the doctor turned to sit back down. She ignored me.

"We've taken up enough of your time, Dr. Harriman." I stood up and Kate followed, handing the handkerchief back unused. "Please give our condolences to Elizabeth."

"I'll be sure to tell her you stopped by when she wakes up." He led us to the foyer—the scent of lilies still thick in the air—and shook our hands, then closed the door behind us.

"Don't say anything until we get in the car." I spoke with a grin fixed on my face, in case anyone watching us could read lips.

"I don't think he can hear us." Kate crossed the street and unlocked the car. I waited until we got inside and closed the doors.

"Okay, now we can talk." I fastened my seat belt snugly as Kate rolled the car off the curb. We tapped the bumper of the SUV in front of us. "What do you think of our suspect being the examining doctor?"

"I think you almost blew it. We're not supposed to know that she may have been poisoned, remember?"

"I know. But why do you think he didn't mention the rash or the possibility that the fall wasn't what killed her?"

"Because he's not supposed to discuss it with anyone, I'd imagine."

"I guess you're right." I put my sunglasses on top of my head to hold back my hair. "Unless he wanted to play down the poisoning angle because he's the one who poisoned her."

Kate weaved her way through traffic as we headed toward Chevy Chase, the sound of car horns honking behind us. "I'll play along. Let's say he poisoned her. How did he do it?"

I threw out a guess. "Maybe he injected her at the crime scene and pretended to be trying to save her life."

"Why poison her when, at least as far as we could tell, she was already dead? Anyway, how could he have pulled out a needle with all those cops around, not to mention the other doctors?"

"Okay, so he injected her earlier in the night." I pressed my foot instinctively against the floor of the car as we approached a yellow light.

"So he just goes up to his ex-wife, jabs her with a needle, and they both go along their merry little ways?" Kate sped up and we burned the red light. "That doesn't sound like the Clara Pierce I knew and loathed."

"So the theory has a few holes." I looked out my window as we passed the National Cathedral. Tour buses were lined up three deep in front, and Kate honked as one tried to merge in front of us. Kate hated when cars tried to get in front of her.

"Listen, Annabelle, I can tell you that Dr. Harriman wasn't as upset as his son-in-law."

"What do you mean? The cleavage test?"

Kate nodded. "He peeked."

"Well for God's sake, Kate, you have to make an effort not to look. I don't even know if I passed your cleavage test."

"I'm guessing that he didn't like his ex-wife, but Dr. Harriman doesn't seem like a sinister murderer to me."

I recognized that tone of voice. "You think he's attractive, don't you?" My mouth fell open as I watched Kate begin to blush. "I can't believe it. You've got a crush on one of our suspects."

"I do not." Kate's voice cracked. "I just think he's polite and distinguished."

"God help me. I've got Mata Hari as a sidekick." My cell phone began singing, and I retrieved it from the side pocket of my purse. Richard's number popped up on the display and I answered.

"Tell me you're having better luck than we are, Richard."

"Didn't you get my message?" He sounded exasperated. "I spent half the morning at the Phillips Collection and didn't get anywhere with that dreadful woman in charge of events. I'm almost grateful she took me off her list of approved caterers."

"So you couldn't find any connection to Mrs. Pierce?"

"Not a thing," Richard said over a lot of background noise. He must have been at the police station. "How's your detective work going?"

"Not bad if Kate would stop eliminating suspects because they're too attractive to be murderers."

"Too bad we don't have any solid female leads," Richard responded. "At least that would cut down on the chances of her dating the killer."

"What's he saying about me?" Kate grabbed for the phone.

"Just that he finds it highly unlikely you'd base a decision on physical attributes alone," I said with a straight face.

"Of course she wouldn't use just physical qualities, Annabelle. Don't forget money. That's at least number two on her list."

I tried not to break into a grin. "You're right, Richard."

"What's he saying now?" Kate sounded suspicious.

"That I was off-base when I implied you judge people by only one criterion."

"Good." Kate threw her chin out. "Tell Richard I'm sorry I assumed he was teasing me."

I tried to keep a straight face. "Did you hear that, Richard?"

"Each delicious word of it."

"Yes, I know you're sorry about all the times you teased Kate."

"Hey, that's not what I said," Richard protested.

"It's about time he apologized for all the cracks he makes about my social life," Kate insisted.

"He feels awful." I mouthed the words to Kate while I listened to Richard's complaints getting louder in my ear.

"That's fine, Annabelle." Richard sighed deeply. "Mock me. Make fight of your dear friend who's stuck in this godforsaken police department with nothing to drink but vending-machine coffee."

"I'm not mocking you." Fabulous. He'd become a martyr in the span of two hours.

"I think the police are looking at me funny, too."

"Why?" I asked. "What are you wearing?"

"Nothing flashy. Just my silver paisley jacket with matching flat-front pants."

Just what I would have chosen for a visit to the police station.

"I'm sure when they finally give me back my equipment and let me reopen my business there'll be a few jobs for me." Richard sucked in his breath. "Perhaps I can specialize in catering for pet funerals."

"Don't be ridiculous." I grabbed the dashboard as Kate made a sharp left into a residential neighborhood.

"You think I'm overreacting to being a prime suspect in a murder case? I feel light-headed, Annabelle. My whole career is flashing before my eyes."

"Put your head between your knees."

"I can't. These pants are too tight."

"Can you lie down?"

"Have you ever seen the floor at a police station?" Richard's voice rose an octave.

"Why don't you go to the bathroom and splash your face with water?"

I closed my eyes so I wouldn't have to see Kate roll through one stop sign after another.

"The bathroom is even worse than the floor. I'm not setting foot in there without a can of scrubbing bubbles and a pair of rubber gloves."

"I've got to go, Richard." I opened my eyes as the car slowed down, then jerked to a stop. "We're at Mrs. Pierce's house."

"Okay, I'm going to go see if I have some handi-wipes in my car." With the prospect of something to fuss over, Richard already sounded better. "Call me later."

I dropped the phone in my purse and let out a long breath.

"I take it things with the police aren't going well." Kate parked the car across from the Pierce home, with the passenger side halfway in a ditch. The massive stone house already had cars lined up bumper-to-bumper in its circular driveway.

"You know Richard. When is he ever not on his deathbed?" I opened my car door and almost rolled out onto the grass.

"I hope this doesn't take too long." Kate extended a leg out of the car and paused. "Do you hear music?"

"It sounds like a party." I nodded toward the house. "I think it's coming from inside."

We watched a woman in a short Pucci dress and stiletto heels step out of a convertible she'd parked in the middle of the street. A valet in a blue jacket appeared as if by magic and took her car keys from her. We followed from a distance as she walked to the marble-columned entrance of the house. The front door flew open and high-pitched laughter spilled outside as the woman exchanged air kisses with someone and disappeared inside the house. My eyes widened. "They've got valet?"

"Now this is more like it." Kate adjusted the neckline of her dress to display ample cleavage. "I knew I picked out the perfect dress this morning."

CHAPTER 12

I stood inside the expansive marble foyer of the Pierce home and tried to stop myself from gaping. "I can't believe I'm saying this, Kate. For once, you're dressed appropriately."

A woman wearing a tight suede pantsuit edged by us, followed by a tall redhead in a black halter dress cut down to her navel. Could anyone ever pass the cleavage test in that dress?

"Wakes sure have changed a lot." Kate stepped out of the way of one of the many waiters bustling around the house.

"Welcome, ladies." A statuesque blonde in a pink silk-shantung suit approached us, beaming from ear to ear. From her accent, I placed her firmly below the Mason-Dixon line. "I'm Bev Tripton. Clara's best friend in the whole wide world."

So this was the best friend.

"Annabelle and Kate." I extended my hand and she gave me the tips of her fingers to shake. "We worked with Mrs. Pierce on Elizabeth's wedding."

Bev grabbed me by the shoulders. "Wedding Belles, right? Precious name."

"We don't mean to interrupt anything." I noticed a string quartet playing in the corner. "We just stopped by to pay our condolences to Dr. Pierce."

"Well, that's just about the sweetest thing I've ever heard." Bev pulled me forward by the elbow. "You must join us, girls. We're celebrating Clara's life. No sense in getting bogged down in sadness, right?"

"I guess not." I motioned for Kate to follow as Bev led me into the sunken living room. The house looked totally different from what I remembered. The pale peach couches had been removed and people sat at cocktail tables covered in red crushed velvet. A bar stood in the corner, and most of the men were gathered there. I spotted Dr. Pierce with a drink in one hand. He didn't seem distraught for a man whose wife had just died. The oversized green martini didn't help his case.

"Clara loved a good party, so I said to myself, 'Bev, what better way to honor her memory than to have a huge blowout?'"

"I won't forget it anytime soon," Kate said quietly enough so only I heard.

"Help yourself to the food stations." Bev stepped away, still smiling. "But don't spoil your appetite. The cherries jubilee display gets wheeled out in twenty minutes."

Kate linked her arm through mine. "So, what's our strategy? Should we hit the raw bar first or the risotto station?"

"We're not here to eat, Kate. We're supposed to be getting information."

"We just got some valuable information. Her friends hated her even more than we did."

"This is some party, isn't it?" I blinked twice as I spotted an ice sculpture of a mermaid rising like Venus out of the center of the raw bar. "Maybe Bev was being sincere and this really is a tribute to . . . Is that a contortionist?"

We craned our necks to see a leotard-clad performer hop through the room with one leg hooked around his neck.

"Did Bev rent the cast of Cirque du Soleil?" Kate took two glasses of champagne from a waiter and handed one to me. "She only sounds sincere because she's Southern. Believe me, this is no tribute."

"After overhearing those people at Richard's party, I knew a lot of people didn't like her," I said in shock. "But you'd think that at least her best friend and her husband would be a little more discreet with their feelings."

"Speaking of being more discreet." Kate nudged me hard and sloshed a bit of champagne on my sleeve. "Look over there."

I followed Kate's gaze and watched Bev nuzzle up to Dr. Pierce, then whisper something in his ear. He laughed and slipped an arm low around her waist.

"The husband and the best friend." I put my glass down on an end table. "So those women at the party were right."

Kate narrowed her eyes. "This isn't a new thing. They're way too comfortable with each other."

"Are you sure?"

Kate crossed her arms and stared at me.

"Okay, I forgot." I threw up my hands. "You're the expert."

"I wonder how long they've been having an affair under Clara's nose."

"This must be what the Pierces were fighting about. I find it hard to believe that Mrs. Pierce didn't put a stop to this."

"Unless she died before she got the chance." A look of panic crossed Kate's face. "Hurry, there's a mime heading our way."

"I can't move." I pointed to the wall of people blocking the path to the foyer. An opening began to appear. Too late. The mime materialized in front of us, and began furtive attempts to free himself from an imaginary box. I hated mimes. Kate elbowed her way through the crowd, and I followed close behind, escaping the silent performer still trapped in his box.

"Dr. Pierce had a pretty strong motive to kill his wife," Kate said as we made our way to the door.

"It could've been Bev. A rich doctor is a good catch for her."

"If Bev is twisted enough to throw a party like this when her best friend dies, she's twisted enough to commit murder," Kate said.

"If we can find out more about the affair between Bev and Dr. Pierce, we'll be one step closer to figuring out who had motive enough to kill our client." I ducked as a stilt-walker stepped over me. "And I know exactly who can give us the dirt."

"Who?" Kate paused with one hand on the doorknob.

"Who's been doing the hair of every rich society lady for the past ten years, including Mrs. Pierce?"

"Why didn't I think of him first?" Kate exclaimed as she pulled open the front door. "I guess this means we aren't staying for the cherries jubilee?"

I rolled my eyes and gave Kate a push out the door. "Let's go talk to Fern."

CHAPTER 13

Fern stopped in mid snip as Kate and I walked into his Georgetown salon. "I don't believe my eyes."

He must have been finishing up the last client of the day because the salon was otherwise empty. The narrow shop always reminded me of a palace rather than a beauty parlor. Instead of the usual wall of mirrors, each of the three stylists had an ornate, gold mirror in front of his chair with a towering, carved wooden credenza to hold their supplies. This is what the "Cut and Curl" at Versailles must have looked like.

"Girls! I wondered how long you would go between appointments." He rushed over and embraced me, taking a handful of my hair and examining the split ends. He turned to hug Kate, and then pulled the top of her head to within an inch of his face. "I hope you don't tell people that I do your hair."

I smiled to the client, who tapped her watch. "Fern, we're not here about our hair. We just wanted to talk."

"Wait just a second." He returned to his client, analyzed her haircut from all angles, then pulled off her smock with a flourish and tipped her out of his chair. I watched in amazement. Fern's ability to stay pristine while cutting and coloring has always baffled me. I've never seen him with a single hair on him. As usual, he wore his own dark hair smoothed back, with not a strand out of place. The only flash of color in his all black ensemble came from an enormous topaz ring on his right hand.

After the customer had left, Fern patted the seats of two shampoo chairs. "Okay, let's fix these disasters."

I brushed away a hair that had landed on my jacket. "Like I said, we're just here to catch up on our gossip."

"Besides, we don't have appointments," Kate said.

"We'll make a deal." Fern pulled two fluffy beige towels down from a shelf. "You let me fix your hair and save my reputation, and I'll tell you anything you want to know. After all the brides you've sent me, a little trim is nothing."

I looked at the clock on the wall. Five o'clock. Well, I didn't have any plans for the evening.

"Fine with me." I shrugged, taking the black smock he handed me and surrendering my suit jacket. "How about you, Kate?"

She lowered herself into a chair and winked at Fern. "As long as I can be out by seven. Hot date."

"When I'm done with you, your date won't be able to keep his hands off you." Fern gave Kate a knowing look and motioned for me to sit in the chair next to her.

Kate rubbed her hands together. "Work your magic."

"If you're good, I'll tell you a secret to drive your date wild." Fern winked. Getting some rather questionable advice on men came with all of Fern's haircuts.

"It's like gasoline to a flame." I groaned as I sat down and let Fern push my head back into a black basin. He stood between Kate and me, and turned on the water for both of us.

"Too hot?"

I shook my head as he wrapped a towel around my neck and began massaging my scalp with his fingers. "Did you hear what happened to Mrs. Pierce, Fern?"

"Don't remind me." He stopped massaging my head and shuddered.

"I'm not sure why you're upset," Kate said. "I'm the one who fell on top of her dead body."

"Who do you think has to do her hair for the funeral?" He turned away from me and started rubbing Kate's head vigorously.

"You're kidding." I sat up halfway in my chair. Fern pushed me back down with one hand.

"Well, I did the woman's hair for almost ten years. They want to make sure she looks good for the viewing."

I wiped some water out of my eye. "Is this something you normally do?"

"The older my clients get, the more time I spend at the funeral home working on dead heads." Fern wasn't known for sugarcoating his words. "I should open a second salon there."

"Who called you about doing her hair?" Kate asked.

"Her best friend, Beverly. They've both been coming to me for years."

"Really?" I started to sit up again, but Fern had a hand on my head. He pumped some shampoo onto my hair, and I heard him doing the same to Kate.

"They were in the salon just a few days before the wedding. This is the mango and chamomile blend to invigorate the scalp. They wanted me to hide their roots."

"I guess they're not natural blondes?" Kate didn't sound surprised. We had watched the women who came out of Fern's salon get blonder by the year.

"Half the 'natural' blondes in this town are my work. Now I'm putting on a coconut and papaya conditioner."

"You're making me hungry. Annabelle wouldn't let me eat a thing today."

I ignored Kate's whining. "So then Mrs. Pierce and Bev were getting along the last time you saw them together?"

"Of course." Fern rinsed my hair with a burst of freezing cold water. "This will make your hair shine."

"Had either one started acting strange recently?" I tried to dance around my real question.

Fern squeezed my hair and twisted it up into a towel. "Not that I noticed. Why all the questions?"

"For God's sake, Annabelle." Kate sat up, holding her towel around her head. "She wants to know if Clara knew that her husband and Bev were having an affair."

"Oh, is that what you're asking?" He pushed us up with a finger on our backs and guided us to two plush red stylist chairs. "She knew about the affair for ages. I thought you were hinting at something big."

"You don't call that big?" I stared at Fern as he towel-dried my hair with one hand and Kate's with the other.

"You have to understand these society tramps." Fern held up a long, wet strand of my hair.

I tried not to let my mouth fall open. I had never gotten used to the way Fern referred so casually to his clients.

"I just tell it like it is." Fern smiled at my surprised look. If I called my clients tramps, I'd be fired. Fern managed to insult people with a big smile on his face and get tips for it. "I think we should do soft layers around your face and get rid of this ridiculous blunt cut."

I tried to sound nonchalant. "As long as I can still pull it up."

"What's the point of having a fabulous haircut if you always wear it in the ponytail?" He started cutting. I closed one eye.

Kate swiveled her chair around to face Fern. "I don't get it. Didn't having an affair with Dr. Pierce give Bev the leg up on Clara?"

"So to speak?" Fern elbowed Kate. "That's not the way Clara saw it. See how these layers frame your face, Annabelle? I don't suppose you'll let me do highlights, too?"

"Don't push it."

"Clara got bored with her husband." Fern measured two sections of hair along my jawbone. "She only married him to get back at her ex, anyway."

"This is getting juicy." Kate rubbed her hands together.

"Dr. Pierce and Dr. Harriman were best friends about seven or eight years ago, girls. Clara found out her husband . . ."

"Dr. Harriman at the time, right?" I asked.

Fern bobbed his head up and down. "He cheated on Clara with one of his nurses. Huge scandal."

"That must have burned her up." I brushed a pile of wet hair clippings off my lap. "Especially since she's so into people's status in society."

"She wanted revenge." Fern ran a hand through my hair and gave an approving nod. He turned to Kate. "What's the best way to get even with a cheating husband? Have an affair with his best friend, Clara thought."

"I hope you didn't give her that advice," I said.

Fern put a hand on his hip. "I would never meddle in someone's personal life. Anyway, that's not the best way to punish a cheating man."

I didn't wait to hear Fern's way. "She did more than have an affair with him, though. She married him."

Fern shrugged. "Clara could overdo it sometimes."

"You don't have to tell us about Mrs. Pierce going overboard." I ran a hand through my hair. I'd have to remember to check the scale later. I'd probably lost at least a pound in hair weight.

"By the time Clara finished getting revenge, she'd married a nice doctor. But that was it." Fern flipped Kate's head forward.

"What do you mean?" I took off my smock and shook the hairs into a gold trash can by my feet.

"Clara loved money, glamour, and power. Her new husband had money, but nothing else that mattered to her. After a while she got bored and just ignored him. I'm going to angle the sides to give you movement, Kate."

"Poor Dr. Pierce." Kate peeked out from under her long bangs. "No wonder he had an affair with Bev."

"Who could blame him?" Fern held a section of Kate's hair up and measured it with a shining, gold comb.

"He certainly had a motive for murder," I said. "There are two things I know, girls. Hair and men. That man didn't have the guts to kill her."

"What about Bev?" I sat back down in my chair and spun around. "Could she have killed her best friend?"

He brushed the back of Kate's neck with a fluffy brush. "I wouldn't put the murder past her, but why bother? Clara knew about the affair with her husband and didn't care."

"I'm still not quite clear on why she didn't care." Kate examined the back of her hair with the gilded hand mirror Fern handed her.

"Simple. She had her own little fling to distract her."

I nearly fell off my chair. "Someone was willing to have an affair with that witch?"

"You didn't know?" Fern seemed gleeful. "With the president's top economic advisor."

"Do you mean the one who's on the news a lot?" I could hear my voice begin to shake.

"She's the kind of woman who likes to trade up." Fern nodded, and then pulled out a blow dryer with a long nozzle. "You know the one, right? He's got just enough gray at the temples to look honest. Boyd, I think."

"William Boyd." Kate met my eyes in the mirror. "Oh, we know him all right."

I could feel a knot forming in the pit of my stomach. "We were just hired a few weeks ago to plan his daughter's wedding."

CHAPTER 14

"So Mrs. Pierce had an affair with a prominent political figure who just happened to hire you. Why didn't you tell me sooner?" Richard had been waiting when Kate dropped me off in front of my building. I'd revealed the latest development in the Pierce soap opera before we even reached the second floor.

"What are you talking about? I just found out about it myself," I insisted.

"Not about the affair." Richard led the way up the narrow staircase. "I mean about being hired by the Boyds. Were you trying to keep it a secret so you could use another caterer?"

"Don't be so paranoid. We were both too caught up with the Pierce wedding to think about anything else. To be honest, I intended to set up a tasting with you as soon as we were through." I stopped at the top of my landing. Nearly a dozen crates and cardboard boxes were stacked around my doorway. A pile of plastic garment bags slid off one of the boxes and onto the floor. "What in the world is going on?"

Richard shifted from one foot to another. "I had the equipment that I took from police storage delivered here. I figured it would be more practical that way."

"Why would it be more practical to keep your cooking equipment here? Why not at your catering kitchen?"

"I don't want anyone to get the wrong idea, since I'm still technically closed and can't use the company kitchens." Richard started pushing one of the boxes forward as I opened the front door.

"When you say that you took the equipment from the police, am I to assume that this is legal?"

"Are you suggesting that I stole my own equipment from the police station?" Richard looked as outraged as he could manage while straining behind the weight of a large brown box. "They gave me everything they no longer needed for the investigation and made me promise not to open my kitchens until the exact cause of death has been determined."

I picked up a milk crate and placed it inside the door. "Why am I getting an uneasy feeling about this?"

"I can't imagine." Richard wouldn't meet my eyes. "I do have an idea I wanted to run by you, though."

"I knew it." I slid another box inside my apartment with my foot.

"Since I'll be staying here until things are safe again, why not do my catering from your kitchen?" Richard scooped up an armload of plastic garment bags.

"Wait a second." I shook my finger at him. "I thought you weren't allowed to cater."

"They asked me not to open *my* catering kitchens." Richard pushed the last box through the doorway by crouching over and getting a running start of a few feet. He stood up and brushed off his hands. "They didn't say anything about using *your* kitchen."

I closed the door and threw my keys on the nearest end table. "I won't have to worry about being killed. You're going to get me arrested first."

"Arrested for what? Illegal flambé? Possession of an unlicensed spatula?" Richard dismissed my concern with a flick of his wrist. "Don't be silly. There's nothing to worry about."

"What happens when the police return and see your little setup?"

"What reason would the police have to come back here?" Richard pulled out what appeared to be an industrial-strength chrome blender from one of the boxes. He disappeared into the kitchen, and then opened the white, wooden shutters that divided the top half of the two rooms and poked his head out. "This counter would be a perfect breakfast bar if you got rid of all this junk."

"That's where I put my mail. I haven't gone through it in a while." I flopped down onto the chair facing the kitchen. "Reese said he'd return the guest list sometime, so I think you can count on him getting a glimpse of your covert operation."

Richard scooped my piles of junk mail and overdue bills into his arms and vanished behind the counter. "He needs to drop something off, right? We'll make sure he doesn't come in the kitchen. That's simple enough."

"This plan is destined for disaster," I moaned.

"I have only a few small parties, anyway. Nothing we can't handle."

"We?" I gaped at Richard. "I hope you mean you and your invisible friend."

"You're so heartless, Annabelle." Richard's voice cracked. Such a faker.

"I'm already harboring a criminal activity, so don't even dream about getting me charged with aiding and abetting, too."

"They don't send people to jail for cooking, darling." Richard popped his head out of the kitchen. "Do they still wear stripes in prison? I would look atrocious in horizontal stripes."

"I think they wear blue now. Or orange." I rolled my eyes.

"I look fabulous in blue." Richard sprayed the counter with cleaner and wiped it away with an exaggerated swipe. "Especially if it's a deep, electric blue. Accentuates my eyes."

I stared at the pile of garment bags that Richard had dropped on the couch. "Let me guess. You even brought uniforms for us to wear."

"That's not a bad idea, but no." Richard stuck his tongue out at me through the space above the counter. "Those are the bridal party tuxedos that you're supposed to return to the shop. I put them in my car the other night and forgot about them until today."

I glanced at my watch. "Well, it's too late to return them now. The place closes at five."

"I would've returned them for you, honey, but I wasn't sure which tuxedo place you used."

I let my hair down. "Don't worry about it."

"Well, knock me over with a feather boa." Richard rushed into the living room and pretended to stagger against the wall. "You finally cut that mop."

"Thanks, I think," I said as Richard recovered from his shock and began examining my hair from all angles. My phone rang while he fluffed the back of my hair with his fingers, and I grabbed it from my purse.

"Miss Archer, this is Mike Reese. Detective Reese. We've made a copy of the guest list you loaned me, so I thought I'd return it to you tonight."

"That's fine." I looked at the boxes of contraband taking up most of my living room. "When should I expect you?"

"I'm already in Georgetown, so it shouldn't take me more than five minutes."

"Perfect." I cursed Richard silently. "See you in five minutes."

I clicked off the phone and tossed it behind me on the chair. Richard held a pocket mirror up so I could see the sides of my hair he had teased straight out. I glared at him. "Detective Reese is on his way and if you don't want me to break down and make a full confession, you'd better do something with all this stuff."

CHAPTER 15

The doorbell rang, and I glanced over my shoulder into the open kitchen where Richard stood amid his neatly arranged supplies. He wore a plaid apron edged in pleats that we'd found wedged in the back of a drawer. "Are we ready?"

"Absolutely." Richard waved a metal spoon at me. The smell of sautéed onions filled the apartment. Richard had found a withered onion sprouting roots in the back of one of my refrigerator drawers and cut it into pieces. Hopefully the detective wouldn't get close enough to notice the lack of any other food. "Just making dinner and minding my own business."

"Good." I paused before opening the door. "Try not to talk too much."

Detective Reese wore a pair of jeans that were broken in. He slipped off a brown leather jacket, and I tried not to notice how great his arms looked in the white T-shirt underneath.

"It sure smells good in here." He walked toward the kitchen. "What are you cooking?"

I opened my mouth, and then went completely blank. Richard and I hadn't planned that far.

"A sweet onion tart with goat cheese." Richard looked up from the stove. Leave it to Richard to pull something out of the air and make it sound delicious.

"It's an experimental recipe." I didn't want the detective to get any ideas about staying for dinner. "We don't know if it'll be any good."

Reese leaned on the counter separating the living room and the kitchen. "I didn't know that the owners of catering companies actually cooked. I thought you had chefs."

"We have several chefs." Richard puffed out his chest. "But you have to know the basics, in case of an emergency."

"Is making dinner for a friend considered an emergency?"

"This is more of a favor," Richard explained. "An emergency is when your chef calls in sick."

"Or when you aren't allowed to use your staff or your kitchens?" Reese leveled his gaze at Richard.

A flush began to creep up Richard's neck. He punched the fan button on the range. "It's getting hot in here."

"Can I offer you anything to drink?" I stepped between Reese and the kitchen, remembering my empty refrigerator as soon as I'd spoken. Please let him not be thirsty.

"No, thanks." Reese turned from the kitchen, seemingly satisfied that he'd scared Richard enough. He sat on the edge of the couch and pulled the folded guest list from his jacket. "We didn't have any luck finding anyone named Phillips on the master list. Chances are that isn't even important, but we're grasping at straws right now."

"Do you have any suspects?" I sat down across from him and watched as he flipped through the list.

He studied me for a moment. "I shouldn't be discussing this with you."

"I'm only asking because I might be able to give you some information you don't have." I cleared my throat. "About some people who aren't upset that Mrs. Pierce is dead."

"From what we've discovered, that won't narrow down the field much." Reese grinned and dimples appeared in both cheeks.

I tried to stay serious. "I just found out that her husband and her best friend were having an affair, and Mrs. Pierce knew about it."

Reese's eyes widened. "Interesting. Are you sure?"

"I saw it with my own eyes." I blushed, and then shifted my gaze away from him. "You know what I mean."

"I know what you mean." He pulled out a pad of paper and a silver pen. "What's the best friend's name?"

"Bev Tripton. Also write down William Boyd."

Reese tapped his pen on the table. "That name sounds familiar. What's the connection?"

"He's the president's economic advisor, and Mrs. Pierce was having an affair with him."

"I won't even ask how you got this information, Miss Archer. You shouldn't be running around playing detective."

"I have no desire to do your job for you, Detective." I crossed my arms tightly in front of me. "All I care about is clearing Richard's name."

"Him?" Reese lowered his voice to a whisper and jerked a thumb behind us where Richard leaned over the counter trying to listen. "We don't consider him a real suspect."

"Then why the big deal about examining his equipment and testing his food? You know all this bad publicity is ruining his business."

"We're not trying to put anyone out of business, but we are trying to solve a murder."

"So now you're sure Mrs. Pierce was murdered?"

"You don't read the papers, do you?" Reese cocked an eyebrow at me. "The article that ran this morning leaked the fact that an overdose of two different kinds of blood pressure medications killed the victim."

"Two kinds?" I had to start reading the newspaper.

"Mrs. Pierce took one medication for high blood pressure, but we found two drugs in her system. One was her prescription and the other wasn't."

I winced. "I guess it's what you'd call too much of a good thing."

"I guess so." The detective gave me a brief smile. "So now we have to determine how the killer delivered the second medication to her."

"By slipping it in her food or something?"

"That's what we're hoping to find out by testing the leftover hors d'oeuvres and plates for residue of the drug." The detective pocketed his notebook, and clicked the silver pen a few times before standing.

"Couldn't she have accidentally taken the wrong medication?" I followed him to the door. "How can you be sure it's murder?"

"It's unlikely that she would have taken two types of pills within a few hours. We checked her prescription and her pill box. No sign of the second medication."

"Which means that someone else knew what medication she took and mixed the two on purpose."

Reese put a hand on my arm. "I appreciate the names, Miss Archer, but let the police do the investigating."

"I'm not trying to . . ." I started, but the detective cut me off.

"Stick to wedding planning." He grinned and gave my arm a small squeeze. "It's less dangerous."

What a condescending jerk!

"That's what you think." I pulled my arm away and swung open the door, making a point not to meet his eyes.

"Thanks again." He gave a wave to Richard, and then stepped into the hallway. He caught the door with one hand as I tried to slam it shut and leaned close to me. "By the way, Annabelle, I like your hair."

CHAPTER 16

I stood in front of the bathroom mirror after my morning shower and studied my haircut. A bad idea. I could never make my hair look as good as Fern did when he cut it. I always spent one day looking great and three months pulling my hair up so I didn't have to attempt to style it. I blew my hair out and attempted to style the smooth layers. Hadn't the ends turned under yesterday?

"Since when do you use a blow-dryer?" Richard poked his head in the bathroom, rubbed his eyes, and then stepped in to stand behind me. He'd slept in the khaki pants and white T-shirt he had on last night.

"Since I got this high-maintenance haircut." I crimped the ends with my hands. "I'm going to have to quit my job to keep up with it."

"That's the price of beauty, Annabelle." Richard yawned and covered his mouth. "Were you planning on using the kitchen this morning?"

"What do you think?"

"Right. Stupid question." He walked back down the hall.

"What's on the menu for today?" I called out.

Richard had brought in bags of groceries the night before and filled the refrigerator and cabinets. My kitchen must still be in shock.

"Just a couple of drop-off lunches for law firms." His voice carried down the hall. "Pesto chicken on focaccia, espresso-rubbed steak salad, fruit with a tarragon glaze. That kind of thing."

I abandoned the bathroom—and any hopes of my hair behaving—and joined Richard in the kitchen. I hoisted myself up on the counter next to the sink and let my feet swing from side to side.

"I just cleaned that, honey." Richard motioned to the Formica counter. He opened the refrigerator and started to pull out cellophane bags.

"I guess there's no chance of getting breakfast around here?" I pawed through the bags he put next to me. All produce. Not my idea of comfort food.

"Do I look like I'm running a diner?" He slapped a Styrofoam package of meat in the sink, and then thrust a paper bag in my direction. "I had a feeling this would happen, so I stopped in the bakery section last night."

I peeked in the bag and sighed. "Blueberry muffins with a crumb topping. I'm in heaven."

"I hope this means you'll be staying out of my way?"

"You bet." I slid down off the counter. "Kate and I agreed to do a little more snooping around, so as soon as she gets here . . ."

"I forgot." Richard snapped his fingers. "Kate called while you were drying your hair to say that she's going to be late."

"How late?"

"She didn't say. Something about going to visit a former boyfriend who works at the White House and getting more information about Boyd."

"Very late." I took a muffin out of the bag and bit into it, sending bits of crumb topping onto the floor. I sighed as I tasted the sweetness of the blueberries.

"Weren't you just saying last night how you needed to catch up with client calls and paperwork?" Richard ignored my mumbled complaints about Kate as he pushed me out into the hall. "Now is your chance."

I finished the first muffin before I reached my office. Peering in the bag, I stepped gingerly over the favor boxes on the floor and sat down at my desk. Only two more muffins. I had to make them last. Richard wouldn't be happy if I came back for more food.

I opened my phone log and started dialing clients. Voice mail on the first three calls. I tried to make most of my client calls early in the morning or around lunchtime, so I could leave a message and not get stuck in hour-long conversations about bridesmaid shoes. Since it was morning, I hoped everyone had gone for a coffee break.

"One more thing I forgot." Richard reached an arm around the door frame, without showing his face. He dropped a piece of paper with a phone number on my desk. "Mrs. Boyd called while you were doing your hair."

That settled it. I would never blow-dry my hair again as long as I lived.

"Anything else you've forgotten to tell me, Richard?" I raised my voice as he scurried back to the kitchen. "Like all my brides have decided to elope?"

I dialed Mrs. Boyd's phone number and counted the rings. After the sixth ring an out-of-breath voice answered.

"Mrs. Boyd?" This didn't sound like the perfectly put-together political wife.

"Yes?" she snapped. "Who is this?"

Oh, no. Not another Mrs. Pierce. I didn't remember her being like this when we met.

"Annabelle Archer from Wedding Belles. I'm returning your call."

"Of course, Annabelle." Mrs. Boyd's voice warmed up. "Thank you for returning my call so promptly. It's been a little crazy around here."

"I understand." I hoped she couldn't hear my tone of relief.

"I called you to talk about selecting a caterer." Mrs. Boyd rustled papers on the other end of the phone. "Now that we've booked the Meridian House for the reception, I hoped we could set up some tastings."

I glanced down at my calendar. "When would be good for you?"

"I know it's short notice, but anytime this week. Next week my husband goes out of town, so if we don't fit it in soon we'll have to wait until the beginning of next month."

"I might be able to get a caterer to do a tasting for you this week. That way we can get the process started."

"Could you?" Mrs. Boyd sounded pleased. "That would be perfect. We want a caterer who does French food well. We want this wedding to have the feel of a garden party in Provence."

"That won't be a problem. There are some fabulous toile linens that would be lovely for cocktails outside."

"As long as they're pink. We want everything to be pink."

I winced. "Everything?"

"Everything," Mrs. Boyd said. "Even the food needs to match."

Great. The wedding would look as though it had been hosed down in Pepto-Bismol. I walked with my phone to the kitchen and waved my arms to get Richard's attention.

"What are you doing tomorrow night?" I mouthed to him.

"Nothing," he whispered back. "Why?"

I walked back to my office. "I'm certain that Richard Gerard Catering would be willing to do a tasting in your home tomorrow night."

"He's supposed to be wonderful, isn't he?" Mrs. Boyd said. "Are you sure he'll agree to such a short notice?"

"I'll handle it," I assured her. "I'll have him put together a menu today and fax it over to you."

"Don't forget our color scheme, Miss Archer."

I thought such rigid color schemes had gone the way of color-coordinating the bridesmaids with the punch. I heard Richard coming down the hall as I said goodbye to Mrs. Boyd.

"What are you up to, Annabelle?" He stood outside my office door, hands on his hips.

"Since you're so gung-ho to cater, I figured you wouldn't mind doing a tasting for Mr. and Mrs. Boyd tomorrow night." I spun all the way around in my office chair. "It'll give us the perfect opportunity to see how much Mrs. Boyd knew about her husband's affair, and if Mr. Boyd had anything to do with the murder."

Richard drummed his fingers on his hips. "And how do you expect to get this information out of them? Should I plan on putting truth serum in the food?"

"I guess I'll just see how they react when I casually mention Mrs. Pierce. People usually give themselves away when they're lying."

"I'm going to go to all the hassle of throwing together a last-minute tasting just so you can see if you get a reaction?" As the doorbell rang, Richard turned on his heel and stomped down the hall. "That detective got it right, Annabelle. You should leave the investigating to the police."

I followed him to the living room. "You might get a catering job out of this, too. It's not a total waste."

"Maybe you can talk some sense into her," Richard said to Kate as he let her in. He appraised her acid-green skirt slit up to midthigh. "Maybe not."

"Just wait until you hear what I found out about William Boyd." Kate tossed her hot pink plaid purse on the couch.

Richard jerked a thumb in my direction. "Wait until you hear what she's gotten us into."

"You go first, Kate." I perched on the arm of the couch and let Kate stretch out across the rest. Her skirt was clearly too tight to sit up in.

Richard went back into the kitchen where we could watch him through the open shutters. "I hope you don't mind if I listen from in here. Not all of us can spend all day playing private eye."

"Somebody is in a lovely mood." Kate kicked off her heels.

"Ignore him," I said. "Tell us what you found out."

"So I went to the White House to visit Jack, that guy I used to date last year. Do you remember me talking about him?"

"The one who laughed like a girl?"

"No." Kate propped her head up against a cushion. "The one who had a shoe fetish."

"I think so." I needed a chart to keep them straight.

"Anyway, I paid Jack a visit this morning. We had a great time catching up and swapping work stories. We even set a date for dinner tonight."

"Please tell me this is going somewhere," Richard said, his voice muffled behind a cabinet door.

"It just so happens that his office is only a few doors down from Boyd's and he filled me in on some pretty interesting fireworks that went on last week."

"Mrs. Pierce?" I leaned forward.

"You got it." Kate swung her legs off the couch and inched herself into an upright position. "Jack didn't hear anything specific, but he said Clara did plenty of yelling when she visited Boyd."

"I wonder what they were fighting about." I stood up and paced the room.

"The rumor around the office is that she must have threatened to tell his wife about their affair. What else could it be?"

"That would do it." Richard heaved a chef's knife up and it landed on the cutting board with a thud.

"No one heard exactly what they fought about, but everyone heard what Boyd said after Clara left." Kate stood up and walked behind the couch to lean over the counter into the kitchen.

I couldn't believe she would tease us like this. "Well, what did he say?"

"Jack said that Boyd fumed all day and stalked around the halls saying that Clara wouldn't get away with it, and that he would shut her up once and for all."

"Anything else?" Richard eyed Kate.

"Just that he would kill that meddling witch." Kate grinned. "That's all."

"Bingo," I said. "I think we've found our murderer."

"Just because he threatened to kill her?" Richard gave a little snort. "If I remember correctly, darlings, you both made similar threats."

"We weren't serious." I walked to the counter and grabbed a strawberry when Richard turned away. "But if Clara had been about to ruin our lives by exposing a secret, maybe we would have been."

"She ruined my life for a while," Kate said under her breath.

"People make idle threats, then get over it all the time." Richard returned to the big, glass bowl of fruit salad and pursed his lips. He glared at me. I stopped chewing and tried to swallow the berry whole. How could he miss a single strawberry?

"Water under the ridge," Kate said.

"Bridge," Richard and I said simultaneously.

"Most likely a lover's spat." Richard moved the salad bowl to the other side of the kitchen. "They probably forgot about it long before the murder."

I wiped my mouth on my sleeve and ignored Richard's disapproving glare. "When was the fight?"

"That's just the thing. They wouldn't have had time to forget about it," Kate said. "It happened the day before the wedding."

I whooped. "See, I told you the tasting would be a good idea."

"What tasting?" Kate asked.

"The one I arranged for Richard to do at the Boyds' house tomorrow night. It'll be the perfect opportunity to sniff out more clues."

"This is getting much too Nancy Drew for my taste," Richard griped.

"They won't know we're there to find information. Mr. Boyd could never expect us to know that he threatened Mrs. Pierce's life the day before she was killed. I don't think even the police know that." I winked at Kate. "What were the chances of you dating someone who overheard all this?"

"With Kate, I'd say the odds weren't bad." Richard blew Kate a kiss.

"Ha, ha." Kate turned her back to Richard and flounced back to the couch. "I wouldn't mind getting to snoop around inside their house. It looks amazing from the outside. Not that I'm thrilled about the idea of hanging around a murderer. If Boyd did do it."

"I'd be willing to bet that he had something to do with her death." I tapped a finger on my chin. "And tomorrow night will be the perfect opportunity to find out."

Richard glanced up from slicing pieces of focaccia and rolled his eyes. "What could possibly go wrong with this plan?"

CHAPTER 17

"Everything that could possibly go wrong today already has." Richard polished a sterling silver knife with the dishtowel tucked into the waistband of his pants, then placed it on the Boyds' long, mahogany dining table. Everything about the room, from the floors to the walls to the claw-foot table, was dark wood.

"That's a good thing." I set an oversized pink-rimmed base plate in front of each of the tall chairs. "If nothing else can go wrong, then dinner will be perfect."

"First, I couldn't get the grade of filet I wanted. I had to settle for choice." Richard set a ruler on the table to see if the silverware was even on both sides of the plate. "Then Party Settings delivered the wrong dessert plates. Wait until you see them. They look like hospital china, which means I'm going to have to paint the plate with raspberry coulis to cover it up. And, of course, I couldn't find the wine that matched the pink peppercorn sauce anywhere in the city."

"Remember that this tasting is just so they can sample your food. This isn't the final menu for the wedding." I patted his arm. "I think you've done an amazing job considering the short notice I gave you."

"I'm almost positive that this is the least amount of time I've ever had to pull together a formal dinner," Richard snipped. "No other caterer would dare to try."

"You get full marks for bravery." I set a white plate with a scrolling pattern on top of the charger. Classic and formal, yet not boring. Richard considered matching people's personality and tableware an art form.

"I'm not the brave one. You're trying to catch a murderer," Richard said. "Where do you think he is, anyway?"

We hadn't seen anyone since Mrs. Boyd let us inside two hours earlier. I glanced at the grandfather clock in the corner. Half an hour left before we were scheduled to start the tasting.

Kate wedged an ivory taper into the crystal candelabra in the middle of the table. "Didn't you hear Mrs. Boyd say he had a doctor's appointment right before this?"

"I bet we have time to snoop around a little before he gets here," I whispered.

"Snoop around?" Kate almost dropped her handful of candles. "That's not part of the plan."

"Mr. Boyd's office is right across the foyer and the door is partly open." I tugged at Kate's arm. "If we're going to do this, let's do it right."

"You're nuts." She pulled away from me. "What if he comes home early and we get caught?"

"Doctor appointments always run late, so there's no way that Boyd will get here on time," I assured her.

"What if Mrs. Boyd comes back downstairs?"

"That's why Richard's going to stand guard for us." I looked tentatively at Richard.

"Leave me out of this." Richard started out of the dining room, and I ran to catch him. "If you think I'm going to be around when you two get hauled off to jail, you're out of your mind. I'll tell you where I'll be. Crawling out the kitchen window."

"Please, Richard. Kate and I will only poke our heads in for a second."

Richard allowed himself to be prodded across the foyer.

"After two minutes, you're on your own," he huffed.

"Stand out here and if you hear anyone coming, give us a signal." I pushed the door to Mr. Boyd's study open the rest of the way.

"Would a flare suffice or were you thinking more along the lines of exotic bird calls?"

I gave Richard my most saccharine smile. "A tap on the door will do nicely."

We stepped into the office, and I could make out the shape of a desk in the corner. I heard Kate sliding her feet across the floor, probably so she wouldn't trip, and I did the same. We reached the desk and Kate turned on a lamp sitting on the edge. I snapped it off.

"What are you doing?" I blinked hard, temporarily blinded by the light. So much for my eyes having adjusted to the darkness.

"How are we going to find anything if we don't have light?"

"Let's try this." I felt my way over to the window and found the plastic bar that adjusted the blinds. I twisted it, and stripes of soft moonlight fell onto the desk.

"Not bad." Kate bent over the desk and picked up a book. "His calendar."

I took it out of her hands. "I wonder why he doesn't have it on him."

"Maybe he keeps one for here and one for the office. Flip to the week before the wedding."

"What's taking so long, girls? Hurry it up."

I cursed Richard under my breath for making me jump. "Two more minutes."

"I'll give you one, and then I'm out of here," he hissed back.

Great. No pressure. I flipped back a page in Boyd's calendar and ran my finger down the record of meetings.

"This guy visits the doctor a lot. He had an appointment last week, too."

"Is Clara's name in there anywhere? Or the initials CP?"

"Not that I can find." I scanned the pages quickly. "Feel around. Is there anything else on the desk?"

"Ugh. I think he emptied his pockets on here. Stick of gum, a few pennies, receipt, ball of lint."

"Where's the receipt from?"

Kate uncrumpled it. "From a pharmacy. For a prescription."

"I wonder what he takes. Does it have a date?"

Kate unfolded it. "The tenth."

"The day of the wedding. Are you thinking what I'm thinking?"

"That I can't believe this guy picks up his own prescriptions?"

"Good point." I tried not to sound too surprised as I took the receipt from Kate. "But he would pick it up himself if he didn't want anyone to know about it. Mrs. Pierce died from mixing two blood-pressure medicines, right? What if the prescription Boyd had filled the day of the wedding was for one of them and he somehow used it to kill her?"

A sharp rap on the door made my stomach drop. "That's Richard's signal." Kate clutched my arm. "We've got to get out of here."

CHAPTER 18

A high-pitched, warbling whistle followed Richard's loud tap on the door.

"Is that supposed to be a bird call?" I stuffed the drugstore receipt into my shirt pocket.

"Who knows?" Kate whispered. "I'm not waiting around to see if he sends up a flare."

I held out my arm to stop Kate from barreling through the door when I heard Richard's voice, much shriller than usual.

"This is the most breathtaking parquet floor I've ever seen, Mrs. Boyd."

I held my breath. They sounded as if they were right outside the door.

"Why, thank you, Mr. Gerard."

"Call me Richard. Everyone does."

Footsteps indicated they were heading away from the office door.

"If you have a minute, Mrs. Boyd, I'd love to show you the china we chose for this evening. I think of it as Martha Stewart meets Louis the Fourteenth."

I cracked the door. "Okay, Kate. It's all clear. Richard has Mrs. Boyd in the dining room with her back to us."

"Where are we supposed to have been?"

"There's a powder room under the staircase. We could be coming out of there."

"Both of us?" Kate asked. "Together?"

"Better she thinks we're weird than she finds us snooping around her husband's office."

"If you say so."

We tiptoed past the dining room, and then made a big production of shutting the door to the bathroom and walking loudly down the hall.

"There you are." Mrs. Boyd turned as Kate and I entered. A petite woman with dark hair cut in a thick page boy, Helen Boyd had a tight smile that seemed to blink on and off again like Christmas tree lights.

"Did we miss anything while we were washing up for dinner?" I asked.

Richard gave me a fake smile. "All we've done so far is review the menu."

"I hope you found the bathroom without any problem, Miss Archer."

I waved her concern away with one hand. "No problem at all. I love the way you've decorated it."

She raised an eyebrow. "Really? Most women don't like the fly-fishing motif."

Fly-fishing? I should have checked out the bathroom before opening my big mouth.

"Annabelle isn't most women." Kate patted me on the back. "She adores fly-fishing."

"Do you, now?" Mrs. Boyd studied me carefully. "Then you and my husband will have lots to talk about. It's his passion."

"You know I'm more of a beginner, Kate." If looks could kill, I'd have been in the market for a new assistant.

"He'll be thrilled that someone speaks his lingo. Heaven knows I don't share my husband's fondness for the outdoors." She bestowed a series of her blinking smiles on us.

Richard looked at his watch. "Are we expecting Mr. Boyd soon?"

"Yes, but why don't we get started without him?" Mrs. Boyd lowered herself into the chair that Richard slid out for her.

"Excuse us for one moment." Richard let me and Kate walk past him into the kitchen. "We'll be back with the first course."

Kate waited until Richard closed the door before collapsing in a fit of giggles. "Good luck chatting with Mr. Boyd about fly-fishing."

"Who decorates their bathroom with a fly-fishing motif?" I leaned over and let my head fall on the wooden kitchen island, glowering at Kate from my inverted position. "You're pure evil squeezed into a Lilly Pulitzer dress."

Richard waved his hands like a bird about to take flight. "Fight it out later, girls. You haven't told me if you found anything in the office yet."

"We found something all right. Show him the receipt, Annie." Kate only used my nickname when trying to get on my good side.

I produced the slightly crumpled yellow copy for Richard to inspect.

Richard took it from me. "He fills his own prescriptions?"

"That's what I said." Kate wore a look of vindication as she opened the lid of the stainless-steel stock pot simmering on the stove and a savory sweet smell filled the air.

"Am I the only person paying attention here?" I snapped my fingers. "He fills the prescription, then attends the wedding. Mrs. Pierce dies of an overdose of blood-pressure medication. Hardly a coincidence."

"The sneaky and suspicious side of your character is really coming out, Annabelle." Richard pushed Kate out of the way, and stirred the contents of the pot. "I like it."

"I've got to agree with Annabelle, it's all too convenient," Kate said. "If Clara planned on exposing their affair to his wife, causing her to leave him, and possibly ruining his political career, I'll bet he'd do anything to stop her."

I nodded. "If they'd been seeing each other, he'd know that she took blood-pressure medicine. It wouldn't take a genius to figure out that giving her a big dose of blood-pressure medicine on top of her own medication would kill her."

Kate rubbed her hands together. "We know he had plenty of motive. He had opportunity, too, because we saw him at the wedding. I'll bet he pulled her aside to apologize for the fight, and then managed to slip her the poison."

"Now we have evidence." I took the receipt and tucked it in the zippered compartment of my purse. One piece of paper I didn't want to lose.

Richard lifted a wooden spoon from the pot and took a taste from it. "We can prove that he got a prescription filled, but we can't be sure that it was the same medication they found in Clara's system."

"I just have a feeling, Richard. The case is coming together."

Kate rocked on the balls of her feet. "Just to play devil's adjective, how did he get a doctor to prescribe it to him?"

"It's devil's advocate." Richard pointed the spoon at Kate.

"What if he takes blood-pressure medicine himself?" I said. "It wouldn't be unusual among political types."

"We can find out if he has high blood pressure." Richard lifted the pot off the stove and set it in the sink.

"Let me guess, Kate and I will sneak up to his bathroom and go through his cabinets?"

"I thought of simply asking his wife. Unless you two didn't get your fill of spying?"

"How are we supposed to work that into casual conversation?" I put my hands on my hips. "Please pass the pepper and the blood-pressure pills, if you have any."

"You'll figure something out, Annabelle." Richard ladled a spoonful of pale pink soup into a shallow bowl and passed it to me. I held it by the rim to avoid burning my fingers on the hot bottom.

Kate took two bowls and put her back against the door. "If not, you always have fly-fishing to fall back onto." She backed out of the kitchen, smirking.

I followed and set a soup bowl in front of Mrs. Boyd, then sat down across from Kate. "Since your daughter's wedding will be next summer, Richard chose an apple chestnut soup to start the meal." Inspiration struck me. "We can lower the amount of salt in case either you or your husband have any health concerns. Like high blood pressure?"

"We both have mild hypertension, but nothing to be concerned about for the wedding."

Jackpot.

"Do you take medication?" I asked.

"Yes, why?" Mrs. Boyd eyed the soup and didn't make a move toward her spoon.

Kate gave a forced laugh. "Don't let Annabelle worry you. She likes to get a full family profile when we start the planning process. Allergies, likes, dislikes, medications."

"Am I too late? Did you start without me?" Mr. Boyd came through the front door, dropping his square briefcase in the foyer and continuing into the dining room. Kate sent her soup spoon clattering onto the table.

"Not yet." Mrs. Boyd turned her cheek when her husband bent down to kiss her.

I'd remembered Mr. Boyd as being taller and more handsome when we'd had our first meeting. I could see why women would be attracted, though. Chocolate brown hair with a distinguished amount of gray. Blue eyes that any woman would die for. Discovering that he'd probably killed my former client in cold blood lowered his overall sex appeal, though.

"We were just about to taste the soup." I pushed my chair back and almost flipped it over. "Let me get you some."

Richard had a filled soup bowl in his hand when I stepped into the kitchen. "Was that Mr. Boyd I heard?"

I nodded. "He's our guy. Mrs. Boyd told us he takes medication for blood pressure. He's the killer." My heart pounded. I needed some blood-pressure medicine myself.

"Okay, Annabelle. Calm down. Maybe we should call the police and let them take over from here."

"Not until after the tasting," I insisted. "Maybe he'll let something slip and incriminate himself even more."

"Fine. But if anything happens, remember that I'm right in here with 911 predialed on my cell phone and my finger on the send button."

Not exactly how I pictured the cavalry arriving, but I could live with it.

I nudged the door open with my toes, and carried the bowl with both hands. I lowered it in front of Mr. Boyd and noticed he'd drained his water glass. "Apple chestnut soup served warm with a dash of crème fraiche."

"Helen cooks like this all the time." He winked up at me. "Right, honey?"

"I would if you were ever home."

"I guess I've held back my wife's cooking ability all these years by working late." Mr. Boyd laughed and took a spoonful of soup.

Mrs. Boyd stared into her soup, stirring it in circles.

"This is one of Richard Gerard's signature warm weather dishes." I felt the need to fill the silence. "It's just crisp enough to be refreshing, but substantial enough for a formal dinner."

Mrs. Boyd didn't stop stirring and didn't look up.

"Could I get a little more water?" Mr. Boyd strained to swallow. I hoped the soup wasn't too thick.

I reached for the silver water pitcher on the sideboard behind me, and Mr. Boyd held out his crystal goblet for me to fill. Mrs. Boyd's eyes flashed as she watched her husband gulp down the entire glass and resume eating his soup.

"We can also serve it in a demitasse cup if you'd prefer to have six or seven smaller courses," Kate offered.

I mouthed a quick thanks for the save, and forgave her for the whole fly-fishing incident.

"That's a thought, Helen." Mr. Boyd put his spoon down, leaving a small pool of pink in the bottom of his bowl. He cleared his throat. "Like the tasting menu we tried at Citronelle."

Mrs. Boyd's voice became a hiss. "I've never been to Citronelle."

Mr. Boyd stood up halfway, knocking his chair to the ground. His hands gripped the table on either side of him, and I saw red blotches creeping up his neck. It looked as if he would explode. Kate's mouth dropped open, and I made a slight motion with my head that we should leave.

As I tried to slide out of my chair without being noticed, Mr. Boyd gasped for breath, his mouth opening and closing like a fish. His arms began to shake, and then he collapsed on the table, his face completely in his soup bowl.

Mrs. Boyd let out a piercing scream and Richard burst through the door, cell phone in hand.

We all stared at Mr. Boyd, purple faced with pink drops of liquid in his hair.

"It's the soup!" Mrs. Boyd turned on Richard, waving her finger viciously, "You've killed him! You've poisoned my husband."

To his credit, Richard didn't faint.

CHAPTER 19

"Well, we can cross Mr. Boyd off our suspect list." I sat next to Kate and Richard at the end of the Boyds' living room sofa, staring at the intricate pattern of the Persian carpet covering the floor. We were waiting for Detective Reese to return and finish questioning us. He'd been called away to talk with Mrs. Boyd before her Valium kicked in.

Richard sat with his head in his hands. "I still don't understand how this happened. At least at the wedding there were lots of people who could have murdered Mrs. Pierce."

"I know." Kate rubbed her temples. "Tonight, we were the only ones in the house, aside from Mrs. Boyd."

I crossed my legs and jiggled my foot in circles. "Mrs. Boyd is the obvious suspect, considering how irritated she seemed to be at her husband, but did you see how shocked she looked when he fell over?"

"You can't fake hysterics like that." Kate pulled her dress down an inch.

"He could have had a heart attack or something." Richard sounded hopeful.

"With all these cops crawling around taking pictures and questioning us?" I shook my head. "Unlikely."

The door across from us opened, and Detective Reese strode across the room. In a dark gray blazer over black pants and a tightly knotted striped tie, he looked far more official than he had the other night when he stopped by my apartment. And far more severe.

"Let me see if I understand this correctly. All three of you thought it would be a good idea to set up this dinner and use it as some sort of trap?"

Richard barely met the detective's eyes. "I wouldn't say trap, exactly."

"What word would you use, Mr. Gerard?" Reese paced in front of us. I had to uncross my legs so he wouldn't hit my foot. "Enlighten me."

I cleared my throat. "We wanted to see how Mr. Boyd would react if we brought up Mrs. Pierce and the murder. Casually."

Reese glanced at the notes he'd made earlier. "You thought he might be the killer because of a fight he and Mrs. Pierce had the day before the wedding, right?"

I could hear sarcasm dripping from his voice. Okay, it didn't sound like such a great reason when presented like that.

"We believe she threatened to tell his wife about the affair," Kate said in a tiny voice.

"That's the only evidence you had?"

We all nodded. We'd told the police what Kate learned from her White House source, but we'd omitted the evening's illegal search-and-seizure operation in Mr. Boyd's office. Our fabulous clue that sealed the case against Boyd seemed useless now. No need to tell the police since we'd dropped Boyd off our suspect list for good.

Reese closed his eyes and rubbed them with one hand. "Each time I turn around, Miss Archer, I find you in some sort of trouble with one or both of your sidekicks."

Richard twitched at the word "sidekick." I elbowed him. "I'm sorry, Detective. I'm not trying to get in these situations. Honestly."

"I asked you to leave the detective work to me. Now I'm ordering you. Stop running around trying to solve this thing on your own."

"Okay." I stared at my lap. I felt awful. We'd only made things worse.

"I hope you realize this is dangerous stuff you've gotten yourself into." Reese touched a hand to my shoulder. "I don't want to see you get hurt."

My face flushed, and I didn't lift my head to look at him.

He pulled his hand back. "I don't want to see any of you get hurt."

I didn't raise my eyes until I heard Reese pull the door shut behind him.

Richard stood up. "I don't know about you, Kate, but I'm a little upset that our safety came as an afterthought."

"You're reading too much into things, as usual." I shook my head.

"Can we get an expert opinion on that, Kate?"

"Definitely interested," Kate confirmed. "Although I don't know why, considering the way she treats him."

"What do you mean?" I went to check that the door had closed all the way.

"You don't give him any encouragement at all. How is he supposed to know that you like him?"

"I don't like him." I tried not to raise my voice. I didn't want Reese to overhear.

"Sure you don't, Annie." Richard came over and put an arm around me. "You always blush when you speak to a man."

"Why not tease him a little?" Kate walked across the room twisting her hips from side to side. "Like I do."

"I don't think tease is an accurate description for what you do," Richard muttered.

Kate made a face at him. "Then it'll work perfectly for Annabelle."

"I'm not going to tease the poor guy, so you two can forget about it."

"Fine, have it your way." Kate walked back to us minus the twist. "People will start talking about the wedding planner who can't find a husband for herself."

"I'm not searching for a husband." My face got warm again. "I don't want to settle for someone just for the sake of getting married."

"I didn't say you had to settle," Kate said. "But don't you want to plan your own wedding one day?"

"Why would Annie need to get married when she has us?" Richard winked at me. If he meant this to be comforting, it didn't work. I thought about what Kate had said and wondered if I should stop focusing on work. Everyone else in the world was getting married. At least it seemed that way to me. My phone began singing and I pulled it out of my purse, glancing at the number on the caller ID. Kimberly Kinkaid. I hoped she wasn't calling about pinning flower petals to the grass again.

"Hi, Kimberly. What can I do for you?"

"What do I do with my purse during the reception?"

I could feel my eye begin to twitch. "What do you mean?"

"Should I put it on the table or under my chair?" Hysteria began to creep into her voice. "What is proper wedding etiquette?"

I was sure Emily Post didn't have a section in her book on purse placement. I tried not to sound irritated. "It's fine to put it next to your chair."

I could hear her let out a deep breath on the other end of the phone. "Okay. I can check that off my list now."

Detective Reese stuck his head back in the door. "Mr. Gerard, I just remembered something."

"I've got to run, Kimberly," I whispered into the phone, and then dropped it back in my purse.

Richard raised a hand to his mock turtleneck. "Yes, Detective?"

"I left a message on your voice mail earlier, but I'll go ahead and save you the trouble. We finished analyzing all your equipment and testing the food from the wedding. It's clear that the poison came from a source unrelated to your food, so we gave the go ahead for you to reopen your business."

"Thank you, Detec..."

"In light of Mr. Boyd's murder, though, you can disregard that message."

My mouth fell open. "You're sure he was murdered?"

"We're sure. We'll focus our investigation on the obvious... the soup."

"Mr. Boyd was poisoned, too?" Kate gulped.

Reese closed the door without another word. So much for our inside source. Richard turned slowly to face me.

"This is all your fault." He jabbed a finger at my nose. "I'm not listening to any more of your brilliant ideas."

"Calm down, Richard."

"I will not calm down. I'm going to end up in prison. I'll spend the rest of my days cooking in the prison cafeteria for people called Tommy One Thumb and Sammy the Weasel."

"You're not going to be arrested." I dodged his finger, which came closer and closer to my face. "Your soup had nothing to do with Mr. Boyd's murder. If he was poisoned, it must have happened before he arrived home. Maybe someone slipped something into his drink at work."

"Stop trying to figure it out." The vein on the side of Richard's head pulsed. "That's how we got into this mess in the first place."

"If I recall correctly, you were just as into solving Mrs. Pierce's murder as I was."

Kate tried to get between us. "She's right, Richard. We both made the decision to try to find Clara's killer."

Richard marched to the door. "If I hear one more word about anyone trying to solve anything, there will be more than two bodies for the police to worry about."

He slammed the door behind him, and Kate turned to me. "He really got his toes out of joint, didn't he?"

CHAPTER 20

"So, did the same person kill Mrs. Pierce and Mr. Boyd?" Kate slowed as we reached the front of my building and looked over her shoulder. The small market across the street had closed, and the streets were dark and quiet.

"It seems too coincidental for both of them to die within days of each other." I found my keys and opened the heavy front door. The tiny foyer held a silver grid of mailboxes and the staircase. No room in Georgetown for a fancy lobby. I checked my mailbox quickly, and then put a finger to my lips. "Don't make any noise. I saw the lights on in Leatrice's apartment."

We started tiptoeing up the stairs, and Leatrice appeared in the hall.

"Don't worry about disturbing me, Annabelle." Leatrice wore a brightly colored peasant dress and what appeared to be a red tissue paper flower in her hair. "Just watching an old episode of *Murder, She Wrote*."

"Sorry to be in such a hurry." I didn't stop climbing. "We've had a long night. We're too tired and hungry to stop."

"Not a problem, dear. I'll tell you what. I'll order us a pizza, and you can tell me all about your night." Before I could protest, she'd run back in her apartment, and I could hear her on the phone.

"This is the perfect end to an already horrible night." I bent forward and dangled my arms over the railing.

"If she's buying, I can put up with a little chatter for a while." Kate shrugged. "It'll be like being on a bad date."

I managed a smile. "You always know how to put a positive spin on things. At least we won't have to worry about her trying for a good-night kiss."

"I'm not so sure. She seems to like you an awful lot, Annabelle."

Leatrice bounced out of her apartment and pulled the door shut. "The pizza will be here in twenty minutes." She held up a kitchen timer. "If they're late, it's free."

I led the way upstairs with Kate behind me, and with Leatrice and her ticking timer bringing up the rear. If only I could tag Leatrice with one of these, I thought, then I'd always hear her coming. I pushed open the door to my apartment and let Kate and Leatrice walk in first.

"Good heavens!" Leatrice dropped her timer and the buzzer went off prematurely. Richard stood in the middle of the living room in a pair of purple silk drawstring pajama bottoms and nothing else. He had a trim waist any woman would covet, and I couldn't help wondering if he waxed his chest or if his skin was really that smooth.

Richard flung his arms over his bare torso. "It's considered polite to knock before barging into a room."

"It's my living room," I protested. "I wasn't aware I had to knock."

Richard picked his pale green angora blanket off the floor and wrapped it around his chest. "I thought it would be easier to stay here tonight and move my things in the morning."

"You don't have to leave." I tried not to sound exasperated.

Richard pulled the blanket up to his neck. "When I'm around you, bad things happen to me."

"I'm sorry I got you in trouble, Richard. But listen, Kate and I have figured out how someone could've murdered Mr. Boyd before he came home."

"Murder?" Leatrice sounded excited.

"I can't believe what I'm hearing." Richard let the blanket slide back down to his waist. "Let me guess. You've concocted a brilliant plan to catch the real killer by throwing a brunch that, of course, I'll cater. We'll assemble all the suspects and then they'll all start dropping dead. Poisoned, naturally."

I rolled my eyes. "I see that you're still upset."

"Why would I be upset?" Richard shrieked. "I'm only under suspicion for murder for the second time in one week. Both your clients, I might add."

"Things seem bad now," I said. "but you'll be cleared in this death just like you were for the last one."

"Not another word!" Richard pursed his lips and held his palm up to me. He turned to Kate and Leatrice and gave a dignified bow. As dignified as you could be with an angora throw wrapped around you. "If you'll excuse me, ladies. I'm going to bed."

"Come on, Richard. We've ordered a pizza." Kate picked up Leatrice's timer and handed it to her. Leatrice just stared at Richard with her mouth agape.

"No, thank you. I'll be on the bedroom floor trying to get some sleep before the police come and drag me away." Richard flounced off down the hall.

Leatrice took my hand and squeezed it. "I don't think things are going to work out with this one, dear."

"He'll get over it." Kate dropped onto the couch. "You know what they say . . ."

"Don't, Kate. I can't handle anything else being murdered tonight, even words."

"What kind of fight did you have?" Leatrice asked.

"Not a fight, exactly." I sat down next to Kate. "He blames me for getting him in trouble with the police."

"The police? Did you see that cute detective again?" Leatrice seemed torn between her love of mysteries and her need to find me a husband.

"Yes, Detective Reese happened to be at the scene of the crime." Did everybody I know have a one-track mind?

"The scene of the murder, you mean?" Leatrice's whole face lit up, then she squeezed my hand. "That detective is just the type of man you need, Annabelle."

"You're not the only one who thinks so," Kate said to Leatrice. The doorbell came to my rescue.

Leatrice frowned at her broken timer. "I think they took more than twenty minutes, but I can't prove it."

I got the idea Leatrice ate a lot of free pizza.

"I'll get drinks for all of us." I walked to the kitchen while Leatrice paid.

"Don't bother." Kate took a six-pack of Coke from the delivery man.

"I ordered drinks, too," Leatrice said. "I've seen the inside of your refrigerator, remember?"

Kate cleared a space on the coffee table for the pizza and drink cans while I brought a stack of LIZ AND JAMES cocktail napkins from the kitchen and passed them around. Leatrice handed me a steaming slice of pizza, its trails of cheese hanging underneath like loose string. I inhaled the intoxicating scent of the pizza and my stomach growled. I thought back to the last pizza I'd tasted at a client's wedding. Thin, the size of a silver dollar, topped with goat cheese and frisee. I took a bite of the gooey sausage-and-green-pepper pie and sighed. Now, that was more like it.

"You were telling me about your run-in with the police," Leatrice reminded me, dabbing at her mouth with a napkin.

"One of our clients died tonight at a tasting Richard did for us." I tried to talk through a mouthful of cheese.

"Another client?"

"You make it sound like they've been dropping left and right."

"Well, they have been," Leatrice said a little too cheerily. "How did this one die?"

"It appears to be poison, again." I popped open a can of Coke and took a sip, the fizzy drink tickling my nose. "Unfortunately, that means that they're looking at Richard's soup as the cause of death."

"He blames Annabelle because she came up with the idea to do the tasting in the first place." Kate picked at a blob of cheese stuck on the inside of the pizza box. "That's why he's madder than a wet pen."

Leatrice nodded at Kate with a puzzled expression on her face.

I barreled on. "I don't think the death had anything to do with our tasting. I think we were just in the wrong place at the wrong time."

"It doesn't look too good to be involved in back-to-back murders." Leatrice pressed her eyebrows together. "That's an awfully big coincidence."

"We're aware of that, Leatrice," I said.

Kate turned to me. "I think you're right, though. Mr. Boyd had such a violent reaction to the poison it must have been something strong. Something that toxic would have smelled so bad he wouldn't have eaten it."

Leatrice's face lit up. "If he was poisoned sometime before the tasting, it could have happened to take effect after he ate the soup. Do you know where he was before he came home?"

"When we looked in his day planner, I didn't look at today's schedule." Kate shook her head. "I focused on what he did the week of the wedding."

Leatrice dabbed at her mouth with a napkin. "Were you girls snooping around?"

"Just a bit," Kate admitted. "We thought this guy who died might have been the person who killed our first client, so we were looking for clues."

"Don't you remember, Kate?" I snapped my fingers. "Mr. Boyd had a doctor's appointment right before he came home. My money says he reacted to something he was given then."

Kate threw her pizza crust back in the box. "Why would his doctor poison him, though?"

Leatrice picked up Kate's crust. "Is he with an HMO?"

Kate and I both gave Leatrice a look.

She shrugged. "Well, that would explain it, dears."

"Maybe his doctor didn't poison him," Kate said. "Lots of people have reactions to medicines."

I dropped my half-eaten slice onto the table. "What if the doctor thought that Mrs. Pierce told Boyd something she shouldn't have? There are two doctors I can think of who might have benefited from Mrs. Pierce's death."

"What are the chances that Boyd goes to one of them?" Kate leaned back on the couch.

Leatrice didn't blink. "Who?"

"It's worth checking out," Kate said as if she'd read my mind.

"Dr. Pierce and Dr. Harriman." I tossed my balled-up cocktail napkin in the pizza box. "The husbands."

CHAPTER 21

"I'm leaving you, Annabelle." Richard stood in the doorway of my bedroom. "I've packed up my things in the kitchen, so your apartment is back to normal."

I sat up in bed, rubbing my eyes. "You're not still mad about last night?" Everything that happened at the Boyd's house rushed back to me. If only it had been a bad dream.

"About the murder you managed to make me the chief suspect for?"

I managed a weak laugh. "I'm sure Reese wasn't serious about that."

"Right, Annabelle. Policemen always joke around at crime scenes. It's part of their charm." Richard turned on his heel and stomped down the hall. I jumped out of bed to follow him.

"Come on, Richard," I begged. "Don't leave like this."

"You're clearly insane if you think I'm going to stick around and get sucked into another harebrained idea that might get me killed or worse . . . sent to prison."

"How could I predict that Boyd would drop dead? This isn't my fault."

Richard flung open the door. "Your idea to do the tasting. Your fault."

"Not my idea to serve soup," I said under my breath.

"I heard that, Annabelle." Richard rolled up the sleeves of his yellow linen shirt in precise folds. "The soup tasted divine. I sampled it myself."

"See? The soup couldn't have been poisoned." I hid behind the door in my tattered red flannel pajamas. Not something I wanted anyone to see.

"Try telling it to the police. On second thought, don't tell anything to the police."

"Maybe I could convince them that you had nothing to do with Mr. Boyd's death if we proved that he'd already been poisoned when he ate the..."

"Stop right there." Richard put his arms out like someone bracing for impact. "Don't talk to the police. As a matter of fact, don't talk to anyone. Especially me. Don't call me. Don't write me."

I sighed. "Richard, you're being ridiculous."

He bent to pick up a box. "If it's ridiculous to want to go one day without being accused of murder, then I'm guilty as charged. You're a trouble magnet. Stay away from me." Richard marched to the top of the stairs and tossed his head back. "Good-bye forever, Annabelle."

I felt as if I were stuck in a gothic novel.

"Come on." I ran after him as he disappeared down the stairs. "Don't go away mad."

Richard sniffed. "I'm going to go where no one can hurt me anymore."

"And where would that be?"

"The Red Door Salon. The one at Fairfax Station next to the Louis Vuitton store." He choked back a sob. "But don't even think of following me."

Oh, for crying out loud. Most of my break-ups with boyfriends hadn't been this dramatic. Halfway down the stairs I remembered the torn seat of my pajama pants and ran back up to my apartment. I listened to Richard's footsteps getting farther away. Fine, if that's the way he wanted it. I started to slam the door when I saw Leatrice's head popping up behind the railing of the staircase.

"I couldn't help overhearing." She walked up to my landing, breathing heavily. For an old lady, she had incredible hearing.

"Come on in, Leatrice." She would, anyway. I slammed the door shut and hoped Richard could hear.

"Don't be upset, dearie. To tell the truth, I've seen this coming for a while."

So much for Leatrice's keen perception. "Richard and I just work together. No romance between us, I promise."

"I thought he'd been staying over." Leatrice moved the plastic tuxedo bags to sit on the couch. I'd forgotten to return them for the fourth day in a row. I hated paying late fees.

"Just as a friend. So I wouldn't be afraid to stay here after the break-in."

"He brought so many things with him, I thought maybe he'd moved in with you."

Who needed a neighborhood watch group when you had Leatrice keeping tabs on you?

I kept my hand over the rip in my pajama bottoms and walked sideways to the kitchen. "Do you want coffee?"

"Not if it's that instant kind," Leatrice grimaced. "I came up to see if you and Kate are planning to question the two doctors today."

"We're going to do a little investigative work at Dr. Harriman's office, but other than that we're keeping a low profile. We don't want people knowing we're still snooping around." I poured the contents of a Nescafe single into a mug. "If Detective Reese questions me one more time, I think he might put me in protective custody."

Leatrice beamed at me. "Protective custody with the detective. That doesn't sound so bad."

I moaned and turned on the electric kettle. I needed coffee to deal with Leatrice.

The phone in my office rang and I looked at the kitchen clock. Ten o'clock. Damn. I'd bet the messages were piling up. If I didn't return their calls right away, my clients would send out a search party. The kind with torches and pitchforks. I skidded down the hall in my socks and grabbed the phone on the third ring, managing a breathless hello.

"Did you get the scan of the cake sketches?"

"Hi, Alexandra." I flipped through the pile of scans I'd printed out yesterday. "I'm glad you're not a crazed bride."

Alexandra laughed. "I sent them to you and the Murphys yesterday. I wanted to know if you'd heard from Mrs. Murphy yet."

I found the cake sketches and sat down at my desk. "I haven't checked my voicemail this morning. Yesterday turned out to be a bit hectic."

"Another deadly client?"

I winced. "You could say that. Okay, I'm looking at the cake designs."

"Do you think I made the bow cake too hideous?"

I studied the drawing of a tall, tiered cake with what appeared to be giant tongues rolling down from the top. "I think it's safe to say she won't choose it."

"Mission accomplished." Alexandra sounded pleased with herself.

"There's my call waiting. I'll let you know what Mrs. Murphy says about the cake."

I clicked over to the other line, half expecting an irate Mrs. Murphy to be screaming about bows.

"What a sexy voice, Annabelle."

Who was this? A pervert who knew my name? I cleared my throat. "Can I help you?"

"It's Maxwell Gray."

The photographer from the Pierce wedding. Famous for photographing society brides and hitting on anything in a skirt. Except his brides. Bad for business, he said.

"Right. How have you been?"

"Swamped with nothing but calls from people wanting to hear about the Pierce murder. I haven't gotten any work done. What have you been up to?"

Setting traps for suspects, sneaking around people's houses for clues, witnessing a client's death. "The usual."

"I wanted to tell you that I rushed the proofs from the wedding. I thought the bride would like to have the portraits of her mother as soon as possible. If you want to look at them before the bride and groom pick them up later this afternoon, stop by the studio."

Most photographers sent me digital images for my website, but Maxwell Gray was old school. Not only did he shoot film, he gave his clients prints. I hoped Maxwell didn't have any ulterior motives in showing me the images.

"Thanks. I'd love to see how the museum photographed. Kate and I have an appointment first, but how about I swing by in a couple of hours?"

"I'll be waiting."

Technically snooping around Dr. Harriman's office with Kate couldn't be considered an appointment, but I shrugged off my little white lie. Seeing the wedding pictures would be just the thing to take my mind off the murder case for a while. And Richard claimed I couldn't stay out of trouble. What did he know?

CHAPTER 22

Kate swung into a parking space in front of the Chevy Chase Cardiology Center, missing the car next to her by mere inches. "So what's the plan again?"

I turned my phone off, feeling less guilty about doing more investigating. I'd spent the entire drive to Dr. Harriman's office on my cell phone with brides and felt completely caught up. I knew that feeling would last five minutes at the most.

"Simple," I explained. "We go into the office and you make a scene to distract the receptionist while I sneak into the records room and see if Dr. Boyd is a patient."

"What kind of scene?"

I slipped on a pair of sunglasses. "Anything you want, as long as it's dramatic."

Kate sighed. "We need Richard for something like this. He's the best at faking illness."

"Well, he's not talking to me at the moment, so we'll have to manage without him." I opened the car door and tried to wedge myself out in the tiny sliver of space Kate had given me.

She stood waiting for me behind the car when I'd finally managed to squeeze out. "Maybe I should go in ahead of you so I can have time to create the distraction, and you can slip by me."

"Sure." I nodded and brushed the dust off my pants. It looked as if I'd polished the entire side of the car with my legs. "The next time I'm going to be the wheelman."

We walked to the front of the steel office building, and I watched Kate go through the revolving glass doors. I looked at my watch and cursed in my head. We should have synchronized. For all I knew, Kate could have run into a cute security guard and not even have been past the front lobby by then.

I watched another couple of minutes tick by and decided to go inside. I found Dr. Harriman's name on the directory in the lobby and got on the elevator to go to the fifth floor. As soon as I stepped off the elevator, I heard Kate's raised voice. Good old Kate. Her distraction sounded very distracting. I felt bad for ever doubting her.

I opened the door to Harriman's offices. Kate stood at the receptionist's desk speaking in a heavy Russian accent that made her sound like Natasha from the Rocky & Bullwinkle cartoons.

"Ma'am, we're a cardiology practice." The receptionist looked as if her patience was wearing thin. "You'll have to put out the cigarette."

My mouth almost fell open as Kate blew out a heavy stream of smoke, then I put a hand over my nose so I wouldn't breathe in the acrid air. Where did she get the cigarette? I knew she didn't smoke. Perhaps I should have been more specific about the type of distraction. At least all eyes were on Kate.

"Look again for name, dah-ling," Kate said to the receptionist.

I slipped through the waiting room and into the back offices as Kate gesticulated wildly with the cigarette. Who knew Kate could do a convincing Russian accent? I would have to give the girl a raise.

I walked down the hall passing three examination rooms and a men's bathroom. Where did they keep their files? I rounded a corner and froze. Dr. Donovan, our groom, stood at the end of the hall, but he appeared to be studying a patient's chart and didn't see me. I took a few steps backward and ducked into the men's bathroom I'd just passed.

I didn't want to try to explain what I was doing creeping around his offices without an appointment. Not to mention why my assistant had suddenly acquired a Russian accent. I groaned to myself thinking of Kate smoking up a storm in the waiting room. I had to get us out of here.

My cell phone began ringing, and I dove into my purse for it. I pushed the talk button and held my breath. I didn't hear anyone in the hall, but I could hear Richard nearly shrieking on the other end of the phone.

"I'm a little busy right now, Richard," I whispered, cupping my hand over my mouth to muffle the sound.

"That's what I hear," he snapped.

"What are you talking about?" I couldn't believe I was arguing with Richard over the phone while hiding in a men's bathroom.

"I went back to your place to make amends and apologize for being a bit sensitive this morning . . ."

"You're forgiven, Richard." I cut him off. "Now can I call you back later?"

"But Leatrice said that you and Kate took off out of here like a shot talking about finding evidence." Richard's voice went up a few octaves. "I know you're not out there getting into more trouble after all that's happened."

I heard voices in the hallway getting closer, and I stepped into one of the stalls and pulled the door closed behind me. "Of course not, Richard."

"Please tell me you have more sense than to get yourself in even deeper trouble than you have already, Annabelle."

I stepped onto the toilet seat and crouched down so my head didn't poke above the stall. My slingbacks would be a dead giveaway if anyone walked in and saw my feet under the door. "Give me a little credit."

"Then why are you whispering?"

I gulped and thought for a second. "Kate and I are at a museum. You know I can't talk normally when I'm in a museum."

"Why are you in a museum?" Richard sounded skeptical. "Which one?"

"The National Museum of Women in the Arts. We're doing a walk-through with a bride."

Richard was silent for a few seconds. "Does she have a caterer?"

I grinned. Always the businessman. "Not yet, but I promise you can do a proposal."

"This doesn't mean I'm not still angry with you," Richard said with a huff. "But send me the information, and I'll work on something for your bride."

He hung up, and I let out a deep breath. I had to get out of there before I got arrested and Kate got dragged off by Homeland Security.

As I stepped down off the seat with one foot, the strap of my other slingback slipped off my heel and the entire shoe dropped into the toilet. Damn. Damn. Damn. I fished my shoe out with one finger and dropped it on the floor, then opened the door to the stall and looked around the bathroom. Two gleaming metal hand dryers were mounted on the walls with not a paper towel in sight. Why was I not surprised?

I slid my foot into the dripping shoe and leaned against the door, listening for voices. Nothing. I poked my head out of the bathroom. The coast was clear. I squished down the hall and dashed through the waiting room, where a group of irritated nurses surrounded Kate. I caught her eye as I slipped out the door and motioned for her to follow me.

I held the elevator until Kate got inside, the two of us breathing as though we'd run a race. We didn't speak until we were out of the building and in the car.

Kate put the key in the ignition and turned to me. "Well, did you find anything?"

"No," I shook my head, coughing from the cigarette smoke that emanated from Kate's clothes. "I ran into the groom before I could find the files."

"What was he doing here?" Kate stared at my feet. "And why is your shoe leaking?"

"You don't want to know." I gave a shudder. "Donovan shares a practice with his father-in-law, remember?"

"I'd totally forgotten." Kate slumped over the wheel. "So all of that was for nothing?"

"Well, it wasn't a total waste." I took a deep breath. "I learned that you can do a decent Russian accent."

Kate grinned. "What can I say? The men love it. Now what?"

"Well, you still have your meeting with Jack from the White House, right?"

Kate perked up. "You're right. Maybe he'll be able to tell me something good. He's a big fan of my accent, you know."

"That may be more than I needed to know. You're going to be subtle, right?" I put on my seat belt as Kate flung the car in reverse. "We don't want word getting around that we're trying to solve this case."

"I'm always subtle, dah-ling," she said in her Russian accent.

I swallowed hard. "Just drop me back at the office so I don't have to watch."

"What are you going to do while I'm pumping Jack for information?"

"I got a call from Maxwell Gray this morning. The pictures from the Pierce wedding are in, so I'm going to look at them before the bride and groom pick them up."

"You're going to see pictures of Clara right before she died? How creepy."

"I didn't think of it that way," I said. "I figured we spent enough time planning the wedding. We might as well get some shots of the decor for our web site."

"Just be careful you don't get more than you bargained for," Kate warned. "You know photographers in this city."

"Not as well as you do, I'm afraid."

There were few straight men in our business and they all seemed to be photographers. Kate had dated enough of them to know to keep her distance.

She arched an eyebrow. "Take my word for it, then."

"Don't worry, Kate. Everything will be fine."

Kate gunned it out of the parking space. "Why does that sound familiar?"

CHAPTER 23

My cell phone rang, and I hunted for it on the passenger-side floor as I merged from M Street onto the Key Bridge. By the time Kate had dropped me off at my car in Georgetown, I was already running late to meet Maxwell. I'd thrown my purse in the front seat and half the contents of my bag had spilled out.

I had one hand on the wheel and one groping among the loose papers on the floor where I'd last spied my phone. I heard the rings slide under the passenger seat and into the back. Reaching behind me, I scooped up the phone, keeping one hand on the wheel. A car honked as I veered into its lane for a moment. Almost as bad as Kate's driving.

"Wedding Belles. This is Annabelle." Office calls were being forwarded to my cell phone, so I wouldn't get too far behind with work.

"Are you at Maxwell's?" Kate asked. I heard car horns around her, and knew she must be in traffic, too.

"Not yet." I took a right off of Key Bridge onto the GW Parkway. The thick green trees created a lush corridor for me to drive through. The perfect day for a convertible. Not that I didn't love my old Volvo, but I dreamed of being less practical. "How's your meeting with Jack?"

"I'm running a little late. I'm not sure how much more he can tell me about Boyd, though. Unless the man ran up and down the halls announcing the name of his doctor, this might be pointless."

"See what you can find out. I'm just curious."

"Don't tell Richard," Kate said. "He'll have a fit."

"This isn't the same thing as snooping. You're just chatting with an old friend." I accelerated on the gentle curves of the road, and then looked out my rolled-down passenger-side window. I watched a crew team practice in the Potomac River, their boat cutting the smooth water, as I breathed in the cool crisp air.

"You keep telling yourself that," Kate said. "Okay, I've got to run. Call me when you're done at Maxwell's studio. And be careful, Annie."

"I doubt the murderer is after me, Kate."

"I'm talking about Maxwell."

I laughed, turned off the phone, and tossed it on the seat next to me. Maxwell Gray proclaimed himself the ladies' man of the wedding industry. Not that he had a lot of competition. He looked like a cover model for a romance novel, only older and much more weathered. I didn't consider his silk-shirt-and-gold-medallion brand of sexiness much of a turn-on, although I'd heard I was in a minority among my colleagues. I cringed at the thought.

I almost missed the exit for the Chain Bridge and had to brake hard not to fly off the sharp curve of the ramp. Too busy thinking about Maxwell and his conquests. I glanced at the directions in my lap to make sure I hadn't passed his studio. I drove by the entrance to the CIA and continued through the primarily suburban area until I came to a cluster of office buildings. I turned into the parking lot and found a space in front of Maxwell Gray Photography.

His studio had large front windows filled with portraits of brides in various dramatic settings. How had he convinced a bride in her wedding gown to lie down in the middle of a wheat field? Most of my brides were afraid a ride in a limousine would wrinkle their dresses. Forget rolling around in a field.

I walked into the studio. A chime signaled my arrival. Maxwell came around a corner and advanced on me, taking my hand and pressing it to his lips. He wore his ash blond hair long and brushed off his face, the back perfectly smooth. He did a better job with a blow dryer than I did. He had an unnaturally thin nose, and teeth so perfect they had to have been capped. He ran his tongue across his top lip as he released my hand. The Pierce photos had better be nothing short of amazing, I thought to myself.

"Annabelle, you're as lovely as ever." He gave me a sticky smile and waved me into the appointment room where he met with all his clients. A low glass table held all his sample albums. Two red velvet chairs flanked a royal blue velvet couch. Fringed lamps, perched on a pair of glass end tables, and palm trees filled the corners of the room. I couldn't shake the feeling of visiting a harem.

Maxwell pulled a bottle of champagne out of a standing metal bucket. "Can I offer you a glass?"

"I'm really here to see the pictures. I'm not much of a drinker. Not at noon, anyway."

"I thought we might get to know each other a little better."

Perfect. Just when I thought the week couldn't get any worse, the slimiest photographer in Washington starts hitting on me.

I motioned to the ornately framed wall portraits around the room. "Beautiful work, Mr. Gray."

"Call me Maxwell." He poured himself a glass of champagne. Obviously he didn't have a problem drinking before noon. "All the other wedding planners do."

I'll bet they do. I forced myself to smile. "It was nice to finally work with you, Maxwell." And to finally have a client with the budget to afford a society wedding photographer.

"I photographed Clara's family for years. Long before she became a Pierce."

Maybe this visit wouldn't be a total waste, after all. It shouldn't be too hard, I thought, to finesse some information about Mrs. Pierce from him. I wished I'd paid more attention to Kate's flirting instruction.

"I changed my mind about the champagne." I tried to bat my eyelashes, hoping that Kate would be proud. "I'd love a glass."

Maxwell filled a crystal flute with champagne and passed it to me. He raised his glass in a toast. "To possibilities."

The possibility that I won't sue you for sexual harassment. I smiled, and took a tiny sip. Maxwell drained his glass.

"So how long did you know Mrs. Pierce?" I sat down on one of the chairs. He chose the couch and reclined on it so that his black silk shirt fell open to one side, exposing the top part of his chest. I'd never seen such impeccably coiffed chest hair. He must have used mousse.

"I started photographing her family for Elizabeth's sweet sixteen party, so it's been about ten years." Maxwell refilled his glass. "Back when she was Clara Harriman."

"I noticed how well you dealt with her." I pretended to take a drink. "Especially when she got upset at you for taking a shot of her bad side."

"I can be honest with you, right, Annabelle?" He didn't wait for my answer. "That woman made my life a living hell every time I worked with her. If she didn't have so much money and so many rich friends with marriageable daughters, I'd have told her to find another photographer."

"But you never seemed upset."

"I work hard to look so calm . . ." Maxwell chugged his second glass. He noticed my nearly full glass and motioned for me to drink.

When he turned to retrieve the champagne bottle, I dumped the contents of my glass in the base of the nearest palm tree. "So I guess you saw a lot of interaction between Mrs. Pierce and her family."

"If you mean did they all hate her, too, the answer is yes."

I leaned close. "Not her daughter, though?"

"No, not Elizabeth." He spilled a little champagne as he reached over to fill my flute. "And not Elizabeth's fiancé, either. Clara adored him, and who wouldn't like someone who adores you?"

"But everyone else hated her?"

"With good reason." Maxwell turned the empty bottle upside down in the wine bucket. "She ignored her own husband and had made her ex-husband's life miserable when she divorced him. Harriman and his new wife were blacklisted from any important social function for years."

"Which husband do you think had the better motive to kill her?"

He leaned over and put a hand on my knee, giving me what could only be called a leer. "Are we playing detective?"

I slid my knee away from his grip. "No, but I thought that if anyone would be clever enough to figure out who killed Mrs. Pierce, it would be you."

He puffed his chest out, making his abundance of chest hair seem even more prominent. "You're quite perceptive, Annabelle. I do have a theory."

"About which of her husbands killed her?"

"I'd pick Dr. Harriman. Clara enjoyed making him suffer during their divorce. She especially loved spreading rumors about the new wife. I heard the new Mrs. H had to go on antidepressants after hearing that half the town believed she had a love child with a televangelist."

Nothing Mrs. Pierce did shocked me anymore. "I can see how the Harrimans might hold a grudge, but I thought the divorce happened five years ago."

"Clara never stopped spreading rumors to get them ostracized from Washington society. She even refused to invite the new wife to the wedding." Maxwell eyed his empty glass, and his mouth curled into a pout.

"I do remember Dr. Harriman's name being on the invitation alone, but I didn't think anything of it," I said more to myself than to Maxwell.

"No one wanted to cross Clara." He leaned over so far he slid off the edge of the couch and caught himself with one hand. "You should've heard her talking the day she came in to review the group photos she wanted for the wedding."

"About her ex-husband?"

"No, even better." Maxwell licked his lips. "She told me about an affair she'd been having with a political big-wig."

I tried to act surprised. "An affair?"

"The last in a long string." Maxwell got to his feet, swaying as though he stood on the deck of a ship. "Why don't I get us another bottle of champagne? I always keep several chilling in the refrigerator."

I'll bet you do. I waited until he left the room, and then twisted around to empty my champagne into the palm tree for the second time. Poor thing would probably die from alcohol poisoning.

"She bragged about the affair, then?" I raised my voice so he could hear me in the next room.

"She always bragged about the men she fooled around with." His voice sounded muffled and far away. Did he have his head in the refrigerator? "This particular one may have been her best work ever."

"What do you mean?"

"Clara relished having power over people and making them squirm. Some people knit for a hobby, Clara did this." Maxwell's voice sounded strained, as though he were wrestling with the champagne cork. "When I saw her, she told me how upset this guy had gotten when she threatened to go public with the affair."

"So she planned to tell his wife?"

"No, his wife already knew." The champagne cork gave a loud pop from the other room. "Clara wanted to leak it to the media and ruin his political career. Apparently he had aspirations of running for office."

I paused with my upside-down champagne glass over the tree. "Wait a second. His wife already knew?"

"That's what Clara seemed most happy about." Maxwell's words slurred together. "The wife confronted her and made all kinds of threats. Clara laughed about it. Said that dried-up prude didn't scare her."

I dropped my glass and it landed with a thud in the potting soil. Mrs. Boyd knew. This changed everything.

CHAPTER 24

I hurried to pick the champagne flute out of the dirt and set it on the table. I brushed away a clump of soil before Maxwell returned to the room holding out a new bottle of champagne like a proud father.

"I've been saving this particular bottle for a special occasion." He sat down on the couch and leaned toward me. "I think today qualifies."

Unbelievable. This guy thought he was getting somewhere with me.

"Tell me about the fight that Mrs. Pierce had with Mrs. Boyd." I held out my glass and tried not to look repulsed. "When did it happen?"

"Did I mention the other woman's name?"

Damn! Hopefully Maxwell would think he'd let it slip instead of me. "You weren't supposed to tell me?"

Maxwell ran a hand over his slicked-back hair. "Not that Clara cared, but I've always prided myself on being discreet."

Right. He might as well have put out a newsletter.

I put a finger to my lips. "This will just be between you and me, Maxwell. Our little secret."

His face flushed, possibly from the champagne. "It happened the day before her daughter's wedding. Mrs. Boyd came to Clara's house in the afternoon and made a huge spectacle of herself."

This sounded nothing like the tight-lipped Helen Boyd I'd met. "Why? What did she do?"

"It started out calmly with Mrs. Boyd asking Clara to leave her husband alone."

"Which Mrs. Pierce refused to do?" I prodded.

"Of course." Maxwell adjusted himself on the couch, stretching from end to end. "Mrs. Boyd got angry and called her all sorts of names. Not that any of them were new to Clara."

I smiled, vicariously enjoying the thought of Mrs. Boyd using every name in the book. "How did Mrs. Pierce react?"

"She laughed at the woman. When Mrs. Boyd threatened to tell Mr. Pierce, Clara told her she didn't care. Said she wanted Mrs. Boyd's husband, not her own."

"Ouch. Poor Mrs. Boyd." I picked up my glass of champagne and noticed clumps of dirt floating on the top.

"That's when things got ugly. Mrs. Boyd started screaming that if Clara tried to ruin things she'd kill her."

"Mrs. Boyd threatened her life?"

"Clara didn't take it too seriously, though." Maxwell tipped his glass back to let the last few drops roll into his mouth. "Called her a noisy little mouse and laughed about the whole thing."

I'll bet she's not laughing now.

"Mrs. Pierce told you all of this?" I covered the top of my crystal flute with my hand so he wouldn't notice the dirt.

He nodded, his eyes drooping. "Here we've spent the whole time gossiping about Mrs. Pierce when you came to see my photography."

I'd forgotten about the pictures. I looked at my watch. "I've got a few minutes to spare."

Maxwell pulled a small, square box from under the coffee table with one arm. He barely shifted from his position on the sofa as he handed it to me, and then closed his eyes. If I'd finished a bottle and a half of champagne, I'd have felt like taking a nap, too.

"So these are all the proofs?" I took the lid off the box and flipped through the enormous stack of snapshot-size prints. There must have been several hundred photos. No way I could go through them all at once. Maxwell didn't answer me, and I glanced up.

His head lolled to the side and his mouth hung open. Passed out. I put my finger under his nose and let out a sigh of relief when I felt his breathing. I couldn't bear another dead body.

"I've got to be running, Maxwell," I whispered so he wouldn't wake up. "I'm going to take the proofs with me and bring them back later, okay?"

No response. At least I asked. I operated on the philosophy that it's better to ask for forgiveness than permission, anyway.

I walked out on my toes, carrying the box of photos in front of me. When I got in my car, I picked up my phone, pressing the speed dial number for Kate's cell.

"Hi, Annabelle." Caller ID. "Did you escape in one piece?"

"He passed out before he could make his move." I heard the sound of clattering silverware. "Where are you?"

"Hold on a second. Let me go outside." The background noise disappeared. "Jack wanted to take me to lunch, and he's been so helpful I couldn't turn him down."

I tucked the photo box into my oversized nylon purse then backed out of the parking lot and pulled into traffic. "You're a true martyr. Where did he take you?"

"The Palm."

One of the places in D.C. to see and be seen. Kate would fit in beautifully.

"Tough life. Be sure to have the crabmeat cocktail."

"Okay, okay. Don't you want to hear what I found out?"

In my excitement over the Clara Pierce and Helen Boyd fight, I'd forgotten about suspecting one of Clara's husbands of poisoning Mr. Boyd. "Of course."

"Jack didn't know anything about Boyd's doctor, but he said that Mr. Boyd seemed fine when he left work."

"Which gives more strength to our theory that Boyd wasn't poisoned until later." I switched the phone to my other ear. "But I'm not convinced that his doctor killed him anymore."

"I'm not done," Kate said. "Since Jack wasn't any help, I called both doctors' offices. I pretended to be Boyd's scheduler and tried to set up an appointment. Dr. Pierce's office had no record of Boyd, but Dr. Harriman's office did. I made an appointment for Boyd for two weeks from today."

"You're kidding." I merged onto the GW Parkway and got in the fast lane. I couldn't believe it had been that simple to find out.

"Hold on. It gets even better. The police were thinking along the same lines we were."

"What do you mean?"

"They arrested Dr. Harriman an hour ago."

"I don't believe it." I swerved out of my lane for a second, and then grabbed the wheel tightly. "Now I'm really confused."

"What do you mean? It makes perfect sense. He had motive and opportunity for both murders, even if he is handsome."

"I guess you're right. But after visiting Maxwell, I'm not convinced that

Harriman is the only one with motive and opportunity." I moved into the right lane to let an SUV pass.

"Spit it out, Annabelle."

"According to Maxwell, Mrs. Pierce told him that she and Mrs. Boyd had a huge fight the day before the wedding."

"About what? I didn't think Mrs. Boyd knew about the affair."

"She knew, all right." The dark SUV stayed right behind me with its lights on. I sped up. What kind of jerk put high beams on in the daytime?

"That explains why she acted so cold to her husband at the tasting. I wonder if he knew about the fight."

"It happened on the same day that Mrs. Pierce fought with Mr. Boyd. I wonder which came first. Mrs. Boyd's fight might have been the reason that Mrs. Pierce went to see Mr. Boyd. Or maybe, Mrs. Boyd found out about the fight with her husband and went over to have it out."

"It's kind of like the chicken or the leg," Kate said.

I rolled my eyes and glanced in my rearview mirror. The SUV had matched my speed and driven so close to me I could see the driver hunched behind the sun visor. I couldn't make out the face. Too much glare.

I changed lanes. Maybe if I could speed up enough I'd lose this maniac. "Mrs. Boyd threatened to kill her when Mrs. Pierce said she'd expose her husband."

"It sounds like Mrs. Boyd got more upset about her husband's political career being ruined than she did over the affair."

The SUV dropped back and merged into my lane.

"I didn't think of it that way. I guess you're right, Kate. She said something about Mrs. Pierce ruining things. Probably not talking about her marriage."

"I'll bet she's one of these political wives who's put as much into her husband's career as he has. There's no way she'd let another woman take that away from her."

"So much for my bright idea of Mrs. Boyd being the killer. She might have killed Mrs. Pierce, but she wouldn't have killed her husband." I stepped on the gas to try to pull away from the SUV. I passed the rectangular brown sign that informed me the Key Bridge exit was a mile and a half away. Not much farther.

"Who's to say there aren't two murderers on the loose?"

"That makes me feel a lot better. Thanks, Kate." I swerved into the right lane as I drove across a short bridge. I jerked forward as something hit my car from behind. The SUV. "That idiot just hit me."

"What? Are you okay?"

I stayed in my lane as a few cars entered the highway from the right. "Yeah. I'm going to pull over at the exit for Key Bridge. I don't know what this creep's problem is."

I lurched forward again, this time much harder, and my head hit the steering wheel. The cell phone fell onto my lap, and I tried to pick it up again while the SUV pulled alongside me. I saw the sign for the Key Bridge ahead and sped up. If I could just make it to the exit. I accelerated, driving under a wide concrete bridge, but the SUV swerved into my lane, knocking me off the road. I barely missed going into the concrete bridge, and my car sped toward a patch of tall grass. I screamed, lifted my hands in front of my face, and slammed straight into the Key Bridge sign.

CHAPTER 25

"I flattened it." I sat up; one hand on my forehead where a throbbing bump had developed. "The sign for Key Bridge is gone."

Even if I couldn't hear the beeping of medical equipment, the antiseptic smell would be an instant tip-off that I was in a hospital.

"Lie back down. The doctor doesn't want you moving, in case you have a concussion." Kate stood next to my bed in the emergency room of Georgetown Hospital. The white curtain had been drawn around us halfway, but we could watch doctors and nurses rush by. Kate looked frazzled. I hated to think how fast she'd driven to get here before my ambulance arrived in the ER.

"Thanks for calling 911," I said. "How did you know where I crashed, though?"

"You told me where you were exiting, and then I heard screaming and scraping metal." Kate shuddered. "I put two and two together."

"Is it my head injuries, or did you say that right?"

"You must be delirious." Kate smiled and handed me a paper cup of water.

I leaned back on the thin pillows. "Maybe this is what heaven is like. No mangled expressions."

"Then you must be dying."

A strangled cry came from behind the curtain, and Richard rushed to the bed. He threw himself across my lap. "If you die, I'll never forgive myself."

"Richard, I'm okay. I'm not dying."

Richard lifted his head from the sheet. "You're not? But I heard Kate say you were."

"We were joking around." Kate patted his back. "She's fine, aside from some scrapes and bruises."

"I don't think it's funny to joke about dying." Richard pulled himself up to his full height, and I noticed that his eyes were rimmed in red. He dabbed at his nose.

"We're sorry," I said. "We didn't know you were there. How did you hear about me?"

"Kate called me on her way here. Hysterical. I drove as fast as I could, but obviously not as fast as some people." He elbowed Kate.

"You two didn't have to make all this fuss. I'm fine. My airbags worked." I touched my tender forehead. "I must have ended up punching myself in the head when they deployed."

Richard threw up his arms. "Will you stop being so damn independent for two seconds and admit that you need us?"

"Sorry." I reached for his hand. "Thanks for coming. Especially after everything I've done."

Richard's eyes watered. "It's not your fault, Annie. Kate's right. You didn't force me into anything. To be honest, I enjoyed trying to solve the case."

"You did?" Kate raised an eyebrow.

"Not the part where the police put me on the suspect list, but the rest of it was a bit of an adventure."

"I don't mind adventure." I propped myself up on my elbows. "I do mind being run off the road and almost killed."

Richard's jaw dropped. "Run off the road?"

"Not an accident?" Kate's voice sounded unsteady.

"That SUV wanted me dead. The driver didn't just bump my car; he rammed it from the back and the side."

"Who would want to do that to you?" Richard held his fingertips over his bottom lip.

"Someone who thinks I'm getting too close to finding out who killed Mrs. Pierce and Mr. Boyd."

"But, Annabelle," Richard glanced at Kate. "They already caught the killer."

"Maybe, maybe not," I said.

Kate pulled the curtains the rest of the way around my bed. "You think the murderer is still on the loose and is trying to kill you, too?"

I raised an eyebrow. "Don't you think it's a little coincidental that my apartment gets broken into and I get nearly killed all in the span of a few days?"

"But the police arrested our number-one suspect," Kate insisted, perching on the edge of the bed.

"Maybe we were wrong." I looked from Kate to Richard. "Maybe the police are wrong."

Richard patted my hand. "Maybe we should leave well enough alone."

"With someone still out there trying to kill me?"

"Why would the murderer want to kill you?" Kate shook her head. "We've just been playing a guessing game. It's not like you have any hard evidence."

"We might know more than we think. The murderer must be aware that we've been hunting around for clues. Maybe they're scared we'll find something or maybe we already have."

"Annabelle, you could be right." Richard poured himself a glass of water from the plastic pitcher. "We weren't scared when someone broke into your apartment because we thought they were after something."

"Exactly, Richard," I said. "If they didn't find what they wanted, they must assume I still have it."

Kate gave me a weak grin. "Instead of trying to get it back again, they're just trying to get rid of you."

"I must have something that the killer considers a threat. But what?"

Richard tapped his fingers on the metal bar of the hospital bed. "Heaven knows what could be in that mess in your apartment."

"So much for the outpouring of sympathy." I frowned at him.

Richard crumpled up his paper cup. "I think we have two options. We can either take these attempts on Annabelle seriously and forget about the murders, or we can put all our information together and find out why the killer considers us a threat."

"Everything has happened to Annabelle. Maybe the killer doesn't consider us a threat." Kate pointed to herself and Richard.

"That's fine with me." Richard let one side of his mouth curl up in a smirk.

"Hey," I cried. "What happened to my loyal side-kicks?"

"I think you should make the decision, Annabelle," Richard said. "After all, you're the one who seems to be in the most danger."

I touched the knot on my head and thought about Mrs. Pierce's twisted body and Mr. Boyd's purple face lying in a bowl of soup. "I don't want to let anyone get away with murder."

BOOK 1: BETTER OFF WED

"Especially when they're killing off our business." Kate winked at me.

"Then we're back on the trail?" Richard went pale behind his smile.

"To be totally honest," Kate admitted. "Annabelle and I were never off it."

"Really?" Richard's smile faltered. "You've been poking around today even after what happened last night?"

"Wait until you hear what Kate and I found out, though."

Richard wagged a finger at me. "You're lucky I'm too happy that you're alive to be mad."

"We've got lots to do." Kate threw back the curtain. "Let's get you out of here."

CHAPTER 26

Leatrice stood underneath a huge bouquet of helium balloons in my living room. The balloons all read GET WELL SOON in various color combinations and bounced around the ceiling, their ribbons hanging down around Leatrice's face. She wore a necklace made entirely of the little metal bells, and she jingled as she ran to greet me.

"Kate called me and told me about your car accident. I've been worried sick."

I pried her from around my waist. "I'm fine, Leatrice. No major damage."

"The doctor did say you need rest." Kate led me to the couch. "Your concussion means no running around."

"He said mild concussion."

"A concussion? Oh, dear." Leatrice wrung her hands. "Don't worry. I can stay with you as long as you need me."

I felt a miraculous recovery coming on. "Thanks, but Kate's going to spend the night to make sure I don't slip into a coma or something."

"Well, I'd be more than happy to keep you girls company," Leatrice chirped. "We could stay up all night and watch my favorite episodes of *Matlock*."

The coma didn't sound so bad. "How did you get in my apartment, Leatrice?"

"You gave me a spare key ages ago in case you ever got locked out, remember?"

I must have had temporary insanity. "Not really, but it's probably the concussion."

"I wanted to surprise you when you came home from the hospital. Do you like the balloons?"

"They're great." I smiled at Leatrice. "It's not like I stayed in the hospital more than a few hours, though."

"I'm glad they didn't keep you overnight." Leatrice sat on the arm of the couch. "The food at the Georgetown Hospital isn't so good. Now Suburban Hospital has decent food, but I hear the service is terribly slow."

No doubt in the Zagat guide under hospital cafeterias. "We're not in luck here, either," Kate said from the kitchen. "Looks like a couple of leftover slices of pizza and a few cans of Coke. Is this lettuce?"

Richard walked in the front door that still stood ajar, plastic grocery bags hanging off his hands. "Don't worry. I thought things in your kitchen might be desperate since I cleared out, so I stopped at the store." He went into the kitchen and began unpacking the bags with Kate. I reached for a cushion, and Leatrice leapt up to put it behind my back. An ideal setup, if my head didn't hurt so much and Leatrice didn't jingle each time she moved.

"Kate mentioned that the car accident may not have been an accident at all," Leatrice said.

"You and Kate had a nice, long chat, didn't you?" I raised my voice to be sure Kate could hear me. She pretended to be busy with the groceries.

"After our pizza party last night, I gave her my phone number. In case she ever needed anything. Good thing I did, too."

"Yeah, good thing." I tried to catch Kate's eye to give her a dirty look.

"So the other car ran you off the road? Were they trying to get rid of you?"

"I don't think you should get caught up in this mess any more than you already are, Leatrice. See where trying to solve these murders got me?"

Her face fell.

"Oh, come on, Annabelle." Kate came from the kitchen and sat on the chair. "Tell her our theories."

"I can help you figure it, too," Leatrice insisted. "I always solve the crime before Jessica Fletcher does."

"See? It can't hurt to run our ideas by someone else." Kate kicked off her heels. "Two heads are better than a nun, anyway."

"Young people today have such colorful expressions." Leatrice giggled and patted Kate on the arm. "I'll have to remember that one."

The thought of Leatrice running around using Kate's garbled sayings made me grin and rub my aching head simultaneously.

Leatrice took a seat beside me. "Do you think the person behind the two murders is the same person who tried to kill you?"

"I'm not sure if the murderer was trying to kill me or just scare me off the trail." I reached for the bowl of personalized candy hearts and popped one in my mouth. My version of comfort food.

"Regardless, your car crash must mean we're getting close," Kate said.

"Who are your suspects?" Leatrice found a pen and legal pad in the piles of papers on the floor next to her feet.

"We keep coming back to Mrs. Pierce's two husbands," I said. "Her ex-husband, Dr. Harriman, who hated her for making his life miserable during their divorce, and her current husband, Dr. Pierce, who had an affair with his wife's best friend."

"We'll call them the Ex and the Sex." Leatrice made a column for each on her pad of paper. "What's the evidence against each one?"

Kate tucked her feet under her. "Well, Dr. Harriman was arrested today for his ex-wife's murder."

"I'd say that's pretty strong evidence." Leatrice dropped the pad in her lap. "You think the police got the wrong person?"

"He'd been one of our top suspects, but he was arrested before someone tried to kill me today," I said. "If we go with the theory that the person who committed both of these murders is also out to get rid of me, then Dr. Harriman can't be the killer."

Leatrice picked up her paper again and gave my shoulder a pat. "Of course I believe you if you say someone tried to kill you, but let's look at the evidence against all the suspects before we eliminate anyone. No stone should go unturned."

"God forbid we skip a step in the private investigator correspondence course," Kate muttered out of the corner of her mouth.

Leatrice ignored Kate. "So let's get back to the two husbands."

"First off, it had to be someone who knew she took blood-pressure medicine." I took the pillow from behind my head and sat up. "Both Dr. Harriman and Dr. Pierce fit the bill."

"We thought Dr. Harriman was the most likely killer," Kate said. "He attended the wedding and examined the body before the paramedics arrived. He also had an appointment with Mr. Boyd less than an hour before he died."

Leatrice kept her eyes on her notebook. "Motive and opportunity."

Kate sighed. "On the other hand, she treated Dr. Pierce horribly. He and Clara's best friend were having an affair and they won't waste any time now that she's gone. Also, they were both missing at the wedding when we found Clara, so they could have planned it together."

"A buddy system for murder." Leatrice tapped her pen on the legal pad.

"Don't forget what you found out about Helen Boyd, Annabelle." Kate sat forward and rested her elbows on her knees. Richard joined us from the kitchen, and I remembered that I'd been too dazed in the hospital to tell him my latest scoop.

"Mrs. Boyd knew all about her husband's affair with Mrs. Pierce. Mrs. Pierce wanted to blow the cover off the whole thing and destroy his career."

Richard drew his breath in sharply. "Why?"

"Because she could," I reminded him. "This is Mrs. Pierce we're talking about, after all. No loyalty. No forgiveness. Maybe Boyd did something to make her angry and she wanted to punish him. Who knows?"

"You're sure Mrs. Boyd knew?" Richard pressed.

I nodded. "The day before the wedding she showed up on Mrs. Pierce's doorstep threatening all sorts of things, including murder."

"I have a hard time imagining prim Mrs. Boyd making threats," Richard said.

Kate's eyes widened. "Where were you when she thought you killed her husband?"

"In a state of catatonic shock, I think." Richard put a hand on his forehead and swayed. "It's all fuzzy."

"She threatened to kill Mrs. Pierce," I assured them. "And called her every nasty word you can imagine."

"How marvelous." Richard smiled. "I bet I'd have thought of a few more choice words for her, though."

"Did anyone hear Mrs. Boyd say she'd kill your client?" Leatrice asked me.

"No, but Mrs. Pierce told Maxwell the whole story."

"Then it's hearsay." Leatrice made a note. "Not enough to build a case around."

"All this thinking has made my head pound." I picked up my purse to retrieve the pain medication the hospital had given me. "Could you get me some water, Richard?"

He went into the kitchen, and I heard him searching for a clean glass. I opened my purse and took out the small box of wedding photos. "I almost forgot. The whole reason I went to see Maxwell Gray. The pictures from the Pierce wedding."

Kate took the box from me. "Are there any good shots of the Corcoran Gallery? We spent so much time designing the event."

I shrugged. "I didn't get a chance to look at them carefully."

"I wonder if we'll find anything in the pictures." Leatrice dropped her pad and pen and ran over to stand behind Kate.

"What are you hoping to find?" I asked.

"That concussion must have really affected you, dear," Leatrice looked up from the pictures. "I'm searching for clues to the murder."

I forgot all about my headache.

"Good thing these photos were in your purse or they'd be at the mechanic's with your car," Kate said.

My car had been hauled off to a Georgetown body shop in the hopes that my crumpled bumper and mangled grate could be repaired. I'd be without a car for at least a week. Not that I felt like driving anytime soon.

Leatrice thumbed through the first few photos. "What kind of wedding pictures are these? Who takes pictures of the food?"

Richard hurried from the kitchen and nudged Leatrice to scoot over. "I asked Maxwell to get a few close-ups of the hors d'oeuvres and my displays. Let me see."

"The best way to find clues will be to find pictures of the victim." Leatrice instructed us. "See who she's with and who's near her. If we're lucky, we'll find some of our suspects lurking in the background."

"Have you ever seen such a spectacular blend of color on a sushi station?" Richard held up a picture. "The sweet sushi is a work of art. All my idea, naturally."

I handed Leatrice a print of Mrs. Pierce being escorted down the aisle by a handsome groomsman. "This is the victim. Clara Pierce."

"That's some hairdo." Leatrice studied the cotton candy helmet. Bold words coming from a woman as old as she was with jet-black hair.

"I've got to hand it to Maxwell," Richard said. "He captured the true beauty of the chive-tied beggar's purse."

Leatrice strained to look at the photo in Richard's hand. "You serve food in a purse?"

Richard groaned and shook his head. "A beggar's purse is a term we use when we fill a crepe and tie it up into a tiny bundle. For these we used a long chive to make the bow on top. Have you ever seen anything so adorable?"

Leatrice took the picture from Richard. "Doesn't look like any purse I've ever owned."

Richard snatched the picture back and muttered under his breath as he continued to admire it.

Kate passed a pile of prints to me. "There are lots of pictures with Clara, but most of them are portraits at the church."

"She looks fine in all of these," I said. "If she'd already been poisoned, it hadn't kicked in yet."

Leatrice held a photo an inch from her nose. "If I wanted to poison someone, I'd do it during a party where it's easier to slip it in food or drink. Not at a church."

"These are gorgeous table shots, Annabelle." Richard held up a square picture of one of the dining tables taken before the guests descended for dinner.

I took the picture from Richard and held it by the edges. Looking at the breathtaking flowers and coordinating Limoges china, I felt a twinge of regret. Each wedding had something go not quite right. Off-key soloist. Mediocre food. Late limousines. But not this wedding. We'd planned for a year so it would be perfect. It had been, except for the dead body.

"Check this out." Kate peered over Leatrice's shoulder. "The bride with Clara and Dr. Harriman."

"Neither parent looks happy," Leatrice said. "Good thing the daughter stood between them."

"I must get a copy of this one." Richard clapped his hands. "The caviar in the quail egg is like a tiny Faberge masterpiece, if I do say so myself."

"Here's a classic." I lifted a photo of Clara and Bev Tripton out of the stack. They held each other around the waist and each had a drink in the other hand. "They seem pretty chummy," Kate said.

Leatrice took the photo. "The victim's eyes are bloodshot. Maybe the poison had started to take effect."

"Here I am setting up the Indonesian satay station." Richard waved a photo in front of me. "Do you think that jacket makes me look hippy?"

I didn't bother to look. "No."

"I don't care for the way the side vents hang. I may have to cycle that suit out of the lineup."

"Another one of Mrs. Pierce with a drink in hand," I said.

"It appears to be the same drink, Annabelle." Leatrice pointed to the glass in Mrs. Pierce's hand. "See? Same type glass and same two little plastic straws."

"What?" Richard snapped his head up. "Hand me those pictures."

"Is there a problem?" Kate asked.

He jabbed at the photos. "You'd better believe there's a problem. These straws shouldn't be here."

"I'm not sure I follow you." I watched Richard stand up and take huge strides around the room, mumbling about straws. Maybe he'd finally lost it.

"I never use plastic straws at my parties. It would ruin the look of the entire event to have guests running around with tiny poles sticking out of their drinks."

"Curious." Leatrice took the two photos from Richard as he sank back onto the couch.

"I have no idea how those hideous things could have landed on my bars."

"Do we have any pictures of the bars?" I asked.

Kate and I sifted through the proofs, fanning them out on the coffee table.

"Right here." Kate held up a shot of a bar draped in white shimmery organza. The glasses were arranged in front with the bottles of liquor behind them. Small glasses of olives, onions, and lime wedges sat on both ends. No straws.

Richard inspected the photograph, and then tossed it back on the table. "Thank God. They didn't come from me."

Kate threw her hands in the air. "Then where did they come from?"

Leatrice slapped her knee. "I'll bet the murderer brought them. What better way to get poison into a drink?"

"If the poison was in powder form, the killer could have packed it into straws, dropped them in her drink, and let the poison dissolve," I said.

Kate leapt up. "Mrs. Pierce wouldn't think twice about it. Who'd notice a detail as insignificant as plastic straws but Richard?"

Richard appeared stuck somewhere between a smile and a frown.

"We've discovered how the murderer did it," I said. "Now we just have one tiny detail remaining."

"What's that?" Kate asked.

Leatrice let out her breath slowly. "Figure out which of the suspects *is* the murderer."

CHAPTER 27

"I think we should call the police in on this." Richard went into the kitchen and poured a glass of water. He remembered my headache. I took two pills out of the orange plastic cylinder then watched Richard drain the glass. Maybe not.

"Isn't the detective going to be upset with us?" Kate asked. "He told us not to go snooping around."

"We just stumbled across this clue." I stood up gingerly and walked to the kitchen. I took an open Coke can out of the refrigerator, and then washed my pain medicine down with a big swallow. Flat but still very sweet. I took another swallow even though I knew flat soda was not medicinal. The caffeine and sugar would make me feel better, if nothing else.

"I'm not going to be the one who calls him," Kate shook her head. "Annabelle should call him. He likes her."

I shuffled back to the couch, moving slowly to keep my head from pounding. "He does not."

"I'll bet you'd get a lot of sympathy, too." Kate mimicked a swoon. "All men love a damsel in a mess."

Richard cast his eyes around my apartment. "In this case, I think mess is the appropriate word."

"If I didn't have a concussion, I'd make you pay for saying that, Richard."

Leatrice picked up the phone and took a card out of her pocket. She dialed while she talked. "I'll call the detective. He's a nice young man. I'm sure he'll be happy to come over and get the evidence."

Come over? I didn't want him seeing me with a red knot in the middle of my forehead like a Cyclops. Couldn't someone drop it off at the station? I waved my arms to get her attention, but Leatrice was chatting away. She put the phone back on its charger.

"Detective Reese is more than happy to come right over and hear about our evidence. He's especially interested in your accident."

"How does he know about that?" I could hear my voice getting shrill. "I didn't hear you tell him."

"News travels fast when you have a police radio."

I couldn't jaywalk without this guy finding out. I got up and headed down the hall to the bathroom, walking lightly on my sore knee. At least I could find some makeup to cover my bump and maybe brush my hair.

"Where are you going?" Richard called after me. "You're the star attraction."

"This star needs to freshen up. I feel disgusting after being in the hospital all afternoon."

"Do you want some help with your makeup?" Kate followed me to the bathroom door. "If we give you full, pouty lips, the emphasis will be off your forehead."

They'd have to be enormous lips for anyone not to notice the lump on my head. "Thanks, but I'm not going to fix myself up for Reese. I just want to wash my face."

"Suit yourself."

I closed the door and rummaged through the contents of the vanity drawers. Powder, mascara, and lipstick were usually the extent of my makeup routine. I knew I had some old liquid foundation in here somewhere, though. I pulled out a handful of perfume samples in their small, paper folders. The plastic stoppers had loosened on a couple and the contents of the vials spilled onto my hands. I choked at the combination of the spicy musk and tea rose scents.

I jammed my hand into the back of the last drawer and found a tube of brown cream concealer. A bit of hard makeup snaked out as I squeezed the tube. It would have to do. I dabbed it on my knot and flinched. Still sore. I patted the brown gently over the surface of the bump until it looked like a beige lump instead of a red one. Good enough.

"I feel much better." I walked out of the bathroom and down the hall.

Kate saw me, and her eyes bulged. "What did you do to your head?"

"Is it too obvious?"

Richard came out of the kitchen and held his nose. "Who's going to notice her head with that awful smell?"

My eyes started to tear. I felt as horrible as I must have looked. "I spilled some perfume on my hands."

"Some?" Richard backed away from me.

Leatrice came and put her arm around me. She scowled at Richard and Kate. "You've had a frightful day. No one expects you to look perfect after being in a car accident. If anyone understands that, Detective Reese will."

I let her lead me to the sofa and put cushions under my head and feet. "I didn't do it for Detective Reese, Leatrice."

"Of course not, dear. I'm sure he won't notice a thing." Leatrice left me, and I could hear her in the hallway scolding Kate and Richard in hushed tones. After a few minutes, she went to the door. "I hear footsteps."

No doubt her superhuman hearing had been developed over years of eavesdropping.

Leatrice flung open the door, but her smile evaporated when she saw Alexandra and not Detective Reese. She gave Alexandra's pink crop pants and pink-and-green plaid purse the once-over. "Who are you?"

"I'm Alexandra." She held out a white box. "I brought some sweets for the injured."

"Come on in," I called out from the couch. "How did you find out so fast?"

Alexandra pointed in Kate's direction.

I raised an eyebrow at Kate. "I don't think you've ever been this efficient."

Kate shrugged. "I made some calls from the hospital. So shoot me."

Alexandra placed the box in front of me. "I brought you samples of your favorite cake flavors."

I rubbed my hands together. "The dark chocolate truffle and the lemon curd?"

She nodded and sat next to me. "Are these pictures from the Pierce wedding?"

Richard ran up and joined us on the couch. "Wait until you see the food shots. To die for!"

"Are there any of the cake?" Alexandra pawed through the photos. She held up a photo of Mr. and Mrs. Pierce. "Who is this man looking so chummy with Mrs. Pierce?"

Kate's eyes widened. "What do you mean? That's her husband. You saw them arguing, remember?"

Alexandra shook her head. "That's not who I saw her fighting with."

My jaw hit the floor. "Who did you see her fighting with then?"

"What's all this about?" Leatrice couldn't contain the curiosity in her voice.

"Alexandra told the police that she saw Mr. and Mrs. Pierce fighting before the wedding, but it seems like it wasn't Mr. Pierce after all."

Alexandra sifted through the stack and held up a photo of the bride with her father. Dr. Harriman. "This is the one."

I exchanged glances with Kate. "Are you sure?" It looked more and more as if the police arrested the right person. The bump on my head made me think otherwise, though.

"Of course." Alexandra looked taken aback. "This one is much better looking than her husband."

"She's right," Kate said. "You could never say that Dr. Pierce is as distinguished as Dr. Harriman."

Richard took the photo from Alexandra. "I have to admit, the silver in his hair is quite striking."

I threw my hands in the air. "This is a murder investigation, not a beauty contest."

"I'm surprised to hear you're still investigating the murders." Detective Reese stepped inside the open door, nodding at Kate and at Richard, who shrank back against the wall. Alexandra brightened at the sight of the detective and didn't notice Leatrice glaring at her.

I had to admit that in his black jeans and leather jacket, Reese looked a bit menacing. In a sexy way. The detective took a seat across the coffee table from me.

"I didn't mean investigation," I stammered.

He nodded, and then changed the subject. "I hear you were a victim of road rage this afternoon."

"Is that what they called it in the police report?"

"I didn't see a police report. You weren't hit in my district," Reese said. "I have friends in Virginia, though."

"You were checking up on me?" I exchanged looks with Kate.

"Miss Archer, I'm a detective." Reese raised an eyebrow. "Checking up on people involved in my cases falls into the job description."

I felt a flush creeping up my neck. "Well, it wasn't a case of road rage, Detective."

"What would you call it?"

I touched a hand to my head. "Attempted murder sounds more accurate."

Reese laughed. "Just because you were a victim of a hit-and-run doesn't mean the driver tried to kill you. These kinds of things happen all the time."

"The car didn't just bump into me and drive away." I swung my feet down. "He rammed me twice and pushed me off the road."

Reese swept a hand through his hair. "Are you sure you aren't exaggerating?"

"Do you think I got a concussion from being tapped on the bumper, Detective?" I pointed to my lump. "It looked even worse a few hours ago."

"I don't see how." Reese stared at my forehead, a puzzled expression on his face. "Maybe you should consider airbags."

"Thanks for the tip, but this is with airbags." It would be much easier to dislike him, I thought, if he weren't so good-looking.

"I find it hard to believe that someone would want to kill you." Reese locked eyes with me. "Murder is serious business."

I threw up my hands. "I'm glad you noticed."

"We think the killer tried to get rid of Annabelle because she knows too much," Kate insisted.

"That's impossible. We arrested Dr. Harriman this afternoon for the murder of Clara Pierce. That was before your accident."

I crossed my arms over my chest. "We heard. Maybe he had an accomplice, though."

"You think you know something the entire police department doesn't?" Reese cast a look at all of us. Richard shook his head vigorously, and Alexandra just smiled.

"We know that Mrs. Boyd threatened to kill Mrs. Pierce the day before the wedding," Kate said. "Maybe she was in on it with Dr. Harriman."

"Please don't tell me how you got this information." Reese gave a weary glance in my direction.

"It just fell in our laps." I shrugged my shoulders.

"I'll bet it did." Reese stood. "I appreciate the call, but I can't run around chasing rumors. I need hard evidence."

Leatrice rushed to his side. "That's why we called you. We do have evidence. We figured out how the murderer administered the poison."

"Go on." Reese sat back down. "I'm listening."

"Take a look at these photos." Leatrice handed him the pictures of Mrs. Pierce holding her cocktail. "Do you see anything out of place?"

He studied them for a moment. "No."

"Exactly." Leatrice danced around him. "The normal person wouldn't think twice when seeing these."

"Luckily, Richard isn't normal," I said. Payback for his comment about my messy apartment.

Leatrice pointed to the photographs. "These aren't Richard's straws. He doesn't use them, and they weren't on the bars. We checked."

"Are you sure?" Reese sounded interested.

Richard peered down his nose at Reese. "Of course I'm sure. I'd die before using a cocktail straw for a wedding."

"Clara is the only one with a straw in her drink." Kate handed him a handful of reception shots. "See for yourself."

"So you came to the conclusion that the straw held the poison?" The corner of the detective's mouth twitched into a grin. "Not bad deductive reasoning."

"You think we're right?" Leatrice's bell necklace jingled as she bounced up and down on her toes.

"I can't say for sure, but it makes sense to me. Do you mind if I take these pictures back to the station?"

"Could you leave the ones of the hors d'oeuvres? The shot of the caviar-filled quail egg should go in a frame." Richard started weeding through the prints spread out on the coffee table, then stopped when he saw Reese's face. "Or you could take them all and bring them back whenever you're done."

"Just because you found this clue, doesn't mean I want you hunting for others." Reese directed his comments to me. "We've got the murderer locked up, remember?"

"You're sure Dr. Harriman did it?" Kate asked.

"He had motive and opportunity for both murders, and now we might know the way he killed Mrs. Pierce." Reese held up the photos.

"And I saw him arguing with Mrs. Pierce at the wedding," Alexandra said, giving Reese a look that was either sheepish or flirtatious. "I got the husbands switched at first, but now I'm sure it was Dr. Harriman."

"What about Mrs. Boyd?" Kate didn't sound convinced. "We just forget about her?"

"Just because someone threatens murder, doesn't mean they did it." Reese met my eyes. "I don't want to hear about any more snooping around from any of you."

I gave him a sugary smile. "I'm going to be taking it easy for a while. You don't have to hit me over the head for me to get the hint."

His eyes flitted to my poorly concealed bump. "At least not twice, I hope."

CHAPTER 28

"I'm telling you, Annabelle. Maxwell sounded upset that you took the proofs." Kate stood outside the bathroom and spoke through the door. We'd survived the night together, but we were having a hard time negotiating time in the one bathroom.

"You talked to him?"

"While you were in the shower just now. He said he left a couple of messages yesterday, too."

"Did you tell him that I got run off the road and had to be taken to the hospital?" I dried off and put on my plush Willard Hotel bathrobe, last year's Christmas gift from their catering department. "Otherwise I'd have returned them right away."

"I tried, but he kept talking about how upset the clients were when they couldn't see the photos. Should I call the bride and explain that we gave them to the police?"

"Don't bother." Not likely to do any good, anyway. A bride would cut you slack only if you produced a death certificate. "I'll be out in a couple of minutes, and I'll deal with it."

I wrapped a smoke-blue towel around my hair like a turban, trying not to make it too tight. The shower had washed off the last bits of makeup and the knot on my head shone like a new penny. Maybe I'd let Kate have a go at downplaying it with pouty lips.

"Thanks for taking this morning's phone calls." I passed the office on the way to my bedroom. Kate sat at my chair with her long bare legs propped up on the desk. Since it was an office work day, Kate had worn her idea of casual Friday—pink silk shorts that left little to the imagination and a black and white striped top with spaghetti straps that tied at the shoulders.

Kate had the phone pressed to her ear and she rolled her eyes, mouthing the words "Alice Freakmont." Mrs. Pierce's death had elevated Alice Freemont to the role of our most demanding client. We called her Freakmont because she called at least once a day to freak out about something.

"What is it this time?" I whispered.

Kate covered the mouthpiece with her hand. "Is it okay for her bridal attendants to go bare-legged in July?"

"Tell her the latest trend is for bridesmaids to wear nothing at all under their gowns."

Kate held the phone at arm's length while she laughed. Just the thought of Alice, arguably the biggest priss on the planet, telling her bridesmaids to go naked under their formal, A-line dresses made me feel better.

I continued into my bedroom and stepped out of my robe. I pulled on a white fitted T-shirt with my favorite jeans and did a deep knee bend to stretch out the seat. A little tight but wearable. I had to stop letting Richard cook. He didn't know how to make anything with less than a stick of butter.

"Yoo-hoo, anyone home?" Speak of the devil.

I stuck my head into the hallway and saw Richard coming toward me in a navy suit. "We're conservative today, aren't we?"

He opened the jacket and flashed the melon-orange lining. "Fooled you. This is my mood-swing suit."

Kate stepped out of the office. "Just what you need."

Richard buttoned the jacket back up. "What are we up to today, ladies?"

"I have big plans to do nothing," I said. "I'm still recuperating from yesterday, and I promised Reese I would stay out of trouble."

"You were serious about that?" Richard followed me into the kitchen. "The other times you promised to stop snooping around you never did."

"But now we have the clue that proves how the murderer poisoned Mrs. Pierce," I said.

"So now you don't care about finding out who killed her?"

"You heard the detective," I insisted. "They caught the killer."

"But you aren't totally convinced, are you?" Richard gave me a suspicious look. I could tell he didn't trust me not to run off and try to solve the murder.

"My gut tells me the killer is still on the loose," I shrugged. "If you have any bright ideas how to figure out who it is without making my head pound, I'm all ears."

"We've talked to everyone involved in the case." Kate squeezed by me and leaned against the counter. "How much more will we really be able to find out?"

"We're the only ones who think the murderer is still at large." Richard shook his head. "Maybe we're wrong."

"To be honest, we can't afford to spend any more time running around looking for clues." I poured myself a cup of lukewarm coffee. "Kate and I have another wedding this weekend, which we've hardly had time to think about."

"Luckily the bride and groom are laid back and the whole thing has been planned for months," Kate said. "I talked to them this morning. The rehearsal is still set for six o'clock tonight."

I smacked myself on the head, then instantly regretted it as my forehead throbbed. "I forgot about the rehearsal."

"Don't worry about it, Annabelle." Kate waved her hand. "I'm going to run it for you. You're not in any shape to deal with rowdy groomsmen at this point."

"Thanks. You're right." I sighed. "But I feel like there's something else I've forgotten about. Something important."

Richard cleared his throat and pointed over the counter to the pile of plastic tuxedo bags stacked on the arm of the couch. "They've been sitting here for almost a week. Are you planning on keeping them?"

I took a sip of day-old coffee, gagging as I poured the rest down the sink. "That's what I forgot to do. Return the tuxedos from the Pierce wedding. The fines will be more than the cost to rent them in the first place."

"Maybe if you explain the whole story, the guy at the tuxedo shop will give you a break," Kate said. "Don't you know him pretty well?"

"Yes, and after all the weddings I've sent him, he should let me have the tuxedos outright."

"Do you want to go now and return them? I'll take you." Richard, sounding eager to have a mission, went to gather up the garment bags. "I don't have anything to do since I'm still under police orders not to work."

"Should you be going out so soon, Annabelle?" Kate asked.

I put my cup in the sink. "I'll be fine."

Richard opened the door and let me pass. "Famous last words, darling."

CHAPTER 29

"Sauro's is two blocks down on the left," I said as we exited Dupont Circle onto Nineteenth Street and drove past a series of formal restaurants catering to business executives. Waiters were sweeping off the sidewalks in front. Warm enough to eat outside if you could handle the exhaust fumes.

"I'll drop you off, then circle the block for street parking."

I'd have been finished before he found a space. Not the easiest place in the world to park. "Why don't you park in one of the garages?"

"No, thank you." Richard shook his head. "The last time I let a parking attendant have my car he readjusted the seats, reprogrammed my radio, and jammed my roof open."

"That's right. I remember it rained that day."

"Exactly." Richard pressed his lips together as he pulled over. "I looked like an absolute fool driving around in a convertible holding an umbrella."

"Fair enough." I stepped out onto the curb, dragging the garment bags behind me. "I'll be waiting."

I pushed the glass door to Sauro Custom Tailor open with my hip. The small shop was cool and quiet, a marked changed from the bustling street outside. Mr. Sauro appeared from the back of the shop and took the bags from me, laying them out across the counter.

"Another successful wedding?" He flashed me a smile as he thumbed through the bags, moving his lips as he counted. Mr. Sauro looked the same as he always did, a tape measure around his neck and silvery hair showing traces of once being dark. His hands were worn from hemming and tucking thousands of suits over the years. I wondered how many grooms he'd seen come through his store.

"You could say that," I said. Most people who knew Mrs. Pierce would call it a great success.

"Almost a week late." He gave a low whistle, and then winked at me. "Don't worry about it."

"Thanks, Mr. Sauro. I promise it won't happen again."

He waved off my apologies and opened the top bag. "Let me check the pockets. Don't want to end up with an extra wallet."

"I haven't even opened the bags, so I hope all the components are there." I sat down on the step stool in front of the wall-length mirrors and watched Mr. Sauro hang the suits on a metal bar as he inspected them.

Mr. Sauro winked at me. "When will we see your groom in here picking out his wedding clothes?"

"Not for a while." I felt myself blush. "I'm too busy with work right now to think about marriage."

Mr. Sauro made clucking noises. "I have a feeling the right man will walk into your life soon."

Richard swung open the glass door and stumbled into the shop. "The best spot I could find is two blocks away in an alley. I'm starting to perspire."

"Well, we're almost finished here." I stood up so Richard could sit on the stool.

"Take your time. I'm not going back out there until I cool down." Richard took off his jacket and fanned himself with a brochure for After Six formalwear. "One drop of sweat and this shirt will be ruined."

"A cigarette lighter and an empty plastic baggy." Mr. Sauro held up the two items. "That's all I found in the pockets."

I took both from him as he went into the back of the store. I rolled the thin, silver lighter in my palm. Not the cheap, drugstore variety. I would need to call around and try to find its owner. I began to wad up the plastic bag when some white powder fell out onto my hand. I opened the bag and shook it, causing a small pile of white to gather in the pointy corner.

"Richard, take a look at this."

"You've never seen a sandwich bag before?" Richard held his shirt away from his body with his fingertips.

"Not one with white stuff like this in it. Besides, why would one of the men have a sandwich baggy in his pocket?"

Richard walked over and took the bag from me "Well, what do you think it is?"

"I think it's poison."

Richard shrieked as though he'd been burned and dropped the bag to the floor. "How could you let me touch it? I've been contaminated. Where's a sink? I need to get this off my hands."

"Not that kind of poison," I said. "The blood-pressure medication that caused Mrs. Pierce to die."

Richard reached down and retrieved the bag, holding it away from him by the edges. "So whoever killed her carried the straws around in this bag, waiting for the right time to drop them in her drink?"

"It makes sense, doesn't it? If only we could determine whose tuxedo this came from, but they're all alike."

"Were Dr. Pierce's and Dr. Harriman's tuxedos both in the pile we returned?" Richard ran a fingertip along the row of hanging black jackets.

I nodded. "The bride wanted all the men to match so she asked her father and stepfather to rent the same style as the groom and groomsmen. I counted eight tuxedos total, so they're all here. It could have been either of them."

Richard jerked his hand away from the tuxedos. "Think about it, Annabelle. The murderer's clothes have been sitting in your apartment all week, and we didn't even know it."

CHAPTER 30

"The question is, does the murderer know I've been sitting on this evidence?" I carried Richard's suit jacket in one hand and the plastic baggy in the other. He walked in front of me, taking up most of the sidewalk by holding his arms out so they wouldn't touch his body.

"That would explain why you've been a target."

"It didn't even occur to me that the killer's clothes were in that pile of tuxedos," I said. "Now I understand why someone broke into my apartment."

"Why did he put his tuxedo in with the others to be returned if he didn't want anyone to find the evidence?"

"Maybe he forgot about the baggy in all the commotion following the murder." We rounded the corner into a narrow alley where Richard's car sat between two TOW AWAY ZONE signs. A white slip of paper peeked from underneath his windshield wiper. "There's no such thing as the perfect crime."

Richard took the parking ticket from the windshield and folded it without looking inside. "Don't they say that when a murder is committed the killer makes a hundred mistakes?"

"Something like that." I opened the passenger door. "Aren't you going to look at the ticket?"

"It's a fake. I always put that out when I park illegally."

I gave Richard a disapproving look. "I wouldn't suggest using it when

BOOK 1: BETTER OFF WED

we park at the police station."

"Don't look at me like that. I know you keep orange cones in the back of your car to block off parking spots on wedding days." Richard opened his car doors with the click of his remote. "You're serious about going there now, Annabelle?"

I decided not to press Richard about his fake tickets since he was right about the collection of orange hazard cones in my trunk.

"We should give this evidence to Reese as soon as possible." I lowered myself into the leather seat. "I'm not crazy about the idea of hanging on to it any longer than I already have."

"But isn't this more evidence against Dr. Harriman, the person we don't think did it?"

I shrugged. "I guess so, but it could've been Dr. Pierce just as easily."

"Or any one of the groomsmen."

"Why would the groomsmen want to kill the bride's mother?" I raised an eyebrow. "They didn't even know her."

"Just a thought," Richard mumbled. "They did meet her, after all. After I met Mrs. Pierce the first time, I wanted to kill her."

I rubbed my temples. "Just drive."

"I'm warning you." Richard eased the car out of the alley and edged his way into traffic. "The District Two police station isn't glamorous, and it certainly isn't clean."

"We won't stay long. I'll just hand this over and leave. I don't want to take up time the police could be using to build their case."

"So now you're admitting that Dr. Harriman might be the killer?" Richard drove around Dupont Circle and headed down Massachusetts Avenue, passing embassy after embassy.

"Finding the traces of poison in the tuxedo rules out our female suspects. Mrs. Boyd may have threatened to kill Mrs. Pierce, and Bev may have wanted her beloved best friend out of the way, but a man carried the poison straws in his pocket."

"Such a shame, too. Helen Boyd would have made a spectacular Lady Macbeth."

"The killer also had to know which medicine Mrs. Pierce took, which drug would kill her when mixed with her medication, and have easy access to prescription drugs."

Richard went around another traffic circle without slowing. "Which both Harriman and Pierce did, since they'd both lived with her and they're both doctors."

"But of the two, only Harriman had access to Mr. Boyd before the tasting, so he could have killed both victims."

"Which means that someone else tried to run you off the road."

"Maybe he sent his new wife to deal with me once he was arrested. But he seemed so pleasant when Kate and I talked to him at the bride's house."

Richard drummed his fingers on the steering wheel. "A real Dr. Jekyll and Mr. Hyde. How did he know you'd have the tuxedos, though?"

"I announced to all the men in the wedding that they should leave their formalwear with the coat check at the end of the night and I'd return them. He must have forgotten all about the baggy when he dropped off his tuxedo."

"Probably too excited about Mrs. Pierce's death." Richard sped through a yellow light to cross Wisconsin Avenue, and then veered off into a neighborhood with alternating colonial and Cape Cod-style houses. After several blocks, he slowed and parallel parked beside a low brick building with several police cruisers in the adjoining lot. Grass covered the front lawn of the building, and a web of tree branches provided shade for the cars. Not how I'd imagined an urban police station.

"This isn't so bad, Richard." I stepped out of the car and crossed the street. I didn't see the bustle of police officers and shady characters I'd expected. It looked almost deserted. "From the way you described it, I thought there would be convicts in leg shackles being dragged away for floggings."

"Where did you get that absurd idea?" Richard strolled across the street buttoning his jacket. "I stand by my assessment of the bathrooms, though."

We walked up the sidewalk to the glass double doors. As Richard reached for the metal push bars, both doors flew open. A group of officers rushed past us. Richard stumbled backward onto the pavement, and I tripped over him, landing cleanly in his lap.

"I don't believe it."

I gazed up at the source of the deep, mocking voice. Reese. Who else? I tried to push myself off of Richard, who made high-pitched gasping noises. Reese pulled me up by one hand with such strength that I bumped against his chest. I'd never been so close to him before. I backed away and felt my cheeks flush.

"We were looking for you, Detective. We wanted to give you this." I held out the plastic baggy.

Reese took the bag and cocked an eyebrow. "Thanks. I can never get too many of these."

"For heaven's sake, Annabelle." Richard stood up and flicked specks of dirt off his hands. "Stop blushing like a schoolgirl and explain what it is."

I shot daggers at Richard. "We found it in the pocket of one of the wedding tuxedos. We think the killer used it to carry the straws filled with poison."

"See the white powder in the bottom?" Richard poked at the bag with his pinkie finger.

Reese held the bag up. "Whose tux did it come from?"

"That's where things get confusing." Richard twisted to dust off the seat of his pants. "Annabelle collected all the tuxedos from the wedding party and the fathers. They've been sitting in her apartment since Monday night, waiting to be returned."

"After the burglary," Reese said.

Richard took a step toward Reese. "We think the killer remembered the evidence in his jacket and came looking for it. But we hadn't yet brought them in from my car, so he didn't find anything."

"Did they all realize that you would have the tuxedos, Annabelle?"

"I told all the men who were part of the wedding that I'd take their clothes back to the shop for them."

"Pretty nice of you." Reese gave me a half grin. "Do you do that for all weddings?"

I returned his smile. "I told you I'm full service."

"Does the bag help at all, Detective?" Richard took off his jacket. I noticed Reese's eyes pause on the orange lining.

"I'll have the lab run some tests on it. I have a feeling you're right about this powder. Combined with the evidence we have from Boyd's murder, this should lock Dr. Harriman away for a long time."

"You determined that he killed Boyd, too?" Richard hooked his jacket on his finger and swung it over his shoulder.

"Mr. Boyd died from an overdose of a cardiovascular drug, not poisoned soup. We found the needle mark." Reese gave Richard a quick nod. "You're off the hook."

Richard gave an exaggerated sigh of relief. "Free at last." You'd have thought he'd been locked in solitary confinement for a month.

"That explains everything but my accident." I looked between Richard and Reese. "We still have to figure out who tried to kill me."

"I don't think you have anything to worry about, Annabelle." Reese squeezed my arm. "You can hang up your detective badge. Our case against Dr. Harriman is airtight."

CHAPTER 31

"That's what he said?" Kate sat on the floor of my office packing small Tiffany boxes into shopping bags. She was barefoot with her high-heel cork wedges tossed in the corner, and I noticed that her pink toenails matched her pink silk shorts.

"I guess they have enough proof to link him to both." I sat down in my office chair. The blue boxes had taken up most of the floor for two weeks, and I was glad to see them go.

"I should have known from when he failed the cleavage test."

"Kate, if we relied on your method of testing suspects, half the city would be in jail now, including most of the police force."

"He still doesn't seem the type to commit coldblooded murder. He sounded genuinely concerned about his daughter that day we visited her."

I shook my head. "You never can tell about people."

"I'm a little sorry the whole thing's over."

"That's because your life wasn't in danger." I used a fat Magic Marker to cross off several days on the wall-size calendar above my desk then waved my hand in the air to clear the marker smell. I'd been so preoccupied with the murder case, I'd fallen behind almost an entire week. "It may have been exciting, but I'll be glad for things to get back to normal."

"I guess we can close the books on the Pierce wedding now." Kate slid one of her spaghetti straps back on her shoulder then reached for more boxes.

"The only thing left is to attend the memorial service tomorrow morning."

"You must be joking!" Kate dropped a handful of favor boxes, and I heard the sound of tinkling glass. I hoped we had extras.

"I think it would be nice of us to pay our respects to the bride. We liked her, remember?"

The corners of Kate's mouth turned down. "I didn't like her that much."

"We'll sit in the back and sneak out as soon as it's over. You have to go with me," I begged.

"Why can't Richard take you?" Kate asked.

"He's going to meet us at the church. He'll be coming straight from a meeting."

"But I have to prepare for our wedding," Kate argued. "I don't have time."

"The funeral is at ten a.m. and the wedding isn't until six o'clock. Do you have any other excuses you want to try out?"

"Give me a second. I'm sure I can come up with one."

I tapped my foot. "I'm waiting."

"You're still recovering from your accident. Too much exertion could be bad for you."

"How much could I exert myself at a memorial service?"

"I don't know. You saw the party Bev had in her honor." Kate wagged her finger at me in warning. "If she's in charge, there could be conga lines and limbo contests."

"No harm ever came from going to a funeral, Kate. The murderer is behind bars, so we're all safe. There's nothing to worry about."

Kate let out a breath. "You keep saying that."

CHAPTER 32

Leatrice knelt next to the tiny flower bed in front of our building and jumped up when I walked out the door. She wore a long denim apron with rows of pockets, each with a gardening tool or a different type of seed packet peeking out the top. I fantasized about getting one for weddings, so I could keep my emergency supplies with me at all times. With brides, you never knew when you'd need superglue, safety pins, or aspirin. The aspirin was more for me.

"Doing some morning gardening, Leatrice?" I held the door open for Kate, who carried two oversized shopping bags full of favors for the evening's wedding.

"Best time to be outside." Leatrice tugged her apron straight. "Where are you two going so early? I rarely see you up and about before eleven."

I took a deep breath, inhaling the fresh air that had yet to be polluted by car exhaust. The morning really was the best time in Georgetown.

"We're going to Mrs. Pierce's funeral." Kate shuffled a few steps down the walk. "Aren't you jealous?"

I knew Kate meant it sarcastically, but I could see that Leatrice didn't. I could just imagine us walking into the church with Leatrice trailing behind in her apron and green-and-pink-flowered gardening hat.

"You won't be missing much, Leatrice," I said. "The case is closed."

"I heard last night."

"How did you find out?" Kate glanced at me and raised an eyebrow.

"The eleven o'clock news. They showed your detective friend making a statement."

I needed to start paying more attention to local news. First I'd missed the leak in the paper, and now I'd missed seeing Reese on TV. I wondered if he wore a uniform or if he always wore street clothes on the job.

"It turns out that Mrs. Pierce's ex-husband killed her and Mr. Boyd." Kate rested the bulging bags on the sidewalk.

"Did the evidence we found help at all?" Leatrice asked. "Do you think they'll call on us to be witnesses at the trial?"

I could just imagine Leatrice taking the stand in the rhinestone tiara she wore for special occasions.

I suppressed a smile. "They have enough physical evidence and probably won't need our testimony."

Leatrice looked deflated, and I patted her on the arm. "I'm sure that Detective Reese won't hesitate to call you if he needs a reliable witness."

"Too bad he won't be coming around any more." Leatrice reached into one of her many pockets for a tissue and dabbed at her nose.

"Don't take it too hard." Kate took a few steps to her car and unlocked the trunk.

Leatrice sniffled and stuffed the tissue back in her apron. "Allergies. It must be all the pollen."

"I'm sure you'll see Reese again." Kate packed the shopping bags into the trunk and slammed it shut. "Annabelle can't seem to stay out of trouble."

"That's true." Leatrice smiled.

I slid into the passenger seat next to Kate. "Sorry Leatrice, we have to hurry if we're going to make it to the funeral on time."

"Sometimes I think she's got hats in the belfry," Kate said as she jerked the car in gear and pulled away from the sidewalk. I started to correct her, then just rolled my eyes and took my cell phone out of my purse.

"I'm going to call Richard and make sure he's on his way."

"Don't worry. We'll know plenty of people at the funeral."

I held the phone to my ear. "Most of them were on our suspect list at one point, remember?"

Kate gripped the steering wheel with both hands. "They don't serve communion wine at funerals, do they?"

"We're not going to be poisoned, if that's what you're thinking," I assured her. "Dr. Harriman is behind bars."

"With this bunch, I'm not going to take any chances." Kate pressed her lips together.

Richard finally answered his phone. "Annabelle, is that you?"

"We should be at the church in a few minutes. Where are you?"

"I've been a bit delayed. I'll try to get there as soon as possible."

"Is anything wrong?"

"All I have to say is that Neiman Marcus shouldn't send invitations to a secret sale if they intend to open it up to everyone and their brother. I might as well be at Filene's Basement."

"That's your important meeting? A sale at Neiman's?"

Kate's mouth fell open. "He'd better be joking."

"This isn't just any old sale, darling. Prada is half price and not last year's line, either." I heard lots of voices in the background. "Oh, dear. I'm being jostled in the checkout line. Do you people have no concept of personal space?"

I assumed he wasn't talking to me. "I didn't think you shopped like the rest of us mortals."

"My Neiman's personal shopper is out sick, if you can believe the rotten luck. Don't worry about me, though. Listen, I've got to run. They're opening a new counter." The line went dead.

Kate narrowed her eyes. "Tell me he's coming."

"Well, the good news is he's next in line."

The sharp asymmetrical spires of National Presbyterian Church jutted into the sky in front of us. Not exactly your typical white clapboard church with a cross on top. We parked in the huge paved lot, but neither of us made a move to open our doors.

"I'm not going in," Kate said. "There's hardly anybody here yet."

Only a few other cars were in the lot with us, mostly European imports. The university stickers in the back windows of the cars read like a Who's Who of colleges. Princeton, Columbia, Duke, Harvard, Yale.

"Get down." I slid down below the dashboard. "Dr. and Mrs. Donovan just pulled up."

"The bride and groom?" Kate ducked behind the steering wheel. "I thought we were here to see the bride. Why are we hiding?"

"See her, yes. But I don't want to have a long conversation with her. She's probably still upset about the pictures." I peeked over the dash. Dr. Donovan drove the navy blue Mercedes into a space across from us. I noticed the stickers on his back windshield. Andover, Princeton, Harvard. His car must feel right at home.

"Elizabeth doesn't look so good," Kate whispered as the bride walked into the church on her husband's arm. "How could she get more frail and delicate?"

"Don't forget, her mother's dead and her father was arrested for the murder."

"Poor girl. She doesn't have anyone left except her husband." Kate pressed her brows together, and a tiny crease formed between her eyes. "But if I had to be left with one person, I wouldn't mind it being him. He's at least a nine."

I groaned. "I'm not sure which is more tasteless, rating the groom or doing it at a funeral."

"Give me a break. This is no normal funeral." Kate sat back up halfway when the bride and groom disappeared inside the building. "Have you ever seen such cheery people in your life?"

Cars were coming in a steady stream by then, depositing black-clad mourners with big smiles on their faces. Couples greeted each other with air kisses and pats on the back.

"Just be thankful there aren't mimes this time," I said.

Just then a sharp rap came on my window. "Problem, ladies?"

CHAPTER 33

I raised my head and saw Fern standing next to the car door. He wore a long black jacket that reached down to his knees and a frilly white shirt that puffed up around his neck.

"What are you doing down there, girls?"

"You scared me to death." I pulled myself up from the floor of the car and opened the door. "I thought you were somebody else."

"You were waiting for someone hunched up on the floor of the car?"

"No. It's just that each time I'm doing something strange the same person seems to catch me." I stood up and brushed off my dress.

Kate came around the car to stand beside me. "A cute detective, no less."

"Tell me about this detective." Fern put an arm around Kate and his eyes widened with excitement. "How cute?"

"What you might call tall, dark, and ruggedly handsome," Kate said.

"Good." He fluffed the ruffles on his shirt. "I don't like pretty boys."

"He's not too tall." I avoided Kate's eyes. "And nothing went on between us, Fern, so you can wipe that grin off your face."

Kate put her foot up on the bumper of the car and straightened her stocking. "She's playing hard to get."

"I'm surprised you've heard of it." Fern arched his eyebrow as he appraised Kate's hemline.

"I didn't say I endorse it." Kate laughed. Somehow Fern could get away with saying outrageous things to just about anyone and make them love him for it.

He winked at me. "Let's not forget why we're here, girls."

I nodded solemnly. "You're right. We're here to pay our respects."

"Wrong." Fern lowered his voice as a group of women passed us. "We're here to critique what all these society tramps are wearing."

I looked around to see if anyone had heard him. "Half of them are your clients," I said in shock.

"Don't worry," he reassured me with a grin. "I call them tramps to their faces."

I believed him.

Kate linked her arms with ours. "This funeral might not be so bad after all."

Fern led us up the sidewalk and into the side door of the church. We walked down a hallway lined with large floral arrangements. Tall, spiky gladiolas seemed to be the flower of the day, with white lilies coming in a close second. The smell of flowers was almost cloying, and I put a hand over my nose.

Fern made a face. "I can never look at a gladiola without thinking of death."

"We should have sent a huge bouquet of birds-of-paradise," Kate said. "That would be different."

"Do you notice anything odd?" I pulled Fern and Kate close to me. "They used the same color scheme as the wedding. All creams and whites with hints of blush."

Fern shivered and rubbed his arms. "You gave me the chills, Annabelle."

"Too bad it's been a week since the wedding or they could have reused the same flowers," Kate added.

"Why not?" Fern smoothed the front of his jacket. "I had to fix Clara's hair the same way she wore it at the wedding."

I winced. "I forgot about that. How awful, working on Mrs. Pierce."

Fern shrugged. "For once, the tramp couldn't talk back."

I stifled a laugh and thought that if I listened hard, I might hear Clara trying to do just that. We hung back as most of the crowd thinned out and went inside the main sanctuary. Elizabeth and her husband greeted people at the entrance, the doctor clearly holding his wife up. Her vacant expression and glassy eyes didn't leave much doubt she'd taken sedatives to get through the service.

"Do you recognize anyone?" Kate tried to hide behind a large fan-shaped spray of flowers.

"There's Bev Tripton." I joined Kate behind the arrangement as Bev entered the hallway. "Can you believe the outfit?"

Mrs. Pierce's devoted best friend wore a black suit with a wide portrait neckline, her ample cleavage protruding. The netting that extended from her black pillbox hat covered her face and came to rest on the exposed part of her breasts.

Kate did a double take. "Well, at least it's black."

"Who is she kidding with the veil?" Fern made clicking noises with his tongue. "And that hat is all wrong for her face."

"Here comes Dr. Pierce," I whispered to Fern through a palm frond. "I'll bet they came together and just walked in separately so it wouldn't look bad."

"This is ridiculous." Fern moved the greenery away from my face. "It looks like I'm talking to a floral arrangement with four legs."

I stepped out from behind the flowers. "I guess you could say we're having a hard time getting out of sleuth mode."

"Do you plan to spend all day out here, girls, or can we go inside?" Fern prodded us forward. We'd only advanced a few feet when loud footsteps approached from behind. I glanced over my shoulder and saw Helen Boyd striding toward the chapel in a fire-engine-red dress. I turned around so she wouldn't recognize me.

"Talk about tramp." Fern's jaw dropped open as Mrs. Boyd passed us. "Who is that?"

"Remember the man you told us that Mrs. Pierce had an affair with?" I said. "That's his wife."

Fern slapped a hand to his cheek. "This is going to be the best social event of the entire year. Hurry!"

As we reached the door of the chapel, my cell phone began singing. I never remembered to set it on silent mode. I answered and cupped my hand around the mouthpiece.

"I'm on my way, Annabelle." Richard's voice echoed as if he were in a well.

"Hold on a second," I said to Fern and Kate, and then ran outside to get better reception. The closer I walked toward the parking lot, the clearer Richard sounded.

"Has the service started yet?"

"No, but we were just about to sit down. How far away are you?"

Richard's voice faded in and out. "I'm on the parkway, not quite at the CIA."

"I thought you were at Neiman Marcus." I walked as far as Kate's car, and leaned against the hood, facing the bride and groom's shiny Mercedes.

"The one in Virginia, not the one in D.C."

"Well, hurry up, Richard. You've got to see what people are wearing to this funeral."

"All Washington women wear is black. How hard could this be?"

"Mrs. Boyd didn't get the memo. She's in red."

"I can't believe I'm missing this," Richard cried. "Don't let them start without me."

My voice caught in my throat. It couldn't be. My mind started racing. "Of course. I can't believe I didn't think of it before."

"What? You're starting to break up, Annabelle."

My hands shook. I tried not to let the phone slip from my grasp. "I just realized something about the case, Richard."

"I'm going by the CIA. I can hardly hear you."

"They arrested the wrong person, Richard. I'm sure of it."

"This again?"

"Now I think I have the proof we need. I just need to check one thing out at home." The phone went dead. I hoped he understood me. I ran back into the church and skidded to a stop in front of Kate and Fern. They stood alone in the doorway to the sanctuary.

"That must have been some phone call," Fern said. "Your face is all flushed."

Kate brightened. "Was it Detective Reese?"

I shook my head. "I'm going to go call him, though."

"It's about time you stopped being coy," Kate said.

"I'm going to call him about the case." I lowered my voice to a whisper. "I have some new evidence for him."

"But the case is closed, Annabelle." Kate's voice almost pleaded. "Let it go."

"I can't let it go." My voice trembled with excitement. "They have the wrong person, Kate. Dr. Harriman isn't the murderer, and I know how to prove it."

CHAPTER 34

The organ started playing inside the sanctuary, and a few people hurried past us through the doorway.

"Go ahead inside," I said, taking Kate's car keys from her. "I have to go home and check out something, then I'm going to call Reese and give him my new evidence."

"Can't you tell us what's going on?" Kate leaned forward on the pointy toes of her high heels.

"I can't say anything out here because someone might overhear me." I gave a quick shake of my head. "You go ahead in without me. It would look odd if we all skipped the service, especially since people have already seen us."

I watched them slip into a pew close to the back, and then I tiptoed down the marble hallway and ran to Kate's car. I got in and put the key in the ignition while I called information for the District Two phone number. I splurged the extra fifty cents to be patched through directly. Driving and talking I could manage. Driving, talking, and writing down a number at the same time, I couldn't.

"I'm looking for Detective Reese," I said when a voice answered. "It's an emergency."

The cop on phone duty didn't sound impressed. "He's out. I can take a message."

"Is there any way you can reach him for me? This is important." I steered with one hand and used my knees to hold the wheel in place.

Luckily Wisconsin Avenue ran through the city in a relatively straight line.

"I can relay your message as soon as he calls in, ma'am. That's as good as I can do." I doubted that, but didn't want to get in an argument.

"Tell him Annabelle Archer called with important information about the Pierce murder case. I was at Mrs. Pierce's memorial service, but I'm heading back to my apartment so he can reach me on my cell phone. Please tell him it's an emergency."

"Will do."

I hung up the phone and felt like screaming. I had to talk to Reese. Where could he be? Too many thoughts were jumbled in my head. I took a deep breath to calm down. Was I right or had I jumped to conclusions?

I dialed Richard's number again and went immediately into voice mail. He must have been driving through every patch of bad reception in Washington. I left him a message telling him my hypothesis and instructing him to meet me at home, and then flipped off my phone.

I passed the "social" Safeway in Upper Georgetown, where singles found shopping nights more exciting than happy hour. I turned off Wisconsin and parked a block away from my building, the tip of the car creeping into someone's brick driveway.

Could I be overreacting? Maybe my new theory was wrong and Dr. Harriman had killed his ex-wife and Mr. Boyd. No. I'd found the missing piece of the puzzle. I felt it in my gut.

Leatrice stood in the same spot we'd left her in earlier that morning. This time she had on rainbow-striped gloves. "Back so soon, dearie? Where's Kate?"

I dashed past her. "At the funeral."

"Did you forget something?" Leatrice watched me throw open the door to our building and start up the steps two at a time.

"My brain," I called out behind me. "I should have realized ages ago."

"I don't understand." Leatrice followed me inside the building and looked at me as though the head injuries had finally kicked in. "What should you have realized?"

"Never mind." I paused at the first landing. "If Detective Reese or Richard come, could you let them in, Leatrice?"

She clapped her hands. "Of course. I'll send them right up."

I ran the rest of the way up the stairs and reached my floor panting. I stumbled into my apartment and dropped the car keys on the floor. I checked my phone again while I turned on my computer. Nothing. That meant Reese must still be out. Didn't cops have to check in regularly?

I sat down at my computer screen and logged on to the Internet. After a few minutes of searching, I sat back and smiled. Bingo. I printed out several pages and left them in my printer while I went to the kitchen. I grabbed a Coke out of the refrigerator. Probably not the best way to calm my nerves, but I didn't care. I poured it over ice and listened to the fizz die down. I paced a few minutes before dialing the police station again.

"I'm calling for Detective Reese."

"Are you the lady who called here earlier looking for him?"

"Yes. I'm Annabelle Archer." My voice still shook.

"Okay, I gave him your message, and he said he was on his way to your place."

I hung up. If I didn't know better, I'd think Reese wanted an excuse to see me. Good thing I'd been at a funeral. My black sheath dress made me look almost thin.

I fluffed the pillows on my couch and dumped my nearly empty glass of Coke in the sink. I found a can of lemon furniture polish in a bottom kitchen cabinet and walked around spraying it in the air. If it didn't look clean, at least it could smell clean. The doorbell rang and I tossed the empty can of polish in the trash.

I undid my hair from the black clip that held it back and shook it loose as I walked to the door. I pinched my cheeks and said a prayer that Richard and Kate couldn't see me. I planted a smile on my face and opened the door. My smile vanished.

It wasn't Detective Reese. It was the groom.

CHAPTER 35

"Dr. Donovan." My voice sounded unnaturally high-pitched. "I'm sur..."

"Surprised to see me?" He stepped into my apartment and pulled the door closed. "I don't know why, Miss Archer."

I tried to keep the tremor out of my voice. "Can I help you with anything?"

"For starters, you can tell me how you figured it out."

"Figured what out?" My eyes flitted to the door, which he blocked with his body.

"Don't patronize me. I overheard you tell your friends that you knew the police had arrested the wrong person." He didn't blink as he stared at me. "You didn't notice me on the other side of the sanctuary door, did you?"

I shook my head, my mouth too dry to open. I stepped back, and my legs touched the edge of the couch

"Your phone has a distinctive ring, Miss Wedding Planner." I cursed myself for picking "Here Comes the Bride," and cursed Kate for being right when she told me it was a stupid idea. "I heard the ring when you came to pay condolences to Elizabeth, then in my office when you were snooping around, and again today. So why don't you tell me how you knew?"

I cleared my throat. "The sticker."

"What?"

"You have a window decal on your car for Andover Academy. *Phillips* Andover Academy. 'Phillips' is the only name we couldn't match up from Clara's notebook. You don't have a diploma from the prep school on your wall, though. I figured there must be a good reason for not putting it up with all the others."

"Which would be?" He sounded like a teacher coaxing a pupil.

"At first I thought you didn't go to Andover and you were willing to kill to keep that secret hidden." I took a baby step away from him. "But when I went on the school's web site, I saw an old photo of you in the alumni section."

He crossed his hands over his chest. "Continue."

"The funny thing is that you're not listed in the alumni directory. At least Andrew Donovan isn't listed, but I suspect *you* are, aren't you?"

The groom smiled and winked at me. "Very good, Miss Archer."

I glanced at the clock on the bookshelf behind him. Where was Richard? Never mind Richard, where was Detective Reese?

"So you changed your name and that's what your mother-in-law discovered?" Mrs. Pierce's comment about changing names during the wedding started to make a lot of sense. "You killed Clara to keep your old identity a secret."

He stepped away from the door and moved toward me. "Not bad for a wedding planner."

"You're the one who left the poisoned straw in his tuxedo jacket, not Dr. Harriman." I pointed a finger at him. Everything made sense now. "You knew Clara took medication for blood pressure and you could easily get a prescription filled."

His eye twitched. "The tuxedo jacket was a mistake."

"You ransacked my apartment trying to get it back, but you couldn't find it." I tried not to sound too victorious. "But why kill Mrs. Pierce? She adored you."

"No, she loved Andrew Donovan, Ivy League graduate. Andrew Donovan, successful doctor. Andrew Donovan, only heir of wealthy parents." His eye twitched faster. "She didn't love Andy Klump of Pittsburgh."

"You made up a fake past as well as a fake name?" I couldn't help being impressed with the extent of his lies.

"Once I got a scholarship to Andover, I promised myself I'd never be part of that blue-collar family again. I created an entirely new life for myself, complete with a family tree and ancestors going back to the Mayflower." His eye twitched in rapid fire now. "I became Andrew

Donovan and couldn't even remember what it felt like to be Andy Klump."

This guy was nuts. I glanced behind me. Could I make it down the hall to the back door before he caught me? "Too bad the diploma gave you away."

"That damn Andover diploma. My future mother-in-law noticed it was missing just as you did. When she asked me about it, I told her I'd misplaced it years ago. End of story, right?" He paused and stared at me, as if waiting for me to answer.

I sidestepped the arm of the couch. "I guess not."

"She decided to surprise me by getting a copy and having it framed. Of course, when she called Andover they had no record of an Andrew Donovan. A little research into the old yearbooks turned up Andy Klump. Andy Klump who'd been dead and buried for ten years."

"So she threatened to call off the wedding and expose you." What a great story. I'd almost forgotten he wanted to kill me.

"Worse. She told me that she'd keep my secret if she had the final say in my life with Elizabeth. Where we lived, who we socialized with, which clubs we joined. Total control."

I could imagine how delighted Mrs. Pierce would have been to realize that she wouldn't be losing a daughter, she'd be gaining an indentured servant. She'd have loved blackmailing her son-in-law for the rest of her life. Part of me didn't blame him for killing her.

"I hadn't come this far and made so many sacrifices to be controlled by a society witch like Clara Pierce. I had no choice but to kill her. Don't you see?" He turned his attention to me.

I took a step backward. "Then you killed Mr. Boyd because of his relationship with Clara."

"I couldn't be sure she hadn't indulged in pillow talk, now, could I?" He furrowed his brow, causing rows of frown lines to appear on his forehead.

"You must have switched needles when Mr. Boyd came in for his appointment with your father-in-law."

He nodded. "Easy enough to do when you share office space and have medications lying around. It's very simple to overdose on normally harmless medications, you know. Do you want to hear something funny, Miss Archer?"

Somehow I didn't think his idea of funny would be the same as mine. "Mmm-hmm."

"I had no idea about your tasting with the Boyds until the next day.

Imagine my surprise when I found out that you and your caterer friend were in hot water again." He chuckled. "You must have figured it out, though, because you came sneaking around my office."

"You thought I was in your office trying to find information about you?" I kicked myself for not making the connection sooner.

"I heard your phone and guessed you must be sneaking around my office for a reason. Then when I saw you come out of the photographer's studio and Maxwell told me you'd taken my wedding pictures, I knew you were too close for comfort."

"You're the one who tried to run me off the road, aren't you?" My voice and courage were coming back. "That wasn't your Mercedes, though."

"Elizabeth's SUV. Not that she'd notice the dents with all the medication I have her on." He removed a pair of surgical latex gloves from his pants pocket. "I thought you'd be clever enough to back off."

"Why bother trying to kill me?" I swallowed hard as I saw the gloves. That explained why he didn't leave any fingerprints when he broke into my apartment. "I didn't know you were the murderer until today."

He pulled the gloves on. "You were getting too close, talking to too many people."

"Why didn't you kill Dr. Pierce, too?" I shouldn't have suggested more potential victims, but curiosity got the better of me. "Couldn't his wife have shared her secret with him, as well?"

The groom arched an eyebrow at me. "You weren't close to Clara, were you? She and her husband barely spoke. I didn't have to worry about her telling him." He took a step toward me and my mind raced with thoughts of how to keep him talking. There was a knock on the door and I almost cheered. That would be Reese or Richard. Just in time, too.

"Yoo-hoo." Leatrice peeked inside. "It's me, dearie." So much for my knight in shining armor.

CHAPTER 36

"I wasn't aware you were with someone." Leatrice gave Dr. Donovan the once-over and skipped into the room. The doctor stared at her without speaking and slipped off the gloves.

"This isn't a good time, Leatrice." I made a quick jerky movement with my head toward the door, praying she'd take the hint and leave before Dr. Donovan decided to kill her, too.

"I'm Annabelle's neighbor, Mrs. Leatrice Butters." She took the groom's hand and pumped it.

He shot me a warning look.

"We're kind of in the middle of something, Leatrice." I darted my eyes in the groom's direction several times. Why didn't she pick up on my signals?

"Did I disturb something private?" Leatrice took a step, and then pulled on Dr. Donovan's sleeve. "You should see her when she doesn't have that red bump on her forehead. She's even prettier."

Perfect. First I'd be humiliated, and then I'd die.

Dr. Donovan put a hand on Leatrice's shoulder. "Mrs. Butters, we'd like a few moments alone, if you don't mind."

"Alone?" Leatrice clasped her hands together in what seemed to be the sheer joy of the moment.

"Thank you for stopping by to check on me," I said, widening my eyes and motioning my head toward the doctor. She nodded, and then gave me two thumbs up before the door closed on her. What did I have to do? Send up smoke signals?

"Nice lady." Dr. Donovan leaned against the door with one hand. "It would have been too much trouble to try to kill you both at once, though."

"How do you plan to get away with all this?" My eyes darted around the room. Any heavy objects I could use to defend myself?

"I've gotten away with two murders so far. The police don't have a clue."

"I've already called the cops." I edged myself against the wall. "They're on their way here right now."

He took a step forward. "By the time they arrive, I'll be gone. I changed my identity once, I can do it again."

"You should escape now before they get here."

His eyes became narrow slits. "I should have killed you days ago. If you hadn't been such a busybody, I would've gotten away with it."

I wished that Reese could hear that. I narrowed my eyes. "You're not going to get away with this."

The doctor clenched and unclenched his fists. "Your bravery is only matched by your stupidity, Miss Archer."

He lunged for me, and I ran around the back of the couch. We stood on opposite sides, poised like animals ready to strike. My only chance would be to reach the back door before him. I picked up an armful of cushions and hurled it at his face, as I took off for the exit.

He swore as the cushions hit him, then I heard his feet behind me. I closed in on the door. Just a few more feet. I felt a hand hit my back and pull me down. I screamed as my elbows hit the floor.

I twisted around onto my back, arms flailing. He raised his hands to clasp my neck as I rained punches on his face. As he tightened his grip around my throat, I heard a blood-curdling sound.

Mouth opened in a high-pitched scream, Leatrice flew through the air above us, clutching a shovel. She brought the metal down on Dr. Donovan's head, and he collapsed on top of me. Between acute hearing and shovel-wielding skills, I decided Leatrice might be a super hero in disguise. Leatrice rolled him off me with one of her brightly colored sneakers. A very good disguise.

I sat up, rubbing my throat. "How did you know, Leatrice?"

She sat down on top of him, his head between her feet. "Like I told you, I read a lot of mysteries."

"What took you so long? He almost killed me! Didn't you see the signals I sent you with my eyes?"

Leatrice reached over and patted my arm. "Yes. Next time don't be so obvious, dear. You almost gave the whole thing away."

Richard ran through the open door, gasping for breath. He saw Leatrice sitting on top of the doctor's limp body holding a shovel inches from his face and slumped against the wall. "Heard screaming . . . double parked . . . left car running . . . ran all the way . . . can't breathe . . ."

"It's over, Richard. Dr. Donovan confessed to both murders."

Richard fanned himself with both hands. "Is he dead?"

Leatrice peered through her legs at the doctor's face and raised the shovel over her head. "I don't think so. Should I hit him again?"

CHAPTER 37

After the police removed Dr. Donovan, barely coherent and mumbling about changing his name to Vanderbilt, I held court in my apartment. With a fresh new lump on my head, I figured I should be calling the shots. Leatrice and Kate sat on either side of me on the couch, taking turns holding the ice pack on my head. Richard had risen to the occasion, preparing an impressive display of cold hors d'oeuvres, considering the contents of my kitchen.

Detective Reese perched on the edge of my over-stuffed chair, taking small bites of a tomato and Velveeta canapé that Fern insisted he try. He wore a black knit shirt that stretched over the muscles in his arms. I concentrated hard on not noticing.

"Can you believe that Richard didn't want to use this perfectly good cheese? Those expiration dates are just guidelines." Fern pointed a thumb toward Richard in the kitchen. Reese stopped in midbite and placed the hors d' oeuvre on a lavender monogrammed cocktail napkin. Fern gave a loud sniff and retreated to the kitchen.

Kate tucked her legs under her. "I can't believe Dr. Donovan was the murderer."

"He covered well, setting up his father-in-law." Reese picked up his notepad from the table. He'd almost filled it when he arrived and questioned us. Now he was on the last page. "We would have discovered him eventually, though."

I lifted the ice pack off my head. "You mean after he'd killed me, changed his identity, and moved to another country?"

"Don't excite yourself, dearie." Leatrice pushed the ice back on lump number two.

"He'd have stayed put if you hadn't gone around stirring up trouble, Annabelle." Reese folded his arms across his broad chest.

I forced myself to look a few inches north and meet his eyes, which seemed to turn greener as we argued. "You're saying it's my fault he tried to kill me . . . twice?"

Leatrice gave a nervous laugh. "I'm sure that's not what Detect. . ."

"If you hadn't stuck your nose in the investigation, he wouldn't have felt threatened enough to kill you," Reese insisted.

"I can't believe this." I sat up quickly, felt a pain in my head, and leaned back. "We solve this case and present the killer to you on a silver platter, and you still won't give us any credit."

He nodded his head at Leatrice. "I'll give credit for the most creatively subdued suspect."

I thought of the groom being carried out with clumps of mulch from Leatrice's shovel clinging to his face and tried not to smile. I wanted to focus on outrage.

Leatrice turned bright pink. "I just worked with what I had."

Richard came out of the kitchen followed by Fern, who carried what appeared to be a plate of pinwheels made out of luncheon meat and something gooey. He gave a weak sigh as I eyed the plate Fern set on the coffee table. "This day has been one disaster after another."

"There, there." Fern put an arm around Richard. "Don't you worry about a thing. Try one of my yogurt pinwheels."

Richard peeked through his fingers at the drippy hors d'oeuvre Fern held up. "Heaven preserve me."

Kate raised an eyebrow at Richard, and then leaned over toward Reese. "I can't believe the groom killed his own mother-in-law. We didn't have a clue before today."

I noticed her neckline hanging low, and pulled her back next to me. "Actually we had plenty of clues. The victims being killed with prescription drugs, the tuxedo with the powder residue . . ."

"I guess you're right," Kate said. "Don't forget 'Phillips' written in Mrs. Pierce's notebook and the missing diploma."

"We didn't even make the connection that Dr. Donovan worked in the same office as his father-in-law," I added. "It never occurred to us that the killer could be someone so charming."

"Or so handsome." Kate grinned at Reese.

I pinched her hard on the leg. She yelped, glaring at me, and I noticed Reese trying to contain a smile. I reminded myself that cocky policemen weren't my type. Reese caught my eye and gave me a small wink. I smiled at him in spite of my best efforts not to and felt my face get warm. Then, again, a little adventure in life wasn't all bad.

THE END

FREE DOWNLOAD!

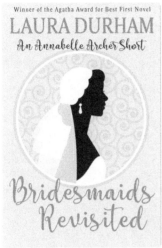

A LUXURY BRIDAL SHOWER.
THE STRESS IS HIGH.
THE PRESENTS ARE GONE.
THE BRIDESMAIDS ARE SUSPECTS.

CAN ANNABELLE UNMASK
THE THIEF?

amazon kindle

nook

kobo

 iBooks

Get your free copy of the short story "Bridesmaids Revisited" when you sign up to the author's mailing list. Go to the back of the book to sign up.

BOOK 2: FOR BETTER OR HEARSE

Annabelle Archer Wedding Planner Mystery
by Laura Durham

CHAPTER 1

"I barely escaped being sliced up like a sushi roll, Richard." My shaking hand pressed the cell phone to my ear as I paced the marble lobby of the Fairmont Hotel. "I'm not exaggerating, either. Chef Henri tried to kill me."

The only thing worse than working with a temperamental bride is dealing with a temperamental chef, and as one of D.C.'s top wedding planners, I'd had my share of both.

"He refuses to serve the Peking duck as a passed hors d'oeuvre, but with all these additional guests, we don't have room to do it as a station." I'd called my best friend, and arguably the city's best caterer, Richard Gerard, for some insight into the mind of a culinary despot. While I had a wedding at the Fairmont Hotel, Richard had one at the Dumbarton House in nearby Georgetown. His guests weren't due to arrive for another hour, and I could hear the clattering sounds of setup in the background.

Richard let out a high-pitched shriek. "We do not throw things, people. If I see anyone else tossing my imported Hungarian salad plates on the tables, heads will roll." He switched to his most calming voice. "Now Annabelle, you know he has a valid point. The real art of Peking duck is in the carving.

I should never have asked for practical advice from someone who matched the food at a dinner party to the outfit he planned to wear.

"Richard, he chased me out of the kitchen with a knife and threatened to walk off the event if I ever set foot in there again."

"He's a chef. They're known for being dramatic, especially this one." A gasp. "Who put this cloth on the sweetheart table? I specifically requested the linen pin-tuck for the bride and groom, not the satin stripe."

I tapped my square-toed black pump in rapid fire. "I've about had it with chefs. I knew Henri had a reputation for being difficult, but I had no idea he would be so evil."

"You think you've seen evil?" Richard gave a low whistle. "You should hear the stories his former employees tell." I didn't have time for Richard's stories now. They usually involved at least one person wearing something "totally wrong for them" and ended up with Richard giving an impassioned speech worthy of an Oscar.

"Okay, I get it, but what am I supposed to do?" I walked to the heavy glass doors leading from the lobby to the Colonnade room and glanced at my watch. The guests would be arriving from the church in a few minutes, and I had a chef who had threatened to walk off the job if I questioned his creative control again.

"Where's Kate? Maybe she could bat her eyelashes at him and he'd be a little more agreeable." Richard referred to my faithful assistant. Faithful to me, that is, not to any man she'd ever known.

"At the church. Anyway, I think it would take a bit more than eyelash batting to calm Chef Henri down."

I walked into the Colonnade and smiled. I often described it to my brides as "dramatic, yet feminine," and it ranked as one of my favorite ballrooms in the city. Walled entirely in glass, it looked out onto an open air courtyard that had a massive granite fountain and brightly colored flowers that were changed according to the season. At the moment, they were vibrant autumn shades of yellow and orange.

Inside, waiters lit votive candles around the ledge of the raised gazebo that took up the center of the room. Garlands of red roses curved around the gazebo's whitewashed columns, and tiny rosebuds strung on transparent thread hung between them to create a delicate curtain effect.

The bride had wanted to use elements from her Chinese background to personalize her wedding, so we'd incorporated lots of red, the Chinese color of celebration, and used signs from the Chinese zodiac in everything from the invitations to the ice sculptures. Huge mounds of deep crimson roses sat in the middle of each square table on crisscrossed red satin runners, and menu cards personalized with each guest's zodiac sign had been tucked into the napkins.

Two giant ice carvings, a tiger and a rabbit, rose up from huge blocks of ice and faced each other across the room. The ice tiger stood on its hind legs with his two front paws extended, and represented the groom's zodiac sign, while the rabbit had been carved in profile on its hind legs and represented the bride's sign. The sculptures were lit from above with beams of white light, and they glistened like fine crystal. Despite my usual distaste for ice sculptures, I had to admit that the room was striking.

"I swear these waiters are going to push me over the edge. I don't think a single one read the look book I put together for this event." Richard's voice crackled at me through static. "Are you still there, darling?"

"I'm admiring my handiwork, that's all." I walked back out into the hallway that led to the Colonnade.

"Is this the same little wedding planner who didn't think she could compete with the grand dames of the industry only a couple of years ago?" A gasp. "Flat fold napkins, people, not fan-fold. This is not a Rotary lunch."

I adjusted the flower arrangement on the marble credenza next to the ladies' room and cradled the phone against my shoulder. Glancing in the mirror above the flowers, I brushed a long strand of auburn hair off my face. I pinched my cheeks to give them a bit a color and noticed that I actually had hollows now. The one advantage to having brides run you ragged —no time to eat!

"I've come a long way under your watchful eye, Richard."

"Don't mention it. Name your firstborn child after me and we'll call it even."

I laughed. "That's a safe promise since I haven't even had a date in months." To be completely honest, I hadn't had a real boyfriend since I started Wedding Belles four years ago.

"Don't be down on yourself, darling. You've had some nibbles," Richard reassured me, and then his voice rose to a shriek. "What are the frosted champagne flutes doing *on* the tables? They're for passing only. Did anyone read their timeline?"

"By nibbles do you mean the pastry chef who had a lisp or the bartender who ended up taking home a bridesmaid?"

"Those are bad examples, Annie. What about the detective we dealt with on that murder case?" Glass shattered in the background. "If they broke my etched-glass water goblets, I'm going to die."

"Detective Reese?" I tried to play it cool, but I felt my face get warm at the thought of the dark-haired cop. We'd met when one of my former clients had turned up dead in the middle of the wedding reception and Richard and I had gotten tangled up in the investigation, much to the detective's dismay. I dismissed the fluttery feeling in my stomach when I remembered that I hadn't heard from the detective in the months following the case. Not that I'd expected to, of course. "When would I ever see him again? It's not like we run in the same circles."

Richard let out a breath. "Why wait for him to make the first move? Maybe you could happen to drop by the station and bump into him."

"That's not my style and you know it," I protested.

"I didn't know you had a style, darling."

I gave a fake laugh. "Very funny. What possible reason would I have to be at the police station? Unless I wanted to report one of my brides for harassment."

"Don't tell me bridezilla is still calling you at home all the time?"

"She called me last night at eleven o'clock to tell me that her honeymoon resort would be featured on a special segment of the news." I rolled my eyes. "I don't know how she got my home number in the first place."

Richard groaned. "I think that qualifies as grounds for a restraining order. When is her wedding, anyway?"

"I'll be rid of her in November, if I survive her neuroses that long. Only a couple more months." My call waiting beeped in, and I recognized Kate's number. "I've got to run. That's Kate on the other line calling from the ceremony." I clicked over and could hear lots of voices in the background.

"I just loaded the last trolley with guests and we're on our way. The first one should be there any minute. The videographer is on it, so maybe she can get room shots before most of the guests arrive."

"Good thinking, Kate." I hurried toward the hotel lobby so I could spot the old-fashioned open-aired trolley when it arrived. "I'll see you when you get here."

I dropped my phone into my jacket pocket and took out my crumpled wedding timeline. The photographer had flown through the formal portraits, the limousines had been on time, and the bride had even been ready early. We were perfectly on schedule. I closed my eyes and let out a long breath. I knew not to trust the calm before the storm.

"Asleep on the job, are we?" A Scottish accent pulled me out of my momentary rest. My eyes flew open. His spiky blond hair and the tattoos that covered his arms were offset by a black muscle shirt and traditional red kilt. I wasn't an expert on formal Scottish attire, but I didn't think that leather, lace-up Captain America boots were usually part of the outfit.

The band. They had declined to go along with our theme, not that I could blame them. It wouldn't make much sense for an all-eighties rock band called "The Breakfast Club" to dress like geisha girls. The band agent had assured me that not everyone in the band wore kilts. The rest of the foursome sported leather pants, feathered hair, and Miami Vice jackets. Not your typical wedding band by a long shot.

He watched me give him the once-over and grinned. "We're dressed and finished with our sound checks."

I glanced at my watch. "That was fast." Usually bands took forever to set up.

Captain America gave me a wink. "We're good." Uh-oh. Cute band guys were always trouble, especially if they knew they were cute. I could see it coming a mile away. By the end of the evening half of the bridesmaids would be all over this guy. I hope he didn't think I was falling for it. Before I could put on my I-mean-business wedding planner face, he reached out and touched my hair.

"Are you by any chance Scottish?"

"A bit," I found myself stammering. My usual composure had clearly abandoned me. "And some Irish."

He nodded and locked eyes with me. "I have a thing for redheads."

He turned and walked out of the lobby, looking back once to smile. My I-mean-business wedding planner face had been shot to hell, and I felt lucky just to keep my mouth from gaping open. The bridesmaids didn't stand a chance.

Usually Kate attracted most of the male attention at weddings with her bouncy, blond hair and come-hither heels. I'd been able to steer clear with sensible shoes and a general disregard for primping. I pulled my hair back into a quick bun as I gave myself a mental shake. I didn't have time to get flustered by a bad boy musician who probably flirted with everyone. Even if he did have a thing for redheads.

"They're right behind me." Fern dashed through the front doors waving a hairbrush. He wore his dark hair in a tight ponytail, and I suspected he'd coordinated his red brocade jacket to go with the decor.

Fern had become known as the wedding hair guru in Washington because of his attentiveness to brides. He insisted on doing the final touches only moments before the bridal processional, and he always waited until after the ceremony to repair his masterpieces. Sometimes I feared that he would actually start walking down the aisle with the bride, hair spraying in time to the music.

Now, the ceremony over, Fern had beat a hasty retreat from the church to the Fairmont. He ran past me, blowing me an air kiss with one hand. "I have to find my equipment case before the bride arrives. I barely beat the trolleys over here."

Sure enough, the orange and gold Old Town Trolley pulled up in front of the glass doors, and guests began emptying out. I met the videographer as she came through the doors, battery packs and wires barely peeking out from under her black suit jacket. One of the few female videographers in the city, Joni was also one of the most talented and the chattiest. I had to be careful or I'd find myself gabbing with her for half an hour.

"Hey, Joni. We're in a big rush. Could you get some shots of the courtyard before the guests wreck everything?" I pointed out the enormous arrangement of red tulips by the door to the outdoor courtyard and the masses of red rose blooms we'd floated in the fountain.

"Then once you've got that, you can go inside to the Colonnade. The bride wants lots of detail shots of the ice sculptures."

"Wait until you see the footage I got of the bird loose in the church. I think the bride's aunt is still trying to get the bird poop out of her hair."

I cringed and made a mental note to look for the wet wipes in my emergency kit. I was sure they could handle bird poop.

"Can you show me later?" I gave her a prod toward the courtyard, where people were beginning to descend.

"Sure, just remind me." Joni also had the attention span of a fruit fly and she knew it. She hurried off past the guests, who were being distracted by the line of waiters offering trays of ginseng lemonade and green tea martinis, the specialty drinks for the evening. The pianist played tunes from *Madame Butterfly* in the background as guests mingled around the bar and moved outside to the courtyard. So far, so good.

Time to deal with Chef Henri. Taking a deep breath, I walked back into the Colonnade and went immediately into the kitchen, expecting to be greeted by the usual bustle of the waiters and grumbling of the chef. Nothing. All the waiters must have been passing hors d'oeuvres, and Chef Henri had probably decided to go off somewhere to pout. Perfect. A hundred eighty guests would be sitting down to dinner in less than an hour and I had no chef.

I stormed out the swinging exit door that led to the far side of the Colonnade and stopped short. Taking a few steps forward, I grabbed the back of a chair to keep my knees from buckling.

I had found Chef Henri.

I didn't know whether the blue tinge on his skin was connected to the blood that covered the lower part of his chef's jacket or was a result of his being impaled on the outstretched claw of the enormous ice tiger. All I knew was that he looked very cold and very dead.

CHAPTER 2

"A horrible crime has been committed!" Fern's shrieks carried across the room. Could he see across the room to where I stood in front of the dead, now dripping chef? "Where are you, Annabelle? My styling case has been stolen."

"I'm on the other side," I managed to call out. I could hear Fern's indignant footsteps, but I couldn't take my eyes off the impaled chef to turn around.

"Who do I speak to about lodging a complai . . . ?" Fern's voice trailed off as he walked up beside me. "Oh dear. Tell me this isn't the chef you had a fight with."

My mouth dropped open. "How did you know I had a fight with him?"

"Kate told me after you called her at the ceremony." He cocked his head to the side. "He doesn't look very good, Annabelle. Is he dead?"

I nodded my head and took a deep breath to keep from getting sick. I usually felt faint when I had to get my finger pricked at the doctor, and the sight of this much blood made my legs feel like cooked spaghetti.

"Poor fellow." Fern's expression was somber, then he nudged me with one elbow. "I must admit, honey, I didn't think you had it in you."

"I didn't do it!" I cried as I looked away from the body. "I found him like this."

Fern put a hand to his temple and slumped against me. "Well, that's a relief. I was going to suggest some anger management courses, but if you're sure you didn't . . ."

I narrowed my eyes at him. "I'm sure."

"Of course I didn't really think you could do something like this. Even with all that stress you've got pent up from a severe lack of sex." Fern shook his head. I knew my lackluster love life scandalized him more than the dead body. "It would take a lot of strength to kill someone this way. What kind of ice sculpture is this?"

"A tiger. The groom's sign from the Chinese zodiac."

Fern walked close to the body. "So he's impaled on the tiger's arm?"

"The claws." I motioned to the sculpture without looking. "You can't see them anymore, but the tiger had big claws."

Fern raised an eyebrow. "That doesn't seem very safe."

"We didn't expect anyone to fall on them," I explained, trying to keep the irritation out of my voice.

"I hate to break it to you." Fern put his hands on his hips. "I don't think he fell. He had to have been pushed."

My head started to pound. "I need to sit down." I walked to the nearest table and pulled out a chair to collapse into. As unpleasant as Henri had been to me, I felt horrible that he had been murdered and a bit guilty for thinking such mean thoughts about him.

"Where is everyone?" Kate's voice carried from the doorway, and then I saw her blond head bobbing toward me. I nudged Fern to stand in front of the ice sculpture, so she wouldn't start screaming at the sight of the corpse.

Kate barely glanced up as she plopped down in the chair next to me and dropped her pink Kate Spade bag on the floor. She shrugged herself out of the jacket that covered the backless dress I'd forbidden her to wear. "Now don't get upset, Annabelle, but we might have to fly into the ointment."

"You mean a fly in the ointment?" Kate's ability to mangle even the most common expression scared me. Lately some of her word concoctions had started to make sense, which scared me even more. "We already have one."

"Why?" Kate's eyes widened. "Is Chef Henri still being impossible?"

Fern stepped away from the ice sculpture. "I wouldn't say that exactly."

Kate saw the body and jumped up, promptly losing balance on her stiletto heels and stumbling to the side. She gave a yelp as she fell, and I lunged to catch her. Fern moved neatly out of the way as the two of us went down, arms flailing. I lay on my back, assessing the possibility of serious injury, until I heard a familiar Scottish accent.

"Should I ask what you're doing down there or assume that you have everything under control?" I looked up at the kilt-wearing bandleader, who had one eyebrow raised and appeared to be stifling a great deal of laughter. Fabulous. He was a smart-ass, too.

"You could give me a hand if you have nothing better to do," I grumbled.

He winked at me as he pulled me up. "I can't think of anything that could be better."

Did women really fall for this? Kate, still on the ground, cleared her throat loudly and stared at the Scottish equivalent of David Bowie. Apparently they did.

Fern ignored Kate's protests as he pulled her up, and then turned to me. "What's with the kilt? I thought you said this wedding had an Asian theme."

"He's with the band," I explained, trying to keep the impatience out of my voice. Fern gave me a knowing look and nodded.

"What's with the kilt?" Kate practically screamed. "How about what's with the dead guy?"

"That's the chef." Fern put an arm around Kate. "The one Annabelle had the fight with, but she swears she didn't kill him. Between you and me, I don't think she has the strength to do it, anyway."

"I'm still in the room, you know." I rubbed my temples where my head had started to pound.

Kilt-boy inspected the corpse closely. "This isn't part of the decor?"

Fern gasped. "What kind of weddings do you have in Scotland?"

"American weddings are supposed to be really different and outrageous. Don't you have Renaissance themes and the like?"

"That's a very small, off-beat part of the population," I explained. "We certainly don't have murder- themed weddings. Not in Washington, at least."

"Can we continue this discussion somewhere away from Chef Henri?" Kate backed away, her voice trembling. "This is horrible. He's blue."

Fern shuddered. "I'm sure the ice is cold."

"I don't think frostbite is what got him." Kate rubbed her arms as if trying to warm herself. "I can't believe he's dead, even if he was impossible to work with."

I glanced at the pale lips and flat, expressionless eyes, then looked away and took a long breath. The man who had been such a terror to me earlier hardly seemed imposing now. Chef Henri had been far from beloved, but I wondered who hated him enough to do this.

"Annabelle, are you in here?"

"Richard?" I didn't know whether to be relieved or concerned. Richard usually didn't decrease the drama in a situation. "I'm on the other side of the gazebo."

"My event doesn't start for another hour, so 1 came over to try to help you out with Chef Henri . . ." His words trailed off as he came into view of the spectacularly lit chef impaled on an ice tiger that was being inspected by a heavily tattooed Scotsman.

"Now, Richard," I said, then stopped. I didn't know where to begin. In this case, it was as bad as it looked.

"Oh my God." He put both hands to his head, without disturbing the dark, choppy hair that I knew he'd painstakingly arranged to look messy. "Can you explain this catastrophe?"

"Don't worry," Fern reassured him. "He's with the band."

Richard didn't take his eyes off the spectacle in front of him. "How long has he been here?"

Fern turned to me. "When did the band arrive?"

"I'm talking about the dead body hanging off that ice monstrosity." Richard kept his voice level, but his face had started to turn an unpleasant shade of pink under his spray-on tan.

"I found him like this a few minutes ago," I said. "I meant to call the police right away but Fern came in, then Kate got here, then the bandleader found all of us—"

Richard held up a hand to silence me. "So the police haven't been notified yet? Shall I help you move him onto the dance floor so guests could dance around him?"

Fern's eyes widened. "Oh, I don't think that's such a good idea."

So much for sarcasm. Richard cast his eyes heavenward and muttered under his breath.

"I'm telling you, Richard, we just found him," I insisted. "He can't have been dead very long."

Richard walked up to the chef as he pulled out his cell phone. "Are you people out of your minds? He's melting. I'm going to call the police before there's nothing left but a body balancing on an ice cube." He leaned in close to the corpse. "Is this Henri?"

"You mean the chef I had the big fight with that everyone seems to know about?" I glared at Kate, who began busily inspecting the carpet. "Yep. You can call me Miss Motive."

Richard closed his phone and the color drained from his face. "I didn't recognize him."

Fern gave a sad shake of his head. "He doesn't look his best, I'm sure. Which is a shame, because with the right haircut I'll bet he could look quite attractive."

"I know he wasn't the most popular chef in town but I didn't know anyone hated him enough to do this." Richard's voice caught in his throat. "This is not good, Annabelle."

"Thank you for noticing. At least no one from the wedding has seen him yet."

"Um, Annabelle." Kate tugged on my sleeve.

I turned around and found myself face-to-face with the bride. Crap. She let the cathedral-length veil that had been draped across her arm drop to the floor, and her dramatically made-up eyes were fixed on Chef Henri. I could be pretty sure this wasn't how she'd pictured her wedding day.

I opened my mouth to reassure her that everything would be fine, but I was too late. For such a petite, demure-looking girl, she could really scream. My hair stood on end as I clutched my hands over my ears, and I feared the glass walls of the room would shatter at any moment.

Richard jumped at the noise, and his phone flew straight up in the air. Reaching back to catch it, he stumbled into the corpse and the ice tiger teetered precariously on its base. As the massive sculpture began to lurch backward, Richard grabbed the chef to keep it from falling. The bride stopped screaming abruptly and her knees buckled as she sank to the floor. Fern caught her by the veil before she hit the ground.

"I think I might be sick." Richard put one hand over his mouth as the other clung to the dark, wet strands of hair that were once part of the dead chef's tragic comb-over.

"Hold on and I'll push from the other side." The bandleader took a few long strides around the ice sculpture.

"Stop right where you are," a deep voice boomed from behind us. I spun on my heels and saw a uniformed police officer with a hand above his holster. "Nobody move."

I looked on helplessly as the bride's veil gave way and she hit the carpet face first with a soft thud, leaving Fern holding a handful of white tulle. Richard let out a barely audible squeak before Chef Henri's hair slipped through his fingers and the giant ice tiger crashed to the ground, corpse and all.

CHAPTER 3

"I say we make a run for it," Kate said under her breath. "I'll create a distraction and you guys sneak out the back."

Kate, Fern, and I sat at a round cocktail table draped in an ivory hotel tablecloth while Richard paced in front of us. The walls of the basement meeting room had been upholstered in a silk cream damask to coordinate with the patterned carpet and match the linens. Hotels were big on neutrals.

We'd been stashed in the Imperial Room while we waited to be questioned, but it had been ages since they'd taken the bandleader to talk to a detective. The silver pitcher of water they'd set out had been empty for an hour, and my stomach had started to rumble.

"One problem with that plan," I replied. "We don't know how to get out the back. I've never been in through the loading dock, have you?"

"What a splendid idea, Kate." Richard's voice had a tone of mild hysteria to it. "I, for one, am all up for adding 'fugitive' to our resumes."

"I'm sure we aren't really suspects." Kate stretched her arms over her head, causing her dress to inch dangerously high up her thighs. Not that she cared. "This is just a formality because we found the body."

"Don't you mean found the body, touched the body, ruined the crime scene, and destroyed evidence?" Richard counted off on his fingers.

She rolled her eyes. "If you want to get really technical about it. . ."

"We're staying right here until this mess is sorted out," Richard said firmly. "Anyway, the four of us would get all of two blocks out of the city before being arrested."

"What do you mean?" Fern protested. "We can blend in."

Richard looked Fern up and down. "Are those Prada loafers?"

Fern nodded enthusiastically and held up his feet so we could all get a good look at his designer shoes. "Do you like them in red?"

Richard folded his arms across his chest. "I rest my case."

Kate slumped back down in her chair. "I guess that plan is up the window."

"*Out* the window," Richard and I said in unison.

The door opened and the uniformed officer we'd met previously strode into the room. A dark-haired man wearing beige pants and a navy blazer followed, closing the door behind him. Detective Reese. He looked exactly as I remembered him, though a little more tan.

"Well, well, well." He pulled a chair out and sat down facing us. "The gang's all here."

Richard looked even more jumpy since Reese had entered the room and he gave a nervous giggle. "You're on this case?" The last time we'd encountered the detective, Richard's business had been shut down and he'd almost been arrested.

"Lucky me, right?" Reese gave me a quick glance then opened his small leather notebook. So much for the sight of me causing him to swoon. I wondered if he even recognized me.

"Would you like me to tell you what happened, Detective?" I felt a hint of irritation creep into my voice. "It might save you some valuable crime-solving minutes."

He looked up and held my gaze with his deep hazel eyes. The corner of his mouth twitched up into a half smirk. "I'm glad to see you're as easy-going as ever, Miss Archer."

I felt a flush begin to move up my neck. "I didn't know you remembered me, I mean, us."

Reese looked from me to Kate to Fern and settled on Richard. "Vividly."

"I had nothing to do with it," Richard burst out. "When I came in the room, they were all standing around the body."

I shot him a look. "Thanks, Richard."

Reese nodded and flipped to a page in his notebook. "So how did you end up holding the deceased 'by the hair' and dropping him onto the floor?"

"I tried to catch him and ended up with a handful of hair." Richard paled a few shades.

"That comb-over was the real crime," Fern muttered.

Reese turned his attention to Fern, who shrunk back into his chair. "When did you enter the crime scene?"

"You see, I'd just realized that my equipment case was missing and went to find Annabelle so I could report it stolen." He took a quick breath and leaned forward. "When I came into the Colonnade, I saw her in front of the ice sculpture."

The detective wrote quickly in his pad. "Did you see anyone else in the room?"

"Well, the chef." Fern shrugged. "But he was dead, so I don't think he counts."

"No, he doesn't count." Reese sighed and turned to Kate.

"I must have come in after that because Fern and Annie were both in the room, but I didn't notice the body at first." Kate adjusted one of the spaghetti straps of her dress. "The band guy came in right after me. Probably not more than two minutes later."

Reese asked the uniformed officer to bring in the lead singer, and then looked at his notes. "So if I have this right, Annabelle came in, followed by Fern, Kate, the band guy, then Richard."

"Ian," the kilt-clad Scotsman said from the doorway. "Not that I mind 'band guy.' "

Reese gave Ian the once-over and turned to me. "This is the lead singer of the wedding band?"

I smiled and nodded. "They're supposed to be very good."

"We're better than good, darling." He came in and pulled up a chair next to me. "It's a shame you didn't get to check us out." Ian didn't seem to be intimidated by the police presence, or even notice it, actually.

I tried not to blush more than I had already.

Reese looked between us for a second, and then went back to his notes. "We're trying to piece together tonight's chain of events. When did you come into the room?"

"After I spoke to this lovely redhead in the lobby, I went to check on how the rest of the band was coming along." Ian turned his gaze from me to the detective. "Maybe ten minutes later I went into the reception room and saw the two girls on the floor and the chap in the great jacket standing next to them. The high- strung fellow didn't come in until after that."

Richard twitched visibly, and Fern puffed his chest out.

Reese raised an eyebrow at me. "What were you doing on the floor?"

"I got startled when I saw the body and stumbled over my shoes," Kate said before I could explain. She held her legs out to show the detective the high heels. Clearly, Kate needed more male attention. "Annabelle tried to catch me, but we both ended up on the ground."

Reese turned back to me. "It seems that you were the only person alone with the body, then."

"Aside from the person who killed him, you mean?" I didn't like the way this seemed to be headed.

"Of course," the detective said quickly. "Did you see anyone leaving the room?"

I shook my head. "But someone could have left through the kitchen and escaped through the back of the house without anyone seeing them. Anyone who worked in the hotel knows how to get around in the back corridors."

Reese arched his eyebrows. "The back of the house?"

"Sorry." I gave an apologetic smile. "That's the term we use for all the behind-the-scenes areas like the kitchen and the corridors that connect everything."

"Have you ever been in back?"

"Sure," I admitted. "I've gone into the kitchens and the employee cafeteria before. But I wouldn't know how to get around easily, if that's what you're getting at."

"Were you in the back at all today?" Reese sounded casual, but red lights started going off in my head.

I sat up on the edge of my chair. "I went into the kitchen to check on things and discuss the setup with the chef."

Reese didn't look me in the eyes. "When did this take place?"

"About half an hour before I found him murdered." My mouth felt very dry. Did they think I killed Chef Henri? "But I stayed in the lobby from the time I left Henri in the kitchen to when I came back in the room. I'm sure lots of people saw me."

"I can vouch for her being in the lobby." Ian gave a firm nod of his head. He looked at Reese seriously and almost appeared fierce. "If you think this girl murdered someone, you're all wrong, mate."

I gave Ian a grateful smile, and then glared at Reese. "See? What does my being in the kitchen have to do with Henri's death?"

"It seems that one of the other chefs overheard you having a huge fight with Henri earlier today and said that you left in a rage." Reese snapped his notebook shut and stood up.

I cringed. "We had a disagreement over one of the food stations. Who said I left in a rage?"

"The same person who called us to report the murder." Reese finally met my eyes. "And named you as the killer."

CHAPTER 4

"That's impossible!" Leatrice Butters, my elderly neighbor who took an overeager interest in my personal life, had been waiting for me at the door of our narrow Georgetown apartment building when I got home from hours of police questioning. She wore a navy sweat suit with green puffy frogs that seemed to squeak each time she pressed against one. Leatrice had a fondness for "action" clothing. "Who could ever suspect you of murder?"

Richard had insisted on making sure I got home safely and had walked ahead of me up the stairs to open my door. I'm sure it had nothing to do with getting out of earshot of Leatrice and her squeaking frogs.

"Apparently some overeager cook saw me right after I found the body and assumed I did it." I already felt weary explaining the night's events and dreaded having to do it a hundred more times. "Once the police pinned him down, he admitted that he didn't see me doing anything but standing next to the body."

"Thank goodness for that." Leatrice looked relieved as she followed me closely up the stairs to my fourth floor walk-up. The building was only four stories high, with two apartments on each floor. Small enough for neighbors to actually know each other, which was rare in D.C. Sometimes I considered it more of a mixed blessing, though.

"How did you know about the murder before we got here?" I turned to Leatrice as we reached my floor. "It hasn't been on the news, has it?" My brides would be less than thrilled to see me on the news involved in a murder. The fact that the murder took place at a wedding would send some of them into comas.

Leatrice shook her head and beamed. "My police scanner. I keep it on all the time."

I felt my stomach drop. So much for keeping this incident hushed up. "You heard my name on a police scanner?"

"No, dearie." Leatrice patted my arm. "I heard that the report came from the Fairmont and remembered that you mentioned the hotel when I saw you leave this morning. To be honest, the scanner doesn't give as much information as I'd hoped."

"Really?" Knowing Leatrice, she'd been expecting color commentary of the crimes. I needed to lie down. Richard held the door open for me and visibly restrained himself from shutting it on Leatrice. According to Richard, Leatrice meddled in my life too much. I don't think he liked the competition.

I dropped my purse on the floor and collapsed onto my slightly worn yellow twill couch. Nudging a pile of wedding magazines out of the way, I propped both feet up on my coffee table. Leatrice sat down next to me while Richard headed off to the kitchen.

"So who do they think did it?" Leatrice's eyes danced with excitement. Sometimes it worried me how much she liked mysteries.

"I have no idea." I let out a deep sigh. "Considering how many people hated the murdered chef, it could have been anyone. Apparently I had the least motive of anyone in the hotel."

"I told you, Annabelle." Richard emerged from the kitchen with a mini wheel of Brie and a box of crackers. "Anyone who ever worked with Henri wanted to kill him. He was the most notorious chef in town. And one of the most talented."

Leatrice put a hand on my arm. "Is that cute detective working the case?"

Richard snickered, and I glared at him. "Yes, Leatrice, but I've told you a thousand times that there's nothing going on there."

"I know." Leatrice's face fell. "It's such a shame."

"Isn't it, though?" Richard gave me a sugary smile as he sat down across from us in the matching yellow armchair. Richard loved seeing me squirm when Leatrice started trying to play matchmaker. I'm sure it was the only reason he tolerated her. He put the box of crackers on the table and started to open the Brie.

"I don't know if I would eat that cheese." I cringed as Richard opened the round wooden box. "I think I've had it for a while."

Richard unwrapped the white paper covering and made a face. "Now you do understand that the refrigeration process does not stop time, don't you?"

"Yes." I rolled my eyes. "I just forgot about it."

Richard stood up, holding the offending cheese in front of him at arm's length. "I will never understand how you can be so detailed and precise with your weddings, yet your own life is a mess."

"It is not a mess," I protested. "Anyway, if I spent all my time shopping and cleaning, I'd never be able to put in the hours to plan all those perfect weddings."

"One word for you, darling." Richard disappeared into the kitchen then poked his head up over the counter that separated the living room and kitchen. "Balance."

"I have balance," I shouted over my shoulder as I sunk into the couch. "I'm even taking a yoga class. If that isn't balance, I don't know what is."

Richard walked back into the living room and planted his hands on his hips. "You're taking yoga? Miss Type A, if-I'm-not-doing-ten-things-at-once-I'm-not-busy? Now this I have to see."

"Fine." I folded my arms across my chest.

"Now, now." Leatrice waved her arms. "You kids stop your bickering. You're just like me and my Jimmy used to be."

Jimmy? Richard mouthed to me.

"Her late husband," I said under my breath. Richard's eyebrows shot up and he opened his mouth to say something, but I grabbed him by the sleeve. I stood and began tugging him into the kitchen.

"Come on; let's go find something to eat." I turned to Leatrice. "We'll be right back."

Once we got into the kitchen, Richard pulled my hand away and started unwrinkling his sleeve. "What was that all about? Doesn't she know by now that the chances of us getting together are slim to nil? Heavy on the nil?"

"I think she forgets things sometimes. I'm not going to be the one who explains things to her again. You do it."

Richard wagged a finger at me. "I have a strict 'don't ask, don't tell' policy."

"People have to ask? I mean, aside from Leatrice?"

"Very funny, Annabelle." Richard narrowed his eyes and looked over the counter at Leatrice, who was happily pressing the frogs on her shirt to make them squeak. "I think the nut-ball has a selective memory."

"Be nice, Richard."

He pressed a hand over his heart and let his mouth gape open. "You wound me, darling. When am I not nice?"

"Well. . ." I began.

Richard cut me off with a raised palm. 'That was a hypothetical." He opened the refrigerator as the doorbell rang. We both jumped at the loud noise.

"Could you get that Leatrice?" I called out as I turned to examine our food options.

"Of course, dearie." She shuffled to the door. "Are you expecting anyone?"

Leatrice opened the door and gave a small scream. Richard and I both froze.

"Good heavens," Leatrice gasped. "We're being robbed!"

CHAPTER 5

I rushed into the living room and saw Leatrice with her hands in the air and Ian standing in the doorway with a puzzled expression on his face. I didn't see a weapon in sight.

"Leatrice, what are you talking about?" I went up and pulled her arms down. I heard Richard's muffled laughter behind me. "Ian isn't robbing us."

"You know him?" Leatrice flushed. "I guess I got startled by the tattoos."

"Sorry about that." I waved Ian into the room. He'd traded in his kilt and Captain America boots for a pair of broken-in jeans and Doc Martens, but he'd kept the black tank top. If it weren't for the tattoos covering both well-muscled biceps, he'd be practically mainstream.

"Are those real?" Leatrice had overcome her embarrassment and stood inches away from Ian's arms.

He nodded. "Do you like them?"

Leatrice cocked her head to one side. "They're interesting. This woman certainly isn't dressed to be riding a dragon like that, though."

"Tattoos are very fashionable now." Richard sank onto the couch, barely taking note of the body art. "Everyone has them."

"Do you think I should get one?" Leatrice brightened.

"No," I said forcefully. I noticed Richard's disappointment that I wouldn't let him egg her on and glared at him. I turned my attention to Ian. "What are you doing here, by the way?"

He produced my boxy, metal wedding emergency kit from behind his back and set it on the floor. "The lads accidentally loaded this in with our equipment. Your address is on the business card you taped to the inside, so I figured I'd return it to you."

"Thanks." I wondered if that was the only reason he'd returned it personally, but I didn't want to take a bit of harmless flirting too seriously. He seemed like the type who did lots of flirting anyway.

Ian took a few steps away from Leatrice and gave my apartment the once-over. "Is this just an office or do you live here?"

"I live here," I explained. "My office is down the hall with the bedroom." My apartment was shaped like a baby rattle with two clusters of rooms separated by a long hallway. I loved the fact that nothing in Georgetown was a standard size or shape.

He strode over to the windows that lined the front of the living room and pulled back the curtains. He peered three stories down to the street. "Great location."

"It's a very safe building." Leatrice followed him across the room. "I'm president of the neighborhood watch." Actually, Leatrice *was* the neighborhood watch.

"How did you get in, anyway?" I asked. The front door was controlled by a keypad. You either had to know the code or have a resident buzz you in.

He gave me a lopsided grin and shrugged.

"On second thought, I don't want to know." I looked at my watch. "Did you just leave the hotel?"

"The police made our load-out a bit longer than usual. At least they didn't make us wait until they'd questioned everyone or I'd still be there."

Leatrice raised herself up on her tiptoes, which still only brought her chest level to Ian. "You were at the murder scene, too?"

"Bit of bad luck, eh?" He flashed her a smile. I could tell that Leatrice didn't think it was bad luck at all.

Leatrice moved in close. "Did you see anything important? Any clues?"

"Lots of people coming and going all day, but nothing sinister." He placed his hands on the back of an oversized armchair and leaned forward. "I don't see how they're going to sort this mess out with everyone looking the same."

"What do you mean?" Leatrice asked.

"Except for me and the lads, everyone at that place is dressed alike. All those waiters are in tuxedos and the cooks are in those white jackets. Who can tell them apart?"

"I never thought of it that way," I said. "But not everyone is a suspect, are they?"

"The police spent a lot of time with the kitchen staff," Ian said.

"That makes sense." Richard picked at a tiny blob of something on my couch. I needed to stop using my couch as a dining table. "They did work with Henri the most and had the easiest access to him."

"But who would benefit the most from his death?" Leatrice tapped her chin. "The killer has to have a strong motive."

'Trust me, Leatrice." I patted her on the arm. "Anyone who knew the victim had a strong motive."

"The only time I saw the chef that day, he was dead." Ian sidestepped around the chair he'd been leaning on and sat down. He propped his feet on my coffee table, then noticed Richard shooting daggers at him and dropped them back to the floor. "So I guess that leaves me out."

Leatrice folded her arms across her chest and her frogs let out a chorus of squeaks. "Not necessarily. You could have a secret motive."

"Oh, please," Richard mumbled, then pointed to the unidentifiable spot on my sofa and whispered to me, "What on earth have you been doing on here?"

"Nothing." I could feel my face warm. "I probably spilled something."

"A secret motive would make you the perfect killer." Leatrice raised her voice to talk over us.

"You do have a dining table, you know." Richard looked behind him at the wooden table covered in paperwork then let out a long breath. "Forget I said anything."

I glanced at Ian and he caught my eyes, then winked at me and grinned. Richard cleared his throat and I looked away.

Don't even think about it, darling, Richard mouthed to me. I didn't have to be an expert lip reader to understand his meaning.

"What if you had a connection to the victim that no one knew about?" Leatrice ignored us and continued. "If no one knows your motive, then you wouldn't even be a suspect."

"I suppose that's true." Ian shifted in his chair, clearly humoring Leatrice. "But the chef was dead when I saw him."

"Ah ha!" Leatrice pointed a finger at Ian. "You knew he was a chef, though."

Ian gave me a panicked look. "He wore a chef's hat and a jacket that said 'Chef Henri' on it."

"Oh." Leatrice sounded deflated.

Richard stood up and brushed trace amounts of lint off his pants. "I'm going to excuse myself before you get out the stretching racks and make this a proper inquisition. I've had quite enough questioning for one day, thank you."

"Do you really have to go?" I motioned to Leatrice and Ian with a jerk of my head as I followed him to the door and gave him a desperate look. Leatrice could continue like this for hours.

"It's nothing you can't handle, darling," he assured me, visibly stifling a laugh. "Anyway, I have to prepare for the bridal open house tomorrow afternoon."

I smacked my forehead. "That's tomorrow?"

"You and Kate told me you were coming a week ago, so don't even think of backing out." Richard wagged a finger at me.

"Why are you doing this again?" The thought of a roomful of prospective brides and their mothers sent a chill down my spine.

"Simple. The brides come to the showroom, they taste the food, ooh and aah over the stunning linens I've chosen, and then realize they absolutely must have me to cater their wedding."

I sighed. "It's in the afternoon, right? I have yoga in the morning."

Richard raised an eyebrow. "I already see problems with this new Zen quest of yours."

"We'll be there," I promised, making a mental note to call Kate as soon as he left. "It slipped my mind with all of this murder business. It's not every day I'm a suspect in a police investigation."

"Welcome to my world," Richard grumbled, picking up his briefcase from beside the door.

"Oh, please," I groaned. "You were a suspect for about half a second and that was months ago."

Richard pressed his hand to his chest. "I may not seem wounded to you, but the scars run deep."

"This isn't the first time you've been involved with the police?" Ian called from across the room. He must have been desperate to get away from his conversation with Leatrice. "You've got more of a past than I imagined."

"Not really." I shook my head and felt my face flush. I could feel Richard's disapproving look. If I didn't know better, I'd have thought he was jealous. "One of our clients was murdered at a wedding a few months ago and Richard was a suspect for a few days."

Richard shot me a look. "For those of us who've been wrongly accused, a few days can feel like eternity. Now, as much as I'd love to stay and exchange criminal records, I've got to run." Richard gave Ian a slight nod, looked at Leatrice and sighed, then leveled a finger at me. "I'll see you tomorrow. And wear something nice. There'll be lots of brides attending."

"Of course." I started to close the door behind him.

Richard stuck his head back in. "Make sure Kate wears something modest. It's an all-ladies tea, so tell her not to waste the cleavage on us."

"Okay, okay." I pushed him out the door and sighed. Just what I wanted to do. Spend a Sunday afternoon chatting up brides. As if I didn't do enough of that already.

CHAPTER 6

"This isn't exactly how I imagined spending a Sunday off," Kate whined as I handed her one of two Grande Skim No Whip Mocha Frappuccinos and got in the passenger seat of her car. She'd double-parked in front of the Starbucks on Georgetown's bustling M Street, and taxicabs honked as they veered around her.

"I know." I'd barely closed the car door and balanced the drink between my knees when Kate careened the car out into traffic. "I'm missing my yoga class for Richard's bridal tea."

"Wasn't that class in the morning?" She glanced at the digital clock on her dashboard. "It's almost two o'clock."

I took a sip as Kate stopped for a red light. "I didn't want to cut it too close. Anyway, it took me forever to figure out an outfit." Actually, the thought of wrapping myself into a human pretzel had seemed far less appealing as I lay in bed this morning than it had when I'd signed up for Beginner Yoga. I'd only missed three classes, I reasoned with myself, ignoring the fact that there had only been four total.

"Annabelle, you're wearing a wrap dress. How hard is that?"

I tugged the beige fabric of the low wrap neckline together. "Well, I had to shave. And not only my ankles like when I wear pants."

Kate made a right turn without signaling and the cars behind us screeched to slow down. "At least that explains why you don't have a boyfriend."

I glared at her as we bounced over the uneven pavement of the latest street construction, and I clutched my drink to keep it from spilling. "Have I fired you yet today?"

Kate stuck her tongue out at me. I noticed that she'd actually taken my advice and skipped the usual cleavage display. Her white cowl neck top was practically prim, although her hot pink skirt had a side slit that revealed most of her thigh. I knew I should be grateful for any nod to modesty, so I ignored the skirt.

We passed a row of tiny restaurants and shops as we headed toward the Potomac. People lingered over brunch on one of the restaurant balconies, and my mouth watered at the thought of Eggs Benedict. I could be sure that the bridal tea would feature pretty, dainty food not even remotely as satisfying.

As we turned up K Street and skirted past Washington harbor under the bridge, I rolled down my window so I could enjoy one of the few days of perfect autumn weather in Washington. We exited off K Street and Kate merged into traffic without looking or slowing down. The wheels screeched against the pavement, and I knew we'd left tire marks and possibly an accident behind us. I sunk a little lower in my seat and clung to the seat belt with my one free hand.

We passed the Watergate Hotel, all retro curves with fabulous views and even more fabulous scandal. On the other side, trees with burnished gold leaves edged the shores of the Potomac and colorful sailboats dotted the water. This was exactly the type of day that brought tourists in droves and made it impossible to get around. I looked at the rows of tour buses as we approached Memorial Bridge and shook my head.

"Richard will kill us if we're late."

"Relax." Kate pushed her sunglasses back on her head. "It's an afternoon tea. It's supposed to be fun."

"You call a roomful of brides and their mothers fun?"

"Good point."

"First a murder and now a bridal tea. I don't know which is worse."

"I'm surprised Richard didn't cancel the tea." Kate burned a red light to make a turn.

"Are you kidding?" I laughed. "The police know he had nothing to do with the murder. And you know Richard. Even if he were a suspect, he'd manage to pull off the event covertly."

"Right. What was I thinking?" Kate flipped her hair out of her face. "The police don't still think you had anything to do with the murder, do they?"

"No. Ian said they seemed to be most interested in the kitchen staff at the hotel."

Kate slammed on the brakes as the car in front of her stopped to take a photo of the Washington Monument out the window. "Ian?"

I pulled myself back from the dashboard. I didn't know whether my heart pounded from the near-death drive or the impending third degree. "You remember. The lead singer from the band."

"The cute one with the tattoos? The one who is so not your type?"

"Why is he not my type?" I turned in my seat to face Kate. "I've dated wild guys before."

Kate raised an eyebrow and accelerated the car. "Who?"

"Steven in college. He was an environmental protester always chaining himself to something."

"Please, Annabelle. I'll bet he wore a ponytail and wrote poetry, too." Kate rolled her eyes at me. "Sensitive ponytail boys are not wild. Moody, maybe. But not wild. Trust me." When it came to men, I usually did.

"I never said I was interested in Ian, anyway."

"But you've talked to him since the wedding?" Kate screeched to a stop to let a tour group wearing identical bright orange T-shirts cross the street next to the Smithsonian Castle. She gunned the engine as the last person crossed.

"He came by my apartment yesterday." I held up a hand when I saw the 'I told you so' look on Kate's face. "Just to return my emergency kit. It got mixed up in the band's equipment."

"Okay, so you're completely uninterested in this hot musician who came by personally to return your stuff. Got it. Please continue."

I ignored her sarcasm. "As I was saying, Ian thought the police spent a lot of time with the cooks."

Kate weaved her way through traffic to make all the green lights, passing the row of massive Smithsonian museums leading up to the Capitol. "Which makes sense. They would have had more motive and opportunity than anyone."

"But there are so many of them, and they all dress alike." I took a final sip of my Frappuccino and put the empty plastic cup in the armrest holder. "How will we tell the suspects apart?"

Kate gave me a sideways glance. "Why would we have to tell them apart?"

"We won't," I said quickly. "I'm a little curious about who hated Henri enough to impale him on an ice sculpture, that's all."

"If the police just cleared me as a suspect, I wouldn't want to cause any more trouble." Kate began scanning the streets for parking as we drove through the Capitol Hill business district. "But that's me."

"I have no intention of stirring up trouble." I pointed to a marginally legal parking space on Eleventh Street right across from Richard's townhouse showroom. "I only said I'm curious. Georgia and Darcy will be able to tell us more."

"You mean Georgia and Darcy from the Fairmont?"

I nodded and looked out the window, pretending to be inspecting the parking space intently. "We're having lunch with them tomorrow."

"Well, well, well." Kate drummed her fingers on the steering wheel. "You didn't waste much time sticking your hose in this murder case."

"It's not my *hose*, it's my *nose*. And I'm not sticking it anywhere. We have lunch with Georgia and Darcy all the time. Georgia is one of my few friends from UVA who ended up in DC, and the only one aside from me who isn't a lawyer or doctor."

"Didn't you meet in 'Wedding Receptions for Fun and Profit'?"

"Very funny. You know there's no such class." I shook my head. Kate loved to joke that UVA had a mythical wedding planning degree. I'm sure the university founders would be spinning in their graves if they could hear. Georgia and I liked to joke that we were living proof that you could make a good living with an English degree as long as your job had very little to do with your major.

"And so what if I'm a little curious about the investigation?" I asked

Kate angled the car into the parking space and turned off the engine. "As long as you're just curious. Promise me you won't get us any more involved in this mess than we already are, okay?"

"Why would you think that I'd get more involved—"

"Annabelle," Kate cut me off and leveled a look at me.

I sighed. "Fine. I promise."

"Thank you." Kate let out a long breath. "I feel much better."

"Ready for a roomful of brides?"

"And their mothers?" Kate examined her lipstick in her visor mirror, and then flipped it up. "Bring it on."

CHAPTER 7

"Where have you been?" Richard met us at the tall double doors of the gray row house. The metal plate next to the door read RICHARD GERARD CATERING and had been added since my last visit. Not surprising. Richard loved making changes to the office decor so he could stay on the cutting edge. I had recently talked him out of repainting the entire building in a greenish brown hue called "Baby's First Summer," and he was still in a snit that I'd referred to his new favorite color as "Baby's First Diaper."

I glanced at my watch. "The party only started half an hour ago. What could possibly have gone wrong yet?"

"Wrong?" Richard gave a falsetto laugh and looked behind him. "Who said anything is wrong?"

Kate lowered her voice. "Are you feeling okay?"

"You've got to help me," he said through a fixed smile. "My best captain, Jim, couldn't come at the last minute because his flying squirrel got sick, so it's just me and the kitchen staff."

"A flying squirrel?" I exchanged a look with Kate. "Is it legal to have those as pets?"

Richard held up his hand and shook his head. "Don't ask. My life is a Fellini film today. Not to mention, these people are out of control."

"The brides or the mothers?" I peeked around Richard to assess the roomful of guests. About a dozen or so women and one stocky man clustered around a table draped in a chartreuse silk cloth and decorated with china teapots full of pink peonies. Trays of open-faced tea sandwiches and miniature pastries surrounded the flowers and were the focus of the oohs and aahs coming from the guests. It was hard to see any reason for Richard's anxiety. Then again, Richard didn't need a reason.

He arched a brow. "Take your pick."

I took another look at the guests. "I hate to burst your bubble, but this is a dream event."

"Oh, really?" Richard jerked his head in the direction of the one man in the group, clearly a Father of the Bride who was built like a fire hydrant and wore a dark, double-breasted suit. "Do you have any idea who that is?"

Kate shook her head. "He doesn't have the look of a politician." Kate kept up with politics by dating plenty of political staffers. She may not have known anything about the issues, but she knew which states had the cutest interns.

"I wish he were a politician," Richard said with a sigh, then lowered his voice and gave me a meaningful look. "He's in trucking."

My eyes widened. "Do you mean . . . ?"

"The family business."

"And?" Kate looked between the two of us. "I don't see the problem with a family-owned trucking company."

"Organized crime, Kate," I hissed.

"Oh." Kate shrugged. "Leave it to DC to have an organization for everything."

"It's not an association," I started to explain, and then thought better of it. "Never mind."

"Mr. Constantino's daughter, Sophia, is getting married next year, and he wants it to be the wedding of the century." Richard dabbed at his brow. "I don't know if I can handle the pressure."

"You're the best, Richard." I gave his arm a squeeze. "Don't worry about it. What's the worst that could happen?"

"I could end up lying facedown in fresh cement, that's what."

"Doubtful. He's in trucking, not construction." I grinned.

Kate nudged him and smiled. "You could end up in a shipment of bananas headed for Canada, though."

Richard glared at Kate. "Now I feel much better."

"That's what we're here for." Kate fluttered her eyelashes.

"And for the free food." I eyed the tray of scones a waiter set out on the buffet. Richard's cream scones were heavenly and usually vanished in a matter of seconds. "I don't have a thing to eat at home."

"Shocking," Richard drawled as he motioned us into the main room. "I'm going to check on the kitchen." He spun on his heel and disappeared down the hall.

"Do you think we can get in, eat, and get out without actually having to talk to any brides?" Kate asked.

"Annabelle Archer?" My name was practically screeched over the conversation, which came to a complete halt. A mother and daughter in matching pink and green plaid headbands and grosgrain belts ran across the room. Debbie and Darla Douglas. One of my upcoming brides and her mother.

Debbie's wedding to Turner Grant III promised to be an event fit for the son of a Mississippi congressman and the daughter of a country club Lady Who Lunches. Darla had happily turned over all the wedding planning to me once she'd negotiated free-flowing mint juleps and a bourbon-tasting bar for the reception. Darla was my favorite mother of the bride because she was usually too soused to care what went on.

"Debbie and I were hoping we'd see you here." Darla leaned in for an air kiss, and I tried to avoid getting splashed by her cocktail. Leave it to Darla to procure a martini at an afternoon tea. I wondered if she'd actually brought her own.

"Mother and I were discussing your idea of using magnolia leaves everywhere for the wedding." Debbie gestured with her matching martini. "We think it's an adorable idea."

Darla rested a hand on my arm. "Do you think we could find a magnolia china pattern or would that be too much?"

The wedding had already passed "too much" months ago.

"Maybe we could use that new leaf plate at Perfect Settings for the salad course," Kate said. "It's shaped kind of like a magnolia leaf."

Darla glanced at Kate next to me and a look of surprise crossed her face. "Kate, dear. I didn't see you there."

How many martinis had this woman already gone through? Kate elbowed me, and I pressed my lips together to keep from laughing.

Debbie put a hand to her cheek. "I didn't recognize you in that turtleneck." I'm sure they'd never seen fabric even remotely close to Kate's neck before.

"You look practically Republican." Darla giggled.

Kate flinched. "It's technically a cowl neck—"

I cut her off in mid-sentence. "Have you tried the scones yet? They're one of Richard Gerard's signature items."

"We haven't gotten to the food." Darla's eyes flitted to the buffet, and then dismissed the bowls of cream and berries with a shudder. Darla would as soon let a scone pass her lips than she would drink her morning orange juice straight.

Debbie raised her glass. "We're on a liquid diet until the wedding."

"But you both look fabulous." I couldn't imagine either woman getting more willowy, and I'd bet the only nutrition Darla had gotten for years came from the garnishes in her drinks.

"I have to fit into my Monique Lhuillier slip dress." Debbie downed her drink in one final gulp.

I had visions of Debbie walking down the aisle in a narrow slip dress holding a bouquet, her father's arm, and a martini. Kate and I would need a drink after this wedding. Or during it.

"Can we get you anything from the bar?" Darla cooed as she peered at the lonely olive in the bottom of her glass. "Our drinks need a little freshening up."

"I think I'm going to start with some food, but thank you."

"Suit yourself, sugar." Darla patted my hand, and then teetered off across the room to the bar with Debbie close on her Ferragamo heels.

"I hope Richard didn't invite anymore of our clients to this," Kate whimpered. "We can't count on all of them to be drunk on a Sunday afternoon. I would hate to have to pull off a coherent conversation."

"I'm going to be incoherent if I don't eat soon," I whispered to Kate as I tried to see through the crowd to the buffet. "Are there any scones left?"

"I can't see." Kate grabbed my elbow and pulled me forward. "Follow me, and don't make eye contact with anyone."

We maneuvered past clusters of chattering brides comparing bridesmaid dress colors and swapping favor ideas. I crossed my fingers no one would recognize us. We reached the food display, and I breathed a sigh of relief when I saw several scones left on the tray. Maybe everyone at the party was dieting to fit into their wedding dresses.

Kate held up a heart-shaped scone. "Is this a theme or has Richard gone soft on us?"

I looked at the trays of heart-shaped cookies and tea sandwiches that filled the table from end to end. I placed a tiny butter heart on my plate and reached for a scone. "It's official. He's finally lost his mind."

Kate laughed and handed me a napkin.

"Can you believe this, Mother?" The girl next to me motioned at the food. I guess she wasn't a big fan of hearts, either.

"What is it now, Viola?" The woman beside her sounded less than patient.

"There isn't a thing here that's vegan."

"You're not still on that kick, are you? Don't think for a second that your father and I are paying for a wedding where you serve nothing but vegetables."

"How can you expect me to use my own wedding to exploit animals?"

Kate raised an eyebrow and edged away from them. I turned to get some whipped cream and saw that the bride had straight dark hair parted down the middle that almost reached her patchwork skirt. She wore no visible makeup and was in serious need of eyebrow maintenance.

Her mother, on the other hand, could've given Tammy Faye Bakker a run for her money. She stood about a head taller than her daughter and wore her shoulder-length dark hair in a bob that was sprayed to within an inch of its life. Her eyelashes had so many coats of mascara it was a wonder she could still blink, and her eyelids were layered in about a dozen shades of blue.

"Viola, you cannot have a vegan wedding. How will you have a wedding cake if you can't use dairy products or eggs?"

"I'm sure they can make wedding cakes with soy."

The mother sucked in air. "If you won't listen to me, then at least listen to an expert. The caterer said that one of the best wedding planners in the city would be here. She can settle it."

I froze in mid-dollop and dropped the spoon back in the whipped cream. This was exactly the kind of wedding that would make me want to throw myself off Memorial Bridge within a week. I turned to Kate and motioned her toward the kitchen. I had to find Richard so I could kill him for giving my name to the Odd Couple.

"But I didn't get any berries to go with my scone," Kate argued as I pushed her down the hall and through the swinging door of the kitchen. A massive chef with salt and pepper hair stood behind a metal table singing an operatic version of the *Green Acres* theme song as he stamped out tea sandwiches with a heart-shaped cookie cutter. Several other cooks scurried around him in matching white chef jackets.

"You can eat as much as you want as soon as you help me murder Richard."

"It's always work, work, work with you." Kate put a hand on her hip. "Fine, then. Let's get this over with."

I realized that the kitchen chatter had died, and I looked behind Kate at the row of cooks staring at us in silence. The head chef's thick black eyebrows had become a solid line across his forehead as he scowled at us. He looked much more menacing when he wasn't singing old TV theme songs, despite the red plastic cookie cutter in his hand.

"Oops," Kate gulped. "Out of the frying pan and into a friar."

CHAPTER 8

"I think there's been a misunderstanding." I backed away from the glaring row of chefs. "We were joking about killing Richard."

"We could never catch him, anyway." Kate laughed nervously. "He's way too quick for us."

I shot her a look. "Thanks. That helped."

The head chef studied us for a moment, and then broke into a smile. "I know you. You're the wedding planner friends." His voice was a deep rumble that filled the room.

I breathed a sigh of relief.

The chef returned to stamping out heart-shaped sandwiches. "He talks about killing you, too. It must be an inside joke." The other cooks smiled along with their boss before returning to work, and the kitchen filled with the sounds of chopping and clattering dishes.

Kate and I exchanged a look. That didn't sound comforting.

"What else does Richard say about us?" I let out a long breath. "And how did you know who we were?"

"I've seen you at a few weddings when you run back in the kitchen for something, but we haven't met officially." He wiped his large callused hands on a dishtowel and extended one for me to shake. "Chef Marcello."

"Right. Sorry." I shook his hand but felt like smacking myself on the head. Marcello. The renowned Italian chef Richard told me stories about. His moods were as legendary as his cuisine. "I get so focused when I'm working at a wedding that I don't remember anyone."

"Isn't that how we all are? My cooks can tell you how I get on a job." Marcello gave a deep belly laugh and looked at his staff. A smattering of nervous laughter followed, and he began humming the theme from *The Addams Family*. Marcello seemed friendly enough, but it didn't bode well that Richard considered him moody.

Kate leaned over the counter and gave the entire line of chefs a flirtatious smile. "He can't be as bad as the last chef we worked with."

Marcello stopped humming and arched an eyebrow. "I know every chef in this town. Let me guess." He grinned and continued cutting. "Someone in off-premise catering? The head chef at Ridgewell's?"

"Nope." Kate rocked back on her heels and shook her head. "A hotel chef."

"Maybe we shouldn't be talking about this," I muttered so only Kate could hear. She ignored me.

"A big hotel?" Marcello held the red plastic heart in midair.

"Pretty big. Not one of the huge convention hotels, though."

I cleared my throat. "I really don't think this is a good idea."

"I'll give you a hint. It starts with an F."

"Henri," Marcello hissed, and slammed the heart down onto the counter. The room went silent.

Kate raised a finger in the air. "Technically that's an H."

"He means Chef Henri," I whispered to Kate. "And from his reaction, I'd say he knew him."

"We all knew Henri." Marcello's voice rose several notches. "Everyone in this kitchen suffered under him at one time."

I looked around the room at the grim faces. "You all worked with Henri?" Nods and scowls.

"Almost every decent chef in Washington passed through Henri's kitchen at some point," Marcello explained, his face reddening. "And every one was grateful when they left. Henri was nothing but a tyrant."

"If everyone hated him, how did he stay in business?" I asked. "Wouldn't it be impossible to keep a staff?"

Marcello gave a rough laugh as low murmurs passed through the room. "He was ruthless. He would ruin anyone who crossed him or tried to leave."

"My experience with Henri is starting to look almost pleasant," I said to Kate.

"How did you know Henri?" Marcello's face was starting to return to a normal color.

"We found his body." Kate gave a small shiver.

Marcello paused and appeared to compose himself. "You were at the wedding where Henri was killed?"

"It was our client's wedding," I said. "And ice sculpture."

"Our thanks to your client, then." Marcello smiled out of one side of his mouth, and his eyes flitted back to his work. So much for an outpouring of sympathy.

Richard burst through the door holding a flowery pink plate and skidded to a stop. He gaped at us. "What are you doing in here? I have a roomful of brides dying to talk to one of the top wedding planners."

"Yes." I folded my arms across my chest. "About that, Richard—"

"No time to discuss." Richard held up the plate of pale yellow cake to the chef. "Mr. Constantino insists that this isn't real Italian cream cake."

Kate jabbed a finger at him. "You tricked us. You didn't tell us you were planning on inviting our clients plus a roomful of the city's most dysfunctional brides."

"I don't know what you're talking about." Richard twitched his shoulders and avoided our eyes.

Marcello drew himself up to full height. "This Mr. Constantino thinks he knows Italian cooking better than I do?"

"Of course not," Richard said. "Let me explain."

"The granola and Tammy Faye?" I said, drumming my fingers. "Explain that."

Marcello slammed his palm on the prep table. "I do not cook with granola. You tell Mr. Constantino that if he wants granola in an Italian cream cake, then he needs to find another chef."

"Oh God," Richard whimpered, putting his hand over his eyes. "I'm going to end up like Jimmy Hoffa. I can see it already."

"Is Jimmy Hoffa in catering, too?" Kate whispered to me.

"This is too much." Marcello threw his hands in the air. "First the talk of Henri, now someone is telling me how to cook. And with granola. My creative energy has been stifled."

"No." Richard dropped his hand from his eyes and his eyes grew wide with panic. "Not that."

"I'll be out back meditating." Marcello turned and marched out the back door. The remaining cooks exchanged helpless looks.

Kate shook her head. "Is there anyone who isn't New Age anymore?"

"What did he mean 'the talk of Henri'?" Richard faced me.

"Nothing really." I shrugged. "Kate may have mentioned that we were at the wedding where Henri died. Apparently Marcello knew him very well."

Richard gasped. "You brought up Henri in front of Marcello?"

"Why is that a problem?" Kate asked.

Richard began rubbing his temples. "Over ten years ago Henri and Marcello were best friends and worked as sous chefs together at the Willard Hotel. Until they had a falling out."

My mouth fell open. "Why didn't you tell us before?"

"It wasn't relevant." Richard narrowed his eyes at me. "I never thought you'd come marching into my kitchen and start chatting about the latest murder."

"But that was over a decade ago," I said. "Chef Marcello can't still be upset. What was the falling out?"

"When the job as head chef opened up, Henri framed Marcello for stealing and got him fired."

Kate swallowed hard. "I guess Marcello holds a grudge."

"He's Italian," I said. "Grudges get passed down for generations." I wondered if the grudge had turned into more than that and Marcello had finally gotten his revenge.

"I resent that," Richard said. "I'm part Italian."

"Refresh my memory, Richard." I put my hands on my hips. "What did you do when one of the other wedding planners made an unflattering comment about your food?"

Richard opened and closed his mouth a few times, then mumbled out of the side of his mouth, "I paid a voodoo priestess in New Orleans to put a hex on her."

"I rest my case."

Kate turned to Richard, her mouth gaping open. "Did it work?"

He suppressed a smile. "She looks awful. Her hair has gotten so thin it looks like cotton candy."

"Remind me not to make you angry." Kate put a hand to her own fluffy blond bob. "I didn't know there were hair thinning hexes."

Richard began to turn red. "It wasn't supposed to be a hair thinning curse, but apparently I wasn't specific enough."

Kate turned to me, looking thoroughly confused. "You think Marcello put a hex on Henri?"

"No." I lowered my voice so the other cooks couldn't hear me. "I don't think he hexed him. I think he may have murdered him."

CHAPTER 9

"Everyone is talking about the murder." Georgia Rhodes downed her champagne cocktail in one long gulp. The blond Fairmont catering executive had shoulder-length flipped-up hair that any Texas debutante would envy and curves that would make Marilyn Monroe jealous. Like Marilyn, she drank only champagne. Today she'd already had two glasses, and we'd just given our lunch orders.

"Any idea who did it?" I'd grown accustomed to asking Georgia for advice and insider information since I'd moved to Washington. Being a few years older than me, she'd taken me under her wing when I decided to start a wedding planning business. After my brief stint planning events for a high-powered DC law firm, I thought weddings would be a breeze in comparison. Little did I know that brides make lawyers look like Mother Teresa.

I sipped my iced tea and waved a bee away from my leg. Because of the almost summery September weather, we'd opted for a table in the Fairmont's courtyard under a green market umbrella that shaded us from the midday sun, but not from the local insect population. Kate dodged as a bee flew across the table to where she and Georgia's assistant, Darcy O'Connell, sat.

I glanced past Kate at the garden courtyard, which had looked completely different only two days ago. The red paper lanterns that we'd suspended from the trees on Saturday were gone, and a single red rose bobbing in the fountain was the only reminder of the wedding. You'd never have guessed there had been a murder only steps away from where we sat.

"Has anyone been arrested?" Kate asked.

"No." Georgia dangled her high-heeled mule off her foot and smiled. "The talk's been about who's going to plan the celebration."

"Georgia, you're awful." Darcy shook her head at her boss and gave her a disapproving look over her wire-rimmed glasses. Darcy was one of those girls who never showed an inch of skin or wore a speck of makeup but managed to attract looks anyway. Kate called it the naughty librarian look, and she couldn't believe that anyone could be as prim and unassuming as Darcy appeared. She thought it must be a ploy to attract men through reverse psychology. She hadn't appreciated when I suggested she try reverse psychology sometime.

Georgia and Darcy were the perfect example of opposites who worked well together. Georgia reeled in clients with her Southern charm, and Darcy attended to all the behind-the-scenes details so the events came off without a hitch. Since Darcy didn't like too much attention and Georgia loved to hog the spotlight, it worked perfectly.

"I'm only telling the truth." Georgia signaled to the waiter for another drink. "No one in this place liked Henri, including us."

"I feel bad saying things about Henri now that he's dead," Darcy twisted a piece of her long dark hair into a spiral with her finger. Her hair was stick straight except for the wispy bits in front that she constantly twirled. I wondered how she fought the urge not to put her hair up. I couldn't go ten minutes without pulling mine into a ponytail.

"At least you're not being hypocritical." Kate shrugged off her suit jacket and revealed a nearly translucent white blouse. She slipped the jacket on the back of her chair. I gave a cursory glance around the courtyard and breathed a sigh of relief that no men were sitting near our table.

"I'll admit that I hated him." Georgia crossed her legs and jiggled her foot in circles. "He never let me change a thing on his menus and he insulted all of my 'pinch-me cute ideas.' Would it have been so hard to match the food to the linens just once?"

"Sounds like he didn't make many friends around here," I said.

"That would be putting it mildly." Georgia cast a glance over her shoulder, and then continued in a hushed voice, "I think Henri's death was the best thing that could have happened to this hotel. Even the housekeepers were afraid to go to the employee cafeteria because they had to pass the kitchens. He tormented everyone."

"Do you think the police suspect anyone in the hotel?" I asked, matching her whisper.

Darcy and Georgia exchanged a brief glance, and then Georgia stared at her empty champagne flute. "We were all questioned, of course. But they questioned me a second time. I don't have a convincing alibi."

"Weren't you here in the hotel?" Kate asked. She sat up as a pair of waiters brought four oversized salads in wide-lipped bowls to the table. One of them almost dropped a bowl in Kate's lap when he got a glimpse of her blouse.

"That's right," I remembered. "I didn't see you much when we set up for the wedding."

Georgia pinched her eyes together, and her forehead creased into deep furrows. She picked up a white ramekin of dressing and drizzled a thin stream onto her salad. "I was in my office with the door closed. I needed to catch up with paperwork."

The table fell silent as we began eating. Georgia hated paperwork and loved being in the middle of an event. I didn't buy it.

"You never do paperwork." Kate shifted to the side and winked at Georgia as a waiter attentively refilled her nearly full water glass. "Are you sure you didn't kill him accidentally?"

I rolled my eyes. "How do you accidentally impale someone on an ice sculpture, Kate?"

"I'm telling you, I was in my office doing paperwork," Georgia insisted, a flush creeping up her neck. "I didn't have a choice."

Darcy cleared her throat. "Our general manager gave Georgia a deadline for all of her financial reports. She had to turn them in by the end of the weekend or she'd get a bad review. I would have helped her but I don't know how to do all the reports yet."

"Mr. Elliott has it in for me." Georgia's eyes flashed with anger. "He's wanted to fire me ever since I took this job. He'll use any excuse to write me up."

"Write you up?" Kate stopped eating and held her fork in midair.

"They can't fire you without cause," Darcy explained. "They have to keep track of your mistakes, then when they get enough they can fire you."

"Yikes." Kate cringed.

I looked at Georgia over the top of my iced tea. "Why does Mr. Elliott want to fire you?"

"I refused to go out with him when I first started here."

"I thought dating someone in the hotel is forbidden," Kate said. Leave it to Kate to know the ins and outs of dating protocol in any locale.

"Who cares about that?" Georgia burst out. "Have you seen him? He has more hair in his ears than on his head. At least before he got the plugs."

I cringed. Not a pretty picture. "So you were a little behind in your work and he put the screws to you?"

Kate leaned over toward me. "She said she *wasn't* dating him."

I decided not to even attempt to explain and turned back to Georgia. "How far behind were you?"

"I hadn't even started. I told Darcy to make sure no one bothered me, and she promised to check on the wedding. I explained all this to the police, but they didn't seem too convinced. Darcy was the only person who can vouch for me, and even she didn't see me for a couple of hours."

"I wish I could give you an alibi." Darcy nibbled the edge of her lip. "If I'd come back up to check on you, the police wouldn't have any reason to consider you a suspect."

"Don't be silly." Georgia smiled weakly. "If only I'd dated our general manager, I wouldn't be in this mess."

"Just because you don't have an alibi doesn't mean you're an automatic murder suspect." I waved a forkful of greens. "The police have to have motive and evidence. If you weren't anywhere near the murder, there's no way they could link you to the crime."

"And if you were in your office then you were nowhere near the murder scene," Kate said. "Annabelle, on the other hand, spent half the day with the dead body and they don't consider her a suspect, even though she had more opportunity to kill Henri than anyone. And a pretty good motive, too."

"Remind me not to call you as a character witness," I said out of the corner of my mouth.

"What's your motive?" Darcy readjusted her glasses. "You barely even knew Henri."

"Not that you had to know him very long to despise him." Georgia took the flute of champagne out of the waiter's hand before he could place it on the table.

"The argument we had about Peking Duck, although it was less of a disagreement and more of him chasing me out of his kitchen."

Georgia took a gulp of champagne. "Welcome to my world. He chased me out of the kitchen almost every day. If that was a reason to kill someone, he'd have been dead years ago." She placed the nearly empty crystal glass on the table and patted my arm. "I wouldn't lose any sleep over it, doll."

My phone trilled and I dug it out of my purse. I looked at the caller ID. Richard. Kate and I had an appointment in half an hour to meet Richard and a bride at the rental showroom so she could select the linens and tableware for her wedding. Richard loved these meetings and could examine every cloth until he found the perfect match, whereas I lost steam after the third ivory damask.

"Don't tell me you're already there," I said into my phone.

"I've put together some looks and wanted to get your opinion before the bride arrives. Do you think she'll go for fuchsia and tangerine iridescent overlays?"

I swallowed a mouthful of salad. "Doesn't this bride want pastels?"

Richard groaned. "If I have to do another pastel wedding, I'm going to kill myself. You need to see these overlays, Annabelle. They're scrumptious, and they have beaded chair caps to go with them."

"You're going to try to sell her on chair caps?" I couldn't imagine my conservative bride going for covering only the top half of the chair back and dangling beads off them.

"They're the latest thing in chair accessories, Annabelle. Not quite a chair cover, but a little something to finish the look. Did I mention that they're beaded?"

"Isn't this a garden party?"

"I thought of making it more 'garden party in the Kasbah.' Do you still have that source for renting a camel?"

Now it was my turn to groan. "We'll be right there." I dropped the phone in my purse and took a final gulp of iced tea.

"Let me guess." Kate put her fork down and pulled her jacket off the back of her chair. "That was Richard."

I nodded. "He's already at the showroom, and they have new cloths. And beaded chair caps."

"Say no more." Georgia laughed. She'd tried to convince Richard to cross over to hotel catering a few years ago, but he hadn't been able to handle the concept of standard beige linens and banquet chairs. "I hope you get there before it's too late."

I shook my head. "With Richard I'd say we're way past that point."

CHAPTER 10

"Tell me this isn't the most delicious fabric you've ever seen." Richard opened the door to Perfect Party Rentals with swaths of shimmery orange and pink organza draped over his shoulders.

"It's like an upscale toga party," Kate whispered to me.

"Be glad it's not." I leaned into her ear. "Those are see-through overlays."

We followed him into the English basement showroom, which had been chosen precisely for its lack of windows and abundance of wall space for displays. Racks of cloths and glass shelves packed with china and crystal lined the walls of the compact space, and small tables were set up throughout the two open rooms, showing possible table vignettes. One table was designed entirely in blue with a hand-beaded turquoise cloth, blue glass base plates, and pale aqua water goblets. Next to it, celadon twill covered a table and pooled to the floor, covered with a Battenberg lace overlay and topped with white leaf plates and green and pink tulip glasses. I ran my finger over the fine gauge cotton of the Battenberg lace and sighed. I always felt decoratively challenged after visiting the rental showroom then returning to my own sparse apartment.

"Well?" Richard spun around, letting the sheer cloths flutter near his legs. "If this doesn't make a statement, I don't know what does."

"I don't think that's the statement Pam is going for." I pulled out a white chivari chair with a turquoise cushion and sat down at the blue table. The bamboo ladder-backed chivaris were my first choice for weddings for their delicate appearance, but they weren't the world's most comfortable chairs. But, as I told my clients, you don't want your guests to be so comfortable that they sit all night.

"If she wants a dull garden party, then fine." Richard rested a hand on his hip. "But at least let me give her the option of being fabulous." Richard made it sound like being fabulous was a God-given right that should be emblazoned alongside life, liberty, and the pursuit of happiness.

"Have at it. I won't stand in your way." I pointed a finger at Richard. "But no camels. If you want camels, you have to clean up after them."

Richard's mouth dropped open, then he glared at me. "Fine. We'll do without the camels." He lowered his voice. "Although they would have been perfect."

Kate joined me at the blue table. "Can I watch? I feel a nap coming on."

"You shouldn't have had lunch." Richard wagged a finger at her. "I never eat during the day. Slows me down. A Red Bull is the perfect liquid lunch."

"We only had salads at the Fairmont." Kate put her head on the table. "I think it's the wine that's making me sleepy."

Richard raised an eyebrow at us. "Aren't we fancy?"

"Don't look at me," I said. "If I had a glass of wine with lunch, I'd be asleep under the table already."

"Speaking of drinking during the day, how is Miss Rhodes?" Richard asked. "And Miss Connell?"

"O'Connell," I corrected him. "They're fine."

"Right." He smirked. "The girl with the Irish name who looks about as Irish as I do." Richard's dark hair and skin favored his Italian side of the family, though he preferred to claim only his French lineage.

"You know, Richard, not all Irish have red hair. Haven't you heard the phrase 'Black Irish'?"

Kate looked up. "That's what that means?"

Before I could make an attempt at an explanation, we heard a rap on the door behind us. Pam Monroe stuck her head inside the room and waved.

A petite girl who wore her ash blond hair swept back in a French twist, Pam taught elementary school in Georgetown and looked the part. She fell on the easygoing end of the bride spectrum, and didn't seem to have an image of the perfect wedding seared in her mind like most girls. Her fiancé, on the other hand, had made partner at one of D.C.'s largest law firms and had a clear idea of the way he wanted things. But since he was too busy to attend most of the wedding appointments, we were left to interpret his wishes. I hoped he'd be happy with our guesswork.

"Sorry I'm late." Pam came into the showroom swinging her oversized, quilted bag filled with rows of tabbed folders. I was grateful these were for her fourth grade class and not her wedding plans, although I'd had brides with wedding binders so complex that they'd required a separate index.

I stood up to greet her. "No problem. We were looking at some of the newest linens. Should we wait a few more minutes for Bill?"

Pam flushed and shook her head. "He can't make it. An important meeting came up at the last minute. You know how that goes."

We knew. An important meeting had come up when we'd gone on site visits, met with caterers, and interviewed photographers. He'd stayed at the invitation appointment long enough to veto the gorgeous letter-press invitation on handmade paper that Pam liked and to insist on traditional Crane's cards with black engraving. I, for one, wouldn't miss him.

Richard cleared his throat. "Annabelle and Kate told me that you want to have a classic garden party."

"Evermay is such a perfect place for our wedding reception," Pam explained. "The mansion is beautiful, of course, but we fell in love with the tiered gardens and the fountains. Since it should still be nice weather in October, Bill and I thought it would be fun to have a jazz ensemble playing as guests wandered around. We want it to be simple and elegant."

Simple and elegant. These were words almost every bride uttered, and each meant an entirely different thing by it. I'd learned early on that what was simple and elegant to one bride was simply awful to another.

Richard clapped his hands together. "Fun you say? I'm getting a vision of something truly fun and fabulous. Envision canopies with huge lounging cushions tucked around the gardens. I'm picturing using hot pink, mango, and yellow as a modern twist on the autumn palette." He unfurled the shimmery pink and orange cloths from his arms. "Tell me this isn't to die for."

Pam rubbed the organza between her fingers. "I never thought of using bright colors. Bill usually likes white for everything. It's simpler, you know."

Kate rolled her eyes at me then turned to Pam. "I'm sure Bill will love whatever you choose. Why not have a little fun with your wedding?"

Pam smiled tentatively and eyed the fabric again. "It's a possibility."

"Or we could go with something totally different." Richard tossed the organza overlays to the side and ran to the racks of linens. He pawed through brocades until he reached a matte gold cloth. "What about an evening in Tuscany? We do lots of rich brocade cloths and use the existing stone tables in the gardens as bars. We can have lemon topiaries and use rustic pottery for serving platters."

"That sounds nice, too. We are going to Italy on our honeymoon."

"Perfect." Richard pulled the gold brocade down and threw it over a bare table. He rushed to the other side of the room and plucked a chunky wine goblet and gold glass base plate from the wall display. "Wouldn't this be divine?"

Pam tilted her head and examined the table. "That's another possibility."

I interpreted her hesitant look. "Maybe something a bit more streamlined, Richard?"

He frowned at me then pulled a green toile cloth from the racks. "Do you have a stopover in Provence on your honeymoon, perhaps?"

"No, but that's pretty." Pam reached out and touched the linen. "It's very gardeny."

Richard threw the toile over the brocade and placed a white grape leaf plate and green glass on top. "You can't get more gardeny that green and white toile. We could use these on all the outside tables."

"Maybe, but the fabric is a little busy. There are shepherds and sheep on it."

Richard's mouth fell open. "That's the whole point of toile—"

I cut him off as I walked over to the linen racks and pulled down a pink and green plaid cloth. "Plaid is simpler, but still has a garden feel to it. Where would you put this, Richard?"

"Right back on the shelf where you found it." Richard made a face as he reached around me for a cloth embroidered with tiny palm trees. "I've got it! We do a British Colonial theme with everything in beige and whites. We bring in tall palms to put in the tent, or better yet, we serve the dinner entirely outside on long narrow tables."

Pam nodded. "That does sound simpler. I think Bill would like beige and white."

"We could still do some canopies outside for the cocktail hour." Richard threw the embroidered cloth over the toile and then hurried to the other side of the room for a woven rattan base plate. He placed it on the table and dabbed his forehead with a white hemstitched napkin. "Instead of colored organza, though, we could do white panels of sheer fabric. They would flutter in the breeze and be divine."

Pam beamed at Richard. "I love the idea of dinner outside. But what about doing the tables in white, as well?"

Richard's face fell a bit, but he pulled a white crinkled fabric down and draped it on the growing stack of table linens. "Like that?"

"Possibly, but what about this?" Pam made a beeline for the cotton cloths at the far end of the wall and produced a white one. She removed the rattan plate and spread the new linen over the crinkled fabric. She pulled a white base plate and a standard issue wineglass from the display shelves to go on top.

"White twill?" A bead of sweat crept down Richard's forehead. "You want a plain cotton tablecloth at Evermay?"

"I think it's perfect," Kate said. "It's simple yet elegant."

Richard shot daggers at her. "Are we still doing the canopies draped in fabric at least?"

"Possibly." Pam slung her tote bag on her shoulder again. "I'll have to see if Bill thinks it's too much, though. He likes things simple, you know."

Richard patted his brow. "I'm beginning to get the picture. So we're going with long tables of white twill with white plates and all-purpose glassware."

Kate fluttered her eyes at Richard. "Should I write that down for you?"

He looked at her and tapped his temple. "It's all in here."

"This was easy." Pam let out a breath, walking to the door. "Now all we have to do is pick a florist who can do simple arrangements to go with our look."

"Not a problem," I said. I already had a minimalist designer in mind.

Pam called over her shoulder. "We were thinking of all white flowers."

White flowers. Why wasn't I surprised? And how much more could we discuss about all white flowers?

Once the door shut, Richard moaned. "White, white, white, white. Remind me to wear sunglasses to this wedding."

"Come on Richard." I patted him on the shoulder. "It sounds very classic and pretty."

"I know." He pulled the crystal off the table and put it roughly back on the display shelf. "But the hot pink and mango tents were going to be stunning. Too bad 'Possibly Pam' is too timid to choose anything but white. I'll have to find another client to use my genius on."

"I don't think that would have fit at Evermay, anyway," Kate said. "Call me crazy, but I don't see camels at a stately Georgetown mansion."

"You have no grand vision," Richard snapped and began pulling the used linens off the display table.

My cell phone chirped, and I dug it out of my purse. "Wedding Belles.

This is Annabelle." I heard muffled sobs on the other end of the phone. "Hello? Who is this?"

"It's Darcy from the Fairmont." A loud sniffle. "They took Georgia away."

"What do you mean? They fired her?" Kate and Richard stopped their bickering and looked at me.

"No," Darcy choked on a sob. "They arrested her for Henri's murder."

CHAPTER 11

"They can't really believe that Georgia would murder someone." Richard braced his arm against the dashboard as Kate jerked her car to a stop in front of the District Two police station. He'd whined so much about the empty Starbucks cups littering the back that I'd relinquished the front seat to him for the short ride across town. "She would never risk breaking a nail."

I eyed the low brick building that was hidden away in a quiet neighborhood near the National Cathedral. "I don't think they took her manicure into consideration."

"And they call themselves detectives." Richard stepped out of the car and smoothed his suit jacket.

"Try to be nice, Richard." I slammed the car door behind me. "And inconspicuous."

"Maybe he should wait in the car," Kate suggested, grinning at Richard.

Richard looked pointedly at Kate's translucent blouse. "Maybe we both should."

Who needed children when I had these two? "Listen. We're here because Georgia asked us to come. Both of you behave in there, understand?"

They grumbled as they followed me up the sidewalk. I pushed through the glass double doors and approached the faux wood counter where a uniformed officer flipped through a stack of papers. A few officers sat behind him at desks that were jammed together with barely enough space between them to walk.

The officer glanced up at me from under thick black eyebrows and reached for the No Parking signs and logbook. "How many do you need this time?" His gravelly voice barely rose above the chatter of the officers behind him.

I usually came in here about once a month to get reserved parking signs to put in front of downtown churches. That way we made sure to have at least a space or two for the bride's limousine if parking was tight. And in DC parking was always tight.

"I don't need any signs today, but thanks." I'd started stockpiling them in my car trunk to cut down on trips to the station. "I'm actually here to see someone you've arrested."

One of his bushy brows rose up at the corner. "Name?"

"I'm Annabelle Archer." I turned to motion behind me. "This is my assistant, Kate—"

The officer cleared his throat to interrupt me. "Not your name. The name of the person you're here to see."

"Georgia Rhodes." My face flushed with embarrassment as the officers behind him looked up and snickered. I hoped I had plenty of signs in my car because I wouldn't be coming back here for a while.

"Are you family?"

This wasn't going well. Kate stepped forward and leaned on the desk. "Can't you tell that they're sisters?"

The officer pulled his gaze away from Kate's blouse and studied me for a second. "Not really."

"Her sister dyes her hair," Kate confided to the cop. "She's not really blond."

"I thought she looked like a bottle job." The officer returned Kate's smile. I crossed my fingers that Georgia wasn't within earshot. "Let me check and see if she's allowed to have visitors." He left the desk and disappeared into the back offices.

"Nice going, Kate," I whispered. "What if they figure out I'm not related to Georgia?"

"Impossible. How could they prove that? You could be her half sister or her stepsister. There are lots of reasons you wouldn't have the same last name."

"Or look even remotely alike?"

Kate shrugged. "Recessive genes."

"What if Georgia tells them she doesn't have a sister?" Richard tapped his foot on the worn linoleum floor behind us.

I narrowed my eyes at Kate. "Well?"

Her cheeks flushed. "I never thought of that. I guess then you'd have some explaining to do."

Richard took a step toward the door. "Maybe we should leave before they find out that Annabelle lied about being Georgia's sister. This place gives me the heebie-jeebies, anyway."

"I'm with Richard." Kate backed away from the counter, her face now a bright pink. "Annabelle could get in big trouble for messing with an investigation."

"Might I remind you that you lied to the officer?" I managed to say even though my mouth had gone completely dry. I wondered if the officer would chase us if we made a run for it. Too late. He was approaching the counter.

"It's okay for you to see her." He pointed a finger at me. "But only you. Your friends will have to wait here." I turned to say something to Kate and Richard, but they were already at the glass entrance doors.

"We'll wait in the car." Kate waved with her keys as Richard held the door open. "Take your time."

I mouthed the word "cowards" to them as I followed the stocky cop behind the counter. He led me to a room with several brown chairs clustered around a wooden table. Georgia sat in one of the chairs with her legs tightly crossed. The officer held the door as I went inside, then closed it behind me.

Georgia looked up and a smile broke across her face. "Thank God you're here."

I leaned in for an air kiss. "How are you doing?"

"I'm sitting in a pleather chair in a police station. How do you think I'm doing?"

"Don't worry, Georgia." I eyed the fake leather chairs with strips of duct tape patching the edges as I took a seat across from her. "This has to be a mistake. They can't really believe that you would kill Henri. What evidence do they have aside from the fact that you hated him and don't have an alibi?"

She shook her head. "There can't be any evidence. I was nowhere near the murder scene. Like I told you, I was in my office doing those damn reports all day."

"But no one saw you?"

"Everyone else was working the wedding. Since Darcy had to do my job of coordinating the setup, I didn't even see her for hours." She tapped a pink, perfectly polished nail on the table. "I'm sure they won't waste any time giving her my position now."

"First of all, I don't think Darcy wants your job. She doesn't like dealing with clients, remember?"

"It doesn't matter. The general manager would love to toss me out and put in someone who won't outshine him." Her eyes glimmered with tears. "What am I going to do?"

I reached out and squeezed her hand. "Everything will be fine. The police can't have any evidence to prosecute you with, and the GM can't fire you just because everyone likes you more than him."

Georgia put a hand over her eyes. "You don't understand. The hotel is my life. I've worked almost every weekend for eight years so other people can have amazing parties. I can't remember the last time I had a steady boyfriend. And I'm going to lose it all."

"You're not going to lose everything. Anyway, there are lots of other jobs."

She gaped at me. "Start over? Do you know how hard it would be to get hired in another luxury hotel after being fired, not to mention arrested for murder?" A tear snaked down her cheek. "Do you know how many weddings I've done at the hotel? How many brides I've watched go down the aisle? I've given up a normal life for this career, and I have absolutely nothing to show for it. No wedding of my own, no kids, no house in the burbs, nothing." Her shoulders began to shake, and she buried her face in her hands.

My jaw hit the floor. Georgia's life seemed so glamorous to me. Beautiful clothes, perfect hair, a chic downtown apartment. Even in college she'd been the golden girl with the cute boyfriend and even cuter clothes. I'd always aspired to what I'd thought was Georgia's life of champagne and caviar. Who would've guessed that she wanted 2.5 kids and a house with a picket fence? "I had no idea..."

"Be careful, Annabelle," she said through sobs. "In this business, you snap your fingers and a decade has gone by."

Tears pricked the back of my eyes as I watched her cry. I swallowed hard and tried to sound upbeat. "It's not the end of the world. This will all blow over and you'll be back at the hotel in no time."

She looked up at me. Tears had muddied the smoky shadow on her eyes, and she wiped dark streaks with the back of her hand. "Will you help me, Annabelle? I can't trust anyone at the hotel anymore, and you've been such a good friend. You remind me of myself when I first started in this industry."

I wasn't sure that was such a compliment now that I had a firsthand look at where years of planning events got you, but I owed it to Georgia after all she'd done for me. "Of course. What do you want me to do?"

She leaned forward and lowered her voice. "No one at the hotel will tell the police anything, but they might talk to you. People there know you. They like you. Could you ask around? Try to find out any gossip that might help clear me. The real killer must be someone in the hotel, and someone has to have seen or heard something."

That sounded simple enough. No danger in eavesdropping. "Don't worry. We'll find out who really killed Henri and get you out of here." I looked at Georgia's swollen, red-rimmed eyes and took both of her hands firmly in mine. I tried to sound more confident than I felt. "I promise."

"Time's up, ma'am." The stout officer stood at the door. I gave Georgia's hands one more squeeze before I followed the cop back out to the entrance. Three men stood talking in front of the glass doors, and I recognized the man in a snug-fitting blue polo shirt. Detective Reese. Great. I put my head down and tried to scoot around the group so he wouldn't notice me and accuse me of meddling in another investigation.

"Miss Archer?"

Crap. He noticed me. I looked up and flashed him a quick grin but didn't stop walking.

"Hold up a second."

I pivoted around and tried not to let the panic I felt creep into my voice. "Hi, Detective."

He took a step to close the distance between us. "What are you doing here?"

I blurted out the first thing I could think of. "I'm picking up some No Parking signs for a wedding."

He looked at my empty hands and raised an eyebrow. "Really? Where are they?"

I dropped my eyes to my hands. No signs. Nice going, Annabelle. I opened my mouth to explain, and then thought better of making up another lie. I wished I had Kate's ability to flirt her way out of any situation, even though she credited the Wonder Bra for a great deal of her success. It would take the mother of all Wonder Bras to get me out of this one.

Reese took me by the arm and leaned close to me. "Does this have anything to do with the arrest we made in the chef's murder? I would have thought you'd steer clear of the case now that you're no longer a suspect."

I tried to pull away, but he held my arm tight against him. "You were mistaken when you suspected me, and you're mistaken about Georgia, too."

"Please tell me this woman isn't a friend of yours." Reese rolled his eyes as he released me.

"I've known her for years, and I can tell you for a fact that she could never murder anyone," I insisted. "Even Henri."

Reese grinned at me, his hazel eyes deepening to green. "You sure know how to pick 'em, sweetheart. She's as guilty as they come."

My cheeks burned. Now I remembered how cocky he was. "Just because she doesn't have an alibi? You're pinning it on her because you haven't found the real killer."

Reese's smile vanished. "We have evidence that links her to the crime scene. The fact that she doesn't have an alibi is icing on the cake."

"What evidence? I was at the crime scene, remember?"

"How could I forget?" He gave me an exasperated sigh. "We found an item belonging to Miss Rhodes with traces of the chef's blood on it. Unfortunately the media got wind of it, too, so you can read all about it in tomorrow's paper."

"What item?" This sounded suspicious. I'd heard about police planting evidence. "How can you be sure it belongs to her?"

"Apparently Miss Rhodes has a scarf that she wears frequently. It's been called her 'signature' scarf by several coworkers. We found it wedged in the back of her desk drawer with drops of dried blood on it."

Georgia's Jackie O Hermes scarf? My heart sank. She idolized Jackie almost as much as she did Marilyn, and the scarf was one of her prized possessions.

"I'm afraid it doesn't look good for your friend." Reese shook his head.

I was afraid he was right.

CHAPTER 12

"You still think she's innocent?" Kate handed her keys to the Fairmont Hotel valet the next morning. We'd made record time from my apartment to the hotel after she picked me up. "They found blood on her Jackie O scarf."

"Of course I believe she's innocent." I stepped out of the car and smoothed out the wrinkles in my blue pencil skirt. Even though Detective Reese had momentarily shaken my belief in Georgia's innocence, I was still determined to help her. "Someone set her up. Someone who wants her out of the way."

Kate came around the back of her car, tucking a white shirt into black boot-cut pants that left little to the imagination. "Who?"

"That's what we're here to find out." I'd convinced Kate to join me in a little hotel reconnaissance on Georgia's behalf only after I threatened to turn the Egan wedding over to her. Our office code name for Hillary Egan was "Hillary Again" because she called ten times a day and her wedding was still seven months away.

I led the way into the lobby of the hotel and made a beeline for the concierge desk when I saw that Hugh was on duty. He looked every bit the proper concierge, standing ramrod straight in his dark blue jacket and gold concierge pin. Despite his formal appearance, he served as DC's command center for gossip. He knew everything that went on in the hotel and the city. The fact that he didn't mind sharing his information made him my favorite concierge.

He smiled when he saw us and held up a finger as he finished making dinner reservations for a guest. When he hung up the phone, he glanced around him. "What are you two doing back here? Run. Save yourselves."

Kate laughed. "That bad?"

"It's like being on the *Titanic*," he muttered, smoothing his tidy brown moustache with one finger. "We're down two people in three days."

"You haven't lost Georgia for good." I tried to sound more confident than I felt. "Once the police realize they've made a mistake by arresting her, I'm sure she'll be back to work."

Hugh gave a quick shake of his head. "I doubt it. The general manager isn't thrilled about having one of his catering sales staff arrested for murdering his head chef."

"But if they find out she's innocent, they have to give her back her job," I insisted.

"They can find a hundred ways to fire her. If Mr. Elliott wants her gone, she'll be gone." Hugh slid a map across to me. "This makes it look like I'm working."

I took the map and flipped it open. "Do you think Georgia killed Henri?"

Hugh fingered the gold concierge pin on his lapel and thought for a moment. "No. She has a bit of a temper, but I wouldn't peg her as the violent type."

Kate put an arm up on the marble countertop. "Annabelle thinks she was framed."

Hugh's eyes widened and he looked positively giddy. "Really? Who do you think framed her?"

"That's where we thought you could help out. You must know who would want to get rid of Georgia." I leaned in for the kill. "You know everything."

Hugh blushed. "Not everything. I mean I do know a lot about what goes on here. Most of it is who's having an affair or who got drunk and made a fool of themself. That kind of thing. Not who's setting up someone else to take a murder rap."

"Forget the murder, then," Kate whispered. "Tell us the juicy stuff."

I frowned at her. "We're not here for random gossip, Kate."

Kate made a face at me.

"I can tell you that Georgia wasn't always the most popular girl in the hotel," Hugh said in a lowered voice as two hotel guests passed us. "The banquet captains complained that she changed her room diagrams at the last minute, and Mr. Elliott had to chase down her paperwork."

"Those don't sound like reasons to frame someone for murder," I said.

"You're right," Hugh admitted. "As much as we all despise Mr. Elliott, I doubt he'd frame someone for murder. He's too spineless to do something like that. I'm sure that Georgia's arrest is a lucky break for him. He'd been searching for a way to get rid of her without looking like the bad guy. And as much as Georgia drove them crazy with last minute changes, the banquet staff really is fond of her. She could make you insane and make you love her at the same time."

I looked pointedly at Kate. "I know the feeling."

"Back to the drawing board." Kate ignored me, squinting at something across the lobby.

I followed her gaze and did a double take. "Is that Ian?"

"Who?" Kate turned back to me, confused. "I didn't notice his face. I only got as far up as his jeans, which he wears very well."

"The bandleader from Saturday." As I watched Ian deep in a conversation with what looked like a hotel cook, I pulled my ponytail holder out and my hair fell loose down my back. "I wonder why he's here again. And who is he talking to?"

"He used to bartend in the hotel and returns to say hi every so often. The guy he's talking to is Emilio, one of the sous chefs." Hugh grinned at me. "What I'm curious about is why you let your hair down."

"What?" I put a hand through my hair. I knew I looked better with it down, even if I rarely wore it that way. "I got tired of it being up, that's all."

Kate folded her arms across her chest. "I do believe you're flustered, Annabelle."

"Don't be absurd. I'm not flustered," I lied. "I'm confused that he never mentioned working here before. He made it sound like he didn't know Chef Henri."

Hugh groaned. "Everyone who worked here during the past ten years knew Henri. None of us were spared."

Kate nudged me with her elbow. "I think he's spotted you, Annabelle. He's coming this way."

Ian wore a white T-shirt that covered most of the tattoos on his biceps, but I caught myself staring at the hard curves of his arms anyway. I tried to smile as naturally as possible with Kate snickering behind me.

"We meet again." Ian kissed my hand and then Kate's, and nodded at Hugh. "You know I have a weakness for redheads."

"I do now." Hugh arched an eyebrow at me, and I could bet that it would be a matter of minutes before the entire city heard the story.

Ian met my eyes with his own blue ones. "And long red hair, too." He winked at me. "I knew you would be trouble the moment I saw you."

"What are you doing here?" I stammered. Not my most eloquent moment.

His eyes flitted to Hugh, then back to me. "The lads left a power cord the other night so I'm picking it up. Lucky for me I ran into you. Wouldn't you call this fate?"

"I don't know." I looked back to Kate for help, but she just smiled at me. For once it seemed like she didn't mind sharing the spotlight. Of course, I knew she'd be teasing me about this for years to come.

"What are you doing on Friday night?" he asked.

My mind blanked for a moment. "I have a rehearsal for a wedding."

"All night?"

"No, but after that I should get ready—"

"Good. Plan on dinner with me, then. You have to eat, don't you?" He kissed me quickly on the cheek and left with a wave to Kate and Hugh before I could say a word. The light scent of his cologne lingered on me, and I inhaled deeply as he walked out the glass doors of the hotel. Kate had been right about his jeans. He looked awfully good in them.

Kate gave a low whistle. "That was impressive."

I raised an unsteady hand to where he'd kissed my cheek. "I think I have a date."

Kate wore a look of admiration. "That guy is smooth. You definitely have a date."

Hugh let out a breath. "I think *my* knees are weak."

"I think I'm going to throw up." I hadn't had a real date in so long, the thought of one nearly brought on a panic attack.

"Don't worry." Kate threw an arm around my shoulders. "I'll bring you up to speed and give you some tips."

I laughed. "Now I'm really scared."

"It's about time you had a little fun. DC women focus too much on their careers," Hugh said, then gave a small wave to someone behind me. "Speaking of all work and no play . . ."

I turned as Darcy walked up, taking short fast steps, her long dark hair swinging behind her. She pushed her glasses up onto the top of her head and rubbed her temples. Her eyes were bloodshot and had dark circles underneath.

"Have you come to help?" She slumped against the concierge desk.

Kate stared at her. "What happened to you? You look awful." Leave it to Kate to be subtle.

"You try doing the work of two people," Darcy complained. "It's impossible to keep up."

"Kate doesn't even do the work of one person." I sidestepped as Kate swatted at me.

Darcy managed a weak smile, and then wrinkled her brow. "Do you guys need anything from catering? Please tell me you aren't one of the twenty proposals that Georgia left in her inbox. And I've only gotten halfway through returning all her messages."

"No, we only came by to find information to help clear Georgia," I said. "We promised her we'd try to help." From the look of things, Georgia didn't need to worry about Darcy wanting her job.

"Yes, please! Did you see her?" Darcy's eyes widened. "They wouldn't let me in because I'm not family."

I nodded. "She swears that she didn't kill Henri, and she thinks someone is setting her up."

Darcy looked at Hugh. "Who would want her gone bad enough to do that?"

Hugh shrugged. "My only guesses were Mr. Elliott or one of the captains."

Darcy frowned. "Not the captains. They're all bark. Mr. Elliott would love any excuse to fire her, but I can't imagine him being involved in a murder. He's more the type to wait for someone to hang themselves."

"Sounds charming," Kate said.

Hugh leaned over the counter. "Does Mr. Elliott know about the fight?"

Darcy leveled a finger at him. "No, and if you tell anyone . . ."

"You know I would never spread rumors that would get Georgia in trouble." Hugh recoiled at the accusation.

"What fight?" Kate asked.

"This is just between us, right?" Darcy motioned for us to come closer. "No one knows about this except for Hugh. If the police or Mr. Elliott found out, Georgia would be done for."

Kate made a zipper motion across her lips. "You can trust us."

Darcy took a deep breath. "Henri came up to Georgia's office. He was steamed about the pricing of a menu she'd done. I didn't hear most of it because they closed the door, but when he opened the door to leave, I heard him threatening to tell Mr. Elliott that Georgia had no idea how to do her job. Georgia yelled back that she wished he was dead and threw a glass paperweight from her desk at him."

Kate sucked in air. "Did she hit him?"

"She missed and hit the wall instead," Darcy continued. "Henri stormed out."

I gulped. "You didn't tell the police?"

Darcy reddened. "I guess maybe I should have, but I know Georgia didn't kill him. She didn't really mean what she said. It was the heat of the moment. We've all joked about wishing Henri were dead. I knew if I told the police, it would look bad for Georgia."

"When was the fight?" I asked.

Darcy cringed. "The morning of the wedding."

Kate put a hand to her mouth. "The same day Henri was murdered?"

Darcy nodded. She was right. Georgia had motive, evidence linking her to the victim, and no alibi. It looked very bad indeed.

CHAPTER 13

"You look like you need a drink, darling." Richard perched on the edge of an upholstered bench as Kate and I collapsed onto the beige sofa in his office sitting room. The couch was a sleek, modern design, more angles than cushion, and my back immediately regretted the choice.

I shifted around, trying to get comfortable. "I wish. Isn't a bride meeting us here, though?"

"Viola Van de Kamp and her mother, Louise." Richard looked at his watch. Ever since he'd gotten a Cartier, he checked the time with a regularity that bordered on compulsive. "They're three minutes late."

"That name sounds familiar." A little red light went off faintly in the back of my brain, but my mind swirled with questions about Georgia and her connection to Chef Henri's death. Was it a coincidence that Henri died only hours after he so enraged Georgia that she threw a paperweight at him? If Georgia was on the verge of being fired, would she do something desperate to keep Henri from threatening her job?

Richard cleared his throat. "So you girls have been out and about already today?"

Kate leaned her head back against the back of the sofa. "Annie wanted to poke around at the Fairmont. Ask a few questions about Georgia."

"Any luck?" Richard looked back and forth between us.

"No," I confessed. "We actually found out that Georgia had an incriminating fight with Henri the day of the murder. She screamed that she wished he was dead and hurled a paperweight at him."

"She missed, though," Kate added.

"Heaven help us." Richard rolled his eyes. "Now I like Georgia as much as anyone, but do you really think you can find anything that will convince the police she's innocent?"

"If I don't help her, who will? She's all alone and about to lose everything." I felt my jaw tighten. "I know she'd do the same thing for me."

Richard put up his hands. "Okay, okay. Just asking. Personally, I think she should plead temporary insanity. Anyone who gets blood on a Hermes scarf has clearly lost her mind. I'd acquit her in a second."

I laughed despite my best efforts not to. "Very funny. But she didn't get blood on the scarf. She was framed."

"You don't say? Who framed her?"

Kate leaned forward and cupped a hand around her mouth. "We're still working on that minor detail."

"You can make all the jokes you want, Richard, but we're going to find out who really killed Henri and set Georgia up."

"As long as you do it after we meet with the Van de Kamps." Richard stood up and unbuttoned the bottom button on his black suit jacket. He never liked his jackets buttoned all the way because he claimed it looked too uptight. "They're interested in wedding planners, not a crime fighting duo. And they haven't signed my contract yet, so a few mentions about how fabulous I am would be appreciated."

"You're sure these are good clients, right?" I asked. "Not a bride who thinks that decorating the reception with origami is a good idea?"

Richard put a hand on his hip. "You're still steamed about that, aren't you?"

"I can make paper cranes in my sleep," Kate complained.

"This is a Potomac family who wants to throw a big bash for their only daughter. I guarantee you won't be doing arts and crafts for them." Richard jumped as the doorbell rang.

The door opened and I heard footsteps in the foyer. Richard rushed forward to greet them, but all I could see as Mrs. Van de Kamp rounded the corner was blue eye shadow and lots of it. It took me only a second to recognize the girl in the shapeless dress behind her mother. I looked at Kate, whose eyes widened in recognition and fear.

It was Viola the Vegan.

"Weren't you two at the bridal tea?" Viola eyed us warily. She looked less than thrilled to be there, and I had a feeling there had been some sort of coercion involved.

"You must be Mrs. Van de Kamp." I stepped forward and took the mother's hand. I turned to Viola and forced a smile. "And you must be the bride."

Viola barely took my hand. "You must be a genius."

Kate and I exchanged glances. The last thing we needed was to deal with Bratty Bride for the next year. Richard laughed nervously and motioned for us to sit down.

I took my seat on the couch. I avoided looking at Richard for fear I might be overcome with the need to bludgeon him to death. "Tell us about your wedding plans so far."

"Isn't that why we'd hire you?" Viola slouched down in an armchair. "To plan the wedding?"

I liked this girl less every second. The faster I could get out of this, the better. I turned to the mother. "Have you set a date?"

"We're looking at next fall, but we want to see what your availability is before settling on a day." Mrs. Van de Kamp sounded desperate, and I could see why. "You come highly recommended from Richard."

So much for saying we were already booked, if she intended to plan the wedding around our availability. Leaving the country to get out of it seemed a bit extreme.

"I need to get married before Jupiter goes retrograde, Mother." Viola gave an exasperated sigh. "So it has to be before October seventeenth."

Then again, maybe relocating the business overseas wasn't such an outrageous plan.

"Come again?" Kate did little to hide her curiosity.

Viola rolled her eyes as if we were idiots for not knowing the star charts. "After Jupiter goes into retrograde, it won't be good for me to enter into any unions. That includes marriage."

"Absolute nonsense," her mother snapped. "I will not rearrange a wedding based on what a telephone astrologer told you."

Viola crossed her arms in front of her. "Fine. Then I won't come."

Richard jumped up and rushed to the wooden sideboard by the window. "I forgot to offer everyone some champagne. We always start off the wedding planning with a toast."

This was new. I suspected Richard had made it up to force everyone to have a drink and loosen up. Not a bad plan.

"Why don't we worry about the date later and talk about general style," I said as Richard briskly tore the foil off a champagne bottle. "What's your vision of the wedding?"

"I want an outdoor ceremony," Viola started before her mother could speak. "Something very rustic. No formal gardens. And I want to use lots of seasonal flowers and leaves."

Okay. Not a bad start. An outdoor, autumn wedding could be beautiful. Maybe this wouldn't be a disaster after all.

"What colors were you thinking for bridesmaids?" Kate asked.

"They're going to be called wood nymphs, not bridesmaids, and I thought they could be in body stockings with leaves sewn on."

I bit my lip to keep from laughing. This would be one bridesmaid—oops, wood nymph—outfit that no one could ever claim to wear again.

Mrs. Van de Kamp gave a muffled cry. "You can't make your friends wear leaf pasties to your wedding."

"Bridesmaids dresses are stupid." Viola squared her shoulders. "So are bouquets. I want them to carry floral tambourines instead."

Now this I wanted to see. Although I doubted she'd have any friends left after she told them they were wearing leotards and shaking tambourines down the aisle. I could see Kate begin to tremble with silent laughter next to me.

"Champagne anyone?" Richard rushed over with a round metal tray of crystal champagne flutes.

Mrs. Van de Kamp took a glass and downed it in one gulp. Even under her tire track blush, I could see her cheeks burn with anger. I didn't blame her.

"Is it sulfite free?" Viola gave the tray a suspicious glance.

"No." Richard spun on his heel away from her. "Better not have any."

"I think we should do this at a later date, once Viola has had an opportunity to rethink her ideas." Mrs. Van de Kamp stood and jerked Viola up by the sleeve. "Thank you, ladies. Richard." She pulled the girl all the way across the room and out the door as Kate and I hurried to stand up. The door slammed behind them.

Richard held the tray of champagne in one hand and downed glass after glass with the other. "What the hell was that?"

"Exactly my question." Kate turned to him, her mouth hanging open. "You call those clients normal?"

Richard hiccupped. "I might have misjudged."

"Might?" Kate and I said in unison.

"Okay," Richard admitted. "They're awful. Can I make it up to you with dinner?"

"This one is going to cost you." Kate walked over and snatched the last glass of champagne off the tray before he could. "I'm in the mood for a French martini at Mie N Yu."

Richard put the tray down. "Shall we end the workday early and try to snag the loft table?"

"Let me run to the ladies' room while you call ahead," I said over my shoulder as I walked down the back hall. I paused outside the doors to the bathroom and kitchen, which were side by side. Whose voice was that? I stepped closer to the swinging kitchen door and pressed on it enough so it opened a fraction of an inch.

"I owe you a debt of gratitude for what you did." Marcello spoke in hushed tones. "We all do."

Why the secrecy and whispering? I leaned forward so I could see through the sliver of an opening. Marcello stood to the side holding a cordless phone.

"After all these years, he got what he deserved." Marcello gave a soft chuckle. "Finally, his career was the one put on ice."

Ice? I straightened up with a jerk. Could he be talking about Henri? Who else?

"I only wish I could have seen the look on his face," Marcello added.

I pressed against the door to see more clearly, and the hinge creaked.

Marcello froze. "Hold on a second. I think I heard something."

With my heart pounding, I let the door go and spun around. I ran back to the front of the house, passing Kate and Richard in the sitting room. I kept running to the foyer, motioning them to follow me.

"Wait for us," Kate cried, grabbing both of our purses.

Richard stood holding an empty glass of champagne as Kate hurried away. "What's the rush? They're holding the table for us."

"Come on." I gave a nervous glance toward the kitchen door. "I'll tell you once we're out of here. It's about Henri's murder."

Richard's shoulders sagged. "Again?"

I nodded. "A suspect just moved to the front of the line."

CHAPTER 14

"Coy does not become you, Annabelle." Richard stepped out of his convertible after parking next to us in the Georgetown lot. We'd taken separate cars to the restaurant so we wouldn't have to drive Richard back to Capitol Hill after dinner. It was early enough that we'd found space in the tiny public lot next to Mie N Yu.

"I'm not being coy. I just want to wait until we're sitting in the restaurant to tell you. Someone could overhear us on the street."

"Who?" Richard looked around us. "A college kid or a Hari Krishna?"

"Less talking, more walking." Kate passed us and strode down the sidewalk toward the brick red and gold facade of the restaurant with sheer yellow curtains fluttering in the doorway. "I'm dying for a martini."

"You shameless hussy."

I recognized Fern's voice immediately. Or maybe it was his vocabulary I recognized. Who else called people hussies to their face? I turned to find him standing behind us wearing a long black Nehru jacket with an ornate silver cross hanging down the front. If I didn't know better, I'd have pegged him for a priest. Although the slicked back ponytail and giant rings on his fingers were a bit of a giveaway.

Kate spun around with a smirk on her face. "Look who's talking."

"I am a man of the cloth." He looked wounded, then grinned at us. "You wouldn't believe how nice people are to you when you're a priest."

Richard shook his head. "You do know you're not really a priest, right?"

"I'm a hairdresser. It's close enough," Fern explained. "I take confessions exactly like they do."

Richard frowned. "But priests don't spread the stories they hear all over town."

"A technicality, I'm sure." Fern dismissed Richard with a wave of his hands. "What I want to know is why you're tying one on at five-thirty? Isn't it a little early?"

"Not after the meeting we just had." Kate sighed. "A nightmare bride."

Fern's face lit up. "Worse than the one who had me put three tiaras in her weave? Do tell."

I looked at Richard, who shrugged his shoulders, and then I turned to Fern. "Would you like to join us for dinner?"

"Only if I wouldn't be imposing," Fern said as he linked arms with Kate and led the way into Mie N Yu without a backward glance.

As I followed them through the opening in the restaurant doorway's sheer curtains, my eyes took a few seconds to adjust to the low lighting inside. Mie N Yu had been designed around the travels of Marco Polo, so there were tons of low tables surrounded by luxurious cushions; tables perched high in cages, and red fabric cascading from the ceiling. Kind of an East meets West meets Kama Sutra. It was also a place where the pretty people of Georgetown came out to play.

After a delay appropriate for one of the city's hot spots, an aloof hostess led us to a table nestled on the landing between the first and second floors and draped with white netting. The table jutted out over the first floor and had carved wooden sides to keep people from falling over. This was the perfect place for talking without being overheard since there were no other tables near us. Kate and Fern began studying the martini menu immediately.

"Well, are you going to tell us now?" Richard tapped his fingers on the round wooden table.

I waited until the hostess had descended the stairs again. "I overheard someone talking to Henri's killer. They were on the phone." I hesitated to implicate Richard's chef. Knowing Richard, he wouldn't take it well.

Kate pulled her eyes away from the long list of martinis. "How could you know that Henri's killer was on the other end?"

"Because they were talking about icing careers," I said patiently. "The person on my end thanked the other person for getting rid of someone they both hated."

"Enough already," Richard said with a sigh. "Who did you overhear?"

I cringed, knowing Richard wouldn't like this one bit. "Marcello. He was on the phone back at your office."

"You can't know that he was talking about Henri," Richard sputtered. "Talk about putting words in his mouth. Just because he has a past with the victim doesn't mean he's on a murder phone tree."

"It may not sound convincing, but you should have heard him," I cried. "He sounded very secretive and sinister."

"I don't think you can prosecute someone for murder because they sound creepy on the phone." Kate looked as skeptical as Richard.

Fern waved a cute waiter over to take the drink order. "Two French martinis and . . . Annie, what are you drinking?"

"A Coke." I turned to Richard. "You said that Marcello was with you at the time of the murder, right?"

"Campari and soda for me." Richard flipped open the laminated menu and nodded. "He was the chef at our wedding at Dumbarton House."

"Give us a few more minutes to look at the menus," Fern said quietly to the waiter.

"Of course, Father." The young man gave a bow of the head as he left the table.

Richard gave Fern a look. "You're out of your mind."

"What?" Fern gave an innocent shrug. "Did I say I was a priest?"

"What if he didn't kill Henri, but had someone do the dirty work for him?" I asked, trying to steer the conversation back to the murder. "I'll bet he knows all the chefs in town."

Richard shook his head. "Why would someone commit murder for him? That seems like a pretty big favor to ask. Don't forget that Marcello was out of the industry for a while. I don't know how much he would have stayed in touch with his old colleagues."

I swiveled around on my cushioned chair. "What do you mean he was out of the industry? I thought you hired him after he left the hotel side."

"Henri didn't only get him fired," Richard explained. "Marcello was blackballed for years. No one would hire him. He went into a tailspin. His wife left him. He lost custody of his daughter. He basically lost everything before I took a chance on him. It was the best hiring decision I ever made, of course. The man is a culinary genius."

I swallowed hard. "That's an awful story. I had no idea." I almost didn't blame Marcello if he wanted to kill Henri. I didn't want Georgia to take the fall for it, though.

"It had to be someone on the inside to get to Henri without being noticed." Richard snapped his menu shut. "Marcello doesn't have the friends in the hotel world that he used to. I doubt he could have done it even if he wanted to."

"That makes perfect sense," Kate said as our drinks arrived. She balanced her martini gingerly as she took a sip from the flared edge. "So many people in the hotel hated Henri that it seems silly to consider suspects who would have had to come from the outside without being noticed. I think people at the Fairmont would have noticed someone as big as Marcello poking around and trying to get someone to commit murder for him."

"Maybe I should tell the police what I overheard just to be on the safe side. Even if Marcello is innocent, he might be able to lead them to the killer because he knows so many cooks who hated Henri."

Kate lowered her drink to the table. "It's true that birds of a feather flock to leather."

Fern giggled. "My kind of birds."

Richard rolled his eyes. "This is ridiculous. You're going to tell the police that you overheard my head chef talking to an unknown person about something that may or may not be connected to a murder? Are you trying to ruin me? And are you sure you don't have an ulterior motive?"

"I don't know what you mean," I said dismissing his accusation.

"I do." Kate waved her hand in the air. "You mean Reese?"

Fern's eyes bounced back between Kate and Richard. "Reese?"

"That cute detective that Annie had a crush on a while back," Kate said.

Fern bounced up and down on his chair. "He's more than cute."

"I didn't have a crush on him," I protested. "We were strictly professional."

"I know," Kate groaned. "Such a disappointment. Leatrice had practically picked out the wedding invitations."

"The one who questioned us at the hotel, right? Dark hair and nice arms?" Fern raised an eyebrow.

Kate looked surprised. "I'm impressed."

Fern pointed to the room below us. "Isn't that him over there?"

We all followed Fern's gaze to a table across the room. Sure enough, Reese was sitting at a low table leaning up against some beaded cushions. He wore a black knit shirt that pulled tight across his chest and showed off his tan arms. My pulse quickened until I looked across from him, then my body went cold.

If she was a day over twenty-one, I'd have been shocked. Her long hair had been streaked blond, and she wore too much makeup and not nearly enough skirt.

"Maybe she's his sister." Kate turned back around with a stricken look on her face.

"I hope not." Fern hadn't taken his eyes off the couple. "I don't think it's appropriate to touch your sister on the leg like that. Even here."

"I never thought he was good enough for you, anyway." Richard made a face. "If those are the type of bimbos he likes, then good riddance. You need someone with more sophistication and polish."

"I wouldn't tell Richard about your date with Ian, then," Kate whispered to me behind her hand.

"Can you believe that outfit?" Fern shuddered. "Who would wear a skirt that short?"

"Hey," Kate cried. "I own that skirt."

Fern patted her on the hand. "And I'm sure on you it looks lovely, but right now we're trashing Annabelle's competition."

"Thanks, guys." I steadied my voice. "I'm telling you, though. I don't have a thing for Detective Reese." Richard was right. If these were the type of women Reese liked, then I could forget about him. I could never compete with Miss Legs. Girls like that didn't work sixty-hour weeks and run around setting up weddings for twelve hours at a time. I reached over, took Kate's martini out of her hand and took a long drink.

"Are you still overcome with the urge to tell the police what you heard Marcello saying?" Richard asked after he returned the glass to a startled Kate.

"Let Reese figure it out on his own if he's such a great detective. He doesn't want our help, anyway." I beckoned the waiter over so I could order a martini of my own. "I'm trying to clear Georgia. The police are on their own."

After I'd ordered a French martini, Fern pulled the waiter down by the sleeve. "Give it wings, my son."

CHAPTER 15

"I've been waiting up for you, dearie." Leatrice stuck her head out of her first-floor apartment as I started up the stairs. "Do you want to watch an episode of *Perry Mason* with me? I found a channel that plays them late at night."

Just when I thought my social life couldn't get worse.

"I'm pretty tired, Leatrice. Kate and I were running around all day. Maybe some other time."

Leatrice pulled her door closed and followed me up the staircase. She wore a black apron that looked like the front of a tuxedo jacket complete with bow tie and ruffled shirt. It gave a whole new meaning to the phrase "black tie optional."

"I heard that they arrested someone for the chef's murder."

I paused at the first landing and leaned against the metal banister. "Was it in the paper already?"

Leatrice shrugged. "I don't read the paper. Too much politics for my taste. I heard it on the scanner."

"Right." How could I forget her scanner? I eyed her apron and tried to change the subject. "So, doing some cooking?"

"Cooking?" She cocked an eyebrow at me and shook her head.

Silly me. I should have known better than to assume anything about Leatrice's choice of wardrobe. I should have been grateful she had clothes on underneath the apron. "Never mind."

"Do you know the girl they arrested?" Leatrice hurried up behind me as I took the stairs two at a time.

"She's a friend of mine and she didn't do it." I reached my doorway a bit out of breath and paused before I put the key in the lock. I thought for a second about how I could go inside without letting Leatrice in, then realized it would be impossible and opened the door anyway.

Leatrice led the way into my living room, bouncing on her toes. It was almost scary how excited she got about crime investigation. "They arrested the wrong person?"

"Definitely." I kicked off my low black pumps and dropped my purse on the floor beside the couch. "Someone framed her for the murder."

"How do you know?" Leatrice's eyes grew wide as she sunk into the overstuffed armchair.

"Georgia isn't a killer," I said firmly. "There are lots of other people who had motive to kill the chef, as well. Better motives."

"Like who?"

"Richard's head chef, Marcello, for one." I moved a pile of papers on the couch so I could sit. "Henri ruined his life by blackballing him from the industry over ten years ago."

Leatrice edged forward in the chair so her feet touched the floor. "That's a long time to plan revenge."

"He's Italian," I explained. "From what I hear, any of the chefs who worked with Henri had strong motive to kill him."

"And you think one of them committed murder and framed your friend for it?"

"That's where I get a little fuzzy," I admitted. "The chefs have the strongest motives, but I don't know why they would want to frame Georgia. The people who would want to get Georgia out of the way—like the hotel's general manager—don't have much of a motive for killing Henri."

"That does present a problem, dear." Leatrice furrowed her brow in concentration. "It's a shame we don't have pictures of the event to search through for possible clues."

"The photographers had barely arrived at the hotel by the time we found the body," I said, then snapped my fingers and began looking around the room. "But the videographer got there early and shot footage of the courtyard."

"Was that where you found the body?" Leatrice stood up and started looking with me.

"No, but the courtyard is right outside the room where the chef was killed, and the walls to that room are all glass." My voice quivered as I dug my hand behind the couch cushions. "The videographer could have shot something in the background without even knowing."

"This is so exciting." Leatrice lifted the chair cushion and peered underneath. "What are we looking for?"

"The phone." I recovered it from under a blue fleece throw at the end of the couch. "I'm going to call the videographer and see if we can look at her footage. I just hope she isn't in a chatty mood today."

Leatrice hurried over and stood next to me while I dialed my favorite videographer's number by heart. Usually I loved gabbing with Joni about the latest industry gossip because she somehow knew the dirt on everyone, but today I didn't have time for chitchat. The phone rang a few times before a soft woman's voice answered. She sounded a little more like a phone sex operator than a videographer.

"This is Joni, how can I help—"

"Hey, it's Annabelle." I cut her off. "Sorry to be so rushed, but do you have the footage from Saturday's wedding?"

Joni's voice switched from professional to relieved. "Hi, Annabelle. I'm glad it's you. I wanted to ask you what you think I should do with this DVD. I have great dressing and ceremony coverage, but after that it's all mostly mayhem. I do have a pretty good shot of everyone stampeding for the front door when the bride ran out into the courtyard in hysterics, but I don't think she's going to want that on her wedding movie."

I cringed, remembering the chaos the bride had created once she came to and saw the dead chef and shattered ice sculpture. We hadn't been able to stop her from running into her cocktail party screaming bloody murder, and it hadn't helped matters that she had an enormous bruise on her cheek from where Fern had dropped her. No amount of editing could make that look pretty.

Joni continued, "I tried to do the last part in slow motion and put some romantic music in the background but it looks like a chase scene in a horror movie."

I groaned. "That bad?"

"Yep. It's going to take some major work to make this look halfway presentable. You don't think they're in a rush for this, do you?"

"No," I reassured her. "I don't think the DVD is their major concern right now." I doubted the bride would be eager to relive her wedding anytime soon since I'd heard that she'd gone to a holistic healing spa "for her nerves" in lieu of taking a honeymoon.

"I wish they'd gotten the short version instead of the long. I can make anything look great in a highlight reel. Maybe they'd agree to the short version, considering what happened."

"You haven't cut any footage yet, have you?" I held my breath for the answer.

"No way. I always keep the raw footage."

I let out a sigh of relief. Thank God she was as paranoid as me about keeping things.

"You never know what you might need later," Joni added. "I've had clients ask me to re-edit their wedding film a year later because their grandmother died and they want more footage of her. Or they want me to take out someone they aren't speaking to anymore. I even had one bride ask me to redo the entire thing without the groom after they got divorced. Then there was the time that—"

"I need to ask you a huge favor, Joni." I knew this would be a hard sell. "I need to see the raw footage of the wedding."

She hesitated. "You know I don't like anyone to see the raw footage. It's like guests walking into the ballroom during setup. It ruins the magic of the finished product."

"You know I wouldn't ask if it wasn't important," I pleaded as Leatrice tugged on my sleeve.

"Tell her why we need it," Leatrice whispered.

"I only gave the raw footage to a bride once, and that was because it was a nudist wedding. I couldn't bear the thought of having to look at all those naked people again."

"You shot a nudist wedding?" I forgot all about the murder for a moment. "Did you have to work in the nude?"

"Of course not," Joni gasped. "It was years ago, when I first started out in the business. I wouldn't take a nude wedding now."

I had no idea there was even a market for nudist weddings in DC. I wondered what the proper wording on the invitation would be. Would Crane's even engrave the words "clothing optional" in the bottom corner? Somehow I doubted it.

Leatrice poked me in the arm. "Well?"

"It's really important that I see the footage before it's edited," I begged. "I promise to return it to you as soon as I look at it."

"What are you looking for?"

If I really wanted her to show me the DVD, I'd need to tell her. "I think you might have recorded something through the glass walls of the Colonnade without knowing it."

"Really?" Joni sounded interested. "Like what?"

I exchanged a hopeful look with Leatrice. "Like the murder."

CHAPTER 16

"Did she agree to let you see it?" Kate's voice crackled through my cell phone as I walked down a side street toward Georgetown's business district. Georgetown already brimmed with energy at ten o'clock in the morning, with box trucks double-parked for their deliveries and boutique owners putting out sidewalk signs. I passed a New Age shop and noticed a sign advertising two-for-one chakra balancing, hanging amid the dangling crystals in the window. The sale would have tempted me if I had any idea what or where my chakras were.

"After I explained our theory about Georgia being framed, Joni was more than happy to help out." I glanced at my watch to make sure I still had enough time to get my morning Frappuccino before meeting Kate. "She's bringing it by this afternoon."

"Our theory?" Kate sounded amused.

"Yes, our theory," I insisted, dashing across M Street before the light changed. "You, me, Richard, and Leatrice."

"Leatrice? How did she get involved in this?"

"You know Leatrice. Do you have to ask how she got herself involved?" I pushed the glass door to Star- bucks open with my shoulder. The M Street coffee shop boasted lots of exposed brick, wood floors, and a large front window perfect for people watching. I sucked in the intoxicating aroma. Too bad I couldn't stand drinking the stuff unless it was mixed with enough chocolate and milk to make it nearly unrecognizable as coffee. With its whipped cream topping and faintest hint of coffee flavor, the Frappuccino had been the heaven-sent answer to my coffee aversion, and now I'd become addicted to them. I ordered a Grande Light Mocha Frap and congratulated myself for not splurging on a Venti.

"This isn't turning into one of Leatrice's amateur sleuth projects, is it?" Kate asked. "Like the time she believed that she saw the old guy in 2B on *America's Most Wanted* and started following him around in a trench coat?"

"Of course not," I lied, knowing full well that Leatrice considered herself an equal partner in finding the real killer and clearing Georgia whether I liked it or not. I took my drink from the counter and walked back out to M Street. "Anyway, she hasn't followed that guy around in ages."

"That's because he moved, Annabelle. Not that I blame him. Who wants to be stalked by a midget in her late seventies?"

I headed down a side street toward the harbor, taking small sips of my Frappuccino. "She's not a midget, and you know it, Miss Smart Aleck."

"Maybe not legally, but she is pretty small," Kate argued good-naturedly. "I think she's shrinking, too."

I arrived in front of the trendy flower shop, Lush. Monochromatic bunches of green and white flowers sat in galvanized buckets in the window. I tried the door. Locked. "How far away are you?"

"Right around the corner," she said as I saw her red car squeal around the curb, clipping the edge of the sidewalk. She parallel parked semi-legally at the end of a row of cars and hopped out. "Are we the first ones here?"

"The boys must be running late," I called out as she strode across the street. By "the boys" I meant the two floral designers, Buster and Mack, who owned Lush and had become our new favorites. Their edgy modern designs were only one of the reasons they weren't your typical florists.

I heard a low rumble in the distance. In a few seconds two shiny chrome Harley-Davidson motorcycles appeared around the corner. They growled to a stop in front of us, and the massive riders, clad almost entirely in black leather, dismounted the bikes. The color of their goatees, one brown and one red, was the only way to tell them apart from a distance. They pulled off black helmets and pushed their riding goggles onto the tops of their heads. The "Mighty Morphin Flower Arrangers," as they preferred to be called in the biker world, had arrived.

"I swear those pants must be special order," Kate said under her breath. "I don't think Big and Tall shops in Washington carry leather. Not stretch leather, at least."

Buster of the dark brown goatee took two long steps to reach us. "Would you believe we got pulled over?"

"Apparently some bike gangs have been causing trouble." Mack joined him, shaking his head. "This one had to tell the cop that we're florists on the way to a meeting with wedding planners."

"The officer wouldn't believe me." Buster took out a jumbled key ring and opened the door to the shop. "We had to wait while he ran our plates. And then he gave us tickets for speeding."

"Imagine," Kate muttered to me as we followed them inside.

They hung their helmets on hooks by the door and flipped on the track lighting that illuminated the window floral displays with colored light. A polished chrome rack held more galvanized buckets of blooms along the side wall, and a high metal worktable ran the length of the back, with several stools tucked underneath. The center of the room was empty. Minimalist, according to Buster and Mack. No stuffed animals, wicker baskets, or balloons in sight. Woe to the unsuspecting person who tried to order a "Pick Me Up" bouquet. The boys would slit their own wrists, then the customer's.

"Remind me why we're meeting with Nadine again." Mack tossed the bride's thick file on the table. "Correct me if I'm wrong, but isn't the wedding this Saturday?"

I hopped up onto a stool. "She's just getting nervous and wanted to take a final look at what you have in stock."

Buster waved a hand at the buckets of viburnum, hydrangea, and calla lilies. "Everything that's green or white in here is hers. I hope she knows that it's too late to chicken out and go with some mamby-pamby blush tone scheme."

"Don't worry," I assured them. "She may be Southern, but she's not a girly-girl."

"She loves the look you boys put together," Kate added. "The lime green and white is going to look amazing in the Park Hyatt's modern ballroom."

Buster ran his finger down a desk calendar and glanced up. "You know where our other wedding is on Saturday, don't you?"

"The Fairmont," Mack chimed in. "People check in but they don't check out."

Buster ignored his counterpart, who giggled with Kate. "We don't know what's going on over there. I'm assuming the wedding is still on, but Georgia won't return any of our calls."

"You haven't heard, then?" I said. Darcy must not have made it to their messages yet. Surprising that the gossip hadn't reached them, though. Georgia had been one of the first big hotel catering execs to recommend the avant-garde florists, and they adored her. "Georgia's been arrested for the murder of Chef Henri."

Both men gasped.

"When did this happen? We've been at a Christian biker rally and only got back last night," Buster said, his face stricken.

"She would never!" Mack's eyes were wide.

"Of course not," I agreed. "She's innocent."

Buster sank onto a stool, his face considerably paler. "Then why did they arrest her?"

"We think she's being set up by someone who wanted her out of the hotel," I said.

Mack blinked back tears. "Who would do such a thing?"

"We're not sure yet." I dug in my purse for a tissue and held it out to Mack. "The GM wanted to replace her, but the general consensus at the hotel is that he's too spineless to frame her for murder."

"Those other chefs at the Fairmont aren't too spineless." Mack blew his nose. "We've heard them talking when we're bringing flowers through the back of the hotel."

Buster nodded in agreement. "The sous chefs are almost as mean as Henri."

"Really?" Kate asked. "Maybe being scary is a chef thing."

"The real killer must have set up Georgia to throw the police off the trail," Buster said.

"Maybe. Kate and I have promised Georgia we'd nose around and see who hated Henri enough to kill him. If we can find the actual murderer, Georgia will be off the hook."

Buster's face relaxed. "If we hear anything interesting, we'll let you know."

"We should send flowers," Mack sniffled. "Do they let you get flowers in jail?"

Kate patted his hand. "I don't think so."

Mack dabbed at his eyes. "It's too horrible to think about Georgia sitting in some drab cell with no decor."

"She'll be out before you know it," I tried to reassure them. "In the meantime, we still have a wedding on Saturday, remember?"

"Come on, you old softie." Buster gave Mack a hard pat on the back. "We won't let this get us down, will we? The bride is counting on us."

Mack bobbed his head up and down. "She's such a sweet little thing, too."

The glass door swung open and a cloud of cigarette smoke tumbled into the room. A waifishly thin woman followed, her brown hair tied up in a messy bun and a cell phone pressed to her ear.

"What do you mean they're bringing their kids?" she screamed into the phone, losing all remnants of her lilting Southern drawl. "This is an adult reception, Mother. That means no kids." A pause while she took a drag on her cigarette, then coughed. "He's your brother. You fix it." She dropped her phone in her Louis Vuitton tote bag and smiled at us. "Sorry about that. Last minute guest issues."

"Hi, Nadine," I sputtered as everyone else stared. "I didn't know you smoke."

"Oh, this?" She looked at the cigarette between her fingers. "I started this week to calm my nerves before the wedding. It doesn't seem to be working, though." Leave it to a bride to try to reduce stress by picking up a habit that could kill you.

Mack grabbed a small glass bubble bowl from the shelf and rushed to hold it under her cigarette's long, dangling ash before it fell.

"Thanks." She took the bowl from Mack and pulled out a stool. "I'm still getting used to these things."

Buster regained his composure and opened her file. "Annabelle and Kate mentioned that you want to go over a few things for your wedding."

"I haven't been able to sleep because of my bouquet." Her slight Southern drawl had reappeared. I noticed that her eyes were bloodshot and rimmed in red. I could see that she was well on her way to a meltdown and wondered if she'd make it to Saturday. Or if we would.

Buster read the proposal. "We have down a hand-tied bouquet of white Casablanca lilies and white hydrangea."

"I'm sure it would be beautiful, but it doesn't seem to fit the modern theme we chose for the rest of the wedding." Nadine waved her cigarette, and Kate ducked as some ash flew her way.

Mack raised an eyebrow. "For the rest of the wedding we have chartreuse arrangements of pods and orchids with touches of lime green viburnum."

"Exactly." Nadine took a drag and blew out a stream of smoke. "I love that look. Can we do something like that for my bouquet, too?"

"Well . . ." Buster and Mack exchanged glances as Nadine slid off her stool and walked to the rows of tall metal flower buckets. She ran her hand along the blooms.

"This is it!" she cried out, pointing to a cluster of puffy green balls covered in soft fuzz. "I love these. They're so untraditional. I want to carry a bouquet that no one has seen before."

"That would do the trick," Kate whispered to me.

"You want to carry a bouquet of only those?" Mack asked, the corner of his mouth twitching up.

Buster jumped in before Mack could say anything else. "Could we add some green orchids to fill it out?"

"That's fine. Just a few, though." Nadine threw her hand back, and her cigarette went flying. We all dodged as it landed in the corner and Buster stamped it out. The bride didn't even notice.

Nadine turned around and gave a long, satisfied sigh. "I feel much better now." She picked up her purse. "I've gotta run to my final dress fitting. I keep forgetting to eat, so they have to take it in again. Where did I put those cigarettes?"

"We should be all set, then," I said, hoping to put closure on her last minute changes. "We'll see you at the rehearsal."

Nadine opened the door and paused. "I'll call you this afternoon, Annabelle. I have a few changes to the passed hors d'oeuvres."

Before I could explain the problems involved with changing the menu three days before the wedding, she left.

"I'd say that went well," Kate said with a smirk.

"Oh, shut up." I pulled the bride's floral proposal out of my bag and turned to Buster and Mack. "So what's the name of the flower she changed her bouquet to?"

Buster grinned. "The bride chose a lovely bouquet of orchids and monkey balls," he said in a television announcer's voice.

I froze. "Excuse me?"

"You heard right." Mack beamed. He and Kate collapsed against each other in hysterical laughter.

I imagined the newspaper write-up in Nadine's South Carolina hometown. 'The bride wore an ivory Vera Wang gown of silk organza embellished with seed pearls and carried a hand-tied bouquet of orchids and monkey balls."

Sometimes my job had its rewards.

CHAPTER 17

"I would have left it outside your door but your neighbor threatened to call the bomb squad on me," Joni said as Kate and I reached the landing to my apartment. She sat outside my apartment door wearing black pants and an untucked black T-shirt, with a paper shopping bag sitting in her lap. Leatrice hovered a few feet away in hot pink cowboy boots, giving her the evil eye.

"I noticed her following me in the building so I pretended to go in my apartment then I tailed her to your door." Leatrice didn't take her eyes off Joni. "I was about to make a citizen's arrest when you showed up."

Clearly, Leatrice had been watching too much true crime TV again.

"I'm so sorry." I hurried to get my keys, giving Leatrice an evil eye of my own. "How long have you been waiting?"

"Not long." Joni got to her feet and held out the brown bag with handles. "I planned to leave the DVD hanging on the doorknob but apparently that's frowned upon in this building."

I looked at Leatrice over my shoulder. "This is Joni. The videographer I spoke to on the phone."

Leatrice began to fidget. "How did I know she was who she claimed to be? That bag could be a high-tech explosive, for all I know."

"Did you explain who you were?" I asked Joni.

"Several times." Joni arched an eyebrow. "I didn't know I needed to bring *two* forms of ID, though."

Kate gave her a nudge. "Well, you do look suspicious. Most terrorists are blond females, you know."

"She's wearing all black and carrying a package," Leatrice insisted. "You can't be too safe."

"This is Washington," Joni muttered. "Everyone wears black."

I pushed open my front door and ushered everyone inside, taking the bag from Joni. "Do you want to stay and watch it with us now that you're here?"

"Why not? It's one of the more interesting wedding films I've shot for pure entertainment value. There was that time that I shot the biker wedding and the bride wore white leather. I don't even know where you could find a leather wedding dress."

Thankfully, I didn't have any idea, either. The day a bride asked me for a leather dress would be the day I hung up my wedding planner hat.

"And how could I forget the circus wedding?" Joni continued. "That couple was a bit off to begin with, though."

"Circus people are odd," I said.

"Oh, they weren't with the circus," Joni explained. "They just wanted a circus-themed wedding. The groom dressed like a ringmaster and the bride wore a tightrope walker's costume. All the guests had to dress up like clowns."

"That's one way to get a lower guest count," Kate muttered.

Leatrice brightened. "I wouldn't mind going to a wedding like that. I already have the outfit."

I shook my head. Why was I surprised?

"I'll put the DVD in." Kate took the bag from me and headed toward my television stand tucked in the corner. "I'm dying to see what happened. We missed most of the action after the police detained us."

"After the bride ran into the courtyard screaming that her wedding vendors had murdered someone, it was pretty much pandemonium." Joni took a seat on the end of the couch and scooted over when Leatrice sat next to her. "I stopped shooting when the police came out. Luckily, I hadn't come anywhere near the crime scene, and they weren't interested in my ceremony footage."

"It didn't occur to the police that you might have inadvertently recorded something through the glass walls?" I stood behind the couch and waited for Kate to finish putting the DVD in the player.

"The officer who took our statements seemed really green," Joni said. "I don't think he'd been to many murder scenes."

Leatrice turned around to face me. "But you'll show this to the police if we find anything, right?"

"Of course. Once we've determined who the murderer is, I'll turn all the evidence over to the cops and let them make the arrest." I sighed. "We have to make sure our evidence outweighs the evidence they have against Georgia or it won't do any good."

"The DVD's starting." Kate hunched in front of the TV. "Where's the remote to this thing?"

"I got it." I reached over to the wooden end table at the foot of the couch and grabbed the silver remote control. Kate stepped away from the television screen as it filled with an image of the bride getting her makeup done in the hotel suite. She wore jeans and a white button-down shirt, and her bridesmaids clustered around her nibbling on bagels and sipping champagne. She looked so happy that I cringed remembering her face when she saw the dead chef. I pushed the fast-forward button and the screen flashed through more dressing footage, shots of the outside of the church, and the world's fastest ceremony processional.

"Those are lovely dresses." Leatrice sniffled. "Do you think we could slow it down and watch some of the ceremony? Weddings are so beautiful, I always cry."

"No way." Kate shook her head. "It's a full Catholic mass. I sat through it once. No way am I sitting through it a second time."

We watched in fast forward as readers zipped up to the podium, the bride and groom exchanged vows in rapid fire, and the priest whizzed through communion. I leaned against the back of the couch wondering how long it would take us to get to the good part. You know you've done too many weddings when you consider a murder the most interesting part of a wedding film.

"Here comes the cocktail hour." Joni reached back and tugged on my sleeve.

I pressed Play and the courtyard came into view. Red lanterns hung from transparent wire and seemed to be suspended in midair. The camera panned the entire space then zoomed in on the bar set up against the Colonnade wall. As the camera slowly tightened its shot on the specialty drink menu in the red lacquered frame, I noticed a flicker of movement behind.

"Stop it there," Kate cried, pointing to the screen. "Someone's moving in the Colonnade."

"You're right." I paused the DVD and forwarded it a frame at a time.

The background was blurry, but I could make out two figures, both wearing white.

"Chef jackets." Kate slid close to the screen. "They must be wearing chef jackets."

I snapped my fingers. "Of course." We watched as the figures grappled in slow motion. Then one pushed the other behind the indoor gazebo. The next few seconds seemed to last forever as we waited to see what happened next. Finally one of the chefs emerged into the camera's view. Only one of the chefs. He left the room through the kitchen exit then came back in twice more, each time disappearing behind the gazebo. The killer certainly was thorough.

Kate turned around, her mouth hanging open. "Did we just see the murder?"

I nodded, unable to form a coherent sentence. I put the screen on freeze frame.

"It's not very easy to tell who it is, though." Leatrice squinted at the out of focus figures on the television.

"But we know two very important things now." My brain started working on overdrive as I focused on the screen. I walked to the TV and pointed to the figure who must have pushed Henri into the ice sculpture. "Whoever killed Henri wore a chef's jacket and had dark hair."

"You're right." Kate studied the screen intently. "That narrows it down some, but at the Fairmont there are lots of folks who work in the kitchen and have dark hair."

"Yes," I agreed. "But Georgia isn't one of them."

CHAPTER 18

"If the DVD clears Georgia of the murder, I don't understand why we don't take it to the police." Kate followed me through the Fairmont Hotel lobby, running to keep up.

After Joni had left and Leatrice went downstairs to get her magnifying glass so she could further inspect the footage, Kate and I rushed down the back fire escape of my apartment building. Before Leatrice could notice we were gone, we'd hopped in my car and sped away. We knew she would have insisted on joining our search for dark-haired men in chef jackets, and it's hard to be inconspicuous with a little old lady in pink cowboy boots tagging along.

"For starters," I said, turning to Kate, "I called Reese, but I had to leave a message. Let's hope he bothers to call me back. I told the officer I talked to that we'd found evidence to clear Georgia, but he sounded like he didn't believe me."

Kate tapped a finger on her chin. "The police don't believe the wedding planners turned amateur sleuths? Shocking."

I ignored her sarcasm and resumed walking. "Even though we helped him solve the murder of our mother of the bride, he doesn't seem to think we're anything but a nuisance. Plus, the police are sure that Georgia is the killer, so it's going to take a lot of convincing for them to admit they made a mistake and let her go." I looked over my shoulder to make sure Kate kept up. "I also think we need to have more evidence about the actual murderer before we turn our information over. Which is why we're back at the Fairmont. To narrow down the list of dark-haired suspects."

"So you want us to build an entire case, and then hand it to the cops on a silver platter?"

I took the stairs to the second floor two at a time. "If that's the only way to be sure that Georgia is cleared of the murder, then yes. Unless Reese deigns to return my call."

"I don't know about this, Annabelle." Kate lowered her voice and closed the distance between us. "Do you think it's smart of us to poke around the hotel? What if the real killer doesn't want to be discovered?"

"We'll be discreet," I assured her. "I promised Georgia that I would ask around the hotel. I'm sure her colleagues will want to help her."

Kate shot me a sideways glance. "Except the one that wanted her fired and the one who framed her for murder."

"Mr. Elliott isn't off my suspect list." I reached the second floor landing and paused to catch my breath. "The charming general manager may not have a lot of hair, but if I remember correctly, it is dark."

"So is Marcello's," Kate reminded me. "Are there no Scandinavian chefs in the city?"

"Believe me, if Richard hadn't been working with him at the Dumbarton House at the time of the murder, Marcello would be at the top of my list. But unless human cloning has come a lot further than I think, it would have been impossible for Marcello to kill Henri. I still think that Marcello might know something about who *did* kill his archenemy, though."

"Too bad he would never tell us." Kate followed me past the executive offices and through the door that led to the back hallways.

"After the way he reacted when we mentioned Henri, I doubt he'd be willing to talk about the murder case again."

"Luckily we don't have to talk to him to get the information we need."

The halls in the back of the hotel were in stark contrast to the ones the guests saw. Painted cinder-block walls and utilitarian tile floors were a far cry from the hotel's trademark gleaming marble and polished glass. I stopped in front of the door to the employee cafeteria and motioned with a jerk of my head. "We have more than enough people right here who can lead us to the killer."

"Good thinking, Annie." Kate patted me on the shoulder. "If anyone is gossiping about the murder, this is the place we'll hear it."

I walked inside the employee cafeteria, which had recently been painted red. We were met by the buffet line, which reminded me of elementary school, with the rectangular metal pans of steaming food lined up behind glass hoods. We passed the hot food offerings and made our way down to the beverage station. The ice dispenser made a grinding noise but produced no ice, so we filled our tall paper cups with lukewarm Diet Coke. Nothing like a nice warm soda.

Once we had our drinks, I motioned for Kate to follow me into the sitting area filled with square tables and wooden chairs. A TV mounted on the wall played *Oprah,* and a cluster of women in housekeeping uniforms watched intently. A tall man I recognized as one of the security staff sat in a corner reading a newspaper. He glanced over his paper as we chose a table by the window that overlooked the roof of the Colonnade.

Kate slid her chair closer to me. "How are we going to get any information out of these people? No one is talking."

"I guess we wait until *Oprah* is over." I peeked at my watch. We had twenty minutes before the talk show queen released her siren's hold on the room.

"Do you ladies work in the hotel?" A deep voice startled me, and I jumped, spilling a bit of my soda on the table. No great loss. The security officer stood over me in his dark suit.

"Not exactly," I started to explain. "We're event planners, and we have an event in the hotel." Technically not for another two months, but not a complete lie, either.

He cleared his throat. "You can't be in the employee cafeteria if you're not an employee."

"Darcy O'Connell told us it would be okay for us to come here for a drink while we're working," Kate explained. Again, technically true. Darcy had said that during our last job at the Fairmont, but she probably hadn't intended for us to stop by randomly and hang out.

The officer narrowed his eyes at us and pulled out a walkie-talkie. "I'm going to have to confirm this with Miss O'Connell." He walked out of earshot and spoke low into the device.

"Don't worry, Annie." Kate took a sip of tepid soda and made a face. "Darcy will cover for us."

"So much for being low-key," I muttered. "The whole hotel knows we're here now."

"If we really wanted to blend in, we should have swiped a couple of housekeeping uniforms." Kate pointed a thumb toward the cluster of women in blue uniforms with white aprons.

I rolled my eyes. "This is not an episode of *I Love Lucy.* Do you really think the two of us would pass as maids, anyway? We're about twenty years younger than those women. And when is the last time you cleaned something?" Not that I was one to talk.

Kate made a face at me. "I can clean. I just choose not to most of the time."

"I'll bet you don't even own a toilet brush."

She gave me a horrified look. "Toilets use brushes?"

Before I could even begin to explain, my cell phone rang. I pulled it out of my purse and recognized the number on the caller ID.

"Hi, Nadine," I said as I answered the phone. "What's up?"

"I'm worried about my dress," she said in a shaky voice.

"What about it?" I kept my own voice calm. "Did something happen?"

"No, but the girls at the salon are concerned about the cathedral-length train getting crumpled when it's transported to my hotel suite. Can we get a stretch limo so the train doesn't have to be folded?"

I heard the unmistakable sound of smoke being exhaled. "You want me to get a limo for the dress?"

"Yes, the longest one they have. I'm going to pay one of the girls from the salon to ride with it."

God forbid the dress gets lonely on the ride across town.

I ignored Kate's muffled giggling. "No problem, Nadine."

"Oh, and one more thing," Nadine said. "Can you make sure the limo is black? Since my dress is technically ivory, I think a bright white limo would clash with it."

I paused to steady my voice and keep from laughing. "You think a white limo will clash with the dress?"

Kate clamped her hand over her mouth and shook with silent laughter.

"Don't you?" The bride sounded shocked that I would question her.

"A black limo is no problem, Nadine. Call me if you think of anything else." I dropped the phone in my purse.

Kate wiped tears from her cheeks. "Ow. My sides hurt."

"It could be worse." I grinned. "At least she didn't insist on a police escort for the dress."

The security officer returned to our table, looking deflated. "Miss O'Connell gave you the okay to be here." He forced a smile before he turned away. "Have a nice day, ladies."

"We're lucky that Darcy is so cool," Kate said.

I bit the edge of my lip. "I'm sure she's wondering what we're up to."

"It's no big deal. She's on our side, remember? Didn't you see how stressed she was trying to keep up with Georgia's workload and her own? Darcy wants Georgia back more than anyone."

I looked past Kate and saw Darcy's face in the cafeteria doorway. She waved for us to come outside and then disappeared from view. I pulled Kate by the sleeve out of the cafeteria. Once in the hallway, I spotted Darcy behind a stack of plastic glass racks.

"What are you doing there?" I asked.

"Me?" she snapped, stepping from behind the racks. Her white blouse was half untucked from her black skirt and her hair looked like it hadn't been brushed in days. She'd gone from naughty librarian to demon-possessed librarian. "What are you doing here? Don't tell me you're actually here for a tasty snack in the employee cafeteria?"

"What happened to you?" Kate stared at Darcy.

"I pulled an all-nighter trying to catch up on work." Darcy rubbed her hands over her bloodshot eyes. "Sorry if I'm a little grumpy, but I'm exhausted. I can't take much more of this."

"Sorry if we took you away from something," I said. "We thought we might overhear something in the employee cafeteria that could help us prove Georgia's innocence."

"Really?" Darcy raised an eyebrow. "Did you have any luck?"

Kate shook her head. "We hoped to find some of the kitchen staff or chefs, but they aren't in there."

"The sous chefs are downstairs getting ready for a party in the ballroom," Darcy explained. "Most of the kitchen staff is probably there as well. Any reason why you want to talk to them?"

I looked at Kate, who nudged me to continue. "We found some evidence that shows that the actual killer had dark hair and wore a chef's jacket."

Darcy's mouth gaped open. "That's amazing. What kind of evidence?"

"The videographer shot part of the murder from the courtyard without even realizing it," Kate said. "We just watched the DVD."

"Did you get a really clear look at the killer?" Darcy's eyes widened with excitement.

"It's fuzzy," I confessed. "We can't make out who did it, but we do know he had dark hair."

"If you're looking for dark-haired chefs, then you should talk to the two sous chefs and the pastry chef first," Darcy whispered. "All of them worked directly under Henri, all of them have dark hair, and all of them hated their boss. Emilio and Gunter should be working on the buffets in the ballroom foyer, and Jean may be setting up the dessert display already."

"Thanks, Darcy." I gave her arm a squeeze. "I know Georgia would be happy to know that she still has friends in the hotel."

Darcy nodded. "Georgia was a great boss, and I never knew how hard she worked until now. If I can do anything else to help, please let me know."

"Thanks," I said. "I guess we're going to go find some chefs."

Darcy took a few steps down the hall and called over her shoulder, "Don't let them intimidate you. They're like most chefs. Their bark is worse than their bite." She began to hum as she disappeared around a corner.

Kate gulped. "If one of these chefs killed Henri, I'm afraid we have more to be worried about than his bark."

CHAPTER 19

"This is a disgrace!" The distinctive disdain of the French accent carried from where Jean St. Jean stood examining a table of desserts on the other side of the ballroom. "Mon *dieu!* Who put the tartlets on a mirrored tile?"

Kate took a baby step back out into the hallway before I caught her by the arm and pulled her into the room. The large ballroom was filled with rows of tables draped in white cotton cloths, and matching napkins stood in fan folds on the white base plates. Each table had the same low glass bowl of red and gold flowers. This party definitely had the feel of a corporate event.

I dragged Kate behind me as I weaved my way through the maze of tables to where Jean stood muttering to himself at the dessert display. He wore a pristine white jacket over dark billowy pants and a tall chef's hat perched on his brown wavy hair.

He jumped when he heard us behind him. "Who are you?"

"Just party planners," I responded, hoping he would assume that I meant we were the party planners for this event. Not a lie, I reasoned to myself. An omission.

"Of course." He gave a curt nod of his head. "I am Jean St. Jean, the pastry chef for the Fairmont Hotel. I was merely inspecting the work of my subordinates before the party begins."

"We've heard wonderful things about your work." I nudged Kate. "Haven't we?"

"Absolutely." Kate bobbed her head eagerly. "The Fairmont is known for having some of the best chefs in the city."

Jean St. Jean gave a smug smile. "It is nice to be recognized for one's excellence." Boy, this guy was full of himself.

"Such a shame that you lost the real culinary genius in the hotel, though." I shook my head and didn't take my eyes off St. Jean.

His smile disappeared and his eyes flashed with anger. "They're saying that Henri was the genius? Idiots."

"Well, he was the head chef, wasn't he?" Kate asked in an innocent voice.

"Not because of culinary skill, I assure you," the pastry chef fumed. "The man didn't have as much talent in his entire body as I do in my little finger. The only ideas he ever had were ones he stole from others."

"Did he steal your ideas?" I pressed.

"He stole from everyone. If any one of his chefs had an idea, Henri claimed it as his own and took the glory." St. Jean slammed his hand down on the dessert display, and the rows of tiny truffles began to roll around.

This guy had some impulse control issues.

"So he wasn't very popular among the other chefs?" I caught a truffle as it headed for the edge of the table.

St. Jean laughed derisively. "We don't miss him, if that's what you mean to ask."

"Were you here the day of the murder?" I said, knowing full well that he had been.

"Of course." He turned his attention back to the dessert table. "I created the wedding cake. Such a pity the guests never saw it. It was quite a masterpiece."

I vaguely remembered the four-tiered stacked cake ornamented with the red Chinese symbol for double happiness on each layer. I knew it had been set up on the baby grand piano in the alcove, but I couldn't recall if I had seen it before or after I found the body.

"So you were in the Colonnade around the time of the murder?" I watched as he realigned the truffles.

The chef stopped what he was doing and looked up at me. "I set up the cake during the cocktail hour, but Henri was nowhere to be seen when I left the room."

"Are you sure?" Kate folded her arms over her chest.

"I think I would have noticed him." His face flushed. "Why so many questions?"

"Just curious," I said. "Did you see anyone else in the room when you were there?"

"Gunter and Emilio came in to check the stations as I left. We were all in and out of the room setting up the wedding. Nothing unusual about that." He narrowed his eyes. "Who did you say you were again?"

"Nobody important." I backed away. "We'll let you get back to your work."

"You might want to rethink the mirror tiles, though," Kate added as she followed me. Jean St. Jean scowled and stalked off through the back kitchen doors of the ballroom.

"Well, that was interesting," I said. "He wasn't shy about hating Henri."

"Did you believe his alibi?"

I shrugged. "I wouldn't put the murder past him, but let's see if anyone corroborates his story."

"So one down, two to go." Kate navigated through the sea of tables toward the doors.

I pressed my lips together. "We'd better find Gunter and Emilio before our French friend warns them. He seemed suspicious of our questions."

"Maybe you should let me lead the next interrogation. I have more experience charming things out of men."

Kate had a point. "Be my guest." I held open the doors to the foyer. Two chefs in matching white jackets stood with their backs to us. Jackpot.

"Why must you insist on making the crudités display so Prussian?" one of the chefs said to the other, rolling his r's and laughing.

"You have no appreciation for the precision of cooking," the other replied in a heavy accent that I placed somewhere between Germany and Eastern Europe. I could only assume this was Gunter. His dark hair was cropped close to his head, and his jacket looked like it had been starched until it could stand on its own.

"And you have no appreciation for its passion."

I'd heard of Emilio's reputation for avidly pursuing passions in and out of the kitchen.

Kate cleared her throat, and both men looked over their shoulders at us. Emilio did a double take, and grinned at Kate like a wolf about to pounce.

"Perhaps these lovely women would give us their opinion." The Latin chef's brown hair fell in curls around his face.

Gunter returned to his straight rows of vegetables with a measuring tape. "I must finish my work without delay."

"We were admiring your artistry." Kate approached a table set with various clay bowls of Spanish tapas and ran a finger languidly around one of the bowls. "I love a man who's passionate about his work."

Emilio raised his eyebrows. "It takes a good eye to recognize culinary beauty. You must appreciate the art of food."

"I appreciate a lot of things," Kate purred. Man, she was pouring it on thick. I wondered if I should remind her to question them, not seduce them.

"Are you staying in the hotel?" Emilio leaned close to Kate. "Perhaps we could meet for drinks after I get off."

"We're actually working, too." Kate explained. "We're party planners."

"So you work here often?" He ran his tongue along his bottom lip.

Kate nodded. "We'll be here more now that Chef Henri is gone."

"Don't tell me he terrorized you." Emilio took Kate's hand with a concerned look on his face. "That man had no shame."

"He got what he deserved," Gunter said over his shoulder.

"Were you here when he was murdered?" Kate asked Emilio in a conspiratorial whisper. "Did you see the body?"

"Of course we were here." Emilio puffed out his chest.

Gunter turned around with a snap. "We checked the stations, and then left the room together before Chef Henri was murdered. Just like we told the police."

"That's right." Emilio bobbed his head in agreement. "We never saw the body."

Kate rubbed her hands together. "How exciting to have been in the room only moments before a murder took place. Did you see anything suspicious? Maybe someone else went into the room after you?"

"The banquet captain, Reg, and the general manager were coming in the main entrance of the Colonnade as we left through the kitchen doors." Emilio darted a glance at Gunter. "We didn't go back to the Colonnade, though, so we never saw when they left."

Kate pressed a hand on Emilio's arm. "I'll bet the police were really interested in your story."

"We were in the kitchens working at the time of the murder, so we couldn't tell them much." Emilio shrugged.

"Was Jean with you, as well?" I tapped my foot on the carpet.

"We were all together." Gunter's face wore no expression. "Excuse me. I must return to the kitchen."

Kate watched the stiff chef walk away. "I hope we didn't upset him by talking about the murder. It's so fascinating that it happened right here in this very hotel."

Emilio dismissed Gunter's behavior with a wave of his hand. "He's not much of a talker. His closest friend is that measuring tape." He glanced at his watch, and his eyes widened. "You must forgive me, ladies. I also must get back to work."

"Of course," Kate said. "Nice meeting you."

Emilio gave a parting leer. "I hope we meet again soon. Perhaps you can give me your number?"

"Sure." Kate turned to me. "Do you have a pen?"

I dug in my bag for a pen and handed it to her.

Kate scrawled something on a page in her purse-size day planner and ripped it out. She folded it in half and tucked it into the pocket of the chef's jacket.

He patted the note and then gave Kate a seductive smile and me a cursory glance before darting through the banquet doors.

Kate sighed. "Sorry that wasn't more helpful. At least we found out that the banquet captain and the GM were in the room around the time of the murder, too."

"Are you kidding? We found out a lot more than that. I think he's hiding something."

"Me, too," Kate said eagerly, and then a puzzled expression crossed her face. "Wait. Which one?"

I rolled my eyes. "Gunter, of course."

"Why?" Kate asked. "He said almost nothing."

"Exactly. His answers were too easy. Almost like he rehearsed them. I think he knows more about the murder than he's letting on."

"Emilio seemed nice enough."

"Are you sure it was a good idea to give him your number, though?" I asked as Kate handed me back my pen.

"Oh, don't worry. I didn't give him my number." She shook her head seriously. "I gave him yours."

CHAPTER 20

"**Y**ou did what?" I stared at Kate in shock.

"Emilio might have gotten suspicious if I refused to give him my number."

"But why give him mine?"

Kate shrugged. "You told me I shouldn't play the field so much."

"But I should?" Before I could launch into a proper tirade, my cell phone rang. "Wedding Belles, this is Annabelle."

"Annabelle, honey. This is Darla Douglas." The voice slurred slightly. "Debbie and I have a quickie question for you."

I looked at my watch. It was already afternoon, so they must be past their first cocktail of the day.

"We're thinking of doing the groom's cake in the shape of Turner's black lab, Binger. Do you know a cake baker who could do that for us?" She paused and took a drink of something. "He just adored that dog."

Past tense? I gulped. "Binger isn't alive?"

"No, but we think it would be a special way to remember him on the wedding day."

By serving him to the guests? I rubbed my head. "Okay, can you send me a picture of the dog?"

"We'll shoot one right over to you. Now, does this baker do a good rum cake?"

I cringed at the thought of the booze-themed wedding that seemed to be solidifying. "Of course, but you can do a tasting to make sure."

"That's a great idea. We want to make sure it's as flavorful as my grandmother's recipe. Most people go too light on the rum."

Nothing like getting drunk off a slice of the beloved deceased Binger.

"I'll set up the tasting for you," I said. "How's next week?"

"Perfect. I'd better run. Debbie and I don't want to miss our court time at the club."

I hung up my phone. "Remind me not to eat the groom's cake at the Douglas wedding."

"Let me guess, martini flavored?" Kate asked.

"Close enough," I groaned. "Rum cake in the shape of a dead dog."

"It must be a wedding." A voice from behind startled me.

I spun around, clutching my hand to my heart. "Reg! Don't sneak up on people like that." My heart raced as I wondered how much he'd heard.

The tall, wiry banquet captain laughed as Kate clutched my arm. "D-Didn't mean to scare you."

"Thanks," Kate said as she walked to a nearby cocktail table and sat down. "I think I lost a year off my life."

"What are you two doing back here so soon?" Reg ran a hand through his unruly brown hair. "I thought you'd steer clear of this place after the police finally let you go."

Kate nodded. "That would make sense, but we're trying to help—"

"Darcy." I jumped in before Kate could mention Georgia and tip off one of our suspects. "We stopped by to see if we could help Darcy since she's so swamped with work now that Georgia is gone."

Reg's face clouded. "Poor Georgia. She didn't have anything to do with Henri's murder."

"How can you be sure?" I took a seat next to Kate. This didn't sound like someone who wanted to frame her for murder.

"Georgia is too s-s-sweet to hurt anyone," he insisted, with a slight stutter. "You can tell about people, and Georgia is no killer."

"Then who do you think killed Henri?" Kate laced her fingers together and rested her chin on them.

Reg pressed his lips together and sank into a chair across from us. "I don't know. If I had any c-c-lue that could help Georgia, I would've told the police already."

"Georgia is lucky to have a friend like you, Reg," I said.

"I don't think she considers me a friend." Reg smiled weakly. "We didn't run in the same circles. She's much too glamorous to socialize with a banquet captain."

I looked at the shy banquet captain with cowlicks pushing his hair in all directions and a stutter that emerged when he was nervous. Did Reg have a crush on Georgia?

"I t-t-tried to visit her in jail, but they wouldn't let me in," he continued, his face flushed pink. "I wanted her to know that some people still care about her."

"Listen, Reg." I grabbed his hand. "Did you see anyone go into the Colonnade before Henri was murdered?"

"I went in to double-check the room setup, but Henri wasn't there. The waiters were at the cocktail hour since we'd set up the room so early, so it was only me."

"Did you see any of the chefs in the room?" Kate asked.

He chewed on his lower lip as he thought. "Gunter and Emilio were leaving through the back kitchen door as I came in."

So they were telling the truth. "What about Jean?"

"Nope." He shook his head. "The cake was already set up, and I didn't see him all afternoon."

"And Mr. Elliott?" I asked. Emilio had claimed that Reg had been with the general manager.

Reg frowned. "The GM followed me in the room. He was on the warpath that day."

"What do you mean?" Kate raised an eyebrow.

"Some days he seemed to look for something or someone to p-p-pick on. Saturday was one of those days."

"Did he find anything?" I pressed.

"I don't know," Reg said. "He told me to leave the Colonnade so that the photographer could get some room shots before the guests came in. The next thing I knew, Henri was dead, and the police were swarming the place."

"Mr. Elliott was setting up room shots?" I exchanged a look with Kate. We both knew the photographer hadn't been in the hotel until after the murder took place.

Reg nodded. "If a wedding made the hotel look good, he always got promotional pictures."

The wheels in my head were slow to turn. What would Mr. Elliott gain by killing Henri? "Reg, is there any reason Mr. Elliott would've wanted Henri dead? Anything at all?"

"No one really liked Henri," Reg explained. Hardly breaking news. "But he was the highest-paid employee, aside from the general manager himself. Henri caused lots of problems in the hotel, but he would have created even more if they tried to fire him."

"Did Mr. Elliot want to fire Henri?" I cast a glance over my shoulder as a bartender brought a rack of glasses to the bar at the end of the foyer. "We heard he'd been looking for a reason to fire Georgia."

"I think he would have been happy to get a troublemaker like Henri out of the hotel," Reg whispered. "He seemed intimidated by Georgia, so maybe he tried to kill two birds with one stone."

My mouth fell open. "You think this was the GM's idea of budget cuts?"

"Well, it does save on a severance package," Kate said.

"As horrible as Mr. Elliott sounds," I said, "I have a hard time believing that he killed Henri just so he wouldn't have to fire him."

Reg grimaced. "You don't know the people in Human Resources, do you?"

"Annie, this would explain why one person would kill Henri and frame Georgia for it," Kate said. "It sounds like Mr. Elliott was the last person in the Colonnade before Henri's death."

I nodded as I processed our clues. Mr. Elliott could have easily gotten a chef's jacket from the kitchen and confronted Henri once he had assured himself that no one would disturb the "room shots." It would've taken only a few minutes to push Henri into the ice sculpture, then ditch the jacket and return to the front of the hotel.

I had one last question for Reg. "Do you think there's any reason why Gunter would have acted strange when we questioned him?"

"Are you sure that Gunter wasn't being himself? He's never been the friendliest fellow." Reg gave an almost apologetic laugh.

"That's putting it mildly," Kate said.

"He's not very social with the staff," Reg continued. "He seems to tolerate his fellow chefs, but that's about it. Never really fit in. And he drives them all crazy with his tape measure. I doubt he'll stay at the hotel once he gets his green card and can change jobs."

"Thanks, Reg." I stood up as I saw a few people begin to wander down the stairs. "You've been a lot of help."

Reg reached out and shook my hand tentatively. "Will you tell Georgia that we all miss her?"

"Of course, Reg." I squeezed his hand. "I'll tell her that you asked about her."

Reg flushed and stepped away. "Tell her I'd do anything to help her."

"Come on." I pulled Kate by the sleeve toward the elevators. "I think we've gotten all the information we're going to get today."

"Don't you want to talk to Gunter again?" Kate asked. "I thought you said he was hiding something."

"I did." I pressed the elevator call button in rapid fire. "I still think he knows more than he said. Maybe he's even covering for Mr. Elliott. But I don't think we're going to convince him to spill his guts."

"What about Mr. Elliott?" Kate followed me into the empty elevator car. "He seems guiltier every second."

"And more dangerous," I agreed as the elevator surged up toward the lobby. We were quiet for several seconds, then I said, "If he planned Henri's murder to get rid of two problem employees, then he won't be very willing to talk to anyone about it."

"So what do we do next?" Kate hurried behind me as I exited the elevator.

"I think it's time to give some of our information to the police." I dug in my purse for my valet parking ticket. "They can question Gunter and Mr. Elliott and get more information than we can."

"I thought you didn't trust the police to keep looking for the killer since they have Georgia in custody."

I pushed through the glass revolving doors that led out of the hotel. "I don't, but we have so much information now that they can't ignore it." I handed my parking ticket to the valet attendant and held up a finger. "First, we have the DVD, which shows that the murderer was a dark-haired man in a chef's jacket. Second, we've determined that all the chefs came in and out of the Colonnade prior to the murder. Unfortunately, they all corroborate each other's alibis. Emilio and Gunter saw Mr. Elliott and Reg come into the room after they left, and I'll bet Gunter saw more than that by the way he clammed up. We have a general manager who everyone knew wanted Georgia fired and apparently also wanted Henri out. He cleared the room for photos that you and I know couldn't have taken place because there was no photographer. That gives him motive and opportunity." I sucked in a breath. "And he has dark hair. Well, some at least."

"You think Gunter is covering for him?"

I nodded. "It seems like all the chefs are concerned with saving their own necks. Turning in the boss isn't the smartest move, especially if your green card is dependent on keeping your job. I wouldn't be surprised if all the chefs know more than they're willing to admit."

Kate gave a low whistle. "What a hornet's vest!"

CHAPTER 21

"Help has arrived," Richard called out as he swung his silver convertible Mercedes into the Fairmont's circular drive with a squeal of tires.

Kate hopped into the backseat and I slid into the front, giving Richard a sheepish smile. "Thanks for coming. I don't know what they did with my car."

"We waited for over an hour, and they still couldn't find it." Kate stuck her head between the two front seats. "At least they didn't make us pay."

"This is a bad sign, darlings." Richard pulled the car back onto Twenty-fourth Street and slid a pair of sunglasses on. "First your car is stolen, next we're all going to find ourselves bound and gagged and being shipped off to heaven only knows. You know I would be a prime target for white slavery."

"I would only assume." I rolled my eyes. What a drama queen. "This is nothing more than bad luck."

"Don't you think it's an awfully big coincidence that when you start your own mini murder investigation your car disappears?" Richard peered at me over his dark glasses. "And that the suspects you're questioning happen to have access to the garage where your car is parked?"

"I think the chances are greater that the valet lost the ticket than that someone intentionally took my car," I said.

"Don't forget the time a parking attendant crashed my car driving it up the garage ramp." Kate raised her voice above the traffic.

I shot a look over my shoulder. "Thanks, that's very comforting. I'm sure they'll find my car."

"You're out of your mind if you think this is some wild coincidence," Richard insisted. "I told you not to stick your nose in this case."

I gaped at Richard. "No, you didn't."

"I didn't?" He looked genuinely surprised. "Well, I certainly meant to. Consider this a slightly belated warning not to meddle anymore."

"I'll consider myself warned." I settled back in my seat and looked around M Street as we entered Georgetown. Narrow restaurants with brightly colored awnings lined the streets, and a row of black sedans and a couple of motorcycle cops sat in front of the Four Seasons Hotel across the street. I wondered which dignitary was in town this time.

"I know that look," Richard sighed. "You have absolutely no intention of minding your own business, do you? Why would this day be any different? Why doesn't anyone listen to me?"

Soap operas had less angst than this. "I'll make a deal with you, Richard. If you give us a ride to the police station, I'll turn over my evidence to Detective Reese and retire from the case."

"Really?" Richard gave me a suspicious look. "What's the catch?"

"No catch." I shrugged. "Let me run inside my apartment and grab the DVD, and then we can go straight to the police."

"What DVD?" Richard made a sharp right on Thirtieth Street and sped around a car trying to parallel park.

"The DVD that shows the murder of Chef Henri," Kate chimed in from the backseat. "The wedding videographer didn't even know she'd filmed it through the glass walls."

Richard's eyes widened as he paused momentarily at a stop sign. "Can you tell who the killer is?"

"It's not totally clear," I confessed. "But you can see that whoever did it has dark hair and is wearing a white chef's jacket."

Richard drummed his fingers on the steering wheel. "So another chef did kill him."

"Or someone who snagged a chef's jacket." Kate waved a finger in the air. "It would have been a great disguise."

Richard pulled to a stop in front of my building. "So, did you narrow down the field of dark-haired people at the hotel?"

"I thought you were against snooping around. I wouldn't dream of sullying you with our ill-gotten information." I opened my door and blew him a kiss while Kate stifled her laughter. "I'll be back in a flash."

I pushed open the heavy front doors of my narrow stone building and ran up the stairs two at a time. I caught my breath when I reached my apartment on the third floor and took a second to listen for footsteps or squeaking clothing. So far no sign of Leatrice. I dashed into my apartment, grabbed the DVD off the top of the player, and shoved it back in the paper bag it had arrived in. I went back down the stairs at a more leisurely pace since apparently I didn't need to dodge Leatrice this time. I walked out of my building and stopped short. I'd spoken too soon.

Leatrice sat in the backseat next to Kate, wearing a hot pink cowgirl hat accented with white rickrack. Richard's lips were pressed together so tightly they'd disappeared entirely.

"Leatrice." I tried to sound happy to see her. "What are you doing?"

"Kate told me that we're taking the DVD to the police station." Leatrice beamed. "You don't think I'd miss that, do you?"

I arched an eyebrow at Kate. Richard looked as if he couldn't decide which one to throttle first.

Kate batted her eyelashes. "I may have mentioned something."

The chances of convincing Leatrice to stay behind were slim to none, and I didn't relish the idea of dragging a little old lady kicking and screaming out of a car in broad daylight. Richard looked like he was pondering the same options.

"No jury in the world would convict us," Richard finally said in a conspiratorial whisper. "Not when we admit the hat as evidence."

I ignored him and got in the car. "Okay, Leatrice, you can come, but we're only going to be a few minutes. We're dropping the DVD off and leaving. I'm afraid it's not going to be very exciting."

"Don't you worry, dearie. It beats watching reruns on the Game Show channel."

Richard adjusted his rearview mirror in a huff. "The hat has got to go. I can't see a thing behind me."

"But it matches the boots." Leatrice raised a hot pink cowboy boot in the air for inspection. They did, indeed, appear to be a matching set. "They'll look silly without the hat."

"I don't think the hat deserves all the blame," Richard muttered.

"How about you take it off for the ride over?" I bargained. "So it won't blow away?"

"Good thinking." Leatrice took off the hat and gave me a pat on the shoulder.

Richard glanced over at me before he gunned the engine. I'd be paying for this for the next decade.

Despite Leatrice's insistence on singing "One Hundred Bottles of Beer on the Wall" during the drive and Richard's noticeable acceleration as each bottle of beer happened to fall, we arrived in front of the police station in one piece.

"No singing," I said as we walked up the sidewalk to the glass front doors. "We're here to turn this over to Reese, explain what we've learned, and leave."

Leatrice nodded silently as she bounced through the door on the toes of her boots. The officer at the desk glanced up, and then did a double take when he saw Leatrice. I guess it wasn't every day you saw an elderly woman in pink cowgirl regalia. Especially in DC.

"Wait here," I said to Leatrice.

She and Kate sat on two plastic chairs lined against the wood-paneled wall while Richard followed me to the desk. Clearly he'd rather take his chances with the cops than be associated with Leatrice.

"I'm here to see Detective Reese. Is he in?" I asked the desk clerk. "I need to drop something off."

"Oh, yeah?" The tall, pasty officer looked past me to where Leatrice sat swinging her legs. "What's her name?"

"No, I'm not dropping off a person," I explained.

Richard elbowed me. "This is a once-in-a-lifetime chance. Don't be a fool. Take it."

I shot him a look and then turned back to the cop. "I'm dropping off evidence in a murder case." I held up the paper bag by its handles.

The officer's eyes widened and he stroked his thin blond mustache. "He's questioning someone, but I'll see if he can be disturbed."

"It's not too late to change your mind," Richard whispered as the cop disappeared in the back. "I'm sure they'd take good care of her."

"Very funny, Richard. You know Leatrice isn't crazy. She's just a bit colorful." I followed Richard's gaze and saw that Leatrice had twisted her boots around so that her feet looked like they pointed in the wrong direction. She and Kate were giggling like fiends.

Richard put his hands on his hips. "I say we leave them both."

"What's this about evidence?" Detective Reese's gruff voice startled me and I spun around. He wore a rumpled shirt and at least a day's growth of stubble. "We're kind of swamped with homicides right now."

My cheeks got warm when I saw him, but immediately cooled when I remembered his bleached blonde cupcake at the restaurant and the fact that he hadn't returned my call from earlier. I cleared my throat. "We didn't mean to disturb you, but we have something that might change your mind about Georgia."

"I doubt it." He ran a hand through his hair. "I'm finishing an interview with another hotel witness, and it's not looking good for your friend."

I held out the bag. "Wait until you watch this. The wedding videographer inadvertently filmed the murder through the glass walls while she filmed in the courtyard."

Reese took the bag from me and pulled out the DVD. "You've watched it?"

I nodded. "It's not crystal clear, but you can tell that the person who killed Henri had dark hair and wore a chef's jacket."

Reese raised an eyebrow and tapped his fingers on the white DVD case. "This might be interesting."

"And we talked to the chefs in the hotel today," I said, pausing to take a quick breath. "They all have alibis, but the sous chef, Gunter, seemed to be hiding something. We think he may be covering for someone. The general manager cleared out the Colonnade for a photographer to take room shots, but the photographer wasn't even in the hotel at the time. Maybe Gunter saw the GM with Henri but is afraid to say anything because he might lose his job and his chance for a green card."

"So much for letting us do our job." Reese leveled his eyes at me. "If you're doing so well on your own, why give this to me?"

"For God's sake, don't encourage her," Richard groaned.

"I left you a message earlier telling you all about what we'd found. Maybe if you'd bothered to return my call, you would have been able to wrap up the case already."

Richard gave a nervous giggle.

Reese glanced over his shoulder at the officer answering phones at the front desk. "I didn't get it."

I felt a twinge of regret for being so short with him. "Really? Well, I actually don't have a burning desire to do your job for you, you know. I wanted to turn over our evidence so you could interrogate Gunter and the general manager and let Georgia go."

"I'm afraid it won't be that simple." Reese dropped the DVD case back in the bag. "Gunter won't implicate the GM."

I balled my hands into fists. "How do you know unless you try?"

"I know because he's dead. We got a call only a couple of minutes ago that one of the Fairmont chefs accidentally electrocuted himself. I was about to head out to join the investigation when you arrived."

"You're sure it's Gunter?" I felt light-headed.

"Yep. It's a hard name to forget." Reese patted me on the shoulder. "Bad luck for him and you, huh?"

I felt numb. Gunter's death didn't have anything to do with bad luck. I felt more convinced than ever that he'd known something about Henri's death. And unfortunately the murderer had made sure he'd never get the chance to tell anyone.

CHAPTER 22

"You don't look so good, dearie." Leatrice watched me collapse onto my couch. "Maybe you need something cool to drink."

"I'll check out the refrigerator," Richard called over his shoulder as he walked from my living room to the kitchen. He pulled open the wooden shutters that created a window between the two rooms. "Make sure she doesn't faint."

"I'm fine," I lied. Richard had threatened to throw Leatrice's hat into traffic if she sang again, so the ride home from the police station had been mercifully quiet, but my head still throbbed. It was hard to believe that we'd spoken to Gunter only a couple of hours ago and now he was dead. I couldn't help thinking that my meddling was the reason.

"You didn't get this upset when you saw Henri's body." Kate tossed her shoes off and perched on the arm of the couch. "What gives?"

"What if we're the reason he's dead?" I asked, my throat dry. "Obviously he was killed so he couldn't talk, and we're the ones trying to get people to talk."

"You can't blame yourself for this." Kate shook her head. "Maybe it was an accident."

"Too coincidental," I said firmly. "I'm starting to think Richard is right about my car, too. Maybe the real killer is sending us some warnings to back off."

"Did I hear you say that I'm right? Will wonders never cease?" Richard bounced out of the kitchen carrying a glass of something brown. He handed it to me. "It's slightly flat Coke, but in this case it'll be good for you."

I took a drink. Sad to say, I was getting used to flat soda. "Poor Gunter. Now we'll never know what he was hiding."

"But we can be pretty sure he saw something that someone didn't want him to share with you or the police," Leatrice said. "You must have struck a nerve with your questioning."

"That's right, Annabelle," Kate agreed. "We must have been on the right track or the real killer wouldn't have felt threatened enough to murder again."

"Is that supposed to be comforting?" Richard shuddered. "You girls are lucky you got out of there alive."

"I don't think *we're* in danger," I said, dismissing Richard's concern.

"Oh really?" Richard began pacing in front of my windows. "A smart killer would go straight to the source. Why not get rid of the two people who are poking around and stirring up trouble? The police aren't looking for more suspects, so the murderer is home free as long as you two don't mess everything up."

I opened my mouth to argue and then stopped. He had a point. Maybe our harmless investigation wasn't so harmless after all. "But who's the most likely killer out of the people who knew we were asking questions about Henri's death?"

"I don't think we can assume that only the people we talked to knew we were there," Kate said. "Word travels fast."

"Why don't we write down all the suspects?" Leatrice began searching for some blank paper on my coffee table. She produced a legal pad from under a pile of magazines and pulled a miniature pencil from her pocket.

Richard let out a long breath. "This seems rather pointless since you're officially retired from your investigation, right?"

"It can't hurt to talk about the case." I shifted in my seat and avoided his eyes.

"There's Mr. Elliott, the hotel's general manager," Kate began. "Nobody likes him, and he wanted to get rid of both Georgia and Henri. He got everyone out of the room where the murder took place under false pretense, too."

Leatrice scratched feverishly in the pad. "That's good. Motive and opportunity. Who's next?"

"I guess the remaining chefs we spoke to. Jean and Emilio. Neither of them was too fond of their boss, and both were in the room prior to the murder. But they have alibis." I downed the last of the flat soda and put the glass on the floor. "Jean is a bit of a prima donna, and Emilio is the in-house Casanova."

"Is he still chasing skirts?" Richard smirked. "He worked for me a few years back. I was always afraid I'd open a kitchen door and find him romancing a prep cook on the counter."

Leatrice's eyebrows popped up. "That doesn't sound very sanitary."

"I doubt Emilio's love life has anything to do with the murder." I tried to change the subject before Leatrice asked for more details. "I would normally list the banquet captain, Reg, as a suspect but I think he's too in love with Georgia to frame her for murder."

"He could have committed the crime without meaning for Georgia to get arrested for it," Kate suggested.

"Good point." I nodded. "That would explain why he's so distraught over her arrest. Maybe he killed Henri to help Georgia, then his plan backfired."

"But do you really think Reg could have murdered someone?" Kate asked me. "He can barely get two sentences out without tripping over his words."

"I know, but if we eliminate everyone we think is too nice to be a killer, our list will only have one name—Mr. Elliott. And Darcy and Hugh swear that he's too spineless to do it."

"Who are Darcy and Hugh?" Leatrice started to write their names down.

"Darcy has been Georgia's assistant for the past three years and Hugh is the head concierge," Kate explained.

"Talk about people who are too mild mannered to kill someone, unless Hugh could get first row Kennedy Center tickets out of it." I grinned. "Neither of them have motives, either."

Leatrice frowned and tapped the notepad with her pencil. "I'll leave them on the list, anyway. Do you have any suspects who don't work in the hotel? It sounds like your victim might have had enemies all over town."

I avoided Richard's gaze. "There is another chef who hated Henri enough to kill him."

"There is no way Marcello could have had anything to do with Henri's death," Richard insisted. "I was with him setting up for a wedding at Dumbarton House at the precise time Henri was murdered."

Leatrice shook her head. "That doesn't make him a very good suspect, then."

"No, it does put a wrinkle in things," I admitted.

Leatrice looked at her notes and then looked up at us. "Someone isn't what they seem to be."

I snapped my fingers. "She's right. What do we really know about these people? We need to research our suspects. Find out about their pasts. Where else they worked in town, their reputations, their personal lives. Maybe that will give us the clues we need to piece it all together."

Richard glared at me. "Might I remind you that you swore off meddling only an hour ago?"

"Annabelle doesn't have to do it." Kate hopped up. "I've got lots of contacts in hotels."

"Do you mean contacts or ex-boyfriends?" Richard batted his eyelashes at her.

Kate stuck her tongue out at him. "Jealous?"

"Hardly." Richard snatched my empty glass from the floor and flounced off to the kitchen.

"Listen." Kate lowered her voice. "I have to run a few errands tomorrow, so why don't I pop by some of the hotels and see what I can dig up?"

"Alone?" I asked. "After what happened today, are you sure that's safe?"

"I could go with you," Leatrice offered.

"No," Kate said forcefully, and then relaxed into a smile. "I'll be fine. None of the other hotels have murderers on the loose, remember?"

"I should stay in the office and get some paperwork done. And it'll keep Richard off my back about meddling." I shook a finger at her. "As long as you promise to call me as soon as you find out anything."

"I'll come back with a full report," Kate assured me.

Richard emerged from the kitchen with his hands on his hips. "I would like to lodge a formal protest against this harebrained idea."

"What harebrained idea?" I gave him my most innocent look. "Kate is perfectly capable of gathering information."

"If she comes back with anything more than a stack of men's phone numbers, I'll die of shock."

Kate stood up and slipped her feet into her shoes. "You wait and see what I find out." She grabbed her purse from the floor and marched over to the door. "Sticks and scones may break my bones .. ."

Richard watched as Kate slammed the door behind her and he shook his head slowly. "I rest my case."

CHAPTER 23

"Have you heard anything from Kate yet?" Leatrice caught me as I stealthily tried to open my mailbox in the building foyer.

"It's barely afternoon." I sighed, looking at my watch. I scooped my mail out of the metal mailbox and snapped the door shut. "She's probably still getting started." Truth be told, she probably just rolled out of bed. Not that I was one to talk. I aspired to make it out of my yoga pants by afternoon. Not that I'd actually made it to yoga class, but I figured getting dressed for it was a step in the right direction. Tomorrow I'd actually attempt a sun salutation.

Leatrice followed me back upstairs. "I've been thinking about the murders. I think we're missing something."

"Like the killer," I replied absentmindedly as I padded up the stairs in my sock feet. I'd spent the morning printing updated "to-do" lists for clients and returning phone calls. For once my mind was focused on marriage, not murder.

As I reached my landing, I heard my business line ringing. It figured the second I left my desk, the phone would ring. I opened the door and rushed down the hall to get the call in time. I snatched the phone off my desk and steadied my voice. "Wedding Belles. This is Annabelle."

Nothing but dial tone.

"Did you miss an important call?" Leatrice stood in the hallway behind me, slightly out of breath.

I looked at the caller ID. The Fairmont Hotel. I wondered who could be calling me from there. Hugh, the concierge, with some juicy gossip? Darcy on the verge of a nervous breakdown? I punched in my voice-mail code.

"Well?" Leatrice rocked back and forth on her heels, making her gold jingle bell necklace ring.

"Isn't that a Christmas necklace?" I asked as I listened to the message.

She gave me a look like I was a simpleton. "On the Style channel they say you should have a signature piece of jewelry, and this is mine."

Somehow I didn't think that was what the Style channel had in mind.

I hung up the phone and put it back on my desk. "They found my car. But it's been scraped up. I'd better grab a cab to the hotel. No way am I calling Richard and having him say 'I told you so' the entire ride there."

"Don't be silly, dear. We can take my car."

I stared at Leatrice for a few seconds. "You have a car?"

"Of course I have a car. I don't drive it much, of course. Not much need when you have everything within walking distance."

"Do you have a license?" I hesitated to ask.

Leatrice gave me a curious look. "Of course. You're not supposed to drive without one, you know."

I didn't dare ask if she'd updated it since the Carter administration. "Okay. Give me a second to get dressed and we can go."

"Perfect." Leatrice clapped her hands. "I'll go warm her up and meet you out front."

I ran into my bedroom as I heard Leatrice close the front door. I tugged on a pair of black pants that I salvaged from the top of the hamper and pulled the plastic dry cleaning bag off a blue silk sweater. I figured the recently cleaned sweater would make up for the not-so-fresh pants. I threw my hair into a ponytail, snatched my black purse from the floor, and headed out the door.

Although the yellow Ford circa 1980 only had four doors, it took up almost as much space as a small stretch limo as it idled loudly in the middle of the street. I didn't see Leatrice at first glance, but I had little doubt that this was her car. They didn't make cars like this anymore. For a reason. I couldn't imagine where in Georgetown she could find a parking space large enough for this monstrosity.

Two loud honks of the car horn made me jump, and I finally noticed Leatrice's jet-black hair poking above the steering wheel. "Hop in, dearie."

I opened the passenger door after a few hard tugs and lowered myself into the car. Leatrice perched on a pile of phone books on the driver's side and wore what appeared to be old-fashioned flight goggles and a flying scarf.

She revved the engine. "I feel the need for speed."

Great. Mario Andretti with cataracts. "We're not in any rush," I assured her.

"Don't you want to see what this baby can do? She's in mint condition." Leatrice rubbed the dashboard. "I only take her out for special occasions, but she corners like she's on rails."

"Mint condition" was a slight exaggeration. The fabric roof of the car had started to bubble and sag in places, making the interior seem smaller than it actually was, even though from the outside it looked like we were driving a small apartment. I rolled down my window by hand as Leatrice stuck her arm out the window and merged into traffic.

"Did you just give a hand signal?" I glanced nervously behind me at the car that had slammed on its brakes to let us in.

"The turn signals are on the fritz," Leatrice explained. "Don't worry, though. I know all the hand signals."

I fumbled for my seat belt and wondered if anyone else in the city knew them. My only consolation was that the Fairmont was less than a mile away. How much damage could we do in less than a mile?

Minutes later I pried my fingers off of the armrest and stepped out of the car in front of the Fairmont. Leatrice was indeed the only person in DC who knew or used hand signals. At least the official ones.

"That was fun." Leatrice hopped out of the car. She handed her keys to a gawking parking valet and strode after me into the hotel, her long scarf fluttering behind her. "Didn't I tell you she handled like a dream?"

I nodded, still steadying my legs. Driving with Leatrice was like riding in a runaway shopping cart. I paused as we walked into the lobby and noticed every person staring at us.

"Don't you want to take off your goggles, Leatrice?"

She pulled them down so they hung around her neck. "Remind me to put them back on when I drive, though. They're prescription."

"This shouldn't take long. Do you want to wait for me while I talk to the front desk?"

"Wait a second." Her eyes lit up. "This is where the murder took place, isn't it?"

"Yes, but we're not here about the murder. We're here to get my car back, so wait in the lobby and I'll be right—"

"I can't pass up a chance to see the murder scene." Leatrice shook her head. "It would be bad investigating."

"We're not investigating. I promised Richard that I wouldn't poke around and cause any more trouble." I lowered my voice. "There's a killer in the hotel who wasn't too happy that Kate and I were asking questions yesterday and wouldn't be happy to see me snooping around again."

"Then you go find out about your car, and I'll do the poking around." Leatrice headed off across the lobby.

The thought of Leatrice snooping around by herself made me cringe. She was incapable of keeping a low profile, and I feared the mayhem she would create on her own. If I took her, at least I could get her in and out as fast as possible.

I chased after her. "Okay, fine. I'll show you the murder scene, and then we get my car and go."

"Agreed." Leatrice skipped after me as I led the way to the Colonnade.

I hurried down the glass hallway and paused outside the room to listen for any voices before walking in. Silence. I craned my neck around the corner and saw that the room was deserted before waving for Leatrice to follow me inside. The Colonnade was set with a handful of round tables and upholstered chairs but was otherwise bare.

Leatrice went up to the raised gazebo. "Where did you find the body?"

"Over there." I motioned to the far side of the room. "Now let's get out of here."

"In a minute." Leatrice walked up the stairs of the gazebo and put a hand against one of the large white columns. "So these blocked the view of the murder on the DVD."

"I guess." I walked around to where the ice sculpture had been. "It would be hard to get a clean view across the room with all these columns."

"So even though the chef was killed in broad daylight in a room with glass walls, it would have been difficult to get a good look unless you were in the room." Leatrice tapped her foot while she thought. "Even if someone saw something, it would be hard to distinguish much because of the obstructed view."

"I suppose you're right, but that doesn't tell us anything we don't already know."

"It tells us that the killer knew the room well enough to know where he would be hidden from view," Leatrice said. "Which means that this wasn't a crime of passion. The murder was well planned. Who arranges the setup of the room?"

"You think the room was arranged for the murder?"

Leatrice shrugged. "Or the killer got very lucky that the ice sculpture sat directly behind a column."

"It must have been a coincidence because Georgia did the room diagram."

"Your friend who was arrested for the murder?" Leatrice raised an eyebrow. "Are you sure she didn't have anything to do with it?"

"Of course I'm sure," I said with more confidence than I suddenly felt. "She was in jail when the second murder was committed, remember?" I gave myself a mental kick for doubting Georgia.

"What if there are two killers? Didn't you say that one of your suspects is in love with her? Maybe he was her accomplice."

"That's ridiculous. We're leaving, Leatrice." I spun around and my breath caught in my throat. A thin man with sparse dark hair stood in my path. Mr. Elliott.

"You two have some explaining to do," he said without changing his stem expression. "Perhaps I should call security."

CHAPTER 24

"Who are you?" Leatrice narrowed her eyes and folded her arms in front of her. I tried not to groan aloud.

"I am the general manager of this hotel." Mr. Elliott looked Leatrice up and down and sneered. His navy suit was perfectly pressed and silver cuff links glinted from his wrists. "Who are you?"

"You're the general manager?" Leatrice looked at me with a glint of recognition. "That's very interesting."

"What I find interesting is what you are doing snooping around my property. Shall I call security to get some answers?"

"We aren't snooping," I said quickly. "Your hotel lost and damaged my car yesterday, and we're here to pick it up." I returned his sneer. "You should be glad I'm not suing."

"Oh." Mr. Elliott's demeanor changed, and I saw his PR smile for the first time. "I'm terribly sorry."

"You should be," I snapped, building up steam. "I do a lot of business in your hotel, and I don't appreciate having my property damaged."

"Are you one of our frequent guests?" He looked nervous and ran a hand over his perfect hairline. "Perhaps we could make this stay complimentary."

"I'm not a guest. I'm a party planner and I do a lot of events here," I admitted, squinting to get a closer look at the precise rows of hair plugs. Did he really think they looked natural?

"Oh?" He raised his eyebrows. "What kind of events?"

293

"She's the best wedding planner in town," Leatrice chimed in. "She had a wedding in this room last weekend."

Mr. Elliott studied me more intently. "That was your wedding? I thought you looked familiar." He returned his gaze to Leatrice. "But who are you?"

"I'm her driver." Leatrice tossed her scarf across her neck and over her other shoulder.

"I was just telling my . . . um, driver what a spectacular wedding it was." I shook my head in feigned disappointment. "Such a shame we didn't get any photos before the unfortunate incident. The hotel didn't happen to take any room shots did they?"

Mr. Elliott gave me a curious look. "The hotel? No, we didn't take any pictures of the room."

"I thought you might have arranged for a photographer on your own. For publicity purposes, maybe?" I furrowed my brow as if trying to remember. "I thought someone mentioned something about some room shots being taken."

Mr. Elliott's eyes went cold and hard. "They were mistaken. The hotel had no photos taken. If we had, I'd have known about it."

"Of course. How silly of me. You probably know everything that goes on in your hotel, right?"

Leatrice put her hands on her hips. "Any idea who killed your two chefs, then?"

His jaw muscles flinched. "I'm afraid I'm keeping you from your car. Allow me to escort you to the lobby."

"No need." I breezed by him, waving for Leatrice to follow me. "We have to see Darcy anyway. More business for your hotel."

Leatrice ran to keep up with my pace as we rushed out of the room and down the hallway toward the elevators. "I didn't like that man," she said. "I hope he's high up on your suspect list."

"He is," I assured her. "It's interesting that he denied knowing anything about photos of the room when he used that as his reason to clear the room before the murder."

"Are you sure the source who told you that is reliable?"

"Why would Reg lie?" I brushed off the question. "No, Mr. Elliott is the one with something to hide."

"So there weren't any photos taken?" Leatrice followed me into the open elevator.

"No, but I think he made up the story about having a photographer come in so that everyone would leave the scene of the crime. That would have bought him about five minutes of uninterrupted time during which he could have killed Henri."

"Really?"

I nodded and pressed the button for the second floor. "Because of the setup involved in events, the room is only ready to photograph about ten or fifteen minutes before the guests are invited in. Sometimes we can't even squeeze room shots in because of the tight timing. But if the photographer does have time, it's crucial that the room be cleared so he can get shots without any people in them. Once the staff has been cleared out, they usually don't come back for five or ten minutes."

"So anyone in the event industry would know that?"

"Definitely." I held the elevator door for Leatrice, and then led the way through the glass doors to the executive offices lobby. Beige chairs clustered around a round mahogany coffee table that held sample wedding albums. I smiled at the receptionist sitting behind a narrow wooden desk. "We're here to see Darcy O'Connell, but we don't have an appointment."

"Annabelle?" Darcy poked her head around the corner. Her hair hung loose around her face and the bags under her eyes seemed to have gotten bigger. She looked like hell. "I thought I heard your voice."

"Darcy, how are you doing?" I asked as diplomatically as possible.

"I'm on my way to check on my cakes for this weekend and get a cup of coffee in the cafeteria. Do you want to join me?" She looked at Leatrice. "What happened to Kate?"

"Oh, we split up today to cover more ground. This is Leatrice."

"I'm her driver." Leatrice stuck out her hand for Darcy to shake.

Darcy shook Leatrice's hand and looked at me. "A driver? I'm in the wrong job."

"She's my neighbor," I explained. "She gave me a ride."

Darcy managed a weak smile and held open the door that led to the back hotel corridors for us. "Should I ask what you're doing back here?"

"This time it's perfectly innocent." I followed Darcy down the wide hallway to the elevators. "Leatrice brought me down to pick up my car since the valets lost it yesterday."

"The valets lost your car?" Darcy looked shocked as she led the way onto an industrial-sized elevator car. "I've heard of them taking a while to bring a car, but not to find it at all?"

"Maybe someone did it on purpose to warn me away from the hotel."

"Like who?" Darcy held the elevator door open for us once we reached the basement.

"Whoever killed Henri and Gunter might not be too thrilled that I was snooping around." I noticed Leatrice lagging behind to read some staff memos tacked to a bulletin board, and I reached back and tugged her forward.

"So, are you any closer to finding out who did it?" Darcy wove her way through the labyrinth of hallways, and I followed closely at her heels, wishing I had breadcrumbs to drop behind me.

When we reached the pastry kitchen, Darcy appraised the trays of miniature wedding cakes lined up on a metal counter. Jean looked up from piping icing on them and gave her a curt nod.

"Looks like we're on schedule." Darcy backed out of the narrow entrance to the kitchen.

Leatrice pulled on my sleeve. "Do you mind if I stay behind and watch him work? I've never seen such adorable little cakes."

"Okay, but don't go anywhere," I warned her. "I'll be right upstairs in the employee cafeteria, and I'll come get you in a few minutes."

"Take your time," she called over her shoulder. "This is better than the Cooking channel."

I caught up to Darcy, who held the elevator for me. "Sorry. She doesn't get out much."

"I wish I had her energy," Darcy sighed. The elevator surged up to the second floor, and we got out as a banquet server passed us with a pile of tablecloths. We passed the dry cleaning counter where all the uniforms were stored and walked into the employee cafeteria.

A few maintenance workers sat at a table in the corner and the TV blared a courtroom drama. Darcy passed the trays of hot food steaming behind glass and made a beeline for the coffee machines. "I don't know how much more of this workload I can take."

"They haven't brought anyone in to help you?" I took the foam cup she offered me and filled it halfway with coffee.

Darcy shook her head. "If Georgia doesn't come back to work soon, I'm a goner. She didn't take great notes, so trying to piece the information together in her files has been a nightmare."

"Georgia was never strong on paperwork, that's for sure." I poured milk into my coffee until it was the color of caramel, then tore open a handful of little blue sweetener packets. "But if everything goes like I hope, Georgia should be released soon."

"Really?" Darcy poured a cup of black coffee and took a sip. "Have you talked to the police?"

"I gave them the DVD of the murder yesterday, and it shows that the killer is a dark-haired man in a chef's jacket. That should be enough to clear Georgia or at least get them to reconsider other suspects."

Darcy shook her head. "Even if she's released from jail, she might not get to come back to work. I've told you that Mr. Elliott has it in for her."

"That's not fair. He can't fire her because he doesn't like her. Anyway, I suspect he might have had more to do with the murder than everyone else thinks."

Darcy's eyes bugged out. "You think our GM is a killer?"

"Why not?" I asked. "Everyone thinks he's too spineless to do it, but I think he's every bit ruthless enough to commit murder. Leatrice and I ran into him before we came to see you, and he got very nervous when we brought up the murders."

Darcy went pale. "You talked to Mr. Elliott about the murders? You're braver than I thought."

"Actually, Leatrice brought it up," I admitted.

"Then she's braver than she looks," Darcy said. "Most people in this place are scared of him, including me."

I grinned and glanced at my watch. "Speaking of spunky old ladies, I'd better get her before she drives the pastry chefs crazy."

Darcy looked at the oversized metal clock on the wall. "And I'd better get back to work. No rest for the weary."

We parted ways in the hallway and I traced my steps back to the elevators and down to the pastry kitchen. I stuck my head in the door expecting to hear Leatrice chattering away, but the kitchen was empty. The long metal worktables had pans full of individual square cakes decorated with marzipan fruits, but no sign of Leatrice or any chefs.

Great. She'd probably come looking for me and gotten lost in the maze of hallways.

"I told her to stay put," I grumbled to myself. "Now I'll never find her."

As I turned to leave, my eye recognized a glint of gold on the floor. It looked like one of the jingle bells from Leatrice's necklace. I picked it up and my stomach sank as I saw more scattered on the ground a few feet away.

I had a very bad feeling that Leatrice wasn't wandering in the hallways looking for me. She was in danger.

CHAPTER 25

"I never should have left her alone with a killer on the loose," I scolded myself, sinking against a narrow metal table. "This is all my fault."

"Talking to ourselves, are we?" The Scottish accent made me jump. "You know that's the first sign of insanity."

"Ian?" I blinked hard. Despite the fact that his extensive arm tattoos were covered up by a black, long-sleeve shirt, he was still hard to miss. "What are you doing here?"

"I happened to be dropping off one of the band's new demos to the catering office and thought I'd say hi to the old gang." He winked at me. "Bit of good luck finding you, I might add."

I sighed with relief that he wasn't stalking me. "Of course. You used to work here."

"In a different lifetime." He grinned. "Before the band made it and I could quit my day job. Would you like to join me for a cup of the world's worst coffee in the employee cafeteria?"

"No." I gave a quick shake of my head, and then saw his face fall. "I mean, I'd love to, but I have to look for my friend, Leatrice. She's missing."

"Your funny little neighbor? Let me help you, then." He pushed up his sleeves to expose part of his tattooed arms. "I know this place inside and out."

"That would be great." I returned his smile. "I left her right here watching the pastry chef about twenty minutes ago. When I came back to get her, she was gone, but I found some little bells from her necklace on the floor."

Ian took the tiny gold bell from my outstretched palm. "These came from a necklace?"

"She likes to wear things that make noise," I explained.

"I don't blame her." Ian grinned at me. A jingle bell necklace was tame in comparison to his stage attire. "Let's look around and see if we can find any more. Maybe they'll lead us in the direction she went."

I dropped down on my hands and knees to get a better view and immediately regretted it. Pastry kitchens weren't known for being spotless. I sat back on my heels and wiped my hands against each other, letting a shower of crumbs fall to the tile floor. At least my black pants hadn't been clean to begin with.

"Any luck?" Ian called from across the room, where he stood next to an industrial ice cream maker.

I sat back up. "Nothing. Maybe she wandered off looking for me."

Ian came over and held out a hand to pull me up. "She could be lost in the hallways. Odd that neither of us saw her, though."

I took his hand and let myself be hoisted up. "I have a bad feeling that she's in trouble."

"Don't worry." Ian helped me brush off the front of my pants. "How much trouble can you get into in a kitchen?"

I raised an eyebrow at him. "How about being electrocuted or impaled?"

"Right. Forget I said that." He snapped his fingers. "Wait a second. Do you think she could have gotten locked in somewhere accidentally?"

"Like where?" I looked around the room.

Ian pointed at a large metal door by the entrance. "The walk-in freezer. It can be clamped from the outside."

We both rushed over, and Ian yanked on the metal handle and heaved open the massive door open.

Leatrice sat on the floor with her aviator's scarf wrapped around her like a mummy and her jingle bell necklace clutched in her hand. My knees felt wobbly seeing her tiny, shivering figure.

I rushed forward. "Are you okay?"

She looked up and smiled weakly. "There you are, dear. I knew you'd find me. I kept ringing my necklace in case you could hear it through the walls."

Ian helped me pull Leatrice up and walk her out of the freezer. He unbuttoned his shirt and slipped it off, revealing a tight black tank top underneath, then draped the shirt around her shoulders.

Leatrice's eyes grew wide as she stared at him, and a little color seeped back into her cheeks. "Oh my. I remember you." She nudged me. "They don't make gentlemen like this anymore, do they, Annabelle?"

I tried to avert my eyes from Ian's naked arms and mostly bare chest. "How did you get locked in there, Leatrice?"

She pulled the shirt closed in front of her. "I watched the chef decorating those precious little cakes, and then he got called out by another chef. I looked around the kitchen while I waited for him to come back. They have amazing gadgets in here, by the way. I didn't even know what half of them were supposed to do."

"The freezer?" I prodded her.

"Right. I was curious about the big metal door, so I opened it and the next thing I knew I was being pushed inside. I tried to resist but I'm afraid I wasn't strong enough. My necklace even got caught on something and it broke in two."

"We found some of them," Ian said. "They must have scattered when they fell."

"Did you see who pushed you?" I asked.

"No. It all happened too fast." She held up her necklace. "Do you think this can be fixed?"

"I'm sure." I patted her on the arm. "I've got super glue in my wedding emergency kit. When we get home, I'll fix it for you."

"You know it's my signature piece," she said.

Ian pulled me back a few steps. "Do you want me to call security?"

I shook my head. All I wanted to do was go home. It was bad enough that I had Kate out hunting for clues, but I'd never forgive myself if something happened to Leatrice. "I think we've made enough of a stir already without getting security involved."

"What do you mean?"

"Why else would someone push Leatrice into a freezer if not to warn me off?" I whispered. "We bumped into the general manager and he practically ran us out of the hotel. Clearly people in the hotel know I'm here."

"That Darcy girl knew we were here," Leatrice said, still shivering. "Maybe you shouldn't be so eager to tell her about the investigation, dear."

"Darcy was with me, Leatrice. She doesn't have a reason to kill either chef, anyway." I turned back to Ian. "Someone must have assumed I was here to poke around about the murder, though."

"Why would they assume that?" Ian furrowed his brow.

I avoided his eyes. "Probably because that's what I've been doing the past two times I was here. I promised Georgia that I'd try to find information to clear her of the murder."

Ian let out a low whistle. "That explains a lot."

"But this time I wasn't here to do any investigating," I explained. "I came down to get my car, which the parking garage lost yesterday, and Leatrice gave me a ride."

"So this isn't the first mishap you've had here?" Ian asked.

"No, but all I wanted to do was pick up my car. Nobody was even supposed to know I'd been here."

Ian cast a glance at Leatrice, who busily inspected her bell necklace with her prescription goggles. "This is your idea of keeping a low profile?"

"My other options aren't much better."

Ian grinned. "You're right. I've met the rest of your posse. It's a bit of a toss-up, isn't it?"

"Shouldn't we get your car?" Leatrice looked back at us through her goggles. "I feel much better now."

"I don't think you should drive." I shuddered, thinking about Leatrice's driving. I'd hate to see what it was like when she wasn't in peak form.

"But I have to take my car home."

"I'll drive your car home for you," Ian offered.

Leatrice beamed. "Isn't that nice?"

"Are you sure?" I asked. Ian hadn't seen the car yet, and I hesitated to ask if he remembered hand signals.

Ian held out a crooked arm for Leatrice. "It would be my pleasure."

Leatrice giggled and took his arm, then glanced back at me. "Why don't you follow us? I have a feeling we're going to burn rubber."

I sighed. Any chance I ever had to be inconspicuous was officially shot to hell.

CHAPTER 26

"Where have you been?" Kate lay sprawled out on my couch wearing faded boot-cut jeans and a pink baby doll T-shirt. Her shoes were scattered on the floor and the new issue of Martha Stewart *Weddings* lay open on her lap. "I've been waiting for ages."

When I'd given Kate a key to my apartment for emergency purposes, I hadn't imagined this being one of the disaster scenarios. "I had to get my car from the Fairmont. Leatrice and I ran into some trouble."

"Leatrice?" Kate sat up. "Why would you take her . . . oh, hi, Leatrice."

Leatrice still held tight to Ian's bare arm as they followed me inside. "Kate, dear. You remember Ian?"

Kate looked at me, then looked at Ian wearing nothing but a tight black tank, and she arched a perfectly penciled eyebrow. "Looks like you had a more exciting day than I did."

Leatrice rushed over to Kate and clutched her arm. "Would you believe that I got locked in a freezer?"

"A freezer? Where were you again?" Kate asked.

Leatrice pulled Kate down on the couch and readjusted Ian's shirt over her shoulders. "I gave Annabelle a ride to the hotel to pick up her car."

"Leatrice insisted on seeing the murder scene," I explained, clearing space on the cluttered dining room table for my purse. "And guess who we ran into while we were there?"

"Not a very pleasant man." Leatrice wrinkled her nose. "What was his name?"

"Mr. Elliott," I said.

Kate sat up straight. "You bumped into the general manager? What was he like? Could you tell he had plugs?"

I shuddered. "Like rows of corn."

"That's what that was?" Leatrice shook her head. "I thought he had a condition that made his hair grow funny."

"Mr. Elliott is pretty much like everyone describes him. Not very likable, and even less so when we mentioned the murders," I said. "I don't see why everyone at the hotel thinks he's incapable of murder. He seems the type to me."

"Elliott is a coward." Ian scowled. "He's known for getting other folks to do his dirty work."

Leatrice touched his hand. "Oh, do you know him, dear?"

"We go back a few years," Ian said. "There's no love lost between us, I can assure you."

Ian seemed to have more connections at the Fairmont than I'd realized. I wondered if anyone knew the whole story behind his past there, since he seemed reluctant to share. I made a mental note to ask Richard. He'd forgotten more gossip about the event industry than most people in Washington had ever known.

"So how did you go from the Colonnade room to being locked in a freezer?" Kate asked.

"We ran into Darcy on her way to the cafeteria." I walked over and moved a pile of magazines out of the seat of a chair so I could sit down. "Leatrice got distracted by the pastry chef and stayed with him in the kitchen while Darcy and I grabbed coffee down the hall."

"Let me tell the rest." Leatrice bounced up and down where she sat. "I watched the chef make these adorable miniature cakes. They looked exactly like wedding cakes, only for midgets."

I'd never heard individual wedding cakes explained quite like that before.

"After he left, I stayed behind to look at all of the fancy appliances," Leatrice continued. "The next thing I knew, someone pushed me into the giant freezer and locked the door. If Ian and Annabelle hadn't found me, I'd be a Leatrice-sickle."

"It was Ian's idea to look in the freezer." I smiled at Ian and noticed that his eyes were locked on me. I felt my cheeks flush and looked away. "We're lucky he knows so much about the hotel."

Kate studied Ian for a second. "Lucky you were in the hotel. You're sure you don't still work there?"

"Ian's in a band, Kate." Leatrice smiled. "He told me all about it on the way over here. Apparently the eighties are really hot now. Just think, in another year I'll be trendy."

I decided not to explain the concept of an eighties cover band to Leatrice. It would take way too long.

"We think someone knew we were in the hotel asking questions and pushed me in as a warning." Leatrice readjusted her aviator scarf around her neck.

I glanced at Leatrice's scarf and goggles and shook my head. "Mr. Elliott, most likely, although I'm sure word got around fast that we were there."

"Or the girl who was asking all the questions about the case," Leatrice said.

"Darcy has been helping us, Leatrice," I explained. "She's on our side, I promise."

Leatrice shrugged. "People can surprise you. Don't you remember that older man with the heavy accent who used to live here? He disappeared only a few days after I saw him on one of those shows about former Nazis who were in hiding."

"He didn't vanish, Leatrice. He moved away. And he was from Russia, not Germany." I turned back to Kate. "So, did you have any luck today?"

"You might say that." Kate stood up and headed to the kitchen. "I'm thirsty. Anyone want anything?" Leatrice and Ian both shook their heads no.

I followed her into the kitchen and stood behind her as she studied the contents of my refrigerator. "Well, are you going to tell me, or what?"

Kate put a finger over her lips. "I'm not so sure we should be telling everyone what we're discovering. First your car disappears, then another chef is murdered, and now Leatrice gets pushed in a freezer? I'm on Richard's side. I don't like the way this is going."

"You're afraid to say anything in front of Leatrice and Ian?" I whispered.

"Not Leatrice, of course. Not that I'd put it past her to create a crime that she could solve." Kate found a can of Diet Coke behind stacks of Chinese take-out cartons and popped it open. "I don't trust Ian. I mean, what do we really know about this guy except that he seems to be at the Fairmont every time we turn around?"

"He did used to work there."

"Exactly my point."

"Not only is Ian the one who helped me find Leatrice, but he doesn't have dark hair." I peeked my head through the opening between the two rooms and saw Leatrice inspecting Ian's tattoos. "He's been nothing but nice since the beginning. I certainly don't believe he has anything to do with the murders. First Leatrice suspects Darcy of being a killer, and now you think Ian might have done it. I think we have enough suspects with real motives to worry about without dreaming up new ones."

"You're probably right. You certainly couldn't mistake that hair for brown, even at a distance."

"I was planning on asking Richard if he knew any gossip about Ian, anyway." I sighed. "Will that make you happy?"

"Good thinking. If he's done anything remotely interesting in the metropolitan area in the past ten years, Richard will know," Kate said. "And you won't see me standing in the way of a possible romance between you and a tattooed rock star who wears a skirt. I wouldn't miss seeing Richard go into cardiac arrest for anything."

She was right. Richard would have a fit if I started dating Ian. He considered himself the arbiter of my nonexistent love life, and I knew Ian wasn't his idea of a suitable match. Not that he'd approved of any of the would-be suitors I'd tried to scrape up in the past few years.

"Is that the business line ringing?" Kate craned her head around the corner.

"I'll get it." I darted out of the kitchen and down the hall. The phone was only on the third ring when I snatched it off my desk. "Wedding Belles, this is Annabelle."

"Annabelle, it's Detective Reese."

"Detective?" My pulse fluttered, and I steadied my voice. "What did you think of the DVD?"

"Not much. The plastic case was empty."

"What?" I stammered. "That's impossible. I know it was there when I brought it to you. Maybe someone at the station misplaced it."

"Another conspiracy theory?" He laughed harshly. "Listen, Annabelle. I appreciate that you think you're trying to help your friend and that you really believe she's innocent, but I think she'd be better off without your help."

I felt like I'd been punched in the gut. "But we found evidence that proves she couldn't have been the murderer. It was on that DVD. You have to find it."

"We don't have time for a scavenger hunt right now." His voice was firm. "We're running a murder investigation."

"I understand that, but—"

"I don't think you do understand. We've been compiling evidence and testimony, and all of it points to Miss Rhodes."

"But she's being set up," I cried. "Don't you see that? How do you explain another murder at the hotel while she was in custody?"

"We found no evidence that Gunter's death was anything more than an accident."

"Oh, come on." I couldn't keep the irritation out of my voice. "Two deaths in less than a week and you think it's a coincidence?"

"I didn't call you to debate this."

"Then don't let me keep you, Detective," I snapped, and hung up the phone. My hands shook with anger and I felt tears prick the back of my eyes.

"Is everything okay?" Kate peeked around the doorway.

"No." I dropped the phone back on my desk. "That was Detective Reese calling to say that the DVD wasn't in the case we dropped off and telling me not to waste any more of his time."

Kate's eyes widened. "You're kidding. Our evidence is gone? Now what do we do?"

"Well, the police won't help us. They won't even listen to us anymore." I shrugged. "It's up to us to find the real killer on our own or Georgia's going to prison for murder."

CHAPTER 27

"Would anyone care to explain to me what those two are doing here?" Richard appeared in the office doorway and jerked a thumb in the direction of Leatrice and Ian in the living room.

Kate jumped. "Don't sneak up on people like that."

"Sorry," Richard said. "The door was open. Leatrice and Ian are debating where she should get her first tattoo, and you're out of your mind if you think I'm going to be a part of that discussion. The idea alone will give me nightmares for weeks."

I glanced at my open desk calendar. "Do we have a meeting I forgot about?"

Richard narrowed his eyes at Kate. "I was summoned for an urgent discussion about some new evidence. I was also instructed to bring empanadas, so this had better be good."

My mood brightened at the sight of the burgeoning white paper bag in Richard's hand. "Are those Julia's Empanadas?"

The hole-in-the-wall empanada shops decorated in neon yellow and red didn't look like much from the outside, but they turned out some of the most decadent savory pastries in the city. I'd developed a serious addiction to the spinach and cheese variety, while Kate loved the one filled with sweet pear. We were lucky they didn't have a shop within walking distance or we'd have to enter a twelve-step program or Weight Watchers.

Richard clutched the bag close. "Yes, but no empanadas for anyone until I know what's going on."

"Yoo-hoo." Leatrice's voice carried down the hallway. "We're going to run downstairs for a second. Ian's never seen a real police scanner before. Anyone want to join us?"

"No, thanks," I called out, sticking my head into the hall. "You two have fun without us."

"Suit yourself, dear." Leatrice had Ian by the hand as she pulled him out the door.

Ian gave me a wink and a helpless shrug as he disappeared from view. I almost felt sorry for him, but better him getting the scanner tutorial than me. Once the door closed, I led Kate and Richard to the living room.

Richard gave my dining room table a cursory glance. "Have you ever actually used this?"

"Don't be ridiculous. Of course I have."

"For dining?" Richard asked.

I stuck my tongue out at him and began clearing the papers off the table. "We can use it now."

Richard dropped the paper bag on the table and disappeared into the kitchen. Once he was out of sight, Kate delved into the bag, pulling out empanadas wrapped in translucent sheets of white paper.

"They're still warm," she moaned.

Richard emerged with a stack of plates, silverware, and paper napkins and began setting the table as I cleaned it off. He pushed Kate out of the way and arranged all the empanadas on a dinner plate in the center of the table, then took a seat at the head.

"Now before anyone takes a bite, I want some explanations," he announced as Kate and I took chairs opposite each other. "Don't think I don't know what's been going on, Annabelle."

I threw my hands in the air. "Nothing has happened with Ian, I swear. Nothing yet, at least. Yes, I agreed to go out with him, but I'm not even sure if we're still on."

"What?" Richard's mouth fell open. "You're seriously considering dating a straight man who owns leather pants? Have I taught you nothing?"

"I can't believe you told Richard," Kate muttered, taking a golden brown empanada from the plate and shaking her head.

"I thought that's what we were talking about." I gulped.

"Well, it is now." Richard shook a finger at me. "I've seen you make some dating blunders, Annabelle, but nothing on this scale before."

"Talk about the pot calling the kettle back," Kate said under her breath.

Richard faced Kate. "Don't even get me started on your dating life. We don't have the time."

"Hey, I'm on your side," Kate said. "I think Ian is all wrong for her."

I picked out a spinach empanada and cut into it, letting the steam escape. "You also think he should be one of our suspects."

"Which is one of the main reasons I think he's all wrong for you," Kate said through a mouthful of food.

Richard stared at Kate. "Why would he want to kill Henri?"

Kate shrugged. "I haven't worked that part out. It just seems like he happens to turn up whenever Annabelle is at the hotel. Including today when Leatrice coincidentally got locked in a freezer."

"I heard you were at the Fairmont today." Richard shook a finger at me. "I thought you were letting Kate do the snooping from now on."

I didn't bother to ask Richard how he knew. He always had his sources.

"I was," I explained. "But they found my car, and Leatrice was the only person around to give me a ride to the hotel."

"She drives?" Richard gasped.

"Sort of," I said. "Anyway, she ended up getting pushed into a walk-in freezer and Ian helped me find her."

"This is exactly why I said you shouldn't meddle in this murder business anymore." Richard rapped his hand on the table. "I hate being right all the time."

"Don't get all worked up," I said. "Ian found Leatrice before it was too late."

"A knight in shining armor," Richard mused, then looked at Kate. "Convenient."

"You two are impossible. Can't someone be nice?"

"Take it from me, darling." Richard took my hand. "If a man seems too good to be true, it's because he probably is. Remember when I thought I'd found Mr. Right and it turned out he liked to sleep naked holding a ceremonial dagger across his chest?"

Kate nearly choked on her empanada. "I thought I'd had some rough dates."

"If that wasn't bad enough, he kept me up all night playing the lyre. And he was an English professor." Richard shuddered. "Imagine what fetishes a rock singer would have."

"If you know anything about Ian, I'm all ears." I tapped my fingers impatiently on the table. "But I say we should be focusing on the most likely suspects, like the remaining chefs and Mr. Elliott."

Kate snapped her fingers. "The chefs. That's what I wanted to tell you before I got distracted by the empanadas."

"What?" I stopped my fork in midair. "Did you find out something today?"

"You know I had to run by the Willard Hotel to pick up some new catering packets. While I was there, I thought I'd chat with some of the waiters as they set up the ballroom."

"Good thinking, Kate," I said. "Some of those guys have worked there for over twenty years. They probably know a ton about the different chefs who've come and gone."

"And guess who came and went from the Willard?" Kate grinned.

"We already know that Marcello and Henri were sous chefs together there. That's not new."

"But we didn't know that Emilio and Jean were prep cooks at the Willard at the same time."

"You're kidding." I sucked in my breath. "So Marcello knows Emilio and Jean?"

"It would seem so," Kate said. "Talk about a coincidence, huh?"

"Don't tell me you're back on this again," Richard groaned. "How many times do I have to explain to you that my chef was working at the time of the murder? He couldn't possibly have killed Henri."

"Maybe he didn't have to," I said. "Maybe he had an accomplice do the dirty work for him."

"I wonder which one did it." Kate wiped her mouth with a napkin. "We should find out how well Marcello knew each of them."

"Stay away from my chef." Richard stood up and threw his napkin down. "We have a huge party at Evermay tomorrow night, and if you upset him, heads will roll. And when I say heads, I mean yours." He picked up his half-eaten empanada and stormed out the door.

Kate sighed. "By the look on your face, I can tell where we're going after our wedding rehearsal tomorrow night."

"Don't worry," I assured her. "Richard will never know we're there."

"We're going to sneak into a private party, question his chef about his connections to a murder, and then leave without Richard finding out?"

"Exactly," I said, with more confidence than I felt.

Kate put her head in her hands. "One good thing about this plan is that we don't have to worry about the murderer threatening us anymore. Richard is going to kill us first."

CHAPTER 28

"This is my least favorite part of the job," I complained the next evening as Kate and I waited in the Park Hyatt ballroom for the wedding party to arrive for the rehearsal. After spending the day confirming Nadine's last minute changes with everyone from the cake baker to the string quartet, we'd gotten there early to make sure that the riser and chairs were set up for our mock ceremony. Now I sat in the front row of chairs with a stack of wedding timelines next to me.

The modern ballroom was a long rectangular room in the basement of the hotel decorated in shades of tan and gold. Modern dome-shaped chandeliers dominated the ceiling and provided the only decor. It was a room that adapted nicely to any type of decorations because it was such a neutral palette, but at the moment it looked naked.

"Why is it that everyone is always late for the rehearsal?" Kate sat on the edge of the riser with her legs sprawled in front of her. I said a silent prayer of thanks that she'd chosen a beige pantsuit and not a skirt.

I looked at my watch. The bride had assured me that everyone would be there at five o'clock, but it was already ten after five and there was no sign of the bride, groom, or anyone remotely resembling a bridesmaid. "They'd better hurry up. We still need to get to Evermay after this."

"I'd hoped you'd forgotten about that." Kate groaned. "I really don't think it's a good idea to provoke Richard when he has a big event. You know how moody he gets."

"I'm telling you, we won't even see Richard. We'll be in and out before he notices us."

"How about I wait in the car? You need a good getaway driver. I can wait on the street with the engine running."

I shook my head. "Nice try."

A woman with fiery orange hair stuck her head in the door. "Is this the Goldman-McIntyre wedding?"

I jumped up. "Yes, you're in the right place."

She opened the door wide and bellowed into the hall, "Harold! I found it."

I motioned for Kate to follow me as I walked to the back of the room. "Are you with the bride's side or the groom's?"

"I'm Doris Goldman, the mother of the groom." The woman with orange hair and equally orange-brown skin held out her hand. Her long fingernails had been painted a metallic copper that miraculously matched her unnatural skin tone exactly, and when she smiled, her teeth almost blinded me. I'd forgotten that the groom was from South Florida until that very moment.

"I'm Annabelle, and this is Kate. We're the wedding planners."

The mother of the groom gave us another brilliant smile. "My husband was right behind me. I'm always losing him." She stuck her head back into the hall and screamed his name again.

"Wonder why?" Kate whispered to me.

A pair of short men, both with thinning hair, came through the door. One leaned on a cane and had less hair than the other.

"We're right here, Doris," the slightly younger man said. "Your father stopped at the water fountain."

"How're ya doing, Dad?" Doris leaned close to her father and shouted into his ear. She turned back to us. "He's legally blind but still gets around like you wouldn't believe."

"Don't fuss over me." He swiped at his daughter with his cane, and then squinted in our direction. "Who are these pretty young fillies?"

Kate gave me a look that said she wasn't fond of being referred to as a filly.

"They're the wedding planners," Doris shouted at a safe distance from the cane.

The grandfather hiked his brown polyester pants even higher around his chest and shuffled over to Kate. He moved pretty fast for a blind guy. "You'll tell me what I need to do, then?"

"Sure." Kate smiled and took a baby step away from him as he slipped a hand around her waist. As his hand drifted south, Kate's eyes widened and she looked to me for help. I bit my lip to keep from laughing.

Doris beamed. "He's quite the ladies' man at his retirement community."

"I can see that," I said.

"Now what's the protocol of escorting single blind grandfathers down the aisle?" Doris rested a hand on my arm.

Did she really think a rule existed for precisely this situation? I imagined flipping through the index of an imaginary wedding protocol book. Grandfathers, blind grandfathers, single blind grandfathers, single blind grandfathers without dates . . .

"There isn't a rule for this, per se—" I began.

"Sorry we're late." Nadine burst through the door with an entourage of bridesmaids scuttling behind her. "We just got out of the salon."

I wondered if the salon had been in Texas, because every girl's hair was teased a mile high. They all wore brightly colored cocktail-length dresses and matching high-heeled sandals, and they were all accessorized out the wazoo. I'd bet money that not a single one of the bridesmaids was from DC.

Nadine's brown hair had been highlighted with blond streaks and she looked especially tiny in her strapless pink dress with a chocolate brown ribbon belt. I caught the distinctive scent of cigarettes as she approached me, and was surprised not to see one dangling from her fingers.

"Nadine, honey." The mother of the bride followed close on her heels, clutching a huge bouquet of bows and ribbons that were tied onto a paper plate. She wore a pastel blue cocktail suit, a single strand of pearls, and a tortured expression. "Don't forget your stand-in bouquet."

"Let's get this over with." Nadine took the ribbon bouquet from her mother and tossed her pink clutch purse on a nearby chair. "I'm dying for a drink."

Her mother gasped, but the groom's mother tossed her head back and laughed, then walked over and flung an arm around the mother of the bride. "Come on, Audrey. I think we could all use a drink."

The mother of the bride pressed her lips together until they vanished from sight. South Florida meets the Deep South wasn't going too well.

"We probably should wait until David arrives," I said to Nadine, who gave me a blank look. "You know, your fiancé."

She looked around the room and her expression darkened. "Where is he?" She tapped the toe of her pink and brown sandal on the carpet. "He'd better not ruin my wedding."

"We can go ahead and put your bridesmaids in order on the stage," I said to pacify her. "That way when the guys arrive, we'll be ready to do the run-through."

Kate extricated herself from the grandfather's grip and rushed forward. "Let me do it."

I'd never seen her so eager to arrange bridesmaids. Usually it was the worst task. Either the girls were too busy gossiping and giggling to listen to our instructions or they thought they knew it all and couldn't be bothered to pay attention. Worse yet were the ones who secretly wanted to be wedding planners and tried to take over. Give me a bunch of clueless guys any day.

"Bridesmaids, follow me," Kate called out as she marched down the aisle toward the stage. The grandfather hobbled forward after Kate, and the girls straggled behind in clusters of twos and threes.

"I hope this doesn't take too long." Nadine sighed, following her bridesmaids. "We need to be at the Occidental Grill by six."

Bold words from a girl who'd breezed in twenty minutes late from the hair salon. I took a deep breath and reminded myself that I hadn't gotten my final payment yet. Be nice, Annabelle.

"I'm worried about her." The mother of the bride came up next to me, her Southern drawl dripping like molasses off every word. "Nadine has always been such a sensitive girl. I think this wedding stress is taking a toll on her nerves."

I looked up at the stage where Nadine stood with one hip jutted out and her hands planted firmly on her hips. Her mother clearly lived in a fantasy world.

"The hard part is almost over," I assured her with one of my meaningless platitudes saved exactly for such an occasion.

"Not that his family has helped matters." She cut her eyes to the groom's family. "They don't care at all about the proper way to do things. It's been most upsetting for poor Nadine."

Poor Nadine chose that moment to bellow across the room. "Mother, do you have the programs that I asked you to bring?"

"Of course, honey." Her mother hurried forward, taking tiny steps and holding out a Crane's shopping bag. "They're right here."

The mother of the groom sidled up next to me and said in a stage whisper, "That woman needs a laxative worse than anyone I've ever seen."

The mother of the bride twitched in mid-walk, but didn't break her stride or her smile. Despite the fact that the groom's mother was brazen, not to mention completely orange, she was starting to grow on me.

I looked up at the stage where Kate had the bridesmaids arranged in an angled line. Nadine stood glaring at her watch, while her mother began handing out programs. I looked at the ballroom doors and tried to will the groom to appear.

My attempt at mental telepathy was interrupted when the mother of the bride shrieked from the front of the room. I spun around and was thankful to see that she appeared to be fine, although her face was flushed red and her lips were set in a white line. The groom's grandfather stood next to her grinning from ear to ear. For a blind guy with a cane, he sure got around.

"That means he likes you, Audrey," the mother of the groom called out, then threw her head back and laughed.

The bride's mother turned an unpleasant shade of purple and stalked out of the room with the groom's grandfather shuffling after her. At this rate we'd all be lucky to make it to the wedding day.

The groom rushed in the door past his future mother-in-law, followed by a group of large groomsmen.

"Where have you been?" screamed the bride.

The groom looked flushed under his tan, and I could see beads of sweat on his brow as he passed me. "The streets are blocked. There are police cars and ambulances everywhere. We had to park six blocks away and walk."

"What are you talking about?" Nadine's eyes flashed with impatience.

"It's true, Nadine." A groomsman with no neck spoke up in defense of the groom. "Something happened at the hotel across the street. It's nuts out there."

Kate and I looked at each other. There were two hotels that could be considered to be across the street from the Park Hyatt. The Fairmont and the Westin Georgetown.

"Which hotel?" I asked, my voice barely above a squeak.

"The big one," Neckless said. "I think it starts with an F."

That's what I was afraid of.

CHAPTER 29

"This is a nightmare." Mack lurched toward me on the sidewalk in front of the Park Hyatt dragging a large wrought-iron flower stand behind him.

I tore my attention away from the swarm of police and emergency vehicles across the street at the Fairmont. I hadn't expected to see the Mighty Morphin Flower Arrangers until the wedding day. "What are you doing here?"

"The hotel said we could load in the heavy things tonight to save us some setup time tomorrow." Mack wiped his forehead with a Bikers for Jesus bandana, and then jammed it back in the pocket of his black leather pants. "But if we'd known the streets were going to be closed we never would've bothered."

"Where's Buster?" Kate looked around.

"He's somewhere behind me with the top of the chuppah." Mack sagged against the iron stand, his face flushed pink. I guess black leather didn't breathe very well. "I lost him at a cross walk."

"You just missed Nadine," I said. "The wedding party walked down the street to catch cabs to the rehearsal dinner."

Mack darted his eyes around him. "That was a close one. I don't know if I could handle the Southern belle from hell right now."

"She's nothing," Kate said. "Wait until you see the mother of the groom."

"Bad?" Mack asked.

Kate shook her head. "Orange."

"There's Buster." I pointed at the approaching florist, who looked like a football linebacker who'd gotten lost in a leather bar. He carried the top of the iron chuppah frame over his head and people scurried out of the way as he approached.

"I should have known this wedding was going to be a disaster from start to finish." He lowered the iron canopy to the ground with a thud. "If we have to rewrite the proposal more than twice, it always means trouble."

"How many rewrites did Nadine ask for?" I'd lost count months ago.

"Eight." Mack didn't smile. "You know that means we're in for wedding Armageddon."

I sighed and glanced across the street at the swarming police cars and ambulances. "Looks like you might be right."

"Don't tell me there's more trouble at the Fairmont." Buster shook his head. "What else could possibly go wrong?"

Kate shrugged. "We just came outside when you walked up. But whatever happened, it must be serious."

"Speaking of serious, did you have any luck finding out who might have killed the chef?" Mack asked.

"Yes, and no," I admitted. "We have some suspects, but we can't prove anything yet."

"Did you have any luck sending flowers to Georgia?" Kate asked.

Mack frowned. "No. But we did the next best thing."

"We sent her our lawyer," Buster chimed in. "If anyone can get her acquitted, he can."

"I didn't know you had criminal lawyers on your payroll," I said. These guys were full of surprises.

"We had a few unfortunate legal misunderstandings in the past." Buster looked at the ground and cleared his throat. "People see leather and motorcycles and think the worst."

"We haven't actually used him in years, but we keep his office full of flowers," Mack explained. "It's good for business. We've done lots of junior associate weddings from his firm."

"The guy is a pit bull," Buster said. "He thinks he'll have her released any day now."

'That's great." Kate sounded relieved. "We haven't been able to prove anything yet, and our witnesses and evidence keep disappearing."

Mack gave a dismissive wave of the hand. "Don't worry. A really good lawyer doesn't need either."

I gulped. So much for the triumph of justice and the legal system.

"Well, we'd better get this stuff in the ballroom." Buster lifted the iron canopy above his head. "There's more where this came from, and I don't want to be here all night. See you tomorrow, girls."

"And we'll come bearing monkey balls." Mack grinned and followed Buster, dragging the wrought iron stand behind him.

Kate rubbed her hands together with a wicked glint in her eyes. "I can't wait to see that bouquet."

"Me, too . . . hey, is that Reg running over here?" I squinted across the street.

The banquet captain hurried toward us, looking back over his shoulder several times. His white shirt hung out the front of his pants and his tuxedo jacket looked like it had been slept in. He scooted behind one of the Park Hyatt's thin columns and motioned for us to join him.

"Reg, what are you doing over here?" I asked as we ducked behind the column.

"Forget that," Kate said impatiently. "What's going on over there?"

Reg took a breath. "Emilio is d-d-dead. Frozen to death."

"The chef?" I asked. "How?"

Kate's face fell. "What a shame. He was cute, too."

"They found him locked in one of the walk-in freezers. He'd b-b-been there for hours and the temperature had been turned as low as it could go."

I felt light-headed when I thought of Leatrice's narrow escape from the freezer. "That's horrible. Do they have any idea how it happened?"

Reg pressed his lips together. "The hotel is t-t-trying to say that he locked himself in accidentally, but that's impossible. Emilio was too clever for that."

"They're probably trying to do damage control." I shook my head. "Accidental death sounds better than murder."

Kate shuddered. "Not much better. Who wants to stay at a hotel where the employees keep accidentally killing themselves? Doesn't inspire much confidence in the staff."

I had to agree with Kate's twisted logic.

"The p-police are questioning everyone." Reg chewed on his thumbnail and glanced around the column at the police cars. "I don't think I can take much more of this."

"Calm down, Reg." I patted him on the arm. "You have nothing to worry about."

"Except for being the next victim," Kate said.

I elbowed her in the ribs and looked back at Reg, who'd gotten a few shades paler. "She's kidding. Ignore her."

Kate rubbed her side and glared at me.

"She's right." Reg jerked his head in Kate's direction. "All the victims were in the Colonnade around the time Henri was killed. Maybe someone is killing off any potential witnesses. That would include me."

"Maybe you should tell the police what you know about the general manager," I said. "He's one of the few suspects left and he had plenty of opportunity when he cleared the room for room shots."

Reg darted his eyes to the ground. "About th-th-that—"

"If there's a chance that Mr. Elliot is the killer, you have to tell the police what you know," I insisted.

Reg buried his face in his hands. "I made it all up."

"What?" Kate and I said in unison.

"The story about Mr. Elliot." Reg peeked at us between his fingers. "I made it up so he would look bad. It never happened. He never even mentioned room shots."

My mouth dropped open. "I don't understand."

"I had to do something to help Georgia." He lowered his hands slowly from his face. "Mr. Elliot had it in for her and wanted to fire her even if she was proven innocent. I thought if I could get him arrested for the murder, she'd go free and get her job back."

"So Mr. Elliot wasn't in the room alone?" I asked.

Reg shook his head. "He took one look at the setup and left. I followed him out and went to check on the cocktail party."

"So much for Mr. Elliot being a suspect." Kate sighed. "What a shame. I really despised him."

"I'm sorry." Reg hung his head. "I've made a mess of everything."

"It's okay. You were only trying to help Georgia." I wondered if Georgia had any idea that the shy banquet captain was in love with her.

"She doesn't deserve to be in jail," Reg said firmly. He looked around the column toward the Fairmont. "I had to tell you the truth, but I'd better get back before I'm missed."

Kate and I watched him scurry back across the street and dart between police cars to enter the hotel.

"I can't believe he made up that whole story." I didn't know whether to be impressed that he went to such lengths for Georgia or angry that he'd led us down the wrong path.

"It was pretty convincing, too." Kate nodded. "I didn't know he had it in him."

"I wonder how many other people are lying to us."

"You mean of the suspects who are still alive?" Kate put her hands on her hips. "We're down two more suspects. Who does that leave at the Fairmont?"

"Well, we still have Jean St. Jean."

"For now." Kate rolled her eyes. "Until he accidentally flambés himself."

"We have another suspect who isn't at the hotel." I started walking toward my car and motioned for Kate to follow me.

"Ian?" Kate asked.

I gave her a dirty look. "No, Miss Smarty Pants. Marcello. I think now is the perfect time to find out what he knows and how involved he is in this whole thing. Come on. We have a party at Evermay to go to."

"If Richard catches us, it's not going to be pretty," Kate reminded me.

"Don't worry." I hunted in my purse for my car keys. "Your workman's comp is all paid up."

Kate gave me a sugary smile. "How comforting."

"How many times do I have to tell you?" I said. "He'll never know we were there. You should be more worried about the fact that a killer is still on the loose."

"Between an unknown murderer and Richard when he gets in a foul mood?" Kate muttered. "I'll take my chances with the serial killer."

CHAPTER 30

"Are you sure it's okay to leave the car here?" Kate asked as I drove up Evermay's steep drive and parked in front of the caretaker's house across from the mansion. "Can't Richard see the car from the front door?"

"I'm sure he's too busy to come outside." I glanced at my watch. "The party starts in half an hour, so he's probably torturing waiters right about now."

"Maybe I should wait with the car in case the valets need us to move it."

"Nice try, but let's go." I stepped out of the car and waited for Kate to join me. "Look at it this way. The faster we get in and talk to Marcello, the faster we can get out."

"Then what are we waiting for?" Kate tugged me by the sleeve as she marched up the historic house's circular drive.

We passed the enormous round marble fountain that dominated the entrance, and I paused to look up at the house. The red brick mansion was classic in design, but nonetheless imposing. Long rectangular windows were stacked in orderly rows across the front of the house and draped with heavy curtains inside. Wings had been added to each end of the square building, softening its edges.

I followed Kate up to the large wooden front door, and we peeked in the side glass panels. No sign of Richard. I turned the brass handle and slowly pushed the door open.

"He's probably in the tent on the other side of the house," I whispered to Kate, waving her into the elongated foyer.

"You didn't tell me my hair was a mess." Kate examined her short blond bob in the large mirror that hung on the wall.

I closed the door gingerly. "You look fine. It's not like we're going to see any eligible bachelors while we're here."

"You never know." Kate wagged a finger at me. "Always be prepared."

Somehow I didn't think this was what the Boy Scouts had in mind when they chose their motto. I led the way through the formal dining room to the kitchen, pausing at the swinging door to the kitchen, and listened to the familiar baritone.

Kate raised an eyebrow. "Is that the theme song to *The Dukes of Hazzard?*

"I think so." I'd never heard an operatic version of the song so it was hard to tell.

Kate rolled her eyes. "Richard sure knows how to pick them."

I put a finger to my lips. "Follow my lead."

I pushed open the kitchen door and ran straight into a stack of plastic glass racks that reached my chest. I edged my way around them, trying not to trip on the heavy plastic sheeting that covered the floor. Marcello stood with his back to us at the counter of the long, narrow galley kitchen.

"The hors d'oeuvres aren't ready yet," he bellowed. "Come back in ten minutes and not a moment sooner."

I cleared my throat. "We wanted to say hello before the event began."

Marcello spun around, and his expression changed from irritation to surprise. "You two. Richard didn't tell me this was your event."

"You know Richard when he gets caught up in things," Kate said with a nervous giggle. "Probably slipped his mind."

Marcello nodded and turned back to his chopping board. "You must excuse me. We're running behind schedule. One of the delivery trucks ran out of gas on the way so the food arrived an hour late."

I groaned. Nothing made Richard more frantic than running late during setup. He would be beyond hysterical, and I knew from experience it wasn't a pretty sight.

"Let's go before he finds us here," Kate said under her breath. She knew Richard as well as I did.

I shook my head and took a step toward Marcello. "Did you hear what happened at the Fairmont tonight?" I tried to sound as casual as possible.

Marcello hesitated for a second before he continued chopping. "Something else happened?"

"Another accidental death," I continued. "The chefs there seem to be very careless."

"A chef?" He held his knife in midair above the counter. "Who?"

"Emilio," I said. "Locked himself in a walk-in freezer."

Marcello lowered his knife slowly and leaned against the counter with both hands. I noticed his fingers turning white from the pressure. So he really didn't know about the murder after all.

"Did you know him?" Kate asked.

Marcello gave an abrupt nod, and then picked up his knife again. "We were colleagues once. In this business you work with everyone at some point."

"I thought he worked under you and Henri when you were sous chefs at the Willard," I said. "So did Jean St. Jean, right?"

Marcello shrugged, but the back of his neck reddened. "Like I said, I've worked with almost everyone in this town."

From his reaction, I'd say he knew Emilio a little better than he claimed to.

"You must admit that it's somewhat of a coincidence for two of your former employees to have worked under Henri, the man you despised, who's now dead." I braced myself for an angry response.

Marcello turned around and began laughing softly. "You think I had something to do with Henri's death? And perhaps the two sous chefs as well?"

"I'm sure Annabelle didn't mean to imply—" Kate began, taking a baby step back.

"I was nowhere near the hotel when Henri was killed, and I have a kitchen full of cooks to prove it, so you'd better come up with something better than a coincidence if you plan to accuse me of murder."

I swallowed hard and put on my best poker face. "You didn't have to actually kill Henri if you masterminded the whole thing. I think you convinced one of your former colleagues, who hated Henri as much as you, to do the deed."

Marcello arched an eyebrow and leaned in toward me. "Interesting idea, but why would someone commit murder for me? I'm afraid my colleagues aren't that loyal. Your theory has a few holes in it, Miss Wedding Planner."

So much for my visions of a spontaneous murder confession a la Hercule Poirot. Marcello actually made a good point. Why would someone commit murder for someone else? I knew I had the pieces to this murder puzzle in front of me, but I couldn't manage to put them together.

"Oh, well. You can't blame a girl for trying," Kate said a little too brightly. "Let's go, Annabelle."

I gave her a withering look.

"Where are my hors d'oeuvres?" Richard's shrill voice carried into the kitchen from the door that led onto the back terrace. He was headed right for us.

"We'd better let you get back to those hors d'oeuvres." I nudged Kate toward the kitchen door. "Richard hates it when food is late."

I caught one final glance of the seething chef before exiting the kitchen and hurrying into the dining room.

"Well that got us nowhere," Kate grumbled.

"Everyone needs to be dressed in five minutes, people." Richard's voice echoed from the foyer. "If I see so much as one T-shirt, heads will roll."

Kate clutched my arm. "He's right outside the room. He must have come through the foyer's door to the terrace. What do we do?"

I turned back to the kitchen, but Kate shook her head.

"I'm not going back in there," she said. "He'll kill us, or worse, turn us over to Richard."

I looked around the sparse formal dining room for a place to hide. Asian art covered the soft green walls and a large wooden table took up the center of the room. I peered up at the crystal chandelier that burned real wax candles. No help there.

"Great," Kate whimpered. "Not even a couch to cower behind."

I eyed the large painted screen that was pressed up against the back wall. "We can hide behind that. Follow me."

We carefully shimmied the screen away from the wall far enough to slide behind it just as we heard Richard's rapid-fire footsteps enter the room. I held my breath as he walked past us. From the corner of my eye I could see him barrel into the kitchen. I let out my breath as I heard the cacophony of Richard's shrieks and Marcello's booming replies.

"We'd better make a run for it," I said.

"I'm not going anywhere with Richard on the warpath like that. I'm perfectly fine right here, thank you."

"Kate, we can't stay here the entire event. Guests are going to start arriving soon. One of them is bound to see us like this."

"As soon as we step out from behind here, Richard's is going to walk out. I know it," Kate whispered. "Why don't we walk behind the screen until we get close enough to the door to make a run for it?"

"You're kidding, right?" I rolled my eyes. "You don't think a screen lurching across the room on its own will attract attention?"

"We'll go slowly and stick close to the wall." Kate edged her side of the screen over. "Work with me, Annabelle."

"Oh for God's sake," I muttered, pushing my end out with my foot. "I'll bet other wedding planners don't do this type of thing."

"We've always wanted to be unique." Kate shuffled sideways. "I think this would qualify."

"Oh, shut up."

We ambled the screen around the outskirts of the dining room until we were almost at the door. I poked my head out and looked into the foyer.

"The coast is clear." I waved for Kate to follow me. "It's now or never."

We abandoned the screen and scurried through the foyer and out the front door. I pulled the heavy door behind me as silently as possible and jumped when I heard Richard's voice on the other side.

"Who moved this screen? Anyone? It couldn't have walked over here by itself, people. When I find out who's responsible . . ."

I started running with Kate close at my heels, and we were both breathing hard when we reached the car. I cast a glance over my shoulder and sighed in relief. No Richard.

"Good thing he didn't see us." I felt a twinge of guilt. "I feel sorry for the poor person who has to suffer his wrath for moving the screen."

"Tell me about it." Kate collapsed against the passenger side. "But better them than us."

CHAPTER 31

"I'd call last night a total bomb." Kate collapsed onto my couch, draping her arm across her eyes. From what I could see, her black suit reached her knee and didn't show any cleavage. I studied her carefully for a hidden side slit or peekaboo back. Nothing. Either everything she owned was at the dry cleaner or she'd finally decided to dress appropriately for a wedding.

"I wouldn't say that." I tucked in my ivory silk shell and zipped up the side of my black dress pants.

"You didn't miss a date with the cutest new senatorial staffer."

"You had a date last night?" I didn't know why I was so surprised. When it came to her social life, Kate was a champion multitasker.

"We were supposed to have dinner at Ceiba, but after the covert mission you dragged me on I was too wiped out to go home, put together an irresistibly cute outfit, and be captivating for a few hours." She peeked at me from under her arm. "I really could have used one of their mojitos, too."

"Our covert mission, as you call it, wasn't a total waste of time." I pulled back my living room curtains and squinted at the bright sunshine, crossing my fingers for some clouds before our outdoor photo session with the bride. Every bride prayed for sunny weather, but photos were more flattering when it was slightly overcast.

"How do you figure that?"

"Didn't you see Marcello's reaction when we accused him of being an accomplice to murder?"

"First off, *we* didn't accuse him of being involved in the murder. That was all you." Kate shook her head. "Personally, I never tick off someone holding a knife."

"Don't you think he was awfully calm about the whole thing?" I hoisted my metal emergency kit onto the table and opened it to see if I needed to restock any wedding supplies.

"Maybe because he didn't do it?"

"I know we can't prove anything, but I just have a feeling that he's involved. Everyone else hated Henri because he was horrible, but Marcello had a real motive. He lost his career, his wife, his kid."

"It's not like he talks about them, though." Kate sat up and adjusted the waist of her black panty hose. "Maybe his wife would have left him anyway. He does have a nasty temper."

I pawed through the contents of my wedding "crash" kit, as Kate lovingly called it. Safety pins, bobby pins, ink pens, hair spray, bug spray, static guard, fake rings, scissors, tape, glue, white-out, sewing kit, buttons, Velcro, ribbon, powder, chalk, extra strength aspirin. We were in business.

"I still have a feeling that Marcello knows something, even if he didn't actually do it," I said.

"Since the police lost our only real evidence, we might never know who did it."

I groaned. "Don't remind me."

"At least Joni hasn't asked for her DVD back yet. If we're lucky, the bride won't even want to see it." Kate gave a small shudder. "Would you want to relive that?"

"Wait a second." I closed the emergency kit quickly and fastened the metal clasps. "Why didn't I think about this before?"

"What? Why do you have that look like you're up to something?"

"I'll bet Joni didn't give us her only copy of the footage. She always copies weddings onto her hard drive so she can edit them, and I'm sure she makes backups."

"You mean in case the wedding planners borrow them and give them to the police as evidence in a murder case?" Kate didn't sound convinced.

"Exactly." I grabbed the phone off the coffee table and dialed the videographer's phone number from memory. Answering machine. I left a long message explaining everything and gave her my cell phone number.

"Anyone home?" Leatrice cooed as she pushed open the door.

I glared at Kate as I put the phone back on its charger. "You didn't close the door behind you?"

"Sorry." She winced. "We're just about to leave for a wedding, Leatrice."

"Lucky I came up when I did." Leatrice bounced into the room wearing a multicolored sweater with three-dimensional puffy penguins sewn all over it. "Ian and I have a theory about the murders that I wanted to share with you."

"You and Ian?" I looked at the door. "He's here, too?"

"Not now." Leatrice laughed. "But he was here last night looking for you. I told him you must be out working so I invited him in and we had TV dinners together."

Kate frowned at me. "Did you stand him up?"

My mouth went dry as I vaguely recalled a previous mention of a Friday night date. Had I missed my only real date in months? "I don't think so. At least I don't remember setting a definite time."

"You need some serious help, Annabelle." Kate gave me an exasperated sigh. "I see that I'm going to have to put some overtime in to bring you up to speed on dating."

"Can I help?" Leatrice clapped her hands.

Just what I needed. Dating advice from an elderly woman in a three-dimensional penguin sweater. I'd have to call Ian later and try to explain, but for now I had to focus on the murder. Not to mention the wedding.

"What's your theory, Leatrice?" I tried to change the subject.

Her eyes lit up. "Ian thinks that it had to be Mr. Elliott, and I have to agree that he's a completely unpleasant man."

"We've been down this road before." I slipped my black suit jacket off the back of a dining room chair. "As much as I'd love him to be guilty, I just don't think he has the motive."

"Did Ian tell you why he's convinced the GM did it?" Kate asked.

"He seems to know everyone at the hotel pretty well. I guess he thinks Mr. Elliott is the most likely person to commit murder." Leatrice blushed. "He's such a nice boy once you get past the tattoos. He even promised to come over and help me with some surveillance this afternoon. Too bad you girls have to go. I'm going to heat up frozen corn dogs."

Poor Ian. This had to be one of his tamer Saturdays. "What type of surveillance?"

Leatrice lowered her voice and darted a glance over her shoulder. "You know that couple that moved into the second-floor apartment?"

I nodded. "The ones from California?"

"Or so they say." Leatrice gave us a knowing look. "I think they're really moles."

"What?" Kate stifled a laugh.

"Sleeper spies," Leatrice continued. "They're planted here by foreign governments and they wait until the perfect moment to spring into action. I've been observing them for weeks."

"No wonder this building has so much turnover," Kate said under her breath.

"You know that Washington has more spies than any other place in the world, don't you?" Leatrice didn't wait for an answer. "We have to stay on our toes, girls."

"Sorry we're going to miss all the fun, but we have to run or we'll be late." I slipped on my jacket and grabbed my emergency kit off the table. "Tell Ian that I said hi and that I didn't mean to stand him up. It's just that I didn't remember . . . no, don't tell him that. I didn't know we had a date . . . no, that doesn't sound good, either. . ."

"Don't worry, dear." Leatrice squeezed my hand. "I'll explain that you've been a bit frazzled what with work and the murders."

Exactly what a man wanted to hear. "Thanks, Leatrice."

She followed us out the door and waved as we hurried down the stairs.

Once we were out of earshot, Kate turned to me. "I hate to be the one to tell you, Annabelle, but she's nuttier than a fruit bake."

CHAPTER 32

"I hope you know that I cannot work under these conditions, Annabelle." Fern grasped my arm as Kate and I entered the bride's suite at the Park Hyatt Hotel. His sunflower yellow shirt was unbuttoned at the collar and his sleeves were rolled up to the elbow. He tapped a round hairbrush nervously in the palm of his hand.

"What now?" I dropped my heavy emergency kit on the floor and sized him up. I'd never seen him so informal or so frazzled.

"Fern!" Nadine bellowed from where she sat across the room by the window. "I'm ready to try again."

"I've already done three updos and she's ripped out every single one." He wrung his ring-laden hands. "I haven't even started on the bridesmaids, and they're all supposed to be ready for pictures in two hours."

I looked at the sullen bridesmaids who sat around the room on plush taupe furniture, silently nibbling on muffins and watching the Weather channel. The dining room table was filled from end to end with trays of fruit and baskets of bagels that looked severely picked over. Celedon green bridesmaid dresses hung off the backs of doors and over chairs, and duffel bags were scattered around the floor. A typical prewedding scene.

"Didn't you do a trial?" Kate asked.

"Two." Fern shot a menacing look over his shoulder at the bride. "But apparently she's been pulling out magazine pictures of other styles since then."

I cringed. If Nadine was as indecisive about her hair as she had been about everything else with the wedding planning, we'd never get her down the aisle.

"How I am supposed to do this?" Fern waved a glossy magazine page in front of us. The bride in the photo had her hair teased up about half a mile, with a snake winding its way around her shoulders and through the top of the hairdo. "Unless you happen to carry a spare snake?"

"Do you want me to check?" Kate motioned to the emergency kit, and then pressed her lips together to keep from laughing.

"I'm waiting," Nadine called in a singsong voice that bristled with impatience.

"I wish I did have a snake," Fern muttered.

"I think what we need is a change of atmosphere." I picked up the phone on the wooden end table, dialed room service and ordered three bottles of champagne. I turned off the television and turned on the clock radio, adjusting the dial to a hip-hop station. "All right, ladies, champagne is on the way, so why don't we start the celebration a little early?" The room quickly filled with excited chatter.

"Not bad." Fern gave me an appreciative nod. "I'd better get back to work. Let me know if you make any headway on the snake."

"This is quite a change." Kate smirked at me. "Usually you're warning brides not to drink so much on the wedding day."

"In this case I think it might help." I heard the muffled ringing of my cell phone and dug into my purse. I crossed my fingers that it wasn't another wedding crisis as I answered. "This is Annabelle."

"It's me. You're not going to believe what I found."

"Me who?" I asked, pressing the phone closer to my ear so I could hear over the giggling of the bridesmaids.

"Joni," she said breathlessly. "I'm watching the footage of last week's wedding again."

I let out a long sigh. "So you made a copy?"

"Of course I made a copy. You think I'd give away my master?"

"Well, no." I felt silly. "So, what did you find?"

"I got this new editing system last week. It's the latest thing on the market. You'd kill me if you knew how much it cost, but anyway, it's the top of the line and it has tons of new features. No one else in town has anything close to this—"

"Does this have something to do with the DVD?" I tried not to sound impatient.

"I'm getting to it." She took a quick breath and then continued. "So I was playing around with some of the new features. You know, getting to know the system. When I heard your message, I thought that I'd put the footage on the new system and see what it could do."

"And?" I urged her on.

"By using the new zoom feature, I was able to home in on the figure that comes into the room with the chef that was killed. I cleaned up the image and focused on the name on the jackets."

"That's brilliant." I held my breath. "So you know the name of the killer?"

"Actually, the *names* of the killers," she said. "Plural."

"What?" I held tight to the phone to keep from dropping it.

"That's right. Three different dark-haired men had a part in killing the chef. I wrote their names down. Gunter, Emilio, and Jean."

"Oh my God." I could barely breathe. "They all did it. Jean must have gotten rid of his accomplices in case they decided to turn on him."

"What?" Joni asked. "You're breaking up a little."

"Nothing." I had to get off the phone so I could call Reese. "I've got to run. This is great, Joni. Thanks for everything."

"Don't mention it. I'm glad I decided to spring for the new system. I'll be paying it off forever, but you should see the things it can do—"

"I'm losing you. I'm going through a tunnel." I ended the call and turned to Kate, who was perched on the arm of the couch reading the wedding schedule.

She glanced up at me and did a double take. "What's the matter? Is the photographer stuck in traffic?"

"That was Joni on the phone. She had a copy of the DVD and used some new system she got to zoom in and read the names of the killers on their jackets."

"Killers?"

"Gunter, Emilio, and Jean. They all did it."

"Tag team murder?" Kate's hand flew to her mouth. "No way."

"Way," I said. "I have to call Reese and tell him."

Kate shook her head. "So Jean killed everyone, then?"

"He must have." I pressed the numbers on my phone screen. "Maybe he thought the others would confess or maybe he was on a roll." I counted the rings and wondered if Reese would be working on a Saturday.

"Precinct Two." A clipped woman's voice answered on the fifth ring.

"Detective Reese, please. Tell him it's Annabelle Archer and it's an emergency."

"Hold on." The phone clattered against something, and I heard voices in the background. I guess their phones didn't have hold buttons yet.

"Reese here."

"Detective, this is Annabelle Archer." The words tumbled out of my mouth. "Sorry to bother you on a weekend, but this is urgent."

"It's okay. I'm working, anyway."

"Champagne for everyone!" one of the bridesmaids squealed as a waiter wheeled a cart with silver ice buckets into the room.

"I won't ask what you're doing." He sounded amused.

"I'll have you know I'm at a wedding." I tried to keep the irritation from creeping into my voice. "But I called you about the Fairmont murder case. I know who killed Henri, and I have solid proof this time."

He sighed. "At this point I'm willing to listen to anything."

"The videographer from the wedding kept a copy of the DVD that you lost. She was able to zoom in and read the names off the jackets of the people who were in the room with Henri."

"I'm listening." Now he sounded interested.

"There wasn't one killer. There were three. Gunter, Emilio, and Jean all had a part in killing their boss. It's on the DVD." I gasped for air and waited for Reese's reaction.

"So Jean must have gotten rid of his accomplices to make sure they wouldn't turn on him."

"That's what we thought, too. Now you have to release Georgia, right? If we've proved that someone else did it?"

"Georgia? We released her last night. That's one hell of a lawyer she got herself."

"She's free?" I felt a weight lift off my shoulders.

"I've never seen anyone as eager to get back to work as she was. She said she hadn't missed one of her weddings in ten years and she wasn't going to miss the one she had today. People in your business really are obsessive, aren't they?"

A chill rushed over me. "She's going back to the hotel today? But Jean is still there. What if he's the one who set her up for the murder? He's not going to be too happy that she's out. He's already killed three people. What's to stop him from killing another?"

"Calm down, Annabelle," Reese said, but I could hear the edge in his voice. "I'm on my way to the Fairmont right now. Whatever you do, don't go in there without me."

"Then you'd better hurry." I hung up and dialed the Fairmont switchboard with shaking fingers. I asked to be put through to Georgia's office, and I held my breath as the phone rang. My heart sank as my call went into voice mail.

"Georgia, it's Annabelle," I said after the beep. "You're in danger. You have to get out of the hotel right now." I hung up the phone and dropped it in my jacket pocket. Kate caught me as I reached the door.

"Where do you think you're going?"

"Georgia's over there with Jean and she doesn't know that he's the killer. If she's walking around the hotel, she won't get my message in time. I have to warn her."

"Are you insane?" Kate grabbed me by the shoulders. "This guy is dangerous. He's already killed three chefs and tried to kill Leatrice."

"It's okay." I shook loose of her grip. "Reese is meeting me over there. I need you to run things for a few minutes while I'm gone. I'll be back before you know it."

Kate darted her eyes to Nadine, who now wore a beehive and tossed back a glass of champagne in one gulp. Kate's eyes filled with panic. "It's too dangerous over there. I'll go."

"Nice try. You'll be fine here," I said. "You've got Fern to help."

Kate looked at Fern, who brandished a brush in one hand and a bottle of champagne in the other.

"I'm telling you girls." He took a swig of champagne. "Sex is the last thing you'll want on your wedding night. After being on your feet all day and seeing all those people? Not on your life! Take it from an expert."

"Right." Kate raised an eyebrow. "Why was I worried?"

CHAPTER 33

"Where's Georgia?" I rushed up to the Fairmont's concierge stand, panting from my dash through the Park Hyatt lobby and across the street. "Has she come in yet?"

Hugh jumped when he saw me, then straightened his formal concierge jacket. "Take it easy, Annabelle. I know you're as excited to see her as we all are, but there's no need to—"

"I have to find her," I pleaded. "She could be in danger."

Hugh leaned over his desk. "What kind of danger? Are you sure?"

"I need to find her before she runs into Jean."

"Do you mean that Jean had something to do with the murder?" Hugh lowered his voice as a guest walked past us.

"I think Jean had something to do with all the deaths in the hotel, and I don't think he'll be too happy that the person he set up to take the fall for killing Henri is free. If he's crazy enough to kill three times, then he's crazy enough to come after Georgia."

"That's such a shame." Hugh shook his head. "He's the best pastry chef we've had in years. I'm going to miss his chocolate decadence cake."

I rolled my eyes. "So have you seen Georgia?"

"She came in a little while ago, but she was running around saying hi to all the departments." Hugh smoothed his moustache with his index finger and looked puzzled. "I don't know where you'll find her, but wherever you do, Reg won't be far behind. He's been following her around like a puppy. Oddly enough, she doesn't seem to mind him. Jail must have had a profound change on her."

"Now that I'd like to see." I grinned at the thought of Georgia reevaluating her life. "Any idea where I should start looking for her, though? I'm not exactly in the mood for a wild goose chase."

Hugh snapped his fingers. "She does have a wedding later today in the Colonnade. I know the tables are down, and Jean was going to start setting up the cake. Apparently it's six tiers and blue."

Blue? Apparently no one wanted a traditional wedding cake anymore.

"So she might be in the Colonnade with Jean? If the police come, can you tell them where I am?" I didn't wait for Hugh to answer before turning and hurrying across the lobby. I leapt the two steps into the sunken lobby lounge and ran on tiptoes down the marble hallway to the Colonnade so my heels wouldn't announce my arrival. I stopped and caught my breath before entering the room.

The tables were set up and covered with pale blue satin tablecloths, giving the room an icy look. I slowly walked around to where Jean stood with his back to me, assembling a giant blue wedding cake on the baby grand piano. A metal pastry cart on wheels stood beside him with piping tubes and extra bowls of blue icing.

"I am not fond of spectators while I work." He shot a disdainful glance over his shoulder, and then resumed piping a pearl border on the cake.

I quickly assessed that the pastry cart didn't hold any knives. "I didn't come to watch you work. I came to talk to you about the murders."

"This again?" He sighed impatiently, but continued his work. "I have told you everything."

"You failed to mention that you and your chef buddies conspired to get rid of Henri together, and then you killed off your accomplices."

"Absurd," he spat out. "You think I killed my colleagues? My friends?"

"Henri wasn't your friend."

He slapped his piping tube down next to the cake. "True enough. His death was well deserved. But I didn't do it."

"Not alone, at least," I pressed. "We have evidence that you, Gunter, and Emilio killed Henri together. It was caught on the DVD."

"I heard about the DVD." He turned to face me. "I suppose it was recovered?"

How did he know about the DVD? And how did he know it was missing?

"The police have it, and it proves that you were involved," I bluffed.

"It's only a matter of time before they find evidence to link you to Gunter's and Emilio's deaths, too."

"I don't have to stand here and be accused of murder." His eyes flashed. "If you'll excuse me, my work here is finished."

I took a step forward. "I can't let you go."

He turned back slowly, one side of his mouth crooked up in a smile. "And what do you intend to do? Subdue me yourself? Arrest me?"

The thought of a citizen's arrest didn't seem realistic at the moment since Jean had a good fifty pounds advantage over me. He fisted his hands and stepped from behind the pastry cart.

"Well, no, but..." I stammered.

"I can handle that part," Reese said as he strode into the room, several uniformed officers following behind him. "We're going to need to take you in for questioning regarding the murder of Chef Henri."

Jean arched an eyebrow but didn't move from his spot. An officer grabbed him by the elbow and started to lead him out of the room. He seemed totally uninterested in the process, but his eyes didn't leave mine.

"Not everything is what it seems," Jean said so quietly that I could barely hear him.

"You okay?" Reese asked, waving a hand in front of me.

"I'm fine." I pulled my eyes away from the chef as the officers escorted him away, and I looked up at Reese. "He never really threatened me. As a matter of fact, he seemed more insulted than angry."

"Some people are like that," Reese said. "Not all murderers are raving lunatics."

"Good thing." I smiled weakly. "I have enough raving lunatics for clients."

Reese laughed. "You know you aren't a typical girl, don't you?"

"You mean your blondie doesn't get involved in murder cases?" I said before I thought better of it.

He raised an eyebrow at me and held my gaze with his hazel green eyes. "I didn't know I had a blondie, but no, I don't know any other women who get involved in murder cases."

"Oh." I felt the heat creeping up my neck. "Well, I don't go looking for trouble, you know."

Reese cocked his head to one side. "That's still up for debate."

"I was only trying to help an old friend who was being framed for murder." I put my hands on my hips. "Anyone would have done the same thing."

Reese studied me for a moment, and then gently brushed a loose hair off my face. "I'm not so sure about that. You have lucky friends."

"Thanks." My mouth went dry and I could feel my heart pounding. I only hoped that Reese couldn't hear it, too.

"Now that your friend has been cleared, I hope you'll stay out of my murder investigations." He winked at me. "You drive me a little bit crazy."

"Oh." My heart sank. "Sorry."

"Don't be sorry," Reese leaned in to me and whispered. "It's not a bad crazy."

"Oh." I tried to keep my knees from buckling.

"There you are," Richard called as he stomped into the room in jeans and a white button-down. "I've been looking everywhere for you."

Reese straightened up, and I jumped away from him. "Richard." I cleared my throat. "What are you doing here?"

"Kate has been calling me nonstop." He waved his cell phone in the air. "Lucky for you I have today off and can swoop in and save the day again." He paused when he saw Reese. "Well, well, it looks like help already arrived."

"Sorry Kate dragged you down here, but everything's fine," I explained. "The police just took Jean away."

"Kate was babbling about Jean St. Jean and a DVD and you being in trouble, but I couldn't make any sense of it." Richard crossed his arms in front of him. "So you aren't in grave danger?"

I shook my head. "Actually, Jean went pretty quietly."

"So I drove down here and valet parked for nothing?" Apparently his mood hadn't improved since last night.

"Not for nothing," I said, my mind racing. "Georgia is out of jail and back at work. Do you want to come find her with me and say hi?"

"I suppose so," he grumbled. "So the trip won't have been a total loss."

I turned to Reese. "I'd better go."

"I'm going to tie up a few loose ends around here, and then head back to the station," Reese said. "I'm glad things turned out well for you and for Georgia."

"Me, too." I nodded. I wanted to say something else, but I could feel Richard's eyes on me. "See you later."

"Count on it." Reese winked almost imperceptibly before he strode out of the room.

Richard raised his eyebrows. "I'm not even going to comment on that."

"I don't know what you're talking about," I said in my most innocent voice.

Richard shook a finger at me. "What's that saying about burning the candle at both ends, or is it playing both ends against the middle?"

"Now you sound like Kate." I started to walk out of the Colonnade. "And I still have no idea what you're referring to."

"Don't think I haven't noticed your little flirtation with tattoo boy." Richard followed me. "Although I've had the good taste to overlook it."

"You're overreacting, as usual."

Richard gasped and stopped in his tracks. "I never overreact."

Classic. Before I could respond, my cell phone began singing, and I reached into my pocket to retrieve it. I looked on the caller ID before answering.

"Hi, Kate," I said as I answered. "Everything's fine. They took Jean away for questioning."

"That's a relief," Kate said over a cacophony of women's voices in the background.

I kept walking through the lobby. "How's everything going over there?"

"Everything was fine until Nadine started rearranging her bouquet and made Mack cry. He and Buster went to repair the damage she did, and I ordered more champagne."

"Good work, Kate. I'll be back in a few minutes." I started up the staircase to the executive offices. "Richard and I are going to say hi to Georgia really fast."

"Okay, but if you see Darcy, don't mention the news about Jean."

"Why not?" I stopped on the landing and waited for Richard to catch up.

"You're not going to believe this, but I just overheard the catering assistants here gossiping about a big secret Darcy's been keeping from everyone at the Fairmont," Kate said. "She and Jean were dating."

CHAPTER 34

"Darcy and Jean?" I almost stumbled up a step. "Are you sure?"

Richard caught me by the elbow. "What about them?"

"That's what the girls over here said," Kate assured me over the phone. "It seems like Darcy went to a lot of trouble to make sure no one at the Fairmont found out."

"I'm sure," I said. "The management isn't fond of employees dating. That's a recipe for early unemployment."

"Who's dating?" Richard hissed, jogging up the steps to keep up with me.

"Hold on," I whispered and pointed to the phone. "It's Kate."

"Exactly," Kate said. "I don't blame her for keeping it quiet, especially knowing what Mr. Elliot can be like. Too bad for Darcy her boyfriend turned out to be a dud."

I laughed. "I'd say that being a serial killer makes you a bit more than a dud in the boyfriend rating system."

"Kate's dating a serial killer?" Richard clasped his hand over his mouth.

"Hey, with some of the guys I've gone out with lately, that'd be an improvement," Kate said.

I shook my head at Richard. "No, Darcy."

"Don't mention anything to Darcy," Kate reminded me. "It might be a touchy subject."

"Got it. I'll see you in a few." I dropped the phone back in my jacket as we reached the top of the stairs.

"Kate's dating Darcy or Darcy's dating a serial killer?" Richard's voice went up a few octaves.

I grabbed Richard by the shoulders. "Keep it down. We don't want the whole lobby to know." I glanced at the bustling hotel beneath us. "Darcy's dating Jean, and Jean just got hauled away for the three murders."

"Oh." Richard pulled himself away from me. "Why didn't you say that in the first place?"

"Sorry." I offered a slightly sarcastic apology. "But don't say anything about Jean if we see Darcy. I don't want to cause a scene."

Richard made signs of locking his mouth and throwing away the key. "You know me. Discretion is my middle name."

"How could I forget?" I pushed open the glass door to the catering and sales offices. The secretary who sat at the front desk was gone, so I peeked around the doorway to the back offices.

Richard crept close behind me. "Do you know where Georgia's office is or are we going to wander aimlessly?"

"It's right down here on the left. She has a window over the alley."

"Pretty."

We walked through the maze of gray fabric cubicles that took up the majority of the floor space. It was eerily quiet since most of the sales staff had left for the weekend and only catering staff with events remained. I heard a soft humming as we reached Georgia's office door.

"Annabelle." Darcy poked her head over the cubicle divider across from Georgia's office. "What are you doing here?"

Richard shrieked and almost leapt into my arms, then glared at Darcy. "Don't jump out at people like that. You almost gave me a heart attack."

"We stopped by to welcome Georgia back to work," I explained, prying Richard off me.

Darcy came around the divider. "I'm not sure if she wants to be disturbed..."

"They aren't disturbing me." Georgia threw open the door to her office. Her emerald green wrap top draped open, showing the edge of her black lace bra; her hot pink lipstick was smeared; and her hair looked like it had been through a wind tunnel. Reg sat in the chair behind her, wearing equal amounts of pink lipstick and a stunned expression.

"Good Lord." Richard averted his eyes.

"Isn't it wonderful, Annabelle?" Georgia pulled me in to her office, tugging her blouse closed an inch. "It took being arrested for me to realize that what I've really been looking for has been right under my nose all this time."

"That's wonderful." I took a step back into the hall. "But we don't want to interrupt anything."

"Nonsense." Georgia threw an arm around my shoulders, causing her shirt to fall open even more. "I have you to thank for everything. Reg told me how you questioned everyone and almost got in trouble with our GM."

"I'm glad everything turned out okay." I looked at Reg, and then nudged her. "Or should I say better than okay?"

"Can you believe he's had feelings for me for all these years and I never knew it?" Georgia whispered to me, and then blew a kiss to Reg.

"We're all happy you're out," I said. "Richard helped us with the investigation, too, you know."

Richard tried to look at Georgia without dropping his eyes to her cleavage. "Hotel catering would have been dreadfully dull without you, darling."

"I'm lucky to have such great friends." Georgia's eyes filled with tears. "And a great assistant, too. Darcy kept the place running while I was away. My office was spotless, and she even caught up with my proposals."

Darcy blushed and shook her head. "I'm relieved you're back. I don't think I could have done your job for one more day, and especially not today's wedding."

Reg stood up and looked at his watch. "That reminds me, I have to start the setup in the Colonnade."

Georgia stuck her lower lip out in a pout, and then turned to us. "Let me walk him to the door, then I'll come back and we can catch up. Make yourself comfortable in my office."

Richard swished past Reg and lowered himself into a chair. "Take your time, honey."

"I'm going to get back to work," Darcy said, stepping back toward her cubicle. "We have a few last minute changes to tonight's wedding timing."

I joined Richard in Georgia's office and walked around her desk to look out the window. It was open all the way and a breeze fluttered in, although the smell from the alley Dumpster below wasn't exactly refreshing. I pressed my nose against the screen so I could look straight down. Employee parking, loading dock, Dumpsters. Not the greatest view, but it beat a cubicle.

"Not a bad office. I like the color." Richard waved a hand at the soft green paint that covered the walls. He craned his neck to look at the shelves behind him that held wedding books, leftover unity candles, cake knives, and stacks of yarmulkes. "She's stocked up, huh?"

I sat down in Georgia's swivel chair. "Next time I'll know where to come when a client forgets the unity candle."

"Speaking of ceremonies, don't you have one to get to?"

"I still have time. They should still be doing pictures right now." I spun around in the chair. "Anyway, Kate can handle it for a few more minutes."

Richard held up a hand for me to be quiet. "Is someone humming the theme song from 'Bewitched'?"

I listened for a moment and realized that the sound came from Darcy's cubicle. I stood up and looked at the perfectly painted walls of Georgia's office. I felt like smacking myself in the head, but instead I reached for a pink paperweight on the desk and hurled it against the wall. It hit the surface with a loud thud, and pieces of plaster and pale green paint fell to the floor with it.

Richard leapt out of his chair. "Look what you've done to Georgia's wall. What on earth has gotten into you?"

"Maybe Darcy can explain," I said, motioning to the catering assistant who stood in the doorway, staring at the hole in the wall.

CHAPTER 35

I walked around the desk and advanced on Darcy. "Maybe you forgot the little story you told me about Georgia's fight with Henri the day he was murdered?"

Darcy remained silent, chewing on her lower lip.

"You claimed that Georgia got so enraged at Henri that she threw a paperweight at him and missed, hitting the wall in her office. One problem, though. No holes in the wall." I took a breath and continued. "Very clever way to cast doubt on Georgia's innocence."

"What's going on?" Richard snapped. "I thought we were finished with all this murder nonsense. Might I remind you, Annabelle, that you just had Jean hauled off to the police station?"

Darcy's eyes flitted to mine and burned with anger before going blank again.

"I thought we'd wrapped everything up, too," I said. "But I thought about something Jean said to me. 'Not everything is what it seems.'"

"How delightful," Richard drawled. "A pastry chef with a penchant for murder and riddles."

"I think he was talking about you." I took a step toward Darcy. "Isn't that right?"

"Her?" Richard shook his head. "But you have evidence that the three chefs killed Henri, don't you?"

"Technically, yes," I admitted. "But I have a feeling that there's more to Darcy and to these murders than meets the eye."

"So I exaggerated the story about Georgia and Henri's fight." Darcy shrugged. "So what?"

"Not only did you not want Georgia to get out of jail, you're the one who fed information and fake evidence to the cops to make her look more suspicious." I leveled a finger at her. "Who better to plant her trademark scarf for the cops to find after your boyfriend put blood on it?"

Darcy raised an eyebrow. "I knew Jean couldn't keep our relationship to himself. Men are so indiscreet."

"Tell me about it, sister." Richard sunk back down in his seat.

"Just because I'm dating Jean doesn't mean I had anything to do with the murders," Darcy said.

"I think men have been your downfall, Darcy." I perched on the corner of the desk. "You've been covering up for your boyfriend and your father all this time."

I watched as Darcy's hands curled into fists, but her expression remained unchanged.

"Her father?" Richard asked.

"That's right," I said. "Didn't you know that Darcy is the daughter that Marcello lost years ago?"

Richard spun around in his chair. "What? Have you lost your mind, Annabelle, or are you determined to ruin me?"

"When I heard Darcy humming the theme song from 'Bewitched,' everything fell into place. How many people do you know who hum old TV theme songs?" I asked.

Richard eyed Darcy. "Well, it would explain why a girl with an Irish name looks so Italian and has questionable choice in music."

"My mother is Irish," Darcy said quietly, her voice steady. "I took her last name."

"I told you." Richard gave me a smug grin. "I knew something wasn't right from the beginning. Black Irish, my foot."

I locked eyes with Darcy and put on my best poker face. "Jean confessed to everything. How he, Emilio, and Gunter killed Henri and you set up Georgia to take the fall for them."

"Jean told you?" Darcy narrowed her eyes at me.

I nodded. "He said he wasn't going down alone."

"I knew I shouldn't have trusted him," Darcy muttered. "Men are weak."

"You father wasn't weak, though," I said. "He was behind this whole murder, wasn't he?"

Darcy burst into derisive laughter. "My father wishes he masterminded Henri's murder. No, he watched from the sidelines, as usual."

"Thank heavens." Richard brushed a hand across his forehead. "It's so hard to replace good chefs nowadays."

"But that doesn't make sense," I said. "Marcello had more motive than anyone. Henri destroyed his life."

"No, Henri destroyed my life." Darcy wrung her hands together. "Do you know what it's like to be eight years old and have your family fall apart? After he was fired, my father became obsessed with getting revenge on Henri. It was all he thought about, talked about. He couldn't find work and he became more and more bitter. Finally, my mother thought we'd be better off without him. I didn't see him for twenty years."

"So you're telling me that after all that time, Marcello didn't have anything to do with killing Henri?" I asked.

Darcy jabbed at her chest. "He may have forgotten about revenge, but I didn't."

Darcy no longer looked like the uptight, frazzled assistant I'd known. She looked calm, controlled, and a little crazy.

I edged around behind the desk. Why hadn't I seen it before? "So you were behind all of this. You came to the Fairmont with the express purpose of killing Henri, and you waited three years to get the revenge your father never could."

"Never send a man to do a woman's job," Darcy said.

Richard started to open his mouth in protest, but took one look at Darcy and abandoned the idea. He slid out of his chair and took a step toward the door. Darcy blocked him.

"You don't understand," she said patiently. "I didn't kill Henri. I was nowhere near the murder scene."

"You convinced Jean, Gunter, and Emilio to kill him for you, though," I argued. "Jean is telling that to the police right this second."

She shut the office door and leaned against it. "Actually, I only had to convince Jean. He got the others on board. They never knew I had anything to do with it."

"Well, if you didn't actually kill anyone, I'd say there's no harm done." Richard gave a nervous laugh. "Don't you agree, Annabelle?"

I ignored him. "You may not have killed Henri, but you conspired to murder him. Was it your idea to get rid of Gunter and Emilio, too?"

"So unfortunate." Darcy frowned and pointed a finger at me. "But they couldn't be trusted not to talk, what with you snooping around and asking so many questions."

"Nice going," Richard mumbled under his breath, as he joined me behind the desk.

"I gave you lots of warnings, Annabelle," Darcy reminded me. "You don't take hints very well, do you?"

"Don't think I haven't said exactly the same thing," Richard said.

I glared at him. "Whose side are you on, anyway?"

He avoided my eyes. "What? She makes a good point."

I turned my attention back to Darcy. "Does your father appreciate that you did his dirty work for him and you're going to go to jail for conspiracy to murder?"

"He has to be proud of me after what I did for him." Darcy's eyes darted wildly around the room. "He has to love me after the sacrifices I made for him. Sacrifices he was never willing to make for me."

Richard gave a low whistle. "Have you ever considered family therapy?"

Darcy's eyes blazed, and she slid a cake knife off the shelf next to her. "You have no idea what you're talking about, and I have no intention of going to jail."

"She's got a knife." Richard's voice came out as little more than a squeak.

Darcy advanced toward us and I backed up, treading firmly on Richard's toes.

"You can't prove that I had anything to do with the murders." Darcy leaned over the desk and swiped the knife at us. "I'm innocent."

Richard shrieked as the blade missed his face by only inches. "May I point out that this is not the behavior of an innocent person?"

Richard and I leaned back to avoid getting cut by the flailing blade and stumbled against the window screen. It bowed with our weight, and we both lurched back into the room. Darcy started around the side of the desk, and I gave Richard a push.

"Move it!" I screamed.

Darcy lunged for us as we ran for the door, and the knife nicked Richard in the arm. He took one look at the drops of blood spreading on the sleeve of his white shirt and collapsed in a dead faint. I stumbled over him, landing on my hands and knees.

"You're not going to get away with this," I gasped as Darcy rounded the desk.

"I keep telling you." She raised the knife over her head. "I'm innocent."

"You're crazy." I scurried around the desk as she dove for me, and got behind the swivel chair. Darcy came around the corner, cursing and panting, her hair hanging in her face. Now she did look crazy. She saw me behind the chair and rushed forward, arms outstretched.

I kicked the chair away from me and it spun toward her, knocking her off balance and sending her sprawling against the window screen. The knife blade pierced the screen, and she flailed for a second before her weight ripped the screen open and she plummeted to the ground below. I cringed when her screams came to an abrupt stop.

I sat frozen in shock for a few minutes, trying to digest what had happened. I could hear shouts and loud voices below me, but I couldn't force myself to move. Darcy had wasted her entire life so she could get revenge for her father and win his love? Dr. Phil would have a field day with this.

I finally tried to stand but my legs felt too weak, so I crawled shakily away from the window until I reached Richard. I rolled him over and slapped his cheeks.

His eyes fluttered open and he sat up. "What happened?"

"The short version?" I slumped against the desk. "Darcy fell out the window. She's gone."

The door swung open and Georgia gaped at us. "What on earth is going on here?" She looked around the room. "You trashed my office."

Reese appeared behind her and called over his shoulder, "The body fell from in here, guys."

"Body?" Georgia jumped when she saw Reese. "What's going on?"

"It's a long story." I took Reese's hand and let him pull me up. "Give me a second and I'll explain everything."

"What happened to your arm?" Georgia asked Richard, pointing to the blood on his shirt.

Reese turned to one of the officers who'd joined him. "Get another ambulance here. Looks like we've got a stab wound."

"Stab wound?" Richard looked down at his arm, then his eyes rolled back in his head and he sagged to the floor again.

Georgia stuck her head out into the hall. "Where's Darcy? She was here a minute ago."

I looked from Reese to the ripped window screen and back again. "I'm afraid she stepped out."

CHAPTER 36

"Where have you been, Annabelle?" Kate rushed me as Richard and I stepped out of the Park Hyatt's elevator onto the ballroom level. Groomsmen in black tuxedos clustered by the door of the ballroom, handing out programs, and the familiar sounds of a string quartet came from inside. "It's ten minutes until they walk down the aisle, and we're missing a mother of the groom."

"I got here as fast as I could," I said as I appraised the setup. A towering glass vase of green viburnum dominated a round table in the foyer and made me do a double take. The Mighty Morphin Flower Arrangers had blown me away again. "Richard had to get stitches and wouldn't let me leave him."

"An exaggeration," Richard spluttered. "But I would think that my life would be a little more important than yet another wedding."

"Stitches?" Kate looked at Richard's shirt and her mouth dropped open.

Richard lowered his voice and made sure no guests were within earshot. "I was stabbed."

"By Jean?" Kate asked.

"No, by Darcy." Richard was relishing every moment of this. "Turns out she was the brains behind the whole operation. It also turns out that she's Marcello's daughter."

"Wow." Kate looked dazed. "I missed a lot."

"Once we find the missing mother, I'll fill you in," I assured her, taking the wedding timeline out of her hands and looking at my watch.

"She was here for pictures, and then she went to her room to freshen up her makeup," Kate said. "Although between you and me if she puts on much more she's going to topple over from the weight of her eye shadow."

"Is that her?" Richard's eyes were wide as he stared behind me.

I turned around and was almost blinded by the copper crushed lame dress advancing on me. I hadn't thought it possible to match a dress to a skin tone as perfectly as she had. She was an unnatural shade of burnished orange from her shellacked hair to her talonlike fingernails. The only spots on her body that weren't orange were her turquoise eyelids.

"What's the mother of the bride wearing?" I whispered to Kate.

"Lavender suit. No beads."

"Have they seen each other?" I hesitated to ask.

Kate nodded. "It wasn't pretty."

"This is better than reality TV," Richard said.

"Well, girls." The groom's mother tapped her watch. "Looks like it's show time. Come on, Harold." Her husband shuffled behind her toward the ballroom.

"What happened to the grandfather?" I'd expected to see the geriatric Don Juan permanently attached to Kate.

"I had him seated early." Kate smiled mischievously. "To give him more time to get down the aisle."

I patted her on the shoulder. "Good thinking."

"Do you want to get the bridesmaids lined up while I deal with the moms and cue the—" I stopped in midsentence as I saw Leatrice, Ian, and Reese get off the elevator. "What are you doing here? All of you?"

Reese rolled his eyes. "I found these two snooping around the Fairmont."

Leatrice nodded eagerly. "Ian and I heard about the latest accident at the Fairmont on my police scanner and he wanted to come down and see what happened."

"We can't have them messing up our crime scene, but I recognized your neighbor right away." The side of Reese's mouth quivered until he could no longer suppress a grin. "When I mentioned that you were over here, they insisted on coming to see you."

"How thoughtful of you." I hoped he didn't miss my sarcasm.

Ian stepped in close to me and took my hand into both of his. "We heard what happened. Are you all right?"

My mouth went dry as I tried to speak. I didn't know which man made me more nervous, but I definitely couldn't handle them together.

Richard sighed. "Oh for heaven's sake, she's fine. I'm the one who nearly died."

"Did you now?" Leatrice bounced over to Richard, the penguins on her sweater jiggling. "Is that blood?"

Reese cleared his throat to get my attention. "I also thought I'd tell you that I got a call from the station. Jean finally confessed to the murders and to Darcy's part in them. Apparently she was the one who managed to lift the DVD when she was giving a statement at the station."

"So she was the one giving you evidence against Georgia that day? She must have overheard us talking about the footage of the murder." I tried to keep my voice steady and sound professional. "I'm glad everything turned out okay."

Reese looked at my hands clasped in Ian's, and then met my eyes for a brief moment. "I have to get back to the crime scene. Try to stay out of trouble from now on, okay, Annabelle?"

I took a tiny step back from Ian, whose gaze was now focused on Reese. I didn't want Reese to think that Ian and I were a couple when we hadn't even gone out yet, but I didn't want Ian to think that I had a thing for the detective, either. I didn't know what I wanted, but I definitely needed an aspirin from my emergency kit.

"The detective knows you pretty well, eh?" Ian said, loosening his grip on my hands.

I could feel my face getting warm. "We've worked together before, that's all."

"Some people have a hard time staying out of trouble," Richard said under his breath, looking pointedly at me as Reese got back on the elevator. "Especially when they juggle too much at one time."

I gave Richard a kick in the shins and felt better when he yelped in pain.

"What time is it?" Kate pulled my hands away from Ian to look at my watch. "We only have three minutes."

I flipped a page in the timeline to bring me to the ceremony page. "Sorry to rush off, guys, but we have to get a bride down the aisle."

"Well, that's another thing." Kate avoided my eyes. "The bride is . . . um, here, see for yourself."

She pulled me by the elbow down the hall to the junior ballroom, with Richard, Leatrice, and Ian trailing behind. The small ballroom had been sectioned off and set up as a holding room for the bridal party. Fern sat in the midst of the celadon-clad bridesmaids dispensing dubious sex advice. The bride wore a dazed smile on her face and looked like she was on the verge of slipping off her chair.

"Is she drunk?" I hissed at Kate.

"I'd say she's snockered," Ian said

Fern jumped up from his chair and ran over to me. "Annabelle! Don't they all look gorgeous? I mean for a bunch of tramps, of course." He burst into laughter, and all the girls joined him.

I had to live vicariously through Fern's insults. Just once I'd like to be able to call a bridesmaid a tramp and live to tell the tale.

I noticed Fern's glassy eyes. "How much champagne did you all have?"

"Oh, it wasn't the champagne that relaxed everyone." Fern cupped his hand and leaned close to my ear. "It was the Valium I crushed up in it that really took the edge off Nadine."

"I've always wanted to try Valium." Leatrice eyed the empty glasses. "I hear it's coming back into fashion."

Sometimes I really wondered where Leatrice got her information.

"You drugged the bride?" I rubbed my temples. Darcy had been a piece of cake compared to this.

"How much did you have?" Richard asked Fern as he watched him lean against the wall with one arm.

"Only a teensy slip or two." Fern slid down the wall to the floor.

I stepped over Fern and walked over to Nadine, shaking her by the shoulders. "It's time to get married."

Nadine raised her head and gave me a huge vacant smile. "Congratulations."

I pulled her up by her arms and propped her against me. "No, Nadine. You're getting married, remember?"

"If you think I should," she slurred.

At least they weren't reciting their own vows, I reminded myself.

"Bridesmaids line up in the order we rehearsed," Kate called from the door in her best drill sergeant voice. "Don't forget your bouquets."

The girls shuffled into line and followed Kate out the door. I grabbed Nadine's bouquet off the table and handed it to Richard as I tried to walk her into the lobby.

Richard stared at the green pod bouquet. "What on earth?"

I held up a hand. "Don't ask."

"This is so exciting." Leatrice clapped her hands. "What can I do?"

"Grab her train so it doesn't get all twisted," I instructed, motioning to the back of Nadine's cathedral-length dress.

"Let me give you a hand with her." Ian winked at me as he took the other side of the sagging bride. "This isn't how I imagined spending time with you, but it's not so bad."

"I'm really sorry that I was out when you came by last night." I tried to keep my voice low so Richard wouldn't overhear. "Kate and I got stuck at work."

Ian gave me a playfully suspicious look. "So you weren't out with another fellow?"

I shook my head and felt my cheeks start to warm.

"I told him that I'd be shocked if you were on a date," Leatrice chimed in.

'Thanks." I turned to shoot daggers at Leatrice, who happily hummed "The Wedding March" as we lurched down the hall. I said a prayer of thanks that the mother of the bride had already been seated and couldn't see the motley crew dragging her daughter down the hall.

When we reached the doorway to the ballroom, Kate was sending the maid of honor down the aisle. She closed the ballroom doors, and I passed the bride off to her startled father, pulling the blusher over her face. Kate and I each held one of the door handles and waited for the music to change while Richard placed the bouquet in the bride's hand.

"Go slow," I whispered to Nadine's father as the trumpet began the processional fanfare and Leatrice unfurled the train behind them.

Kate and I threw open the double doors simultaneously and watched the bride and her father shuffle diagonally down the aisle before we closed the ballroom doors behind them. I slumped against the door.

Ian leaned next to me. "Boy, your weddings sure are something special. Dead bodies, drunk brides—"

I elbowed him lightly. "Hey, all our weddings aren't like this."

"Sometimes there are drunks *and* dead bodies," Richard said, smirking at me.

"I wouldn't mind being a wedding planner." Leatrice stood on her tiptoes to look through the peephole in the ballroom door. "And I'll bet it's even easier when the bride is awake."

"Not always." Between confronting a murderer and getting a doped-up bride down the aisle, I felt like crawling in bed for a week.

"That wasn't so bad," Kate said. "Why didn't we think of sedating our brides before, huh?"

Richard stared at Kate. "Because it's illegal?"

"You know what they say." Kate grinned. "All's fair in love and war."

Richard and I exchanged a look of amused relief.

"You're right about that," I said.

BONUS EPILOGUE

I breathed in the cool night air as I stepped outside the Park Hyatt hotel, walking a few steps away from the glass front doors to lean against a square stone column. The valets stood to one side talking and laughing to each other, and I heard the sound of car horns from the corner intersection. I let my hair out of its ponytail and sighed as it fell down around my shoulders.

"I thought your wedding would be in full swing by now."

I straightened up and followed the sound of Reese's voice until I spotted him crossing the street toward me. "It is, and it isn't."

He raised an eyebrow as he reached me. "Oh?"

"The ceremony and cocktail hour are over, and we just finished announcing the bridal party into the ballroom for dinner," I explained, happy the darkness masked the flush I felt on my cheeks. "It's all downhill from here."

Downhill was a relative term considering the bride had been so intoxicated she'd passed out on her groom's arm and started snoring during her own wedding ceremony.

"After what happened earlier, I sincerely hope not."

I knew Reese meant Darcy trying to kill me and then plunging out the window to the sidewalk.

"Speaking of that," I said, nodding toward the Fairmont Hotel. "How goes it at the crime scene?"

"We're wrapping it up," Reese said, shoving his hands into the pockets of his jeans and leaning against the column next to me. "I should be able to take off soon. How much longer are you here?"

"Until the bitter end," I said, fishing in my pocket for the packet of gummy bears Kate had given me earlier and shaking out a few candies into my hand. "Last dance isn't until midnight."

Reese shook his head when I held out my hand. "I'm trying to cut back."

"Ha ha." I popped a red bear in my mouth. "You should try them. They're great for a late-night sugar rush."

"I'll bet." Reese cleared his throat. "So is your entire team still here?"

I glanced over at him. "You mean my actual wedding day team or all my crazy friends who crashed the party?"

He laughed. "You do have a colorful bunch of friends. Is the guy with the spiked hair a friend of yours?"

"Ian?" I tried to laugh, but it came out more like a squeak. "He's a bandleader."

I made a point not to specify if he was the bandleader for tonight's wedding or not, and hoped Reese wouldn't notice.

"So he's one of your usual wedding vendors?"

I paused before I answered. "I wouldn't say that. We work with a lot of bands. His band is an 80s cover band, so they're not everyone's cup of tea. Why do you ask? Are you looking to hire someone to play Duran Duran covers?"

"Nothing like that," he said. "You just seemed to know him well."

I shrugged. "Being in the wedding trenches together can create fast friendships. Almost everyone I know works in the wedding industry, including all my closest friends."

"Like Richard?"

I ran a hand through my hair. "He was the first caterer who met with me when I started my company. Everyone else blew me off, but he actually took me to lunch and gave me advice on other vendors to call. It was because of him I was able to crack into the business. Naturally, I sent him all my clients, which meant we were working together every weekend and bonding over crazy brides. We've been best friends ever since."

"It's clear he's devoted to you," Reese said.

I smiled as I thought about the many times I'd bailed Richard out of wacky situations and the time he'd secretly moved his catering operations into my apartment. "It's mutual."

We stood without talking for a few moments and, since we were close to a park, I could hear the faint sound of crickets between the blaring of car horns on nearby M Street.

"Was I imagining things or does Richard not like your punk band-leader friend very much?" Reese asked.

"Richard isn't crazy about competition," I said, choosing my words carefully. "It's not personal, but he's gotten used to having my undivided attention for years."

"So he dislikes all your boyfriends?"

I shifted from one foot to the other. "I hate to disappoint you, but I haven't had a real boyfriend since I moved to Washington. For one thing, I've been way too focused on building my business to date and for another, I don't meet many men in my line of work who aren't grooms or gay."

Reese chuckled. "What about the groomsmen or wedding guests?"

I gave a firm shake of my head. "It's a hard-and-fast Wedding Belles rule not to date groomsmen or wedding guests."

"Does your assistant know that?"

Now it was my turn to laugh. "Kate believes the rules are more like guidelines."

Reese's hand brushed mine. "So you're not currently involved with anyone?"

I didn't know how to best answer that, so I took a page out of Kate's playbook and responded with a question of my own. "Are you?"

"No one in particular," he said. "Like you, I don't meet many women in my line of work unless I decide to widen my horizon and start dating felons."

I took a deep breath. "So the blonde you were cozying up to at Mie N Yu the other day wasn't anyone in particular?"

"Please tell me your nutty neighbor doesn't have me under some kind of illegal surveillance," Reese said, turning to face me.

"Of course not," I said, trying to sound indignant on Leatrice's behalf even though I knew it wasn't out of the realm of possibility. "Don't flatter yourself. I was out with Kate, Richard, and Fern, and we happened to see you."

Reese gave me a look like he wasn't completely convinced. "If you must know, I was on a blind date."

"Really?" I said, failing to keep the surprise out of my voice. "That was a set-up?"

"And not a very good one."

I crossed my arms in front of me. "You seemed to be enjoying yourself to me."

He let out a breath. "She may have been pretty, but after an hour I was bored to tears."

I felt a flush of pleasure.

"It's actually your fault, you know," he continued.

I put a hand to my throat. "My fault? How do you figure that?"

"Ever since you started interfering in my cases, other women have seemed dull by comparison."

I felt my face warm as he leaned in closer. I looked up and locked eyes with him, glad I was leaning against a pillar so my knees wouldn't buckle.

"Annabelle?" Kate's voice jerked me out of my momentary daze. "Is that you?"

Reese took a step back as I twisted to see Kate holding open one of the hotel's glass doors.

"They're about to cut the cake, and Nadine is insisting that she wants to cut it with a sword," Kate said.

"But this isn't a military wedding," I said. "There is no sword."

"*I* know there's no sword." Kate let her breath out with a whoosh. "Can you come help me convince the bride of that?"

"I'd better let you get back to work," Reese said, giving my hand a small squeeze before turning and heading toward the Fairmont Hotel.

I watched him go for a moment, enjoying the retreating view and wondering when I'd see him again. Chances were slim that I'd bump into the detective unless I stumbled across another dead body. And what were the chances of that?

THE END

I HOPE you enjoyed FOR BETTER OR HEARSE! To read a sneak peek or order the next book in the series, turn the page!

FREE DOWNLOAD!

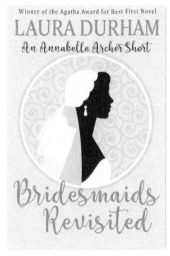

A LUXURY BRIDAL SHOWER.
THE STRESS IS HIGH.
THE PRESENTS ARE GONE.
THE BRIDESMAIDS ARE SUSPECTS.

CAN ANNABELLE UNMASK
THE THIEF?

amazon kindle

nook

kobo

 iBooks

Get your free copy of the short story "Bridesmaids Revisited" when you sign up to the author's mailing list. Go to the back of the book to sign up.

BOOK 3: DEAD RINGER: A NOVELLA

Annabelle Archer Wedding Planner Mystery
by Laura Durham

CHAPTER 1

"Where are you?" I asked, holding my phone against my ear and carrying a pair of overstuffed canvas bags in my other hand. The hotel elevator had deposited me on the basement level of the W Hotel and I sidestepped cardboard boxes, bolts of gold sequined fabric, and bright orange buckets of flowers as I made my way to the ballroom.

"We're in the middle section about halfway down," Kate's voice crackled through the phone. The W Hotel sat right across from the White House, and I wondered if this had anything to do with the dodgy cell reception or if it was merely a basement issue.

The modern hotel had once been one of the oldest historic hotels in the city, the Hotel Washington, but after declining for many years, had been snapped up by a ritzy hotel group and refashioned into a sleek W Hotel. The classic lobby with brocade settees had been replaced by the Living Room with a black-and-white tile floor, a 360-degree bar that pumped out club music, and a virtual fireplace projected onto a flat screen. The rooftop, with its impressive open-air view of the White House and frequent sightings of the president's helicopter detail, had become a highly selective spot for cocktails, featuring willowy women in skimpy black dresses as gatekeepers. I never felt quite hip enough to be at the W.

"Okay, I'll see you in a second." I slipped my phone into the pocket of my jeans and shifted one of the heavy bags to my now-free hand. I stepped carefully down the staircase that led from the elevator bank to the ballroom level, avoiding the lighting crew on tall ladders at the bottom. Almost every inch of the floor was covered in boxes, crates, or tables yet to be unfolded.

"A bridal show is even more chaotic than a wedding," I muttered to myself as I snaked a path through the ballroom foyer. And as the owner of one of Washington DC's top wedding planning firms, I knew firsthand how chaotic weddings could be. I passed through the propped-open double doors to the ballroom and peered across the room, which had already been divided into thirds with panels of ivory fabric that reached from floor to ceiling. A pair of modern crystal chandeliers shaped like massive, glittering cones dominated the ceiling in the long rectangular space and drew my eyes away from the set-up clutter covering the dark carpet. I spotted my assistant's blond bob about halfway down the center, as promised. She waved at me with both hands and what appeared to be a to-go coffee in each one.

"I hope one of those is for me," I said to Kate, dropping the bags on the floor once I'd maneuvered across the room to reach her.

She held out a cup ringed in a brown cardboard holder. "The Annabelle Archer signature drink: a mocha with mint."

"You're the best." I took a sip and let the warmth and caffeine do their work. "But you know that not every person needs a signature drink." Sometimes the signature drinks and custom signage and personalized details that had taken over the wedding world were too much for me.

"Well, you've got one," she said. "And I've got doughnuts behind the bar."

"District Doughnuts?"

She grinned at me. "Yep. The cinnamon sugar ones."

My stomach growled, reminding me that I hadn't eaten breakfast yet. I glanced at the eight-foot-long gold bar with mercury glass panels set against the tall fabric wall. A white-framed mirror with our Wedding Belles logo painted in gold on the reflective surface hung in the middle of the drape.

"You're sure about the bar?" I asked as I ducked behind it to search for the box of doughnuts. Kate had convinced me that instead of a tablescape like all the other DC wedding planners would do for their display, we should have a bar. Even though I'd started Wedding Belles five years ago and was no longer considered the new kid on the block, I still wasn't completely comfortable being a trailblazer.

I found the white box, grabbed a doughnut, and took a bite. The cinnamon sugar atop the warm cake doughnut made me glad I'd skipped breakfast. Not that I'd had any food worth eating in my apartment.

"Of course I'm sure. What bride doesn't want to belly up to a bar?" Kate hopped up onto one of the ornate gold bar stools and crossed her legs, exposing most of her legs as her black miniskirt slid up her thighs. Most people wore jeans and T-shirts to setup but Kate considered every time she stepped out of her apartment as an opportunity to meet Mr. Right. Hence the miniskirt, snug red sweater, and full makeup. I actually had to think hard to remember if I'd put on mascara after throwing my long auburn hair up into a ponytail this morning.

"Frankly, I'm hoping for sober brides." Richard walked up and gave me a peck on the cheek. "It would be a nice change."

"You're only saying that because our last drunk bride got up on the stage and started rapping as the band was breaking down," Kate said.

He shuddered. "Girls that white should never rap."

"Doughnut?" I offered and motioned to the box.

Richard shook his head. "I don't need sugar all over my shirt." He picked at a piece of non-existent lint on his crisp lavender button-down shirt. Richard was another one who didn't do jeans and T-shirts for setup.

Richard was the owner of Richard Gerard Catering, one of the top caterers in the city, and had been my go-to caterer and best friend since I'd hit the wedding planner scene. Richard prided himself on impeccable taste and was a stickler for good behavior. I was amazed he'd survived in weddings as long as he had.

"Where are you set up?" I asked, giving a cursory glance around. From the pile of foliage on one side of me and the glass case on the other, it seemed like we were between a jeweler and a florist but, I didn't see a catering setup.

Richard swept a hand through his spiky brown hair and motioned behind the drape wall. "I'm on the dark side of the moon."

I patted his back. "I'm sure it won't be so bad once all the lighting is on."

"You must be out of your mind, Annabelle. Anyone who's anyone is in the center."

"I'm sure that's not true," I said.

Richard narrowed his eyes at Kate. "Who did you flirt with to land a space in the middle of the room?"

"Hey," Kate said in her affronted tone. "I'll have you know that the show staff is all women."

"And Kate would never use her feminine wiles to get us a better spot in the show," I said with more conviction than I felt.

"Thank you," Kate said, then put a hand over her mouth and lowered her voice. "But you know I'd take one for the team if they had a hot guy in charge."

I nodded even though I didn't think flirting with an attractive man was the strict definition of "taking one for the team." Especially since I couldn't seem to *stop* her from flirting with hot guys.

Richard lowered his voice to a hiss. "I have a cosmetic dentist next to me."

"What's wrong with dentists?" Kate asked. "I've dated several nice ones. They make good money." Kate probably knew the average salary of every man she met off the top of her head.

Richard tapped one foot on the carpet. "Nothing. Unless you're trying to convince people to sample your crème brulee tartlets and profiteroles wrapped in spun sugar."

I could see his point. Sugar was a hard sell next to photos of yellowed teeth.

He began fidgeting with one of his silver cuff links. "The only thing worse would be someone next to me offering on-site colonics."

Kate put her cup down on the bar. "And I'm done with the coffee."

"Brides are coming here to drink Champagne and eat cake," I said. "They want to indulge. And no one can say no to your brownie meringue pops."

Richard allowed himself a tiny smile. "Of course they can't. Those babies are like heaven." He gave me a quick hug. "You always know what to say."

"That's what they tell me." I'd honed my skill of calming down skittish brides and their nervous mothers by being the voice of reason for my neurotic colleagues.

"Well, I'd better return to my side before those dental assistants run out of sugar-free gum and start eyeing my sweets display." He disappeared around the corner of the drape.

I stepped back and gave our bare bar a once-over. "Speaking of setting up..."

"Don't worry." Kate slid off the bar stool. "Buster and Mack promised to drape the rose gold branches over our bar for us."

I gaped at the huge pile of leafy, spray-painted tree branches that nearly covered the floor next to us. "Is all of that for us?"

"Not all of it. Buster and Mack are using some of it. The canopy will cover both of our displays."

"So the Mighty Morphins will be next to us?" Buster and Mack's flower shop was called Lush, but everyone called them the Mighty Morphin Flower Arrangers.

Kate nodded. "Isn't it going to be fun?"

I sipped my warm mocha, then took a bite of doughnut. Kate was right, I thought. We were hanging out with our friends, we were stocked up on sugar, and we didn't need to get anyone down the aisle. Today was going to be fun.

"Annabelle!" I heard my name shrieked across the room. Fern, short for Fernando, was headed my way. He'd pulled his dark hair up in a man bun and wore a velvet-green smoking jacket with a green and yellow paisley ascot. No one could say that DC's top hairstylist didn't make a statement.

"Thank heavens you're here," he said when he reached me. His breath was ragged from either exertion or hysteria.

"What's wrong?" I asked.

He pressed a hand to his chest. "I can't work under these conditions. It's a disaster."

"Take a breath." I led him over to a bar stool to sit down. "What do you need me to do?"

"I'm so glad you asked." Fern collapsed onto a stool and peered at me from under the arm he'd slung across his eyes. "You and Kate are so good at organizing. I need you to help me stage a coup."

So much for our fun day.

CHAPTER 2

"And who are we overthrowing today?" I asked Fern as he fanned himself with a monogrammed handkerchief he'd produced from the breast pocket of his smoking jacket.

"Christopher."

Kate tilted her head to one side. "Who's Christopher?"

"Exactly." Fern pointed at her. "Who is he? Why is he here? Why do I have to work with another hairstylist for the fashion show?"

Things began to click into place for me. "So you're doing the models' hair for the fashion show?"

Fern flung the handkerchief over his face and tilted back on the bar stool. "Of course. I always do the hair for the show. Alone."

"And now you have to work with another stylist." Fern didn't like to share the spotlight with anyone so double billing on the biggest bridal show of the year could push him over the edge.

He peeked at me from underneath the handkerchief. "Not just another stylist, Annabelle. A newbie. A nobody."

Kate rolled her eyes. Talking Fern off of the ledge was nothing new for either of us.

"But you're the senior stylist, right?" Kate asked. "The veteran must be the one to call the shots."

"Veteran?" Fern let the handkerchief fall off his face as he sat up. "That makes me sound so old and . . ." He raised an eyebrow and grinned. "So butch."

BOOK 3: DEAD RINGER: A NOVELLA

"You know what Kate means." I sat down on the stool next to him. "You can use your wealth of experience to guide him. Be a mentor."

Fern shook his head. "Too late. He's taken over and changed my entire style concept for the show."

Kate leaned one elbow on the gold bar. "How did that happen? Do the show directors know?"

It was hard to imagine a personality as forceful as Fern's getting steamrolled into anything. Even the most hardened bridezilla became putty in his hands once he told them to sit down and be quiet. It was a transformation I relished watching, even though I knew I could never get away with talking to brides the way he did. He was famous for lovingly calling his brides tramps and hussies, and they adored him for it. I had a pretty good feeling that I would be fired if I attempted the same tactics.

Fern nodded, then picked up his handkerchief from his lap and dabbed at his eyes. "They'll go along with anything this Christopher suggests."

Kate expression told me that she felt as perplexed as I did. Something wasn't right about this story. Fern was a legend in the wedding-hair world and had been doing the hair for this bridal show for years.

"What aren't you telling us?" I asked

"It's too horrible." Fern pressed his fingers to his mouth. "I can't say it. You'll have to meet him."

What could possibly be so terrible that Fern couldn't even say it out loud? Before I could press him further, Kate looked over my shoulder and gasped. I spun around on the bar stool and saw what had caused her mouth to drop open. Diamonds.

The jeweler next to us was putting the finishing touches on a glittering display of engagement rings inside a waist-high wood and glass case. The rings lay on cushioned black-velvet trays in perfect rows. A stack of cream-colored business cards sat on top of the case along with a bunch of pink roses bursting out of an opaque white vase shaped like a fish bowl. A sign that read "Goodman & Sons" in black swirling letters hung behind the display.

The petite dark-haired woman who'd been arranging the rings slid the glass door to the back of the case closed and locked it with a small key. She glanced up and started when she saw Kate gaping at her.

"Sorry," I said. "My associate can't help ogling your diamonds."

Fern whipped around in his stool, his tears seeming to dry instantly. "Diamonds?"

"You're welcome to look," the woman said.

She didn't need to tell Kate or Fern twice. In mere seconds, they both were leaning the case. I slid down from my stool and joined them.

"I'm Annabelle. I own Wedding Belles."

"I know." The woman took the hand I held out. "I'm Lorinda Goodman. We met at the Hay-Adams Hotel's Love Brunch."

As soon as she said her name I remembered sitting next to her at the annual wedding planner's party. She'd told me about the jewelry shop she'd taken over from her father because, despite the company name, he'd never had any sons. At the brunch her long dark hair had been down, but now she wore it pulled back in a bun at the nape of her neck.

"Of course," I said. "I thought you looked familiar. How funny that we ended up next to each other today."

Lorinda smiled as she walked out from behind the display case. "I have to thank you, actually. You're the reason I'm doing the show. You said such great things about it that I signed up."

"Well, I hope it goes well for you. The brides who come here are usually well-qualified." That was wedding lingo that meant they could afford luxury items like big diamonds and pricey wedding planners.

"Excuse me, sweetie." Fern took Lorinda's hand and led her back to the glass case. "How many carats is that one?"

Fern's love of big gemstones was almost as legendary as his reputation. He owned several rings with stones large enough to make waving an ordeal. Even now he wore a blue topaz ring larger than some robin's eggs.

Lorinda peered into the case. "The one in the middle? That's a three-carat cushion cut."

Kate and Fern both sighed and leaned in closer to the case.

"That would look gorgeous on me," Fern whispered to Kate, and she nodded.

"Do you want to try it on?" Lorinda asked.

Fern swooned against Kate and squeaked out a yes.

Lorinda unlocked the case and gently pulled out the sparkling ring. Fern slid it onto his right ring finger.

"It's perfection," he said.

I shook my head. "Shouldn't we be setting up, Kate, and shouldn't Fern be doing hair?"

Fern frowned at me. "Don't ruin this moment for me, Annabelle."

I mouthed the words "I'm sorry" to Lorinda, but she only smiled.

"I feel like he could be a very good customer," she said.

Fern winked at her. "And I feel like you and I are going to become best friends."

BOOK 3: DEAD RINGER: A NOVELLA

I looked past Fern and Kate and the jewelry case as a collective wave of whispers passed through the room. A tall broad-shouldered man had walked in, and it seemed like every woman had sensed his presence and now stared in his direction. He had wavy brown hair that curled around the nape of his neck and dark eyes that, even from where I stood, drew me in with their intensity. This man belonged on a movie set, not at a bridal show. For a moment I wondered if he was a groom trying to sneak in early before I saw a hairbrush in his hand and a model with her hair done up in a jet-black beehive standing next to him. If this was Christopher I could understand why Fern hated him. He was stunning. I almost hated him and I was a woman.

"Is that Christopher?" I asked.

Fern followed my gaze and sucked in air. "What is he doing down here?"

"That's the other hairdresser?" Kate's face registered surprise, then admiration. The only thing that could pry her away from a case filled with diamonds was a man as beautiful as Christopher.

"You didn't tell us that the models were wearing beehives," I said. "How retro."

"Don't look at me." Fern made a face of disgust as he ran his eyes over the bouffant hairdo. "That's all Christopher. I wanted to do beachy waves."

"You've been known to do big hair before," Kate said.

Fern held up a finger. "There's big and then there's hive. I only do hive if I've had too many cocktails."

Christopher and his model walked to the far side of the room, and then our line of vision became blocked by the drape walls. Kate craned her neck until she stumbled a few feet.

Fern sniffed. "The worst part? He's actually a ladies' man. I can't compete with that."

"Really?" Kate smoothed her hair as her eyes scanned the room, presumably to find out where the hunky hairdresser had gone.

"Why do you think he's getting his way with all the women who run this show?" Fern threw back his shoulders and fluffed his colorful ascot with both hands. "But if that's the way it's going to be around here, maybe I'll leave. They won't have Fern to push around any longer."

He strode out of the ballroom, one hand on his hip, without a backward glance.

"Is your friend always so dramatic?" Lorinda asked.

"Yes," I said. "Always."

"Do you think he'll bring back my ring?" she asked.

Great. Fern had been wearing her three-carat cushion cut when he flounced out. "I'll get it back for you."

"I'll come," Kate said. "It may take both of us to pry it off his finger."

We'd only made it a few feet away from the jewelry display when the lights in the ballroom went out and the entire room was engulfed in darkness.

Strike one for the bridal show.

CHAPTER 3

A few screams then low murmuring followed the plunge into darkness.
I reached out for Kate and grabbed her arm. She yelped and tried to pull her arm away.

"It's just me," I told her.

Her arm relaxed. "Warn me next time you grab me in the dark."

"Who else would it be?" I asked. "I'm the only person standing next to you."

"I don't know," she said. "What do we do now?"

My eyes searched in the dark for the emergency exit signs, but since we were in the middle of the room with fabric walls down the sides, we couldn't see any doors. Even the main doors were blocked by fabric that was still being hung.

So this was why the fire marshal had a fit about us blocking exit signs with décor, I thought.

"Do you think the whole hotel lost power or did we blow out a fuse down here?" Kate asked, now clutching onto my arm.

"No clue." Chances were good that the musicians, caterers, lighting crew, and sound engineers had plugged in enough equipment to short out the city not to mention a renovated hundred-year-old hotel.

I could hear people fumbling and bumping around and a few yells on the other side of the room about a fuse box. The closest person to us was the jeweler, but she hadn't made any noise since the lights had gone out. "Lorinda?"

"I'm over here." Her voice came from where I guessed the jewelry case stood a few feet away from me. "Hey!" she yelped, and I heard a thump followed by some clattering and scuffling.

"Are you okay?" Kate asked.

"Someone knocked me over," Lorinda said.

Who was walking around pushing people in the dark? "Hold on. We're coming." I shuffled my way toward her voice in the dark, pulling Kate along with me. "Where are you?"

"Here, but I'm already up."

I groped a few feet in front of me and found her arm. The lights came on, and I blinked at the brightness. Kate, Lorinda, and I stood together in a tight circle holding each other's arms. We all took a step back, then joined the rest of the vendors in the room in clapping.

"Well, that was a little scary," Kate said.

"I'm sure this building wasn't wired to handle an over-the-top bridal show," I said. "At least they came back on."

"Can you believe that?" Buster walked up and dropped an armload of leafy gold branches next to us, making the pile nearly waist high. His partner, Mack, came behind him with a tall gilded vase filled with a cascade of white orchids.

Mack placed the arrangement on our gold bar. "We were in the hallway from the loading dock when the power went out, if you can imagine that."

Buster, the taller and wider of the two floral designers, adjusted the motorcycle goggles on top of his bald head and brushed some flower pollen off his black leather vest. "It was terrifying. We only had the exit sign for light. Not that I could see over those branches anyway."

Mack came up and gave me a quick kiss on the cheek, his goatee tickling me and the chains on his leather motorcycle pants jingling as he moved. Aside from owning one of the city's top floral-design shops, Buster and Mack belonged to a Christian motorcycle gang. This meant they rode top of the line Harley-Davidson bikes, wore lots of black leather, and did not approve of swearing.

"At least you didn't drop the flowers." Kate motioned to the arrangement they'd made for us.

Mack's sucked in air. "Of course not. Do you know the street value of all these phalaenopsis orchids?"

"I can't thank you enough for doing our space for us," I said. Lush was providing all of our flowers for the show as well as the gold branches that would hang over our two spaces.

Buster waved off my thanks. "We're happy to do it. As long as you keep bringing us more brides wearing huge rocks."

"That reminds me." I turned to Lorinda, who still stood next to her glass case. "This is Lorinda Goodman from Goodman & Sons Jewelers."

Buster and Mack both stepped over to shake her hand, but Lorinda stood staring down at her case without looking up.

"Lorinda?" I said. "Are you okay?"

When she raised her head, her eyes were wide, and her mouth hung open. I wondered if maybe she'd hit her head when she'd fallen.

"My diamond rings," she said, her voice hollow. "They're gone."

CHAPTER 4

Kate and I rushed over to where Lorinda stood, staring down at her jewelry case. She was right. It was empty. The black velvet trays no longer held rows of glittering rings. The back of the case stood open and the trays were askew, as if they'd been emptied and tossed back in. The business cards on top of the case were scattered and some were wet from where water from the flower vase had spilled out.

"But, how?" Kate asked.

Lorinda rubbed her head, seeming dazed. "Whoever pushed me down must have taken them."

"But wasn't the case locked?" I asked. "I thought you had to open it with a key."

Lorinda shook her head. "I unlocked it to take the ring out for your friend to try on. I didn't close it back before the lights went out."

I glared at Kate who made a point to ignore my gaze. This was all because she and Fern had to try on rings. Then I remembered that Fern still had one of Lorinda's rings. Maybe the only ring that hadn't been stolen.

"Should we call hotel security?" Buster asked.

I nodded. "The thief couldn't have gotten far. If we can have the hotel lock this place down, maybe there's a chance of finding them."

Buster hurried off while Mack came over and put an arm around Lorinda. "Why don't you sit down?" He led her to one of our bar stools.

"This has never happened to me before." She perched on the edge of the stool, her shoulders slumped. "And I know it never happened to my father. What is he going to say when he finds out?"

"Maybe he doesn't have to find out." Kate slid onto the stool next to Lorinda.

"I don't think I can hide the fact that I lost a quarter of a million dollars in diamond rings."

Mack mouthed over Lorinda's bent head, "A quarter of a million dollars?"

"I know," I mouthed back. I couldn't imagine walking around with that much worth of anything. I could only hope she had good insurance.

"I think what Kate means is that he won't need to hear about it if the diamonds can be recovered." I glanced at my assistant. "Right?"

"Exactly," Kate said. "Solving crimes is kind of a hobby of ours."

"Well," I started to correct Kate. I didn't want anyone to think that we enjoyed getting caught up in criminal cases. It was purely bad luck that had caused us to be involved in the past. I didn't need to get involved anymore. Weddings were challenging enough without throwing murder and theft into the mix.

Lorinda sat up. "So you could get my diamonds back?"

I gave Kate a pointed look that said I would kill her later for offering us up as makeshift detectives. "We might have been involved in a few cases . . ."

"You have to help me." Lorinda clutched my hands. "If my father finds out that inventory was stolen under my watch, I don't know what he'll do. He still owns the company, and he's not very pleased with me right now as it is. Sales are down. That's why I'm doing the show. I have to get the business back in the black and prove to him that I can run the store as well as any son would."

No one spoke for a moment, and I wondered if Lorinda regretted confessing so much to people she barely knew.

Buster ran back up, breathing heavily. "Okay, the hotel is locked down, and security is right behind me."

"Security will know what to do," I told Lorinda as I spotted two tall men approaching us in black suits and carrying hand-held radios.

As long as we didn't have to involve the police. I did not want my name mentioned alongside another crime. With my bad luck, Detective Reese would hear about it and show up. I wasn't sure if I was up to seeing him again. Things with the handsome detective were always too confusing.

CHAPTER 5

"So tell me what happened when the lights went out," the taller and darker of the two security guards asked Lorinda. His partner, who had hair so pale I wondered if he was part albino, inspected the jewelry case without touching it while we sat on bar stools at the gold bar. Mack and Buster had returned to designing their space while we were being questioned.

Lorinda took a shaky breath. "I was behind the case when everything went black. Annabelle and her assistant were on the other side a few feet away. Then I got pushed to the ground, and I heard some noises. That must have been when they took the rings. Then the person must have run off because by the time I stood up and felt around, no one was there."

The guard questioning us looked to Kate and me. "Is this what you heard, too?"

"It all happened pretty fast, but I definitely heard some scuffling and clattering, which I now know must have been someone messing with the case," I said.

"There was a lot of bumping around all over the room. It was hard to know what was going on or where the noises came from," Kate added. "But I heard noises near the jewelry case, too."

"And your case was unlocked?" The other security officer called from where he hunched over the jewelry case.

Lorinda flushed. "I'd opened it to show a ring and hadn't closed it again before the lights went off."

"So anyone could have taken the rings," the pale guard said, more of a statement than a question.

"I suppose so," Lorinda admitted. "The sliding door to the back of the case was wide open."

"But you could only see that if you were standing close enough," Kate said.

The guard doing the questioning nodded. "And how many people were close enough to see that?"

Kate glanced around her. "Fern had walked off, Buster and Mack were still in the back, and Richard had returned to his booth. So at that point it would have been the three of us."

I glared at her. She'd just implicated us as possible suspects in the burglary. She cringed as she realized what she'd done.

"But we don't have any motive to steal the rings." Kate jerked her head in my direction. "Annabelle barely wears jewelry and can't accessorize to save her life."

"Thanks, Kate," I said. "Very helpful."

"Do you mind if we search your bags?" The pale security officer joined us.

"Be my guest." I waved toward the canvas bags sitting on the floor.

Kate walked behind the bar and handed over her black Longchamp bag. "Knock yourselves out."

"What's going on?" Richard asked as he walked up.

"Lorinda's diamond rings were stolen when the lights went out," Kate said, coming out from behind the bar.

Richard's eyes widened. "What? Who?"

"Richard, this is Lorinda Goodman of Goodman & Sons Jewelers." I touched Lorinda's shoulder. "Lorinda, this is Richard Gerard. He's a caterer."

Richard gave me a cutting glance, which told me I'd given him too perfunctory an introduction. "We've actually met before."

She shook his hand, her face puzzled.

"I catered your father's retirement party two years ago," Richard said. "You probably don't remember."

"I'm sorry. I wasn't very involved in planning the party. My mother handled that," Lorinda said. "But I'm surprised you remember a small party from over a year ago."

Richard seemed pleased with himself. "I never forget a client's name or face. Considering some of my clients, it's both a blessing and a curse."

"All right, ladies." The taller security guard passed Kate her bag. "We've searched all your bags and didn't find anything."

Richard raised an eyebrow. "They think you took the rings?"

I shrugged. "We were closest to the case when the lights went off."

"I mean maybe Kate," Richard said. "But you've never known how to wear jewelry, Annabelle."

Kate grinned. "That's what I told them."

I folded my arms over my chest. "Very funny, you two."

"We're going to search all the booths and bags in case the thief is still in the ballroom," the other security guard said. "And no one is stepping foot out of the hotel without being searched."

"What about the show?" Mack asked. He'd sidled over from the Lush display, where Buster stood on a ladder attaching branches to a metal arch.

One of the guards glanced at his watch. "It doesn't start for another three hours. That should give us enough time to do a thorough search."

"So there's no chance you'll cancel it, is there?" Mack asked, his eyes darting to the piles of gilded branches being suspended overhead and the massive orchid cascade on the bar. I knew he was mentally calculating how much money they'd lose if the show was rescheduled and they had to order all new flowers.

"I can't make any promises," the blond guard told him. "Once three hundred brides come in here, the chance of finding those rings goes right out the window."

Lorinda put her elbows on the bar and let her head drop. "My father is going to fire me for sure."

"Don't worry." Kate rubbed her back. "I'm sure we'll find them."

"Please don't call the police yet," Lorinda said to the security guards. "I don't want to have to file a report if I don't have to."

The guards both eyed her. "Why not?"

She lowered her eyes. "My father. I'd rather he not find out unless he absolutely must."

"It's our policy to call the police for something of this magnitude," the dark-haired guard said. "But we can postpone calling them until after we've made our preliminary search and investigation."

Lorinda beamed at him. "Thank you."

"But that won't take long so if you don't want to file a police report or have the show canceled, you'd better hope those rings turn up sooner rather than later."

With that, the security guards walked away from us and started talking to the photographers who were two booths down.

Mack's face fell and a branch crashed to the floor behind us. We looked over to where Buster stood on the ladder.

"Canceled?" Buster looked like he'd been punched in the gut. "Impossible. Not after all the work we've done, all the money we've put into this."

"I have several hundred profiteroles in spun sugar cages," Richard said, his face turning pink. "And don't get me started on the brownie meringue pops that took me forever to arrange standing up in a bed of colored sugar."

Mack hurried over to the base of Buster's ladder and retrieved the fallen branch. "That's only a worst-case scenario. That's not going to happen, right?" He stared at me, his face begging me to back him up.

"If it does, the hotel is getting a bill from me." Richard stomped off.

I thought of the two options. Option one: the police. The thought of filing a police report clearly upset Lorinda. If her father was as tough on her as it sounded, I understood her wanting to hide a mistake like leaving the jewelry case open and getting robbed.

Option two: canceling the show. Even if they could find another weekend where all the vendors were free before wedding season picked up, Buster and Mack couldn't afford to buy all the flowers again and Richard would bust a gasket if he had to throw away all of the food he'd prepared. No. The show must go on.

"Of course it's not going to be canceled," I said. "Because we're going to find out who took those diamonds."

CHAPTER 6

"Don't we need to set up our display?" Kate asked as I pulled her by the sleeve toward the middle of the room.

"We can't do much until Buster and Mack hang the canopy of branches," I said. "Unless you want to find us helmets to wear as we work underneath them."

Kate shook her head, no doubt thinking back to the large branch that had crashed to the floor under Buster only minutes ago.

The setup of the show had resumed after the blackout, and the ballroom bustled with activity. The makeup artist across from us had suspended an ornate silver-framed mirror in front of her stool and bent over a long narrow table arranging the rows of brushes, shadows, blushes, and pencils she would use on the brides-to-be. She wore her black hair naturally curly and short and always rocked a perfect winged cat eye.

"Let me know if you ladies want a touch-up before the show," she called to us.

I felt Kate start to drift in the direction of the MAC and Bobbi Brown logos, and I tightened my grip on her arm. Since the makeup artist hadn't been at her booth during the blackout, she didn't make my list of people to interview. "Later, I promise."

Next to the makeup artist, stood a space designed entirely in shades of blue from the turquoise backdrop to the navy-blue linen covering a long rectangular table to the thick garland of indigo flowers running the length of the table and touching the floor on either side.

"Are those spray painted?" I whispered to Kate. Not a huge number of flowers found in nature actually came in blue, and I felt reasonably confident that carnations were not one of them.

Kate grimaced. "A better question is are those carnations?"

"Carnations in mass can be pretty," I said.

"Then this needs more mass."

I elbowed her in the side as the florist turned from putting the finishing touches on her spray-painted carnation runner. I glanced up at the sign over the table: Tamara's Flowers. "You must be Tamara."

The woman smiled and pushed a strand of brown hair out of her face. She dropped a pair of clippers into the front pouch of her Tamara's Flowers apron. "Tammy Roland. Nice to meet you."

"I'm Annabelle and this is my assistant, Kate." I shook her hand, then Kate did the same. "It seems like the blackout didn't slow you down much."

Tammy laughed. "Nah. I came in here real early setting up. It's my first show, and I wanted to get it just right. Have you two done this show before?"

"I few times," I said. "It's the best one."

"Is it always in this hotel?" Tammy asked.

"No, it moves around," Kate said. "But this is the first year we've lost power during setup."

"Wasn't that something?" Tammy shook her head. "I was unpacking my garland when it went black."

"So you were behind the table?" I asked.

"Nope. Right in front of it." She motioned to some empty boxes near us. "I had my boxes outside of my space a bit."

I glanced at the long white flower boxes jutting out into the center of the room. "So did you hear anyone moving around or running past you during the blackout?"

Tammy tilted her head to one side. "Running past me? No. But there were definitely folks moving around and bumping into things. I almost fell over trying to find my table."

"I'll bet." I thought back to when Kate and I groped our way over to Lorinda in the dark. It made sense that we weren't the only people trying to move around the room.

"Are you asking because of the lady who got her diamonds stolen?"

I must have appeared surprised because Tammy grinned and rested her fingers on my arm. "It's not a huge room, and eavesdropping is one of my hobbies."

I couldn't help liking Tammy. "Well, if you hear anything that might help us find out who took the diamonds, we're right over in the booth with the gold bar."

Tammy's eyes darted over my shoulders to where our gold bar sat underneath an ever-growing canopy of gold branches. Mack stood on the ground directly underneath Buster and passed up another branch. "You know the boys from Lush?"

"Buster and Mack?" Kate said. "Sure."

Tammy's cheeks flushed. "Would you mind introducing me? Whenever you get the chance or even after the show."

"Of course," I said. "Stop by after all the brides leave, and we'll introduce you."

We left Tammy excited for her meeting with Buster and Mack, but we hadn't gained much new information.

"What the . . ." Kate stopped short in front of the next booth and I bumped into her back.

I stepped around Kate to see what had caught her attention. A pink sign for Brianna's Bride's Wedding Planning hung over an all-white display. A deathly white woman in a white lab coat stood between a Plexiglas swivel stool and a narrow table that held a row of syringes. "Is that what I think it is?"

"Botox," Kate whispered to me. "This wedding planner is giving out free Botox injections."

"That can't be legal," I said, imagining the fits my insurance company would have if I told them I'd be performing medical procedures.

Kate dug an elbow into my side and motioned to the sign on an easel next to the woman. *Erase your worry and your worry lines by becoming one of Brianna's Brides today!* The words were emblazoned in hot pink and surrounded by pictures of hearts and wedding rings.

Kate shook her head slowly. "We can't compete with this."

"Are you kidding me?" I asked. "What kind of crazy person would want to be injected with a toxin at a bridal fair?" I held up a finger "Aside from you."

"Brides," Kate reminded me. "They're exactly this kind of crazy."

"Who is this Brianna anyway? Have you ever heard of her?"

"Never," Kate said. "Do you think she's the one in the lab coat?"

"No." I jerked my head toward a tall blonde who'd appeared from behind the drape in the back of the booth. She wore a fuchsia cocktail dress and sparkly silver shoes that seemed out of place next to a woman in a lab coat. Or at a bridal show.

She spotted us and beamed. "Hey, y'all."

"Hi," I said. "I'm Annabelle and this is Kate. We're from Wedding Belles."

She nodded but didn't register any recognition. "I've never heard of your company. Are you new, too?"

Kate made a noise of indignant protest, but I talked over her. "We've been around for about five years."

"Really? Well, I'm Brianna. I recently moved up from Charleston."

"So you're doing Botox today?" Kate asked.

Brianna leaned in to us. "Isn't this fun? One of the first things I noticed about DC was how serious it is." She made an exaggerated pouty face. "And so many girls have worry lines already. This is just me doing my part to make Washington pretty again."

Kate and I stared at her.

"Y'all are more than welcome to get your foreheads done before the brides get here."

"That's so sweet of you," I said before Kate could come back with what was sure to be a tart reply. "We're actually asking around to see if anyone heard a person running out of the ballroom during the blackout."

Brianna's eyes widened but her eyebrows didn't move. I suspected she'd already sampled her own wares. "How mysterious. Now that you mention it, I do remember hearing someone pass by me awfully fast."

"During the blackout?" I asked.

"Mmm-hmm. Maybe a minute or so after everything went black."

I made a mental note that Brianna's Botox display stood only one booth away from the door to the ballroom.

"Thanks," I said. "That's very helpful."

"Y'all don't forget to come back here for your Botox," she said as I moved Kate away from her. "I promise it will take ten years off your face."

"Ten years?" Kate hissed as I propelled her out of earshot. "How old does she think we are?"

"I'm sure she meant to be nice," I said.

Kate rolled her eyes. "I'm sure she didn't. And what about that line that she'd never heard of us? We're in every magazine and on every vendor list in the city."

"That's assuming she reads."

Kate allowed herself a smile. "Touché, Annabelle. I love it when you're snarky."

We'd reached the propped-open double doors to the ballroom. I spotted the two security officers we'd met earlier coming across the foyer toward us, propelling a struggling man between them.

"I'm telling you, this is all a misunderstanding."

Kate turned around when she heard the voice. "Well, we've found Fern."

CHAPTER 7

"I promise you, I did not steal this ring," Fern protested as he entered the ballroom with a security guard on each side. "I was merely making a dramatic statement."

"That's true," I said, walking up to the two security officers. "He was trying on the ring right before the blackout."

Neither officer seemed convinced. "Then why did we find him getting on an elevator?"

"He was in the middle of flouncing out of the ballroom in protest when the power went out," Kate said.

The taller officer loosened his grip as he gave Fern the once-over. "Protesting what?"

"The indignity of having to work with a marginally talented stylist." Fern's voice cracked as he let his head flop forward. "The horror of being eclipsed before my star has been allowed to fully shine."

"Okay." The blond officer shook his head. "How about I take the ring and return it to the jeweler for you?"

Fern snapped his head back up. "That works for me." He slid the diamond ring off his finger and dropped it into one of the officer's opened palm. The two men released his arms and Fern smoothed his velvet smoking jacket. "I hope these creases in the velvet aren't permanent."

"Looks like you're having a bit of trouble, buddy." Christopher clapped a hand on Fern's shoulder as he came around the drape wall.

Fern stumbled forward a step then righted himself. "No. A little misunderstanding is all."

Kate rested a hand on my arm to steady herself as she took in Christopher at close range. I stared pointedly at Kate, hoping she'd get my message to take her gaping down a notch. Either she didn't notice the message or pretended not to. "I'm Kate. A friend of Fern's."

Christopher gave her a spectacular smile. "Any friend of Fern's is a friend of mine."

I had to admit that not only was this guy gorgeous, he seemed charming. I could tell why Fern despised him. If I met a female equivalent, I'd want to pull out her hair.

Fern had a forced smile on his face, but I could practically hear him seething inside. "What are you doing down here, Christopher?"

"Taking a peek at the ballroom before it all starts." He swept his arms wide. "But I was headed back up. Don't want to fall behind in glamming up these models, do we?" He placed a hand on the back of the model standing next to him, a picture in her beehive, nearly sheer wedding gown, and matching elbow-length sheer gloves. The dark-haired waif made quite the contrast to his bulk. Her bored gaze passed over us, but she didn't spare even the hint of a smile.

"If the show isn't shut down," I said.

"Why?" Fern and Christopher asked simultaneously.

I pointed to Fern's now-bare finger. "The ring you had on your finger wasn't the only one that walked off. Goodman & Sons Jewelers was robbed."

Fern gasped. "During the blackout?"

Kate nodded. "Someone got all of her diamond rings."

Fern staggered into Kate, who nearly buckled under his weight. "All those diamonds are gone?"

I ignored Fern's mock swoon and turned to Christopher. "You were here when the lights went out, right?"

He motioned to the right side of the drape wall. "I wanted to inspect my booth before the fashion show started. You know we're given a free booth for doing the hair for the show?"

I glanced at Fern, who gave a small nod and said under his breath, "I asked to be on the opposite side."

"I'm next to the bespoke tuxedo booth all the way at the end." Christopher grinned. "They're interested in having me model for them."

"I'll bet they are," Kate said. This time Fern stepped on her foot, causing her to yelp and glare at him. At this rate, they would be in a full-on brawl within five minutes.

"Did you see anything?" I asked Christopher, doing my best not to pay any attention to Kate and Fern.

"Well it was pitch dark," Christopher said and laughed at his own wit.

"Hear anything then?" I corrected myself. "Or notice anyone running around?"

Christopher cocked his head at me. "In the dark? No. I mean, people were talking and trying to find their way to an exit but no one was crazy enough to run around. The floor is still covered with boxes. They'd break their neck."

He made a good point. The ballroom remained pretty chaotic and messy. It would be difficult to take a step without having to dodge a crate or a pile of branches or a rack of glassware.

"What about when the lights came back on?" I asked.

He smiled at the model next to him. "I spent a few minutes talking to the tuxedo guys, and now I'm here talking to you."

"Right," I said. "I'm only asking to help find the missing rings. If they have to call in the police, that could mean the end of the bridal show."

Christopher's face fell. "But we've been working on these models since eight a.m."

"We've all been here for a while," Kate said. "That's why we're asking around. We find the diamonds, the show goes on."

"Well, you know where I was," Fern said.

"Had you made it to the elevators when the lights went out?" I asked.

Fern tapped a finger to his chin. "No. I was on the stairs from the foyer to the elevator bank. When everything went black, I froze."

"Who else was in the foyer and stairs with you?"

"Lots of people." He shuddered. "The poor lighting team still on ladders."

"Did you hear anyone running past you for the exit?"

Fern pursed his mouth while he thought. "Running? I don't think so. But someone could have walked past me. There was a lot of noise with the guys trying to come down from the ladders. One of them slipped and yelled pretty loud."

"Well, we'd better head back upstairs. We have a dress rehearsal for the show in a few minutes." Christopher thumped Fern on the back as he moved toward the door, guiding the model with a hand resting on the small of her back. A security guard stopped the pair, giving Christopher a pat-down, then seeing the tiny girl in the form-fitting gossamer gown and waving her through. There wasn't room between her skin and the fabric for a tissue much less a tray of diamond rings.

"Can you believe him?" Fern hissed once Christopher walked out of earshot.

"No." Kate stared after him. "He's almost too good to be true."

Fern glared at Kate. "So this is what betrayal feels like."

Kate slipped an arm around Fern's waist. "You know I love you the most."

He sniffed. "Talk is cheap, darling. But I suppose the beefcake is right. I'd better go back upstairs. You'll come see our dress rehearsal, won't you?"

"When is it? We still need to talk to a lot of people down here about the theft." I spotted the security officers walking toward us and tried to change the subject. "But text me before it starts, and we'll come upstairs."

"If we can," Kate said. "This crime isn't going to investigate itself."

I stared at her, willing her to be quiet, but as usual, she missed my signal. How could she pick up a single guy's signals from miles away yet miss all of mine?

"Very funny." I gave Kate a playful shove as the security officers got within earshot. "You're such a kidder."

"I wish it was a joke," Kate said. "You know that there are few things Annabelle loves as much as poking her nose into a crime when she's told not to."

"Is that so?" The stern expression on the tall officer's face told me that he wasn't amused.

CHAPTER 8

"Do we have a problem here?" The security officer folded his thick arms across his chest.

Kate and Fern had been struck dumb once they'd realized that the head of security had walked up behind them. Fern's eyes had bugged out to fish-like proportions while Kate's mouth hung open.

"No problem," I said. "We were only joking."

He didn't appear convinced. "It sounded like this isn't the first crime you've been involved in."

"What? No, I mean, like we mentioned earlier, we've been involved in one or two incidents before," I said.

"One or two?" His gaze narrowed.

"Or three," I added.

He snapped his fingers. "Wait a second. Did you have anything to do with the murder at the Fairmont Hotel?"

"The Mayflower Hotel was the last one, actually," Kate said. "The Fairmont was the time before."

Now it was the officer's turn to appear surprised.

I glared at Kate. "You're not helping."

"He should be glad to have wedding planners like us around," Kate said. "We always helped the DC police solve the cases. Mostly by almost getting killed but, still, it was a help."

"Sometimes I got to wear a costume," Fern said. "I make a very convincing priest."

Both officers shifted their eyes from Fern to Kate and then to me. The darker one cleared his throat. "Let me be very clear. I do not need wedding planners running their own investigation. I do not want wedding planners running their own investigation. I do not want anyone wearing a costume."

Fern dismissed him with a glance. "Your loss. My performance was Oscar-worthy."

The blond officer leveled a finger at all three of us. "No investigating. I have this completely under control."

"Fine," I said. "We were only trying to help by asking people if they noticed anyone running—"

The darker officer cut me off. "Let us do the questioning, okay?"

I nodded but didn't respond.

He took a deep breath. "We called this in to the police—"

"What?" I cried. "But you promised Lorinda you'd wait."

The officer leveled his eyes at me. "If you'd let me continue, I was going to say that they can't send a team right away. Some sort of incident across town has most of their officers tied up so they won't be here right away."

I sighed with relief. There was a still a chance to save Lorinda's skin and keep the show on schedule.

"But my team is combing every inch of the building until the police arrive." He paused. "And we're questioning everyone."

"I'm glad to hear it," I said.

Fern cleared his throat. "If that's all, I need to go upstairs to finish the models for the fashion show."

"You'll have to be patted down by my guys if you leave the ballroom," the paler of the two officers said.

Fern eyed the two burly men posted at the doors. "Don't mind if I do." He winked at Kate and me over his shoulder as he headed toward the doors.

Once the security duo had walked off, Kate let out a breath. "What a killjoy. He's not nearly as fun as Detective Reese."

"No, he's not," I agreed. Detective Reese would have warned us off, as well, but he would have done it with a flirtatious smile. "And I doubt he has as much experience catching real criminals."

"As a hotel security guard? Doubtful," Kate said. "The only hotels that have had serious crimes are the ones we've done weddings in."

I cringed at the truth of that statement. "Thanks for reminding me that we're the wedding planner angels of death."

"No one calls us that," Kate said. "Well, maybe Richard. But he's one to talk."

"Do you really think this hotel security team has any chance of catching a jewel thief who seems to have planned out their crime pretty well?" I started walking down the side of the room and Kate followed me. We passed a DJ in a tuxedo setting up his laptop. Gone were the days of turntables or boxes filled with CDs. All a DJ needed these days was a laptop, a digital library of music, and a pair of speakers.

"Not really. But you heard what he said. We can't be involved in this." Kate paused at an unmanned booth displaying bridal veils and put a lace mantilla on her head.

I shook my head. "Too virginal for you. Even if we can't investigate, they can't stop us from putting together what we know so far."

Kate replaced the veil on the mannequin head. "Which is?"

"When the lights went out, someone made their way to the jewelry case, pushed Lorinda down, took the rings out of the open case, and hurried out of the ballroom." I continued down the colonnade of wedding booths until I reached the one for Richard Gerard Catering.

"We think they left the ballroom," Kate corrected me. "They could have stashed them somewhere in the room to retrieve later. The lights weren't off for very long."

Richard came around to join us from behind his tiered food display. Frosted glass shelving filled with confections covered the back of his space. Tarts, brownies, cookies, towers of profiteroles. The table in front held small bowls and tiny plates of shrimp and grits, shredded duck tacos, and vegetarian beggar's purses all displayed on Plexiglas cubes with the name of the food written in lavender calligraphy.

"The lights were off long enough, thank you very much," Richard said. "I was terrified that people were going to start running and knock over my glass shelving."

Kate glanced at Richard, then his food display, then him again. "Did you match the calligraphy on the Plexi food stands to your shirt?"

"Well done." He smoothed the front of his lavender button-down. "I hoped one of you would notice."

"Sorry," I said. "My mind is on this robbery."

"Any luck so far?" Richard asked.

"I can't figure out how someone could cut the power and make their way around the room to the jewelry case before the lights came back on," I said. "The Goodman & Sons booth is in the middle of the room."

"Well, one of the lighting panels is right there." Richard pointed to a panel on the wall across from him covered in the same fabric as the hotel walls.

"Did the security team check it for prints?" I asked.

Richard put a hand on his hip. "This is not *CSI*. That thing is covered with prints. Everyone who works in this hotel uses it to adjust the lights not to mention the lighting crew for the show. I doubt they'll find anything useful."

"Good point," I said. "But even if someone killed the lights from here, they didn't have time to walk all the way around the room."

"You're forgetting the possibility that two people pulled off the heist," Richard said. "One to cut the lights and the other to snatch the diamonds."

"So the person who took the diamonds could have been near us when the lights went off. The fastest way would have been to go past Buster and Mack's booth, snatch the rings, then leave the same way," Kate said.

"Except that Brianna said she heard someone run past her," I reminded her.

Kate wrinkled her nose. "Right. I forgot about Botox Barbie."

"So who has the booths closest to the end of the room?" I walked beyond the Richard Gerard Catering space. "There are only a few more down here."

We passed the cosmetic dentistry display, which was devoid of dentists for the moment.

Richard giggled. "I think my sugar is getting to them. They've gone through so much sugarless gum that I'm afraid lockjaw will set in before the show starts. I think they finally had to step outside."

Next to the dentists stood Christopher's booth, near the end of the row. Instead of the ivory drape that everyone else used, he'd draped his space in crushed red velvet. A black velvet tufted stool sat in the center of the space, and an ornate gold mirror hung in front of it with the words "Hair by Christopher" written in a flowery script around the top of the glass.

Kate took a step back. "Wow."

"It's like Vampira meets Versailles," Richard said.

"The questionable choice of beehives is starting to make more sense." I peered around to see if any of the security team was nearby. "Let's see if there's anything suspicious about our hunky hairstylist."

I lifted the edge of one of the black velvet cloths covering his table. Nothing underneath save an empty crate. And nothing on top of the table except for bottles of hairspray and clear glass jars of brushes and bobby pins. "Nothing. Not that I expected to find anything."

"Well, this may be something," Kate said.

I straightened up and focused on Kate holding back a panel of red velvet drape. Christopher's booth backed right up to Buster and Mack's booth on the other side of the fabric wall.

"All you would have to do is pull back this material and voila," Kate said. "You'd be on the other side and only a few steps away from the Goodman & Sons display."

Now things were getting interesting.

CHAPTER 9

"So he had easy access to the other side," I said after Kate had dropped the drape. "But what's his motive?"

"Lots of pretty diamonds?"

I gazed around me at the gaudy but sparse space. "Okay, I'll go with your theory that the cute but dumb hairdresser managed to cut the power, pass through the drape to our side, and snatch the diamonds. But then where did he put them? We saw him get patted down when he left the room."

"Don't forget that his accomplice could have cut the power," Richard said. "Giving him more time to grab and then stash the rings."

"What accomplice?" I pulled my phone out of my jeans as it pinged to let me know I had a text.

"He's a hairdresser," Richard said. "What about the model?"

"That waif in the too-tight, see-through dress? She can barely move in that thing, so I doubt she'd be much help. Besides, she's a model the show provided. I doubt he's laid eyes on her before today." I read the text from Fern. "The dress rehearsal for the fashion show is about to begin."

Richard's face perked up. "I'm up for a fashion show. Anything to save me from the DJ's sound checks."

"Well, you're wrong there," Kate said.

I held out my phone. "I don't think so. He says to come up ASAP."

"No, about Christopher and the model. He's definitely dating her."

BOOK 3: DEAD RINGER: A NOVELLA

"How can you know something like that?" I asked Kate as we walked with Richard toward the ballroom exit. We paused to be cleared by the security team that was frisking everyone leaving the ballroom with Richard complaining loudly that they were wrinkling his shirt.

"The real question is when have you ever known me to be wrong about something that involves dating?" Kate asked.

"You make a good point." Kate did boast an uncanny ability to determine if a couple was involved and even *how* involved with a single glance. She considered it her superpower.

"And you know that Christopher is dating the model because . . . ?"

Kate reached over and rested her hand on the small of Richard's back.

He took a step away. "I beg your pardon?"

"Exactly." She snapped her fingers. "That's not something you do to a colleague or a friend or a model you just met this morning. But Christopher did that to this model, and that tells me that he knows her. Very well."

I nodded at Kate in admiration. "You're like Sherlock Holmes meets Tinder."

"Look at you talking about Tinder," she said. "I'm swelling with pride."

"Just because I've heard about swiping right on your phone to meet Mr. Right doesn't meet I have any intention to ever use the app." The thought of dating being distilled down to an app on my smartphone that offered me pictures of men to either accept (swipe right) or reject (swipe left) horrified me. I'd convinced myself that I'd rather stay single than resort to finger swiping.

"Too bad," Kate said. "I'd be happy to help you swipe."

I pushed the call button for the elevators. "That's what I'm afraid of."

"Richard, tell Annabelle that she's being ridiculous about dating apps."

"Annabelle, you're being ridiculous if you're using dating apps," he said.

"That's not what I meant, and you know it." Kate swatted at him as the far elevator doors pinged and then opened.

Richard held his palm against the motion sensitive elevator doors as Kate and I stepped on. The elevator closed, and I pushed the button for the top floor.

"Remind me again why you care so much about these diamonds?" Richard asked as the elevator surged upward.

I forgot that he'd stomped off before I'd promised Lorinda that we would find out who'd taken her diamonds. "So Lorinda can recover her diamonds and the show won't be canceled."

Richard crossed his arms over his chest. "And why, pray tell, are the police not involved? Wouldn't things go faster if there were detectives here?"

"The police are busy with something else," I said. "Plus, Lorinda doesn't want to file a police report if she can avoid it. She says her father will crucify her if he finds out."

Richard nodded. "Well, she's right about her father. He's awful, and he'd most certainly blame her."

"You seem to know a lot about the man," Kate said.

"I only met him once, but he falls into my top ten list of unpleasant clients," Richard said.

"Wow, that's saying something." I'd worked with enough of Richard's clients to know that those were bold words.

Richard studied me. "So you're determined to find the diamonds before the police arrive because you and Lorinda are such good friends?"

"Not entirely," I said, stepping out of the elevator the second it arrived at the top floor of the hotel. "I do want to help her. I feel bad for her as another businesswoman who's working hard to get ahead. I also don't want to police to shut down the show."

"Are those the only reasons?" Kate asked.

Richard chased after me as I strode down the hallway to the right. "Are they?"

I stopped in front of the large white doors leading to the Altitude Ballroom. "There may be a small part of me that isn't eager to run into Detective Reese."

Richard darted a hand out and held it against the doors so I couldn't open them. "You know he isn't the only officer on the force. The chances he'd show up to a burglary are small."

"Not with my luck," I muttered.

"Anyway, how hard could it be to find a few diamonds?" Kate asked. She pulled open the door to the Altitude Ballroom and we all stared open-mouthed. The ballroom had a wall of windows on the left side with the window shades drawn up to highlight the view and let in light. Funky petal-shaped light fixtures hung from the whitewashed beamed ceiling, and a transparent, illuminated runway extended halfway down the length of the room. Rows of clear Plexiglass chairs surrounded the runway and filled most of the floor space. A white drape embedded with crystals created a backdrop to the runway, and above the runway were thousands of clear wires strung with crystals and suspended so that the room appeared to be dripping in diamonds.

Kate met my eyes. "Well, this could be a problem."

CHAPTER 10

I walked a few steps into the room so that I stood underneath the suspended crystals. I reached up and touched one of the two-inch-long clear crystals dangling overhead. A hole had been drilled into the top so it could be strung. "No one would mistake these for a diamond."

"Not when you get up close," Kate agreed with me.

Richard stood next to me, his head tilted back. "And I seriously doubt the thief would have had to time to transport the rings out of the downstairs ballroom and up to the top floor of the hotel. Much less string the diamonds up over the catwalk."

"If they got the rings out of the ballroom, a smart thief would have walked out of the hotel with them," I said.

"Unless they couldn't." Kate continued walking up to the stage backdrop and fingered one of the gems in the white fabric. "What if their plan was to leave the hotel but they didn't make it and they had to hide the rings somewhere until things cool off?"

Richard cocked an eyebrow at her. "Things cool off?"

"You know," Kate said. "Until the heat is off and they can sneak the diamonds out without security busting them."

Richard motioned his head at Kate. "I hear Godfather but I see Barbie."

Kate stuck her tongue out at him.

The doors on the right side of the room opened and a statuesque woman with a severe blond bun and a clear clipboard stepped in, followed by a row of models in wedding gowns.

"This is a dress rehearsal, ladies," she called as the models walked single file to the back of the stage behind the drape wall. "That means I want you to imagine the room filled with brides."

"Should we leave?" Richard asked.

"You, there." The woman pointed at us. "I need you to be my audience. Sit in the front row."

"I guess not," Kate said.

Richard saluted the woman's back as we scurried to seats facing the runway. We picked up the Tiffany-blue show programs from our chairs and scanned them as the models lined up behind the stage and the lights came on from the corners of the room. I turned around to see a sound and lighting tech standing at a narrow control board in the back right corner.

Kate nudged me. "There's Fern."

I stared up at the stage and could see flashes of his green velvet jacket through the drape. I knew he must have been doing final touch-ups to the models before they hit the runway. Fern always considered himself more than a wedding hairstylist. He helped brides into their gowns, he fluffed their veils, and he calmed their nerves. I often joked that with Fern around, I didn't need to lay eyes on the bride until she was ready to cut the cake.

The music began and the light changed to blue as the first model hit the runway.

"What is that music?" Richard asked.

I cringed. "It sounds like 80s hair-band music played on the violin."

"That's what I thought." Richard nodded. "Interesting choice."

The first model, a blonde in a high beehive, hit the end of the runway and paused so that the A-line skirt of her gown swirled around her legs. She pivoted and, without breaking a smile, tossed two handfuls of iridescent confetti in the air, turned, and walked back down the runway as another model came out. The second model had a smaller beehive and wore a lace fit-and-flare gown.

"Am I losing my mind or are these girls wearing beehives?" Richard said over the strange violin music.

Kate leaned across me to Richard. "Those are two separate questions."

"Charming." He made a face at Kate, then said to me, "I never knew Fern went in for sixies hair."

The second model hit her mark at the end of the runway, threw her confetti and spun around.

The blonde with the clipboard stuck her head through the drape and clapped her hands. "Where is my wind?"

"Wind?" Richard and I mouthed to each other as two fans attached to the ceiling began blowing on the runway.

"Didn't you hear?" I cupped a hand over my mouth and talked into his ear. The music and the fans made it nearly impossible to hear each other. "This wasn't Fern's doing. It was the other hairdresser's idea."

The lights changed to pink, and the music switched. The next model appeared in a tulle gown with a full skirt and a sheer bolero jacket.

"Is that AC/DC?" Kate mouthed.

The model strode down the runway, flung her confetti over her head and it promptly blew into our faces.

"This is the strangest fashion show I've ever seen," Richard yelled over the fans as he spit confetti out of his mouth. "And I had to sit through a swimwear show at my nana's nursing home once."

Kate poked me in the side as another model emerged from behind the drape wall. "There's the model who's dating Christopher."

"She seems familiar," Richard said.

"She's got an Angelina Jolie thing going on," Kate said. "Without the tattoos and six kids, of course."

As the lights changed to a bright white, the dark-haired girl strutted down the catwalk in the form-fitting organza gown we'd seen downstairs. She was pretty in an unusual way with full lips and wide-set eyes. Kate was spot-on with her comparison to Angelina Jolie. The girl reached the end of the runway and paused.

I grabbed both Kate and Richard's knees on either side of me and squeezed. "Look at her hair."

"I'm looking. It's a beehive. The car crash of hairstyles," Richard said. "I can't pull my eyes away."

"Ouch." Kate rubbed her leg. "What wrong with her . . . ?"

Richard sat up, staring at the model more intently. "Wait a second. Is that what I think it is?"

The bright lights were concentrated at the end of the runway, and before the model could toss her confetti in the air, we could see all the diamonds glittering inside her beehive.

CHAPTER 11

"You find a security guard, and I'll make sure the model doesn't leave," I yelled in Kate's ear.

"What if it isn't only one model's hair?" Kate yelled back. "What if the diamonds are spread out through all of them?"

I groaned. I hadn't thought of that. Just because we hadn't seen them, it didn't mean they couldn't be tucked away under layers of extensions and hairspray.

"Then I'll make sure none of the girls leave," I called out.

Kate nodded and slipped out of the room as the fashion show continued.

I leaned in close to Richard so he could hear me. "You keep watch on the doors, and I'll go backstage and tell Fern."

I hunched over as I crept down the row of chairs and behind the drape backdrop. I scanned the group of models for Fern. He wasn't hard to spot, as one of the few people not wearing a beehive. I wiggled my way through the models until I reached him.

"We found the missing rings," I said.

"What?" He made hand motions to indicate that he couldn't hear me over the music.

"The rings." I gestured to my ring finger, then pointed to the nearest beehive. "They're in the hair."

Fern squinted at me, then shook his head. I could understand his confusion. The idea sounded ridiculous. But still not as ridiculous as having beehives in a bridal fashion show, if you asked me.

"I'll show you." I tugged him behind me as I made my way through the models to the dark-haired girl coming off the runway. I grabbed her by the arms and reached up for her hair. She pulled away.

"Who are you?" The woman with the clipboard spotted me. "You can't be back here."

"What are you doing?" Fern eyes darted from me to the woman.

I made another grab for the beehive. "Help me reach in her hair."

The woman with the clipboard closed the few feet between us and swatted at me with her clipboard, connecting with my knuckles. I jerked my hand back and yelped. The model took advantage of the distraction and hurried back onto the runway.

"Richard," I yelled as the music paused between songs. "Don't let her escape."

As the first few chords of "Rock You Like A Hurricane" blasted from the speakers, I pushed a redheaded model to the side and ran onto the runway with clipboard lady screaming at me to stop. The dark-haired model glanced behind her, and her eyes filled with panic as she spotted me giving chase. She hiked her skirt and hopped off the end of the runway. I followed. For a girl who seemed like she could blow away in a stiff breeze, she could run fast. She'd almost reached the back ballroom door when Richard dashed from the other side of the room and knocked her over. She tried to scramble up, but Richard sat on her back.

"Get off me," she shrieked, struggling underneath his weight.

I reached the pair and stopped to catch my breath. "Nice tackle."

Richard arched a brow. "I've watched football."

"Cut the music," clipboard lady said from the runway, where she leveled a finger at Richard and me. "You ruined my dress rehearsal."

The music stopped, and the models came out onto the runway, staring at the scene of Richard in his perfectly pressed lavender button-down shirt and black pants sitting on top of a model half his size. Christopher and Fern both ran over.

Christopher's face flushed red. "What are you doing? Get off her at once."

Richard held up a finger and ticked it back and forth like a metronome. "Not until we retrieve the diamonds."

"What are you talking about?" Christopher asked.

Richard leaned over the flailing girl, put one hand on each side of her head, and shook her like a Magic Eight Ball.

Clipboard lady and several of the models screamed. Christopher's mouth dropped open, and Fern swooned against me. Before I could tell Richard to stop, the first ring dropped from the model's hair. Then another and another and the room went silent.

Richard stopped shaking and picked up a diamond ring from the floor. "Does anyone have any questions now?"

The model raised her head from the floor. "I didn't know they were in there. Christopher said he added crystals to my hair. I had no idea they were actually diamond rings."

"That's not true," Christopher said, gaping at the girl on the ground. "I never said I added crystals to her hair."

"Who else could have done it?" Fern asked. "It certainly wasn't me. And the beehives were all your idea."

Christopher shook his head. "No, they were her idea."

Richard put his hands on his hips without getting off the model. "You expect us to believe that this model picked the hairstyles for the fashion show and managed to hide the diamond rings inside her own hair?"

"Stella," Christopher said, his voice now barely a whisper. "Tell them."

The girl didn't meet his gaze. "I had nothing to do with this."

The double doors opened, and Kate came inside followed by Detective Mike Reese and the scowling head of hotel security. All three paused when they saw Richard perched on top of the tiny model with several diamond rings scattered around her head.

Detective Reese stared at Richard, then at me, and shook his head slowly. "Why am I not surprised?"

CHAPTER 12

"I suppose that's that," Richard said as we made our way through the ballroom foyer on the basement level. He'd been peeved that Detective Reese had not wanted him to shake the remaining rings from the model's head. "I suppose Fern will do a fine job, but my way would have been faster."

The woman with the clipboard had declared the dress rehearsal to be over and had stalked back to the hair and makeup room with the rest of the models. I'd barely spoken to Detective Reese before he'd gone off to question Christopher in the hotel security office. I'd been proud of myself for acting normal around him. Well, as normal as could be expected after he walked in on my best friend pinning down a model and shaking diamonds out of her beehive. I felt a little disappointed that he hadn't said more when he saw me, but at least I hadn't embarrassed myself.

"Your face is still flushed," Kate said.

I put my fingers to my cheeks. "Flushed?"

"You turned red the second Reese walked in the door," Richard said. "Even I noticed from the floor."

I groaned. Great. So much for playing it cool.

"Don't worry." Kate patted my arm. "I doubt the detective noticed. He was too busy dragging Richard off that poor model."

"He did not drag me off. He merely assisted me in standing up. But he should have thanked me for trying to be thorough."

"You promise me you had nothing to do with him being here?" I asked Kate again as I dodged the one remaining ladder in the foyer.

She drew an X over her heart with one finger. "You know I didn't. Only a few minutes passed from when I left the room to when I ran into Reese and the security guard coming up in the elevator. Hotel security had already called the police."

I studied her with suspicion. "And the detective just happened to be the one assigned to the case?"

Kate shrugged. "The hotel may have mentioned that it was a bridal show and there were nosy wedding planners."

I closed my eyes. "Perfect."

"At least the show can go on." Kate glanced at her phone. "And we still have thirty minutes before the brides arrive."

"Thirty minutes?" I said. "We've barely done any setup."

We passed through the open double doors of the basement ballroom and I stopped. I shouldn't have been surprised by how dramatically the room had transformed during the half hour we'd been upstairs because it happened with every event setup, but the change still startled me.

Like all major events, this one had come together quickly at the end. The lighting stands had been tucked out of the way and now illuminated the ceiling with swirling patterns of pale pink and lavender light. The carpet had been cleared of all boxes and crates so we could walk freely down the middle of the room. The vendor displays on either side were finished and a string quartet sat tuning their instruments on the stage at the far end.

"Am I seeing things or is that wedding planner offering Botox?" Richard said to me as we passed Brides by Brianna.

"Interested?" Kate asked.

Richard gave her a venomous look. "I would as soon get Botox at a wedding show as I'd get a massage at the airport."

"Well, I'll bet you she has a line out the door for the entire day," Kate said.

Richard sniffed. "There are some things one does not do in public."

I was with Richard on this one. If I ever got to the point where I felt the need to shoot toxins into my face, I certainly wouldn't pick the middle of the Hotel W ballroom as the place to do it. But, then again, I also knew about the powerful lure of freebies and that some of the brides at the show came to drink as much Champagne, eat as much free cake, and collect as many free gifts as possible.

"I wish we had something as tempting as Botox to give away," Kate said.

"We have the chocolates covered in gold dust," I reminded her.

She held up her two hands like scales. "Botox. Chocolates. Which would you stand in line for?"

"You forgot the gold dust," I said.

Kate eyed me. "Unless we're offering to spray the brides in gold dust from head to toe, I don't think there's much competition."

I waved to Tammy from Tamara's Flowers, who still wore her apron and stood misting her flower garland from a green spray bottle. She waved back.

"Since when are there blue carnations?" Richard asked once we'd passed the florist's booth.

"Since she painted them," Kate said in a lowered voice.

Richard wrinkled his nose. "Well, I hope all that misting doesn't make her spray-painted flowers run."

"Be nice you two," I said. "It's her first show."

"At least she's set up," Kate said as we reached the Wedding Belles display. Although the gold branches were no longer piled on the floor and now created a lush, leafy canopy over the entire ten-foot square space, our gold bar stood bare save the orchid arrangement on the far right side. A light sprinkling of gold paint from the branches dusted the floor. "Our space is a ghost town."

"It won't be once we set out the chocolates." I hurried behind the bar to where my bags had been hidden. I pulled out a pair of gold and white cake stands and placed them on the bar. "See? Better already."

Richard stood back and tapped a finger to his chin. "How many more cake stands do you have under there? A hundred?"

"I have these." I produced a pair of three-tiered dessert displays ornamented with gilded birds and set them next to the cake stands.

"And?" Richard said.

I stood up and put my hands on my hips. "And the chocolates to go on them."

"This can't compete with Botox Barbie down there," Kate said, flailing an arm in the direction of our competition.

"She's right," Richard said. "As ridiculous as I find jabbing needles in people's foreheads in public, you can't deny that the idea is good for buzz."

I reached under the bar for one of the boxes of gold-dusted chocolates in the shape of jewels and resisted the urge to slam it on top. "Buzz?

Since when did being a good wedding planner become about creating buzz?"

"Since forever." Richard came up to the bar and sat on one of the stools. "But now the buzz isn't about the actual weddings you plan, it's about the hype. The fake wedding you design for a styled shoot, the absurdly elaborate tablescape at a wedding show that no bride could afford, the birthday dinner you throw for yourself so you can post perfect Instagram pics. Buzz, buzz, buzz."

I made a face. "Fake, fake, fake." Richard knew how much I detested the idea of designing fake events for photos, even though it seemed to be the fashionable thing to do. I maintained that I didn't have time to make up a fake wedding and book a photographer to shoot it. Not when I was busy planning actual weddings.

"Smoke and mirrors, darling. Smoke and mirrors." He twisted around on his stool and gestured to the woman in the lab coat across the room. "Sadly, now the smoke and mirrors have needles and liability waivers."

"We can't compete with that. No bride will bother coming over here now." I felt tears pricking the back of my eyes. What was wrong with me today?

Richard slipped off his stool and walked around to me, draping an arm around my shoulder. "Of course they will. Not everyone getting married has the skin of a fifty-year-old."

"I have an idea." Kate tapped away at her phone.

Richard and I exchanged glances. Kate's ideas usually involved hot guys, skimpy clothes, and cocktails. I didn't see how any of those could help us now.

Kate tore her eyes from her phone long enough to meet mine. "Trust me."

Before I could protest, Lorinda rushed up to me with Fern only a few steps behind her. "You did it. You got my diamonds back!"

Her excitement snapped me out of my funk. "That was fast. I thought it would take a lot longer to pick them out of that girl's hair."

"I might have used Richard's technique to speed things along," Fern said.

"You mean you shook them out?" I asked.

Fern shrugged. "Maybe once or twice. But I got them all out."

Lorinda held up a black velvet roll of fabric. "And just in time, too."

Over her head, I could see that brides were already gathering in the lobby. Where had the time gone? I felt like I'd arrived a few minutes ago, and already it was showtime.

"You need to change." Richard eyed my jeans and T-shirt.

I glanced down at myself. I'd forgotten that I still had on my set-up clothes.

"Good thing. You've got gold all over the bottom of your jeans." Kate pointed to the layer of gold dust on my calves. Then she pointed to Richard's pants legs. "You, too."

"Perfect." Richard wiped at his pants and came away with gold on his palms.

I pointed to the gilded canopy of greenery above our heads. "It's from the branches that Buster and Mack spray-painted gold. I must have brushed up against them. And it got all over the carpet."

Fern kicked a leg up behind him. "The bottoms of my shoes are gold. How fun!"

"Don't worry. Brides won't notice your legs," Kate said to Richard.

"I don't care about that," Richard said. "These are Prada pants, and they aren't supposed to be gold. My days of wearing gold pants are long over."

"Richard in gold pants." Kate smiled. "Now that's something I'd like to see."

"Not on your life." Richard made a face at her, then walked off.

"Come on." Fern scooped my garment bag from where I'd hung it off the edge of the bar. "You can change and I'll fix your hair."

I put a hand to my ponytail as Fern pushed me out from behind the bar.

"Yes, for heaven's sake do something with her hair," Kate said.

I glanced back as Fern pulled me away from the Wedding Belles space.

"Don't worry," Kate said. "By the time you come back, this booth will be a bride magnet. Trust me."

Knowing Kate the way I did, I wasn't so sure if her idea of attracting brides would fit our brand. Or be legal.

CHAPTER 13

Once I'd changed into my sleeveless turquoise sheath dress and black peep-toe heels, Fern draped a black smock around my shoulders and steered me onto a stool. The "Hair by Fernando" space consisted of a square silver mirror suspended below his sign, a stool for brides to sit on, and a table that held his brushes, sprays, clips, and bobby pins. A pair of magazine covers of models he'd styled had been blown up and placed on metal easels to flank the space. It was simple and clean, which seemed like the complete opposite of Fern's dramatic personal style. But, then again, Fern didn't need a lot to draw in brides since his personality and wardrobe already filled the room.

Fern's space stood on the left side of the room near the entrance doors, almost as far away from Christopher's space as possible. I wondered what the show organizers would do with the disgraced hairstylist's booth now. Fern couldn't work fast enough to do hair for the several hundred brides who'd be streaming through the doors in a matter of minutes. I could only imagine the stampede once brides realized there was only one hairdresser doing free updos.

Fern pulled the black elastic from my hair so that it spilled over my shoulders and down my back. "Let's do something with this perpetual ponytail look you have going on."

"I don't always wear it in a ponytail," I said. "I put it in a bun on wedding days."

He patted my shoulder. "Way to shake things up, girl."

"Were you surprised about Christopher?" I asked.

Fern tugged a round brush through my hair. "Well, you might have noticed that he wasn't my favorite colleague."

Talk about an understatement. "Yep. I noticed."

"But between you and me." Fern leaned close to my ear. "I'm surprised he had the brains to pull it off. He might have been somewhat attractive." Another understatement. "But I never pegged him for being clever."

In the reflection of Fern's mirror, I spotted Detective Reese as he walked into the ballroom. He wore jeans topped with a sky-blue button-down shirt and a brown blazer that was just rumpled enough to look cool. He was one of those infuriating men who looked good in just about anything he put on without even trying. He stopped and surveyed the room until he saw me, then he crossed over to us in a few strides. "Just the woman I hoped to find."

"Well, that sounds promising," Fern muttered so only I could hear him.

"How can I help you, Detective?" I asked, trying to keep my voice steady. *Act nonchalant*, I told myself. *Pretend like he doesn't faze you at all. Did he grow his hair out a bit?*

Reese took a small notebook out of his blazer pocket and tapped his pen on it. "How long has it been?"

"Since?" I said, even though I knew perfectly well what he meant. *That's right. Play it cool.*

"Since you've shown up at one of my investigations?" he said. "A month?"

"More like two," I said a bit too quickly. Fern yanked at my hair as he pulled a strand from one side to the top. I recognized the signal.

Reese grinned. "Two, huh? Well, it's been a pretty dull two months then."

"We've all been staying out of trouble," Fern said.

Reese studied him. "Somehow I doubt that."

"You're so bad." Fern swatted at him with his hairbrush. "Tell him he's bad, Annabelle."

I glared at Fern in the mirror, but he didn't see me. Now who was making a fool of themselves? I tried to crane my neck around, but Fern yanked me back by my hair.

"How did you get assigned to this case? Don't you do homicides?" I asked Reese. I caught his eyes in the mirror and tried hard not to notice how they deepened from hazel to a moss green.

BOOK 3: DEAD RINGER: A NOVELLA

"We had a terror threat across town this morning so they called me in on my day off."

"Sorry about that," I said.

He shrugged and grinned. "I've had worse assignments." He cleared his throat. "You're one of the witnesses to the crime, correct?"

"Kate and I were a few feet away when it happened."

Reese scribbled in his notebook. "Did you see anything?"

"Well, the lights were out so no," I said. "But we heard fumbling with the jewelry cabinet and then Lorinda yelled. Or it may have been the other way around."

"Did you hear the burglar when they ran off?"

I started to shake my head, but Fern held it straight as he fastened my hair at the top of my head. "I didn't but Botox Barbie heard someone run by her."

"Botox Barbie?" Reese asked, grinning.

"Sorry," I said. "I mean Brianna. She's the wedding planner doing Botox injections in her booth."

"You can't miss her." Fern fluffed my half-up half-down hair around my shoulders. "She's extremely blond."

Reese met my eyes in the mirror again and held them. "Is there anything else you'd like to tell me?"

Like that I think your longer hair is sexy and I'd love to run my hands through it? I rubbed my palms on the front of my legs as I forced myself not to stare at him. "Not that I can think of. It happened pretty fast."

Fern unfurled the smock from my shoulders. "You're all done. I've saved you from Ponytail Purgatory."

I mentally added Fern to my list of people to kill if Washington ever opted for a purge.

"Okay. I guess I'll talk to the Botox girl then." Reese leaned in and tapped his notebook on my knee. "I like your hair down. You should wear it like this more often."

"Don't think I don't tell her that all the time," Fern called after him.

I stood up, then pivoted and smacked Fern on the arm. "Ponytail purgatory?"

He rubbed the spot where I'd hit him. "What? He said he liked your hair, didn't he? He came over to talk to you, am I right?"

"About the case," I said.

"Frankly, I don't know why everyone's making such a big deal about these diamonds." Fern folded the black smock over his stool. "I know they're part of Lorinda's display, but it isn't like they're real."

"I'm sorry, what?"

"The diamonds I fished out of that model's hair were not real," Fern said. "If there are two things I know it's hair and gemstones. Well, I know more than two things, but I definitely know jewelry. And those were not genuine diamonds."

I stared at Fern. If he was right, none of this made any sense.

CHAPTER 14

"Where are we going?" Fern asked as he hurried behind me, weaving through booths and around people. I passed the Brides by Brianna booth and saw her being questioned by Detective Reese. I ignored the fact that she had her hand on his arm and his back pressed up against the table of Botox needles. A part of me hoped he'd get a needle in the backside for smiling back at her.

"To see those diamonds," I said. As I approached the Goodman & Sons display, I slowed to a stop.

"Well, that's a new approach for you," Fern said.

The Wedding Belles area had transformed from simple and elegant to gawk-worthy. Club music emanated from somewhere behind the bar and provided the beat for a pair of hunky guys in skin-tight black T-shirts who were tossing bottles of booze in the air. Kate stood in front of the bar arranging gold-flecked martini glasses into an impressive tower.

"What's all this?" I asked.

Kate swept her arms open. "This is our bride catnip."

I had to admit that I had a hard time taking my eyes off the men behind the bar with their very large and very tanned biceps.

"We may not be able to deaden their foreheads," Kate said. "But we can give them some eye candy and cocktails."

"Boys and booze." Fern nodded his appreciation. "Two great things that go great together."

"Do I want to ask how you found these guys so quickly?" I said.

"Kurt and Alex are craft bartenders downtown," Kate said. "I've known them for years. You know how you go home after weddings and crawl into bed? Well, I go have a cocktail or two."

"She's one of our best customers." The brawny blond from behind the bar said and winked at me.

I did not find this surprising in the least. "So what are we serving?"

Kate clapped her hands. "They're creating a custom cocktail for us called the Wedding Belle. Don't you love it?"

I tried not to cringe. It was one thing for our brides to have custom cocktails with cutesy names but I could have gone years without having a drink named after my company. The dark-haired bartender passed me a martini glass across the bar with a light blue concoction inside and a curl of lemon peel dangling from the lip of the glass. "Try it. It's something new and something blue."

"Look at you with the wedding lingo." Fern batted his eyes at the bartender.

I took a sip. The drink was good. I took another sip. Very good.

"Kate asked us to make it a little sweet and a little tart," the blond bartender said.

"Like us," Kate said. "Get it?"

"Subtle." I passed the drink to Fern.

"Don't mind if I do," he said, then downed the drink in one gulp.

"Another?" the blond beefcake asked.

"That's a hard no." It would not pay for me to be tipsy when brides started streaming through the doors. Plus, I needed to keep my wits about me if Lorinda's diamonds really were fakes.

"I'll have another," Fern said. "And don't go light on the liquor."

I tugged on his jacket. "You can't get drunk. I need you to inspect those diamond rings again on the down low."

Fern giggled. "The down low?"

"You know what I mean." I jerked my head in the direction of the Goodman & Sons booth where Lorinda stood wiping off the top of her glass jewelry case. "Casually admire the rings and see if they're real."

Fern sighed. "Then can I have another cocktail?"

I gave him a push. "Yes, but one more and I'm cutting you off. If you drink too much, you start calling all the brides tramps."

"He does that anyway," Kate said.

"Au contraire." Fern shook a finger at her. "I call them all hussies. I only call them tramps when I drink."

I watched as Fern sidled up to Lorinda's jewelry case and began gushing over the rings. His act looked extremely convincing, probably because it wasn't much of an act. Fern was like a bird when it came to shiny objects.

"What's this?" Brianna's voice pulled my attention away from Fern. Her hands were on her hips, but her eyes were on our bartenders. "I thought you were giving out chocolates."

"Change of plans." Kate leaned her elbows back against the bar and stared at Brianna. "How did you know what we were doing anyway?"

Brianna arched a brow. "I do my homework, and I always know my competition."

I exchanged a glance with Kate. "I thought you'd never heard of us."

Brianna opened her mouth, then shut it again. She turned to leave and walked into Detective Reese. She spluttered and giggled and clutched his arms a little too hard before walking back to her booth.

Kate smiled when she recognized Reese. "Fancy a drink, Detective?"

Reese took in our booth with an amused expression.

I felt my face flush. "Don't look at me. This is all Kate."

"Guilty." Kate curtsied.

"It makes a statement. I'll give that to you," he said.

"So how's the questioning going?" I asked, flicking my eyes over to Fern trying on a ring and holding his fingers up in the air. No one could say he wasn't playing his part to the hilt. I didn't want to tell Reese what Fern had told me until I was absolutely certain.

Detective Reese stepped closer to me. "Not bad. It's mostly a formality for the report."

I tried to think of something clever to say to prolong the conversation, but my mind went blank. All I could think of was how close we were standing to each other, and my pulse quickened. Kate backed away, leaving me standing alone with the detective.

"I wanted to ask you something." He lowered his voice and leaned into me, resting a hand on the small of my back. "Do you remember the last time we saw each other at your apartment? I wanted to ask if—"

"Mission accomplished," Fern said as he walked back over to me.

The detective dropped his hand from my back.

"Wait," I said, not sure if I was talking more to Fern or Reese.

"Yes, don't go." Fern grabbed Reese's elbow. "You're going to want to hear this, too."

I tried to meet the detective's eyes to mouth an apology or an explanation, but he focused on Fern.

"What do I need to hear?" he asked.

"That I was right." Fern said. "Those diamond rings we found in the model's hair are as fake as Kate's winter tan."

CHAPTER 15

Detective Reese tilted his head as he stared at Fern. "So you think that the diamond rings that were stolen were fake?"

Fern shook his head. "I think the diamond rings we found were fake."

"Meaning?" I said.

Fern glanced behind him at Lorinda. He had nothing to worry about. There was no chance she could hear us over the music coming from behind the bar. "I tried on the same ring two times today. The first time, before the blackout, the diamond was genuine. The second time, right now, it was fake."

"You're positive?" Reese asked.

Fern leveled a withering stare at him. "I know my jewelry, sweetie. Those were different stones. I'm not saying there aren't some very convincing synthetic stones on the market but these are more along the lines of cubic zirconia, so it's not hard to tell if you know what you're looking for."

"I don't understand," I said. "Why would there be two sets of diamonds?"

"And bad luck for the thief who snatched the wrong ones," Fern said. "Is it still a crime if what you steal isn't worth anything?"

"I'm thinking yes," I said to Fern under my breath.

Detective Reese pulled out his notebook and began scanning his notes.

"The real question is where are the real diamonds if the ones we recovered aren't real?"

"Richard," Kate called. "Come have a cocktail!"

I turned around to see Richard walk up holding a floor sweeper. He glanced at his Gucci watch. "Brides will be coming through those doors in five minutes. I don't think now is the time for drinking."

Kate held out a frothy blue drink in a martini glass. "It's the perfect time. I promise you it will take the edge right off."

"Off him or the brides?" Fern asked, and I hushed him.

Richard waved off the drink. "I popped over to bring you this." He propelled the floor sweeper forward. "Unless you want every bride who walks by your space to leave dragging gold dust with her."

I took the sweeper and ran it over the section of carpet with the most gold covering it. Some of the dust vanished but a good deal remained. "This may take more than a sweeper."

Richard frowned. "Well, I didn't bring my carpet shampooer."

I pointed to the sweeper. "Wait. Did you bring this with you?"

"Of course," Richard said. "Hotels never have enough brooms, and finding someone to run a vacuum at the last minute is next to impossible, so I brought my own cleaning supplies."

I reminded myself to have Richard over to my apartment more often. With his supplies.

"How did you get gold all over the floor?" Reese asked, stepping closer to the gold patch that covered most of our space.

I pointed above our heads. "See all those leaves? Buster and Mack spray painted them and some of the paint got onto the floor."

"Leaves don't grow gold," Mack called over from his booth, where he stood placing the final few palm fronds into a large arrangement. "Not that I'm complaining about the metallic craze. It could be worse."

"We all got it on our pants and shoes earlier," Richard said. "Luckily, I also brought stain-remover wipes so my Prada pants were saved."

"And I wasn't wearing pants." Kate gestured to her short shirt and exposed bare legs.

"I wonder." I pulled Reese to the side. "Can you find out if Christopher and the model have gold dust on their shoes?"

His expression seemed confused, then he nodded. "I can do that. Let me call my guys."

While the detective walked away from the Wedding Belles booth and pulled out his phone, Buster and Mack joined us.

BOOK 3: DEAD RINGER: A NOVELLA

Kate swept her arms wide. "Care for a drink?"

Both men, confirmed teetotalers, declined her offer but gazed appreciatively at the bartenders flipping bottles and pouring their blue concoction into gold-flecked glasses.

"This is a departure from the original design, no?" Buster asked me.

"You could say that," I said. "Kate amped it up a bit."

"We have to compete with the likes of Botox Barbie over there." Kate gestured to Brianna's booth with her drink, and a bit of blue liquid sloshed over the side of the glass.

"That girl?" Mack said. "You don't need to worry about her. She doesn't have a clue what she's doing."

"You know her?" I asked.

"She came into the studio for a 'meet and greet.'" Buster made air quotes with his fingers. "Claimed she wanted to get to know us but then spent the entire time asking questions about other planners, mostly you two."

"Really?" Kate glared in Brianna's direction.

"You two have come up so fast that now you're the ones to beat," Buster said.

It felt nice to think of all our hard work paying off but not so nice to think that we were now the planners that other people wanted to knock off. So much for our moment in the sun.

"She asked us to design her booth for the show," Mack said. "Can you imagine? And she's never even sent us a scrap of business."

"I doubt she has a scrap of business," Richard said. "Smoke and mirrors, I tell you."

"Smoke and mirrors and Botox," I reminded him. "But why would she make a point of saying she'd never heard of us earlier?"

"Maybe she has memory issues. Have you seen how blond she is?" Fern asked. "And that's a bottle job, too."

"Hey." Kate tapped her foot on the floor. "Don't knock all blondes."

"Not you, darling." Fern walked over and fluffed her hair. "You never let your roots go."

I wasn't sure if that was the compliment Fern meant it to be and could tell by Kate's face that she wasn't sure, either.

"Annabelle?" Detective Reese tugged on my elbow.

I followed him out of earshot of the others. "So, was my hunch right?"

"You were right. Neither Christopher nor the model had gold paint on them. Not the bottom of their shoes, not their pants, not her dress."

"So neither of them could have been near the jewelry case to steal the diamonds."

He shook his head and gave me a half grin. "Would it do any good to tell you to leave the crime-solving to the police?"

I returned his smile. "What do you think?"

CHAPTER 16

"Not only is there no direct evidence that the hairdresser stole the rings, he swears up and down that he had nothing to do with it," Detective Reese told me.

"Since my theory that he snuck through the back of his booth to the Goodman & Sons booth is shot, maybe he didn't take the rings," I said.

"The fake rings," Reese corrected me.

I held up a finger. "But Fern swears that the rings he looked at before the blackout weren't fake. He's sure there are two sets of rings."

The detective cast his eyes around the room. "Okay. Then where are they?"

I glanced around me. The first few brides were being let in through the tall double doors at the front of the room. They carried canvas tote bags with the show's blue logo splashed across the side, and I knew they would soon be filling the bags with everything from pamphlets to business cards to favors. I hoped they wouldn't try to make off with our martini glasses. Or our bartenders.

"Well, if the diamonds in the model's beehive were fake and the guards have searched every person leaving the ballroom, then the rings must still be here."

Reese watched the brides entering with their new totes and groaned. "Don't tell me we're going to have to search every bride when she leaves."

I agreed that this was not an appealing prospect. Not only would it take forever but the brides were sure to raise a fuss.

"You planning to join me?" Kate asked as she came up to me. "I don't know if I can sell all these brides by myself."

Richard and Fern had disappeared, no doubt off to their own booths. Buster and Mack stood in front of their elaborate tablescape ready to talk to potential clients. Our hunky bartenders were flashing gold cocktail shakers and preening for the small group of brides who'd already gathered. I didn't have much time before I needed to begin passing out our cards and giving our spiel.

"Two seconds," I said to Kate.

Reese shook his head. "I should let you go. And I should remind you which one of us is the detective."

"Well then, Detective, I suggest you talk to Brianna again. She's the only person we found who heard someone hurrying past her in the dark." I leaned back to check out the Brides by Brianna booth. "And it doesn't appear that any brides have accepted her needle-in-the-forehead offer yet so she's free to talk."

"Thanks." Reese did not seem pleased by this information, and I felt pleased that he hadn't fallen under the blond bridal consultant's spell.

I joined Kate and pulled a small stack of my cards out of my dress pocket. "It seems like our boys and booze are more of a draw then Brianna's dead foreheads."

Kate gave our bartenders a thumbs-up as they tossed two cocktail shakers in the air to each other, then poured the contents out into a row of martini glasses. The cluster of brides around the bar clapped. "What did you expect? These girls may be engaged, but they're not dead. A cocktail from a hot boy will win out every time versus a needle in the face."

"It serves her right for lying about knowing us."

"Maybe she's too ditzy to remember that she'd heard of us. Fern did say all that hair bleaching could fry her brain."

I rolled my eyes. "I'd take anything Fern tells you with a grain of salt. Or a sack of it. I think she's an opportunist. She says what she needs to say at any given moment."

A bride approached us holding a blue drink. "I'll take her," Kate said to me, then turned on her brightest smile for the potential client. "I see you have your something blue already."

The girl giggled. "These are so yummy. This is my second."

Already? I hoped this girl signed contracts as fast as she downed cocktails.

"Developing signature drink concepts is one of the services we offer in our full planning package," Kate said. "Can I tell you more about full planning?"

"Well, I'm actually getting married in Ohio, but I wondered if I could have the recipe for this drink."

Kate's face froze, and I stifled a laugh. Strike one for brides. I hoped this wasn't another bad omen for the day. I glanced over at Brianna, who stood talking to Reese. I averted my gaze so I wouldn't feel irritated watching her flirt with him. Then something occurred to me. "She made it all up."

"What?" Kate asked.

"Who made up the drink?" the Ohio bride asked.

"Not the drink." I patted the bride's arm. "Brianna. Brianna lied."

"Who's Brianna?" The bride sounded slightly buzzed and very confused.

"We already went over this, Annabelle," Kate said in a low voice.

"Not about that." I clapped to focus her attention. "About the blackout. She didn't hear anyone running past her. I'll bet she made that up for the attention or to feel important or to sound more interesting."

"I'm sorry." The bride eyes moved from me to Kate. "What blackout? Is that the name of the drink? I thought it was called the Wedding Belle."

Kate peered down the row at Brianna who chose that moment to toss her head back in a fake laugh. "You might be right."

"I'm sure I'm right." The bride took another sip and glanced back over her shoulder at the gold bar. "The bartender said 'the Wedding Belle.' Oh, is that your company name, too? How fun!"

I ignored the bride. "It makes sense. Especially since she was the only person who was adamant about hearing a person rushing past."

"Whipped cream vodka, blue curacao, drop of lemon juice, lemon twist," Kate said to the bride while steering her out of our area with one hand and taking the empty martini glass with the other. "So if that's true, the only person who had any contact with the thief was Lorinda."

I focused on the jeweler, who stood a few feet away from us showing off her rings to a pair of women. "If the rings were fake, at least one set of them, what's to say the thief wasn't fake either?"

CHAPTER 17

"What do you mean the thief was fake?" Kate pulled me a few feet farther away from Goodman & Sons Jewelers. "You think Lorinda made it up?"

"It's clear that Lorinda was in on it because otherwise why wouldn't a second-generation diamond expert notice the rings are fakes? Originally I thought she'd arranged for the burglary but it actually makes sense that there never was a burglary. Think about it. No one else had any encounter with a thief who supposedly ran up in the dark, snatched a tray full of rings, and left. Doesn't that strike you as odd?"

Kate set the empty martini glass on a nearby cocktail table. "So you think she made up the thief and took her own jewelry? But where did she put it, and how did a complete set of replica diamonds end up in the beehive of a model?"

"I haven't worked all of that out yet. And I hope I'm wrong." I chanced a glance at Lorinda as she laughed with a bride and her mother. She didn't seem like the criminal type and, as far as I could tell, she had no motive to fake a robbery. To tell the truth, I wasn't fully comfortable with the idea of Lorinda setting up the crime. For one, she'd been the person to ask me to find the rings. Would she do that if she'd planned the heist herself? And for another, I liked her. She was a fellow female businesswoman, and she seemed sensible. That wasn't always easy to come by in the wedding world.

"Where did Detective Reese go?" I asked.

I scanned the room, now filled with brides. Some had come in pairs, some had mothers with them, and some had brought reluctant grooms. I could barely see the heads of our bartenders over the crowd that had accumulated around our bar.

"I'm going to go find the detective," I told Kate. "I need to tell him my theory and see if he can poke some holes in it."

Kate clutched my arm. "You're leaving me alone?"

"Why are you complaining? The brides are busy with the show." I gestured at the girls cheering the bartenders as the two men shook their cocktail shakers in unison.

"What happens if they get rowdy?"

"Well, what happens when you get rowdy at a bar?" I asked, knowing that this probably happened more often than I wanted to know.

"I go home with one of the bartenders," she said. "I don't think that's such a good idea here."

"Let's hope it doesn't come to that." I pointed to a girl dropping an empty martini glass in her tote bag. "Those glasses are rentals, right?"

"Why do people think that everything at a bridal show is up for grabs?" Kate headed off to fish the martini glass out of the bride's bag while I snaked my way through the ever-growing crowd.

I waved at the makeup artist who was misting a setting spray over a bride's face. Her line for complimentary "lashes and lips" held at least a dozen people. I cut through the line and passed by Tammy the florist whose voice had gone up several octaves as she pitched herself to brides. I understood her nerves. I'd felt faint and nauseated the first time we'd done a bridal show. I gave a cursory glance to Brianna as I walked by. She had what appeared to be a mother of the bride in the Botox chair and a handful of brides pausing to watch. Brianna's smile appeared unnaturally bright and forced, and she made a point not to notice me.

I rounded the corner of the drape wall and headed down the next row of displays. A videographer who looked too young to shave, a DJ behind a raised metal booth wearing oversized headphones, a wedding cake baker passing out samples of chocolate hazelnut cake and vanilla sponge with Grand Marnier. But no detective.

I passed the cosmetic dentist with his two pretty assistants in crisp lab coats who were distributing coupons for teeth whitening. Right next to them, Richard stood behind his towering display of confections with a handsome waiter in front holding a silver tray with cocktail napkins. A group of women loaded their napkins with sweets while Richard passed them his card. He motioned for me to join him behind his table.

"Of course you can do a brunch for your reception. We do a fabulous sweet and savory crepe station."

One of the women dabbed at her mouth with a lavender cocktail napkin. "I thought more along the lines of waffles with flavored syrups."

Richard's face froze and his gaze moved to the woman next to her. "And when is your wedding?"

"I'm a bridesmaid."

He pulled back his cards. "Enjoy the show, ladies. Don't miss the teeth whitening next door."

They wandered off, and Richard put the back of his hand to his forehead. "Waffles? Does it look like I'm running a Waffle House here? Do I seem like I've ever set foot inside a Waffle House?"

I shook my head. "I'm surprised you even knew they existed."

"I have to tell you, Annabelle, I'm not so sure this crowd is our clientele. I've had one bride asking about a cookout with hotdogs and hamburgers, one who asked if I could recreate Chick-fil-A nuggets as an hors d'oeuvre, and now Miss Waffle House."

"So far we've had an Ohio bride who wanted our drink recipe and another who tried to steal the glassware."

Richard slumped forward on his elbows. "I'm worn out, and it's only been thirty minutes."

"Has Detective Reese passed by here?"

"I think I saw him heading toward Christopher's empty booth. Why?"

I told Richard my theory regarding Lorinda and my misgivings about it. "I can't think of why should would do it. She doesn't have motive."

"Money," Richard said. "The oldest motive there is. She'd receive an insurance payout if the rings were stolen."

"But she has a successful business. Goodman & Sons is one of the biggest names in town."

"Maybe, but I know old Mr. Goodman is tough on her. He always wanted a boy and never got one, hence the company name. But it isn't only her he's awful to. He's never satisfied with anything anyone does. I'm sure she's under a lot of pressure to increase profits."

"How do you know all this?" I asked.

"I catered that party for them, remember?" Richard said, pulling out his cell phone. "I'm sure I have pictures in my phone. We did all the stations themed after a gemstone. My idea, of course. The entire extended family showed up and the old man didn't appear to like any of them very much. The feeling seemed mutual from the whispering I heard. Not that I blame them."

Knowing this made me even more sympathetic toward Lorinda. I couldn't imagine trying to live up to a father who always wanted you to be a boy.

"So receiving a big insurance payout but still having the diamonds to sell would mean more profits?"

"I'm sure." Richard scrolled through the photos on his phone. "All she'd have to do is report that the recovered diamonds were fake after the show. Maybe claim she didn't have time to inspect them in all the hustle and bustle. She'd be able to move the real rings off the property without the tight security since the rings had been found. It would be pretty believable."

I eyed Richard. "Have you ever thought about becoming a master thief?"

"All the time, Annabelle. All the time." He held up his phone screen. "Here's a photo from the party. We did one station all in green to represent emeralds. All the food was green, the linen was green, and the flowers were green."

I inspected the photo and tried not to make a face at the sight of all the green food. "That's green all right."

He took back his phone and flipped to another image. "And the diamond station. All white, naturally."

He passed me the photo of a buffet table covered in a shimmery white cloth with a massive white floral arrangement in the center dripping with crystals.

"Who's that behind the table?" I asked, pointing to a dark-haired girl in the background.

Richard glanced at the photo. "Some niece, I think. The entire family shares the same features—dark hair, pale. Very Morticia Addams."

"Well, either we have a serious doppelganger situation going on here or that girl in the picture is the model who had all the diamonds in her hair."

CHAPTER 18

"I knew I recognized her from somewhere." Richard snapped his fingers.
"So Lorinda and the model were in cahoots. Now it's all coming together."

"That pretty-boy hairdresser may not have known anything after all," Richard said over the buzzing of conversation and strains of string music from across the room. "He never seemed bright enough to hatch a jewelry heist to me, anyway."

I searched the sea of women and the occasional bewildered groom. "I need to find Reese and tell him. Do you mind if I steal your phone?"

"As long as you bring it back. I may need it to send out SOS messages if these Waffle House brides continue."

"Sorry," I mouthed as I left him with a stunned expression on his face at an approaching couple wearing matching burgundy and yellow Redskins jerseys. I wound my way through the crowd, jumping up every so often to peer over the heads. No Reese. Where had he gone?

I followed the thumping music and cheers back to the Wedding Belles display, which was now body-to-body with brides. I couldn't even find Kate until I stood on my tiptoes and spotted her blond hair behind the bar. I pushed my way through the crowd until I reached her.

I held up Richard's phone. "I found a new clue."

Kate pointed to her ear and shrugged. I realized she couldn't hear me over the music and the chanting brides. "The drinks are a hit," she yelled.

"The guys can't pour them fast enough so I'm helping." She had a row of cocktail shakers lined up in front of her and a bottle of vodka in one hand and blue curacao in the other. She poured in the liquors. "Can you add the ice?"

I slipped Richard's phone in my pocket and wiggled behind the bar. My revelation could wait a few minutes. After all, I was here to promote the company, not solve crimes. I grabbed the metal scoop in the ice bucket and added ice to the cocktail shakers, causing some of the liquid to splash out the top. "Oops."

"Don't worry." Kate clamped the tops on the cocktail shakers and slid them down the bar to our shirtless bartenders. "It takes practice to add the perfect amount."

My eyes searched for a cloth to wipe up the spill, and I felt the gears in my brain clicking into place. Where had I seen someone else wiping up a spill? Lorinda. She'd been cleaning up water from the vase of flowers on her display. And if I remembered correctly, the spill had happened after the robbery. What if the spill wasn't a spill from the vase being jostled but water that overflowed the vase once something was added to it?

I peered over the sea of heads to Lorinda's display and spotted the vase, a white bubble bowl. Opaque enough so you couldn't see inside and large enough to hold plenty of diamonds along with the flower stems.

"I think I know where the diamonds are," I said to Kate and motioned to the jewelry case.

Kate tilted her head to one side. "I thought those were the fake ones."

"Not inside the case. On top."

Both of Kate's eyebrows went up, then her eyes caught something behind me. "Weren't you looking for Detective Reese?"

I turned around and saw the detective standing at the back of our crowd, his arms crossed and a crooked grin on his face. I waved both arms at him so he'd see me. He waved a single finger in response.

"I've got to go tell him what I found out about the model and the vase."

"I have no idea what you're talking about, but I'm right behind you," Kate said.

We pushed our way through the throng of thirsty and boisterous brides until we reached Reese.

He grinned. "That's quite a crowd you've got. I'm surprised no one's dancing on top of the bar yet."

"It's a bit more interactive than we expected," I said. "I've been searching all over for you."

"I've been avoiding your colleague." He glanced over his shoulder in the direction of Brianna's Botox booth. "She's... a lot."

"Not in the mood for a forehead full of toxins?" Kate asked.

"Among other things," Reese said.

I couldn't help feeling a wave of pleasure that the ditzy blonde hadn't charmed him. "Well, I'm pretty sure she lied about hearing the thief running past her."

"I agree," Reese said.

"You do?" I thought I'd have to lay out my reasoning to convince him.

He nodded. "She displayed obvious signs of deception when she told me her story and it changed from one telling to the next."

"Well, good," I said. "That means you might believe my theory that there was no burglar at all."

Reese took a step closer to me. "I'm listening."

I laid out my theory, showing him the iPhone photo and explaining about the connection between the model and Lorinda.

He cocked his head to one side and studied me for a moment. "Not bad, Annabelle. It seems like I need to bring a couple of ladies in for questioning."

Kate paled. "Not us, right? Because I don't think it's safe for us to leave the bartenders alone with this crowd."

"Not you," Reese reassured her.

"But you haven't heard the best part yet," I said. "I know where the diamonds are hidden. At least I think I know where the diamonds are hidden."

I pulled the detective behind me through the crowd with Kate following. I tried not to notice how nice his hand felt, warm and solid. Before we reached Lorinda's display, he maneuvered his fingers so that his enveloped mine. I felt my pulse quicken and hoped he wouldn't notice.

"Annabelle, Kate." Lorinda smiled when she saw us approach and faltered only slightly when she noticed me hand-in-hand with Detective Reese.

I dropped Reese's hand. "I'm so sorry, Lorinda." I took the pink roses out of her vase and laid them, dripping, on the glass of her display case.

She stepped back as water dripped onto her shoes. "What are you doing?"

I flipped the vase upside down and water gushed down over the case and the carpet below. Kate jumped back as water splattered all of us. I shook the vase harder, and a torrent of diamond rings fell out, clattering onto the jewelry case.

"Oh, now I understand what you were talking about." Kate thumped me on the back. "Nicely done, boss."

Lorinda's face darkened, and she set her mouth in a hard line.

Reese pulled out his phone and called for backup, then took Lorinda by the arm. "You need to come with me."

"Should we stay here?" I asked as a uniformed officer walked up and began gathering the diamonds in an evidence bag.

"Definitely." Reese paused in front of me. "I'm going to take her to the squad car, then come back in and take statements." He leaned close. "Don't even think of running out on me."

"I'll be right here." My voice came out much breathier than I'd intended.

After Reese and Lorinda left, Kate turned to me. "And you said bridal shows were all the same."

CHAPTER 19

"That was, without a doubt, the most memorable bridal show in history," Richard said as he leaned against the sleek black bar in the hotel's lobby, club music pulsing in the background. Oversized geometric crystals studded the sides of the bar and created a stark contrast with the intricate European detailing on the walls and ceiling that had been retained during the remodel.

Kate leaned back on her shiny red leather bar stool with her legs crossed. "Memorable for the fake jewelry heist or for the fact that the police had to shut down the whole thing only an hour into it?"

"I had a bride in mid-updo when they cleared out the room." Fern shook his head and took a sip of his dirty martini. "Some poor girl is walking around with half her hair done up and the other half hanging out."

"If you ask me, it happened in the nick of time." Richard swirled the ice in his rocks glass. "A mother of the bride had almost talked me into a buffet themed around her Precious Moments figurines."

I pushed the two canvas tote bags filled with our leftover show props underneath a bar stool Kate had saved for me and hopped up. The bar was crowded with brides who'd been exiled from the show but who didn't want to go home, and I felt lucky that we'd snagged a corner of the bar. I peered down the length of the lobby and noted that bridal show attendees occupied all the contemporary armless chairs and ornate French-inspired settees that made up the furniture vignettes throughout the room. The

BOOK 3: DEAD RINGER: A NOVELLA

ones who weren't sitting were standing, some swaying close to the massive Grecian urns topped with ball topiaries.

I ordered a gin and tonic and saw an expression of surprise and pleasure cross Kate's face. Usually I'd have been the first one to be heading home instead of bellying up to the bar, but I hadn't seen Detective Reese since he'd left with Lorinda, and I'd promised him that I wouldn't leave.

"Cheers to the oddest bridal show ever," I said once my cocktail arrived. After we clinked glasses, I asked Kate, "Did our bartenders escape unscathed?"

"I snuck them out the loading dock. Two shirtless men wouldn't have made it five feet in this crowd." She gestured to the inebriated women around us. I didn't remind her that part of the reason the women were so tipsy in the first place might be our bar-themed booth.

"Should I ask what happened to their shirts?" I said.

Kate took a sip of her cocktail. "Suffice it to say that a few brides got overly excited and the shirts got damaged in the melee."

"Basically, the women ripped their shirts off?" I asked.

"In a nutshell, yes," Kate said. "Who knew engaged women could be so wild?"

Richard gave a small shudder and drained his glass. "I think you mean terrifying."

"Just because someone wants to serve local wine does not make them terrifying," I told him.

"Agree to disagree," Richard said.

"I don't know about the rest of you." Fern nibbled on an olive. "But today has restored my faith in bridal shows."

"We were shut down," I said. "And vendors were arrested."

Fern nodded. "Wasn't it the most fun you've had in ages? I wish we hung out like this all the time."

"You're only saying that because you got to drink, watch our hunky bartenders, and shake a girl's head until diamonds fell out," I said.

"Exactly." Fern winked at me. "If I could shake some of our brides' heads like that I'd be in heaven."

Richard scanned the crowd. "Are Buster and Mack still downstairs?"

"The branches are harder to take down than they were to put up." I sipped my gin and tonic. "Plus, the police needed samples as evidence, so I doubt they'll be done for a while."

"Having the police at our event breakdowns is starting to become a very bad habit," Kate said.

435

I wagged a finger at her. "Technically, a bridal show isn't a wedding so it doesn't count."

"You keep telling yourself that, Annabelle," Richard said. "But how many other planners have a detective on speed dial?"

"Speaking of other wedding planners." And detectives. I let my eyes wander around the lobby. "What happened to Brianna? I saw her when we started to break down, but then she disappeared."

Kate shrugged. "Who knows? I'm surprised she isn't here at the bar passing out business cards."

"Wasn't our hot detective questioning her?" Fern asked.

"Reese?" I said. "You saw him questioning Brianna after the show?"

Fern plucked an olive out of his martini glass. "Very intensely if you ask me."

I took a gulp of my gin and tonic. So much for waiting for Reese. I bet he'd forgotten all about telling me not to leave the second Brianna batted her eyelashes at him. And I'd probably imagined the spark I'd felt between us and read too much into his actions. When it came down to it, he'd still never made a move. I felt a wave of irritation at myself for getting my hopes up again. I drained my glass and stood. "I think I'm going to head out."

"What?" Kate said. "I thought you promised to hang out with us and debrief."

"She did finish her drink," Fern said. "That's a first."

"I'm sorry." I scooped the tote bags from the floor. "But it's been a long day."

"You can say that again." Richard kissed me on both cheeks. "Call me later."

I nodded and then gave Fern an air kiss, trying to ignore his pout. My heels clicked on the black-and-white-tile lobby floor as I made my way to the valet parking stand on F Street, which was as crowded with brides as the bar. I fished my valet ticket from my bag and gave it to the nearest attendant.

"You might as well wait inside," he said. "It's going to be at least ten minutes."

Great. I went back inside and ducked into a side room off the lobby with a cluster of black leather and metal slope-backed chairs. The walls were covered in a paper that made it appear that the room had floor-to-ceiling bookshelves. Uber-chic hotels didn't have walls of books, I reminded myself. They had wallpaper that made it seem like you were surrounded by walls of books.

The room was tucked away enough that it was free from brides, so I set my bags on the floor and sank into a chair to wait, closing my eyes to avoid looking at the concentric prism pattern on the brown and beige carpet and enjoying the relative quiet.

"I thought you promised not to run off."

My eyes snapped open to find Detective Reese standing in front of me.

"Me?" I stood up, the gin and tonic giving me more courage than usual. "You're the one who disappeared."

He angled his head at me. "It took longer than I expected to question Ms. Goodman and her niece."

"So they were in on it together?" Curiosity overpowered my irritation.

Reese nodded. "It was pretty clever. Ms. Goodman planted the fake rings in her niece's hair before the blackout, and then the girl shut off the power while her aunt dumped the real rings into the vase and acted like a burglar had made off with them."

"So they planned for the fake rings to be discovered?"

"Apparently the plan included setting up the hairdresser. The model could claim innocence, and they could make off with the real diamonds after the show ended."

"And then report them as fakes afterward?" I asked.

"And claim they hadn't noticed in the chaos of the show," Reese said.

"Good thing Fern can spot a fake gemstone at a hundred paces."

Reese gave me a half smile. "Your friends do have their uses."

"Please." Now it was my turn to cross my arms. "You never could have cracked this case without us."

Reese stepped closer to me. "It wouldn't have been so hard if you hadn't sent me on a wild goose chase."

"Wild goose chase?" This was some gratitude considering I'd solved his case for him.

"The eyewitness who claimed to have heard the burglar run past her?"

I rolled my eyes. "Brianna? Don't blame me for that one. And it's not like you seemed to mind questioning her."

Reese unfolded his arms from across his chest. "What are you talking about?"

I felt my face flush. "Never mind. It's none of my business who you like."

Reese shook his head. "For your information, I spent the past fifteen minutes reading her the riot act for giving a false police report and impeding an investigation. Do you really think I'd like someone like that?"

I opened my mouth but shut it again, not sure how to respond. It made me happier than I wanted to admit that Brianna got in trouble with the police and even happier that Reese didn't like her.

"For someone who's pretty good at uncovering clues, you can be pretty clueless," he said.

Before I could revel in Reese admitting I had crime-solving skills or react to being called clueless, he leaned down and slipped one hand around my waist and flattened it into the small of my back. My irritation melted as I pressed against him.

"I'd say it's very much your business who I like," he whispered into my ear, his mouth brushing against my earlobe and sending shivers down my spine.

I gripped the back of the nearest chair to keep my quivering knees from buckling. If I'd been in any state to speak, I would have told Reese that, for once, I agreed with him.

FREE DOWNLOAD!

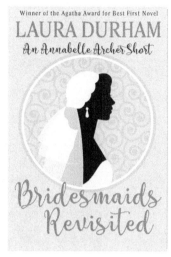

A LUXURY BRIDAL SHOWER.
THE STRESS IS HIGH.
THE PRESENTS ARE GONE.
THE BRIDESMAIDS ARE SUSPECTS.

CAN ANNABELLE UNMASK THE THIEF?

amazon kindle

nook

kobo

 iBooks

Get your free copy of the short story "Bridesmaids Revisited" when you sign up to the author's mailing list. Go to the back of the book to sign up.

BOOK 4: REVIEW TO A KILL

Annabelle Archer Wedding Planner Mystery
by Laura Durham

CHAPTER 1

"This rain is going to ruin the view of the White House." I threw open one of the french doors that led to the Hay-Adams Hotel's narrow balcony overlooking both Lafayette Park and the most famous address in Washington, DC.

The gray clouds that hung over the city had been sending a steady mist of rain since the morning and, as it was now midafternoon, my hopes for a sunny wedding day, along with my hopes for a happy bride, were dwindling fast. I stepped onto the balcony and let the fine droplets settle on my skin. I breathed in the fresh scent of rain and felt glad it had washed away the pollen haze that had been hanging over the city for the past week, even if it did have to happen on the one day I needed clear skies. I ignored the clattering noise of the wedding band setting up behind me and took a moment to soak in the relative peacefulness of standing nearly ten stories above the city on a sleepy, rainy Saturday.

I reached into the pocket of my dress and felt for the packet of gummi bears my assistant, Kate, had given me earlier in the day. I popped a few into my mouth and savored the sugar rush. They were probably the only calories I'd get until much later that night so I didn't feel guilty about them. I held up the Cellophane candy packet to Buster, one half of my floral designing duo, and jiggled it.

He shook his head, pulling at his brown goatee with his fingers. "I'm too stressed to eat right now."

"Don't worry. It might clear up," I said, dropping the candy back into my pocket and patting Buster on his thick tattooed arm. I didn't fully believe what I said but, as the owner of Wedding Belles, one of DC's top wedding-planning companies, I'd learned that is was crucial to keep my creative team positive on the wedding day. Even if that meant lying to them.

Buster raised his eyebrows and the motorcycle goggles he wore on his forehead followed. "It's hard to pull off a springtime in Paris theme when it looks like a hurricane's brewing outside."

"Don't you think you're exaggerating a bit?"

Buster was usually the more even-keeled half of the floral design duo from Lush. His partner, Mack, was equally tattooed and leather-clad with a dark red goatee instead of a brown one but, generally speaking, the more emotional of the pair. I hoped Buster's nerves didn't mean that Mack was in a full-scale meltdown.

I turned from the view to look for Mack and glanced over the ballroom that had been transformed into springtime in Paris. One of the biggest selling points for holding a wedding at the Top of The Hay, the name for the iconic hotel's rooftop ballroom, was the two walls of glass french doors that wrapped around the L-shaped room and provided both natural light and a stunning view. It was the perfect pick for a bride wanting any type of garden theme, and it had been a natural fit for our bride who wanted to recreate Paris in the spring. Whitewashed Eiffel Towers were interspersed between the towering arrangements of pink tulips on a runner of grass that extended the length of the long, rectangular tables. A tiny easel sat at the top of each place setting with a guest's name painted over a pastel impressionist background, and white ladder-backed chairs wore pale-pink tulle skirts.

"There you are," I said as I spotted Mack walking toward us under the hanging flower garden that Buster had installed in the ceiling alcove over the dance floor.

Mack dodged a hanging tulip. "Well, I delivered the bride's bouquet."

"And?" I asked, not sure if I wanted to know the bride's reaction.

Mack flopped down in a nearby chair. "Let's just say that if I cursed, now would be the time I'd pick some choice words about our bride."

I cringed. Mack and Buster were members of a Christian biker gang, and I'd never heard a swear word leave their lips.

Buster closed the french doors. "She didn't like the collar of nerines around the tulips?"

"Who knows what she hated more?" Mack tugged at a loose thread on his black leather vest. "She said it gave her a headache."

"The scent of it?" I asked. "I thought you specifically chose flowers with no scent."

"I did," Mack said. "She approved every flower in the whole wedding, remember?"

"How could I forget?" I recalled every painstaking moment of the planning ordeal with Tricia, from bringing blooms to her house for her to sniff test to sending her MP3 files of every song the band played so she could eliminate songs that were in a key she found irritating to having the chef forward her the ingredient list for every bite that would be served so she could identify offending foods.

"So she's not going to carry it down the aisle?" Buster asked.

"She's not going to walk down the aisle." Kate stood in the open doorway across from us, her hands on her hips and the toe of one high heel thumping on the carpet.

I closed my eyes and dropped my head for a second. "Not this again."

"Yep. She claims the stress has made her too sick to attend her own wedding." Kate strode across the room, her blond bob bouncing with each step. She had long legs that she preferred to show to their full advantage with short skirts, even on a wedding day, so her fitted black dress stopped several inches north of her knees. When she reached Mack, she sat in the chair next to him, crossing her legs so that her dress rose even higher on her thighs.

"How can she be stressed?" I asked. "We've done everything for her."

"Beats me." Kate shrugged. "But I never understood all the syndromes she claims to have."

Buster held up one finger. "There's the hypersensitivity to light."

"And migraines brought on by the scent of lilies," Mack said. "And garden roses and peonies and lily of the valley."

Kate snapped her fingers. "And don't forget that anything louder than a speaking voice can make her swoon."

"Why is she having a wedding in the first place?" Buster asked. "It's filled with all the things she claims make her sick."

"I'm sympathetic to the girl if she really has all these problems," Mack said. "I know what it's like to get a migraine. But her symptoms seem to come and go."

Kate lowered her voice. "She's an attention whore. Why else would you be such a hypochondriac?"

Mack swatted at her. "Language, young lady."

Kate rubbed her arm where Mack had made contact. "Sorry, but I stand by my assessment. Annabelle and I caught her doing one of those

Insanity workout DVDs when she claimed to be too exhausted to get out of bed."

"It's true," I said. "She cancelled one of our first meetings so we decided to drop her welcome box off at her house as a surprise."

"The surprise was us catching a glimpse of her working out like a maniac through a gap in her front curtains." Kate shook her head. "I knew she couldn't look as buff as she does by staying in bed all the time."

"Did you call her on it?" Buster asked.

"No. We mentioned it to her mother but she said that Tricia was in therapy to work through her hypochondria and need for attention and that we shouldn't say anything or it would make it worse."

"Worse than this?" Buster's motorcycle goggles lifted with his eyebrows.

Kate touched Buster's thick forearm. "That's what I said."

"Since she's a rich hypochondriac who needs a lot of attention, her mother thought the wedding would actually help," I said. "What better way to get more attention than a big wedding?"

"Not if you don't show up for it," Mack said.

I shook my head. "I'm sure she's bluffing."

"She probably needs some of the patented Annabelle Archer Zen," Kate said. She loved to tease me about being able to calm down even the most nervous brides just by being around them. So far, though, Tricia Toker had pushed the limits of even my Zen energy.

I sighed and mentally steeled myself for the bride's histrionics. "I'll go check on her. Fern should be done with everyone's hair by now."

"Fern is not done because Fern can't work under these conditions." The hairstylist to Washington's most elite, and all of our brides, stood in the doorway of the ballroom with a can of hairspray in one hand and a round brush in the other. Since Fern always tried to dress to the theme of the wedding, he wore a navy and white striped boatneck T-shirt with white pants and a navy beret. I noticed that his beret had slipped from its earlier jaunty tilt, and strands of dark hair had escaped from his low ponytail. He threw his brush on the floor. "Fern quits."

CHAPTER 2

I held Fern's hand as we rode down the hotel elevator, listening to the soft pings as we passed each floor. It had taken a significant amount of convincing to get him into the elevator with me, and I held his hand partly to comfort him and partly to make sure he wouldn't make a dash for it when the doors opened.

I took a deep breath to brace myself for the impending interaction with the bride and inhaled the scent of designer hair products that surrounded Fern. I knew it was a mixture of the ones he wore on his own hair and the ones he used on his clients. The only time I ever smelled like expensive hair product was when I allowed Fern to do my hair, which wasn't often enough for his liking.

I squeezed his hand. "I'm sure it's not so bad."

Fern arched an eyebrow at me. "How am I supposed to put her hair in a high bun if she doesn't like to feel pressure on her head?"

"Haven't you been her stylist for years?" I leaned against the brass rail that ran the short length of the elevator's back wall and stepped out of my black heels. I'd left my flats upstairs and would switch back into them once I'd seen the bride. I liked to look dressy for the client but couldn't bear to be in heels for an entire wedding day as Kate could.

"Yes, but she only gets her hair cut once every six months or so, and I basically go to her house, wave the scissors over her head, fluff it up, tell her she looks divine, and leave."

"And she pays you for that?" I shook my head. "I'm in the wrong business."

Fern squeezed my hand. "I could have told you that a long time ago, sweetie."

"How do you deal with a client who's making up all these issues?" I asked Fern. His years as a hairdresser to the elite had given him an incredible level of patience and insight into people.

"Her mother clued me in years ago and asked me to play along, so I do." Fern twitched his shoulders. "I have clients with genuine sensory issues and actual chronic fatigue syndrome so it's not hard to tell that Tricia's illnesses are fabricated. It's sad she feels like she needs to do it."

"I guess." After a tortuous planning process, I had a hard time feeling too sympathetic but I knew Fern had a point. A person had to be seriously damaged to pretend they were always sick. Plus, I'd learned early on in planning weddings that the most difficult people usually were the most unhappy with themselves.

"I'm sure we can figure this out," I said as the elevator door opened and we faced a wooden accent table with a white orchid plant. "Can you convince her to wear her hair down?"

Fern led me to the right and down the hall to the very end where the largest suites in the hotel were situated. He paused in front of a cream-colored door with an engraved gold plate that read the Jefferson Suite in cursive. "I suppose I could be persuasive if I wanted to be."

"Trust me." I knocked lightly. "You want to be."

A woman with a silvery-blond helmet of hair opened the door. "Thank heavens you're here, Annabelle." She pulled me inside. "Where have you been?"

I reflexively glanced at my watch even though I knew I'd been upstairs for less than thirty minutes. "I had to check on the ballroom setup, remember?"

The bride's mother nodded. "That's right. You told us that, didn't you? It's just that Tricia is having such a hard time dealing with all these disasters."

"What disasters?" I asked. I looked around the spacious suite, which was decorated sumptuously in shades of ivory and cream. Twin sofas topped with oversized fringed cushions were flanked by a pair of soft chairs. A mahogany dining room table surrounded by upholstered chairs sat behind them. A wooden sideboard held the remains of breakfast. Champagne chilled in an ice bucket. And the maid of honor, and only attendant, sat in the makeup chair by a row of tall windows.

BOOK 4: REVIEW TO A KILL

So far every vendor had been on time and every delivery had been accurate. We weren't missing flowers or dealing with late makeup artists or even a late breakfast delivery. After the challenges of the planning, everyone was on their toes. And counting down the minutes until it was over.

Fern dropped my hand and took a few steps toward the closed door that led into the attached bedroom, where I assumed the bride was resting. "Why don't I check on her?"

As Fern walked away I took Mrs. Toker's hands in mine. Sometimes mothers needed someone to listen to them, and I could validate feelings until the cows came home. "So tell me about these disasters."

The mother of the bride gnawed at her lower lip. "Well, the rain for one."

"You know I can't control the weather, Mrs. Toker," I said. "And we chose an indoor venue for the precise reason that Tricia didn't want to worry about the weather if we did a tented wedding."

The mother nodded like her head was attached to a trip wire. "We just wanted this day to be perfect. After her illness and her father's death, Tricia deserves a day all about her."

From what I'd seen over the months of planning, every day was all about Tricia. And I had a hard time believing that the girl had become as spoiled as she was only after her father's death a little over a year earlier. A girl had to be indulged all of her life to be ruined as badly as Tricia Toker.

Even though her extreme hypochondria was clearly something she'd honed over years, this was the first time I'd had a bride use undiagnosed illnesses to get attention, controlling every person she knew and manipulating them with equal parts guilt and pity. But even so, she'd alienated almost everyone she knew so that only a few diehards like her mother, fiancé, and maid of honor remained at her side. That was also the reason that her guest count was less than one hundred and a decent number of the guests were from her late father's company. I assumed they were attending out of respect for the parents and to stay on the mother's good side as she'd taken over the running of his business.

Fern poked his head out of the bedroom. "The bride's asking for you."

I left Mrs. Toker chewing on her thumbnail and went into the dark bedroom. I could make out the form of the bride reclining on the king-sized bed, and as my eyes adjusted to the lack of light, I saw that she still wore her bathrobe. I tried not to focus on the fact that, according to my schedule, she'd be walking down the aisle in less than an hour. We'd never had a bride get married in a bathrobe, but there was a first time for everything.

"Did you want to talk about the flowers?" I asked.

She waved a hand at me. "No. They're fine. It was the florist's cologne that set off my migraine."

I knew Mack didn't wear cologne, but I didn't dare argue with her if she'd made peace with her bouquet. That put us one step closer to walking down the aisle.

"Get Madeleine in here, too," the bride said to Fern.

I heard him sigh as he called to the maid of honor. I leaned back so I could see through the open doorway and into the living room. The petite strawberry blonde hopped down from the makeup stool and hurried into the bedroom.

"Do you need anything, Tricia?"

The bride took a deep breath and exhaled. "I know you hate wearing your hair pulled back because it makes you look like a ferret, but I need you to wear it up since I'm going to have my hair down now. I want to be the only one with loose hair."

Fern and I exchanged a look. This was officially the first time I'd ever heard a bride tell a bridesmaid that she looked like a ferret. It was not the first time I'd had a bride try to make a pretty bridesmaid look worse than her, though. Tricia wasn't plain. Her dark hair and ice blue eyes made her striking, but she wasn't delicate and pretty in a feminine way like her friend.

I glanced at Madeleine, who looked nothing like a ferret, and whose eyes were unblinking. Madeleine nodded and forced a smile. "Of course, Tricia. Whatever you want. It's your wedding day."

Tricia beckoned her only attendant over and grasped her hand. "Madeleine has been my best friend since our freshman year in college. Madeleine and Dave and me. The Three Musketeers, remember?"

Madeleine laughed. "All for one and one for all."

Fern and I laughed politely, but I wondered why either of us needed to be present for this moment.

Tricia sat up slowly, propping herself on her elbows. "By the time Fern finishes your bun, I should have recovered enough to do my hair."

"Do you need me?" I asked, taking a step toward the door. "I was going to check on the ceremony setup downstairs."

"You can go." Tricia rubbed her temples. "But don't send me Kate again. Her bouncing makes my head pound." She reached for her phone on the bedside table and began typing with her thumbs.

For the thousandth time since answering Tricia's initial phone call, I regretted ever meeting her.

Fern walked me to the door and kissed me on the cheek. "At least this hussy doesn't have a problem with flouncing."

"I'll be back up in thirty."

"She'll be ready or she'll be dead," Fern whispered in my ear.

"Talk about a Sophie's Choice."

He winked. "You're telling me."

As I pulled the door to the suite closed behind me, my cell phone starting singing "Pachelbel's Canon" from inside my pocket. I pulled it out and answered before I noticed the name of the caller.

"Wedding Belles, this is Annabelle."

"It's me." Me was Richard of Richard Gerard Catering, my best friend since I'd started my wedding-planning business more than six years earlier and he'd taken me under his wing. Richard was known for his impeccable style, his cutting-edge cuisine, and his love of designer clothes. I must have brought some sort of balance to his life because I didn't own one clothing label that met his approval, I could subsist on Diet Dr Pepper and takeout Thai for weeks, and my style would be called casual at best. "How's it going with Too Tired Tricia?"

"Very funny," I whispered as I walked down the hallway to the elevator. "I think we're going to get her down the aisle."

"I'd hope so considering the budget on this one."

"You know I would have brought it to you if I could have," I said. "But the hotel was the best fit." Richard's catering company only did catering for mansions, museums, and historic sites that didn't have their own kitchens.

"Don't mention it. It's nice to have a weekend off for once. Anyway, I don't think I could take the stress of waiting to see what she writes."

I paused in front of the elevator bank. "What who writes?"

"The bride," Richard said. "Didn't I tell you that she has quite the reputation in the culinary world?"

"She's a culinary writer?" I didn't think she did anything since she was both wealthy and busy pretending to have chronic fatigue syndrome.

"No. She's famous for her poisoned-pen reviews. She's panned just about every restaurant in town."

I felt lightheaded and put my hand out to the wall to steady myself. "Why didn't you mention this earlier?"

"I just put two and two together." He paused and cleared his throat.

"But I'm sure that's just restaurants. I don't think she'll write bad reviews about her own wedding."

I glanced back at the door to the Jefferson Suite and remembered her typing away at her phone. "I hope you're right."

CHAPTER 3

"She's an internet troll, too?" Mack clutched Kate's arm for support.

Kate staggered a few steps since Mack had a hundred pounds on her, and then she steadied herself. "Just when I thought the bride couldn't get any more charming."

I'd texted Kate, Buster, and Mack to meet me downstairs in the Hay-Adams Room. We were using the smaller downstairs room for the ceremony, and then guests would go upstairs to the rooftop for the reception. I wanted to put the finishing touches on the ceremony and drop the latest bombshell in person. I needed to be sure none of them were standing on the balcony when they heard that our difficult bride had a penchant for the poisoned pen.

Kate and I had placed the ceremony programs on the chairs while Buster and Mack had draped ribbon across the back of the aisle we'd created using rows of rustic chairs with woven cane backs. Earlier in the day, they'd laid an aisle runner made out of jute and had lined the sides of it with a thick carpeting of moss and colorful tulips that appeared to be growing out of it. At the front of the aisle, they'd created a canopy out of branches and ivy in front of a solid wall of boxwood that was dotted with wire-basket window boxes crowded with lavender tulips and pink hyacinths. Candles had been lit, and the smell of burning wax mingled with the fresh smell of greenery.

Guests were gaping and angling for pictures with their phones as they entered the room, so I pulled my crew off to the side. "All we have to do is make sure that everything is perfect, and she won't have any reason to write a bad review."

Buster crossed his arms over his chest. "You know trolls don't work that way. They do it for the attention, not because they're actually trying to give an honest review."

"Maybe I misspoke when I referred to her as an internet troll," I said, keeping my voice low so the guests, also the troll's friends and family, wouldn't hear.

"You didn't." Kate looked up from scrolling on her phone. "I already found one of her reviews on the Wed Boards and it's not good."

The Wed Boards were an online forum where brides compared weddings, offloaded used wedding accessories, and shared what they called "picks and pans" of wedding vendors.

Mack craned his neck to see Kate's phone. "How could she have a Wed Boards review yet? We're in the middle of her wedding."

"She's one of those Weddies," Kate said, referring to the brides who lived on the Wed Boards and thought that obsessing about weddings made them qualified to be wedding planners.

"You're sure it's her?" I asked.

She looked up at me. "The username is TriciaandDaveatTheHay."

Mack gave a low whistle. "That's pretty specific."

"She trashed a florist she called before she hired us. Gave them one star," Kate said.

Mack looked affronted. "She called another florist? I'm glad I didn't know that before you brought her to us."

Kate cleared her throat and began to read the review. "Even though we didn't hire this florist, I was disappointed that they couldn't bother to return my call within the same afternoon. Clearly this business can't manage their time well."

"The same afternoon? Are you kidding me? I can understand twenty-four hours but the same afternoon?" Buster said. "What if we have a long meeting with a bride or a walk-through off-site?"

I dug in my suit pocket for my stash of gummi bears and popped a handful in my mouth, savoring the comforting rush of sugar. "Well, she does spend most of her time in bed pretending to be ill, so I'm sure an afternoon feels like forever."

"I can't believe she hired us," Kate said. "We've certainly let calls go for more than a few hours."

"I think I just happened to pick up the phone the day she first called," I said.

"Good thing, right?" Kate said.

"Is it?" I couldn't help wondering if the florist who got the review for not returning a call got off easy. Were we all in for one-star reviews by a bride who loved getting attention for bad behavior?

Buster nudged me. "Groom at six o'clock."

I turned around to see the tall, handsome groom in his white dinner jacket scanning the room.

"Are you ready to get married?" I asked as I approached, giving him my best "let's do this" smile.

Dave rubbed his hands together and smiled without meeting my eyes. "Sure. It looks great in here. Very French."

"I'm glad you like it." I took in the room alongside him and had to admit that it looked spectacular.

"Not that I'm the one you have to please." He laughed and went back to rubbing his hands.

"We try to make everyone happy on a wedding day," I said. "Can I get you anything before we start the processional? Water? A beer?"

I hoped the groom held some sway with his future wife, and I hoped it wasn't too obvious that I was kissing his ass. What I really felt like offering him was a new identity and a one-way ticket to Papua New Guinea so he could run away from Tricia Toker forever.

He shook his head and a brown curl came loose and dropped onto his forehead. "No, Tricia would be livid if I drank before the ceremony."

My phone vibrated with an incoming text and I pulled it out of my pocket to look. Fern had the bride ready and was bringing her and the maid of honor down.

I put my hand on the groom's elbow. "Why don't I go ahead and get you tucked away with the officiant for the ceremony?"

He jumped at my touch. "It's time?"

I nodded and felt like apologizing. But I reminded myself that it wasn't my fault this nice guy was marrying an awful woman or that he'd gone all in and worked for her family company, too. I was only the wedding planner, not the idiot who'd proposed to her. Whenever this scenario played itself out in my work, I told myself that the seemingly terrible bride or groom must have some wonderful qualities they kept hidden from the world and only their betrothed saw. In Tricia's case, the qualities must have been hidden very deeply.

I steered the groom back to his holding room then pulled Kate outside the ballroom with me to wait for the bride. "Where are Buster and Mack?"

"They went back upstairs when I told them the bride would be coming down soon."

"Cowards," I said.

"Lucky cowards," Kate said under her breath.

I recalled the bride's aversion to Kate's bounciness. "Why don't you go stand next to the harpist, and I'll give you the cues from the door?"

"And avoid an encounter with Tricia the Troll? You don't have to tell me twice." Kate headed back into the Hay-Adams Room before I could tell her not to call the bride that out loud.

I heard the lobby elevator doors ping open and rushed around the corner to meet it. The small elevator was filled with a mass of netting with a navy blue beret peeking behind it. Tricia stepped out, her full tulle ball gown rustling as she moved. Her dark hair spilled over her bare shoulders in waves and she carried the white tulip bouquet ringed with green nerines. If she weren't such an unpleasant person, I would have thought she looked beautiful.

She clutched my hand in a grip surprisingly strong for someone always so weary. "The wedding needs to start now. Right. Now."

I darted a glance at Fern, who was nodding vigorously behind her. "You got it."

I ran to the door of the Hay-Adams Room and caught Kate's eye next to the harpist, giving her the signal to start the processional. Luckily, the processional consisted only of the maid of honor followed by the bride walking with her mother. I pulled the maid of honor to the doorway as I heard the harp begin to play and spotted the groom and officiant moving into place under the floral canopy. I smiled at Madeleine in her pink satin Vera Wang sheath, noticing that her hair had been pulled back so tightly her eyes now turned up at the corners. I didn't think she looked like a ferret, but it didn't look comfortable. I gave her a nod, and she set off down the aisle.

I turned to the bride and her mother. Fern had draped the blusher over the bride's face and stood behind her fluffing the thick layers of tulle in her skirt. The mother of the bride, her pale green dress hidden almost completely by the wedding gown, held her daughter by the arm and kept her nervous eyes trained on her face.

I smoothed the blusher so that it fell behind her bouquet. "Are you ready?"

She let out a breath, and the single layer of tulle that was the blusher quivered. "I don't know if I can make it down the aisle."

Oh, no, I thought. *We did not work this hard and get this far to have the bride flake out at the last minute.*

I put my hands around hers on the bouquet stems. "I know you can do this."

The mother raised her bitten thumbnail to her mouth. "Maybe we should postpone for an hour or two."

Was she crazy? If we postponed, we wouldn't be starting the reception until ten o'clock at night and we had to be out of the rooftop ballroom by midnight. Even I couldn't squeeze a four-course dinner, dancing, toasts, and cake cutting into two hours. I shot Fern a desperate look.

He dropped the back of the bride's dress and came to stand next to her, linking his arm in hers. "You're going down that aisle right now if I have to drag you myself. Understood?"

Tricia and her mother both nodded mutely, and I stepped aside as the threesome walked through the door and down the aisle, with Fern jerking the bride forward every time she slowed down.

Kate had edged her way to the back of the room and joined me outside where we could watch the ceremony through the glass panes of the wooden doors.

"I can't look," I said. "Is he still up there?"

"I think he just gave away the bride," Kate said. "I did not see this one coming, although I like Fern better as the father of the bride than as the priest. He was blessing me for weeks after that wedding. Now he's shaking the groom's hand. You've got to see this, Annabelle. The groom looks so confused."

I looked up to the ceiling. "Why can't we have one normal wedding? Just one?"

"Because there's no such thing," Kate said. "Weddings are crazy. Period."

I hated when Kate was right.

CHAPTER 4

"I'm coming," I said as I padded down the hallway of my apartment in my socked feet. I surveyed the living room, still littered with remains of the weekend's wedding: my boxy metal emergency kit sitting next to the couch, my black Longchamp bag filled with the wedding files slumped against the dining table, a pink shoe bag with my change of shoes flung on the rug, the folded-up wedding schedule covered in check marks laying where it had fallen onto the hardwood floor by the door, and samples of the program, menu card, and escort cards for me to file later tossed on the glass coffee table. I tried to ignore the mess, and my aching feet, as I opened the door.

"It is Monday morning, right?" Kate asked, giving my outfit of jeans and a Wedding Belles T-shirt the once over. "Don't we have a meeting with a prospective couple?"

I held the door open wide, letting Kate come inside as she extended the nubby brown coffee holder in front of her with one hand. "They canceled. Left a message last night."

Kate waved a hand over her blue paisley dress and high-heel slides. "And you couldn't let me know?"

"Sorry." I took the paper cup she offered me, feeling the warmth of the beverage through the cardboard sleeve, and motioned her to follow me back to the office. I knew without taking a sip that she'd brought me my favorite hot mocha, and I felt a wave of affection for my assistant. "I didn't check it until an hour ago."

BOOK 4: REVIEW TO A KILL

Kate dropped her pale pink purse on the floor of my home office, which consisted of a white IKEA sawhorse desk, a rolling leather chair, and a tall filing cabinet. "That doesn't seem like you."

"I'm still recovering from Saturday." I took a sip of the rich coffee and closed my eyes as I swallowed. "Thanks for this. It's just what I needed."

Kate took my black desk chair and kicked her shoes off under my desk, setting her own drink, a nonfat soy latte if it was her usual, on the wooden surface. "I think we'll all be recovering from that one for a long time."

"Fern's the only one of us who seemed to have a good time." I sat down cross-legged on the carpet.

"Maybe we would have had fun if we'd led a conga line when the band played 'Dancing Queen.'"

I groaned. "Don't remind me."

"You have to admit that he embraced the father-of-the bride role. And he may have been the only reason Tricia stayed for her entire reception." Kate spun around in my chair. "Plus, he gave a great toast. It didn't have anything to do with the couple, but it was better than a lot I've heard."

"I missed all the toasts after his but I can't imagine they were as good." I set my cup next to me and dug into a cardboard box, pulling out a pair of white cubes with clear lids and handing one to Kate. "Leftover doughnut favors."

Kate opened the lid to her box. "So they're only two days old?"

"Something like that." I took a bite of the strawberry frosted doughnut, letting the slightly stale crumbs of pink icing fall onto my lap.

"Did you do anything fun on Sunday?" Kate asked, nibbling on her own doughnut.

"Aside from sleeping in and ignoring my throbbing feet?" I took a drink of mocha and followed with a bite of doughnut. This was my ideal breakfast although I knew if I did this every day, I'd gain twenty pounds.

"No date?" Kate wiggled her eyebrows up and down. "Maybe a visit from a cute bandleader or a hot cop?"

My cheeks flushed, and I mentally cursed the fair skin that betrayed my emotions. "You know I'm not dating Ian or Mike Reese."

"Too bad. They're both cute in different ways." Kate leaned back. "And remind me why you aren't dating them?"

"For one thing, Ian's band is on tour, and for another, we were never officially dating." I didn't add that I found the tattooed Scottish singer of the eighties band the Breakfast Club unnerving. I wasn't sure whether I was attracted to his bad-boy persona or if the butterflies he gave me were a subconscious warning sign that I should not date men with body art.

"And the hot cop?" Kate asked.

"You know we've never gone out." I'd never told Kate about the intense moment we'd had the last time I saw him, and I felt some measure of relief since I hadn't heard from him since. "I don't think he has time to date, anyway."

Kate studied my face for a moment before shrugging and taking a swig of her latte. "His loss." She spun around in my chair. "So now that our meeting is cancelled, what's on our agenda for today?"

"The usual postwedding routine. Thank you notes to all the vendors. Filing the contract and paperwork. Moving Tricia's client folder into the Past Clients folder on the computer."

"I love that part." Kate wiggled the mouse on my desk and the computer screen came to life. She found the folder on my desktop that read "Tricia Toker" and dragged it to our virtual version of long-term storage. "So long, Tricia."

"We should check in with Buster and Mack and see how the late-night floral drop-off went."

"That's right." Kate snapped her fingers. "They had to refresh all the centerpieces and put them in different vases for the brunch the next morning. They must have been at the hotel all night."

"They were still there when the valet finally brought my car." I stood and brushed crumbs off my jeans, making a mental note to find my Dustbuster. "Do you want a banana?"

"What time was that?" she asked, and cocked her head to one side. "You have bananas?"

"Two a.m.," I said as I walked down the hall to my kitchen and scanned the counter. Kate was right. No bananas. I opened my refrigerator out of habit and noted that it was virtually bare unless condiments, beverages, and salad dressing counted as food. I eyed the leftover takeout boxes shoved in the back and decided it was too early for cold cashew chicken. The first thing I needed to do after I found my Dustbuster was shop for groceries.

"Is it too early to call them?" Kate yelled.

I headed back down the hall. "They're florists. They're always up early to scout the flower markets. Anyway, it's past nine."

Kate tapped on my computer as I walked back in the office. "I just got a notice from the Wed Boards on my phone."

I pulled my phone out of my jeans pocket with one hand. "You check that, and I'll call Buster and Mack."

"I'm logging in now," Kate said.

I punched my speed-dial button for Lush flower shop and listened to it ring.

"We have a new review," Kate said.

"Lush Floral Designers, this is Mack."

"It's Annabelle," I said, then covered the phone and asked Kate, "Who's it from?"

"Annabelle, thank goodness you called. Buster's going crazy. I'm afraid he's going to hurt someone."

"What? Why?" I asked.

Kate swiveled the chair to face me. "It's from Tricia."

I felt my stomach clench. "Mack, what's happened?"

"Have you been on the Wed Boards? That horrible woman has ruined us." His voice shook as he spoke, and I heard Buster bellowing in the background. "She's ruined all of us."

I looked at Kate's face and I knew, without reading a word, that Tricia the Troll had trashed us online.

CHAPTER 5

Not more than an hour later, I rubbed my arms briskly for warmth, wishing I'd worn more than a T-shirt as I pushed through the heavy plastic flaps leading to the refrigerated area of the flower market. I held the flaps back for Kate, who had her bare arms crossed tightly in front of her. Rows of industrial orange buckets filled with cut flowers covered the cement floor in front of us—roses bundled tightly together with thick Cellophane, unopened lilies hiding their pink throats, and white orchid sprays bursting in all directions.

"I thought you said Buster and Mack would be here." Kate stamped her high-heeled feet for warmth as we surveyed the room.

"This is where they told me they'd be." I backed out of the room, wishing I hadn't left the hot mocha at my apartment. The coffee would be the perfect thing to warm me up. "Mack said they were selecting flowers for Jessica's sample centerpiece on Friday."

"Is that this week?" Kate shook her head. "I'm losing track of time."

"That's what happens during wedding season. The days and weeks start to run into each other." I wound my way around buckets of filler flowers like Queen Anne's lace and baby's breath as we walked back through the unchilled area of the warehouse.

"Why do I never feel that way about vacation?" Kate asked. "Oh, wait. It's because I never get vacation."

I gave her a push. "You do, too."

"Only in the dead of winter or maybe one week in August when it's a thousand degrees."

"You're a wedding planner," I reminded her. "That's one of the hazards of the job. Working every perfect weekend of the year and only getting free time when no one wants to be outside."

"This job has a lot more hazards than you'd expect." She held up the fingers on one hand. "A bad vacation schedule, mentally unstable clients, paper cuts galore—"

"There they are." I interrupted Kate's laundry list of complaints when I spotted our friends Buster and Mack—or the Mighty Morphin Flower Arrangers, as they liked to be called—at the far end of the warehouse floor.

Mack waved his arms when he spotted me, and the chains on his leather vest jingled. Buster barely cracked a smile as we approached, but he hugged us when we reached them. Even though Buster and Mack always wore black leather, they usually accented their pants, vests, and jackets with colored T-shirts, but today both men were in black from head to toe and their faces looked just as somber.

"So these are the flowers for Jessica's sample?" I asked as I looked over the selection of peonies, roses, and blooming branches in the buckets at their feet. "I know she's going to love it."

Buster furrowed his brow, and his black goggles rose. "I hope so."

"Look who it is!" A petite woman with red hair and so many freckles that they all ran together walked up holding a clipboard. She was a sales assistant for the floral wholesaler, but it was well known that she wanted to use the job as a springboard into wedding planning.

"Hi, Callie." Kate gave her an air kiss. "You missed happy hour last week."

Callie was a part of the group of younger wedding assistants that Kate went out with from time to time. They were all single and looking, some more successfully than others. Kate had confided in me that Callie had dated nearly all the guys who worked at the floral warehouse, including her boss. I concentrated very hard on not judging her.

Callie beamed. "I had a date with Jonathan."

Kate had mentioned that Callie had gotten very lucky when she'd gone home with a lawyer after one of their girls' nights a few weeks ago but she hadn't mentioned that she had a boyfriend.

"Well, well, well." Kate put her hands on her hips. "You go, girl."

Callie bounced on her toes. "I think he might be the one."

Kate scrunched up her nose. In all her dating adventures and misadventures, she'd never used that phrase and usually dismissed it when other people did. Sometimes it amazed me that Kate had ever wanted to work in weddings considering her tenuous belief in "happily ever after."

Callie leaned into us. "I think he might propose."

Kate rolled her eyes, and Buster and Mack muttered a few half-hearted congratulations. Callie's face fell.

"Ignore them," I said, shooting daggers at my friends. "We're coming off a rough wedding and some bad reviews from the bride so we might not be in the happiest wedding mood right now."

"I've been reading the Wed Boards all morning. For work research, not for my wedding," Callie added quickly before Kate could chide her. "Some of the girls on there are brutal. They call themselves the Weddies."

"Oh, we know all about the Weddies," I said.

Kate and I had decided long ago to avoid the Wed Boards if we could. We knew it would make us crazy to read amateurs giving each other incorrect advice, and we didn't want to read snarky comments about our friends in the wedding business.

"Any chance you've seen a Tricia Toker on there recently?" I asked. "Maybe under the user name 'TriciaandDaveattheHay?'"

She looked up while she thought, and she snapped her fingers. "She's the one who posted a long rant about the lack of customer service in the wedding industry and how it's a racket. A lot of brides jumped on and agreed with her."

"I'm sure they did," Buster said. "Brides can't understand why it costs them more to have us create a rose centerpiece for them than for them to grab a dozen supermarket roses."

"Come to think of it, that bride did complain a lot about floral designers," Callie said. "She claimed that because she was rich, her planner had taken her to the most expensive one in town and they were gouging her."

"Are you kidding me?" I said. "She told me she only wanted the best and not to bother showing her anything less than the most high-end."

"Gouging?" Buster's face reddened, and he looked as angry as I felt. "We cut out half of the original proposal."

"Oh, no." Mack wrung his hands. "Here he goes again."

"Listen," I said, linking my arm through Buster's. "You can't let one bad egg get you down. Tricia Toker is a horrible person and she was never going to be happy. That's not your fault. Your work for her wedding was beautiful. I know it, you know it, even she knows it. Even if she won't admit it."

Mack reached up and put his arm around Buster's massive shoulder. "She's right, you know. We can't sulk about one bad review all week."

Kate hooked her arm around Mack's tattooed bicep. "People like that will get what they deserve in the end. It's karma. Just you wait and see. There's a special place in hell for people who write nasty reviews just to be mean."

"And if we're lucky, Tricia will get there sooner rather than later," I said.

"I'm not sure how I feel about that." Buster's face looked conflicted. I doubted he was supposed to wish people to hell, but maybe his Christain biker buddies would make an exception if they knew Tricia. "I'd like to be there when karma slaps her upside the head, though."

"We'd all like to be there," I said. "But the fact that she spends most of her life in bed pretending to be sick already tells you what kind of life she's going to have."

"If you think about it," Kate added, "we really should feel sorry for her."

Buster raised a pierced eyebrow at Kate. "I'm not at that place yet." He managed a weak grin. "But thanks for cheering me up, girls."

"And promise me you won't read the review again," I said. "It won't do anything but make you mad."

"And I'd advise you not to go on the Wed boards," Callie added.

"Annabelle hasn't even seen our review yet," Kate told them. "I wouldn't let her."

Mack's mouth dropped open. "You didn't see what she said about you?"

Kate dug her elbow into his side, and he grimaced.

I narrowed my eyes at her. "I thought you said it wasn't so bad."

Kate swept a hand through her blond hair. "I said it wasn't worth worrying about. And that's true. It won't do you any good to get upset by it now. Take the advice you just gave Buster."

I agreed with Kate for the moment but vowed to read the review the second we got back to the office.

"Well, if it isn't the Wedding Belles team and the boys from Lush." A tall woman with blond hair approached us, her Louis Vuitton purse swinging on her arm and her southern drawl dripping like molasses off her words.

"Brianna." Kate said her name like a curse. Brianna, owner of Brides by Brianna, was a new wedding planner but not what we would consider a friendly colleague. We met her at a recent bridal show, where she pretended not to have heard of Wedding Belles before Buster and Mack clued us in that she'd been asking all over town about us. Since then we'd learned that she was one of the few planners who talked badly about her competition when she met with potential clients and what she said about us always reached our ears.

"Hi, Brianna," I said, my voice flat.

Brianna gave us an exaggerated frown. "I was so sorry to see that you got those bad reviews."

I wanted to be surprised that she would find out so quickly, but I pegged her as the type of person to have Google alerts on all her competition.

Brianna ran her eyes over Buster and Mack. "You, too."

Buster and Mack were silent. Word had reached their ears that she thought the Mighty Morphin Flower Arrangers were too dramatic and expensive. She'd steered more than one couple away from using Lush so there was no love lost between the three.

"You know what they say." She looked me up and down. "Out with the old and in with the new."

She spun to leave, and her Louis Vuitton hit Kate on the arm.

Buster glared after her. "Just because she's brand new and as clueless as they come does not mean you're old, Annabelle."

"Thanks." I appreciated Buster's words and the fact that he said them loud enough for Brianna to hear as she flounced off, but the insult still stung.

Kate rubbed her arm as we stared after Brianna. "That woman is the worst. I'd like to kill her."

"Add her to the list," I said.

CHAPTER 6

"The entire review is lies," I said as I paced back and forth in my living room. Kate and I had driven back from the floral warehouse to my apartment, and I'd peeked at my computer screen while Kate was in the bathroom. I'd then attempted to drown my sorrows in sugar by eating all the remaining doughnut favors as I read and re-read the reviews.

"I know, I know. It doesn't even make any sense," Kate said from where she lay sprawled across my pale yellow couch with her phone in one hand. She'd opened the Wed Boards app so she could continue reading the library of bad reviews Tricia had unleashed only hours after her wedding. "She blames us for a level of stress that made it impossible to enjoy her wedding day."

I paused in front of the couch. "Who is she kidding? She was never going to enjoy her wedding day. People like that are too caught up in their own pity party to enjoy anything."

"At least she didn't accuse us of giving her a severe allergic reaction that nearly had her rushing to the hospital, like she claims in her review of Buster and Mack," Kate said. "Her words, not mine."

I sat on the arm of the couch and took a deep breath. "We'll be lucky if Buster and Mack don't end up in the hospital after this." When we'd left the boys at the warehouse, they'd been planning to ride their Harleys and clear their heads. I wasn't convinced that two livid bikers should be on the road, but I also knew that bikes were their version of therapy.

"The hotel got crucified because she claims the staff didn't refresh her suite enough times on the wedding day." Kate shook her head. "Ridiculous. I personally saw waiters clearing dishes twice, and I wasn't in her room that long. Does she expect the hotel staff to be like a Roomba and walk around her room all day long picking up lint from the floor?"

"You and I know it's ridiculous and petty, but brides won't when they read these reviews." My phone began trilling from inside my pocket, and I wiggled it out of my jeans and answered.

"This is one time I hate being right," Richard said.

"How did you find out so quickly?" I asked as I mouthed Richard's name to Kate. Kate nodded then headed for my kitchen.

"Fern."

Of course. Fern knew most gossip in town before it even happened, usually because he started it. I wondered if he'd gotten a bad review, as well. Kate and I had only made it through three reviews—ours, the hotel's, and Buster and Mack's—but we knew it was the tip of the troll's iceberg.

"So you've read it?" I asked.

"I'm afraid so. But look on the bright side. It's your only one-star review, and you have dozens of five-star reviews."

"It still brings our star rating down. Now we're averaging four and a half stars. That means we'll show up under all the planners with five-star ratings. It bumps us two full pages down the list." I rubbed my temples. "We get a lot of referrals from the site. At least we used to."

Richard didn't reply for a moment. "I know it seems bad now but you'll feel better once you eat a little something."

I looked over at Kate, who stood peering into my nearly empty refrigerator. "Do a dozen doughnuts count?"

"She's already eaten a dozen doughnuts," he said, his voice sounding muffled.

"Who are you talking to?"

"No one," Richard said. "You are decent, aren't you?"

"If you mean am I dressed, then yes. What's going on?"

My front door flew open and Richard and Fern stood in my hallway, their arms laden with canvas grocery sacks.

"Ta-da!" Fern cried. "The cavalry has arrived!" He rushed past me, giving me an air kiss on both cheeks.

Richard came inside and closed the door behind him with one foot. "Fern insisted that we come over and lift your spirits, so here we are." He lifted the bags in his arms, and I spotted two bottles of wine and a wheel of Brie. My spirits felt a little better already.

Fern had dumped his bags on my kitchen counter, and he and Kate stood side by side unpacking them.

"This is an unusual selection of food." Kate examined a pineapple and a pint of mint chocolate chip ice cream.

Richard glanced at his Gucci watch. "We would have been here sooner, but Fern insisted we stop and get all your favorites."

"Chocolate croissants from Pâtisserie Poupon and cupcakes from Baked & Wired." Fern held up a paper bag and a white pastry box.

Kate peeked into another paper bag. "Are these what I think they are?"

Fern grinned and nodded. "Julia's empanadas."

I gave Richard a hug, and my voice broke. "You two are the best."

"Now, now." Richard patted me on the back then cleared his throat and pulled away, making his way to the kitchen. "Today is not only going to be a carb-fest. I also brought healthy food because you know you don't eat right, Annabelle."

I didn't usually welcome Richard's scoldings about my admittedly lousy eating habits, but today I'd let it slide. I walked over to the counter that separated my kitchen and living room and pushed back the wooden accordion shutters so I could see fully into the kitchen. I'd been meaning to remove them entirely since I liked being able to see in each room from the other but hadn't gotten around to it.

"You seem pretty upbeat," Kate said to Fern. "Did you escape Tricia's poisoned pen?"

Fern folded one of the fabric grocery bags and laid it on the counter. "Only because she's afraid I'll make all her hair fall out the next time she has her hair done."

"Why does she think that?" I asked.

Fern pulled open a bag of salt-and-vinegar potato chips—Kate's favorite—and popped one in his mouth. "Because I told her I would."

"I hardly think threatening a client is a good business practice," Richard began, but Fern cut him off.

"I told her if she wrote even one bad word about me I'd shampoo her hair with enough Nair to leave her bald as a coot." Fern's face darkened. "I feel bad that I didn't include the rest of our team in the threat, though. I should have warned her off trashing you, and I didn't. I'm sorry, girls."

Kate threw an arm around his shoulders. "It isn't your fault that our bride is an awful human."

"And you didn't know she'd pan us," I said. "The wedding was beautiful after all."

Fern smiled as he put a four-pack of my favorite bottled Mocha Fraps in the door of the fridge alongside a six-pack of Diet Dr Pepper. "It was. Any normal bride would have been over the moon with it. Even if the best man's toast was disastrous. Then, again, he had to follow me so the expectations were high."

"All toasts are painful," Richard said. "I had one that went on for forty minutes with the best man recounting every year he'd known the groom."

"This is why I need my sedative dart gun," I said. "If someone start talking too much, I could casually shoot them with a dart then drag their inert body away."

Kate looked at me askance. "I'm pretty sure that would be illegal."

"But effective." I walked around to join my friends in the kitchen. "We should eat. Because I have big plans after lunch."

Kate lifted the lid to the cupcake box. "Dessert?"

I shook my head. "I'm going to Tricia's house to tell her exactly what we all think of her."

CHAPTER 7

"Did I mention that I think this is a horrible idea?" Kate asked as she tried to navigate the Georgetown sidewalk beside me in her heels.

"Several times," I said.

We'd walked from my apartment to Wisconsin Avenue then turned to head up to Glover Park, where the bride lived. Since it was a weekday afternoon, we had to dodge not only people on the sidewalks but sandwich boards placed outside shops to beckon customers inside. I passed a woman talking on her cell phone then edged around a double-sided chalkboard advertising a mani/pedi deal for a nail salon. I slowed to let Kate catch up.

"Are we even sure she'll be home?" Kate grabbed the sleeve of the white cardigan I'd thrown over my T-shirt.

"Well, they don't leave for their honeymoon in Paris for a week, and I'm sure she's too worn out from writing nasty reviews to leave her house." I waved the white envelope in my hand at her. "And if she's not there, we'll leave this."

"It's a good letter," Kate said. "But are you sure you want to respond to her at all? Couldn't we just wait for Fern to make her hair fall out?"

"Normally I'd be all for taking the high road." I paused at an intersection. "We've had plenty of high-maintenance brides, and I've never called any of them on their bad behavior. I know it's all part of the job."

Kate hitched her pink purse over her shoulder. "The bad part of the job."

"But this girl wrote reviews specifically to damage people who worked really hard for her. You, me, Buster, Mack, the hotel staff—we put up with way more abuse than anyone should. And our reward for that is a review filled with complaints that simply aren't true?" I shook my head. "Not this time. Those reviews can hurt our business and that business is how we all survive."

"You're right." Kate balled her hands into fists. "I'll bet she doesn't even care if my clothing and cocktail budget gets slashed."

I glanced at Kate as we crossed the street, with her taking two short steps for every one of mine. "I don't give you a clothing and cocktail budget."

"I know. I give myself one." She winked. "When I've been very good, I get a shoe bonus."

We reached the bride's street, and I turned left. We'd come to her house so many times during the planning process, for meetings and dress fittings and to pick up guest RSVPs, that I didn't even need to glance at the numbers on the row houses.

The Glover Park neighborhood sat right above Georgetown and consisted of narrow brick row houses pressed tightly together, nearly all with wooden porches jutting out front. The houses alternated between redbrick and those painted shades of yellow, cream, green, and blue.

"You're sure about this?" Kate asked as we got closer to the house. She paused for breath and leaned against a car parked at the curb.

"What's the worst that could happen? She already wrote us a bad review. You can't go lower than one star. At least we can have our say and tell her what we think of her."

We reached the yellow-brick house with gray concrete steps, and I led the way up the stairs to the porch, grasping the metal handrail. Most houses on the street had rocking chairs or swings on their porches, but this one was spartan. I remembered the bride's mother telling me that Tricia couldn't be outside because of her allergies, and the groom wouldn't sit outside without her. I had a feeling the bride had decided that her fiancé couldn't be outside without her, and he'd had to go along with her scorched-earth policy regarding porch furniture.

I knocked firmly on the door, and it eased opened. The last person who shut it must have been in a hurry and not pulled it closed all the way. I turned back to Kate. "Should I poke my head in and call their names?"

I called the bride's and groom's names. No answer. I called out again, this time a bit louder. Silence.

"Maybe they're upstairs." Kate nudged me. "Maybe they're too occupied to hear you."

I cringed. "It's completely quiet. Unless they're mimes, I doubt they're 'occupied.'"

"Maybe the bride also suffers from narcolepsy and fell asleep?"

"That's one lucky groom," I said under my breath.

"Should we drop off the letter and leave?" Kate craned her neck around me to look into the hallway of the house. "There's a hall table right there."

I spotted the whitewashed table with a matching mirror hanging over it. It held a shallow crystal bowl with a set of keys, a photo in a silver frame, and a miniature boxwood topiary shaped like an inverted cone. I stepped inside the house and Kate followed closely behind, her heels making clacking sounds on the hardwood floors. I leaned my letter up against the topiary, briefly touching the greenery to ascertain that it was, in fact, fake.

"Let's go," I said. I didn't want to admit it, but the heavy silence of the house gave me the creeps. Where were they?

Kate held up the framed photograph of the bride, groom, and maid of honor in Georgetown sweatshirts. "The bride is actually smiling in this."

"She didn't start having her issues until after college, remember?" I whispered, even though there was no one around to hear us.

Kate shook her head and replaced the photo. "You know I never retain personal facts about our couples. There isn't enough room in my head. Plus I don't care."

We'd started toward the door when we heard a sound behind us. Kate spun around and grasped my arm. "What was that?"

My heart pounded, but I tried to breathe calmly. "I think it came from the kitchen."

"Tricia? Dave?" I called. No response.

Kate relaxed her grip. "Maybe a window blew open."

A faint moan came from the kitchen, and Kate slapped both hands over her mouth.

"That wasn't a window," I said. "We should check it out."

Kate dropped her hands from her mouth. "Are you kidding me? Have you watched no horror movies? This house is haunted, and you and I need to get out of here as fast as humanly possible." Her eyes darted around her. "Especially me. I'm blond. The blondes are always picked off first."

I took Kate's hand and pulled her forward. "It's not haunted. Come on."

"If we get attacked by evil house spirits, I will never speak to you again." Kate hunched behind me as I walked slowly down the hall.

"You've already threatened to quit twice this week. Your quota is up."

"Oh, I won't quit. I just won't talk to you," Kate said as we shuffled along.

"Well, that should work well."

When we reached the kitchen, I poked my head around the opening that led into the room and dropped Kate's hand. "Oh, no."

"What is it?" Kate looked over my shoulder then sucked in her breath. "I'll call 911."

Now I knew why the groom hadn't answered me. He lay facedown on the black-and-white tile floor in a growing pool of blood.

CHAPTER 8

"The ambulance is on its way." Kate came back into the kitchen but stood far away from the body on the tile.

I rose from where I'd knelt down next to the groom, glad to get some distance from the metallic scent of blood. I took a slow breath and let the sudden wave of nausea pass, the taste of bile bitter in the back of my throat. I didn't normally react to the sight of blood, but the smell was another matter entirely. "He's still breathing."

"Should we do something?" Kate wrung her hands. "CPR? Mouth-to-mouth?"

I shook my head and pointed to the round hole in his shirt over his shoulder. "It looks like he was shot in the back. I don't think we should move him."

"Who would shoot him in the back?" Kate's eyes darted around the kitchen like she expected the shooter to jump out from the contemporary white cabinets at any second. "Do you think it was the bride and that's why she's not here?"

"I don't know." I steadied myself with one hand on the cool alabaster-and-gray marble countertops and tore my eyes from the body. "Why would she shoot him?"

"You're right. She's the one with all the money. He should be the one knocking her off. And it's not like she could find another guy as hot as him who would put up with all her crap."

I motioned to the groom on the floor. "He can probably still hear you, you know."

Kate cringed. "Right." She put both palms on the counter and let her head fall between them. "Sorry."

"Don't touch anything," I said, pointing at her hands on the counter. "We don't want to mess with the crime scene."

She jumped back like she'd been burned. "You're right. You don't think we'll be suspects, do you?"

"I'm sure we'll be witnesses." I snatched my hand from the counter and walked gingerly around the room, looking for something to use to wipe off our prints. A roll of paper towels sat tucked in a corner on a standing metal holder. I pulled off a few sheets without touching anything but the paper and proceeded to wipe the spots on the swirled marble where we'd made contact. I balled the used paper towel up and shoved it into my pocket.

"Great." Kate began pacing in a small circle again. "Just what we need."

I had to agree with Kate that this day was going from bad to worse very quickly. The warmth of the room and the sight of the growing puddle of blood began to make me feel dizzy. I looked out the back kitchen window and breathed deeply, trying to imagine that I could smell the small fir tree outside in their postage stamp of a yard. I'd never fainted, but there was always a first time.

"Maybe we should leave." Kate motioned to the front door. "No one knows we were here. I even gave a fake name to the 911 operator."

"You gave a fake name to 911?" I stared at her, my dizziness overshadowed by my surprise. "Why?"

She shrugged. "I'm used to giving fake names to guys at bars. It popped out before I could stop myself."

"Do I dare ask what name you gave?"

"My fallback. Erica Kane."

"Great. That doesn't look suspicious at all," I muttered. "A soap opera character placing a 911 call shouldn't raise any red flags."

"Hey," Kate said. "I was flustered."

"Tricia?" a woman's voice called from the front hallway. "Dave? I'm here with the cake top."

Kate and I exchanged a glance then peered around the doorway of the kitchen and into the short hallway. The bride's maid of honor stood a few steps inside the house, holding a small white box. Her strawberry-blond hair was swept into a messy ponytail, and she wore almost no makeup.

BOOK 4: REVIEW TO A KILL

Quite a contrast from her wedding day look of a tight bun and dramatic, smoky eyes pulled so high it had looked painful when she blinked.

I stepped out of the kitchen to greet her and to keep her from coming any farther into the house and disturbing the already-disturbed crime scene. "Hi, Madeleine."

Her eyes widened when she saw me. "Hi. What are you doing here?"

Kate joined me in the hall. "Just dropping off some final paperwork."

Madeleine nodded but didn't seem convinced. "Where are Tricia and Dave? I'm doing Tricia's mom a favor and delivering the cake top from the wedding."

The concept of saving cake for the first anniversary always baffled me since no food tasted good after a year's worth of freezer burn.

"Dave is in the kitchen," I said. Kate twitched.

Madeleine took a step forward. "Hey, Dave. I'm here with the cake."

There was no answer, and the maid of honor narrowed her eyes. "What's going on?"

"Listen, Madeleine." I took a step toward her and held out a hand. "Something has happened to Dave. An ambulance is on the way."

She shook her head. "An ambulance? Why?"

"It looks like someone broke into the house and surprised Dave," I said. "He's been shot."

Madeleine released the cake box, and it fell to the floor, making a dull splat as the top popped open and icing splattered onto the hardwood. Before we could react, she pushed past us into the kitchen and screamed when she saw the groom lying on the tile floor.

"Maybe we should call Detective Reese," Kate said to me out of the corner of her mouth. "This could get ugly."

Madeleine had dropped to her knees and had her hands over her mouth, her shoulders shaking as she cried.

"The police should be here any minute. We don't need to call Reese every time we hit a bump."

Kate's mouth opened as she stared at me. "Hit a bump?" She waved a hand at the body, the growing pool of blood, and the sobbing strawberry blonde next to them.

I had to admit that none of this looked good. I stepped around the crying girl, bent over the groom, and placed a finger on his neck. The pulse was faint but steady, and I felt a wave of relief. "He's still alive. Technically this isn't a homicide. Reese is a homicide detective."

Kate took out her phone. "You're nuts. I'm calling him."

"Home invasion isn't his division." I reached for her phone.

She dodged me. "So what? I'd rather have a cop we know on site than a bunch we don't. What's the big deal with calling him?"

"Nothing." I closed the gap between us and grabbed for her again. If I was being honest with myself, I didn't want the handsome detective to think I was chasing him. I hadn't seen him since the moment we shared a couple of weeks ago at a bridal show. We'd texted a few times. Then he'd gone radio silent. I'd rather not have to deal with in-person rejection the same day I had to find one of our grooms shot in the back. "I don't think we need his help."

Kate backed away from me, punching numbers on her phone with one thumb. "You know it's okay to ask for favors? Or help? Even from a hot guy."

"I'm telling you, we don't need help. At least not from him." I heard her phone dialing and the wail of an approaching ambulance's siren. "Everything is under control."

I hated the thought that Detective Reese might think I needed him. I was no damsel in distress, I told myself, and I didn't need any guy to rescue me. Especially one who had a habit of going AWOL. I swiped for the phone again and knocked it out of her hand. It flew into the air then bounced off the groom's back before landing faceup in the pool of blood. The maid of honor gasped, the groom groaned, and the ambulance sirens grew louder. It knew it must be right outside the house.

"Hello?" Reese's voice came out of the phone as Madeleine, Kate, and I all stared at it. So much for not tampering with the crime scene.

"Nice going," Kate said. "How are you going to explain this?"

"It is *your* phone."

"*Was* my phone. I'm never touching that again."

"Hello?" Detective Reese's voice came from the phone and behind us simultaneously.

I turned around and saw him standing next to a uniformed officer in the doorway to the kitchen. A pair of paramedics with large red cases pushed past them into the room.

Reese clicked off his phone and narrowed his eyes at us. "Which one of you is Erica Kane?"

CHAPTER 9

"Do you want to tell me why you and Kate and that blonde were standing over a man who's been shot?" Reese asked once he'd taken me outside to the front porch. "And why Kate gave a fake name to 911?"

I leaned back against the white wooden railing of the porch and crossed my arms. I was grateful to be out of the house and felt sorry for Kate, who was being questioned inside. I took in a long breath of cool air, letting it fill my lungs completely before I blew it out. "That part's easy to explain. Kate was nervous and that's the name she gives to guys in bars if she's not interested. She said it without thinking."

Reese raised an eyebrow. "That's not completely unbelievable."

"Trust me. If you knew Kate better you wouldn't think twice." Out of the corner of my eye I saw the flashing lights of the ambulance and squad cars that had double-parked in the middle of the narrow street and a small group of curious neighbors gathering on the sidewalk. The sirens had been turned off, but I could hear the wailing of more in the distance.

The detective rocked back on his heels. "That doesn't explain why you're here in the first place. And who's the blonde?"

I tried to ignore the fact that he looked really good in jeans, a blue button-down shirt, and a brown blazer. "The guy on the floor in there is one of our grooms. We came by to talk to the bride, and the door opened when I knocked. We called both of their names and were about to leave when we heard some noises in the kitchen. That's when Kate and I found the groom. The strawberry blonde crying hysterically is the bride's best friend and maid of honor from the wedding, Madeleine."

Reese took a pocket notebook out of his blazer and flipped it open, writing the name 'Madeleine' on a blank page. "Was she here when you arrived?"

"No. She came in with the top of the wedding cake after we'd been inside the house for about ten minutes. Right after we called 911."

Reese jerked a thumb at the cake box that had been kicked out of the way when the paramedics rushed in. "That cake box?"

I nodded and felt a twinge of guilt over the cake smeared across the floor.

"So he'd already been shot when you arrived?" Reese asked.

"Of course he'd already been shot," I said. "We certainly didn't shoot him."

Reese wrote in his notebook. "Do you have any idea how long he'd been on the floor? Did he say anything? Could you already see blood?"

I thought back to the moment when I'd first seen the groom lying on the black-and-white tile floor. "There was definitely blood already, but he wasn't conscious. I had to check his pulse and breath to even know he was still alive."

Reese looked up. "So you did touch the body?"

"Only to determine if he was breathing. We didn't move him."

"Did the blonde touch the body?"

I thought back to Madeleine kneeling next to the groom. "I don't think so but maybe."

A police cruiser pulled up behind the ambulance and flipped off its lights. A uniformed cop got out and came up the front steps of the house, nodded to Reese, and went inside. I moved so I could see into the house where Kate stood talking to one of the policemen in the front hallway.

"So you find the body, determine that he's still alive, and then what?" Reese tapped his pen on the notebook.

I took a breath and replayed the events in my head before answering. "Kate called 911, Madeleine walked in, I checked for a pulse, then you arrived."

Reese looked at me. "That's your whole story?"

I did not want to admit why Kate and I had been fighting over her phone. "Those are the pertinent facts."

"How about the less pertinent facts, like how a phone ended up in the victim's blood?"

I shrugged. "It slipped."

"And Kate was calling me because?"

"She thought you might be able to help." I sighed. "She thought it looked bad for us to be at another crime scene and that you could keep us out of the report."

The detective closed his notebook. "What did you think?"

"I thought that you're a very busy man and we didn't need to bother you."

He took a step closer to me. "You think I'd be bothered if you called me and asked me to help."

I avoided his gaze. "You're busy. How do I know what you'd think? It's not like we know each other that well."

"Ah," he said. "Is this because we haven't talked lately?"

"No." He was standing much too close for comfort. I walked to the other side of the porch. "I know you're a busy man and probably one of those types who says they don't have time for anything but work."

He followed me, closing the distance between us again. "One of those types? Sounds like you think you've got me pegged."

"I don't think I've got you pegged." I started to feel flustered. This was not going the way I'd imagined it. I was coming off bitter and whiny, not cool and nonchalant. "I'm saying I don't expect anything from you."

He pressed his lips together and nodded. Before he could respond, one of the uniformed officers came out on the porch and pulled him aside. They spoke briefly, but I couldn't make out the conversation. Whatever it was made Reese's face turn grim.

"I wish you had called me sooner," he said once the officer went back inside.

"Why?"

"Because I could have told you not to leave a letter outlining your grievances to Tricia Toker at the scene of the crime."

The letter. I felt like smacking myself in the forehead. I'd completely forgotten that I'd left it sitting on the hall table propped against the fake topiary. "She left us a nasty review online so I wrote her a letter telling her what I thought of her. I was just getting it off my chest."

Reese studied my face. "And that's all you did?"

"To get my anger off my chest?" I asked. "Of course. Why?"

It was Reese's turn to look away.

"You don't think I killed the groom to get back at his awful bride, do you?" I stepped closer to Reese and touched his arm. "Because that doesn't make any sense."

481

He met my eyes. "I don't think that at all but, like it or not, I have to consider you person of interest in the murder investigation."

"Murder?" I stepped back until my legs hit the porch railing. "Did the groom not make it?"

"I don't know about the groom. The paramedics are still working on him. I'm talking about the bride. My officers found her upstairs in bed with a bullet hole between her eyes."

CHAPTER 10

"This is not good." Richard folded the newspaper and laid it on the foot of my bed before walking over and opening my blinds.

I raised my head a few inches off the pillow, shielding my eyes from the daylight streaming in and eyed the paper. "If you're talking about the article in the *Post* that names me as a person of interest in the murder of a bride, then 'not good' is an understatement." I flopped back onto my pillow. "How did you get in, anyway?"

Richard flicked a hand through his spiky dark hair, which, thanks to the miracle of designer sculpting cement, never had a strand out of place. "Your nutty neighbor has her uses."

My elderly downstairs neighbor, Leatrice, had a key to my apartment not because I'd given her one but because she'd made a mold of my key using her amateur spy gadgets before I'd taken my spare key back. Leatrice considered herself a hair's breadth away from being a supersleuth but Richard considered her only moments away from being committed. And if he had his way, he'd be the one committing her.

"She's a terror," I said. "She started a Go Fund Me page for my criminal defense, and I haven't even been charged with anything. And I won't be because I didn't touch Tricia Toker, and the police know it."

Richard shook my foot through the beige duvet cover. "Well, you're not going to be able to fix anything from your bed."

I produced my cell phone from under the covers. "That's where you're wrong. I can monitor everything from right here. If I play my cards right, I never need to leave this room again. Look, I can access the *Post* article here and read all the nasty comments. And if I go on Instagram, I can see where Brianna reposted it and tagged Wedding Belles in the image." I threw my phone down and reached for the now nearly empty bag of gummi bears on my nightstand, shaking the remaining few sticky bears into my palm. I tossed them into my mouth and began chewing. "See? I don't need to move a muscle. The haters will come right to me. And did you know that those Weddies have already started a tribute page for Tricia, and they're all posting things about losing a member of their Weddies family? I mean, obviously they never met her."

Richard snatched the empty candy bag out of my hand then cast a glance around my bedroom and made a face. "If this is what you're like after only one day of self-induced exile, I shudder to think of the disarray after a week."

I sat up, jamming a pair of pillows under my back and pulling my auburn hair into a ponytail. "Give me one good reason to leave. It's not like the phone is ringing. The two potential clients I was scheduled to meet this week canceled. I'm assuming they read about the murder and decided not to hire a wedding planner embroiled in a scandal. The clients we do have on the books have gone radio silent, no doubt waiting to see the degree of fallout before they decide to jump ship or not. And Detective Reese pretty much threatened my life if I so much as breathe in the direction of the investigation."

Richard used two fingers to lift a pair of jeans claw-like from where I'd tossed them on the foot of the bed. He dropped them on the floor and took a seat on the side of the bed next to me. "And you're going to roll over and take it? What happened to the fired-up Annabelle who tore out of here yesterday with a list of grievances in defense of her team and her colleagues? Where's that person?"

"She walked into a murder scene. That's what happened."

Richard grabbed me by the shoulders. "We've had worse. The important thing is that you get up again and fight back. They may take your brides, but they can't take your freedom."

"Are you quoting *Braveheart* to me?"

"Too much?" Richard asked, dropping his hands. "It felt like I brought it out too soon."

"A touch," I said.

"At the very least, why don't we start with getting up and showering?" Richard patted my hands. "Baby steps."

BOOK 4: REVIEW TO A KILL

I groaned as he flung back my wrinkled duvet and grasped both hands to pull me to my feet.

"That's what you sleep in?" He narrowed his eyes at me.

"It's Pink Floyd. It's vintage."

He wrinkled his nose. "It's a concert T-shirt. The only vintage that's worth wearing is vintage Armani, vintage Versace, or vintage Dolce & Gabbana."

I had to admit I couldn't remember the last time I'd seen Richard in a T-shirt. He wouldn't be caught dead in a graphic tee. Even to come over to my apartment and drag me out of bed, he'd worn a black polished-cotton dress shirt and perfectly pressed flat-front chinos.

"Is she up yet?" Leatrice poked her head in my doorway, and I jumped at the sight of her. She'd recently tried to go from her bottle-black hair to red, and the results had been a shade more akin to an electric burgundy than any red found in nature. Not that her black hair had been convincing since Leatrice had recently turned eighty, but at least I'd been used to the jet-black Mary Tyler Moore look.

"I'm coming," I said. Then, when Leatrice disappeared, I whispered to Richard. "You let her loose in my apartment?"

He grinned at me. "More motivation to get out of bed, wouldn't you say?"

"This is domestic terrorism." I snagged the white terry-cloth bathrobe off the hook behind my door and wrapped it around myself as I walked down the hall.

"I'm glad you're up." Leatrice took me by the elbow and steered me toward my dining room table. I looked down at her since she only reached my shoulder and took in her outfit. Compared to her some of her unusual ensembles of the past, the bright blue skirt and suit jacket with scalloped hems were positively tame. And retro.

"Nice suit," I said.

Leatrice beamed at me. "Do you like it? I'm channeling Kitty O'Day."

"Who?"

"She was a detective in the movies played by Jean Parker," Leatrice said.

I eyed the matching blue hat perched on the back of her head. "I'm assuming a while ago."

"The forties."

"Ask her why," Richard said as he came up behind me. The amusement in his voice made me nervous.

"To get me in the right frame of mind to work on your defense."

Leatrice swept a hand over the papers she'd arranged on the wooden dining room table.

I leaned closer to read them then turned to her. "This is all information about Tricia's murder."

Leatrice nodded. "The police reports, the autopsy, the media clippings. It's all here."

"Should I ask how you got all of this?" I put my fingers to my temples. "And how long have you two been in my apartment anyway?"

They both ignored my last question, but I imagined it had taken at least an hour to set out all the documents in such organized piles. How had I not heard them?

"She's gotten very good at computers," Richard said, grinning like the Cheshire cat from where he sat perched on the arm of my sofa.

I stared as Leatrice put on a pair of glasses. "Do you know how to hack into computer systems now?"

"Hacking?" Leatrice laughed. "No, but I made some friends online in my noir chat groups who do."

I glanced back at Richard. "Do I want to know about the chat groups?"

He shook his head. "Definitely not."

Leatrice swatted at Richard. "This one is such a worrywart. But I do have some concerns about the police's investigation."

I sat on the chair Leatrice pulled out for me.

"For one, they don't have any leads on potential suspects. Other than your letter. And two, you and Kate are the only people of interest so far."

"That can't be right," I said. "Tricia must have had plenty of enemies. Just think of all the people she panned online. Plus, all the people she abused in person. The list of suspects should be a mile long."

"You forget that she comes from a filthy rich family," Richard said. "Maybe no one wants to come out and say they hated her. That's probably why none of the people panned ever responded to her reviews."

I put my head in my hands. "Except me."

CHAPTER 11

"So now can you tell me where we're going? You were vague on the phone," Kate said as she slid into the passenger seat of my black Volvo and shut the door. "Don't get me wrong. I'm glad you're up and about. The way Richard talked, I thought you were going full hermit."

Leave it to Richard to turn staying in bed for less than twenty-four hours a call for an intervention. I craned my neck around to check oncoming traffic as I pulled away from the curb in front of Kate's high-rise apartment building. "It's a client."

I thought all the prospective clients for this week canceled." Kate tugged her seatbelt into place then lifted her dove-gray shirt over the lap belt and smoothed it out so it wouldn't wrinkle.

"They did." I slowed as I entered Dupont Circle and took the exit for P Street, grateful that traffic was light and the circle wasn't backed up. "This is a past client."

Kate twisted in the car seat to look at me. "Since when do we have meetings with past clients? Who was it who taught me to keep a firm line between business and friendship?"

"I know," I said. "This is a special case."

"Because?"

I ignored her question as we entered Georgetown and passed a bakery. "Did you have breakfast?"

Kate flipped her phone over in her lap. "Do you mean did I have lunch? Yes, I did. Now do you want to tell me who we're meeting?"

"You mean who I'm going to meet while you act as lookout?" I turned onto Reservoir Road.

"Lookout? I got all dressed up to be a lookout?" Kate motioned to her black pencil skirt and fitted button-down shirt. "This is a waste of a perfectly good outfit. Now I know why you didn't ask Richard to come with you. He hates playing the sidekick."

She was partially correct. I hadn't asked Richard because I knew he'd disapprove and try to talk me out of it plus I knew he got flustered under pressure. Kate was a skillful charmer and had talked her way out of plenty of sticky situations and bad dates. Being a lookout played right into her wheelhouse.

I swung into the squat, industrial parking garage for Georgetown Hospital and rolled down my car window to take a ticket.

"The hospital?" Kate said. "You aren't actually visiting who I think you're visiting, are you?"

"You mean our groom who was shot?" I found a spot on the first level with just enough room for us to squeeze out. "That's exactly whom I'm visiting."

"I thought the detective told you to stay out of the investigation. Isn't this the exact opposite of that?"

I wiggled out of the car, being careful not to hit the other vehicle with my door or rub against the side of my dusty car in my black pants and pale blue silk tank. "I fully intended to stay out of things until I found out that not only do the police have no other persons of interest except for us, they haven't found a single real suspect."

Kate inched out of her side then released the breath she'd been holding in. "How did you discover that? Detective Reese?"

I led the way to the main entrance of the redbrick hospital, holding open the glass doors for Kate. The lobby reminded me of every other hospital lobby I'd been in. Lots of muted primary colors and blond wood with miles and miles of cream-colored tile. I took a breath and wondered if there was a secret *"eau de* hospital" air freshener that gave the buildings their antiseptic scent.

"I wish." I felt annoyed at Reese for not letting me know just how much hot water I was in with the police, and I was no longer convinced that his top priority was looking out for me as he'd claimed. "Leatrice used some new hacker friends to get the police files."

"I beg your pardon, what?" Kate stumbled in her black peep-toe heels as we reached the elevator bank.

"I know. Her hacker network is a whole other story I haven't delved into but, suffice it to say, Leatrice has appointed herself in charge of our defense team." A chime indicated that an elevator had arrived, and the metal doors in front opened.

Kate leaned against the wall of the elevator once we'd stepped inside. "That's terrifying."

"Tell me about it." I pressed the button for the third floor. "But she was able to get me the groom's hospital room number and determine that the police aren't providing security for him."

"So the plan is for you to go into the room and for me to stay outside in case anyone shows up?" Kate asked as the elevator doors slid open. "How long do you need to talk to him?"

"Not long, I hope." I led the way to the right side of the hospital wing. More beige-and-cream walls broken up by nurses' stations made out of faux pine. "I just want to ask him a few more questions than the police did."

Kate put a hand over her nose. "You read their interview of the groom?"

I nodded. "Reese didn't do the questioning. I think his new partner did, and it seemed pretty cursory to me. That or the groom wasn't in the right frame of mind to answer questions. But since nothing of value was taken from the house, the intruder must have had a personal reason. And if anyone would have an idea about the reason, it would be the groom. I'm hoping he's more talkative now that he's out of surgery and recuperating."

We reached the room number Leatrice had given me. I glanced at the name on the door and confirmed it was Dave's room. As I pushed it open, Kate grabbed my sleeve. "What's the signal in case someone shows up?"

I shrugged. "I don't know. A whistle? A knock?"

"I'll think of something." She pushed me inside.

As I stepped into the private room, my eyes adjusted to the low light after the brightness of the hallway. The blinds to the large window were closed so the only light came from the attached bathroom.

"Could I get some water?" The voice coming from the bed was hoarse and quiet.

I hurried over to the wheeled swing-arm table and poured a cup from the plastic pitcher. I took it over to the groom and held the cup for him while he sat up and sipped from the blue bendy straw.

"Thanks," he said, lying back on the inclined hospital bed then sitting up again. "Wait. You're not a nurse."

"No, it's me. Annabelle Archer. Your wedding planner," I said. "You probably don't remember, but my assistant and I found you after you were shot."

He shook his head slowly. "I remember you, but I don't remember you finding me. Thanks, I guess."

"I'm so sorry about what happened." I glanced at his bandaged shoulder. "Did you have to have surgery?"

He nodded. "They removed the bullet. The doctors say I'll be fine. My dreams of being a major league pitcher are shot, though."

I laughed with him once I heard him chuckle.

"You probably don't remember much about that day." I offered him the water again and he drank.

He cleared his throat and winced. "I remember having my morning coffee. I like to sit at the kitchen counter and check news on my phone while I drink my coffee." He paused. "Tricia was upstairs in bed. She'd been worn out by the wedding and was trying to build up her strength for our honeymoon."

"That's right. You were going to Paris. When were you leaving?"

He pressed his eyebrows together like he was trying to recall the date. "A week after the wedding. Tricia wanted time to rest and tie up loose ends."

More like she wanted to write all her horrible reviews, I thought, but I kept this to myself. "So you were downstairs and Tricia was upstairs. Do you remember hearing anyone come inside?"

"No. But I'd already stepped outside that morning to check the temperature so I might have left the front door open when I came back in. Our neighborhood is usually very safe."

"Were you sitting with your back to the kitchen doorway?"

He moved his head up and down slightly. "The only thing I remember is hearing a loud noise and getting knocked off the barstool onto the ground. My face hit the floor and that hurt more than being shot. At least at first. Then everything went black."

"So you didn't see the shooter?"

"No."

I walked over to the pitcher and refilled the plastic cup. "Dave, do you have any idea who would want to shoot you?"

"No clue," he said, turning his face away from the light spilling out from the bathroom. "None of it makes any sense. The cops said that nothing was stolen."

"Do you and Tricia have any enemies?" I asked. "Anyone who would want you both dead?"

"Enemies?" He paused.

I heard Kate's voice from outside the door. "Whip-poor-will! Whip-poor-will!"

As odd as it was, I was pretty sure that was my signal to get out. I put down the plastic cup and pitcher.

The groom sat up. "Wait a second. Why are you asking if someone would want us both dead?"

I opened my mouth and closed it again. Had no one told him that his wife had been shot and killed? I backed toward the door. "I'd better let you get some rest. Again, I'm really sorry."

"Did something happen to Tricia?" he called after me. "Tell me!"

I pushed the door open and closed it behind me so people in the hallway wouldn't hear the groom yelling after me. Kate stood next to the door wearing a white doctor's coat and a surgical mask over her face.

"MOB and MOH at two o'clock," she hissed at me and handed me a green surgical mask.

I glanced at the nurse's station and saw the bride's mother and her best friend with their backs to us. We would need to pass by them to leave. I took the surgical mask and tied it around the back of my head. "You don't happen to have an extra lab coat, do you?"

"Sorry, Charlie." She handed me a clipboard. "But this will make you look more official."

I took it. I could hear the groom still yelling inside his room, and I felt a knot begin to form in my stomach. That was not how I'd intended that interaction to play out. I knew I should go back in and calm down the groom but I also knew that I could not get caught talking to him. "Let's go."

We walked briskly by the nurse's station and down the hall. As we turned the corner, I chanced a glance behind me. The maid of honor had turned her head to watch us and before she disappeared from view, I saw her red-rimmed eyes grow wide.

CHAPTER 12

"Wait!" A hand shot into the elevator before it closed, and the doors opened back up. Madeleine stood in front of us breathing heavily from chasing after us down the hospital corridor. She wore the same clothes she'd had on yesterday, and I noticed flecks of dried blood on the sleeve of her pink cardigan. Her eyes were bloodshot, black mascara lines trailed down her face from crying, and lose strands of hair had fallen from her ponytail into her face.

Kate pulled the surgical mask down from her mouth as we stepped out of the elevator. "Hey, Madeleine. Imagine running into you like this."

Madeleine ran her eyes over the white doctor's coat Kate wore and the clipboard I clutched to my chest. "Do you two moonlight here?"

"No," I said, wondering how to explain away Kate's odd attire. "Kate's just . . ."

"Very germ conscious," Kate finished my sentence for me. "I have a phobia about germs in hospitals. They're breeding grounds for all sorts of infections, you know. So I always wear a mask and coat when I visit."

Madeleine's eye twitched when Kate mentioned infection.

Kate reached out a hand and placed it on her sleeve. "But I'm sure you'll be fine."

Madeleine nodded then pulled her eyes away from Kate to look at me. "We didn't get a chance to talk after the police arrived yesterday. I'm afraid I fell apart a bit."

"That's perfectly understandable," I said. Now it was my turn to put a hand on her arm.

"We would have been just as hysterical as you were if we weren't so used to being at crime scenes," Kate said.

Madeleine looked confused, and I shot Kate daggers.

"Not that you were hysterical," Kate said after seeing my expression. "That was the wrong word. Upset. You were just upset."

"Why have you two been at so many crime scenes?" Madeleine asked, her gaze moving between us.

I sighed. "We've had the misfortune of being around a few mishaps at our weddings."

"Mishaps?" Madeleine asked. "Like accidents?"

Kate snapped her fingers. "Accidents. Exactly. Accidental deaths." She hesitated. "Not really accidental so much as murders, though."

I closed my eyes and tried not to groan out loud. When Kate got nervous, she had a habit of rambling and sharing way too much information.

"You've been involved in murders?" Madeleine's voice barely rose above a whisper.

"We've never killed anyone," I said.

"No way." Kate shook her head. "We're the ones who solve the cases."

A look passed across Madeleine's face. "So you could find out who killed Tricia?"

Even though I was admittedly poking around in the case, it was only to clear Kate's and my name. I did not want to promise anyone that I could track down a killer for them. I jabbed Kate's leg with my foot. "Kate's joking. We leave the investigating to the police."

Madeleine frowned. "That's too bad. I was going to tell you something I forgot to mention yesterday in all the chaos."

"Did you see something?" I asked. "A clue?" I may not have wanted to be tasked with tracking down a murderer, but when push came to shove, I couldn't resist information that could help my cause.

She shook her head. "It wasn't something I saw, it's something I know. Tricia and Dave had been having a feud with their next-door neighbor for months. The one who lives in the redbrick house with the white door."

My shoulders sagged. Another person Tricia antagonized? This wasn't exactly breaking news.

Madeleine looked behind her then continued. "It started when they both put up political signs. For opposing candidates. Words were exchanged. It got heated."

"But this is Washington," I said. "Politics is everywhere. You won't last long in this town if you get worked up about every person who disagrees with you."

"Their neighbor hadn't been here long." She waved a hand. "I don't remember. All I know is he took their politics very personally. And you know Tricia when she's challenged."

Or even when she's not, I wanted to say.

"So you think this feud was bad enough that the neighbor walked into their house and shot them?" Kate asked, her voice sounding unconvinced.

Madeleine shrugged. "I know it sounds extreme, but this guy had serious anger-management issues. And he was armed to the teeth. Or at least that's what he told Tricia and Dave."

"So he has guns?" I asked.

"According to him, he has lots. I think he waved a handgun at them once from his porch."

I tapped my shoe on the floor as I thought. "I'm happy to pass this information on to the detectives working this case. Do you know the guy's name?"

"Frank something. I remember because Tricia used to call him Effing Frank."

I allowed myself a small smile. "That sounds like Tricia."

Madeleine put a hand to her mouth and gave a combination of a laugh and a sob. "It's pretty classic Tricia." She dropped her hand. "Listen, I know you probably think the same thing everyone else does. That Tricia was difficult. That she was unpleasant. That she could be mean."

I looked at Kate, who looked at her shoes.

"All of those things are true," Madeleine said. "She was an unhappy person and she took it out on everyone around her. Trust me, I know. I've known her longer than anyone except her mother. But she didn't deserve to be murdered in her bed like that. And Dave certainly didn't deserve to be shot in the back."

"Of course you're right," I said. "No one deserves that."

Madeleine met my eyes. "It's important to me that Tricia gets justice."

I heard a loud throat clearing and saw the bride's mother staring at us from the other end of the hall.

"I'd better go." Madeleine began backing away from us. "I thought my duties would be over after the wedding, but I'm still chauffeuring Tricia's mom around in her car. Not that I mind. It beats my Honda Civic. And she doesn't critique my driving like Tricia did."

"At least we never have to drive our clients around," Kate said once

Madeleine was out of earshot. "Your critique of my driving is bad enough. If I'd had Tricia rating me, I might have driven her off a cliff."

"But think how much pain and suffering you would have saved us."

Kate shrugged off the doctor's coat. "I'll keep it in mind for the next bridezilla."

CHAPTER 13

"Did you get any good intel?" Leatrice asked when I walked in my apartment. She sat on the dining room table with her legs crossed and swinging beneath her.

"Not from the groom." I dropped my purse on the couch and headed for the kitchen. "He didn't see whoever shot him. He didn't even hear anyone come in. But the maid of honor made a point of telling us about a feud they had with their neighbor."

Leatrice tapped a finger to her chin. "Interesting. Was the feud bad enough to kill over?"

"She says the guy waved a gun at them once." I opened the fridge and plucked a cold bottled Mocha Frappuccino from the door.

Leatrice slid off the table. "Our first alternative suspect. Aren't you glad you went to the hospital? Even if the groom wasn't helpful, the maid of honor made up for it."

I took a long swig of the cold coffee drink and rested the bottle on the counter. "I'm pretty sure the groom isn't glad I went."

I replayed the sight of the groom's face when I let it slip that his wife was also a victim. He'd been shocked and upset. Not that I blamed him. It was bad enough to find yourself in the hospital with a bullet wound but then to be told by a virtual stranger that your wife of one day had also been shot? I hated to think what he was going through now.

Leatrice poked her head over the chest-high opening between the living room and kitchen and pushed back one side of the wooden accordion shutters that divided the two rooms. "What do you mean?"

Before I could explain, a pounding on my door caused us both to jump. "Annabelle! Open up!"

"Goodness." Leatrice put a hand to her throat. "If that's the UPS man, he needs to work on his customer service."

I came out of the kitchen and sighed. "It's not the UPS man." I knew exactly who it was and why he was pounding on my door and yelling. I opened the door and Detective Reese stood in the doorway, his arm up ready to recommence pounding.

He strode into my living room, tossed his blazer over a dining room chair, and spun on his heel. "Are you completely insane?"

Leatrice looked from him to me, her eyes wide. "Which one of us is he talking to?"

I closed the door and turned to face him. "He's talking to me."

"You're damn right I'm talking to you." He took a few long steps across the room, raking his fingers through his dark hair. "Do you have any idea what you've just done?"

"I know I shouldn't—"

"Not only have you interfered with an ongoing police investigation that I specifically asked you to stay out of. For your own good, I should add. But you snuck into a hospital room of a man who was recovering from a gunshot and told him that his wife was dead."

Leatrice sucked in a breath. "He didn't know his wife was dead?"

I shook my head. "I didn't say dead."

"Correction. That his wife was also a victim." Reese interlocked his fingers behind his head and looked up at the ceiling. "Now he's hysterical, the hospital is upset because they had to sedate him, the family is upset because they didn't get to break the news to him at a more appropriate time, and my boss is screaming at me because a person of interest in the case is terrorizing victims."

I tried hard not to roll my eyes. "I would hardly classify this as terrorizing."

Reese stretched his arms out wide. "And do you want to know the cherry on top?" He didn't wait for a reply. "The bride's mother saw your blond sidekick outside the groom's room disguised as a doctor."

"Doctor?" Leatrice mouthed when the detective turned away to start pacing, and she gave me a thumbs-up.

Great. The last thing I wanted was for Leatrice to approve of a disguise and Reese to be mad at me. "I mean, when you put it like that it sounds bad but I didn't visit the groom intending to do any of that."

Reese stopped his pacing to look at me. "Why did you go over there in the first place? I told you to stay out of the investigation and let me do my job."

"Well, you've done a bang-up job already," I said.

"Excuse me?"

Leatrice shook her head slightly but I ignored her.

"Meaning that Kate and I are the only persons of interest in the case." I walked toward the detective. "You haven't found any suspects, even though every person who ever met Tricia Toker wanted to kill her. So if I don't start trying to find some suspects for you, I'm afraid I'm going to find myself being charged with a murder I had nothing to do with."

Reese took a deep breath and rubbed his forehead with one hand. "Do you think I want that?" His voice dropped a few octaves. "I'm doing everything I can to get you two out of this mess, and you keep crawling back in it."

"I'm not trying to screw up your investigation. I'm trying to save our necks."

Reese closed the gap between us and took my hands. "Why can't you let me help you?"

I shrugged and didn't meet his eyes. "I'm doing what I know how to do. Solve problems. Fix things. I'm not used to sitting back and getting rescued."

"No kidding." Reese gave a weary laugh. "You didn't read the fairy tales where the knight slays the dragon for the princess, did you?"

"Sorry, I'm not much for fairytales."

He tilted his head to one side. "A wedding planner who doesn't believe in fairytales?"

"You want to know why I don't believe in fairy tales? Too many Type-A princesses, evil queens, and knights who want to add clauses to my contract."

"Well, I promise not to be any of those if you promise to stop getting mixed up in my investigation." He leaned down and met my eyes. "Deal?"

I wanted to promise him, but I felt torn. On the one hand was the handsome detective looking into my eyes and holding my hands and making my heart race, and on the other hand was the prospect of sitting back and doing nothing to get Kate and myself out of trouble. He leaned in until our lips were inches away. I nodded yes.

He let out a breath and smiled, running a finger down the side of my face. "I'd better get back to work. I've got to clear a wedding planner and her assistant of a murder they didn't commit."

Leatrice stood only a few feet away from us grinning and rocking back and forth in her vintage lace-up heels.

I ignored her and cleared my throat. "Before I forget, I did manage to find out one bit of info you may not have. Apparently, Tricia and Dave had an ongoing feud with their next-door neighbor. And their best friend Madeleine says the guy threatened them and has a thing for guns."

Reese pulled a small flip notebook out of his back pants pocket. "Did she give you a name?"

"Frank. Tricia called him Effing Frank because she hated him. But I know he lives right next to them in the redbrick house."

He scratched a few words into the notebook. "That's actually helpful. But don't let it go to your head. I'll handle checking out this guy, okay?"

I held up both hands in a gesture of surrender. "He's all yours."

He smiled again and reached for the blazer he'd tossed over a dining room chair.

"What's all this?" he asked, staring down at the table covered with police documents. "How did you get these?"

Leatrice hurried over to him. "This is all me, detective. I'm practicing my sleuthing skills."

"Stealing police documents is a felony." He held up a paper and waved it at me. "And you knew about this? You knew these were illegally obtained?"

"Not before she did it," I said, hating how weak the excuse sounded.

Reese shook his head and dropped the paper. It fluttered down to the table. "I can't be involved with this." He walked to the door, not looking at me as he passed. He opened the door then turned. "I want to believe you, Annabelle, but as long as you're working against the police department, against me, I can't be involved. With you. With any of it."

"He'll cool off and come around, dear," Leatrice said once Reese had closed the door behind him.

I'd seen the hurt in his eyes as he'd left. I wasn't so sure.

CHAPTER 14

"You're sure you'll be fine, dear?" Leatrice asked as I gently pushed her out my door. "You don't want me to keep you company after that unpleasant scene with the detective?"

"I'm okay. I promise." What I really wanted after my shouting match with Detective Reese was to be left alone. As well-meaning as Leatrice was, her unrelenting chatter about the murder investigation had started to wear on me.

Her bright burgundy bob wedged into the crack in the doorway as I closed it. "I'm right downstairs if you need anything. Tweet at me. Shoot me a text. Facebook message me. Send me a Snapchat."

"You got it." I wasn't sure if her obsession with crime or her newfound fondness for technology disturbed me more. It seemed wrong that an eighty-year-old tossed around social media lingo more casually than I did.

I leaned against the door once I'd closed it and listened to the clicking of her heels on the stairs as she walked down to her first=floor apartment. I knew it would be pointless to try to lock her out since she had a key to my place and clearly was not shy about using it, but I figured I had a few hours before she concocted a reason to come upstairs again. I congratulated myself for giving her an assignment before I'd sent her away. Tracking down all of Tricia's online review profiles should keep her busy for the rest of the afternoon. Maybe all night if I was lucky and if Tricia had been very prolific with her poisoned pen.

I flopped onto my overstuffed couch and leaned back, stretching my feet under the glass coffee table. I rolled my head to the side so I could see out the window, where the sun's rays began to drop below the Georgetown rooftops. Even though the rent was more of my monthly budget than it should be, I loved living in the classic, residential area of DC. It might not be as hip as the U Street area or as modern as the Clarendon neighborhood just over the bridge in Virginia, but I loved the classic townhouses and occasional cobbled streets of Georgetown. Not to mention my favorite bakeries were only blocks away from me.

I remembered I hadn't had lunch, so I got up to scour what was left of the bounty Richard and Fern had brought over the day before. I found an uneaten spinach empanada in the fridge and began munching on it without heating it up as I walked back into the living room.

My phone trilled from the side table, and I picked it up to check the caller, hoping that it wasn't Leatrice telling me she'd finished her task already. It was Richard.

"Meet me downstairs," he said when I answered. "But don't let Leatrice hear you leave. I'm not in the mood to deal with that pint-sized Jessica Fletcher."

I walked to the window that overlooked P Street, but I couldn't see him. "You're outside? Why don't you come up?"

"I can't. Just come down." He disconnected.

I slipped on a pair of black ballet flats I kept by the door and shoved my keys in the pocket of my black pants then headed downstairs, being careful to walk on my tiptoes the entire way and holding my breath as I passed Leatrice's apartment door. Even though she was elderly, she had hearing that could rival that of a bat. I eased open the heavy wooden door of the building and held it so that it didn't shut with a bang. I spotted Richard standing at the corner.

"What are you holding?" I asked.

"Don't be cute, Annabelle. You know it's a leash."

"Yes, but what are you doing with it and why is there a dog attached to the bottom." I gestured to the Yorkie weaving its way around Richard's legs then lowered my voice. "You don't do dogs."

Richard lifted his feet one at a time to untangle himself from the leash. "I know I don't usually do dogs but there's a first time for everything."

"Is this your dog?" I asked as the brown-and-black dog sniffed my ankles. Richard had always been very clear how he felt about dogs and children—two types of creatures he felt were far too messy and needy for him.

Richard flinched. "Of course not. Have you lost your mind?"

"Maybe," I said. "Leatrice is on Snapchat, and you're walking a dog. Should I be checking the skies for flying pigs?"

Richard began walking down the street and motioned for me to follow. "This is P.J.'s dog."

I ran a few steps to catch up. "And P.J. is—?"

"I've mentioned P.J. before. The bartender who paints portraits."

I racked my brain. Had he mentioned a bartender who was also a painter and had a dog? If so, he'd never mentioned a name. Or that they were close enough that Richard would assume dog-walking duties. "So how long have you been seeing P.J.?"

"A month. Maybe two." Richard paused at the end of the block then hurried across the street with the Yorkie running to keep up.

"Two months?" I said when I caught up. "And you're just mentioning this now?"

Richard's cheeks flushed, and I doubted it was from the scamper across the street. "I didn't want to make a big thing out of it."

"I think it's kind of a thing if you're walking his dog." I tried not to sound petty but I couldn't help feeling hurt that he'd been dating someone for two months without telling me. Ever since I'd moved to Washington a few years ago and opened Wedding Belles, Richard and I had been tight, working together almost every weekend and getting into and out of more than a few scrapes together. "Does the dog have a name?"

"Butterscotch," Richard said.

I leaned down and scratched the dog's head. "Nice to meet you, Butterscotch."

Butterscotch wagged his tail and piddled a bit on the sidewalk.

Richard shook his head and tugged the dog in the direction of the park across the street. "Don't take it personally. He wets himself every time I come into the room."

"Don't worry, Butterscotch," I said to the dog as we entered Rose Park. "You're not the only one who wets himself when he sees Richard. Most of his waiters do the same thing."

Richard glared at me. "Hilarious."

"When do I get to meet this P.J.?" I asked. "I already know his dog."

"Do you really want to start meeting boyfriends?" Richard followed Butterscotch as he explored a patch of bushes.

"Well, you've met all of mine. It only seems fair," I said. "Not that I have either guy at the moment."

Richard raised an eyebrow. "I know you cooled things off with Tattoo

Boy so you could see where things were headed with the detective. What's happened now?"

I gave a shake of my head. "I didn't exactly cool things off with Ian on purpose. His band went on tour. And Reese and I just got in a big fight."

Richard put a hand on his hip. "Spill, girl."

"He found out that I went with Kate to the hospital to talk to the groom, that I accidentally told the groom his wife had been shot when he didn't know yet, and that we posed as doctors to sneak out. Then, after he'd stopped freaking out about that, he saw Leatrice's hacked police documents all over my dining room table and got mad all over again."

Richard's eyebrows shot up so high they almost merged with his hairline. "That would do it."

"Basically, he said that I need to trust him to solve the case and stay out of it or he can't be involved with me." I blinked hard as I felt tears prick the backs of my eyes.

"But you can't," Richard said as a statement, not a question.

I shook my head and swiped at my eyes. "I've been fixing things for people for so long that I can't let go and let someone else take care of it. What's wrong with me?"

Richard patted my arm. "It's a hazard of the job, Annabelle. The people who take care of everything don't know how to be taken care of."

"So I should sit back and let Reese handle it?" I asked.

Richard tugged on Butterscotch's leash as we walked, and the dog tried to inspect every stick and pinecone he passed. "Probably. It is his job, after all. And how do we feel when the overbearing mother tries to do our job for us or the annoying bridesmaid tells us everything we could be doing better?"

"We want to gouge their eyes out." I said. "But this is different."

"Because it's a man you have the hots for?" Richard grinned at me. "You know that if you actually like this guy you're going to have to trust him at some point."

"Easier said than done." The thought of playing the damsel in distress to Detective Reese's knight in shining armor still didn't sit well with me. I didn't know if I was ready to give up control, especially if there was a chance I might be charged with a murder. Besides that, I wasn't sure if Reese had earned my trust. Not when he hadn't even been clear on where we stood.

"Believe me, girl. I get it." Richard nodded at Butterscotch sniffing the flowerbed. "One day you let someone in your life just a little bit, and the next thing you know, you're on dog-walking duty."

"It must be worth it," I said, knowing Richard and his feelings about pets in general.

"All I can tell you, Annabelle, as your slightly older and wiser friend, is to be careful. In this business, you snap your fingers and a decade has gone by and you have nothing but a bunch of pretty pictures to show for it."

I'd never heard Richard talk about his life with anything close to the regret I heard now in his voice. Would I feel the same way if I let things with Reese fall apart?

"Come on, dog. Let's go home," Richard said. Butterscotch wagged his tail, trotted over to Richard, then promptly piddled on his shoe.

"Can I make a suggestion?" I asked as Richard cursed and shook his foot. "Maybe don't wear the Prada shoes when you walk the dog?"

"Are you suggesting I wear pleather?" Richard sucked in a breath. "I might have to walk this dog but I will not lower my standards."

"Fine," I said, taking a few steps away from him. "But do me a favor. Don't wear those shoes to our next wedding together. If we have a next wedding together."

"Of course we'll have more weddings together." Richard walked a few steps then shook his foot again. "This murder thing will blow over and everyone will forget that you were ever involved."

I knew he was saying that to make me feel better and I hoped he was right, but I had a sinking feeling that Tricia Toker was the kind of bride who could do as much damage from the grave as she had in life.

CHAPTER 15

"Explain to me again why I'm here if all our appointments have been canceled." Kate sat cross-legged on the floor of my office in a pair of black-and-white striped silk shorts and a lime-green silk tank top, her idea of casual clothes. My idea of casual consisted of black yoga pants with traces of carpet lint and a pink fitted T-shirt.

I handed her a stack of gold polka-dot file folders. "Because we still have old clients and upcoming weddings even if all the prospective clients got scared off. Besides, I'm not supposed to be meddling in the investigation and if I don't do something to keep busy, I'll lose my mind."

"Aha." Kate flipped open the first folder. "Now the truth comes out. Let 'Project Keep Annabelle From Being Thrown in the Nut House' begin."

I made a face at her. "I thought we could go through these weddings and pull all the proposals the client didn't accept and double-check that we have signed contracts for every vendor."

"I hate paperwork days," Kate said. "How long until you think people will forget about the murder and start calling?"

I sat down next to her with my own stack of folders and swept my hair up into a ponytail. I rarely bothered styling my hair unless it was a wedding day so "ponytail" was my default setting. "People have short memories. Not more than a few weeks, I'd guess." I knew that estimate was very optimistic, but there was no need to drag Kate's mood down by telling her what I really believed.

"Memories may be short, but social media is forever." Kate scrolled through her phone with one hand. "Have you taken a look at Tricia's Weddies tribute page? Who are all these people posting about how amazing she was and why weren't they at her wedding?"

I glanced over at the list of comments as Kate dragged her thumb down the screen. "Some people flock to tragedy. It probably makes them feel good to write something nice and completely untrue. Especially if they didn't bother to show up to her wedding."

"I'm surprised more of these tragedy seekers didn't flock to the Hay-Adams Hotel for filet mignon."

One of the many things Tricia had complained about during her wedding planning was the low response rate. Usually we estimated about ten to twenty percent of the invited guests would RSVP no, but Tricia's no rate had been closer to half. Instead of worrying about squeezing two hundred guests into the rooftop ballroom, we'd had to rent trees so the room wouldn't look empty with eighty. I'd told the bride her wedding weekend was a busy one and people were probably traveling, but that had been a lie intended to keep her calm. The truth I'd known from nearly the first time we'd met was that the bride was a supremely unlikable person and had almost no friends. I'd been amazed she even had the one friend close enough to be her maid of honor.

"Unbelievable," Kate said. "The Weddies are even getting together to share memories of Tricia. Should we go? I'll bet we'd have better stories than any of those posers."

I tapped Kate's folders. "Let's try to forget about Tricia for a day and focus on the upcoming weddings."

Kate put her phone on the floor. "You're right. I feel like we might have neglected some of them because Tricia sucked up so much time."

"Yoo-hoo!" Leatrice called out, and I could tell she was already inside my apartment.

"Maybe if we're quiet enough she won't know we're back here," Kate whispered.

"Impossible," I told her. "She has superhuman hearing."

Leatrice appeared in the doorway wearing a beige trench coat belted at the waist and a matching fedora. "There you are. I thought I heard two voices back here."

"Told you," I said to Kate then smiled at Leatrice. "What's up?"

"I finally did it." She held up a handful of papers. "I found all the reviews that your bride wrote."

Kate raised an eyebrow. "That must have taken a while."

Leatrice walked over to my black office chair and sat down, her feet, clad in old-fashioned black lace-up heels, dangling a few inches above the floor. "It did. I was up half the night."

"This didn't involve any hacking, did it?" I asked. I'd felt guilty after Detective Reese had seen all of the documents that Leatrice's hacker friends had pulled off the police computer system, so the fewer illegal actions taken on my behalf, the better.

She shook her head. "Just lots of searching. Luckily the bride used her real name or some variation of 'TriciaandDaveattheHay' for all her user profiles, so her reviews weren't tough to track down. She must not have cared who knew she wrote them."

"I'm sure she wanted people to know who wrote them," Kate said. "I'll bet that was part of the fun for her."

Leatrice tilted her fedora back. "Well, she was the only one having fun. There wasn't a nice review in the bunch, and there were hundreds."

"Hundreds?" I'd had no idea our bride's poisoned pen had been so prolific. I made a mental note to do a better job of researching our clients before we signed on. A decent Google search could have avoided a year's worth of suffering on our part, not to mention the fact that I wouldn't have been named a person of interest in a murder investigation.

Leatrice handed me the stack of papers. "I put them in chronological order with the most recent ones, the ones from the wedding, on the top. But they go back eight years."

Kate whistled. "That's a lot of hate mail." She slid closer to me so she could read over my shoulder. "There's ours."

I didn't have the stomach to read it again, so I put Tricia's review of us facedown on the floor. I flipped through the review of Buster and Mack, one of the hotel, and then reached one of the bridal salon where Tricia had bought her wedding gown. I scanned the text and shook my head. "She ripped Caroline's boutique to shreds."

"What?" Kate snatched the review from my hands. "But those women bent over backwards for her. They even sent gowns to her house. When have you ever heard of a salon doing that?"

"None of her reviews were justified," I reminded Kate. "Just remember the one she wrote about us. Nothing but lies."

Kate threw the paper onto the floor. "I know, but it just makes me so mad that people think nothing of tearing apart something that someone's worked so hard to build. If Tricia wasn't dead already, I'd want to wring her neck."

Leatrice patted her on the shoulder. "Good thing someone beat you to it, dear."

I continued to page through the reviews. "And here's one for her rehearsal dinner restaurant."

Kate's mouth dropped open. "She panned Charlie Palmer? Come on, it's a DC institution."

"And we recommended it," I said, feeling bad the moment I remembered that we'd been the ones to talk up the steak house. "I guess we owe the manager an apology."

"From the looks of it we owe a lot of apologies." Kate gestured to the pile of papers in my hand then ran a hand through her blond hair. "Is there any vendor we recommended that didn't get trashed?"

"I would say Fern, but we didn't recommend him. And the only reason he missed being a target was because he threatened to shampoo her with Nair."

"Goodness." Leatrice put a hand to her own violently burgundy locks. "That's a scary thought."

"Wait a second." Kate snapped her fingers. "Didn't Fern recommend us for the wedding? Isn't he the reason Tricia called us?"

I tried to think back to a year ago when we got the wedding. "I'd have to look in my lead log, but you may be right. But I'm sure Fern didn't know about the reviews or that things would turn out this way."

"I guess so." Kate slumped back. "And if we get mad at Fern he may shampoo our hair with Nair."

"I don't think the two of us being bald would help the situation," I said.

"But if that ever happens, you're welcome to my wig collection," Leatrice said. "I mostly use them for undercover surveillance, but I'm happy to share."

I didn't want to know what type of undercover surveillance Leatrice meant, and I scanned my memory to see if I could recall any extremely short women following me.

"So what are we going to do with these reviews?" Kate asked. "Give them to the police?"

Turning them over to the police wasn't my first instinct, but I knew I should be trying to let them handle the investigation. I also knew that giving Detective Reese any evidence would only convince him I was meddling again. And telling him that Leatrice gathered them might send him over the edge.

"This is our list of people to visit," I said. "You were right when you said we owed a lot of apologies. And I think we should do it in person."

Kate narrowed her eyes at me. "Are we going to apologize or question them? Because this feels a lot like what we'd be doing if we were trying to investigate the murder on our own."

"You're so suspicious. I think Leatrice is rubbing off on you."

Kate gave me a dirty look, and Leatrice beamed.

Even if I wouldn't admit it to Kate, I knew that we'd be able to learn things from our wedding colleagues that the police never would. And even Detective Reese couldn't fault me for wanting to commiserate with my fellow wedding vendors and victims of Tricia's poisoned pen. Especially if he never found out.

CHAPTER 16

"Tell me again why this isn't a terrible idea." Kate closed the passenger door to my Volvo and walked around to my side. "And are those the same black pants you wore yesterday?"

I glanced down at the black pants and pink button-down I'd thrown on before we left. "No," I lied. "I own lots of black pants." That part was true. But what was also true is that I'd grabbed this pair—the same I'd worn the day before—from where I'd draped them over the chair in my bedroom the night before.

"That, I believe."

It had taken less than thirty minutes to drive from my Georgetown apartment to the DC suburb of Potomac, which meant we'd been very lucky and traffic had been unusually light. The bridal salon Love held a prominent spot in a row of high-end shops and boasted something DC salons could never claim—free parking and lots of it. I'd found a spot directly in front of the salon and reveled in the fact that I hadn't been forced to circle the block or try to wedge my car into a quasi-legal space on the street. I might adore living in Georgetown, but the 'burbs had their perks.

"How could commiserating with a colleague ever be a bad idea?" I asked.

Kate studied me. "I want to believe you, but I feel like we've been down this path before, and it always ends up in us getting busted."

"Busted?" I laughed, but it sounded manufactured, even to my own ears. "The police can't get angry at us for visiting friends. And Caroline Love is a friend."

Kate hiked her pink Kate Spade purse onto her shoulder. "Whatever you need to tell yourself but I still say we're biking up the wrong tree."

"That I would like to see," I said, but Kate didn't catch my meaning. If I was honest with myself, the visits were as much about my need to get myself off the potential suspect list for Tricia Toker's murder as they were about reaching out to our wedding colleagues. I'd had enough dealings with the police to know they wouldn't be as motivated to find an alternate suspect as I would be, and they didn't know the wedding industry like we did. Anyway, visiting wedding friends was not the same as hacking into police computers so, as far as I was concerned, this was a step in the right direction.

I followed Kate as she led the way up to the tall glass doors. The entire front of the salon featured floor-to-ceiling glass. Flanking the double doors were rows of couture wedding dresses suspended by transparent wires, giving the effect that the dresses floated in midair. When we opened the doors, a white half-moon receptionist's desk sat underneath a massive sign that read "Love" in swirling white letters on a dove-gray background. The salon extended in both directions with racks of gowns covering the walls interspersed with full-length mirrors.

"Kate? Annabelle?" A slender woman with glossy brown hair that fell straight to her shoulders came from behind the desk. "Do you have a bride coming today?"

"Not today." Kate reached the salon owner first and gave her a quick hug. "This is a social visit."

I extended the box of pastel, French macarons we'd picked up on our way. "We're here to commiserate."

Caroline Love took the box and gave me a hug. "I'm assuming you mean about that horrible girl." She waved us into the back of the salon, and we followed. Several cream-colored tufted couches clustered around a small stage surrounded by mirrors. This was where brides came to model the gowns they tried on and where their family and friends watched. We each took a spot on a couch around the empty stage.

"You saw the reviews," I said more as a statement than a question.

Caroline opened the box of macarons, removed a pistachio-green cookie with a white filling, and passed the box along to Kate. "I only read ours. Then I had to shut down my computer before I threw it out the window."

Kate selected a pink macaron and slid the box over to me. I passed the box back to Caroline without taking one. Even though macarons were stylish and pretty and seemed to be omnipresent in weddings and bridal styled-shoots, I'd rather save the calories and have a chocolate chip cookie any day of the week.

"You didn't miss anything," I said. "They were all equally awful."

"What makes me furious is that we bent over backwards for that woman. We took dresses over to her house. We've never done that before."

"I know." I felt a twinge of guilt remembering that I'd set up the appointment and worked with Caroline to have a selection of gowns delivered along with a dress consultant to assist the bride. "You and your staff were amazing."

"I should have known when I heard how she treated her mother and maid of honor." Caroline craned her neck toward the door to the back rooms. "Elaine, do you remember that sickly bride?"

A middle-aged woman with short dark hair popped her head out of the door. "The mean one who couldn't get out of bed?"

She had a slight accent that made it sound like she was singing all her words.

"That's the one," Kate said.

"Elaine is our top seamstress." Caroline beckoned the woman to come out and join us. "You remember Annabelle and Kate from Wedding Belles."

We all nodded to each other in greeting.

Caroline patted the space next to her on the couch. "Tell them what happened at the final fitting with the bride."

Elaine sat but kept her hands folded in her lap. "I don't normally talk about our brides, but after I read what that woman wrote about us . . ." The smile dropped from her face.

"It's okay," I said. "She trashed all of us, so you won't get any judgment here."

Elaine looked to Caroline, who nodded. "What she wrote online about us ruining her alterations was completely false. When I went to her house for the final fitting, she didn't fit into the dress because she'd gained weight."

"That's a change," Kate said. "Usually brides get so nervous before the wedding day that they forget to eat and drop weight."

"Not if you have everyone running around and doing things for you," I said. "Tricia didn't lift a finger for her wedding despite claiming in her review that she was stressed."

Kate grinned. "I'll bet she wasn't happy she'd put on some pounds."

"She blamed me for altering the dress wrong even after her mother reminded her that she'd been eating ice cream every day," Elaine said. "Then when I said I'd have to let the dress out, the bride threw a tantrum."

"I'm glad we missed that one," I said to Kate, even though we'd witnessed our share of Tricia's meltdowns.

"At you or at her mom?" Kate asked.

"At her mother and her girlfriend," Elaine said.

"Must have been the maid of honor, Madeleine," I said. "She didn't have any other friends."

Elaine nodded. "Yes, Madeleine. That's the one. Well, the bride accused her of being jealous and trying to upstage her at the wedding. Screamed that Madeleine blamed her for everything and was out to ruin her special day."

"By force-feeding her Ben & Jerry's?" Kate rolled her eyes. "That bride was a loon."

"Her mother tried to calm her down, but the bride turned on her and said that it was her mother's fault that her father was dead." Elaine pressed her hands together in her lap. "I'd started to sneak out with the dress by this time, but the last thing I heard was the bride yelling over and over to her mother, 'You killed him. And I'm going to tell everyone what you did.'"

"She accused her mother of killing her father because her dress didn't fit?" I knew that the bride's very wealthy father had passed away just over a year ago, not long before the bride had gotten engaged, but I'd never heard even the slightest whisper that the death hadn't been from natural causes.

"This was no normal bride," Caroline said.

She made a good point. "Did it sound like she meant it when she accused her mother or do you think she was just blowing off steam?"

Elaine raised her eyebrows. "I've never heard anyone 'blow off steam' by accusing them of murder, but after reading the lies she wrote about us, I believe she'd say anything to hurt someone."

I wondered if Tricia's accusations were another instance of her being horrible or if there was truth behind them. Did Tricia's mother have a reason to silence her own daughter?

CHAPTER 17

"That's ridiculous," Kate said after I'd told her my theory of the bride's mother as murderer. "Tricia's mother was devoted to her. Too much, if you ask me. She never would have killed her only daughter."

We'd left Potomac and were heading to Charlie Palmer restaurant, one of Washington, DC's iconic power-lunch spots and the site of Tricia's rehearsal dinner. I'd rolled down the car windows after we'd merged onto the GW Parkway to head back into the city. The tree-lined road was a welcome respite after the beltway traffic, and I breathed in the cool air scented by evergreens as I mulled over what we'd learned at the bridal salon.

"But what if her only daughter was about to expose her for killing her husband?" I rested my elbow on the open window and held up my hand to be buffeted by the breeze as I accelerated on the open stretch. Driving helped me think, as long as it wasn't bumper-to-bumper traffic. Unfortunately, uncrowded roads in DC were getting harder and harder to find.

Kate brushed her hair off her face and switched on the radio, flipping through the stations until she found the perky pop music she favored. "I think she'd go to jail."

Maybe Kate was right. It was tough to imagine Mrs. Toker doing anything to harm a hair on her daughter's spoiled head.

"But why would Tricia accuse her mother of killing her father?" I asked as we rounded a bend and the Potomac River came into view below us with rowing teams cutting across the dark blue water. "Doesn't it seem suspicious that she blurts it out during a wedding meltdown and then ends up dead a few days later?"

"You mean after she writes horrible reviews about half a dozen businesses and treats every person she comes in contact with on her wedding day like garbage?" Kate tapped her fingers to the sounds of Katy Perry. "What's suspicious is that she survived as long as she did. I hope you're not going to share this idea with Reese."

"Of course not." I wasn't going to tell Reese because to tell him I had a theory would be admitting that I'd been gathering evidence, even if I could claim it was inadvertent. In addition, I felt like my theory was falling apart by the second.

My phone began ringing "Pachelbel's Canon," and I reached a hand behind me to dig it out of my purse.

"You have got to change that ringtone," Kate said. "Isn't it bad enough that every other wedding sends their bridesmaids down the aisle to that song?"

"At least I changed it from 'The Wedding March.'" I glanced down at my phone before I answered it. "Hi, Richard."

"Are you at home?" he asked.

I looked to my left and could see the buildings of Georgetown across the Potomac River, a single church spire jutting up from the rooftops. I was close to my Georgetown home even if I wasn't going there. "Why? Is it time to walk the dog again?"

"Dog?" Kate said. She knew Richard's feelings about pets as well as the rest of us did.

I put a finger to my lips to quiet her and put my phone on speaker so I could hear without holding the phone to my ear. Then I dropped the phone in the cup holder.

"Is that Kate in the background?"

"Yes," I said. "We're in my car."

"Car? Where are you going?"

We crossed the glittering Potomac and merged with other traffic onto Constitution Avenue. "Nowhere special. We just popped by Love Bridal Salon to apologize to Caroline for sending Tricia her way, and now we're on our way to Charlie Palmer."

"To eat?"

Kate bobbed her head up and down. "Let's eat there. I've been having a craving for their crabmeat cocktail."

"No," I said to both Kate and Richard. "Tricia held her rehearsal dinner there. We owe the manager an apology, as well."

"So you want me to believe that you're driving all over town for no other reason than to apologize to your murdered bride's wedding vendors?" Richard's voice rose. "Are you out of your mind?"

"What?" I tried to sound as innocent as possible. I stayed in the middle lane as we drove past the imposing government buildings that lined the left side of the street along the approach to the White House.

"You know very well 'what.' You're trying to dig up some information you can use to clear yourself, aren't you?" Richard asked. "What happened to our conversation about trusting people and not having to be the person to fix everything all the time?"

"I'm considering it," I said. "But we did discover that Tricia accused her mother of killing her father during a dress-fitting meltdown."

"I don't see what good that does you. Didn't the bride have regular meltdowns and insult every person she came in contact with?"

"Well, yes." I passed the White House and stopped at the traffic light. "But don't you think there's the possibility that her mother killed her to keep her quiet?"

Kate shook her head vigorously next to me, but I ignored her.

"The bigger questions are," Richard said. "will the police think it's worth pursuing and is that tidbit of information worth getting you in even deeper trouble for poking around in the case when you've been told not to?"

I hated when Richard was right. "Fine. But don't you think it's the least bit interesting that the mother of the bride might have killed her husband?"

"Annabelle, if I had a dollar for every wife who's knocked off her rich husband I'd be on the beach in St. Barts, not brainstorming a menu for an Alice in Wonderland-themed brunch. You don't happen to have any ideas, do you?"

"What about Cheshire cat canapés?" I said.

Kate snapped her fingers. "Queen of Romaine Hearts salad."

"Not bad," Richard said. "I had mini Queen of Clubs sandwiches and Mad Hatter cookie batter ice cream cones."

I merged onto Pennsylvania Avenue, making a right onto a wide street lined with cars. This was usually my best bet for finding a spot near Charlie Palmer. Kate pointed at a tight parking space at the end of the row, and I swerved into it, backing as close as possible to the car behind me so only the tip of my car extended past the parking zone sign. Kate gave me a thumbs-up.

"Don't forget that the groom was shot, too," Richard said. "So the killer was someone who wanted them both out of the way."

"And if I was going to kill my daughter," Kate said. "I'd certainly do it before I spent all that money on a wedding, not after."

"Spoken like a true mercenary," Richard said.

Kate took it as a compliment and smiled.

"We've got to run." I took the phone out of the cup holder and grabbed my purse from the back seat. "I'll call you later."

"I would tell you two to stay out of trouble, but I think I'd be wasting my breath." Richard clicked off.

I stepped out of the car and onto the sidewalk. "It's not like we can get in trouble on a weekday in broad daylight."

Kate walked over to me in her cork wedge heels and adjusted her silk tank top so her cleavage showed. "Speak for yourself."

CHAPTER 18

Kate pulled open the tall metal-and-glass doors leading into the upscale steakhouse. Charlie Palmer didn't have dark wood or burgundy leather or any of the clubby touches you might expect of a steak house. It was all glass walls and natural light and clean lines, which made it an easier sell for brides. I ran my eyes over the sunken dining room with its row of fabric doughnut-shaped chandeliers suspended over square tables draped in white cloth. A pastel landscape took up most of the far wall and a tall arrangement of white calla lilies and twisting branches sat on a sideboard in the middle of the room.

A lean dark-skinned man in a black suit and matching black shirt looked up from the host stand when we walked in and smiled when he recognized Kate. "You're back already?"

Kate had set up the private dining room for Tricia's rehearsal dinner the previous Friday night while I had been running the ceremony rehearsal. Even though she'd only been on-site for an hour before guests arrived, Kate had a way of sticking in people's memories. Especially if the people were men.

"I missed you already." Kate squeezed the man's arm. "Topher, this is my boss, Annabelle Archer. Annabelle, this is the man to know at Charlie Palmer. He's one of the assistant managers but he does everything on-site for the private parties."

Topher tried to suppress a grin. "She exaggerates."

"It's nice to meet you." I held out my hand. I didn't go for kisses as quickly as my assistant did. "Kate's been talking about you nonstop since the rehearsal dinner on Friday." A lie, of course. She hadn't mentioned a word about this Topher fellow. But hopefully it was a lie that would pay off.

Topher shook my hand. "A table for two today?"

Kate linked her arm with Topher's and rested her other hand on his chest. "Not today, sadly." She made a pouty face. "We came about the review."

Topher's smile dropped away. "Our first one-star review on the Wed Boards."

"We feel awful about it." Kate rubbed Topher's arm, and I felt like an intruder being so close to them. I rarely got to see Kate's charm in action and when I did, it felt like I'd stumbled onto a late-night cable channel.

"The bride panned all of us," I said, as much to remind Kate that I was standing right next to her as anything. "But we're really sorry we brought her to you in the first place."

Topher shook his head and broke eye contact with Kate to look at me. "It's not your fault. And, like you said, she wrote bad reviews on everyone."

"Isn't he the greatest?" Kate asked, leaning into Topher.

He cleared his throat and glanced around him, perhaps remembering that he had a restaurant filled with guests in full view. "Come. Let me buy both of you a drink." He led us to the L-shaped, polished wood bar that stretched along one side of the restaurant.

"Two Bombay Sapphire and tonics," Kate said to the heavyset bartender as she hopped onto a high-backed upholstered barstool and crossed her legs. I took the stool next to her and Topher stood between us.

"Did you have any idea the client was unhappy before the review came out?" I asked. "Were there issues on the night of the dinner?"

Topher rested his elbow on the back of Kate's barstool and stole a glance at her long legs, which were barely covered by her striped silk shorts. "Aside from the bride not mentioning any dietary restrictions until we took her order and then telling us she was gluten-free and vegan."

I winced. "At a steakhouse?" I'd also personally seen Tricia put away more than one cheeseburger, so I knew she'd pretended to be a gluten-free vegan just so she could claim the service had been slow in her one-star review.

Topher shrugged. "We get it all the time. The chef managed to pull something together, but it did take him a few minutes."

"But everyone else was happy?" I picked up the gin and tonic that had arrived in front of me and took a sip.

"To be honest, I wasn't in the room the entire time. It was a busy night."

"And Topher was keeping me company while I ate at the bar," Kate said.

"You stayed?" I asked. "I thought you went home once the guests arrived." Our usual rehearsal dinner MO was to set up the private room with the place cards and any favors, check in with the client when they arrived, and then leave the dinner service in the hands of the private-party manager.

Kate sipped her gin and tonic. "Tricia seemed to be on the warpath when she arrived, so I thought it might be smart to stay."

I agreed. It was what I would have done.

"But she was fine the rest of the evening?" I asked.

"Aside from the fight with the groom," Topher said. "That was some scene, but at least they took it outside."

Kate's eyes widened. "How did I miss that?"

"I think you'd gone to the ladies' room," Topher said. "It was almost at the end of the dinner when I heard the bride and groom arguing in our foyer. When she raised her voice, he told her to be quiet and pulled her outside."

"I can't believe I missed that," Kate said. "I barely heard the groom give one opinion during the entire time we worked with them. I would have loved to see him argue back to her."

I leaned forward in my stool. "Did you happen to hear what the fight was about?"

"Only a minute of it but I remember that she said she couldn't take it anymore."

I looked at Kate. "Take what? It wasn't like she put up with much."

"And then the groom told her to calm down, that it would all be over soon."

Kate sucked in her breath. "You don't think they had a suicide pact, do you?"

I gave her my most withering look. "No, I do not. They were shot in different rooms."

Kate shrugged. "Maybe the groom had to do both parts of the pact. Shoot her and himself."

I pressed a hand to my forehead. "The groom was shot in the back, remember? How could he shoot himself in the back?"

"Well, the argument doesn't make any sense." Kate drained the rest of her gin and tonic.

"The groom probably meant that the wedding would be over soon and all of her imagined stress with it."

Even though that made the most sense I wondered about the timing. Was the bride worried about something else unrelated to the wedding? And did that something else get her killed?

CHAPTER 19

"There you are, dear. I'd started to worry." Leatrice looked up from her laptop as I walked in the door of my apartment. She still wore the beige trench coat and fedora she'd had on when I left her earlier in the day, and I wondered if she'd moved an inch since I left.

I dropped my keys in the crystal bowl on the table by the door. "Our visit to Charlie Palmer turned into drinks and that turned into appetizers. I left Kate there after she insisted she would only have one more drink and then get an Uber home."

I noticed the air had a musty smell, so I crossed the living room and cracked open one of my large windows. The wooden panes were original to the building, and they stuck in the summer heat and let in cold air in the winter, but at least I got a bit of a breeze being four stories up. I glanced around my living room, taking in the dust gathering in the corners and made a mental note to clean soon. Or at least spray some lemon Pledge so it smelled clean.

"I'm assuming there was a man involved," Leatrice said. Kate's weakness for attractive men was legendary.

I thought back to how cozy Kate and Topher had been when I'd left them. "You assume correctly."

"How did your visits go?" Leatrice stood up from the dining room table where her research into Tricia's murder still laid strewn around her laptop.

"You mean did I find any clues that might help clear our names?" I asked. "Not really, although I learned that Tricia accused her mother of killing her father and that the bride and groom had a big fight the night before the wedding at their rehearsal dinner."

Leatrice followed me into the kitchen where I opened the refrigerator and removed the last two cans of Diet Dr Pepper. I handed one to Leatrice then popped open the other and took a drink, leaning back against the Formica countertop as I swallowed the fizzy sweetness. Diet Dr Pepper was the only diet soda I could drink without cringing. Truth be told, I preferred my carbonation with full sugar, but too many regular sodas and I'd have to cut out food to make up for the extra calories.

"Do you think the bride's mother killed her husband?" Leatrice asked.

"Who knows? Probably not. Tricia said a lot of things that weren't true just to hurt people. I wouldn't be surprised if she said it just as a dig at her mother."

Leatrice wrinkled her nose. "The more I learn about this girl, the less surprised I am that someone shot her."

"Join the club. I'm shocked someone didn't do it sooner." I walked back out to my living room, sitting on one end of the couch and pushing a pile of wedding books to one side on the glass coffee table to make space for my soda.

Leatrice sat across from me in the pale yellow armchair that matched the couch, and her feet dangled above the floor. "What about the fight at the rehearsal dinner?"

"It doesn't make any sense. The bride apparently said she couldn't take it anymore and the groom told her it would all be over soon."

"Wedding jitters?" Leatrice suggested.

"Maybe," I said. "But it doesn't fit their pattern. I never saw the two of them fight once the entire time we worked with them. The groom let Tricia say awful things and never made a peep, but the night before the wedding he snaps back at her and tells her to be quiet. The worst part is that I missed it. I would've given good money to see someone tell that bridezilla to shut up." I reached down and grabbed my Diet Dr Pepper. "Did you have any luck online?"

Leatrice clapped her hands together and jumped out of the chair. "You could say that." She hurried over and picked up her laptop. "You know how I was researching all the people and places she trashed online? Well, I found one person who fought back."

I sat up. "You mean someone responded to her reviews?"

Leatrice nodded so energetically her fedora nearly flew off her head. "A French baker. She panned his profiteroles, and he responded saying that an American palate couldn't possibly appreciate a French pastry and that if they ever crossed paths, she'd be sorry."

"What was his name?" I asked, feeling my stomach do a preemptive flip.

Leatrice looked down at her screen. "It doesn't have a name for the baker, but his shop is called Pastries by Philippe."

"It couldn't be," I said, pulling my phone out of my pocket and dialing Richard, who answered on the first ring.

"I was just about to call you," he said. "Are you home?"

There was a knock on the door.

"I'll get it, dear." Leatrice put her laptop back down on the living room table and crossed the room.

"Before you start," I said to Richard, guessing he was about to launch into a long and dramatic story. "Who did the Hay-Adams Hotel hire to do all of their wedding cakes?"

Leatrice opened the door and Richard walked in still holding his phone to his ear. "The new one? Pastries by Philippe. Why?"

I hung up my phone. "Because Tricia had an online feud with him over a bad review she wrote about his profiteroles a year ago."

Richard arched an eyebrow as he stepped closer. "Interesting."

Leatrice looked from me to Richard. "Why is that interesting?"

"Because Tricia had her wedding at the Hay-Adams Hotel, and they subcontract out all their wedding cakes," I said. "They used to use a sweet lady who lived on the Eastern Shore, but she got tired of the drive, so I heard they hired a new baker."

"And the new baker is this Philippe fellow who threatened the bride?" Leatrice asked.

"But would the baker ever know the name of the couple getting married?" Richard adjusted his black leather cross-body bag. "Doesn't the hotel give him the design and size and he delivers it without ever meeting the couple?"

I shook my head. "They identify the wedding cakes by the couples names in case they have two weddings on a weekend with a similar design but different flavors on the inside."

"So the baker would have seen the bride's name on the order sent by the hotel?" Leatrice tapped her chin. "The plot thickens."

"But why would a baker shoot the bride when he could have poisoned her with wedding cake?" Richard asked.

"Maybe because he would have had to poison all the wedding guests?"

I shook my head. "I don't think any review is bad enough to warrant a mass murder."

"Clearly you've never spent much time on Yelp." Richard shifted his black messenger bag in front of him, tugging the tab closure on the side that had popped open.

I eyed his bag. "The baker had motive. If the order the hotel sent him listed the couple's address, then he also had opportunity. I think we should go talk to him."

Richard did not look convinced. "It's a stretch."

"Of course it's a stretch." I threw my hands in the air. "Just like the mom is a stretch. But whoever killed her had a reason and, so far, Tricia's online victims have the most compelling and public reasons."

Leatrice held up the pile of reviews she'd printed out. "And we have over a hundred of them."

"Including one of Wedding Belles, might I remind you." Richard slipped the wide leather strap of his bag over his head and set it on my couch, where it promptly rolled over to one side and barked.

I gaped at Richard. "Are you carrying that dog in your bag?"

Before he could answer, a brown-and-black mop of fur pushed open the top flap of the bag. Richard raised a hand. "Not a word, Annabelle."

I rolled my eyes at him. "Only if you agree to come with me to talk to Philippe."

Richard put his hands on his hips. "And if I don't?"

I shrugged. "I post a photo of you and your new dog on Instagram and tag you with the hash tag #puppylove."

He staggered back a few feet. "You wouldn't dare."

I pulled my phone out. "Wouldn't I?"

"You're evil," Richard grumbled. "I'm starting to think you may be the murderer after all."

CHAPTER 20

"I'm surprised you didn't leave Butterscotch with Leatrice. They seemed to take to each other," I said as we made our way up Wisconsin Avenue towards Pastries by Philippe. As one of two main arteries running through Georgetown, the street was a long series of row houses that held boutique businesses and restaurants. Everything from trendy day spas that filled the air with the scent of eucalyptus to shops selling shiny men's suits with even shinier salesmen standing out front dispensing compliments and slick smiles to lure in customers.

Richard dodged a salesman in a double-breasted suit. "Are you out of your mind?" Butterscotch's brown-and-black head poked out the front corner of the bag and bobbed along with every step, his tiny black nose sniffing the air. "You've seen the way she dresses. She would have dressed the dog up in some sort of ridiculous costume, and then he would have refused to take it off."

Leatrice had insisted on taking Butterscotch out of his bag and rubbing his belly while Richard and I had discussed our strategy for visiting Philippe. We hadn't come up with much beyond asking the baker questions—my suggested questions were more pointed than Richard's—but Leatrice and Butterscotch had bonded.

I glanced at Richard out of the side of my eye. "You do know this is a dog, not a toddler."

Richard flicked a strand of hair off his forehead. "He requires constant supervision, he isn't toilet trained, and he drools when he sleeps. I fail to see the difference."

I reached back and rubbed my finger under Butterscotch's chin, and he licked my hand appreciatively. "I think he suits you. I've always thought the one accessory you were missing was a purse dog and now you have one."

Richard glanced down at the dog, muttered something unintelligible under his breath, and took a couple of long strides to pass me.

"Here it is." I stopped in front of a brick townhouse tucked between a nail salon and a custom seamstress with a dusty mannequin in the window. Pastries by Philippe boasted a bright yellow door and black-wire window boxes spilling forth with brightly colored flowers. A towering croquembouche, a pyramid of profiteroles held together with a cage of pink spun sugar, took center stage in the picture window, flanked by two small wedding cakes.

Richard gestured to the tower of cream puffs. "And there are the profiteroles that your bride panned online. Front and center."

"Ready?" I asked, squaring my shoulders and tugging the front of my pink button-down shirt to straighten it. Even though I wasn't in a suit, my slim-fit black pants and silk shirt were freshly dry-cleaned and unwrinkled, so I considered the outfit a win.

Richard looked at Butterscotch and held up a finger. "Best behavior, young man." The dog gave Richard's finger a quick lick and disappeared into the bag. Richard sighed and reached for his antibacterial gel while I watched and waited, tapping my foot on the sidewalk.

When Richard had sufficiently disinfected himself, I pushed open the door to the shop and a bell rang above us. The scent of sugar and butter surrounded me, giving me a slight head rush. The shop was as yellow as its door and boasted bright walls, a glass pastry case that spanned the length of the right side, and white cafe tables with matching wire chairs dotting the rest of the room.

"Hello," I called out.

A man emerged from the back in a pair of black jeans and a baggy white linen shirt; the sleeves were rolled up to reveal arms roped with muscles and covered in a swirl of dark tattoos. His brown hair curled down past the collar of his shirt, and it was easy to imagine him on the cover of a romance novel with said shirt ripped open. *"Bonjour."*

"He-llo," Richard said under his breath, and I elbowed him. At least Kate wasn't with me. She would have been completely useless in the presence of such an attractive man.

"Are you Philippe?" I asked.

The man nodded as he gave us the once-over, probably trying to determine if we were an engaged couple or not.

"I'm Annabelle Archer, and this is Richard Gerard."

Philippe's eyes registered recognition, and he looked at Richard. "The caterer?"

"The one and only." Richard gave a mock bow.

The baker picked up a pad of paper from the nearby counter. "You want to order for your parties?"

"Maybe." Richard glanced at the contents of the long glass case. Perfect éclairs sat in rows beside tiny fruit tartlets that glistened in the light, and French macarons in a rainbow of colors were arranged on ceramic cake stands. "Can you do miniature palmiers?"

I cleared my throat and gave Richard a pointed look. We were not here to shop, even though the display of pastries looked and smelled heavenly. "Do you make all the wedding cakes for the Hay-Adams Hotel?

Philippe shrugged as if it was a matter barely worth mentioning. "Oui." He looked at the two of us again, studying us closely for a moment. "You two get married there?"

I waved my hands in front of me, laughing nervously. "No, no, no, no, no. We're not getting married there. We're not getting married at all. What I mean is we're not together." I realized I was babbling. "We're just friends."

Richard let out a huff. "You could do a lot worse, you know."

Great. Now I'd hurt his feelings. I saw Philippe's eyebrows dart up as he put the pad of paper back on the counter. He'd probably witnessed his share of lovers' spats but maybe not one quite like this.

"You know I didn't mean it like that," I whispered to Richard to mollify him. "If I had to pick anyone right now, it would be you."

Come to think of it, Richard was the most consistent and loyal man in my life. Not to mention the fact that he was a successful business owner, a sharp dresser, and a great cook. He was right. I could do a lot worse.

Richard darted a glance at me then reached out and squeezed my arm. "You're forgiven."

"Do you want to order a wedding cake or no?" Philippe asked. He'd taken a seat at one of the bistro tables and crossed his legs, looking extremely bored with us.

"Actually, no," I said. "We wanted to ask you about a wedding cake you made this past weekend." Philippe's face didn't change expression so

I continued. "For a wedding at the Hay-Adams. You designed it to look like the Eiffel Tower. But a smaller version."

"I think that's a given," Richard said.

I ignored his comment and made a mental decision not to marry him after all.

"I remember," Philippe said. "The tower lattice I made in gold."

"Exactly," I said. We'd decided that doing a cake in the actual color of the Eiffel Tower—gunmetal-gray—would be hideous. "Do you happen to remember who the cake was for?"

Philippe leaned back in his chair. "The names of the bride and groom? No. I don't need to know names to create a masterpiece."

Oh, boy. "But the names are on the order you get from the hotel, right?" I pressed.

"Maybe. But it doesn't matter to me. I'm not making a birthday cake." He waved one hand in the air. "I don't write the names on the top in blue icing."

I could see Richard nodding out of the corner of my eye, but I wasn't ready to give up yet. "So you had no idea that the bride was Tricia Toker?"

"No," he answered without missing a beat.

"Do you happen to have the cake order from last weekend?" I asked.

He sighed loudly, rose, and went to the counter, reaching underneath and pulling out a stack of papers. He flipped through them and found the one he'd been searching for then walked back and handed it to me before sitting down. I scanned the paper, ignoring the cake description and sketch at the bottom, and saw the bride's name as well as the groom's in a box in the top corner with their billing address directly below. So he did know where they lived and, conveniently, it was only a few blocks away from his bakery.

Richard peered over my shoulder. "I need to get the name of his sketch artist."

"The sketches, they are mine." Philippe flipped his hair off his shoulder.

"Really?" Richard took the paper from me. "You're very good."

I snatched the paper from Richard and scowled at him.

"What?" He gave me a sheepish look.

I turned back to Philippe. "The name Tricia Toker doesn't ring a bell? Or, should I say, username?" I focused on the baker's face for any flicker of recognition, but there was none. I decided to go for broke. "Would you be surprised to know that the bride from last weekend was the same person who trolled you online last year for your profiteroles?"

Philippe sat up. "The one who said they were dry and tasteless?"

"The very same," I said. "You were pretty upset when she wrote those reviews and called her some choice names in your response."

"Because she doesn't know the first thing about French pastry. Not that it is surprising for an American." His eyes flicked to us. "No offense."

"None taken," Richard said. Butterscotch wedged his head out the back end of the messenger bag, and Richard angled the bag behind him so it remained out of Philippe's view.

Philippe stood, his chair scraping loudly against the floor and nearly toppling over. "What? Now does she want to say my cake was dry?"

"Well, no," I said. "She didn't mention the cake."

"Then why are you here? You ask about the cake. I tell you. You want to discuss old reviews? Fine. We discuss."

I took a breath and plowed forward. "Did you want to get revenge on Tricia Toker for those bad reviews?"

"Revenge?" Philippe laughed. "I don't understand. By making her a gorgeous wedding cake?"

"By killing her," I said.

Philippe backed away from me. "Killing her?"

"She was shot at her home not far from here." I held up the paper. "And you knew her address."

The baker slashed his hands through the air in front of himself. "That is absurd. I never met the woman. And to kill a person over a review? No. I am an artist. I create, not destroy." He stalked to the back of the shop, and I heard a door slam.

"Do you think he's telling the truth?" I asked Richard.

Richard drummed his fingers across his lips. "I can't tell. He could be covering up the fact that he did it, or it could just be that he's French. The accent's throwing me off."

"And the fact that he looks like Fabio?"

"Oh, girl," Richard slid his bag around so Butterscotch faced front, his glossy nose twitching as he took in the rich scent of French pastry. "He's much better looking than Fabio."

"Very helpful," I said, my tone telling Richard that it was not. I felt my phone vibrating through my purse and took it out.

"Hi, Leatrice," I said. "What's up?"

"I had to tell you as soon as I found out." She sounded out of breath but it could have been excitement. "My hacker team did a little research on the neighbor, Effing Frank. His real name is Ferguson, and he works in security for a big company in Virginia."

"Okay," I said, wondering what was so earth shattering about this.

"And the bride's friend was right. He is a gun guy. He's a member of the NRA and has been for twenty years."

"Interesting," I said.

"Even more interesting?" Leatrice said. "When your detective went to talk to him earlier, he was gone."

"Gone?" I asked, feeling a tingle of excitement.

"Not at home and not at work. He called in sick. He's been out since the day of Tricia's murder. Reese filed a report that said so."

I felt a twinge of regret that Leatrice's hackers were still hacking into the police system, but I also felt pleased that Reese had followed up on the lead I gave him so quickly. "Good work, Leatrice. If this guy had something to do with shooting Tricia and Dave, he may be lying low or on the run. Did Reese's report mention how they're following up on him? Are they staking out his house in case he returns?"

"The report doesn't mention anything."

I heard the beep that indicated someone else was calling in, and I held the phone away from my ear so I could read the name on the screen. I blinked a few times, not quite believing my eyes.

"I've got to go, Leatrice. Someone is calling me on the other line."

Leatrice hung up, but I didn't switch over to the new call right away.

Richard glanced at my face then at my phone. "Who is it?"

"You're not going to believe this, but it's the groom."

"The one who got shot?"

"The very same," I said. I'd asked him to call me if he remembered anything about the attack, but I hadn't actually thought he'd contact me. I wondered if he'd remembered something or if he was calling to tell me off for spilling the beans about his wife being shot. I stared down at the phone, too nervous to answer.

CHAPTER 21

"Why is the groom calling you?" Richard asked as we stepped out of the bakery and onto the sidewalk, the scent of sugar dissipating into the air as we shut the glass door behind us. Both he and Butterscotch stared at me intently.

I decided not to tell Richard that the two of them had the same expression. I didn't think my friend was one of those people who would welcome the fact that he shared certain characteristics with his dog. Or, in this case, his boyfriend's dog. I glanced back at the phone as the voice mail notification window popped up then vanished. "No idea but he left a message."

Richard arranged the flap of his black bag so it nearly covered Butterscotch's head, but the dog wiggled his head out again. "I don't like this one bit."

"Which part?" I asked, pressing the icon on my phone to listen to the message. "Being a dog nanny or being sucked into this murder investigation."

Richard glared at me. "I'm going to let the first one slide. But regarding this investigation, I have not been sucked into it. I've been dragged kicking and screaming."

I held up one finger and pressed the other to my ear to try to block out the noise of the passing traffic while I listened to the groom's message. Then I dropped the phone back into my purse. "He wants me to come to the hospital. He says he has some new information that might be connected to Tricia's murder."

"Why is he calling you?" Richard tucked his bag under his arm as we walked down Wisconsin Avenue, Butterscotch leaning out the front of the bag as he tried to sniff the passing pedestrians. "Shouldn't he tell this to the police? Why doesn't anyone I know ever go to the police?"

"Maybe he finds me more trustworthy than the police," I said. "I did ask him to contact me if he thought of anything. Maybe it isn't a big thing, and he feels silly bothering the detective."

Richard ignored a pair of preteen girls making googly eyes at the dog in his bag. "Didn't you accidentally spill the beans about his wife being shot?"

"Accidentally being the operative word. I'm sure he's over that by now but, of course, I'll tell him how awful I feel that I was the one to let it slip."

"Wait a second." Richard clutched my arm and brought us both to a full stop. "You're aren't seriously considering going to see him, are you?"

I shook Richard's hand off and kept walking. "It would be rude to ignore a client who's asking for help."

Richard ran a few steps to catch up. "A *former* client. And it is not considered rude to follow the directives of the DC police department and stop meddling in this case."

"I think you're being overdramatic."

When am I ever dramatic?" Richard shifted his grip on the black bag and Butterscotch gave his hand a lick. "Oh, for the love of God, it's licked me again. Where's my antibacterial hand gel?"

"Dog saliva won't hurt you." I paused at the corner while Richard tried to rummage through the outside pocket of his bag without getting licked again. I rubbed Butterscotch's head. "Just ignore him. He's harmless."

Richard squirted some pale pink gel in his hands and sighed. "I'm trying."

"I was talking to the dog." I raised my hand to flag down a cab.

Richard eyed the yellow cab as it slowed in front of us. "You really can't make it the few blocks back to your apartment building?"

"I'm not going to my apartment. I thought we'd go to Georgetown Hospital since we're out already and only a few blocks away." I opened the taxi door. "Are you coming?"

"I still say you should let Detective Reese handle this." Richard shook his head.

"So that's a yes?" I got in the cab and leaned my head out.

Richard motioned for me to slide over and put his bag with Butterscotch on the car seat next to me before he got in. "Only to make sure you don't get in even bigger trouble."

I gave the cab driver our destination then turned to watch Richard holding the black bag up to the window, the little dog letting his tongue hang out as the car accelerated and the wind blew in his face. "Does Butterscotch need a view?"

"The dog gets car sick if he can't look out the window."

"Have you and Butterscotch taken a lot of car trips together?" I asked.

Richard made a face at me. "I was given a list."

"A list?"

"Of things to remember about the dog. As if I'd forget to feed him without written instructions."

I thought there was a decent chance Richard would forget to feed him if he wasn't reminded. Or that he'd try to feed him tarragon chicken salad cups and individual carrot soufflés. We drove through the narrow streets of Georgetown and around double-parked cars until we arrived at the entrance to the redbrick hospital. The square building had been expanded with more modern buildings that spread out behind it, but the main entrance still had an old-school feel.

"He's on the third floor," I said when we'd walked from the cab to the lobby, passing through automatic glass doors. "The elevators are over here."

My nose twitched reflexively at the distinctive hospital smell. Quite a change from the luscious scents of the bakery we'd just left. I wished I'd packed some pastries in my purse to combat the antiseptic air.

"Excuse me," a nurse with dirty-blond hair called out as we passed by the front desk. "You can't have a dog inside the hospital."

Richard shoved Butterscotch's head inside the bag with a move of his elbow and looked wildly around the lobby.

The nurse leveled a finger at him. "Yes, you. The man with the pink shirt and black purse."

Richard let out an exasperated sigh. "This shirt is salmon, not pink, and anyone who follows fashion knows this isn't a purse. It's a man's messenger bag, and it's Hermès."

The nurse shook her head. "I don't care what you call it. You still can't have Hermès in the hospital. No dogs allowed. You'll have to wait down here."

"For heavens sake, Hermès isn't the name of the dog." At this, Butterscotch wedged his head out of the bag and looked up at Richard, and I could swear the dog was smiling.

"Maybe you should wait here," I said. "I'll be right back."

"All right." Richard looked down at Butterscotch. "You know, Hermès isn't such a bad name. I wonder if P.J. would mind if I renamed him?"

I didn't want to be the one to tell Richard I was pretty sure his boyfriend would mind very much having his dog renamed, so I left him perched on a celadon-green chair trying to get Butterscotch to answer to the name Hermès. I took the elevator to the third floor and stuck my head out before stepping into the hallway. I didn't want to run into the bride's mother or maid of honor this time even if the groom did ask me to stop by. I found the groom's room and pushed the door open, calling his name at the same time.

"Who's there?" he answered back.

I stepped fully into the hospital room. The groom sat up in his bed with all the lights on and the wall-mounted television tuned to ESPN. He looked much more alert than he had the last time I'd visited and, aside from the bandage across his shoulder, didn't seem to belong in a hospital.

"It's Annabelle Archer," I said. "You left me a message asking me to stop by."

He waved me inside. "Right. Thanks for coming so quickly. The last time you visited you asked me to let you know if I remembered anything. And Tricia told me you were a miracle worker so many times during the wedding planning, so I figured you might be able to add to what the police are doing. Plus, I had your number in my phone, and I thought it was worth a shot. You actually knew Tricia, so you have a reason to want to know who killed her, right?"

"Right," I lied. Even though Tricia had been a nightmare to work for, I couldn't help feel a rush of pride that she'd called me a miracle worker. The groom never needed to know that I didn't want to solve her murder because I'd known her. Most people who had known her had wanted to kill her. But it was true I was probably more interested than the police. The desire to save your own skin could be very motivating.

"So is this about your neighbor?" I asked.

"My neighbor?" The groom's brow creased.

"Madeleine told me that you and Tricia had a feud with the guy who lives next door, and he threatened you."

The groom readjusted himself in the bed and made a pained face. "Frank? I mean, he wasn't the friendliest guy but do you think he hated Tricia enough to walk in our house and shoot both of us?"

I noticed he said that Frank hated Tricia, not him. That meshed with what I knew of Tricia but wasn't consistent with how Madeleine had described the situation. Then again, Tricia telling the story to cast herself in a better light wasn't surprising in the least. It probably made her feel better to tell people that the neighbor hated both of them instead of just having a problem with her.

"I don't know. But I do know the guy likes firearms."

Dave nodded. "Not surprising. Have the police talked to him?"

"Not yet." I didn't feel the need to tell the groom that the man who potentially shot him was running loose. "But if you weren't calling me about your neighbor, why did you call me?"

"Oh, right. I found something that may be important." He held up his cell phone. "I haven't had much to do since I've been in here, so I decided to clean out my phone."

I really hoped he was going somewhere with this.

"The day before Tricia and I were shot—" His voice hitched and he paused. "Sorry. It's hard to get used to her being gone." He took a deep breath and continued. "Anyway, I found an email in spam that was sent to both of us. I think you might want to see it."

He held out his phone, and I took it from him. The email had, in fact, been sent the day before the murder from what looked like a random account with no name attached. There was only one line.

You will pay for your lies in blood.

CHAPTER 22

"Where are you?" I asked as I stood in the lobby of the hospital holding my phone to my ear. I'd left Richard sitting on one of the upholstered chairs in the waiting area, but now he was nowhere in sight. The nurse who'd scolded us earlier had her head down at the front desk, and only a couple of people sat in the chairs reading worn magazines.

"Outside," Richard said. "Hermès doesn't like the smell of hospitals."

I looked out the glass double doors and saw Richard waving from the sidewalk. "So now the dog is Hermès?" I asked as I walked outside to meet him. "That was fast."

Richard stood with a leash in his hand, the tiny brown-and-black Yorkie scampering around on the other end. "If I didn't let him out of the bag, he was going to piddle all over the insides, and calfskin does not do well with moisture."

"I'm not sure much does well when soaked in dog urine."

Richard grimaced. "What did the groom have to say? Was his information worth you dragging me here and banishing me to wait for you?" He fanned a hand at his face, and I noticed that it felt more humid than it had earlier.

I looked up at the thickening clouds and wondered if we were about to get rained on. I had the bad habit of not checking the weather unless it was a wedding weekend, so I rarely carried an umbrella. If Richard worried about his man bag getting damp, he really wouldn't like it getting soaked in a rain shower.

I opened up my email on my phone and scrolled to the threatening message the groom had forwarded to me. "Check this out."

Richard leaned forward and squinted at the screen. "Very dramatic. But how does that help anything? We've established that Tricia wrote lies about a lot of people. You can add this person to the list."

I knew Richard was right, but this email seemed more violent and vengeful to me. "No one else threatened her with violence like this. Or sent her a direct email that I know of. This is an escalation. Plus, it was sent the day before the murder, almost like the killer wanted to scare her first."

"Okay, but do we know who sent it?" Richard switched the leash into his other hand as Hermès née Butterscotch crossed between his legs.

I slipped my phone back into my purse. "No, but that's where Leatrice and her hacker friends come in."

"If I've said it once, I've said it a thousand times." Richard shook his hand at me, and the leash quivered. "Do not encourage her."

"At least this new hobby of hers is helpful," I said. "Her hobbies used to include trying to set me up with the FedEx guy and running surveillance on all our neighbors. Why do you think old Mr. Provovitch moved? Because Leatrice was convinced that he was a Russian sleeper spy and followed him anytime he left the building."

"I'd say that was helpful. The old man cooked way too much cabbage and made your hallways smell awful."

"Well, I, for one, am thrilled that her paranoia finally has practical applications," I said.

Richard allowed himself to be tugged forward a few feet by the leash. "Then don't come crying to me when Crazy Lady gets you busted by the Feds for running an illegal hacking operation. If you want my advice, you should ignore this email, and let the groom turn it over to the police."

"For your information, I did tell him to show it to the police. But unless they have a more sophisticated cyber division than I think they do, I doubt they'll do much with it."

"When did you advise the groom to give the email to the police?" Richard asked.

I motioned to the redbrick building behind me. "Just now. After I made him swear not to tell Detective Reese that he called me or showed me the email. I'm trying to take your advice and let go more."

Richard scooped up the dog. "Great. *Now* you take my advice. Are you insane? That means the cops could be on their way here at this very moment. Do you really want to have to explain what we're doing here?" He spun around and walked straight into a man rounding the corner, Richard giving a yelp at the same time as the dog in his arms.

Detective Reese took a step back and stared at the excited Yorkie in Richard's arms. Then his gaze shifted to me and disappointment replaced the puzzled look in his eyes. "I'm almost afraid to ask what the two of you are doing here."

Richard opened and closed his mouth a few times, reminding me of a hungry goldfish.

Reese took a step close to me and grasped my elbow. "I know you aren't trying to sneak in to talk to the victim again without authorization."

I stared up at him and couldn't help thinking how attractive he looked when he was upset. His green eyes deepened and flashed with heat, and I felt my heart begin to beat faster. There were times when I really wished the detective didn't have the dark hair and light eyes that seemed to be my Kryptonite. "Absolutely not."

Richard's head snapped toward me. Technically, this wasn't a lie. I hadn't snuck in to see the groom because he'd asked me to come. And since he'd asked me to visit, it wasn't unauthorized, either.

Reese narrowed his eyes at me, and I could see he was trying to decide if he believed me or not.

"I do live in Georgetown, you know," I said, my voice not much more than a whisper since he stood so close to me.

Reese didn't let go of my elbow but, instead, pulled me closer. "All the way on the other side of Wisconsin Avenue. It's a long walk from your place to here."

Richard cleared his throat. "We're walking my dog."

Now it was my turn to snap my head over to look at Richard. I wasn't sure if I was shocked more by the fact that he'd lied to the detective or the fact that he'd claimed the little dog as his own.

Detective Reese dropped my elbow. "This is your dog?"

Richard gave the Yorkie's head an awkward pat. "Well, I didn't steal him." He jerked a thumb in Reese's direction and laughed. "I mean, honestly. Do you believe this guy, Annabelle?"

Reese eyed Richard, whose mouth was drawn back in a tortured smile that would give the Joker a run for his money as Hermès freely licked his hand. I wondered if Reese was deciding which was stranger, Richard stealing a dog or having one in the first place. He shook his head, either giving up or trying to forget the scene, and turned back to me. "I want to believe you. I really do."

I nodded as I met his eyes and felt guilt wash over me. Here was a guy who wanted nothing more than to keep me out of trouble, and I could not seem to stop lying to him. What was wrong with me?

I reached out and took one of his hands. "I'm sorry I keep giving you reasons to doubt me." I meant every word of what I said. I hated that I had such a hard time trusting him, or any man who wasn't Richard or Fern, and I wished I didn't feel like I needed to solve every problem on my own. It was a wedding-planner curse.

Reese met my eyes. "You like driving me crazy, don't you?"

"It does seem to be my talent," I said.

The detective squeezed my hand. "I'm sure you have other talents, as well," he leaned over and whispered into my ear, sending shivers down my spine. "And when this case is over . . ."

Richard coughed and the dog yipped, bringing me back to reality.

Reese stepped back but kept hold of my hand. "You'd better finish your walk or your friend might nip someone."

I grinned at Reese. "To date, Richard's never bitten a single person."

"Hilarious," Richard drawled, setting the dog back on the ground and heading down the sidewalk away from me. "Come along, Hermès. We know when we're not wanted."

Reese shook his head. "You'd better follow him."

I mouthed an apology to Reese as I ran to catch up to Richard. I looked back and saw him watching me for a few seconds before walking into the hospital.

"Thank you," I said to Richard once I'd reached him. "You didn't have to lie for me."

"Of course I did." Richard tugged Hermès away from a flowerbed. "You would have done the same for me."

It was true I'd gotten myself into more than a few compromising and dangerous situations to help save Richard's skin, but when you're best friends you don't keep score.

I rested a hand on Richard's arm. "I could do a lot worse than you."

He patted my hand as awkwardly as he'd petted Hermès then cleared his throat. "What are you going to do about the email?"

"I already forwarded it to Leatrice, but that is the last thing I'm doing." I made a gesture of wiping my hands clean.

Richard gave me a side-eye glance. "When have I heard that before?"

My phone vibrated in my pocket and I pulled it out, stopping and frowning as I read the text.

"Problem?" Richard asked, pausing next to me.

"It's Leatrice. She says that her hacker guys are working on the email but that she's busy at the moment."

"Dare I ask what she's doing?"

"Apparently, she's on a stakeout."

CHAPTER 23

"Let me see if I understand this correctly," Richard said as we piled into the backseat of another cab, this one a rickety station wagon painted brown. "Your neighbor, whom most would consider eccentric on a good day, is presently parked outside the house of a guy who is currently the only decent lead in a murder investigation?"

"Correct." I gave the address to the cabbie and sat back on the cracked vinyl seats. The taxi had seen better days. Silver slashes of duct tape held the cushions together with bits of crumbling foam peeking out the ends. A cardboard pine tree air freshener, faded from the sun, swung from the rearview mirror but did little to battle the odor of mildew. I made a mental note to wait for an Uber next time. Their black car service may be more expensive but the air quality made up for it.

Richard wrinkled his nose as he lowered Hermès, née Butterscotch, from the window and let him sniff the seat. "And I'm assuming she doesn't have any training in surveillance?"

"You mean aside from stalking me for the past few years and tracking every person in our neighborhood whom she thinks is even remotely suspicious?"

"You make a good point." Richard reclined onto the bench seat and cringed when it crackled against his back. "She's been training for this for her entire life."

"I still don't think it's safe." I drummed my fingers on the car seat as

BOOK 4: REVIEW TO A KILL

we idled at a traffic light, the engine rattling in protest. "This guy supposedly has guns. What if he decides to take a shot at her?"

"Normally, I'd say having a gun doesn't necessarily mean one will use it but in this case . . ."

"Meaning?" I sat forward, resting my hand on the back of the driver's seat and twisting to look at Richard.

He shrugged. "Let's just say that Leatrice is lucky some days that I don't own a gun."

The car jerked forward as the driver pressed the gas, and I was jolted back against the seat as the dog yelped. "You know she means well. She's just . . ." I paused as I thought of words to explain my downstairs neighbor.

"Mentally imbalanced, overbearing, meddlesome?" Richard finished my sentence for me. "Take your pick."

"I was going to say lonely. She doesn't have any family I've ever heard of, and I think most of her friends are dead."

"Coincidence?" Richard tapped a finger on his chin. "I think not."

"You know she's obsessed with solving crimes, not committing them." I grabbed the door handle to keep from sliding into Richard as we made a turn without slowing. The Yorkie tried to regain balance as his four feet skittered across the slick seats. Richard scooped up the tiny dog with one hand before he landed on the floor.

"Who's to say she isn't some criminal mastermind who's secretly been plotting all of these crimes to give herself something to do?" Richard said, tucking the Yorkie back in his man bag.

Now it was my turn to arch an eyebrow at him. As we drove down the bride and groom's street, I pointed a finger at the mideighties Ford Fairmont up ahead. The yellow car stretched out over two parallel spaces along the street and was anything but unobtrusive. The top of a beige fedora barely reached above the steering wheel. "Does that look like a criminal genius to you?"

Richard passed a few bills to the driver as the car slowed to a stop. "That's what's so brilliant. No one would ever suspect her."

I slid across the seat and exited the car from Richard's side, being careful not to slam the door too hard for fear it might fall off. Leatrice's hat bobbed up for a moment when we tapped on the window. Then it began lowering.

"Hurry," she said. "Get in the back seat before anyone sees you."

I pulled open the door to her car, giving it a yank when it stuck, and got into the back seat. Richard followed, setting his messenger bag

543

between us and letting Hermès pop his head out and begin his sniff inspection. Although Leatrice's car was old, it had rarely been driven so no air fresheners needed to dangle above the dashboard and no duct tape marred the cloth seats. Despite the fact that Leatrice rarely drove her car, the dash appeared to have gotten a recent coat of Armor All, and the carpet looked vacuumed. Our cab driver could have taken a lesson. The only indication that time was not on the car's side was the sagging beige ceiling fabric that bloused over our heads.

"Coffee?" She held up a Thermos without turning around.

"No, thanks." I leaned forward so my head poked between the two front seats. "Are you sure this is such a good idea?"

Leatrice turned her head and our faces were inches apart. "I thought coffee was typical on stakeouts. Should I have brought something else instead?"

"Not the coffee." Richard sat forward so his head was next to mine. "She means this stakeout is a bad idea."

"But this guy is your only suspect," Leatrice said. "And someone should be here in case he comes back. In the movies, the bad guy always comes back."

"So what happens when he comes back?" I asked, trying to ignore the dog head that had wiggled between Richard and me.

Leatrice's face lit up, and she rubbed the Yorkie's head. "I call in reinforcements."

Richard glanced at me. "I hope she doesn't mean us."

I sat back. "Promise me you won't leave this car or approach the house or try to be a hero."

"Of course not." Leatrice patted the armrest next to her, and Hermès jumped up on it with a happy yip. "I'm strictly a surveillance operation."

That made me feel somewhat better but didn't completely allay my nerves. "This guy could be dangerous, Leatrice. We know he has guns." I eyed the bright red smart car parked tightly in front of us. "Can you even drive away if you need to?"

"Don't worry about me," Leatrice said. "If I need to, I can drive *over* the car in front of me."

Given the size of her car and the minuscule proportions of the smart car, I believed her. I looked up and down the residential block, cars filling every inch of the parallel street spaces. Most were compacts or small SUVs. A smattering of BMWs and VWs. Nothing like this boat-sized Ford that stretched out the length of the row house it sat in front of.

"Won't you need to move after a certain amount of time?" Richard asked. "The ticketing in Georgetown is the most efficient part of the DC government."

Leatrice pointed to a sticker on her windshield. "I have a zone permit. But speaking of parking tickets, guess what popped up when my guys were searching the police database for Toker?"

Richard's eyebrows rose, and I shook my head. "I know, I know." Now wasn't the time to go into all the questions Richard had about that sentence.

"A parking ticket given out the morning of the murder right on this block to a Toker," Leatrice said.

"I would have thought if the bride lived here she'd have gotten a resident parking permit," Richard said.

I shook my head. "Tricia didn't drive. Too stressful."

"It was given to a silver Land Rover registered to a Constance Toker," Leatrice said. "One hour before you and Kate found the groom lying in a puddle of blood."

"Constance? You mean Connie?" I raised a hand to my mouth. "That's the bride's mother."

Richard looked at me. "Weren't you telling me the mother might have had a motive?"

"The bride accused her of murdering her husband. But we dismissed that as Tricia being her awful self. And we couldn't imagine her mother ever killing her."

"Well, now you have the mother's car at the scene of the crime, which is what we call opportunity," Leatrice said. "It might be time to revisit that motive."

"Hello in there!" A sharp rap on the car window made me jump. "Open up."

I could only see legs in dark pants from where I sat, and my heart raced as I imagined that it was the police. Or, worse, the gun-happy neighbor.

Leatrice smiled, leaning over to pull up the manual lock on the passenger side door. "My reinforcements have arrived."

The passenger door opened, and Fern stuck his head inside. "Am I too late to the party?"

CHAPTER 24

Fern sat in the passenger seat and closed the door behind him, placing a pair of white paper bags on the floor between his legs. From the smell that filled the car, I could tell the bags contained something with plenty of sugar, and my stomach rumbled. When had I last eaten? I thought back over my day. Had my daily food intake really consisted of a gin and tonic, half an empanada, and a Diet Dr Pepper? No wonder I felt light-headed.

"What's in the bags?" I asked as Hermès hopped down from his armrest perch to sniff the bags.

"First things first," Richard said. "What are you wearing?"

Fern twisted around to face us and tipped his brown fedora up so we could see his eyes. "This is a stakeout, right?"

Since Fern always dressed to the occasion, the beige trench coat with the collar flipped up around his neck made perfect sense to me. "What do you have on underneath?"

Fern grinned at me. "I'm glad you asked. Just in case we need to investigate the target's house covertly, I wore clothes that would blend in." He opened his trench coat.

"A catsuit?" Richard gaped at him. "You think a black skintight unitard on a man in Georgetown is blending in?"

Fern made a face at Richard and pulled his trench coat closed. "At night it will."

BOOK 4: REVIEW TO A KILL

I glanced outside where the sun peeked behind the tops of the trees. It would be dark soon enough.

"I think you look perfect," Leatrice said. "Thanks for coming and bringing supplies."

Fern patted Leatrice's arm and reached for one of the white bags being inspected by the dog. "Who wants a hand pie?"

Richard flopped back on the seat and put a hand over his eyes. "This may be the only stakeout in history where the supplies are hand pies."

"What are hand pies?" Leatrice asked as Fern handed her a pastry wrapped in wax paper.

"If you ask me, they're the perfect food for a stakeout." Fern passed one back to me. "They're like pies—pastry with a fruit filling—but they're made into enclosed pockets, so you can eat them with your hands."

I pulled back the white paper covering my still-warm hand pie to reveal a half-moon shaped pocket of pastry crimped around the edges. They'd been deep fried so bits of the grease dotted the wax paper. "What flavor did you get?"

"Some cherry, some strawberry rhubarb." Fern passed a wax-paper bundle to Richard.

Leatrice inspected her pastry. "Isn't this clever?"

I bit into the edge of mine, and warm cherry filling oozed out. The combination of the flaky crust and the sweet cherries was heavenly. I closed my eyes to fully savor the sensation, and it took effort not to moan out loud. I felt tiny paws on my leg and opened my eyes to find a pair of dark doggie eyes inches away from mine as he inspected my dessert.

"No people food, Hermès," Richard said, wagging a finger at him.

The dog ignored him, either because he didn't recognize his new name or because Richard's command sounded more like one of his style suggestions. No white after Labor Day. No flip-flops unless you can see water. No people food. Richard clearly hadn't learned how to be an alpha dog yet.

"So I've got the outfit and the supplies," Fern said. "Who are we staking out and why?"

Leatrice produced a small spiral notebook and flipped it open. I couldn't help noticing that the notebook looked strikingly similar to the ones Detective Reese used to take notes.

"His name is Frank Ferguson," Leatrice said. "He lives next door to the victims. The unpainted brick house. His alias is Effing Frank."

I thought about telling Leatrice that Effing Frank wasn't an alias, just what the bride called him because she was a crappy person but I decided not to bother.

We all turned our necks to look at the redbrick house. Even though it wasn't fully dark yet, I could tell the lights were off inside. My eyes slid to Tricia and Dave's house, which stood mere feet away. The yellow crime-scene tape had been removed from the doorway, but the house looked still and foreboding. A shiver ran through me as I thought back to only a few days earlier when Kate and I had walked into through the front door and found the groom in a pool of blood. I tried not to think of the fact that the bride had also been upstairs with a bullet hole in her head.

As Leatrice told Fern what we knew about Effing Frank—mostly that he worked in corporate security and belonged to the NRA—I tried to put our new clues into place. We had a neighbor who hated the victims and had supposedly threatened them. The fact that he owned at least one handgun and seemed to have disappeared made him the most obvious suspect on our list. I thought about the email the groom had shown me. Did it come from this guy?

Then I thought about what Leatrice had told us about Tricia's mother being at the scene of the crime. Even though the mother had seemed devoted to her daughter, I'd been wrong about clients before. If the mom really had knocked off her wealthy husband and the bride had evidence on her, she could kill to keep it quiet and to keep from going to prison for life. Especially if she'd already killed once before.

"Annabelle?" Richard's voice snapped me out of my thoughts. "Earth to Annabelle."

I gave my head a small shake. "Sorry. I was thinking about the two new suspects. Both of them could be guilty for different reasons, but I'm not convinced by either one yet."

"I know about the guy we're watching, but who is the second new suspect?" Fern asked, crumbling his wax paper into a ball and dropping into the empty bag.

"The mother of the bride's Land Rover was parked on this street the morning Tricia was killed, but it wasn't here when Kate and I arrived. That puts the mom at the scene of the crime at the time of the murder."

"You're sure you didn't see her car?" Richard asked.

"I'm sure. We went to enough meetings with Mrs. Toker to recognize her silver Land Rover from a mile away, and I know it wasn't parked on the street when we arrived at Tricia's house that morning. That means Connie Toker was here and then left."

Fern put a hand to his chest. "That doesn't look good. But do you really think Connie is the type to shoot someone?"

I remembered that Fern knew the bride's mother because he'd also done her hair for years. "I still don't swallow the idea of the bride's mother shooting her own daughter, especially after she'd just shelled out over a hundred grand for her wedding."

Fern shook his head. "She's too skittish to kill someone."

"But why was she here?" I asked. "And if she just popped by for a visit, why didn't the groom mention his mother-in-law when he told me the morning's events?"

The more we learned, the less this murder made any sense at all.

CHAPTER 25

I thanked the doormen as they held open the two sets of heavy wooden doors leading to the Hay-Adams Hotel lobby. I'd made good time to the hotel even though it sat in the heart of downtown directly across from the White House. It helped that I'd missed the morning rush hour. I glanced down at my phone. I even had a few minutes to spare before the ten o'clock meeting. Not enough time to grab a bite in the hotel restaurant, my favorite spot in the city for a really luxurious breakfast, but maybe if the meeting went quickly I'd be able to eat afterward. I'd only had a bottled Frappuccino and a banana on the drive in.

I hesitated inside and scanned the small interior. Rich wood walls extended at least twelve feet high then became ivory plaster that soared upward in a series of arches leading to the intricately carved ceiling. A round mahogany table sat in front of the pair of elevators directly across from the front entrance. It held a massive urn packed with an abundance of white lilies. I breathed in the heady scent of the flowers as I caught my breath. To my right and left were small groupings of maroon upholstered wing chairs arranged around dark wood coffee tables on thick carpets. I spotted Kate in one of the chairs, her legs crossed and her oversized black Kate Spade tote at her feet.

"So what's this about?" I asked as she saw me and stood. I noticed that Kate wore one of her more conservative looks, a pink sheath dress with a scoop neck, although the hemline still ran shorter than anything I owned.

Kate slipped her feet into her nude heels. "So you know how you're a little bit obsessed about clearing our name with the police?"

"You mean so we don't go to jail for a crime we didn't commit? Yep. That rings a bell."

Kate waved a hand at me. "And that's all great, but while you're doing that, our reputation is going down the toilet. I, for one, would like to have a job once this is all over."

I let my shoulders sag. I had been ignoring social media because I couldn't bear to read what was being said. "Is it that bad?"

Kate shrugged. "It's not good. I've been thinking of ways to fix it, and I may have come up with a great one. Do you remember that I told you the Weddies were getting together to pay tribute to Tricia?"

I glanced around me. Aside from the concierge and the front desk attendant, who both spoke low into their phones, Kate and I were the only people in the lobby. "Yes?"

"Well, they're meeting here."

I tried not to let the irritation show in my voice. "I drove across town to crash a meeting of Weddies?"

"Not crash exactly," Kate said.

"Well, we can't announce we're wedding planners, can we? Aren't they very strict about being brides-only?" I rummaged through my purse, found a MAC lipstick, and applied it by memory, pressing my lips together and dropping the black tube back in my bag. "I thought perhaps this was a meeting with the hotel catering ladies. I would have dressed up if you'd told me we were hanging with women who've elevated judging to an art form."

Kate passed her eyes over me and twitched one shoulder. "You're fine. I mean, it wouldn't kill you to take out the orange ponytail holder but the dress is ironed."

I felt relieved that I'd picked up a huge load of dry cleaning before Tricia's wedding and that the navy fit and flare dress I wore had been in that load. I pulled out my hair elastic and tossed my head upside down, shaking my hands through the back of my hair before flipping it back up. "Better?"

Kate gave me a thumbs up. "The hardcore Weddies are meeting in the private dining room at the back of the Lafayette Room."

"Don't tell me they picked the Hay because Tricia held her wedding here."

"You got it," Kate said. "These girls are full-on wedding groupies.

They're the ones who stay in the forum after they get married to give half-baked advice to the new girls."

I cringed. "It sounds awful. Are you sure there isn't a tank of great whites we could jump in? You know, something less terrifying."

Kate stood up. "Come on. This is the best way to find out what's being said about Wedding Belles and nip it in the bud. If we can get these girls on our side it will go a long way to repairing our reputation."

"Fine." I sighed. "But what if they recognize us? Our picture is on our Wed Boards profile and our website."

Kate slid on a pair of oversized sunglasses and handed another pair to me. "Voilà. Instant disguise."

I put on my pair and eyed Kate. The large squared-off frames wouldn't have confused someone who knew her well, but they hid enough of her face that she wouldn't be instantly recognized. I hoped my round tortoise-shell pair did the same.

Kate nudged me as we walked up the short flight of carpeted stairs leading to the Lafayette Room. "And since all the Weddies are in mourning for Tricia the Terrible, no one will think twice when we keep them on to hide our tears."

We reached the top of the stairs and paused. The Lafayette Room was laid out like an L with the long side stretched out along the wall of the hotel facing the White House. Floor-to-ceiling windows covering the far side of the restaurant allowed sun to pour into the room. Upholstered chairs surrounded tables draped in cream linens and set with glittering crystal and white bone china. I inhaled the rich aroma of gourmet coffee and buttery pastries and wished we were sitting down to eat.

Kate said a few words to the maître d' and we were led through the restaurant toward the back. Even at a midmorning hour between breakfast and lunch, the Lafayette Room buzzed with political luminaries drinking cappuccinos and making deals. Political bigwigs weren't as easy to recognize as Hollywood celebrities, but I felt sure I'd seen some of the faces on cable news.

The energy changed once we reached the glass doors of the private dining room at the far end of the restaurant. The rectangular room had a crystal chandelier and white-shaded sconces on the walls. Women stood talking in small groups, some holding flutes of Champagne, and I guessed that not a single one of them was over thirty.

When Kate opened one of the glass doors, I heard the hissing of whispered conversations, one on top of the other. A few women paused to glance at us then resumed talking when they realized they didn't know us.

BOOK 4: REVIEW TO A KILL

"These sunglasses are working like a charm," Kate said.

A waiter passed us holding a silver tray of Champagne. Kate plucked off two glasses and passed one to me.

"Now what?" I asked.

Kate slid her glasses down her nose and peered over them. "Just follow my lead."

She sidled up to a group of four women in sundresses with designer bags swinging from their arms. Instead of joining them, she turned her back on the group and faced me. She took a sip of bubbly then tapped her ear to indicate that she was listening to them.

"It isn't the first time they've been involved in a murder," one of the women said. "The girl over there told me their clients get knocked off all the time."

I fought the urge to correct the woman. We'd only had one client get killed before, thank you very much. Well, Tricia made two.

Kate must have read my mind because she gave a slight shake of her head. "That's right," she said in a voice loud enough to carry. "I heard that Wedding Belles just signed a celebrity from the West Coast."

I tried not to spit out my Champagne.

Kate raised her voice. "From what I hear it's a very well-known actress."

The women behind her paused their conversation. Kate nudged me to say something.

My mind drew a blank. "Really?"

Kate nodded as if I'd just said the most fascinating thing she'd ever heard. "And they say the groom is from Europe. Twelfth in line for the throne."

I noticed Kate hadn't specified which throne but the women behind her didn't seem to notice or care. From the snatches I could hear of their urgent whispers, they'd taken the bait.

Kate tugged me by the arm across the room. "A little help would be nice."

"Sorry," I said. "I choked."

Kate patted my back. "That's okay. We've got a whole room to go."

As we approached another group, I whipped a hand around Kate's waist and spun her around.

"What's going on?" she asked.

I moved us through the women until we stood in front of the ornately carved white fireplace with an massive mirror hung above it. "Didn't you see who was in that group?"

553

Kate craned her neck to look, and I jerked her back. "Brianna," I said.

"What?" Kate raised her voice and a plump brunette glanced at us. Kate smiled sweetly, raising her Champagne flute at her, then leaned in close to me. "What is she doing here? This is a brides-only event."

I tilted my head at her. "Well, we're here."

"Yes, but we have a good reason. I'll bet she's doing nothing but spreading rumors about us and all her other competition. I'll bet you she's the one telling people our clients get knocked off all the time."

Knowing what I did of Brianna, Kate was right about her. Dropping little nuggets of negative information about her colleagues was right up her alley. I allowed myself to peek at our willowy blond competitor. Overdressed, as usual, in a black satin skirt that belled to her knees and a tight black-and-white striped top. "What can we do about it?"

Kate tapped a finger to the arm of her sunglasses. "I'm thinking." She downed her remaining Champagne in a single gulp. "We've got to fight fire with fire."

"Meaning?" I asked as Kate positioned us in front of another cluster of brides.

"That's what I heard," Kate began. "Brides by Brianna was shut down by the police."

I gaped at her as the conversation around us stopped. "What?"

Kate put a hand on my arm in a conspiratorial gesture. "That's right," she said in a stage whisper. "Brianna was actually running a high-priced call-girl service. The weddings were just a cover."

I spluttered at her but didn't manage to get any words out. If Brianna ever heard that we'd started these rumors she would kill us in our sleep. I noticed the women's faces behind me. They were as shocked as I was but more delighted.

One woman actually leaned over to Kate. "So she was a madam?"

Kate nodded. "They're calling her the Marrying Madam."

I had to give Kate credit. The girl could think on her feet.

"Remind me never to tick you off," I said. I surveyed the crowd and could see and hear the ripple of the salacious gossip as it passed through the room. It was only a matter of minutes before it reached Brianna. Not that she could defend herself without revealing that she was a wedding planner crashing a Weddies event. Better to go down as a disgraced madam than have these women tear into you for pretending to be one of them.

"We should probably leave." I kept my eyes on the back of Brianna's head as we maneuvered through the crowd toward the glass doors. "I don't want to be anywhere near Brianna when she hears that she's running a network of hookers."

"High-priced call girls." Kate corrected me. "And there's probably good money in that."

I pushed open one of the doors and held it for Kate. "I'm sure there is. But let's consider that as a last-resort business plan."

"You know, you wouldn't be half bad as a madam."

I cast a glance back at her as I led the way through the restaurant. "Thanks, I think."

Kate looked me up and down when we reached the stairs leading to the lobby. "No one would ever suspect you."

I narrowed my eyes at her. "Why do I think that's not the compliment it should be?"

Kate grinned and held out her hand. "Do you have your valet ticket? I'm going to go charm the guy at the front desk and get them comped."

I pulled the ticket from my purse, handed it to her, and watched her make her way to the front desk. If anyone could sweet talk their way into free parking, it was Kate. I didn't think she'd paid for a drink, meal, or parking since she'd moved to DC.

The elevator doors opened and a woman exited in a bright green floral-print dress. I felt a jolt as I recognized her silvery-blond hair and backed a few steps into the restaurant so she wouldn't see me. She glanced around the lobby but didn't look up toward me before she turned down the short hallway to the side of the elevator bank.

What was Tricia's mother doing here?

CHAPTER 26

I walked down the stairs and looked down the short hallway where the bride's mother had disappeared. Like the lobby, the walls were paneled in a rich brown wood and three doors clustered together at the end: the door to the express elevator to the roof; the door leading downstairs to Off the Record, the hotel's bar; and the double doors leadings into the small ballroom called the Hay-Adams Room. But no sign of Mrs. Toker.

What was Tricia's mother doing here so many days after her daughter's wedding and death?

I walked down the hall. I glanced up at the illuminated numbers that indicated the elevator's movements. It seemed to be waiting at the lobby so I could assume she hadn't gotten on. So she'd either gone down to the bar at ten thirty in the morning or she was in the hotel's smaller ballroom. Luckily the ballroom door had been propped open, so I checked that first, peering around the open door.

While the rooftop ballroom was light and airy, this smaller space felt like an English gentleman's club. The walls shared the same wood paneling as the hallway and lobby as well as the ornately carved ceiling. Multi-tiered brass chandeliers hung down over the room in several places. A fireplace with a large mahogany mantle dominated the near end of the room with a grouping of masculine wing chairs surrounding it. It looked very different than it had on Saturday when we'd covered up everything so that the ceremony room looked like Paris in the springtime as well as the upstairs reception.

The ballroom had been set with round tables draped in gold damask cloths, and savory smells drifted from the catering kitchens that led off of the back of the room. I could safely guess they were prepping for an event.

I spotted the mother of the bride standing next to a bald man considerably taller than her. Aside from the two of them, the room was empty of people. They stood in front of the fireplace, which did not have a fire laid, and she faced away from me. I studied his face for a moment but it wasn't one I'd seen before. Except for a nose that verged on bulbous, his face was unremarkable. But I knew he hadn't been a guest at the wedding.

I pulled my head back and flattened myself against the door so I could listen to their conversation without being seen.

"We shouldn't be meeting here," the man said.

"Well, I don't want anyone to see you coming into my hotel room," Mrs. Toker replied, her voice quavering.

So she had stayed at the hotel. But why? I felt my heart beat faster, and I tried to slow my breath. I didn't want them to hear me hyperventilating.

"Do you have it?" Mrs. Toker asked.

I heard the sound of fumbling paper. "Right here."

The mother of the bride sighed. "I hope the payoff is worth all this effort."

I put a hand over my mouth without thinking. What was going on here? Payoff for what?

"Are you sure this is the route you want to take?" the man asked.

"For now."

I heard a rustling of paper and then a sharp intake of breath that I assumed to be the mother's. What had she seen?

"You know how to find me if you want to take the next steps," the man said.

I heard his heavy footsteps on the carpet as he exited the room from the door on the other side. I sidled a few feet so that I could watch him cross the lobby and exit the hotel. A moment later, Mrs. Toker followed him, a manila envelope tucked under one arm. But instead of leaving the hotel, she turned and walked in my direction—either heading for the elevators or for the Lafayette Room. I scurried back toward the Hay-Adams Room in case she was bound for the restaurant. Then I pushed open the door that led to the downstairs bar, slipping into the stairwell.

My mind raced with conflicting thoughts as I took in deep breaths.

What had I just heard? Why would the dead bride's mother be meeting someone in secret?

"Think," I told myself. "There has to be an explanation."

The door to the stairwell opened, and I yelped. Kate stood holding the door. "Whoa there, jumpy. It's only me."

I put a hand to my chest. "You scared me to death."

I thought you wanted to get out of here." She held up the valet tickets with validation stamps on them. "Or is this your way of telling me we should go downstairs to the bar and start day drinking?"

I stepped out into the hall. "I heard something very strange just now."

Kate peered into the stairwell. "In here?"

"No, not in there. Out in the hall." I jerked a thumb toward the door. "I followed Mrs. Toker and listened in to a conversation she had in the Hay-Adams Room with some man."

Kate held up her hands as if to brace herself. "Wait a second. Tricia's mom is here? Did she never check out after the wedding?"

I shrugged. "I don't know. Maybe she doesn't want to go home after her daughter's death."

"Do you think the hotel is still comping her? You know, because her daughter was killed?"

I thought about it for a moment. I could easily imagine the luxury hotel wanting to appear sympathetic to a guest but, if they weren't careful, Mrs. Toker might move in permanently.

"So what did you hear that made you so nervous?" Kate asked.

"He gave her something in a manila envelope. Something important. She said she hoped the payoff was worth it."

Kate and I both fell silent as a waiter passed between us and went inside the ballroom.

"That's so strange," Kate said once the waiter was far enough away not to hear. "It must be connected to her daughter, don't you think?"

"Are you thinking that between this and her car being outside Tricia's house the morning of the murder, she's looking pretty suspicious?"

"That wasn't what I was thinking, but it is now," Kate said. "Do you think this guy had something to do with Tricia's murder?"

"I doubt seriously that a wealthy Georgetown mom hired a back-alley hit man to off her daughter. And why do it after you've dropped over a hundred thousand dollars on her wedding?"

Kate nodded. "I've said it before. Any sane parent would knock off their kid before they paid for a wedding."

"I don't know if 'sane' would be the right word," I muttered.

"So if we're dismissing the idea of Mrs. Toker hiring an assassin to kill her horrible daughter—which I'm not totally ready to do, by the way—then why was she meeting someone secretly?" Kate stopped her pacing.

I gnawed at the corner of my lip. "I don't know. Tricia's mother must have hired this guy to dig up something for her. He gave her something. The question is what was it and what does it have to do with her daughter's death?"

"Well, I know one way we can find out." Kate paused as she rummaged in her black purse before holding up a Hay-Adams keycard. "I still have a key to the mother's suite."

CHAPTER 27

"And why do you still have a key to the mother's suite?" I asked, staring at the white plastic card emblazoned with the hotel's insignia.

"I haven't cleaned out my bag since the wedding," she said. "And I had it from delivering the money envelopes to the mom's room at the end of the night."

I couldn't reprimand her since I was famous for finding old hotel keys in my pockets after weddings. Not to mention hotel pens, notepads, and matchbooks.

"Do you think it still works?" I asked.

"If she's in the same suite it should." Kate flipped the card around in her hand. "If she moved rooms then we're out of luck."

I eyed the keycard. "Technically, this would be breaking and entering, and I just promised Richard and Reese that I would back off the case."

"It's not breaking and entering if we have the key." Kate waved the card at me and hiked her purse up on her shoulder. "Come on."

I followed Kate down the short hall and around the corner to the lobby elevators then put a hand on her arm to stop her. "What if the mother catches us?"

"We'll explain that we were here for Tricia's tribute. It's completely legitimate. Admirable even."

"That explains why we're in the hotel," I said. "Not why we're in her hotel room."

"We're delivering..." Kate ran her eyes over the lobby then picked up a small vase of yellow roses from a nearby side table. "Condolence flowers."

I looked down at the vase of four roses and then looked up at Kate. "We're big spenders, aren't we?"

Kate pressed the elevator call button. "It's just a gesture. But we're not going to need it."

"Because we're going to waltz right into her hotel room without her noticing?" I asked after we stepped into the dark wood-and-brass interior of the elevator car.

"You forget that I'm the queen of distractions," Kate said as the elevator doors closed and we surged upward. We stepped out onto the seventh floor and she picked up the black house phone resting on a polished wooden credenza across from the elevators. "Yes, the room for Toker, please." She held her hand over the receiver. "Watch and learn."

I sighed and shook my head.

"Yes, Mrs. Toker?" Kate said into the phone in a clipped, British accent. "We have a delivery for you at the front desk. No, I'm afraid you need to sign for it." She replaced the receiver. "Voilà. Empty room."

"Impressive," I said. "Your Russian accent is better, but I like the British."

"Thanks, I've been working on it. People take you more seriously with a British accent. Now let's hide."

We ducked around the corner and listened for Mrs. Toker to leave her room and get in the elevator. Once the elevator doors had closed, we dashed down the hall. Kate put the vase of roses in one hand while she swiped the card key. The green light on the door blinked, allowing Kate to push the door handle down and enter the room.

I glanced around the suite after I'd closed the door behind us. The room looked eerily similar to how it had on the wedding day. The his-and-hers Champagne glasses that I'd rinsed and dried after the toasting sat on the same mahogany foyer table where I'd left them Saturday night, along with the long Waterford box that held the cake knife. The collection of white and ivory envelopes that held cash or checks—not that this couple needed the money—fanned out across the living room coffee table next to the large envelope that contained their signed marriage license.

"She hasn't touched a thing," Kate said, her voice low even though we knew we were alone in the suite.

I took a few steps into the room, passing the grouping of cream sofas topped with oversized fringe pillows. A copy of the *Washington Post* from the wedding day was still folded neatly on one of the couch cushions. "It's creepy. I don't think we should be here."

"Let's look for whatever it was that the man gave her and get out," Kate said, still holding the yellow flowers out in front of her. "We won't have long before the front desk figures out there isn't a delivery for her."

I pawed through some papers on the oval dining room table but found them to be proposals and contracts from the wedding. Kate took the bedroom, and I could hear her opening drawers.

"I may have found something," she called to me.

I hurried into the adjoining bedroom to where she stood at the dark wood desk. She held up a large manila envelope and had placed the yellow roses on the desk.

Kate pulled open the metal butterfly clasp and started to wiggle the stack of papers out of the envelope when we heard a beep at the door and a click of the handle being pressed down.

Despite my desire to see what was inside, I motioned to Kate to put the papers back in the envelope. "Leave it," I whispered. "We need to hide."

Her hands shaking, she shoved the contents back inside, fastened the metal clasp, and set the manila envelope on the desk. She snatched up the vase of yellow roses and darted her eyes around.

I pointed to the closet across the room, and we both rushed over to it as Mrs. Toker came into the suite, grumbling about incompetent hotel staff. I opened the closet door and slipped inside with Kate right behind me, pulling the door shut behind her. I crouched low and tried to bury myself behind a pair of terry-cloth hotel robes as I heard the mother of the bride enter the bedroom. Kate clutched my hand. Mrs. Toker was right in front of the closet doors when her cell phone rang. I could feel Kate jump next to me but the ring of the phone drowned out any sound.

"I'm glad you called me back," Mrs. Toker said when she answered. "I assume you got my message about meeting?"

There was a pause as the person on the other end spoke.

"I thought you might. I'll meet you there in five minutes." Mrs. Toker hung up and walked out of the room, the front door slamming shut as she left.

I could feel Kate relax next to me. She pushed open the closet door and stepped out. "Let's grab that envelope and get out of here before she comes back."

"Agreed." I followed her out and straightened up.

Kate crossed the room to the desk. "It's gone." She opened the desk drawers and looked around her. "The envelope is gone."

"She must have taken it with her," I said, scanning the room and not seeing any place she could have stashed it in the short time we'd heard her inside the bedroom. "Maybe the person she's meeting has something to do with the papers in the envelope."

Kate followed me out of the bedroom. "We were so close to seeing. Should we come back later to see if she returns it?"

"No way. We should thank our lucky stars that she didn't catch us this time." I opened the front door and glanced up and down the empty hall before Kate and I stepped out of the suite and walked to the elevator. As I pressed the call button, I hoped that we wouldn't run into the bride's mother. "Where did you leave those flowers?"

Kate slapped her forehead. "In the suite."

"It's okay." I pulled her into the elevator with me and pushed the button for the lobby. "It's not like they had our name on them. I doubt she'll notice."

Kate cringed. "She may notice. I left them on the floor of the closet."

I crossed my arms and tapped one foot on the elevator floor. "Your accents are great, but your overall spy skills could use some work."

The elevator doors pinged open, and I gave a cursory glance around the lobby to be sure there were no Weddies and no Mrs. Toker before walking quickly through it. I let out a breath of relief as we reached the outside of the hotel. Kate handed the doorman our valet tickets.

"We did it." I gave a subdued high five to Kate when the doorman looked away. "Mrs. Toker never saw us."

"Well done, Miss Archer," Kate said, giving me a mock bow. "Shall we catch a cab?"

Before I could answer her, a piercing scream came from above us. We both craned our necks to look up as a body came hurtling down from the hotel's roof and landed with a vicious thud in the front bushes.

Kate stumbled back a few feet, and I clapped a hand over my mouth as the uniformed doorman ran over to the body. He didn't need to tell us that the woman was dead. No one survived a fall from almost ten stories like that. And he didn't need to tell me who'd plummeted to her death. I recognized the distinctive green floral dress that Mrs. Toker had been wearing earlier.

CHAPTER 28

The wail of sirens grew louder as they approached. Guests of the hotel had drifted outside in response to the screams, and passersby from the street began to gather around the front bushes where Mrs. Toker's lifeless body lay sprawled faceup. Thankfully, I couldn't see her face, but I could see her feet protruding from the greenery, the toes of her beige heels pointing to the sky.

As a sudden wave of nausea passed through me, I put a hand over my mouth, grateful that I didn't have anything in my stomach but a banana and coffee. I turned and focused on the brightly colored flowers in the front beds on the opposite side of the hotel, trying to erase the vision in my mind of the mother of the bride hurtling to the ground. I gave an involuntary shudder. I hated heights and the thought of falling off a high balcony ranked right up there on my list of fears.

"We should get out of here," I said, pulling Kate with me as I backed away from the hotel's entrance and down the sloped drive. "Before the Weddies start coming outside."

Kate tugged me back up a few steps. "Do you think we should leave the scene of a crime. We were one of the few eyewitnesses."

A feeling of panic replaced the nausea. "But we were just leaving the hotel. We can't tell the police anything of value."

"People have already seen us."

I cast my eyes over the growing crowd, phones out to record the tragedy, and the hotel staff trying to keep them away from the body. I tried to keep my gaze away from the dead mother of the bride but my eyes continued to be drawn back to her shoes, one of which had slipped off the back of her heel. If I focused on the shoes and ignored the fact that the woman had plunged over one hundred feet to her death, I could keep the meager breakfast I'd had on the way to the hotel from coming back up. I leaned over and put my hands on my knees.

"Are you okay?" Kate leaned her head over next to mine.

I nodded without speaking and took a deep breath, concentrating on the coolness of the midmorning air and not the dead woman merely feet away from me. From my upside-down vantage point, I saw the ambulance stop in the street with its lights flashing, and a trio of paramedics leaped out. I felt like telling them not to rush, that no medical training could save Mrs. Toker at this point. I closed my eyes to block out the lights.

"I wish I could say this is a surprise."

I opened my eyes to see a pair of khaki pant legs. I didn't need to look up to know who they belonged to. I straightened to standing. "Good to see you, Detective."

The detective didn't look pleased to see me. In fact, he looked angry, his hazel eyes flashing as he glared at me. "What in the name of God are you doing at another crime scene? Please tell me you two just happened to be walking by when the lady fell off the roof."

Kate put her hands on her hips. "If you must know, Annabelle and I were attending a networking event here."

As long as he didn't confirm our alibi with the Weddies and mention our names, we were golden.

Reese's shoulders relaxed a bit, and he had the good sense to look apologetic. "Sorry I jumped to conclusions."

I didn't meet Kate's eyes. She knew as well as I did that he'd be singing a different tune as soon as he discovered the name of the victim. "No problem."

"Were you witnesses to what happened?" Reese asked, looking between Kate and me.

"We'd just walked outside when she fell from the roof," I said, trying to keep my eyes from shifting over the detective's shoulder to the body and the paramedics now hunched over it.

"You knew she fell from the roof?" Reese asked, pulling a notepad from his inside blazer pocket.

"Well, I think I saw her coming from the roof." I looked at Kate who nodded her agreement. "Plus, I'm pretty sure the windows to the guest rooms don't open, but the roof has an open-air balcony with just a railing."

Reese scratched a few words in his notebook. "And that was all you saw?"

"Aside from the scream," Kate added. "We heard her scream all the way down."

The detective looked up. "Really? Interesting."

I didn't know why that would be interesting. Most people I knew would scream if they were falling over a hundred feet.

Reese flipped his notepad closed. "I'm going to need you two to stay a little longer."

"Are we suspects?" Kate asked.

Reese gave her a half smile. "No. Why would you be?"

"We've been suspects before when we were innocent," Kate called after him as he walked away from us and toward his colleagues who had clustered around the victim.

I let myself breathe normally again. "I guess that wasn't so bad."

"Don't you think it's rude to keep us here?" Kate asked. "I might have a lunch date, you know."

"When do you not have a date?" I asked.

Kate winked at me. "A single girl's got to eat."

"A single girl can also get takeout," I said.

"Takeout Chinese food every night is not my idea of a good time," she muttered, turning her head away from me.

Truth be told, it wasn't my idea of a great social life either, but I'd never had the ability to date for sustenance as Kate could.

I took in the bustling scene around me. Several uniformed officers had set up a barricade to keep people farther away from the crime scene, and a police photographer knelt in the bushes taking shots of the body. News crews had decamped to the sidewalk in front of the hotel, and some of the cameras already had bright lights pointing at unrealistically attractive reporters. Detective Reese seemed deep in conversation with a pair of uniformed policemen and another plainclothes detective.

I nibbled on my lower lip. It was only a matter of minutes before Reese discovered the name of the woman who lay dead in the bushes and had some serious questions for us. And it couldn't be long before brides from the Weddies event began to come outside. If Brianna spotted us here she would know it was us who spread the call-girl rumors.

My phone vibrated, and I pulled it out of my pocket, looking at the name on the display. Richard. I pressed the talk button. "What's up?" I tried to sound casual. No use working him up if I didn't have to.

"I should be asking you that question," he said, his voice shrill. "Do you want to tell me why I'm watching you and Kate on the news right now?"

CHAPTER 29

"Hurry, get in," Richard called out through his open car window only twenty minutes after I'd hung up the phone with him. He wore a blue baseball cap pulled down low and, if I hadn't recognized his silver Mercedes convertible with its hard top up and Hermès perched on the console next to the driver's seat, I might not have known it was him. Baseball caps were not a part of Richard's fashion repertoire.

Kate and I stood on the sidewalk in front of the Hay-Adams Hotel where H and Sixteenths streets met, behind the police barricade but still within a few yards of the crime scene. The paramedics had given up their futile attempts to save the victim, and now the medical examiner crouched over the body with a cluster of uniformed officers nearby. Detective Reese had disappeared into the hotel, and I had a feeling he would soon know the identity of the victim. Then things would get sticky for us.

"What are you doing?" I asked as I hurried over to the car. Richard had pulled up in the far left-hand lane of the one-way street, and other cars now had to go around him.

He glanced behind him as a car honked. "I'm your getaway car. Now hop in before I get a ticket."

I motioned Kate over, and she leaned in to look at Richard, resting her elbows on the open window of his car. "What's going on? Is that a dog?"

"It's P.J.'s dog." I gave Kate a meaningful look. "His name is Butterscotch, but Richard calls him Hermès."

Kate shrugged. "Makes sense."

Richard gave an exasperated sigh. "Now do you want to get out of here or not?"

I scanned behind me. I didn't see Reese, but I knew he'd come out of the hotel any minute looking for us. Technically, we'd given our statements, but that was before he knew the name of the victim and made the connection to the other murder and to us.

"Come on, Annie," Kate said from inside the car where she and Hermès now shared the back seat.

I decided I'd rather deal with the detective once he'd had a chance to cool off a bit. Anything was better than getting busted by Brianna and dozens of Weddies. I opened the front passenger door and got in. "Hit it."

Richard stepped on the gas before I'd fully shut my car door, and we flew through the green light and down H Street until we came to a stop at the intersection with Fifteenth.

"Do you want to tell me what happened?" Richard twisted in his seat to look at me, and Hermès jumped up to sit on the console between us.

"You saw the news, right? A woman fell off the roof of the hotel."

Richard cocked his head at me, and Hermès copied him. "Come on. Do I look like a rube?"

"Well, with that hat . . ." Kate began but let her words fade away when Richard gave her a withering glance.

"Fine," I said. "But let me first say that Kate and I were at the hotel for a completely legitimate reason."

"One hundred percent unrelated to any murder," Kate added.

Richard drummed his fingers on the steering wheel. "I'm listening."

"We crashed a Weddies tribute to Tricia," I said.

Richard held up a hand to stop me. "A what?"

"The Weddies," Kate said. "You know. Those girls from the Wed Boards. They had a get-together as a tribute to Tricia since she was so active on the forums. I thought it would be the perfect time to combat the negative press we've been getting by planting some positive press."

"Did it work?" Richard asked, and I knew he was considering it as a possible marketing strategy to adopt.

"Don't even think about it," I said. "You have to be a bride."

"That's discrimination," Richard said with a huff. "But you're not brides."

Kate waved her sunglasses at him. "We were in disguise."

"And that worked?"

"Shockingly, yes," I said. "Kate was able to spread some positive PR about us and combat some of the negative rumors being passed around."

Kate leaned forward. "Did you know that bimbo Brianna was telling brides that our clients get killed on a regular basis?"

Richard made a clucking noise. "You've only had two clients murdered. I wouldn't call that a regular basis."

"That's what we said." Kate flopped back against the car seat. "So we told everyone that she'd had her business shut down because it was a front for a prostitution ring."

Richard's mouth fell open. "You didn't."

I nudged him as the light turned green. "Oh, she did."

"I take back every snarky thing I ever said about you, Kate." Richard looked at her in his rearview mirror. "You're a genius."

Kate blew him a kiss.

Richard gunned it through the light as it turned red. "So you hung out with the Weddies and accused a colleague of being a madam. And then?"

I paused as I considered whether to tell him everything or dole it out in need-to-know morsels. I decided to tell him enough without admitting to full-fledged meddling. "I happened to see Mrs. Toker, the mother of our recently deceased bride, and overhear her make an exchange with some man."

"Happened to see?" Richard shot me a side-eye look.

I held up three fingers and hoped I'd remembered the Girl Scouts salute correctly. "Honest. It was completely random. She must not have checked out of the hotel after the wedding."

Kate leaned forward between the seats. "We had no idea she'd still be there."

"And what do you mean 'an exchange?'" Richard asked as he gunned it to make a yellow light.

"A man give her something in a manila envelope."

Richard didn't take his eyes off the road. "But you don't know what it was?"

"Nope." If I admitted that we'd almost seen what was in the envelope then I'd have to tell him how we'd managed to sneak into the room, and I wasn't ready to get a scolding from Richard.

"No clue," Kate added with more vehemence than necessary.

"That certainly makes the mother of the bride seem suspicious. Do you think she was getting info to protect herself or to find out who killed her daughter?"

"Your guess is as good as mine," I said and meant it. I didn't know what proof she'd been so desperate to get her hands on. It could just as easily have been something to protect herself if she'd indeed killed her husband and daughter or something related to her daughter's killer if she didn't."

Richard paused at the intersection with Constitution Avenue before turning right. "So then how did you get caught up in the roof-jumper drama?"

"Oh, she didn't jump," Kate said, inserting her head between us again.

Richard sneaked a look at her. "What do you mean?"

"Jumpers don't usually scream bloody murder all the way down." Kate sat back, and Hermès leaped into her lap.

I shuddered, remembering the sounds Mrs. Toker made as she plummeted to the earth. Kate was right. They weren't the noises someone resigned to suicide would make.

"You think someone was pushed off the hotel's roof?" Richard gaped at Kate in the rearview mirror.

"Maybe it had to do with the exchange," I said.

Richard slammed on his brakes, and we all jerked forward, Hermès yelping as Kate caught him from flying into the front seat. "The woman who died was the mother of the bride?"

"Didn't we mention that?" I asked, lowering my arms from where I'd braced myself against the dashboard.

Richard sucked in air. "Are you telling me that I just aided and abetted two witnesses to a second related murder?"

Kate patted Richard on the shoulder. "I think this technically makes you our wheelman."

Richard spun around to face Kate as cars honked and swerved around him. "You'd better hope that if I get sent off to prison it's to one of those Martha Stewart-style setups where I can teach inmates how to make frittatas in their toaster ovens."

"They'd be lucky to have you," Kate said as Hermès yipped in apparent agreement.

Richard sniffed. "Damn right they would." He turned to me. "They don't make you wear jumpsuits in those prisons, do they? Jumpsuits don't work on me."

"You're not going to prison," I said. "None of us are."

"Is that a yes or a no on the jumpsuits?" Richard asked.

I shook my head. "I'm going to say no."

Richard let out a long breath and took his foot off the brake so the car began moving again. "I feel much better. Now tell me more about this mother of the bride getting murdered."

CHAPTER 30

"Where's Leatrice?" Kate asked as I pushed open the door to my apartment. "I'm used to her greeting us at the door to the building or waiting for us inside your living room."

"She's on a stakeout."

Kate sat my couch, dropping her black tote on the floor and setting our brown Chopt take-out bag on the coffee table. "Another one of her neighbor surveillance projects?"

I joined Kate on the couch, moving a stack of *Inside Weddings* magazines onto the floor to make space. "Actually, she's staking out the neighbor Madeleine told us about. The one who had a feud going with Tricia and Dave."

"I'm assuming Reese knows nothing of this?"

"You assume correctly," I told her.

I pulled my plastic salad bowl out of the bag and leaned back on the couch cushions, resting the bowl on my lap. I'd insisted we stop for food before Richard dropped Kate and me off at my apartment, and Richard had insisted it be healthy, which eliminated most of my favorite spots. I took the lid off my Santa Fe salad with grilled chicken. It wasn't a box of doughnuts but the chipotle dressing did smell good.

Kate kicked off her nude heels and opened her shrimp Caesar, handing me a plastic fork. "So that makes how many things you're keeping from him at the moment?"

I made a face at her. "You make it sound like I do it on purpose."

BOOK 4: REVIEW TO A KILL

"You don't?" She arched an eyebrow at me.

I swallowed a bite of salad, making a mental note to always get the tangy chipotle dressing. "Of course not."

"Don't worry." She waved a forkful of lettuce at me. "I get it. You're the boss lady. The big kahuna. You're used to being in charge. He's used to being in charge. It's hard for you to let go and let anyone help you. He's used to being the guy who helps people. It's oil and water."

I speared a piece of chicken. "You think we're like oil and water?"

"Well. The two of you have been arguing since you met. I mean, it's cute arguing. Like Sam and Diane."

"From *Cheers*? How do you know about *Cheers*, Miss Millennial?"

Kate winked at me. "Miss Millennial has Netflix."

I mulled this over while we ate in silence. Sam and Diane from *Cheers* may have been funny on a sitcom, but I doubted Reese found any of this amusing. I felt bad that my overwhelming instinct to save my business and my neck, and admittedly my reluctance to trust other people to do things for me, meant I ended up running a secret investigation behind his back. I knew Reese wanted me to trust him to find the real culprit and clear my name, but I found it almost impossible to let go.

My phone buzzed in my purse and snapped me out of my mental musing. I leaned over to where I'd dropped my bag on the floor, pulled out my phone, and glanced at the name on the screen. I pushed the button to accept the call.

"Hey, Leatrice. How's it going?"

"Not bad," Leatrice whispered.

"I don't think anyone can hear you from outside the car."

"I'm trying not to wake up Fern," she said.

"He's still with you?" I asked.

Kate sat up and mouthed, "Who?"

"Fern," I mouthed back.

"He dashed over to his salon for a couple of appointments this morning then came back," Leatrice said.

I wondered what his tony Georgetown hairstyling clients thought about his black cat suit. Not that it was even close to the strangest outfit he'd worn. That was a toss-up between his geisha girl phase and the summer he dressed like Jackie Kennedy, complete with pillbox hats for every outfit.

"Any movement inside the house?" I asked.

"Not yet."

"You know you don't have to stay there. It may be a dead end." I felt

573

bad that Kate and I were relaxing in my living room, eating lunch while Leatrice sat in her car next to a sleeping hairstylist dressed like a cat burglar.

"No trouble at all, dear. I'm happy to do it."

"Can Kate and I bring you some fresh coffee?" Kate frowned at me, but I ignored her.

"No. Fern and I decided to slow down on the coffee since the closest available bathroom is three blocks away in a bakery." Leatrice paused, and I heard some mumbling. "And we have to buy a muffin every time we use it, so Fern's afraid it's ruining his waistline."

Not surprising. Fern was so slim we could probably share clothes. Not that I had the moxie to pull off his ensembles.

"I called you because Dagger Dan narrowed down the IP address from that email you gave me," Leatrice said.

I didn't consider myself a computer whiz by any means, but I did know that an IP address was a computer's unique identifying code. "Dagger Dan?"

"One of my hacker friends. Boots helped him, though."

Boots? Dagger Dan? "Should you be hanging out with these guys, Leatrice?"

She giggled. "Don't be silly, dear. We don't hang out in person. Only online. I've never actually met them, but I think they live on the West Coast. And they're lovely boys."

I was pretty sure lovely boys didn't hack into police departments, but since I was the beneficiary of their illegal actions, I decided to keep quiet.

"They were able to get me an address of where the email originated from. It's a networked computer in an office building in Virginia."

I dug in my purse for a pen and found a black one from the Hotel Monaco. My bad habit of pocketing hotel pens had its benefits. "Can you give it to me?"

She read the street address to me, and I wrote it on my palm.

"This is great, Leatrice. Kate and I will go check it out now."

Kate frowned at me but slipped her feet into her shoes as I hung up with my neighbor.

"Let me guess?" she asked. "Something else we don't want Reese to find out?"

I explained to her about the threatening email the groom had shown me and then, at my suggestion, had shown the police. "The police have the same information we have."

"They probably don't have a team of sketchy hackers working on it, though."

"We aren't hiding anything from them," I said with more conviction than I felt.

Kate shook her head at me. "Talk about following the better of the law and not the spirit."

Kate's mangling of expressions had improved over years of being corrected by me and by Richard, but sometimes she slipped up. I grabbed my purse and keys by the door. "In this case, I think I like the way you say it."

CHAPTER 31

The drive to the nearby Virginia suburb of Falls Church hadn't taken long as the early afternoon traffic was light, and Kate directed me through some back streets using the Waze app on her phone. Spring seemed to arrive earlier each year, and the neighborhoods we wound through were a riot of blooming cherry blossom trees, dogwoods, and tulip beds. I'd rolled down my car windows to breathe in the cool air that hadn't yet become humid and oppressive as it soon would. Summer came earlier each year, as well, and the sticky heat stayed longer, making driving with the windows down unpleasant if not impossible, so I reveled in these few days of perfect temperature and fresh, breathable air.

I rapped my fingers on the steering wheel and hummed along to a pop song by a singer I'd never heard of who was probably half my age and couldn't legally drink. I'd let Kate select the radio station because she hated listening to the news station that gave traffic and weather updates. If it wasn't a wedding day, she didn't pay much attention to either. The drive was so pleasant I almost forgot our mission.

"The entrance should be up here on the right," she said, pointing to an office building that rose about six stories and was covered with mirrored panels.

I slowed and pulled into the parking lot, reading the large silver sign for Cogent Technologies as we passed. This seemed vaguely familiar, and I tried to remember if I'd ever met a client here or just passed the building before. The lot was filled with cars since it was a workday so I circled until I found a spot at the end of one of the closer rows.

Kate leaned forward and peered up at the building. "An email was sent to our clients from someone in this building?"

"According to Dagger Dan and Boots."

"But there must be hundreds of people in there. How do we narrow it down?"

"I don't know." I'd never expected the address Leatrice had given me would be to an enormous office building. "I don't know if the guys can narrow it down further without being in the building."

"I wonder what they do here."

"Something to do with technology."

Kate gave me a withering look. "I got that much from the sign. But that could mean just about anything."

Kate was right. Technology was a word that could encompass anything from software to telecommunications to biomedical.

I pulled out my phone, and tried to search for the company name. "Ugh. The signal here is awful. I guess we'll have to go inside and find out." I rolled up the car windows with a flick of my finger then turned off the car.

"What's the strategy?" Kate asked when she'd joined me outside.

"I'm not sure. I think we'll have to play this by ear when we get inside."

"Do you want me to provide a distraction while you sneak in?" Kate asked, taking long strides next to me as we walked toward the glass front doors. "You know I do some killer accents."

It was true that Kate could do a very distracting Russian accent that both captivated and confused people. She'd used it to great advantage previously so I could sneak past gatekeepers.

"Not this time," I said. "I'm afraid someone might recognize us. I could swear that I've been here before."

Kate pulled on the long metallic door handle when we reached the building and held the door open for me. "Then you came here without me because I've never set foot in this place before."

Our shoes clicked on the gleaming white tile as we walked across the expansive lobby to a black desk guarding a line of elevators. An older man in a blue uniform looked up as we approached.

"Can I help you?"

I looked around the minimalist lobby for anything that could give me a clue about the company. Aside from a grouping of black leather chairs arranged in front of a large portrait of a man I could only assume was the company founder, there was nothing to go on.

Kate leaned forward against the high desk and gave the security guard a dazzling smile. "We've got an appointment."

He handed her a clipboard. "All guests need to sign in."

Kate took the clipboard and nudged me. I leaned over it and scanned the names of the visitors who had come before us as Kate wrote down a fake name and contact number. I knew she had an arsenal of made-up names and phone numbers in her head. She claimed it was the fastest way to get rid of an unappealing man at a bar. I glanced at the fake name she'd scratched on the list and wondered just how many drinks a man had to have to not question a name like "Poppy C. Muffin."

The guard held up two guest badges but paused before handing them over. "Who did you say you were here to see again?"

Kate and I looked at each other. Here was where a fake name didn't work so well since the guard no doubt had an employee list at the ready.

"The CEO." I gestured to the painting on the wall. "We're meeting him about a charity gala he's sponsoring."

"The CEO?" The security guard raised an eyebrow.

"Yes," Kate said. "We're event planners."

That, at least, was the truth.

The guard gestured toward the portrait on the white wall. "You don't have a meeting with him. He's dead."

Well, this was a problem.

Kate put a hand to her heart and gasped. "This is so shocking. We must have made our meeting before he died."

I nodded, deciding to go all in with Kate. "I wonder why no one called to tell us before we drove all the way out here."

"Listen, ladies." The man sighed. "I don't know who you're here to meet but it's not Mr. Toker. He died well over a year ago."

Kate opened her mouth then shut it, and I felt her stiffen next to me. My eyes flew to the portrait of the old man. Mr. Toker? That's why something seemed so familiar. Cogent Technologies was the name of the company Tricia's father owned. The one her mother had taken over. I felt lightheaded as it hit me that someone inside Cogent Technologies had threatened the bride and groom before they were shot.

CHAPTER 32

"We've got to tell Detective Reese," Kate said as we drove back into the city.

"Agreed." I squeezed the steering wheel as we sped along the wooded GW Parkway, which skirted the Potomac River. I was still processing the information we'd learned and trying to fit it in with what we already knew, but nothing seemed to match up. I tried to calm my mind by letting my eyes wander below us to the kayaks and crew teams that cut across the water, leaving ripples behind them. I reached behind me with one hand and dug my phone out of my purse, handing it to Kate. "Can you text him for me?"

"Should I look in Contacts or Recent?"

I ignored her smirk. "Contacts."

She tapped at my phone. "Is he under 'Detective Reese' or 'Mike Reese' or 'Hot Detective?'"

I gave her a side-eye glance. "Should I do it?"

"No, no." She waved me off. "I'll find him. There we go. You have him as 'Detective Mike Reese.' Very thorough."

"Tell him that the threatening email the groom showed him was sent by someone at the Toker company. Be sure to tell him that we don't know who in the company, though."

Kate tapped some more. "Okay. It's sent." She put my phone next to hers on her lap.

I turned the radio up and flipped to the news station before Kate could complain.

"Police are still investigating the death of a woman who fell off the top of the Hay-Adams Hotel yesterday," the voice from the radio announced in nasal tones. "Police have not said whether it is being investigated as a homicide, suicide, or an accident."

"Well, we know it wasn't a suicide," Kate said.

I turned off the radio. "They probably aren't announcing that it's a homicide because they have no leads."

"It's not going to take long before the media connects Tricia's murder with her mother's rooftop death."

I knew Kate was right, and I dreaded the thought of the media connecting us with the second death. If we were lucky, our names wouldn't come close to the news reports on Mrs. Toker's fall. If we weren't lucky, we could kiss our careers good-bye.

I drove over Key Bridge and veered right onto M Street, thanking the traffic gods that it wasn't gridlocked. Sometimes I had to wait through multiple cycles of the traffic light at the end of the bridge before I could actually merge onto M. I sped up to make the left turn signal at the Georgetown Cupcake corner and shook my head at the line of customers that snaked out their door and almost a block down the street. I liked cupcakes as much as the next girl, but hour-long waits struck me as excessive.

"I thought we were going back to your place." Kate looked over her shoulder at the street I'd driven past which led to my apartment building.

"I want to drive by and check on Leatrice. I think it's time to pull her off the stakeout."

Kate shook her head. "I still don't understand why she's there. If this guy had anything to do with shooting Tricia and Dave, I'm sure he's long gone by now."

"Maybe. But it's kept her out of my hair for over twenty-four hours."

"You're right. Maybe we should send her on stakeouts more often."

I wove my way through the residential streets of Georgetown, passing blocks of elegant row houses broken up by the occasional patch of green park, and passed into the Glover Park neighborhood, where the houses went from ritzy to cozy. When we reached Tricia and Dave's street I slowed down to look for parking. I spotted Leatrice's tank-sized yellow Ford still taking up two parallel parking spaces in the middle of the block. The closest thing to a legal space was half a spot at the very end of the street. I pulled as close as I could to the car in front of me and hoped that the back end of my car didn't protrude too far past the No Parking sign.

"Nice," Kate said as she got out and inspected the distance between my car and the one in front. "You could barely fit a sheet of paper between these two. I couldn't have done it better myself."

"Thanks, I think."

We walked the slight incline up to Leatrice's car, and I rapped on the driver's side window. I could see a blur of electric maroon as Leatrice jerked her head toward the noise. Then she rolled down her window a crack.

"Hop in, girls."

The door to the back seat creaked as I opened it, got in, and slid over so Kate could join me. I noticed Leatrice was alone in the front seat. "Where's Fern?"

"He had some appointments so he left about an hour ago," Leatrice motioned to the open laptop on the passenger's seat. "I've been surfing online since then."

Kate looked around her at the dated interior of the car. "You have Wi-Fi?"

Leatrice winked. "Dagger Dan has me piggybacking on a signal from one of these houses."

Kate grinned. "In the real world we call that stealing wifi."

"How's it been going?" I asked. "Any movement in the house?"

She shook her head and looked dejected. "Nothing. I think this may be a dead end."

I leaned forward and patted her shoulder. "Don't worry. I was going to suggest pulling the plug anyway."

"What have you two girls been up to?" Leatrice asked.

"Do you want this morning's news or this afternoon's news?" Kate said.

Leatrice's eyes lit up. "What happened this morning?"

I groaned to myself. So much for keeping it a secret from her. "The bride's mother was pushed off the roof of the Hay-Adams Hotel. We saw it happen." I hoped my voice sounded nonchalant.

Leatrice looked at me like Christmas had just come early.

Kate leaned forward. "And Mrs. Toker was acting very suspicious before she died."

Leatrice sucked in a reverent breath. "You saw her before she died? Were you following her?"

"Of course not," I said. "Not officially at least."

"And we went to the location of the IP address you gave us," Kate said. "Turns out that email was sent from Cogent Technologies."

Leatrice cocked her head. "That sounds familiar."

"I thought the same thing," I said. "The reason it sounds familiar is that Cogent Technologies is owned by Tricia's father, well now her mother, wait . . ." I paused to think. "Who does own it now that all the Tokers are dead?"

"That's not why I recognized it." Leatrice tapped on her laptop's keyboard. "I saw the name when I was on LinkedIn."

"You're on LinkedIn?" Kate and I said at the same time.

My phone rang in my purse, and I fished it out. Reese. I debated whether to answer it but finally decided to get it over with. I'd have to explain myself eventually. Why not now?

"I got your text," he said when I answered. "I'm not even going to ask how you got this nugget of information."

"Okay." This was going better than I'd expected.

"I'm still waiting for an explanation of why you and Kate ran off yesterday."

Uh-oh. "You were busy, and we'd already given our statements."

"But you left something out, didn't you?" Reese's question was telling me, not asking me.

"To be honest, I wasn't one hundred percent sure it was the bride's mother." I'd been 99.9 percent sure, but he didn't need to know that. "But I'm sorry. I probably should have given you the heads-up."

"You think?"

I tried not to pay attention to Kate and Leatrice mouthing to each other so I looked out the car window to avoid being distracted. A silver blur caught my attention. No one drove that fast on these narrow residential streets. Before I could turn around to see who was driving like a maniac, I heard breaking glass.

"What was that?" Kate whipped her head around, and her mouth fell open.

"Should I call 911?" Leatrice's voice came out as more of a shriek.

"Is everything okay?" Reese asked.

"Not really," I said, jumping out of the car and staring at the flames at the end of the block. "My car is on fire."

CHAPTER 33

"How on earth did this happen?" Richard asked as he stood next to me and watched the fire department extinguish the last few flames on my smoldering remains of a car. He wore his black messenger bag across his chest, this time without a dog inside. Richard had been my first call after hanging up with Reese, who had dispatched the fire department himself.

"I told you already," I said. "I heard breaking glass, and when I turned around my car was on fire."

"Have you been having car trouble?" He held the back of his hand in front of his nose to block the acrid smoke billowing off the burning metal. "You know you're terrible about getting your car serviced on time."

"If you're late on an oil change, your car should not burst into flames." I gave him a side-eye glance. "I mean, it's an eight-year-old Volvo, so it needed tweaks here and there, but, no, I didn't have any indication that it would spontaneously combust."

"At least you weren't inside it when it blew." Richard's eyes watered, but I didn't know if it was from his concern for me or from the smoke.

It hadn't occurred to me that I could have been inside the car when it caught on fire. The thought chilled me.

"At least you can finally get a new car." Richard's tone of voice became more cheery. "That Volvo really dragged down your image. It was too soccer mom for you."

"Well, there's the silver lining to the rain cloud," I said. Car shopping was the last thing I needed to add to my plate, but I wouldn't survive long as a wedding planner without some way to transport the boxes of favors and dozens of welcome bags that brides handed over to me the week of their wedding.

"Why were you here in the first place?" Richard wrinkled his nose. He'd been very careful not to touch anything since he'd arrived, and he'd applied antibacterial gel to his hands twice already.

"Checking in on Leatrice's stakeout." I tore my gaze away from the charred hull of my car. "Where is she, anyway?"

"Over there with Kate." He jerked a thumb toward the fire truck, its lights flashing. "And the rest of the firemen."

I turned to see Kate leaning against the truck with a cluster of firemen around her. "I wondered where Kate had gone." Asking Kate to ignore a group of cute firemen would be like asking Leatrice to wear normal clothes. Speaking of Leatrice, I didn't spot her next to Kate but found her a moment later sitting in the driver's seat of the fire truck, pretending to drive. I guessed I should be grateful that she hadn't convinced one of the men to let her wear his suit.

Out of the corner of my eye, I noticed a familiar figure talking to one of the firemen. Reese walked over to where Richard and I stood.

"Fancy seeing you again so soon," Richard said.

Reese nodded at him. "No dog today?"

Color crept up Richard's neck. "He's with my . . . I mean he's with his . . . he's at home."

"Aside from the dog, it looks like most of your posse is here," Reese said. "Did you all come here in your car?"

"No. Only Kate." I didn't mention that Leatrice had already been here because she'd been staking out a potential suspect in the murder case I was supposed to be avoiding. I felt my face flush and not from the residual heat of the fire. "Why the third degree? Do you always investigate car fires like the driver robbed a bank?"

Reese smiled at that. "I'm trying to figure out why someone might want to target you."

"Target me? What do you mean?"

"What I mean is that your car didn't just catch on fire. Someone set it on fire on purpose. With a Molotov cocktail."

Richard's hand flew to his mouth. "This wasn't because Annabelle doesn't get frequent oil changes?"

"I'm afraid not," Reese said. "This was arson."

My mind flashed back to the silver car that sped past and the breaking glass I heard right before my car burst into flames. Someone in that car had tossed a Molotov cocktail at my car and torched it. Of course. I felt a bit slow for not making the connection right away. Then again, Molotov cocktails weren't something wedding planners usually dealt with.

At this point, bridezillas were starting to look pretty appealing.

CHAPTER 34

"That settles it." I dropped into the front seat of Richard's convertible. "I'm out of the crime-solving game."

"Well, I'm glad to hear it." Richard fastened his seatbelt and adjusted his rearview mirror. "It only took having your car torched to convince you."

Leatrice popped her head between the two front seats. "We don't know that the arson is connected to the murder case."

"You said I wouldn't notice she was there," Richard said to me. "I believe the word you used was 'invisible.'"

"I had to say something or you wouldn't give her a ride home, and the cars parked in front and back of her car are too close for her to get out. She's boxed in."

Richard grumbled as he started his car. Kate had declined Richard's offer to drop her off and had, instead, accepted an invitation to grab a drink with one of the firemen. None of us were the least bit surprised.

"I'll come back later for it," Leatrice said. "And if I can't move my car, maybe I'll resume my stakeout."

I turned around to face Leatrice in the back seat. "No more stakeout. You did notice that my car got firebombed, right? Don't you think that's connected to me trying to find Tricia's killer?"

Leatrice tapped a finger on the brim of her fedora. "Perhaps, but that means you're on the right track and you're making the killer nervous."

"The feeling is mutual," I said.

Richard stopped at a red light and twisted to face Leatrice. "Annabelle's car was set on fire. Torched. Flambéed. Burned to a crisp."

"But we can't let that stop us, can we?" Leatrice asked.

"Yes," I said. "We absolutely can."

The light turned green, and Richard shifted his eyes back to the road. "When the walls start running with blood, you run out of the house. When your car gets set on fire, you abandon the case. Haven't you ever watched a horror movie, Leatrice?"

Leatrice shook her head. "Too unrealistic."

"Who knew she was a realist?" Richard said to me under his breath.

I shifted in my leather seat. "Do you have the seat warmers on or am I having a flashback from the fire?"

Richard winked at me. "Warmers. Too hot?"

"I don't think I'll be cold again for a very long time," I said as Richard adjusted the controls. "Even if it wasn't an issue of safety, I'd want to drop the investigation."

Leatrice pulled herself forward using the back of my seat. "I thought you needed to clear yourself as a person of interest?"

"I know I had nothing to do with Tricia's murder, and the police won't be able to find any hard evidence that says I did. Anything they have on me is circumstantial. I've been making myself"—I glanced at Richard—"and everyone around me crazy by running all over the place trying to piece this whole thing together. But you know what I realized as I watched my car burn? I don't have to let this be my problem."

Richard raised both hands in the air. "Hallelujah, she's seen the light!"

"I've put my relationship with Reese, whatever that may be, at risk by meddling in his job. And what good did it do me? We may have more clues but we're no closer to putting them together and finding out who killed Tricia than we were the day we started. The only difference is now I'm down one car and one potential boyfriend."

"When you put it like that," Leatrice began.

"The worst part is that this awful bride is still making me miserable from the grave." I looked out the window. "I couldn't wait for her wedding to be over, and the second I'm finally free of her, she gets herself shot, and I get sucked into her toxic world again."

Richard wagged a finger at me. "What did I tell you about the dangers of wishing your life away in this job? You keep thinking 'I just need to get through this wedding' each time and then, before you know it, a decade has flown by."

"I know." I put a hand on Richard's shoulder. "You were right. You're much wiser than I give you credit for."

Richard paused to let a mother cross the street pushing a stroller that had more features than my late car. "That's what I keep telling people."

"And because one horrible woman spent her life tearing other people down, my business is threatened, a guy I might otherwise be dating is mad at me, and my car gets barbecued." I held up my fingers and ticked them off. "But it ends right now. I refuse to let Tricia do any more damage to me."

"So what will you do?" Leatrice asked.

"For starters, I'm going to change out of these clothes." I lifted the collar of my navy dress to my nose. "I smell like a chimney sweep."

"Thank goodness," Richard said. "I didn't want to mention it earlier since your car was on fire, but that dress isn't the greatest on you, darling. The cap sleeves make your arms look like sausages."

I suppose I should have been touched that Richard resisted the urge to comment on my fashion choice when I was in the middle of a catastrophe. I was less touched that he'd just referred to my arms as sausages.

"Thanks," I said. "I guess I'll just get rid of it entirely then."

Richard nodded. "That would be best. You know if you want me to give the rest of your wardrobe the once-over, you just have to say the word."

I knew exactly what Richard thought of my pragmatic and classic clothes. I also knew that if I gave him free reign in my closet, I'd end up with exactly three items left. I ignored his offer as I always did.

"Then I'm going to get back to work," I continued as Richard slowed to a stop in front of my stone-front apartment building. "We still have weddings coming up and a social media reputation to repair."

Leatrice didn't look convinced. "If you're sure...."

"I'm positive," I opened the car door and stepped out onto the sidewalk, taking a deep breath. "I want nothing more to do with this case. Ever."

CHAPTER 35

"Are you sure you're all right, dear?" Leatrice asked. She'd followed me upstairs after Richard drove off and stood behind me while I opened my apartment door.

"Perfectly fine," I said as the lock caught and I pushed the wooden door with my hip. "I actually feel recharged. Having my car destroyed cleared my eyes."

Leatrice studied me. "You look a bit manic."

"That's just because I'm excited to get back to work. This case has bogged me down for days, and now I'm free." I flung my arms open wide and Leatrice's look of concern intensified.

"Are you sure you aren't nervous after the arson or afraid the same person who set your car on fire will come after you directly?" Leatrice asked.

I paused. That possibility hadn't actually occurred to me, and I didn't like the feeling of panic that fluttered in my stomach.

"Not with you downstairs," I said.

That was a lie, but I was eager to get to work and even more eager to keep Leatrice from coming inside and distracting me with her running patter about suspicious activity in the building and the latest Perry Mason rerun.

Leatrice beamed. "You can count on me. No one is getting in this building unless they've been thoroughly vetted."

I knew the Department of Homeland Security had nothing on Leatrice, and I felt bad for the other residents of the building. The chances of their pizza delivery reaching them just dropped dramatically.

I closed the door as Leatrice went downstairs to assume her guard post, and I drank in the silence. My eyes wandered over the apartment, and I couldn't help cringing at the disarray. It was easy to tell when wedding season had hit full swing or when I was meddling in an investigation. The piles of paperwork grew to dangerous heights and the dust bunnies began amassing in the corners.

My salad bowl sat in the same spot where I'd left it, the food untouched albeit a bit wilted. I sat on the couch and took a bite. No longer crispy but not bad. The tangy chipotle dressing made up for the fact that the tortilla strips, arguably the best part of the dish, had become limp. I finished the salad and took the empty plastic bowl to the kitchen recycling bin.

I pulled my smoky dress over my head as I walked back to my bedroom then tossed it in my hamper by the door. I pulled on the jeans lying on the foot of my unmade bed and grabbed a UVA T-shirt from a dresser drawer. This was more like it.

Feeling a burst of cleaning energy from either the food or the weight of the murder investigation being lifted off my shoulders, I selected an eighties playlist on my phone, pulled the can of Pledge out from under my kitchen sink along with a roll of paper towels, and sang along with Journey as I tackled the police reports spread out on the dining room table. I gathered them up into a pile and dumped them in the recycling bin then sprayed the table surface and buffed it. The sight of so much clean tabletop and the fake scent of lemons gave me a rush, so I started on the papers piled up on the coffee table.

One of my favorite things to do after a wedding was clean out the contents of the client's file, but I often let it pile up when I had one wedding after another during the busy months. The past three wedding files sat in a stack in front of me. I flipped through the contracts and emails, finding nothing I didn't have on my hard drive, and then added them to the police reports in the recycling. After I'd cleared off the glass coffee table, I headed for the kitchen. I needed some energy before I took out my Dustbuster and started sucking up dustbunnies so I grabbed a Mocha Frappuccino from the fridge and flopped on my living room couch to drink it and give myself a break.

The apartment looked better already. Smelled better, too. I set the glass bottle on the coffee table and reached for a magazine from the metal rack at the end of the couch. I ignored the issues of *Martha Stewart Weddings*—I needed a break from all things bridal—and grabbed an old issue of *Vanity Fair*, letting myself get lost in an article about Australian hunk Chris Hemsworth.

I jumped when my door handle rattled, followed by a loud knock that verged on pounding.

"Open up, Annabelle!" The voice was female, but I couldn't determine who it was over the sound of the eighties playing from my phone.

"Who is it?" I yelled over the music.

"It's Kate." Her voice was quieter now. "Let me in."

I glanced at my phone. Had I really been reading for that long? So much for my short break from cleaning. I paused the music on my phone, opened the door, and stood back to let her inside.

She walked in, dropped her purse on the couch, and sniffed the air. "Have you been cleaning?"

"Don't sound so surprised," I said. "I clean sometimes."

"O-kay." Kate spun around to face me. "I found out something really interesting about the case."

"Tricia's murder case?" I shook my head. "I don't want to know."

"What do you mean you don't want to know? Haven't you spent the past few days sneaking around behind Detective Reese's back? Hasn't Leatrice been hacking into the police computer system for you?"

I held up a finger. "Correction. Leatrice did all that on her own."

"But you were using the information, right? The last I checked we were questioning suspects and hunting down an IP address."

"That was before," I said.

"Before what?" Kate asked.

I gaped at her. "Before my car got burned to a crisp."

"You think that had to do with us poking around in the case?"

I nodded vigorously. "Yes. Either that or it's the world's biggest coincidence. Regardless, I don't want to take the chance that whoever torched my car will do something even worse."

"So you're just going to let the police suspect us of the murder even when we had nothing to do with it?"

"We're 'persons of interest,'" I corrected her. "Not suspects."

"That's very comforting. I just hope they make you work the fryer when Wedding Belles has to close its doors and we're forced to work at McDonald's. The heat would be murder on my hair."

Richard's drama was definitely wearing off on Kate.

"We're not going to have to sling burgers," I said. "But I'm done trying to solve this on our own. It's not worth the risks."

"Annabelle, you know you have to break a few legs to make an omelet."

I rubbed my temples. "God, I hope not, but the way things are going today..."

My phone vibrated, and I took it out of my pocket, glancing at the text message that popped up and fighting the urge to scream. "You have got to be kidding me. Leatrice went back to get her car on her own and spotted lights on in Effing Frank's house." I grabbed Kate's purse from the floor. "Come on, let's go."

"Where are we going? I thought you didn't want anything to do with the case anymore."

I opened my front door. "I don't. We're going to drag Leatrice back here before she tries to make a citizen's arrest and gets herself killed."

CHAPTER 36

"Leatrice," I hissed into the dark.

Kate and I had arrived on the quiet street to find Leatrice's car empty. Against my strong objections, Kate had parked in front of a fire hydrant, reasoning that we'd only be a few minutes. Now we found ourselves walking along the sidewalk in front of the houses, peering into bushes, and trying to find Leatrice without attracting too much attention. I almost wished I had Fern's black catsuit so I could blend into the night.

"Over here." The voice came from behind a bushy tree in front of Tricia and Dave's yellow house, which looked abandoned in the dark.

I crept to where Leatrice sat hunched behind a branch, and Kate followed me. "What are you doing?"

Leatrice pointed to the house next door. "This gives me a good view without being noticed."

I looked up at the light spilling from the downstairs windows of Frank Ferguson's house. Since none of the shades had been pulled down all the way, I could see a pair of legs moving around inside.

"Maybe the person inside that house won't notice you," Kate whispered. "But what about people walking by on the street?"

I could only imagine what a homeowner across the street would think if they looked out their window and saw three women crouching behind a bush, one of them in a trench coat and fedora. We would be lucky not to get shot.

Leatrice ignored Kate's comment. "Effing Frank must have a garage in the back because the lights went on a few minutes after I arrived, and I didn't see anyone go in through the front door."

"I thought we agreed that you weren't going to watch him anymore," I said.

"I wasn't. I was in the process of moving my car when I noticed the lights. I called you right away."

"I appreciate you calling me, but we should leave," I said.

"What?" Leatrice's voice rose above a whisper. "But we can't leave now. The suspect just arrived. This is what we've been waiting for."

"Not me." I shook my head. "Not anymore. I told you. I'm done with this case."

"But, Annabelle," Leatrice began.

"I'm serious." I waved my arms. "No more investigation. No more."

Leatrice studied my expression. "Your arms say no, but your eyes say yes."

"My eyes are not saying yes. They're still bloodshot from the smoke of my incinerated car."

"Good luck talking her out of it, Leatrice," Kate said. "I already tried. She doesn't care that we might go to jail or end up asking people if they'd like to supersize their meal."

I let out a breath. "Of course I care, but poking around in this case hasn't helped us. It's made things worse. We shouldn't waste another second thinking about Terrible Tricia or her murder. We hated her. Almost everyone who met her hated her. Effing Frank hated her. She's dead. Her mother's dead. My car went up in flames. I think that's enough for me."

"Even if our business gets completely destroyed before the police clear us?" Kate held up her phone and the brightness of the screen blinded me for a moment.

The headline read, "Local Wedding Planners Involved in Arson."

I snatched the phone from her hands. "Involved in? How about 'were victims of'? Who wrote this hit piece?"

Kate shook her head. "It's one of those gossip sites that gets about half the facts right but prints the lies in bold and the retractions in small print."

I handed Kate back her phone and dropped my head in my hands. "Just when I thought things couldn't get worse."

Kate tapped away at her phone then slipped it into her purse. "I'm not saying we go full-force investigation, but why don't we pass this info to Detective Reese?"

"That Effing Frank is in his house? Fine, but that's not much of a windfall clue."

"We can tell him more than that," Leatrice said.

Kate pivoted on her heels toward her. "What do you mean?"

"That's what I forgot to tell you earlier, girls." Leatrice said. "This is who I was researching on LinkedIn. Effing Frank works security for Cogent Technologies."

CHAPTER 37

"This is huge," I said for the tenth time since Leatrice dropped the bombshell on us.

We'd moved from underneath the tree to the sidewalk next to Leatrice's car to wait for Detective Reese to arrive. I'd successfully argued that it wouldn't look great for us to be hiding in someone's front yard when the police drove up, although even relocated to the sidewalk we'd gotten some curious glances from people walking dogs. Leatrice's trench coat and fedora combo did not help.

Kate leaned against the yellow Ford Fairmont, her bare legs stretched out in front of her and crossed at the ankles. I was impressed that her legs weren't covered in goose bumps considering that the evening temperature had dropped a few degrees since we'd arrived and she hadn't changed out of the short pink sleeveless dress from earlier in the day. Then again, Kate was used to having more of her legs and arms exposed than I was.

"So he could have sent the threatening email to Tricia and Dave," she said.

"Who else?" I asked. "No other suspect has any connection to the building."

"That means he planned to kill them." Leatrice looked up at me from under her fedora. "First-degree murder."

I shivered from both the nip in the air and the thought of Tricia and Dave's neighbor plotting to kill them because of a feud that started over political yard signs. If everyone started shooting each other over political opinions, DC would become a war zone.

"What about the mother's death?" Kate asked. "It doesn't make sense that this guy pushed her off the hotel roof if he shot Tricia and Dave because of a personal feud."

"I don't know," I said. "Maybe she jumped after all."

Kate raised an eyebrow at me. "Do you really believe that?"

"We're still missing the connection," Leatrice said.

"Maybe not," I said as a police cruiser turned onto the block followed by an unmarked car. "Sometimes things don't get wrapped up with a perfect bow. Anyway, that's what Detective Reese can figure out."

Leatrice's frown told me she wasn't happy with my answer.

Both cars rolled to a stop in front of us. Detective Reese stepped out, leaving his partner in the driver's side as he approached us.

"I think it's pretty clear that you can't get enough of me," he said.

I rolled my eyes, and Leatrice giggled.

"I expected another lecture about not meddling," I said.

"I'm saving that for your friend here," he motioned to Leatrice with his head and she ducked her eyes beneath her fedora. "It hasn't gone unnoticed that her car has been sitting in front of this house for nearly two days, mostly with her in it."

So much for her covert operation. Leatrice shuffled her feet and didn't look up.

"I guess I should be grateful that you called us," Reese said. "And that no one from our department had to sit out here in a car for so long."

"I'm sure we could think of some ways you could thank us," Kate said. "Any ideas, Annabelle?"

If I could have reached her skinny leg from where I stood, I would have kicked her. Instead, I had to settle for shooting daggers at her with my eyes.

Two uniformed police officers came up behind Reese so Kate, Leatrice, and I stepped back as he led them up the steps of the porch and knocked on the door of Frank Ferguson's house. After a moment, the porch lights switched on and the front door opened.

"Maybe we shouldn't be in the line of sight," I said, tugging Kate and Leatrice by the arm down the sidewalk.

Once we were half a block away, Leatrice sighed. "Now I can't see a thing."

"Do you really want a guy who may have shot his neighbors in cold blood to get a good look at you?" I asked.

Kate craned her neck to see through the tree we'd been hiding behind earlier. "Did they go inside his house?"

"I don't know," I said.

Leatrice wrung her hands. "Maybe we should move closer in case Effing Frank got the drop on the police and they need help."

Before we could debate whether the police needed an assist, the two uniformed officers appeared with the suspect between them. They walked down the stairs and the paved walkway with Detective Rees bringing up the rear. Frank seemed not to be cuffed, so I assumed they hadn't arrested him and were merely taking him in for questioning.

When Frank reached the sidewalk, he turned his head for a moment, and I got a look at his face before the cops hustled him into the squad car. I felt a jolt of recognition, and I clutched Kate's arm.

"Ouch," Kate said, pulling her arm away then looking at my face. "What's wrong, Annabelle?"

"That's the man I saw Tricia's mother meet with at the Hay-Adams Hotel the day she died."

CHAPTER 38

"Are you sure?" Kate asked, rubbing her arm where I'd squeezed it when I'd recognized Frank.

The squad car had pulled away with the suspect in the back seat, and I stood on the sidewalk with Leatrice and Kate, staring after it. My heart raced from the shock of realizing that the neighbor who may have murdered Tricia was the same man who met with her mother right before the woman plummeted to her death. I put a clammy hand to my chest and tried to breathe slowly to calm myself.

"Shouldn't you tell Reese?" Kate motioned to where the detective stood next to his unmarked car talking through the driver's side window to his partner.

"No way." I kept my voice low. "Then I have to explain that I was eavesdropping on the bride's mother. He already got upset that I didn't tell him we knew the mother when he saw us at the Hay-Adams. Can you imagine what he'll do to me if I tell him I had some potential evidence that I hid from him?"

"Throw you in jail for obstructing justice?" Leatrice asked.

Kate gave her a look. "He is not going to arrest Annabelle. But don't you think keeping this from him is a big deal?"

"Why?" I said. "They already have him in custody. We don't know that his meeting with Mrs. Toker is in any way connected to Tricia's death. Plus, I saw him leave the hotel before she fell off the roof."

Kate frowned. "But we still don't know why he was meeting Tricia's mom."

He did work for Cogent Technologies," Leatrice said. "That's the family company, right?"

"From what I overheard, it sounded like he'd been working for Mrs. Toker. Maybe as part of his job for Cogent," I said.

"Then why wouldn't they meet at the headquarters?" Kate asked. "Why meet secretly in a hotel ballroom?"

"You know our rich clients, Kate. They don't lift a finger if they don't have to. How many times have we met clients at their homes or at their country clubs because they don't want to come into the city?"

Kate shrugged an acknowledgement. "True. I'm sure the mom didn't want to leave the hotel if they were still comping her room." She snapped her fingers. "What if Mrs. Toker and Frank met through the company, at a holiday party or something, and they were having an affair. Maybe what you heard was the end of an affair."

I rolled my eyes. Leave it to Kate to make every situation into a sex scandal. "Trust me. It was not the end of an affair."

Leatrice cleared her throat loudly as Reese approached us.

"I'm headed back to the station to interview this guy and process the paperwork." He ran a hand through his dark hair. "Thanks again for calling us."

"Anytime, Detective." Leatrice bounced up and down on the balls of her feet.

He gave a weary grin before turning away from us. "That's what I'm afraid of."

We watched the detective get in his car and drive away. Leatrice tucked her fedora under her arm and pulled her car keys out of the pocket of her trench coat. "I think we can call this stakeout a success."

I patted Leatrice on the shoulder. "The most likely suspect is now in custody. All thanks to you."

"I'm glad I could help, dear."

So, wait," Kate said. "Did we just help solve another murder?"

"Maybe." I turned toward Kate's car. "The clues seem to point to Frank. He had motive, opportunity, and access to a gun. Who else could have done it?"

Kate started walking down the sidewalk. "I guess you're right. But it doesn't feel as satisfying as the other cases."

I agreed. Even though we'd seen the suspect we'd been gathering evidence on taken away by the police, the case had an unfinished feel to it.

There were still so many unanswered questions and so many threads we hadn't connected. I pushed those thoughts out of my head.

"It doesn't matter," I said. "The police have a guy in custody, which means we are officially in the clear."

Kate let out a breath. "That's a relief. No more dark cloud of doom hanging over our business. And now that the word is out that Brianna is actually a madam, people should have plenty else to talk about."

I felt my entire body relax, and I rolled my head from side to side, hearing my neck crackle. I knew I'd been tense the past few days, but as my shoulders and back released I realized just how much stress I'd been holding in. "I think I need to go to a spa for a week after this."

Leatrice clapped her hands together. "A girls trip. Wouldn't that be fun?"

The image of soaking in a mud bath with Leatrice flashed into my head. Not my idea of relaxing. "For now I want to go home and crawl in bed and not think about Tricia Toker and her wedding ever again. Actually, I'd like to never think about another bride ever again."

"Until our next wedding in a week," Kate said.

At least that bride is sweet. No nasty reviews from her."

"And no murders?" Leatrice looked disappointed.

"Definitely no murders," I said. "From now on, our weddings are going to have zero drama."

Kate raised her eyebrows. "Then which one of us is going to tell Richard and Fern they can't come?"

CHAPTER 39

"Yoo-hoo!" A voice sang out from my living room, and I sat up in bed. I grabbed my phone from my nightstand, looked at the time, and flopped back on my pillows. It was only ten a.m. I'd barely slept after all the excitement the day before, and I'd hoped to get a few more hours of shut-eye.

I heard thumping from the front of my apartment and swung my feet over the side of the bed. Knowing Leatrice, she might let a complete stranger inside if they were cute enough and asked nicely. I tugged on a pair of jeans from the floor and grabbed a white Wedding Belles T-shirt from the drawer, noticing as I slipped it over my head that my hair still smelled like smoke from yesterday's fire. I pulled it up into a high ponytail and hoped no one else would notice the faint scent of charred car emanating from my head.

I stepped into the hall and heard a familiar voice. "Fern? What are you doing here?" I walked to the front of my apartment to see him and Kate dropping several canvas shopping bags onto my couch. I immediately regretted giving Kate a key.

He straightened up and rubbed one of his shoulders. His dark hair was slicked back and in a low ponytail, and he wore his version of casual clothes: black flat-front pants paired with a black button-down shirt and accented with a silver Ferragamo belt buckle. "Hair products are heavy."

Kate began pawing through the bags, examining bottles of serum and cans of spray. "This should do the trick."

"It's not that I'm not thrilled you both stopped by," I said. "But what are you doing here?"

Fern crossed over to me and ran his hands through my hair. "Kate told me about yesterday." He leaned close and took a whiff of my head and gasped. "It's worse than I thought."

"I know I need to wash it," I said. "But I was too exhausted to shower last night."

"A wash isn't all you need, girl. When was your last cut?"

"My last haircut?" To be honest, I couldn't remember the last time I'd been in his salon for a trim. I was notorious for getting caught up in wedding season and forgetting to maintain my hair. That was one of the reasons I wore my hair in a ponytail or a bun most of the time. Easier to hide the fact that I neglected my hair.

"It's a good thing you called me when you did," Fern said to Kate, who nodded absently as she squirted a blue gel into her palm.

I glared at Kate, noticing that her red miniskirt was very mini. "So this is all your doing?"

"You're welcome." Kate rubbed her palms together and began working the gel through her bob. "I knew you wouldn't do it, and I don't think you've had your hair done since the Simpson/Moskowitz wedding, and that was nine months ago. Besides, after yesterday, you deserve to take your mind off things."

I opened my mouth to protest but realized she was probably right.

Fern began arranging his bottles and brushes on my dining room table. "I can't believe someone threw a cocktail at your car and set it on fire."

"A Molotov cocktail," I said.

Fern tapped a finger to his lips. "Now is that a vodka drink?"

"It's not a drink," I said. "It's an explosive."

Fern steered me to a dining room chair and sat me down, unfurling a black smock around my shoulders. "It sounds like a craft cocktail to me. Regardless, a neighborhood with real-estate prices this high should not have car fires."

"Whoever torched my car was warning me off Tricia's murder investigation. And it worked."

"I'm surprised your clients aren't talking about her," Kate said as Fern pulled the black elastic from my head. "I would have thought the murder of a rich girl would have been prime gossip."

Fern eyed my hair as he combed it down my back. "I'm sure they want to, but I've had the receptionist tell everyone I'm in mourning and not to bring up her name." He waved a hand in front of his clothes. "Hence the all-black."

Kate grinned at him. "Brilliant."

"If I sense one of those two-bit hussies is getting close to the topic, I reach for a tissue and excuse myself for a moment. Then I go to the back and sneak some Champagne from the bottles reserved for clients."

"Even more brilliant," Kate said.

"How much Champagne have you had today?" I asked, aware that he would soon be cutting my hair and hoping very much that he wasn't drunk.

Fern waved a hand to dismiss my concern. "A glass or two."

"It's only ten a.m." I hoped I wouldn't end up with a Mohawk or a pixie cut. I knew I couldn't pull off either. I tried to turn my head to give Fern a look, but he held it straight as he sprayed my hair with water. "And how are you in mourning? You couldn't stand Tricia."

"Of course I couldn't, and neither could any of the people who are dying to talk about her." He picked up his pointy scissors from the table. "Are you okay with losing a few inches? Otherwise you'll be sitting on your hair by the time you come see me again."

"That's fine," I said. "But nothing crazy."

Fern leaned into my ear. "Darling, would I ever do something crazy?"

I thought back to the time he dressed like Little Bo Peep for Halloween and carried a toy poodle as a sheep, and I declined to answer.

"So I don't suppose you've learned anything juicy about Tricia then?" Kate asked. Fern's salon had been a good source of intel during past investigations.

Fern snipped, and from the corner of my eye I saw a clump of hair fall to the floor. "Sorry, girls. Was I supposed to be getting information? I did hear a juicy one about Brianna, though. Did you know she's been running a call-girl service through her business?"

I looked at Kate, but she wouldn't meet my eyes. "We should probably tell you the truth before this gets way out of hand."

Fern dropped his scissors, and they clattered onto my hardwood floor. "Don't tell me you two are running a call-girl service, too?"

I waved my hands wildly in front of me. "Of course not. But we might have planted the information about Brianna."

Fern let out a breath as he bent to pick up his scissors. "Well, that's a relief."

"The only reason we said it was because she was spreading awful rumors about us," Kate said.

BOOK 4: REVIEW TO A KILL

"You don't have to explain to me," Fern said. "That one has been jealous of you two since she blew into town on her blond broom. I'm not surprised she was the one behind all the nasty rumors about Wedding Belles."

"Do you think she'll be too embarrassed to stay in the city?" Kate asked, her face hopeful. "Now that she's been outed as a pimp."

"Doubtful," I said. "We aren't that lucky."

"At least we're officially out of the crime-solving business and our names have been cleared," Kate said. "It's a relief that the police have a suspect in custody."

"Who?" Fern asked.

I cut my eyes to Kate. "Didn't you tell him?"

Sorry. I forgot. We were busy packing up his salon to bring here."

"The guy you helped Leatrice stake out," I said.

"Effing Frank?" Fern sounded delighted. "Did he finally show up?"

"When Leatrice went to move her car, she saw lights on inside, so we called the police."

Fern paused his cutting. "Just think of all the crazy things that have happened in the past week, girls."

Kate began ticking off on her fingers. "The wedding where you had to drag the bride down the aisle. The awful reviews. The bride and groom get shot. The police suspect us. Annabelle sees Mrs. Toker meeting with a guy who we later discover is Effing Frank, her daughter's gun-happy neighbor. Mrs. Toker dies. Annabelle's car gets torched. We discover that Frank works for the Tokers. The police catch him."

"It puts the wedding day disaster in perspective, doesn't it?" Fern asked.

I tried to turn around again. "What wedding day disaster?" Aside from Tricia being a nightmare, the wedding had been disaster-free.

"The best man's toast," Fern said. "Don't you remember? When he said the maid of honor's name instead of the bride and then stammered something about how he thought he would be giving his toast for Dave and Madeleine's wedding and not Dave and Tricia's?"

Kate dropped a plastic bottle of styling serum. It bounced on the floor and rolled under my couch. "What?"

Fern shook his head in exasperation. "You two never listen to the toasts, do you?"

CHAPTER 40

I grabbed Fern's wrist as he attempted to resume cutting my hair. "The best man said what?"

Fern sighed and pulled his hand out of my grasp. "I thought you cued all the toasts. How did you miss it?"

"Once we cue them, we go off and start gathering all the items to give the couple at the end of the night," Kate said. "After you've heard a couple hundred speeches, they all start to sound the same."

"Did you miss my toast?" He narrowed his eyes at me.

"Of course not," Kate said. "It was amazing." She was telling the truth since she'd heard his toast even though I'd only listened to part of it.

"Thank you. I thought the bit I did from *The Sound of Music* was inspired, if I do say so myself. " Fern put his hands on his hips, the pointy scissors jutting out on one side and the comb on the other. "But you should have stayed for the best man. It was something special."

"How did Tricia react?" I asked. Our former bride had not been known for her under-reactions or for letting things go.

Fern drew his comb across his neck as if he were using it to cut his throat. "She looked like she wanted to kill him, which made it even worse. He started stuttering about it being an easy mistake to make since Dave had started out with Madeleine."

Kate began pacing. "Started out with her? Like they dated first?"

Fern shrugged and turned my head forward. "That's what I assumed, but you know I would never gossip."

BOOK 4: REVIEW TO A KILL

Kate and I exchanged a look. Fern loved nothing more than juicy gossip and his salon was one of the main conduits in Georgetown.

"Make an exception," I said, twisting toward him again.

Fern screwed up his face like he was debating. Then he continued. "Before the best man could say anything else, the bride elbowed the groom, and he jumped in."

"Did Madeleine seem upset?" I asked as Fern straightened my head and tipped it down so that I stared into my lap, snippets of hair covering the black smock.

"Upset?" Fern said. "Her face turned bright pink, so I think she was embarrassed. But who wouldn't be if an entire wedding was looking at you and wondering about your relationship with the groom?"

"Poor thing." I could imagine how it must have sounded to the guests. Everyone had heard too many stories of best men sleeping with brides and bridesmaids sleeping with grooms not to jump to conclusions.

"I can't believe we missed that," Kate said. "After hundreds of boring speeches, we finally get a juicy one and what are we doing? Packing up the wedding presents."

"I'm thinking sideswept bangs," Fern said. "Are we onboard with this?"

"As long as you're onboard with her pinning them up with a bobby pin everyday," Kate said.

I looked up to protest but realized that she was completely correct.

Fern clutched his hands to his heart. "Bobby pins? Why don't you use a banana clip and finish me off for good?"

"I promise not to use bobby pins," I said. "What happened after the groom cut off the best man?"

Fern's foot tapped beneath me. "The groom made some sort of joke so that everyone laughed, and the little strawberry blonde ran off to the bathroom. I think the bride's mother went after her."

"The bride's mother?" Kate said. "That's interesting."

"So what does this mean?" I asked as Fern combed my hair down so it created a wet curtain around my face. "What kind of relationship did the maid of honor have with the groom?"

"The bigger question is how did I not pick up on it?" Kate asked. "Sensing secret relationships is my superpower." Kate did have an uncanny ability to look at people and know if they were involved romantically and how deeply.

I parted the hair in front of my eyes so I could see her clearly. "To be fair, you never saw those two together, did you?"

Kate tapped a finger to her lips. "Maybe not. When the groom attended a meeting, Madeleine didn't, and when the bride brought her maid of honor with her, Dave never came."

"And does your power even extend to past involvement?" I asked Kate. "You can't tell if two people used to date ages ago, can you?"

She raised an eyebrow. "Are you doubting my powers, Annabelle?"

I let the hair fall back in front of my face. "Forget I asked."

Fern raised my head and pulled his fingers through my hair. "You aren't allergic to fish, are you?"

"What? No. Why?"

He held up a silver tube. "Caviar hair serum."

"Will I smell like fish eggs?" I asked.

Fern squirted a gold gel into his palm and shrugged. "Beauty has a price, darling."

"We need to find out about this thing between Madeleine and Dave." Kate walked down the hall toward my office and returned with my laptop as Fern worked the gel through my hair.

"And you're going to do this how?" I wrinkled my nose at the salty scent of the serum. This caviar potion had better be worth me smelling like sushi.

Kate set the laptop on the table and flipped it open. "The same way we find any good dirt. Facebook."

She tapped away at the keyboard while Fern plugged in his industrial black hair-dryer and picked up an oversized round brush. He began tugging the brush through my hair as he dried each wide strand. I could see Kate's fingers flying along the keyboard, even if I couldn't hear them anymore over the roaring in my ears.

"Nothing on Tricia's page," Kate screamed. "I'm going to try Dave's page. Did he friend us, too?"

"I don't think so," I yelled back, putting a hand over my nose to block out the aroma of cooking fish that emanated from my head. "But Madeleine did. I think Tricia made her."

Kate nodded and didn't look up from the screen.

"When is the last time you updated your profile pic?" Fern asked, stopping the dryer to fluff my hair with his hands. "Aren't you still using your first headshot?"

"Maybe," I said. "It's not like I look any different than I did six years ago."

"Mmmmhmmm." Fern turned on the blow-dryer.

"Did you just roll your eyes at me?" I yelled over the noise.

He shook his head. "I can't hear you."

"Bingo." Kate turned the laptop around so I could see the screen.

I sat up to get a better look and cracked my head on the barrel of the dryer. "Could you turn that off for a second?"

Fern clicked off the hair-dryer, set it on the table, and leaned over with me.

Kate pointed to the images of Dave and Madeleine wrapped around each other, holding hands, kissing. "These are from their freshman year in college."

"And they're on Madeleine's page?" I rubbed my head where it had hit the hard plastic of the hair-dryer.

Kate nodded. "Yes, but they're actually other people's photos that she's tagged in. She must have taken down all of her posts."

"Or Tricia made her remove them," I said.

"They look happy," Fern said. "Happier than Tricia ever did."

"When did Tricia and Dave start dating?" I asked.

Kate spun the laptop around to face her again, typed a few keystrokes and began scrolling. "It looks like the first photo of Tricia and Dave appears a month after the last photo I could find of Madeleine and Dave." She angled the screen so Fern and I could see the photo of Dave and Tricia cheek to cheek. Tricia's smile looked desperate it was so bright.

I sat back in my chair. "So Tricia stole her best friend's boyfriend."

"And married him," Kate added.

Fern whistled. "I'm surprised Madeleine didn't kill Tricia."

Kate gave a low whistle back. "Hell has no fury like a woman's thorn."

Fern raised a hand in the air. "Preach, girl."

CHAPTER 41

"Well, who's to say she didn't kill her?" I stood up so I could walk around the room. Walking helped me think. If only I could walk away from the smell of my own head. I wasn't sure if smelling like fish was better or worse than smelling like roasted car.

"Probably the cops." Kate twisted in her chair to face me. "Since they have the neighbor in custody and there's so much evidence linking him to both murders."

"Knock, knock," Leatrice said as she opened the door and came inside.

"Hi, Leatrice," I said before replying to Kate. "It's just shocking to learn such a big secret about the bride's best friend and her husband. I mean, we did work with the couple for a year."

"Was that only a year?" Kate asked. "It felt like a decade."

Leatrice looked at the array of hair products and appliances on the dining table. "Are you doing makeovers?"

Fern's eyes went to Leatrice's burgundy hair, and he patted the chair in front of him. "Step right up."

"You'd think we would have gotten some hint of this bombshell before now," I said.

"Well, to be fair, the rest of the world heard about it at the wedding." Fern shook his round hairbrush at me.

Leatrice bounded over to Fern's empty chair and let him unfurl a black smock around her shoulders. "Heard about what?"

"Are you open to a new color?" Fern asked Leatrice as he held up a

BOOK 4: REVIEW TO A KILL

strand of her electric burgundy hair. When she gave a distracted nod, he grinned and began poking through a canvas sack at his feet.

Kate angled the laptop so Leatrice could see the images on the screen. "Heard that the groom and the maid of honor dated before the bride and groom did."

Leatrice pressed her eyebrows together as she studied the photos. "And you didn't know about this before?"

"I did." Fern misted Leatrice's hair with his pink plastic spray bottle. "The best man let it slip during his wedding toast, but these two missed it."

"We were packing up the wedding presents," I said. "It's not like we were off taking naps."

"And I had to get the mother of the bride's car out of valet since she was taking all the gifts, remember?" Kate asked.

I thought back to the end of the wedding and how my feet had ached as we'd loaded the boxes and gift bags into the back of Mrs. Toker's Land Rover. "But she wasn't taking them that night, remember? Madeleine took the car because the mom wanted to stay in her suite."

Kate snapped her fingers. "And she asked Madeleine to take the gifts to her house that night."

Fern tilted Leatrice's head forward as he combed out her damp hair. "Being maid of honor really is the worst job."

Things began to click in my brain. "Madeleine had the mother's car the whole time. She mentioned having to chauffeur her when we were at the hospital after the shooting."

"So it wasn't the mother at the bride's house at the time of the shooting?" Leatrice looked up, and Fern pushed her head back down. "Remember how the mother got a parking ticket that morning?"

"So it was just her car," I said. "With the maid of honor driving it."

Kate's mouth opened, and she shook her head. "But the cops have enough evidence to charge the neighbor, right? Otherwise, why is he in custody?"

Leatrice looked up from under the curtain of wet hair in front of her eyes. "He's not. That's what I came up here to tell you. Boots did a little poking on his own and found out that they released Effing Frank late last night."

"What?" Kate and I said simultaneously.

"Apparently, he has an airtight alibi for Tricia's murder and all of the other evidence is circumstantial," Leatrice said.

"But the feud." Kate stood up, and began pacing the same path I'd used. "And the guns. And he works at Cogent. And that's where the threatening email came from. And he had a suspicious meeting with the mom."

"I know," I said. "So much points to him. That's why we need to find out what his role is in all of this."

Kate stopped pacing. "I thought you were sworn off this case."

"I am. I was. That was before we found out all this new information. It's all starting to make sense. We just need to find out why Frank met with Tricia's mom. That's the last piece of the puzzle. I can feel it. Once we find that out, we can put this case and bridezilla behind us for good."

"Okay. How do we do find out what Frank knows?"

"Can you ask your hacker friends to get Frank's statement for us?" I asked Leatrice.

She shook her wet head. "My guys are off-line for a while. They had to pull up their operation and go underground before the authorities found them."

I exchanged a look with Kate. "You said they were on the West Coast, right? Of which country?"

"That's a good question, dear. I'm starting to think they aren't American."

Just perfect. Leatrice had probably gotten in bed with Russian hackers.

"Then I guess we'll have to ask Frank ourselves," I said.

Leatrice snapped her head up and hit Fern in the chest. "An interrogation?"

Kate tapped her foot on the floor. "You do remember the part where he has guns, right?"

I grabbed my purse from the floor. "He's not going to shoot us. We're just going to ask him a few friendly questions."

"We?" Kate and Leatrice both said.

I pointed to Leatrice. "You stay here and finish your hair." I motioned to Kate. "You're coming with me."

Fern squirted some golden gel into a small plastic mixing bowl. "Call us if you need anything."

Kate snatched her purse from the couch and looked at Fern. "You know how you said being a maid of honor is the worst job? You forgot about assistant wedding planner."

CHAPTER 42

"I don't suppose it would help if I lodged a formal complaint regarding unsafe working practices?" Kate said as we walked up the concrete steps leading to Frank Ferguson's porch.

"Who would you be lodging this complaint with?" I asked, pushing my sunglasses to the top of my head. The sun sat high in the sky, the mild spring morning having given way to the midday heat. I knew our days of spring were numbered as I felt the humid air settle on my skin.

Kate crossed her arms. "Isn't there a league of wedding planners I could complain to?"

I knocked firmly on the front door. "Wedding planners are not unionized."

"Well, maybe we should be. I for one, think we should get workmen's comp for undue stress."

I imagined a thick-armed union negotiator sitting across the table from a bride and outlining all the things we could not be forced to do. Maybe Kate didn't have such a bad idea.

"I give you free reign to start a wedding planners' union, Norma Rae."

Before Kate could respond, the front door opened and we stood face to face with Effing Frank. This was the man I'd seen meeting with Tricia's mother the day she'd fallen to her death. He was tall with the bulbous nose I remembered, and up close I could see that he wasn't bald but, in fact, shaved his head. He wore brown pants and a white button-down shirt, which he'd rolled up to his elbows.

"Can I help you?" That deep voice. The same one I'd heard when he and Mrs. Toker had made their exchange.

"I'm Annabelle Archer, and this is my assistant, Kate. We were Tricia Toker's wedding planners."

He nodded and stepped back, holding the door open wide. "Come on in."

Kate and I exchanged a look then stepped inside the house. A sparse living room held a matching tan sofa grouping and a round light-wood coffee table with nothing on it. The fireplace mantle boasted no frames or decorative items and the only art on the wall was a framed print of a landscape over one sofa. It looked like the entire room had been purchased from a furniture showroom.

"I imagine you have some questions." He motioned for us to sit on the couch.

"It seems like you know who we are," Kate said, following me into the living room.

He nodded but didn't elaborate.

"I saw you with Mrs. Toker at the hotel the day she died." I stood in front of the couch but didn't sit. Even though this guy seemed cooperative, I didn't feel comfortable letting down my guard quite yet.

"Have a seat," he said.

"We're fine," I said as Kate started to lower herself on the couch then stood back up.

"Suit yourself." His voice sounded weary, although I reminded myself that he had spent most of the previous evening at the police station.

"What was your relationship to Mrs. Toker?" I asked.

He sighed. "I might as well tell you. I already told the cops everything. All the Tokers are dead, anyway." He leaned his forearms against the back of a tan chair. "I work security for Cogent."

"We know that much," Kate said.

He gave a small lopsided grin. "You're pretty well informed for wedding planners."

"That tends to happen when you're considered persons of interest in a crime you had nothing to do with," I said. "We had to go looking for the real killer to clear ourselves."

"And you came up with me."

"Motive and opportunity," Kate said. "You lived right next door, you hated the victims, and you had guns."

Another half smile. "I have guns because I'm former military and a licensed P.I. And who told you I hated Tricia and Dave?"

"The maid of honor." My voice came out as a whisper. "She's the only reason we suspected you in the first place."

Kate nudged me. "She lied to us. She set this whole thing up."

I held up my hands. "Wait a minute. You're telling me that it's a coincidence that a security guy who works for Cogent just happens to move in next to the bride and groom."

"I'm not saying that at all. I was hired to watch them."

"By Mrs. Toker," I finished for him.

He nodded. "She wanted me to watch the groom and make sure there was nothing funny going on. Tricia was inheriting a huge fortune, and her mother wanted to be one hundred percent sure that the groom had the right motives."

"Anyone who could put up with that girl for as long as he did deserves a huge fortune," Kate said.

Frank made a face that said he agreed with her. "I don't think her mother felt that way."

"So you watched them and discovered what?" I asked.

"Nothing until after the wedding. The next day I followed the groom to the office after he'd left the house with an armful of wedding tuxedos."

"I forgot that the groom works for Cogent, too," I said, more to myself than to Frank.

"I'd been so focused on tracking his moves outside work that I hadn't thought to track what he did when he was at Cogent. So I got into the system and found the email he sent to himself and Tricia from someone else's computer. I did some more digging and pulled up his work phone records filled with calls to Madeleine."

"And that's what you gave Mrs. Toker, and that's what got her killed. Evidence that the bride's husband and best friend planned her murder." The pieces fell into place in my mind. Madeleine had been driving the mother's car when it had gotten a ticket in front of Tricia's house the morning of the murder because she was the killer. She'd fed us misinformation about Frank to send us off on a wild goose chase. She'd driven Mrs. Toker's silver SUV when she threw a Molotov cocktail into my car. She must have been the person Mrs. Toker met on the roof of the hotel and who'd pushed her off.

Kate sucked in air. "He was involved with Tricia's maid of honor? After all these years? But I don't get it. He was one of the victims."

"They set it up to look like he was a victim," I said. "The threatening email. The false information about a feud with the neighbor. Dave being shot in the shoulder so he would be injured but not killed."

A muffled pop came from behind us, and Frank crumpled to the ground.

"Not bad," Madeleine said as she pushed the front door the rest of the way open and leveled a gun at us.

CHAPTER 43

"Is he dead?" Kate whispered to me, her voice shaking, as we walked across the grass that separated Frank's house from Tricia and Dave's.

Frank had looked pretty dead to me when Madeleine shot him from the doorway, but I hadn't gotten close enough to check before the maid of honor announced that we were moving the party next door.

"Quiet," Madeleine said from behind, the gun trained on us from the pocket of the cropped denim jacket she wore over a floral-print maxi dress.

I glanced around me without moving my head but didn't notice any neighbors walking dogs or doing yard work. I suspected that at this time of day most of the residents were at work and any children were at day care or school. I cursed our bad luck.

The air seemed to have gotten warmer and stickier in the time we'd been inside Frank's house. I tried to take a deep breath, but it caught in my chest, and I fought a wave of dizziness, remembering that I hadn't eaten a thing all day. I clutched the metal railing as Madeleine nudged us up the porch stairs and into the yellow house.

"Go on back to the kitchen," she said. Her voice had lost every bit of its sweetness, and I had to remind myself that this was the placid girl who had been so devoted to her best friend.

"How did you manage to pull this off without Tricia suspecting?" I asked, taking a seat on one of the barstools.

"You want a full confession?" She pulled the gun out of her jacket without lowering it, and I noticed that her usually neat strawberry-blond hair looked unkempt. "All right. Why not? In less than three hours, I'll be on my way to Brazil and you two won't be talking to anyone."

Kate twisted on her barstool next to me and made eye contact. She looked as worried as I felt. Leatrice and Fern were the only people who knew we were here, but even they thought we were next door. The police might be looking for Madeleine, given the information Frank said he provided them, but I doubted they would look in Tricia's house.

"It was my idea. Have my boyfriend romance the rich girl. She had access to a world neither of us did, so it was perfect. As the boyfriend and the best friend we got to go with her to the beach house and on the ski trips."

"Tricia went skiing?" Kate asked.

"Before she got 'sick.'" Madeleine made air quotes with her fingers.

"You knew her illnesses were fabricated," I said.

Madeleine rolled her eyes. "Of course. It started in college. She would fake a headache to get Dave to stay in the dorm with her while everyone went out. She was never good at socializing and getting people to like her. I guess when you're that rich, you don't need to be likable. When the headaches worked, she moved on to other things. By the time we graduated, she had me bringing her notes from class, and she barely left the room."

"She sounds like a treat," Kate mumbled to me.

"Yeah, it was a drag."

I thought the word *drag* was a massive understatement to describe Tricia. "So you put up with her for all those years for the money?"

"It wasn't so bad. If Dave and I wanted to be together, he'd just put a sleeping pill in with the pile of medications she took." She leered at us. "Do you know how many times I had him when she was sleeping in the next room? We never had to sneak off to a hotel because we did everything right under her nose."

Kate shook her head. "Well, that's just tacky."

"I did what I had to do," Madeleine snapped. "Keep your friends close and your enemies closer. And make no mistake about it, Tricia was an enemy to everyone she came in contact with."

I couldn't argue with her there.

Madeleine took off the denim jacket, and I noticed that her face looked flushed. "Judge me all you want, but do you have any idea how much money she had?"

I shook my head. I didn't. Most of our clients were well off, but we never knew their net worth.

"Millions." She spread her arms out wide. "Hundreds of millions now that Dave will inherit the company."

I didn't want to be the one to burst her bubble but since Tricia died before her mother, she didn't inherit the company from her. That meant Dave wouldn't be inheriting from Tricia.

"Not when they find out he conspired to have his wife killed, Kate said.

"They'll never know," Madeleine pointed the gun at her. "Everyone who knows anything is dead. Or will be."

"Wrong again," Kate said. "Frank told the police everything he knew about you."

I shot Kate a look. Why was she antagonizing the woman with the gun?

Madeleine's face darkened. "So I was too late?" She shook her head. "It doesn't matter. Dave already cleaned out their joint accounts. We'll be set for life."

"You think you're going to get away with killing your best friend and her mother?" Kate asked.

Madeleine looked at us with a curious expression. "Mrs. Toker was an accident. We wrestled for the evidence, and she ended up flipping over the railing. But you think I shot Tricia in cold blood?"

I didn't have a bit of trouble believing she could shoot her so-called best friend in cold blood and the look on Kate's face told me she didn't either.

I heard heavy footsteps coming down the wooden staircase. "It was Dave, wasn't it? He shot Tricia, and then you shot him to give him an alibi." I remembered the flecks of blood on Madeleine's sleeve after the murder. "Then you touched Dave's body and got blood on you to explain away the blood spatter. He must have been the one Tricia's mom called when she got the evidence from Frank."

"Not bad for a wedding planner," Dave said as he entered the room. He looked like he was dressed for the golf course and held a black duffel bag in one hand. "But I think it's time for us to go, Madeleine." He handed her the duffel. "The car's in the back alley. Go ahead and put this in the trunk. I'll meet you there in a second."

She nodded, handed him the gun, and left through the back kitchen door. So he was the one tasked to do the dirty work. Before I could think too much, I lunged for Dave, knocking his arm up. The gun fired and Kate screamed. Dave released his grip, and the gun clattered to the tile floor. I dove for it, scratching at the groom's hands as he tried to take it from me.

Kate jumped on his back and pulled his hair back with both hands. He roared in pain and reached his arms over his head to yank her off.

"Freeze," I said, stepping back and leveling the gun at Dave.

Kate rolled off him and joined me on the other side of the marble island. He stood up, breathing heavily, his expression murderous.

"What do we do now?" Kate whispered to me. "Shoot him?"

I didn't know what to do since our cell phones were in our purses and those were still at the house next door. I focused on keeping my hands steady, but the gun felt heavier than I expected, and my arms begin to shake.

Before I had to shoot the groom or lower the gun, the front door burst open. "Police! Drop your weapons and put your hands up."

Several uniformed officers rushed into the house as I lowered the gun to the floor by my feet. Dave raised his arms in the air.

Detective Reese pushed past the uniformed cops as they snapped handcuffs the groom, pausing at the door of the kitchen. "Are you two okay?"

I nodded and fought the sudden urge to cry. "How did you know we were here?"

The corner of Reese's mouth twitched into a smile. "Your neighbor called me. She said you'd come over to talk to Frank Ferguson, but you weren't answering her calls. She said she would have come herself, but she was in the middle of a makeover."

My legs felt weak, and I leaned against the countertop. "But how did you know we were here at Tricia's house?"

Reese walked over and picked up the gun from the floor while a uniformed cop led Dave out of the room. "We were walking up to the neighbor's house when we heard the gunshot."

I put a hand to my mouth. "We need to call an ambulance for Frank." I looked at Reese. "Madeleine shot him. I don't know if he's dead or not."

"We have an ambulance on the way already since we heard the gunshot over here," Reese said. "If I run next door to check on him, will you two be okay?"

"We're fine." I put my shaking hands on the rounded edge of the counter.

"Look." Kate pointed out the kitchen window. "Madeleine's driving away."

I followed Kate's gaze out the back kitchen window to the silver Land Rover careening down the alley. "Loyalty really isn't her strong suit."

Reese directed one of the officers to chase down her car as he strode out of the kitchen. Once he'd gone, I allowed myself to slide down to sit on the floor.

Kate sat next to me and put her hand over my shaking one. "We always say bridesmaids can be worse than the brides."

"Yes, but I never thought we'd have one threaten to kill us," I said.

"I know, right?" Kate shook her head. "I always thought you or I would snap and kill one of them first."

I gave a weak laugh. "Talk to me in another five years."

CHAPTER 44

"Unhand me at once." Richard's voice carried from the direction of the front door, where a police officer was likely standing guard —and apparently holding Richard back. "You're wrinkling my Thomas Pink shirt."

"How did Richard know we we're here?" Kate asked.

"I'm assuming the same way Reese found out. The Leatrice phone tree."

"Annabelle," Richard called out. "Are you in there?"

"Back here," I yelled. "In the kitchen."

I heard more muffled arguing, then Richard rushed into the kitchen, his eyes darting around the room until he spotted us on the floor. His hand flew to his heart. "Are you hurt?"

"We're fine." I slowly pulled myself up then put a hand out to Kate. "It's just been a stressful couple of hours."

"Don't I know it?" Richard leaned against the marble counter and flapped his beige suit jacket open and closed, flashing his bright orange shirt as he tried to cool himself down. "I left those Colonial Dames and drove over here like a maniac."

"Colonial Dames?" Kate asked as I pulled her up.

"It's a monthly luncheon I cater for some very sweet and very old southern ladies. Mostly chicken salad," he said. "But as soon as Leatrice called and said you might be in danger, I tore over here."

I touched Richard's arm. "Thanks. We're fine now."

BOOK 4: REVIEW TO A KILL

"Leatrice said that you were coming to talk to the neighbor. Did he do it?"

"No," Kate said. "The groom and maid of honor were in on it together."

Richard's mouth dropped open. "The husband and best friend killed the bride? How twisted."

"It was twisted all right," I said. "And planned for years."

Kate hopped up on the counter. "So the long game must have been for Dave to marry Tricia for the money, kill her, and inherit her part of the company, marrying Madeleine after a suitable period of mourning."

"You have to admire that level of dedication," Richard said. "Most millennials don't stick with anything very long."

"Hey," Kate said. "I've been through thick and thin with Annabelle for almost six years and you don't see me going anywhere."

"You're special." I put an arm around Kate and elbowed Richard before he could make a snarky comment.

"You're alive," Leatrice said as she rushed into the kitchen with Fern close on her heels. She shook her phone at us. "When you're alive you answer your phone."

"Sorry," I said. "Our phones are over at Frank's house."

"Leatrice," Kate gasped. "You're blond."

"I know. Isn't it glamorous?" She patted her platinum flip, releasing a burst of ammonia scent into the air. "Fern thinks it makes me look like Marilyn Monroe."

"If Marilyn Monroe had been put through a fruit dehydrator," Richard muttered.

I shot him a look as his phone rang and he stepped away to answer it.

"Thanks for calling Detective Reese," I said to Leatrice. "And Richard, I guess."

"Well, when we couldn't reach you, Fern and I got worried." Leatrice looked up at Fern, who nodded.

"We wanted to come ourselves, but her head was covered in hair color and tinfoil," Fern said. "I had to rinse and dry her. But after that we rushed right over."

I'd seen Leatrice go out in stranger headgear than tinfoil, but I didn't say so. "No, calling the police was the right move." Not that Leatrice bursting in with a head decked out in foil wouldn't have been a decent distraction.

Fern pulled out a pocket brush and began touching up Leatrice's hair.

623

"So the groom and the maid of honor were in on it together after all. See? I told you she was a tramp."

"You call every bridesmaid a tramp," Kate said.

Fern winked. "I'm playing the odds, sweetie."

"How did you find out?" I asked.

"We saw the cute detective on our way in," Fern said. "Double yum."

"Such a nice boy," Leatrice said with a meaningful look to me.

I felt my face flush. Why did the mention of the detective have such an effect on me? It wasn't like we'd been involved and every time I saw him I was replaying a night of passion in my head. We'd never done anything more than flirting. I shook my head and tried to think of something other than the admittedly yummy cop.

"I told you not to let them get into the wine," Richard hissed into his phone a couple of feet away. A pause. "What do mean you had to step out for a few minutes?" Another pause. "How many times have I forbidden you to bring that flying squirrel to work?"

"Sounds like a dustup with the Dames," Kate said to me.

Richard sucked in his breath. "Well did you catch him, or is he still running loose in Edith Partain's kitchen?" He let out his breath. "Then keep him in the pantry for now, and take the wine away from the women. I'll be there as soon as I can."

Richard disconnected and dropped his phone in his jacket pocket, then turned to us. "I have to run. The Colonial Dames drank too much, and apparently some of them are falling out of their chairs, and one of them took off her girdle."

"In the middle of the lunch?" Kate asked. "Maybe weddings aren't so bad after all."

Richard squeezed my hand. "Call me later, darling."

I nodded and watched him walk out of the house as Reese stepped in, the two men acknowledging each other with a nod. Richard had never lost his initial nervousness around Reese after being a suspect in a murder investigation, and he'd uniformly disapproved of any man I'd ever been interested in. Even though nothing had ever happened between the detective and me, I knew that Richard didn't like the idea that something could.

"How's Frank?" Kate asked as Reese joined our group in the kitchen.

"Alive." Reese ran a hand through his dark hair. "The bullet got him in the shoulder, but he should make it."

I felt a wave of relief. I couldn't help feeling guilty for suspecting the man and encouraging Leatrice to stake out his house, so I was grateful that he would be okay.

Reese's eyes widened for a moment when he spotted Leatrice. "That was quite a makeover."

"Do you like my new look?" she asked.

He smiled at her. "It's the most unforgettable transformation I've ever seen."

"That's one way to put it," Kate said.

Leatrice either ignored Kate or didn't hear her. She elbowed Fern. "Unforgettable. What do you think about that?"

Reese beckoned for me to step outside with him, so I slipped away as Fern started explaining how he'd taken Leatrice's hair from neon cranberry to blond.

On the front porch I could see police cruisers with flashing blue lights jamming the street and an ambulance with its back doors hanging open. I assumed the paramedics were inside the house working on Frank.

Reese cleared his throat. "I wanted to ask you something important before I need to leave for the station to process the groom."

"Anything," I said.

He paused as an officer walked past us into the house. Then he closed the distance between us until we were inches away. He put one hand on my arm as he leaned down until his mouth almost touched my ear. "I've meant to ask you this for a while. Are you free for dinner this Saturday?"

I couldn't help smiling as I realized that Mike Reese had finally asked me out on a real date and, for once, I didn't have a wedding on a Saturday night. Things were looking up.

THE END

BONUS EPILOGUE

I dropped my black purse on the floor as I stepped into my apartment and surveyed the scene. Aside from the piles of papers and client folders blanketing my glass coffee table, the living room wasn't a total disaster. The pale yellow couch cushions could use some fluffing, and it was time to recycle the pile of wedding magazines accumulating in the rack beside the overstuffed chair, but these were fixable problems. Not so bad, as long as I ignored the dust bunnies gathering in the corners of the hardwood floors and the faint musty smell that told me I needed to open a window, even though it was a hot, sticky summer day in Washington DC.

"Nothing a little lemon Pledge can't fix," I muttered to myself as I headed for the rarely touched cleaning supplies under my kitchen sink.

I glanced at the clock above the stove and felt a flutter of panic. I had less than an hour before Detective Mike Reese was supposed to pick me up for our first official date. I'd intended to have plenty of time to tidy up my apartment and get dressed, but my meeting to pick out wedding linens with a bride had run long.

As the owner of Wedding Belles, one of the city's top wedding planners, I should have known that meetings with brides were rarely short. I hadn't counted on my tough-as-nails lawyer bride having a complete meltdown when I asked her to decide between a pintuck cloth and a damask pattern. Two hours later, we'd been no closer to a decision and the bride had been approaching butterfly net territory.

I'd finally left my assistant, Kate, to wrap up the meeting and console the bride.

"Go," she'd whispered to me as she put an arm around the sniffling bride. "I am not letting you miss your date because of another attack of the bridezilla." The bride had looked up, and Kate had rubbed her arm. "Not you, honey. You're a delight."

Kate was the biggest advocate of my burgeoning relationship with the hot detective and seemed to be as excited as I was we'd finally made a date. Truth be told, I was more nervous than excited since Reese and I had been dancing around our mutual attraction for months. I hoped our chemistry didn't fizzle once we actually went out.

I grabbed the lemon Pledge from under the sink and set it on the counter while I took a bottled Mocha Frappuccino from the door of my fridge. Even though it was almost evening, I'd been rushing around since early in the morning and needed the pick-me-up so I wouldn't be yawning in an hour. I took a swig of the chilled coffee and felt instantly refreshed by the combination of sugar, caffeine, and cold.

"Let's do this," I said to myself, setting the bottled drink on the counter and taking up the can of Pledge as I walked back into the living room, spraying the lemon furniture polish in the air as I went. I cracked a window and felt a faint breeze—the only advantage I'd ever found from being on the fourth floor of a walk-up building—before arranging my client files into neat piles on the coffee table and taking the overflowing magazines to the recycling bin down the hall in my office.

My home office was its own personal disaster area, but I fixed that problem by closing the door. No need for Reese to see the evidence of an insanely busy spring wedding season manifested all over the floor of Wedding Belles HQ.

"Yoo hoo," a voice warbled down the hall from the front door. "Are you home, dear?"

I groaned. My nosy neighbor, Leatrice, must have heard me come in the building even though I'd taken off my flats and tiptoed up past her first floor apartment on my way up. Even after living in the building for six plus years, I hadn't mastered the ninja skills necessary to slip by an octogenarian with ears like a bat.

"Right here." I walked down the hall to where she stood by my front door and blinked a few times as I took in her outfit.

"What do you think?" she asked me, spinning around.

Leatrice's Mary Tyler Moore flip was still platinum blond from a recent hair styling session with my friend, Fern, and her lips were painted her usual bright coral. What was not normal was her outfit.

"Are you dressed like a Keystone Cop?" I asked, appraising her small stature and wondering if she was wearing a child's Halloween costume.

"Do you like it?" She produced a vintage-looking police helmet from behind her back and placed it on her head. The long, dark jacket reached mid-calf and was buttoned up to her wrinkled neck.

"You do know Halloween isn't for four months, right?"

She swatted a hand at me. "Aren't you funny? This isn't for Halloween. I thought this would make me look more official."

I rubbed a hand to my temple. "More official for what?"

She sank onto my couch and her jacket nearly touched the floor. "I figured we're doing so much crime-solving, we should look the part. What do you think Detective Reese will say?"

I put one hand on my hip. "That you're impersonating a police officer."

Leatrice pushed her helmet back so I could see her wide eyes. "Is that a crime?"

"I'm pretty sure it's a felony."

Leatrice stood up "Oh, dear. Would that carry jail time?"

I doubted the courts would throw a little old lady in jail for wearing an absurd costume, but I didn't want her to know that. "I'd guess about five years."

She paled under her bright coral blush. "Perhaps I shouldn't let the detective know I have this then."

I held open the door for her as she rushed through. "That would probably be best."

I watched Leatrice's oversized helmet disappear down the stairs and closed the door behind her. If I didn't want Reese to see me sweaty and frazzled, I needed to get in the shower now. I undressed as I walked down the hall, tossing my clothes in the hamper just inside my bedroom door and ducking into the bathroom. I didn't even wait for the water to warm up, stepping into the shower and relishing the cool water as it spilled over me. After a few minutes of lathering up with my favorite mango body wash, I noticed a humming noise that wasn't coming from me.

I turned off the water and stepped out of the shower, wrapping a fluffy beige towel around me. Someone was definitely in my apartment, and they were singing. I paused to listen more carefully. It didn't sound like Leatrice, but who else would let themselves into my apartment? I doubted a burglar would sing while they robbed me, but I grabbed the toilet brush for protection anyway and opened the bathroom door as silently as I could.

Water dripped onto the wood floor as I tiptoed down the hall toward the noise, toilet brush high in the air. I paused at the kitchen doorway, from where the sound seemed to emanate. Were they singing Beyoncé?

I peeked into the kitchen and nearly dropped the toilet brush and my towel.

Richard stood with his back to me, singing as he unpacked a paper sack of groceries. "If you like it, then you should have put a ring on it. If you like it, then you should have put a ring on it." He bent over and began snapping his fingers as he bobbed his hips. "Oh oh oh oh oh oh oh oh oh."

"What on earth are you doing?" I asked, causing him to shriek and spin around with his hand pressed to his chest.

"Annabelle." His cheeks flushed. "You must be out of your mind to sneak up on me like that."

"Me?" I waved my toilet brush at him. "This is my apartment. What are you doing here?"

Richard seemed to regain his composure and gave me the once-over. "Do you always wear a towel when you clean your bathroom?" He inhaled sharply. "Or are you one of those hippies who cleans in the nude?"

I took a deep breath. "I do not clean in the nude. I was taking a shower when I heard you singing and thought you were an intruder. The toilet brush was to beat you with."

"Interesting choice of weapon." He eyed me. "Why are you taking a shower so late in the afternoon? Please tell me you haven't been working in your pajamas all day and are just showering."

Now it was my turn to flush. "Of course not. I haven't worked all day in my PJs in years."

He arched an eyebrow, but didn't say anymore and turned back to his groceries.

"You still haven't told me why you're here." I readjusted the towel around my chest.

"Didn't you get my message?" He opened the refrigerator door and slid a container of strawberries onto a shelf. "I told you I was coming over to cook you dinner. I realized we hadn't had dinner together in weeks, and I have a new Brussels sprouts salad I want to test out on you. "

I felt my stomach tighten. "I was with a bride most of the afternoon and didn't check my voicemail."

"No problem. I used the key you gave me to let myself in." Richard folded the empty paper bag. "Go ahead and get dressed while I start cooking."

I shifted from one foot to the other. "The problem is I already have plans for tonight."

Richard pivoted from where he stood at my Formica counter. "You have an evening meeting?" He shook his head. "What have I told you about setting boundaries with brides? They'd never expect a doctor or lawyer to meet them at night."

"It's not a meeting. It's a date." I let the words out in a single rush of breath.

"A date?" Comprehension dawned on Richard's face, and he dropped his voice as if someone was in the next room. "With that detective?"

"Of course with the detective," I said. "You know things didn't work out with Ian."

"Thank heavens for small favors," Richard said, unwrapping produce from transparent plastic bags. "Since when do you bounce from man to man, Annabelle? I'm starting to think you're spending too much time with Kate."

"I'd hardly call going out with two guys in as many years 'bouncing from guy to guy,' and I have to spend a lot of time with Kate," I said. "She works for me."

A sniff from Richard. "So when does Prince Charming arrive?"

I flicked my eyes to the clock overhead and gave a small yelp. "Any minute now."

I spun on the spot and hurried down the hall, avoiding the puddles of water I'd left earlier. I could hear Richard complaining as I hopped into a casual mint-green sundress and slipped on low, strappy sandals. I brushed out my long hair with a bit of baby powder so it looked cleaner than it was and dabbed a bit of shimmery beige eye shadow on my lids. I gave myself a quick check in the mirror as I heard a knock at the door and hurried down the hall.

Richard hadn't made much progress packing up his groceries, and I tried not to let impatience creep into my voice as I paused in the kitchen doorway. "We can have dinner tomorrow night."

"You're assuming I'm free tomorrow night," Richard said, wrapping a fresh stalk of cauliflower in plastic and dropping it into the paper bag.

I decided not to press it, since Richard was clearly miffed with me. I took a breath to steady myself before opening the door.

"You've got to be kidding me," I said when I saw it was Leatrice and not Detective Reese.

BOOK 4: REVIEW TO A KILL

My pint-sized neighbor had changed out of her Keystone Cops costume and wore a pair of pale blue Mom jeans (in this case, Grandma jeans would have been more like it) and a T-shirt covered in images of what looked like cats in powdered wigs.

"I took your advice and changed," she said, coming into my living room without an invitation.

Richard poked his head through the open space between my kitchen and living room, pushing back the accordion-style wooden divider to get a better look. "You changed into that? What on earth were you wearing before?" Richard wrinkled his nose. "Are those cats on your T-shirt?"

Leatrice beamed. "Not just any cats. Cats dressed as historical figures." She pointed to a tabby cat on her shirt with a white ruff around his neck. "This is Henry the VIII." She pointed to a ginger cat in a black scoop neck dress. "And this is Mona Lisa."

"I must be going mad," Richard muttered as his head disappeared back into the kitchen.

"I'd love to chat, Leatrice," I said, putting a hand on her back and steering her toward the open door. "But I'm actually on my way out."

Leatrice craned her neck to the kitchen. "But he's here."

"And he's leaving," I said, turning my head to face the kitchen and speaking loud enough for Richard to hear.

"Because he knows when he's not wanted," Richard called back.

I knew I would pay for this later, but at the moment, all I wanted was to get Leatrice and Richard out of my apartment before Reese arrived.

"Did I get the wrong night?"

Too late. Reese stood in the doorway in dark jeans and a white button down shirt worn open at the collar. For a moment I forgot about Richard in my kitchen and Leatrice in her crazy cat shirt as I locked eyes with him. His hazel eyes deepened to green and the corner of his mouth curled up in a half grin.

"No," I said, prodding Leatrice forward. "They're leaving."

"Are those flowers?" Leatrice asked, resisting me as I urged her forward.

Reese glanced down at the bundle of yellow and orange Gerber daisies in his hand, clearing his throat as he handed them to me. "These are for you."

"Thank you." I felt my face warm as I looked down at the brightly colored flowers. No man had ever brought me flowers on a first date, and I had to fight the happy tears I felt pricking the backs of my eyes.

Leatrice nudged Reese. "Well, aren't you the gentleman?"

Richard appeared behind me and took the flowers from my hands. "These should go in water and have their stems trimmed. I'm assuming you have a decent vase somewhere in your kitchen, Annabelle."

He vanished into the kitchen again without acknowledging Reese.

"Do you like sushi?" Reese asked, taking a step closer to me. "I thought we might try a cute place down by the canal."

"I do." I didn't tell him that I stuck to the rolls, as I wasn't a fan of chewing big pieces of raw fish.

He smiled and took my hand. "Good. Should we go?"

I scrapped my plans of offering him a drink before our date since I didn't think I had anything decent to offer him, and my apartment was more crowded than I'd expected it to be. I picked up my purse from the floor and nodded.

"Don't wait up," I called out, and heard Richard give an indignant squeak of protest.

Reese opened the door wider so I could walk out, following me and pausing at the top of the stairs when the phone in his pocket trilled. He pulled it out and looked at the number, his face darkening.

"I'm so sorry," he said. "I have to take this. It's the precinct."

I heard him answer and respond in monosyllables until he hung up and jammed the phone roughly back into his jeans pocket.

"That didn't sound good," I said.

He looked down and shook his head. "I have to reschedule our date."

"You're kidding. I thought you were off-duty." I couldn't help the shocked tone in my voice, but instantly regretted it when I saw Reese flinch.

He met my eyes. "A triple homicide. My captain called me in. I'm really sorry, Annabelle." He gave a mirthless laugh. "Trust me. I'd much rather have sushi with you than go to a murder scene."

I tried to smile. "It's not your fault. I'm sorry about the triple murder. Do they have a suspect yet?"

He raised an eyebrow at me.

I put up my hands. "Not that I'm trying to get involved with your case."

"Let's keep it that way." He kissed me on the cheek. "I'll call you later."

I watched him disappear down the stairs and sighed as I walked back in my apartment and dropped my purse by the door. I noticed that the flowers were already in a vase on the coffee table.

Richard came out from the kitchen and handed me a glass of white wine. "Dinner should be ready in thirty minutes."

"How . . . ?" I started to ask.

Richard jerked a thumb in the direction of the kitchen. "Leatrice overheard." He patted my arm brusquely. "I hope you don't mind she's staying for dinner."

"As long as you don't mind," I said. Richard wasn't a big fan of Leatrice.

He shrugged. "It's fine. I'm making her wear an apron over that terrifying shirt."

Leatrice appeared from the kitchen doorway in a red-and-green-ruffled Christmas apron she'd gotten me one year. She put a spindly arm around my waist.

"At least you got some pretty flowers out of it, dear."

I looked at the blooms spilling out of the top of the glass container, and breathed in the savory smells of Richard's cooking as they began to fill the air. Not exactly how I'd envisioned the evening going, but also not my worst date.

My mind went to the triple homicide, and I couldn't help wondering about it. Even though Reese had warned me at least a dozen times not to poke around in his investigations, I hoped he'd share a few details with me. Considering how many times I'd helped him solve crimes, he should know that my skills went beyond wrangling bridesmaids and pinning boutonnieres.

"Hey, Leatrice," I said. "Do you still have your police scanner?"

"You know I do. Why?"

I gave a half shrug. "Want to see what we can hear about a triple homicide?"

Her eyes lit up as she bounded toward the door. "I thought you'd never ask."

FREE DOWNLOAD!

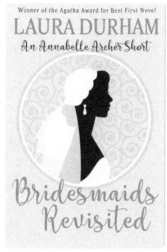

A LUXURY BRIDAL SHOWER.
THE STRESS IS HIGH.
THE PRESENTS ARE GONE.
THE BRIDESMAIDS ARE SUSPECTS.

CAN ANNABELLE UNMASK
THE THIEF?

amazon kindle

nook

kobo

 iBooks

Get your free copy of the short story "Bridesmaids Revisited" when you sign up to the author's mailing list.

Get started here:

BookHip.com/XSZKPG

PREVIEW OF BOOK 5: DEATH ON THE AISLE

"We're going to get killed out here." Kate's voice barely carried over the furious sounds of the storm.

"Hold on to the rope," I said, pushing my wet hair off of my face with one hand and holding an umbrella over us with the other. The rain pelted me from the side and made the umbrella useless, but I still held it up.

"You've got to be kidding," Kate said as she slid down the metal ramp in front of me, clutching the thin rope railing to keep from falling overboard.

When we reached the dock, we both ran to the catering tent a few feet away and pushed our way through the clear plastic sides.

"Well, it's about time," Richard said, his hands planted firmly on his hips. "I rushed everything for you and now it's been sitting." Richard's usually perfect hair was curling around his temples like it did when it rained and he didn't use enough styling cement.

"We're ready," I said, shaking out my umbrella on the rubber mats covering the floor. "Sorry for the delay."

Richard wagged a finger at me. "Whose idea was it again to hold a wedding on a yacht, Annabelle? This is a disaster."

As the owner of Wedding Belles, one of Washington D.C.'s most up and coming wedding planning companies, I'd done a few weddings on boats before. The kind of boats with giant paddle wheels that get rented out for the afternoon. But nothing like the 164-foot luxury yacht, *Mystic Maven*, that was the setting for my latest wedding.

PREVIEW OF BOOK 5: DEATH ON THE AISLE

"It's a super-yacht," I corrected him, propping my wet umbrella against the white plastic sidewall of the tent. "And it would have been a perfect idea if it hadn't rained."

"This isn't rain," My assistant, Kate, wrung out the hem of her skirt. "It's a monsoon. Speaking of disasters, Richard, what are you wearing?" Bold words from someone who had on one of the tightest black evening suits I'd ever seen. I was surprised that she could bend over without the whole thing ripping in half.

Richard glanced down at the black trash bags he'd taped around his body with silver swaths of duct tape. "If you have a better idea for protecting my Prada suit, I'm all ears."

Kate's mouth fell open. "You're wearing Prada on a night like tonight?"

"You must be out of your mind if you think I'm going to caterer a wedding on the most luxurious yacht that's ever docked in Washington DC's harbor and not wear designer."

Richard Gerard Catering was known for the impeccable style of its owner just as much as for its world-class cuisine, and Richard would never dream of wearing off-the-rack for a six figure wedding.

"Speaking of designer, did you see the dresses on the women in there? And the jewelry?" Kate nudged me with her elbow. "Do you think it's all real?"

"Of course," I said. "The stylist from Paris was telling me how many carats the stepmother of the bride is wearing. P.S. It's a lot."

Richard's eyebrows popped up. "All these stylists are really overkill."

"Oh, you think that pushed it over the edge?" Kate ran her fingers through her short, usually bouncy blond bob that had deflated in the rain. "Not the cake designer we flew in from Scotland or the stepmother's personal designer from New York who redid the entire ship in the wedding colors?"

Richard made a face at Kate, and then turned to me. "Are the waiters getting the drinks through the crowd?"

"Yes. I just wish we didn't have to open the bars before the ceremony, but what can you do when this many people are stuck on a boat during a rainstorm?"

"Nothing like cocktails to keep people occupied," Kate said. "And we still have a lot of time to occupy."

"Food or booze," Richard said. "I just hope we have enough food. I know we have enough booze."

He meant the massive ice bar that we'd craned onboard. The huge slab of ice had been carved to hold half a dozen different bottles of the world's finest vodkas, which meant that the guests would be able to get very drunk very fast.

A figure draped in a dripping tangerine orange tablecloth burst through the tent sides. "Did someone say booze? Because I don't think I've had enough."

Kate and I jumped back as the tablecloth splattered to the floor and Fern emerged. His dark hair was pulled back into a low ponytail, and he looked remarkably dry considering that the rest of us appeared to have swum to the wedding.

"Where did you get that cloth?" I eyed the mound of orange fabric in a wet, wadded mound on the floor.

Fern shrugged. "It was lying around, and I couldn't find a slumbrella."

"Slumbrella?" Kate asked. "How much Champagne have you had again?"

Fern hiccupped. "Just a few."

Kate eyed him. "Glasses or bottles?"

"Was the tablecloth lying around as in lying over a table to cover it?" I wasn't as concerned about Fern drinking bubbly with the bridesmaids as I was about him snatching a cloth off a table. I didn't remember having extra linens just sitting around and had a horrible vision of the bride catching a glimpse of a now-naked catering table with its knobby metal legs and particleboard top.

"Of course not," Fern said, and then bit the edge of his lip. "At least I don't think so. But I was in too much of a hurry to notice."

"If those people sent you down here for food, you tell them they'll have to wait . . ." Richard began.

"Is it the bride?" I swallowed hard remembering how nervous she'd been as Fern had done her hair earlier in the day. Fern had a talent for loosening brides up, usually by sharing raunchy gossip of questionable origin, but this one had been a challenge even for a seasoned wedding hair stylist like him.

"No, no, no," Fern waved his hands around his face like he was shooing off a swarm of mosquitoes. "No one slent me. I came to tell Annabelle before anyone else did."

"Tell me what?" I said, immediately running through the list of possible wedding catastrophes in my head. At least it wasn't the bride; I mentally ticked her off my list. My mind leapt to the next natural problem. "Is it the stepmother-of-the-bride? The stylist?"

Fern hesitated. "Maybe you should see for yourself." He snatched my

PREVIEW OF BOOK 5: DEATH ON THE AISLE

umbrella from where I'd propped it against the tent wall and slipped out between the plastic flaps.

"Great." I grabbed a yellow napkin from a nearby pile and draped it over my head. I'd learned this trick by watching the wait staff attempt to keep their heads dry while carrying trays onto the boat.

"I'm right behind you," Kate said, picking up her own napkin.

Richard threw his oven mitt down on the prep table. "Don't even think about leaving me behind." He turned to one of his chefs. "Get all the platters for the buffet ready, and I'll be back to garnish."

I adjusted my napkin so I could see through the dangling points and pushed my way out of the tent. The rain still beat down wildly and it stung my cheeks as it blew from the side. I groped the few feet to the ramp and pulled myself up by the rope, my feet slipping on the slick metal. I was surprised we hadn't lost a waiter or two to the dark water below and was grateful when I reached the top. Jumping onto the boat, I ducked in through one of the heavy glass doors, and then held it open for Kate and Richard to follow.

I pulled the sopping wet napkin off of my head and slicked back a dripping strand of hair. I usually wore my auburn hair pulled back in a bun, but the rain had ruined my simple hairstyle and it kept falling into my eyes. I could only imagine that any trace of makeup had run off my face hours ago. I reminded myself that I wasn't here to look glamorous and meet men. Surprisingly, I had enough of those in my life already.

Fern stood in the hallway that led to the informal dining room on one side and the spacious main salon on the other. We were using the casual dining room to stage the food and, as the door swung open, I could see one of Richard's cooks touching up a silver tray of hors d'oeuvres that a waiter held in front of him.

"This way." Fern motioned us in the other direction and we followed him across the salon to the marble entrance foyer and gleaming gold staircase that led to the lower decks.

The client had indeed redecorated the boat in the wedding colors: lemon, turquoise and tangerine. The couches had orange throw pillows and the entire boat had been carpeted the color of frothy, beaten egg yolks. It felt like walking into a sunset. Or an egg.

"Where are we going?" Kate said from behind me. "The party isn't down there."

Fern placed a finger over his lips like all the guests weren't on the two decks above us putting away vast quantities of vodka. "You'll slee."

PREVIEW OF BOOK 5: DEATH ON THE AISLE

I wasn't convinced that Fern was sober enough to be leading a posse, but curiosity outweighed the voice of reason in my head.

We formed a silent procession down the twisting staircase to the lower deck. I recognized this as the level with all of the guest bedrooms and the indoor gym. This was also where we'd shoved the furniture from the upper decks when we realized that the entire wedding would have to be inside the boat. The original plan had been to have the ceremony, desserts, and dancing on the top deck's helicopter pad, but when we'd seen the forecast for the biggest rainstorm DC had seen in over 100 years, we'd had to change strategy.

Fern opened a door and I saw deck chairs stacked up to the ceiling.

"Oops," he said. "Wrong one."

He opened the door next to it, and I felt the rush of humidity. The glass door to the steam room hung open across from us and had filled the gym with a warm haze. Like everything on the boat, the gym used space efficiently with one elliptical machine, one treadmill, and one universal weight contraption filling the room.

"I couldn't find the switch to turn it off," Fern explained with a cough. The steam smelled like eucalyptus, and I couldn't resist taking a deep breath.

Kate waved a hand in front of her. "Why is the steam room on during the wedding?"

"Is someone in there?" I narrowed my eyes and could just make out a figure slumped against the tile bench. "And are they fully dressed?"

"All right, buddy." Kate called into the room and clapped her hands. "Party's over. This floor is off-limits."

I felt my skin go cold despite the heat billowing from the steam room. "Oh, no," I said as the body slipped off the bench and rolled onto the floor with a splash and a thud. I could see the water on the floor was tinged pink. "Not again."

Richard jumped back as droplets of warm water hit our legs. "Is that . . .?"

I splashed over to the limp body and turned him over to feel for a pulse. "Yep."

Kate gave a small scream when she recognized his face. "Is he . . .?"

"Dead." Fern said. "I checked already."

I pulled my fingers away from the dead man's neck and stepped back. "But what's he doing down here?"

No one had an answer for me so I rubbed my temples and tried to convince myself that this wasn't happening. You'd think it would be easy

PREVIEW OF BOOK 5: DEATH ON THE AISLE

to avoid dead bodies at weddings, but either I had the worst luck in the world or the universe was telling me that I should quit wedding planning and become a coroner. And the week has started off so well.

To continue reading, click the buy link for DEATH ON THE AISLE on the next page . . .

ALSO BY LAURA DURHAM

Read the entire Annabelle Archer Series in order:

Better Off Wed

For Better Or Hearse

Dead Ringer

Review To A Kill

Death On The Aisle

Night of the Living Wed

Eat, Prey, Love

Groomed For Murder

Wed or Alive

To Love and To Perish

Marry & Bright

The Truffle With Weddings

To get notices whenever I release a new book, follow me on BookBub:

https://www.bookbub.com/profile/laura-durham

Did you enjoy this book? You can make a big difference!

I'm very lucky to have a loyal bunch of readers, and honest reviews are the best way to help bring my books to the attention of new readers.

If you enjoyed this boxset of Annabelle Archer Mysteries Books 1-4, I would be very grateful if you could spend just two minutes leaving a review (it can be as short as you like) on Goodreads, Bookbub, or your favorite retailer.

Thanks for reading and reviewing!

AUTHOR'S NOTE

This box set contains two novels from the original series (which debuted in 2005) as well as two new books that were written and released in 2017. A bit of the old, and a bit of the new. This set also contains a couple of exclusive epilogues that add to the intrigue with Annabelle and Reese (including their first "date"). I hope you enjoy them!

It's always hard to read books you wrote a decade ago, and it's impossible not to want to rewrite them constantly. I do think the characters have developed and "come into their own" as the series has progressed. So even though I'll always love the first books because they were my first, I love Annabelle's crew as the series continues (and the later books are my favorites). I hope you'll continue to read the series and follow me along on the journey with these fun characters.

I enjoy hearing from readers—what you like, what you don't like, and any ideas you may have for future books. Please email or reach out via social media anytime (contact details on the next page). Happy reading!

ABOUT THE AUTHOR

Laura Durham has been writing for as long as she can remember and has been plotting murders since she began planning weddings over twenty years ago. Her first novel, BETTER OFF WED, won the Agatha Award for Best First Novel.

When she isn't writing or wrangling brides, Laura loves traveling with her family, standup paddling, perfecting the perfect brownie recipe, and reading obsessively.

She loves hearing from readers and she would love to hear from you! Send an email or connect on Facebook, Twitter, or Instagram via the icons below.

Let's Connect:
www.lauradurham.com
laura@lauradurham.com

Copyright © 2018 by Broadmoor Books

Cover Design by Alchemy Book Covers

All rights reserved.

No part of this book may be reproduced in any form or by any electronic or mechanical means, including information storage and retrieval systems, without written permission from the author, except for the use of brief quotations in a book review.

This is a work of fiction. Names, characters, places, and incidents are the products of the author's imagination or are used fictitiously and are not to be construed as real. Any resemblance to actual events, locales, organizations, or persons, living or dead, is entirely coincidental.

Made in United States
North Haven, CT
23 January 2023